everything

everything

carole wolf

Bink Books
Bedazzled Ink Publishing Company • Fairfield, California

978-1-939562-56-2 paperback
978-1-939562-57-9 ebook

Cover Design
by

TreeHouseStudio

Bink Books
a division of
Bedazzled Ink Publishing Company
Fairfield, California
http://www.bedazzledink.com

For Kyle Mason a.k.a "DyingTomorrow", "Mr. Sic", and both of their families. Thank you for your sharing your stories, for your honesty, and for your creative advice. R.I.P

Special thanks to:

Karen Williams, RN, BSN, CIC, CRNI
Kathy Stelmack, RN
James Jones, RN
Kathy Revell, RN, MS, NCAC II
Delano Koh, RN
Elizabeth Cox, LD, RD
David Wallace, LPC
Fred Cohen, Ph.D, CSU Philharmonic
Det. Quridsha Gilliam

also:

"John," "Kennie," Sophia DeLuna, Tarra Thomas, Alyssa Farmer, Nesrin Houser, Latisha Witherspoon, Kim Diggs, and Jordan Manley

"Do not take my devils away, for my angels may flee, too."
—Rainer Maria Rilke

Part I

chapter one

SEVEN YEARS AGO, today, I broke my mother's heart. Literally. I stood on the bed and cursed her to hell with all my fourteen-year-old might, screamed it into her face like a zealot at a protest rally. The next day, my Uncle Cameron showed up at the school office, signed me out on the grounds of a family emergency, and walked me to his Maxima in a cold, gray silence. He sat for a very long while with the keys in his hand, staring at the dashboard as if it contained all the truths of the cosmos, but there was really only one to be told that day as the words fell from his lips like stones.

She was a musician, a classical violinist by profession, had been playing since the age of six. She was rehearsing for a Christmas performance when her solo suddenly crumbled, and she dropped to a knee, clutching her chest, struggling for breath that wouldn't come. Someone from the brass section tried CPR until paramedics arrived, and she was whisked away through Atlanta's morning rush hour to St. Joseph's Hospital.

It was a Tuesday. 10:46 a.m.

She was thirty-nine but didn't look it. Few people believed her. Some even jokingly requested to see her driver's license for proof. She'd present it with a sly smirk, chuckle, and wave them off when asked to spill her secret. She looked like a young Sophia Loren, they'd say, and I guess that's what attracted my father, back when they were both just out of college. Not her beauty so much as her humility, because he admired that most in a person. "Carry yourself with confidence but always speak with prudence," he would say. And she most certainly did, so much that I never really knew her until she was gone.

Jolán De Carlo Edmunds was an anomaly, a finely sketched piece of work that most people thought they could appraise at a glance, but that was only because she'd designed herself that way. There were only two people in the world who had seen everything beneath the recitals and curtain calls, the guest solos and afternoon private instructions, all the shifts and tones and colors between the first and final movements of her life.

My father was hardly among them, contrary to what he still thinks. Fifteen years of marriage brought him no closer to who she really was than would thirty or seventy-five more.

Some might say she'd tangled herself up in a lattice of lies and feel sorry for him, the unwitting victim of a woman who had the audacity to try to find herself at thirty-eight. Because I did. I spit on her growing, relentless desire to break free of her own constraints and reconnect with a woman long forgotten, promising to destroy our family.

I demanded to live with my father after the divorce, but I was to begin high school that fall, and North Springs was closer with a better music program. So, my future was mutually decided upon by two people who couldn't even find a way to hold onto their own.

As a fifth-year violin student, myself, I was to follow directly in my mother's path. Or, was I? That had all been up for some very passionate, awkward debate after her passing, mostly between my father, Uncle Cameron, and the woman who probably knew her better than any of us.

And so this is where I must digress.

THREE MONTHS BEFORE I killed her, my mother and I were invited out with her best friend Jackie to a poetry reading in Buckhead. Poetry had completely escaped me then. I couldn't have cared less about it, never understood a word of it and, in fact, pouted all the way into town, buckled into the backseat of Jackie's Camry while Mom and Jackie complained about the music selections on the radio—manufactured mainstream trash, the decline of innovation, the death of the true artist.

Jackie kept switching stations. Every time a song I liked burst through the back speakers, either she or Mom would stab the seek button for something else because my thirteen-year-old opinions were weightless as feathers on the moon. They finally found something from the '70s, chugging mid-tempo rock guitars, a young woman singing about magic hands and summer love spells. They would have both been in grammar school then.

Mom turned in her seat and smiled at me. "This was when *real* musicians actually made it to the radio," she said, her eyebrows naturally arched, like soft sculpted dark brown check marks.

Most of the time they gave her the appearance of great wisdom, unless she was irritated or angry. Then they would sharpen like half-folded switchblades, her green eyes almost electric as she leveled you, making you feel smaller than an atom with those eyes, or larger than love itself, depending. Tonight they flickered with a kind of amusement, the clever creative sage, eager to fill my *tabula rasa* with poetry and nostalgia that had nothing to do with me.

"You'd be surprised how many rock stars in our day were classically trained." Jackie glanced at me through the rearview and nodded once. "It was rock, but they made the *good* stuff, the stuff that lives forever, music that meant something."

Mom settled back in the passenger's seat and looked out the window, watched the city go by. "Changed people's lives," she said to no one in particular as the women on the radio sang. "Changed the world."

We were to meet Linda Morgan for dinner before the reading, an older woman and fellow musician my mother had known since I was in diapers, and she waved us over to a lucky parking spot on Roswell, not far from Giovanni's Books.

WE ATE AT a fancy Thai restaurant with a long blackwood liquor bar and transparent, amber-lighted wall fountains that trickled in the dining room corners. The waiter brought menus to our table and presented a wine list. He suggested the Cabernet, but my mother had a Pinot Noir preference for the red wines, Riesling for the white.

She ordered the California Pinot at the consensus of the table and a Coke for me, then browsed her menu while Mrs. Morgan and Jackie discussed venue options for the Civic Orchestra's first Christmas performance. The Catholic Shrine of the Immaculate Conception. Chastain Park Amphitheater, weather permitting. Emerson Concert Hall at Emory University.

They liked best to play in churches and basilicas for the acoustics, Mom always said, but they never rehearsed in them because she said a grand and empty sanctuary blurred the tonality of polyphonic music. Only when filled with an audience did the sound resonate properly, and all the subtleties could be intimated to perfection.

She had an ear like a hawk owl, perfect pitch. If a train whistled somewhere in the distance, she could place every dissonant note and tell you the key if it had one, much the way an artisan might find hues of burgundy in the shadows of a willow tree, or a gourmet chef connoting a trace of licorice in a spoonful of brisket, just by wafting it past his nose.

It was a game she played with her surroundings, always testing herself and testing me, but I didn't have her gift and often wondered how it didn't drive her crazy, the world and all its sounds, so many aural textures hiding in the spaces between. My talent was mediocre at best, and I couldn't tell the difference between a G-sharp and a B-flat without first finding them on my violin. I shared half her genetics, but so far only the physical features, her dark auburn hair in long natural ringlets, the hazel eyes, her mouth. Everything else seemed to have been bestowed upon her, and only her, by the diatonic Lydian gods of some melodic otherworld.

I scanned my menu but didn't find anything appealing. Pearl onions. Cashews. Okra and eggplant. Bamboo shoots in hot mustard marinade. I folded it shut and sat slouching, wishing she would have sent me to Dad's for the weekend so he and I could go out for root beer and pizza, then maybe downtown to The Bodies Exhibition and browse roomfuls of cadavers dancing ballets and playing poker, one of them even conducting an orchestra.

Mom poked me in the shoulder and gave me a look. It said, "Sit up. Now. Do not embarrass me." And so I did. "Find something you like," she uttered into the entrée page. "There's shrimp, chicken, rice, and noodles."

"And all of it swimming in goo from another planet," I mumbled.

"Another *country*. And it's sauce, not goo. What is up with your manners?"

"Everything's smothered in onions."

"Then don't eat the onions, Myla. Pick them out." She was growing weary of me, and she glared at me sideways and pointed to the menu.

I wrinkled my nose.

After a while the waiter returned, and so she ordered for me, as if I were four. Pad Zee Eu—white meat chicken and rice noodles with broccoli in an herb sauce, the only item I would even consider eating; sometimes I forgot how well she knew me. She got the Panang Nuea, braised beef short ribs with curry and kaffir lime, ordering with explicit pronunciation because, to her, that was the respectful and fitting thing to do, and she handed our menus back to the waiter with a courteous smile. The societal etiquette *extraordinaire*.

"I imagine you must be excited, Myla, starting the ninth grade this year," Mrs. Morgan said. She was a cellist in the Civic Orchestra, a twice-sponsored artist in residence for the National Endowment for the Arts and Chamber Music, just like my mom. She poured herself a glass of wine and said to my mother, "The school's got a wonderful orchestra, one of the best in Atlanta, so I'm told."

"You were told right," Mom said. She looked at me, trying to decide what she thought of my future there, my future anywhere. I had been drifting since the divorce, floating farther away from her ideals than she would have liked, and I could see the tiny lines at the corners of her eyes begin to gather with uncertainty. She didn't say what she was thinking, that she had no idea if I'd even be in the orchestra at all, come spring, that she wondered if her accomplishments still inspired me like they once did and if I would eventually just abandon her dreams altogether. She'd been pushing me toward all the things she wanted for so long, and now I was pushing back.

Linda Morgan had no business peering through that lens into our lives, and so my mother draped an arm across the back of my chair and poured herself a glass of Pinot Noir with the other, smiling thinly. "I'm sure she'll make the most of it." She swirled the wine in her glass and watched the pale pink runnels slide down the Bordeaux crystal and took a sip. "What kid of mine wouldn't?"

"Have you thought yet about sending her to Richard Bernadeaux?" Linda asked, and I held my breath and waited for Mom to break into a bitter diatribe. Dr. Richard Bernadeaux was a violin teacher up in Kennesaw, the most sought after by those who hadn't yet learned of my mother, a transplant from the Curtis Institute of Music, my mother's alma mater. The competition, for all rights, and a subject she disliked because it challenged her authority over me.

Mom set her glass down on the table and didn't look at Linda. "No, I haven't."

"I know you've been teaching her for the past few years, Jolán," Linda said, "but objectivity is key if you want her to improve. Studies show—"

"I know what the studies show, and I'd just feel better that she learns from me. At least until she's further into high school. We've been over this." Mom stopped there, held her tongue because we were in public, but I could almost see her eyes changing color, pleasant golden-green to a dark, agitated emerald, like mood rings forever bound to her psychological chemistry.

Linda gave her a scolding glance over the brim of her glass. "He's a good teacher, a phenomenal musician," she pressed, unmoved by my mother's distaste for this topic. "Objectivity. Distance," she reminded her again.

No one had even considered asking me what I thought, but had they ever?

"I heard he's a recluse," Jackie muttered, scrolling through her cell phone. She always knew just when to douse the fire. "A total shut-in when he's not teaching. Never even performs anymore, hasn't done a show in six years. He's gotta be about a hundred now, anyway, isn't he?"

Mom gestured to Jackie with conclusive shrug. "So there you go," she told Linda. "I'm not carting my kid off to Kennesaw to learn from a hundred-year-old hermit, even if he was once the artist chair of performance studies at Curtis. Sometime during my parents' childhood."

"The man's my age, which would be nearly a half century from a hundred, thank you," Linda said. "And so what if he's an eccentric? Does it really matter? This *is* art we're talking about."

"Jolán's plenty eccentric." Jackie waved her off. "Never know what you're gonna get with this one." She gestured to my mother. "I've known her for a decade and still can't figure out whether she's a closet hippie or just a straight with a flair for breaking all the right rules."

"I'm no hippie," Mom said with a grin. "Way too many responsibilities for that."

"You know all the words to 'Voodoo Chile,'" Jackie taunted. She had taken out a compact mirror and sat primping, and she glanced at my mother with a guiltless shrug.

"Who over the age of thirty-five doesn't?" Mom insisted. "Hell, for that matter, so do you, Lotus Moonbeam. We weren't even old enough to be hippies then, anyway, and by the time we were, it was the eighties, and that was the end of that."

"The beginning of the end of music as we'd known it," Jackie muttered. She snapped the compact shut and dropped it into her purse. "The dawn of the button pushers. Thank God classical never fell victim. I can still perform Stravinsky as it was intended, work a little, *earn* my spot in that woodwind section."

"Hear, hear," Linda declared, and she raised her glass. "To tradition." But then she reconsidered and pulled her drink away and raised an eyebrow at my mother. "You're sure you want to toast to that, Ms. De Carlo? Queen of creative license, sower of the misplaced grace note? It just might fly in the face of your aesthetic liberties."

Mom lifted her glass and looked intently at Linda. "It's called improvisation. And the name's still Edmunds. I'm keeping it for professional reasons. How's that for tradition?" And she gave her a wink. "Cheers."

Jackie grabbed my soda and handed it to me. "You, too, kiddo. Come on." And the four of us clinked our glasses to all the musical rules my mother so loved to break.

GIOVANNI'S BOOKS WAS a new place, its grand opening heralded by a reading from up-and-coming poet, Rachel Kingsley. Mom remained rather indifferent about the event and was there only to replace Jackie's husband who'd been called away on last minute business. I was hoping maybe we'd forego this and stay at the restaurant so I could listen to Mom eviscerate Linda Morgan in a debate about classical improv, but they'd dropped it when our food came and spent the meal talking about politics, something they all agreed on.

Mom was unfamiliar with Giovanni's guest reader and shook her head when Linda asked if she'd seen Ms. Kingsley's feature in *The New Yorker* that month.

"Never heard of her," she confessed with a simple smile. "But then again, she might turn up in the reading I plan on doing when things slow down a bit."

"Interesting young woman," Linda said as we found seats in the back of a surprisingly crowded little shop. "In fact, she's about your age, been struggling for years to get published, but you know it's more difficult for poets. It's a genre for a dying breed, I think, trying to breathe life into a lost art, gifted as some may be."

Mom gave that a nod and a half smile. Something in her eyes

scrutinized Linda for a microsecond, but she kept that fleeting judgment to herself and instead turned to me.

"Must you mope?" she insisted. "You've been doing this all evening. What is your deal?"

"I'm not. I'm here, aren't I?"

"Well, Myla, it wasn't as if you had a choice, now was it?"

"Exactly."

She opened her mouth to say more but then reconsidered and let it lie.

Soon the place fell silent, and the poet Rachel emerged from the back room and took a seat before a store full of patrons. She was sandy blonde, her hair pulled up into a casual twist, and she wore a cream-colored, peasant-style, bohemian shirt but was otherwise difficult to see around the heads and hats in my view line.

" 'Forgive me if I've interrupted your journey,' " she began over the hush. " 'But it seems my muse has taken a shine to you. She's cast herself down upon you, spinning the embers of your sparkle spirit into a thousand diamonds, diamonds that melt into raindrop perfection and shower me with a fascination for everything that moves you . . .'"

I heaved a deep sigh and propped a foot across my knee and toyed with a loose thread at the cuff of my jeans, secretly hoping this subtle display of discourtesy just might prick my mother's nerves. But this time she said nothing. There was no peripheral ominous glare, no hand reaching over to swat me from my fidgeting, and so I picked at the scuffed rubber soles of the Birkenstocks she asked me not to wear tonight but hadn't yet noticed either.

" 'Out here, in your universe, your smile commands the stars to dance a glittering ballet for you to watch from a mountaintop on Venus. And I am spellbound. Earthbound. Listening to your smile. Wondering if there is enough room on that mountaintop for an imagineer and her muse. Or, would you flutter away on frightened wings, like a dove, fearful of my approach. In slow motion flight . . .'"

I dared peer at Mom again to see if she saw my insolence, to see if she could intimate the quiet loathing I had for the absolute power she held over me since Dad left, the disdain I felt for being dragged here against my will.

Rachel's first presentation ended, and Giovanni's filled with applause. But my mother didn't move. She just sat there, still as stone with her hands in her lap, and she scarcely issued a breath. I watched her for a long moment as the applause settled. That was when I realized her olive complexion had gone suddenly pale as she stared out at the poet at the front of the room.

I frowned and craned my neck around the man in front of me for a better look at Rachel Kingsley who smiled at the audience and began a personable and enthusiastic preface to her next work, a story of her time as a student at USC in Los Angeles, which had inspired her next poem about emotional resolve.

Mom shifted in her seat. She inhaled a gentle but shuddering breath, then brushed imaginary dust from her jacket sleeve and looked back at Rachel Kingsley. A very small droplet of sweat beaded beneath the wavy auburn baby hairs at her temple, and I thought I'd been transported into some other galaxy, some parallel universe where self-assured, dauntless women came quietly undone at the mention of celestial mountaintops and raindrop diamonds. She looked as though she were facing execution by firing squad as her eyes swept anxiously around the room and stopped at the exit.

"I really do hope she does the one from *The New Yorker*," Linda leaned in and whispered to her. "Such a great piece. I'm surprised you're not familiar with it, as much as you read that thing."

My mother shot her a glance that could have seared the lashes from her coral-shadowed lids, but it went unnoticed, and I couldn't figure what Linda Morgan said to deserve that one.

Many thought Linda was pretentious, the haughty first cellist in an orchestra over which my mother was concertmaster. Professionally, they had always been on fairly equal footing, so I never understood the subtle, ongoing battle of wills that served as a friendship. Linda indeed made my mother twitch with irritation, and my mother brought out the arrogance in Linda Morgan, but that wasn't what that look was for. Linda had spoken amid some other kind of turmoil, a turmoil that wrung my mother's hands in her lap as Rachel Kingsley told pining love stories in syllabic meter under golden-amber track lights.

"'I've got no tales of glory,'" she recited, peering into the faces before her with an honesty I thought inappropriate for a roomful of strangers. "'I've got train wrecks and midair collisions and sinking ships. And as I crawl from the wreckage, away into the weeds to watch it all burn, you find a wildflower and place it in my hair.'"

I looked to my mother again, and she was following along with profound ambiguity, her knee bouncing as if her heel was on a loaded spring. I stretched my neck for another glimpse of Rachel Kingsley, the voice behind my mother's sudden, inexplicable anxiety.

"Sit back, Myla, please," she uttered lowly, and so I did.

Jackie handed me a program to share for distraction. I took it and perused seven glossy pages filled with several short six line poems, apparently her signature style. There was a biographical blurb on the back with a black-and-white head shot. She was beautiful, really. Brown eyed with full lips and a warm smile that pulled you in close. I offered it to my mother, but she didn't take it. She stared down her nose at it instead, like an idle grenade, as if taking it from my hand might cause it to detonate and blow us all to hell.

She shook her head and looked away. "I don't need that."

SHE SPENT THE next thirty minutes in a peculiar daze, her legs crossed, then uncrossed, another smudge of invisible dust on a pant cuff, overwhelmed and trapped there by an invitation we wouldn't have even accepted if her evening student hadn't canceled.

When the reading concluded, the audience rose from wooden folding chairs and turned to one another for good-byes and small talk. Some wandered to a table of Gouda cheese hor d'oeuvres and tiny lemon cake squares. A second table was lined with sparkling sommelier glasses of pink Chablis. Mom took one, and I followed as she worked her way through the crowd, heading for an inconspicuous spot by the door, but someone stopped her. It was Gabe Neale, a French horn player in the Civic Orchestra, and she switched on a smile and turned to him with a friendly embrace.

She was very good at that, good at giving people what they wanted, at keeping in step with everyone's expectations, even when she was so unimaginably distressed that she wanted to dive through the front bay window to escape. Jackie was immersed in conversation over by the refreshment table, so Mom indulged Gabe Neale for several unending minutes while he discussed music selections for their upcoming performance at Emory. He was frumpy and balding, older than she, and he had the continuous habit of pushing his glasses up onto the bridge of his nose as he spoke, but I think she just made him nervous.

" . . . and I was thinking we could finish with Paganini," he finally suggested. "Violin concerto in D minor? It'll certainly give *you* a chance to shine, but of course it's up to you and the conductor at the end of the day. Just some thoughts." He sipped his wine and gave my mother a smile that hovered between kindliness and flirtation. It might have been thought this kind of swooning began the first time Jolán Edmunds' ring finger was noticeably bare. But in truth it had always been this way and merely peaked when whispers of "irreconcilable differences" fluttered around rehearsal sessions and out into the concert halls.

Dad was absent for most of my mother's musical events. He dressed me up and shuffled me along to the major performances, and only if they hadn't fallen on a school night. He would otherwise offer his complimentary seat to a neighbor or co-worker, and Mom and I would find him fast asleep in his recliner when we got home. He was a jazz man, a fair-weather fan of Pat Metheny and Manheim Steamroller, an executive mechanical engineer for LMI Products in Adamsville who blamed the majority of his disinterest in my mother's career on an exhausting daily commute.

He had our neatly packaged suburban life covered with a healthy six figures, so my mother never needed to work, but she couldn't be dragged away from the classical community by a Peterbilt semi and a sixty-foot towing chain. Music was oxygen to her, and so my father left her to her "hobby" and waved her away to the ogles of other men, to the Ph.D.'s in crisp Oxford button-downs and salt-and-pepper sideburns, and the post-graduate neo-hippie boys who longed to impress her with experimental improv on Schubert or Liszt. Gabe Neale fell somewhere in the middle of that spectrum, too old for clever innovation and too young not to undress her with his eyes, hoping to disguise it with shoptalk.

"I'll see what I can do, Gabe." She smiled with a wink and touched his forearm with manicured fingertips, just enough to send him on his way without condescension. There was a wisp of her Omnia Crystalline cologne on his jacket from their embrace as he turned away, which would linger for days until he saw her again at rehearsal. Subtle traces of her presence. Like lipstick on a wine glass.

Jackie joined us at the door and asked if we were ready to leave.

"You have no idea," Mom breathed as we turned for the exit. But then Linda Morgan called from the back of the shop, waving a hand above her head to flag us down. She had someone by the arm, leading her to where we stood at the threshold to freedom, just paces from the sidewalk.

"I've got a surprise before you go," she sang and commenced a rather formal introduction between my mother, Jackie, and Rachel Kingsley herself. "Rachel, this is Jackie Lembke, second clarinetist in the Atlanta Civic Orchestra."

Jackie offered a hand. "Wonderful to meet you. Beautiful work, just beautifully written, like painting pictures with words. A pleasure."

Rachel Kingsley nodded her thanks, but her eyes now darted between Jackie and my mother, and her expression dampened and went flat, as if she'd swallowed something sharp. But she kept her professional bearing as Linda presented a rather stiff and unresolved Jolán Edmunds.

"She's our concertmaster and premier violin soloist," Linda boasted, not so much for my mother's benefit as for her own, for having lassoed the star performer from the exit door and into a personal chat.

Their eyes met and locked, and it was like an iceberg dropped between them, the very same iceberg that sank the Titanic.

"She's been performing here in Atlanta for . . . What has it been, now, Jolán? About twelve years?" Linda prattled on. "Recently she was a guest soloist for the Atlanta Symphony, performed Shostakovich's First Violin Concerto with the grace of a magician, I'll tell you. And now she's all ours with the new Civic Orchestra." She beamed. "Now that you're living in the area, Rachel, you should try to make it to one of our concerts. I do think you'd enjoy yourself."

Linda was the only one in our slowly dilating circle who hadn't noticed the stale air.

Mom broke the tension and extended her hand. "How've you been?"

Rachel Kingsley stared at my mother for several long moments, as if she'd lost something in those hazel eyes that she didn't know how to get back. Finally, she reached for my mother's handshake, slack with misgiving. "Um, fine. I've been fine. I didn't . . . I mean . . ." Her lips began to form what looked like an apology but she stopped short and smiled strangely instead. She flitted a glance down to my mother's empty wedding finger, then across to me—Jolán Edmunds' little mirror image, and her eyes narrowed with subtle bewilderment.

"You two know each other?" Linda chuckled, at once thrilled and perplexed. "Well, now doesn't that beat all!"

"Been a long time," Rachel uttered, and my mother nodded, much the way a surgeon might respond when asked if he did everything he could before pronouncing someone's mother, sister, daughter. Then she snapped out of it and remembered me.

"This is my daughter, Myla." She rested her hands on my shoulders and urged me to mind my manners with a nudge to offer my hand. Rachel took it into hers and gazed at me like a delightful mystery. Her hands were warm and soft, and her smile was the sincerest I'd seen all night.

"Well, you are just beautiful," she said and looked at my mother as if she'd done very well, though it puzzled me as to why that came as such a moving surprise to Ms. Kingsley. "And you're how old?"

"Thirteen and a half. I'll be fourteen in two months." I wanted her to know that I wasn't a child, that I could handle whatever was looming between them like a radioactive dust cloud, but then my mother suggested that I go with Jackie who had excused herself to mingle, leaving Mom and Rachel to some reluctant privacy. Linda Morgan finally took that cue and wandered off as well.

From an empty folding chair I watched them, tried to read their lips as they muttered awkward explanations, shrugging away a clearly inscrutable history. Whatever it was, even I knew this wasn't the time nor the place.

College alumni? Grade school classmates, perhaps? No. It wasn't that simple. Not the way my mother did quick and cagey scans of the room for scrutiny as she spoke, the way she shoved her hands into her coat pockets, insecure, sniffing the air for danger. I'd never seen her so shifted off her axis, so utterly rattled while struggling to keep face, the woman whose very presence was required on stage before a single symphonic note could crack the air, who garnered applause just for showing up to work.

No, this was something much more complicated than losing an old address or searching hopelessly for an unlisted number. I couldn't have been more certain of that as Rachel Kingsley bid my mother a good evening with a lonely smile and left her standing by the door, lost in a flurry of troubling thoughts.

chapter two

IT WAS ALMOST a month before we saw her again. In that time my mother had forgotten two scheduled violin lessons, left the house and drove all the way into the city with the garage door wide open, all our Pensacola beach vacation gear, our camping equipment, the alternate storage freezer, and all its bulk-packaged Costco contents exposed for the taking, if any of our cookie-cutter subdivision neighbors were so inclined. She'd burned her wrist on the oven door and shattered a wine glass on the dining room hardwood and lost her iPhone somewhere between rehearsal on Thursday morning and the grocery store that afternoon.

When a fellow orchestra mate returned it at the following evening's rehearsal, she pecked the screen for several minutes while we sat in the Land Cruiser outside North Atlanta High School where they practiced, refreshing her memory, updating herself on that week's agenda.

Somewhere in her plans was a ride into the Virginia-Highland district the following Sunday afternoon. We crept through post-church-service traffic along Highland Avenue and pulled onto Briarcliff to park. From our vantage point we could see the main strip, an earthy day spa where plastic twenty somethings and taut-cheeked cougars gathered over-priced provisions. A Starbucks. The huge bay window of a bar café called Zorna's. Behind Zorna's window was a drum set and a couple of microphone stands on what I imagined was a small stage, but it was empty at one in the afternoon, awaiting players that probably wouldn't crawl out of bed until dusk.

Rachel Kingsley strolled into view. She took a seat at one of the sidewalk umbrella tables, dug through her purse, pulled out a pocket mirror, and sat checking her reflection for flaws.

"So, what? Are we going to lunch or something?" I asked my mother, but she didn't answer.

She just sat there, the way she did at Giovanni's, peering out at an invitation she was apparently quite reluctant to accept, but *did*, and so it struck me as odd that she would lose her nerve now, with an irresistible enigma just twenty yards away. I began to think she should have done this on her own time and let me stay in Marietta, left me in my room with a house key and a selection of TV dinners. I could have practiced etudes in G-sharp and finished my report on *The Metamorphosis*, rather than being toted along like a fashion accessory.

Rachel checked her watch, browsed through a menu. Then I had the slow but undeniable realization of my purpose there; I was a barricade. A safe and impenetrable buffer between my mother and all the mounting consternation Rachel Kingsley seemed to represent. With the precocious thirteen year old at her side, Jolán Edmunds could avoid any topic that threatened to pick the lock on her lips and crack her surface, and I couldn't understand what would make her run for cover with such fierce desperation because my mother wasn't afraid of anything. Was she? I instantly felt like a co-conspirator.

Mom pulled the keys from the ignition and let the seat belt zip behind the headrest. She gave me a quick once-over as we walked toward Zorna's, inspecting me for oversights in my appearance and demeanor.

"You should've worn a belt," she said of my hiphuggers and cupped a hand under my chin.

I gave her an exasperated eye roll and deposited a moist wad of gum into her palm. She tossed it into the bushes and tucked the tag from my baby tee into the collar.

"Better. But you could look a little more enthusiastic. It's not gonna kill you to have a meal and hang out with a couple of old ladies for a while, is it?" She tried on a smile, looking to me for levity, but her eyes flickered with something I'd never seen before, a vague mixture of regret and longing. I couldn't return the smile with that foreign concoction churning in her emerald gaze, but she just waved it away and draped an arm around my shoulder, donning me like battle armor as we approached the umbrella tables.

Rachel grinned and rose from her chair and hooked an arm around my mother's neck that made her rigid at first, surprised and unwilling, and my mother's eyes fell shut for the briefest moment, and in that moment she seemed to dissolve.

"I wasn't sure you'd show," Rachel told her as we took seats.

Mom shrugged. "Well, I already had errands down this way, so it worked out."

No, she didn't. We were miles from any other plans for today.

Mom tore her eyes from Rachel's and straightened her silverware, took a sip of ice water, and peered out at passersby, at the faces in the cars that sat idle at the red light.

I imagine she felt grateful. None of them knew her. They were all oblivious to how many times she'd changed outfits in front of the mirror that day, how she'd set the alarm for six a.m. for an impromptu trip to the gym and busied the rest of her morning with inane tasks to pass the time, over watering all the plants, rearranging the patio furniture, organizing her sheet music in alphabetical order by composer. She finally chose a pair of olive green cargo pants, a black Old Navy tank top, and a pair of gray

Patagonia hiking sneakers. She didn't want to seem over eager, wanted to send a message to Rachel Kingsley that this was informal, immaterial, just another stop along the winding, busy road through her daily life.

We ordered tall glasses of sweet tea and snacked on warm tortilla chips until our food arrived—sun dried cherry chicken salad, Reuben sandwiches, and sweet potato sunspots. We relaxed under the umbrella shade and watched early autumn pluck burgundy leaves from the southern sugar maples.

Through their dialogue I discovered Rachel Kingsley was actually Rachel Cole, Kingsley having been a professional pen name for over a decade. She and Mom kept the conversation light and uncomplicated while we ate.

I was the central topic, much to my disinterested dread. We talked about school recitals and music camp, whether my mother should continue as my violin instructor or send me to Dr. Bernadeaux, about my grades, my favorite books, my first steps, the tooth fairy. I had done everything early, including being born, which, according to Rachel, was an indisputable indication that I was gifted, and my mother agreed before I could say anything in contrast. It was true I had begun to walk at nine months, lost my first tooth at five, could read basic phrases long before kindergarten, and had already decided on Berklee College, not so much for the music program but to get as far away from Marietta, Georgia as the wind could carry me.

"Got a few friends from Berklee," Rachel told me with a quick glance at my mother. "They're some of the most beautifully inspiring people I've ever met. They said the Berklee experience changed their lives. Not a bad choice. Not bad at all."

Mom gave that a half nod and didn't look up from her plate as she spoke. "It's a fine school for certain things. But I thought we talked about Curtis." She looked at me expectantly and sipped her tea.

"Curtis is where *you* went," I insisted lowly. "Maybe I wanna do something different. Maybe I wanna meet beautifully inspiring people and play jazz or something, be like Linzi Stoppard and work with subharmonics." I dared look her in the eye through the crunch of a tortilla chip. She was so silent I might as well have bitten into a stick of dynamite.

She kept a cool but dissatisfied gaze and tried to smile. "And if playing amplified trash for Hugh Heffner in a bunny outfit and opening Vegas casinos is the pinnacle of your goals, then sure, be my guest. Knock yourself out."

"She also learned the Suzuki Method," I defended, "and she played at the Cannes Film Festival. I thought only smart people did stuff like that."

"The Suzuki Method? Yeah, well, you're very wrong about *that* one, kiddo."

"Speaking of the Cannes," Rachel stepped in without missing a breath, "they're looking at Michael Moore for the Palme d'Or this year. Seems he's got it cornered for conspiracies and scandals, doesn't he?"

My mother left our debate for future discussion and went back to her meal, but not without cutting her eyes at me because I'd embarrassed her. I was supposed to giggle about clothes shopping, climb onto her pedestal like a minion to Aphrodite, and agree with everything she said, the way the orchestra cronies did until she turned her back. That's when the gossip would percolate, like little captions beneath her life that everyone could read but her.

"Well, conspiracies and scandals aren't really that hard to dig up." Mom shrugged and gave Rachel a quick smile. "Not if you know where to look."

"Who's looking?" Rachel said.

"Never know." Mom took the last sunspot from her plate and tossed it into her mouth.

We spent the rest of the meal avoiding conspiracies. Rachel spoke of her days as a post graduate from USC and how she couldn't find work with a literature degree, couldn't find work anywhere and dreaded going home to Ohio, to the tyranny of her own mother who still harbored contempt for her unbridled spirit, particularly for the trouble it'd gotten her into during her last years of college.

She and Mom shared a familiar glance over that one, but all the details were omitted because of me. She eventually found a proofreading job for a local music magazine in Akron, and then her estranged father passed away two years after that and left her a large and disproportionate inheritance, which she never touched, mostly because she had trouble accepting a half-million dollars from a dead man whom she'd never really known.

My mother seemed familiar with Mr. Cole's estrangement, with all the arbitrary details of Rachel's personal background, and she listened like a priest in confession as Rachel admitted to having made a desperate dip into her inheritance three years ago. That was when she had moved to Atlanta with a friend and business partner, with whom she had opened a restaurant and bar in Buckhead, just before landing a coveted publishing deal with Autumn Hill Press.

"I had to take stock. Had to be practical and set myself up, invest in something real. It was either Atlanta or D.C., and we literally flipped a coin." Then she smiled a little. "I guess finding a publisher can be a lot like finding a soulmate—stop looking, and there they are."

"Go figure." My mother didn't say anything more. In fact, she offered very little of her own travels until the story caught up to her and Dad's wedding, my birth in '94.

"I went back to school, to Curtis," was all she offered of anything before that.

Rachel nodded. She understood everything that wasn't said, and I wished I could see into their heads, be a synaptic neuron for just five minutes and leap from thought to unspoken thought.

"Well, I'm glad you did." Rachel smiled thinly. "I'm glad you did what made you happy."

"I needed to change," Mom concluded. "Still do, I guess."

She mentioned the divorce, but it was a side note, as if marriage and divorce were just by-products of something much more complex and meaningful, and I wanted to throw my glass into the traffic. She never considered how it would affect me, how it would shake my world until everything rattled loose and spilled out onto everything else, that maybe I was buried under there, tapping on the twisted girders in Morse code, wondering how long it would take before I suffocated.

The afternoon began to wane, and she and Rachel parted ways with promises to call. Mom was quiet for the drive back to Marietta. She was quiet all the time since Rachel Cole showed up. It was as if she'd awakened from a very bad dream and couldn't get it out of her head, though she rarely slept much after that day. I would stir beneath my blankets on any given night, open an eye at two-thirty in the morning to Bach's *Chaconne* for solo violin, realizing it wasn't just the unusual score to a dream about dragons with butterfly wings; it was her, playing in the downstairs den, venting, purging something toxic, something that had slipped under her skin and coursed through her veins like molten lava.

But my mother never cried—she didn't have to. That custom-built Joseph Curtin did it for her.

BETWEEN THE MIDDLE of October and early November, something shifted, or misaligned, or perhaps fell away. Jackie called it a Mercury retrograde, when everything in the cosmos was out of sync. The messenger Mercury backtracked his path, which threw communication, particularly that of the written word, into an upheaval.

"But it's also a good time to redo things," she appended over a sip of Riesling out on our patio on Halloween night. "You take advantage of it and make it work for you, rather than against you."

She was waiting for my mother to get out of the shower so they could discuss the formation of a quartet, featuring my mother, Linda Morgan, a young violist from UGA named Jessica Walker, and Jackie, whose second instrument was the flute. She played all sorts of wind instruments. Peruvian pan flutes, the Turkish zurna, the Armenian duduk. The four of them could play private gigs around town, weddings, charity functions, funerals.

Jackie checked the time on her cell phone and eyed me strangely. "Shouldn't you be out trick-or-treating or something? It's almost seven. Doesn't that sort of thing start about now?"

I shook my head. "Mom says it's for little kids, that it's not fair for someone my age to be out hogging all the candy. I'm gonna be fourteen in a couple months, so she's probably right."

"So, you're just gonna hang around here with the adults all night? That's kind of a drag. What about your friends? Surely you should be having a sleepover somewhere, with all the goriest, scariest movies you can find. *Carnival of Souls*." She nodded with a sly smile. "That's an old one, but you should still check it out. It's a psychological thriller. Kind of a mindfuck, really. Or *Carrie*. Another classic."

She was the only one of my mother's friends who used profanity in front of me, which I liked because she never treated me like a porcelain doll, like the others. I wasn't on display when Jackie came around. I was real, tangible, and tough, destined for the same womanhood, so why sugarcoat it?

My mother only allowed her to speak to me in that brusque vernacular because she was my godmother and they had been friends for so long, and it was just Jackie's way. If it were anyone else, she would level them with her golden-hazel glare and slice them open with a tongue sharper than a Masamoto knife.

Mom appeared on the stairs, tying her hair back as she crossed the living room toward the patio in bare feet, wearing a pair of gray sweats and a blue form-fitting muscle tee. She was fit, had a swimmer's build and great legs, and I could only hope to be genetically fortunate enough to look like a twenty year old at forty. Jackie was heavier set, but they were often mistaken for sisters with their shoulder-length auburn ringlets like coiled Christmas bows, each with olive skin that baked to a caramel-cinnamon in summertime.

But my mother's eyes were prettier than Jackie's, like gemstones that commanded your attention even when she wasn't looking at you. Jackie trumped her in wit and warmth, but that hadn't always been the case. It had been a slow and steady decline over the years for Jolán Edmunds, a decline in which she had begun to implode. The only one who stood by with an open mind, who knew when to reach for her and when to let her crumble, was Jackie. Lately, however, Mom had been in an upswing.

She poured herself a glass of wine and dropped onto the settee across from us, curled up with a contented sigh and a half smile. Jackie's Kaki King CD played quietly through speakers mounted in the corners of the living room. "So, what'd I miss? What are we talking about?"

"Classic horror," Jackie said. "I think your kid should be somewhere getting the shit scared out of her on Halloween night, don't you?"

Mom shrugged with a smirk. "I thought I provided enough of that around here to last all year." And she smiled at me warmly, amused. "She's been a pretty good sport, though."

"Has to be, with your temperament," Jackie told her. "You've gotten better, here of late, I must say. Not quite back to your old self. More like a revamped version. You've got a spark of something going on, something both sinful and agreeable. Can't really put my finger on it, though."

I suspected it might have been all the time she was spending with Rachel since our lunch at Zorna's. They had gone to dinner twice since then, and now they spoke on the phone at least three times a week. The dialogue was benign and uninteresting if I was within earshot. Then Mom's tone would soften as she wandered out to the back yard or disappeared down into the den, and she'd return with a warm, distant smile and more mysteries than the Kama Sutra temples of India.

The two of them had even gone with Uncle Cameron to a Falcon's game while I spent that weekend at Dad's. She had also begun to keep a journal again. She spent more than an hour a day on her laptop, the way she had when I was little. During those days, she would sit me on her knee and weave my interpretations of our daily adventures into her thoughts, cut and paste corresponding photos into each entry. She let me pick the font—comic sans. And the colors—lavender and yellow. But now, it was a solitary task under the glow of a single Tiffany lamp, at odd hours after dark, Schoenberg's *Variations* seeping from the stereo in surround sound.

She didn't know this, but some nights I watched her from the staircase, between the wrought iron rails, Schoenberg scoring her work like a mad scientist in the dark quirky throes of self-discovery.

Mom gave Jackie a thin cryptic smile but said nothing. Jackie eyed her sideways and wagged a scolding finger.

"You're into something, lady," she muttered, and I could assume that none of it was up for discussion over a bottle of Riesling on this late October evening with Linda Morgan on her way up from Buckhead. "Maybe I don't wanna know what it is."

My mother shrugged, couldn't be pried open. Kaki King plucked complex pretty arpeggios on an acoustic guitar, a minor key, 7/8 time. Mom sipped her wine. Then the doorbell rang. Linda Morgan let herself in, calling through the house from where she hung her coat by the front door.

"Sure you're up for this?" Jackie asked my mother.

"Yeah, I think I can handle Linda," Mom said. "Always do, don't I?"

Jackie topped off Mom's glass. "This oughta help."

"Cheers." Mom raised her drink to Jackie's, and with a clink of the crystal and a sip, Linda Morgan appeared in the doorway.

She was seventeen years older than Mom and Jackie and concealed it poorly with too much makeup and a strawberry blonde Clairol kit, but she always smelled good. Her Acqua Di Gio mingled with the honeysuckle incense that burned on the fireplace mantle, preceding her onto the patio as she took a seat next to Jackie.

She grabbed my hand and reeled me over. "You just seem to grow a foot every time I see you," she remarked, then said to Mom, "If she's not Jolán Edmunds all over again, then I'm not Linda Morgan."

Mom smiled and admired me, but I could see a glint of hesitation in her gaze, as if something about that statement made her a little uneasy. "Well, she's definitely got her father's sense of independence," she said, and I felt my stomach tighten.

My *father's* sense of independence? Who was it that so desperately needed her freedom, who just couldn't breathe anymore after fifteen years of all the creative autonomy a woman could ask for? By the time I was eleven, she was acting as if her wedding band was throttled around her throat, and now she accused Dad of being insensitive? She should have her head examined, and I opened my mouth to say so but knew infinitely better, made mute by all the battles I'd lost on that subject. She was armed with legions of explanations, excuses that she called reasons for the disintegration of life as we'd known it, and so I surrendered as not to be sacked all over again.

"She's got straight As this year," Mom added. "Not too shabby for her first year in high school. And she beat out a tenth grader for third chair in the orchestra last week, too. Just might have to find some rewards for all these accomplishments."

"Dad said I could have a piezo and a preamp for my violin, maybe for Christmas," I told them and gave my mother an unabashed stare because I knew how she'd hate that with every musical fiber, but it was one of the few weapons I had left in my arsenal.

"Really?" She cocked her head and smiled for the sake of Jackie and Linda, but beneath it was a layer of broiling magma that seemed to turn her eyes to an indignant emerald, and she took a sip from her glass, thinking before she spoke. "Well, he hasn't said anything to me about it. Didn't realize he took enough interest in music technology to suggest something like that."

"He didn't. I told him," I said. "I found some on the Internet, and they sell them at Maple Street Guitars."

"Oh, sweetie, you don't want to use those things." Linda waved the idea away with a jeweled hand. "Trust me. You think amplification and special effects will enhance the sound, but in reality you're just taking a step backward. After all, Vivaldi never needed that, Paganini, Tartini, they were all masters and made use of the natural acoustics. And you should do the same."

Mom glared at her. She had taken my mother's thoughts and put a voice to them, the wrong voice, because this wasn't Linda Morgan's crusade. Shattering my wishes was a duty reserved exclusively for Jolán Edmunds, and she had spent a good portion of my life sharpening that skill to razor perfection.

"You should've come to me as well," Mom said. "Asked me what I thought of it before cornering your father. You know he doesn't think like a musician. He'd say yes to glow-in-the-dark strings and a strobe light dangling from your music stand, too, if you asked for it, because he just doesn't know any better."

"Well, I didn't come to you because—"

She held up a hand to suspend the dispute until our company was gone. "Myla, we'll discuss it later. Please." And that was the end of that. Jolán Edmunds had spoken and the earth trembled.

I said nothing more and dropped into a Koozie chair, vanquished again.

"I don't see what's wrong with a little innovation, so long as it doesn't compromise the music itself," Jackie commented because she could get away with it. "It's part of progress, keeps music moving forward. Hell, you should know that better than anyone, Jolán, with as many risks as you take."

"Well, I don't know if you'd call improvising Bach a risk or risqué." Linda raised an admonishing eyebrow as she sipped her drink. The battle was beginning again. "Some things are just better left as they always were, I think."

My mother, already stirring with irritation, told her quite pointedly, "Bach *was* an improviser. So was Schubert, Brahms, Mozart. Would you like me to go on? It's at the core of what being a musician has always been about, so sue me if I've taken a few creative liberties on occasion."

Linda gave that a scolding grin and pointed a blood-red polished nail to the ceiling. "You forget your audience. Those pieces are the very foundation for what we do as classical artists, and the audience knows them as well as we do. As a listener, I want to be able to rely on convention. And as a musician, I respect it, and I don't deviate from it, just because . . . well . . . my own arrogance suggests that I should."

"Here we go." Jackie chuckled. "Welcome to round one of the ongoing improv deliberations, ladies and gentlemen." And she dinged her wine glass with a fingernail to simulate a boxing bell.

"Arrogance?" My mother laughed but her eyes were scorching, ripe with conflict, and so I kept silent and watched her dissect Linda Morgan with surgical efficiency.

I at once feared and admired her predatory bravado, so long as it wasn't directed at me.

"Arrogance is thinking that our understanding of the evolution of Western music hasn't been relentlessly skewed. Simply because composition has been the only thing to leave an indelible record in what we presume to be music history? Give me a break with that shit, Linda." She waved her off. "We only know what we know because specific renditions were written down, encased in glass, and canonized, with nothing to suggest there were any other versions performed except word of mouth. In the meantime, we've sucked all the life and vitality out of whatever historical conceptions there once were about improv, which, in my humble opinion, is beyond disrespectful. I think it borders on disgraceful, in fact. I think Mozart would do back flips in his grave if he knew his creativity had been boxed up and regurgitated to death, every night, performance after performance, by a hundred generations of symphonic drones who call themselves musicians."

"Be careful, young lady," Linda warned with a devilish grin. She loved the combat as much as my mother and tipped her glass in Mom's direction. "Some of us drones have been *vomiting* Beethoven and Mozart since before you could read your own name, much less the first two bars of *Moonlight Sonata*, so peddle your goods elsewhere, dear. I'll never budge on this issue, and you've known that for a decade. As concertmaster in particular, it is your job to represent those works as they're written, and for the most part, Jolán, you do. But, if a misplaced trill or a wayward grace note undermines the historical integrity of a particular piece, then you damn well know it, and so do I, and so does your audience." And she turned up a palm with a shrug.

Mom looked at Jackie. "So, should I just let her have this one? I'm really too tired to do this tonight."

"Yes," Jackie said decisively. "You two have been at a stalemate since before the turn of the century. Concede, for God's sake. One of you, *please*, call it a draw so we can all move on. Jeezus."

"You don't have to concede to me." Linda shrugged. "Concede to your own conscience, because in your heart of hearts you know I'm right."

Mom smiled. "In my heart of hearts I know you're as stubborn as I am, and nearly as opinionated. So, we'll let this one lie for a while. How's that?"

Linda waved her off and took a sip of Riesling. "Whatever makes you feel better."

"It makes *me* feel better," Jackie mumbled. "You two get on that subject, and it's like my friggin head's gonna burst."

THEY TALKED UNTIL well after midnight about everything except improv. I had long excused myself to the downstairs den where I'd opened my mother's laptop to browse the Internet. But as I scrolled through the search results, I noticed her latest journal entry minimized at the bottom tool bar. It was unintentional. An oversight. Her secret soul on display, not meant for my eyes. She had surely gotten distracted, her cell phone tucked into her shoulder while she searched her private teaching calendar, keyed in a new student, checked her watch, and realized she had a Pilates class in thirty minutes. Then she must've shut the laptop, trotted upstairs with her gym bag and car keys . . . and left all her thoughts behind, unlocked.

I googled Guitar Center, priced their preamps to give Dad some options, jotted down the figures. The arrow cursor slid across the bottom tool bar, and today's date glared in bold black on the Word tab beneath the page. Behringer XENYX, $69.95. A little out of Dad's intended range. Maybe the Boss AVA for $19.95. It wasn't as if I were going on tour with Moby, right?

October 31, Microsoft teased.

She would cross the room in two, maybe three purposeful strides and be at my back with daggers in her eyes and bullets on her tongue, an admonishment that my grandchildren would recount to their children around campfires in the dark. This wasn't ice cream flavors and Garanimal shopping at Sears, play dates and garden flowers. It was the quantum physics of her psyche, it was introspective turbulence, decaying particles, the uncertainty principles that quantified Jolán De Carlo Edmunds. And I was a layman, a curious trespasser at the open latch of a brand new box of secrets.

I slid the pointer over the forbidden tab. Laughter crept through the house from the patio. I checked over my shoulder to be certain she hadn't followed after it. The den was still, the doorway empty.

I tapped the mouse but couldn't bring my finger down with the necessary pressure to see it through. And then I did. And my mother's hidden world sprawled out before me, glowing white and Arial black.

chapter three

ON THE FIRST Saturday night in November, I had a front row seat at Symphony Hall to watch my mother perform Bartok's *2nd Violin Concerto* as a guest soloist for the Atlanta Symphony Orchestra. My father had business out of town in Charlotte, North Carolina, and so my chaperone for the evening was Rachel Cole.

She showed up at our house an hour before the show, stunning in a beige silk halter dress and a black cashmere wrap, her golden highlights pulled into a casual twist, like the first night we'd seen her, big shiny dishwater curls falling around the diamonds on her neck. No wonder my mother hesitated as she wandered into the living room from the kitchen, hurriedly slipping on an earring. She wore a black Ann Taylor pants suit with a simple white blouse, uncustomary attire according to some in her profession, but my mother railed against wearing a dress on stage, thought it chauvinistic and oppressive, an inequitable distraction from her talent.

"My goodness," she uttered, her eyes traveling over Rachel's image as if she had never seen beauty before. Then she snapped herself out of it with a quick smile, suddenly self-conscious for my having noticed how Rachel Cole left her breathless. "Well, we should get going."

She picked up her violin case, turned off her cell phone, and handed it to Rachel for keeping during the show, which had always been my father's function until the divorce. Then it had become mine.

I tried not to feel slighted by such an insignificant gesture, but just who did Rachel Cole think she was? How she walked through our front door, glistening like mythic royalty, with a face that could stop a clock and arrest my mother in mid stride. It wasn't so far beyond my thirteen years that I didn't know exactly what was going on.

I TOOK THE backseat in the Land Cruiser. Their hands touched while they spoke, my mother in the driver's seat, Rachel brushing a stray ringlet from my mother's face, doting after her like a devoted concubine, drawing the most tender smiles from beneath Mom's otherwise granite exterior, smiles that had gotten lost while she sank for months into her own introspective quicksand. Had she been so terrified at the thought of drowning that she reached for any hand that reached for hers? They weren't even trying to hide it. Didn't my presence count for something? Had they not considered what I thought of them, together, fingertips brushing, their eyes filled with private recollections, smirking like high school kids secretly proud of having set off the fire alarm during fifth period.

Mom's journal had been cryptic, much like Rachel's poetry only less metaphorical. The most I could infer was that a spell had been cast years ago and then abandoned, but not necessarily broken, because it had persevered for decades, lying dormant. And now, my mother looked at her in a way I'd never seen her look at anyone, as if Rachel Cole had whispered some splendid revelation into her ear that had awakened her from a coma.

WE PARTED COMPANY with Mom at Symphony Hall. She kissed my forehead and touched Rachel's arm with another one of those private smiles, then disappeared backstage.

"This will be the first time in many years that I've heard your mom play," Rachel told me as we found our seats. "In fact, she's only ever played the violin for me once or twice. And that had to be, gosh, about seventeen years ago, so I'm eager to hear what she's done since then."

"You don't look old enough to have known my mom for seventeen years," was all I could think to say.

Rachel laughed lightly. "Well, believe me, I am. But thank you," she said with an appreciative smile. "The idea is to be able to say that seventeen years from *now*. So, we'll see." And she gave me a wink.

"How did you meet?" It just tumbled out of my mouth. There were particulars about their story that hadn't been shared with me for a reason. It wasn't my business yet. But I was too captivated by the spell she had over my mother not to ask.

Rachel thought about it for a long moment, choosing her words carefully, censuring the truth for what might suffice under the circumstances. "Well, let's see. We met in Los Angeles, long time ago, over drinks with some mutual friends."

"How come you guys didn't keep in touch?" I heard myself ask again, unable to reel the words back in as they drifted out between us.

Rachel peered at me. She seemed to be contemplating whether to change the subject or toss out another ambiguous reply. "Sometimes life just takes people in different directions, you know?" she suggested, choosing the latter as not to summon my mother's wrath upon either of us. "And sometimes people's paths cross again when they least expect it." She shrugged, as if there was nothing more to tell, but I suspected there was enough story between them to fill the Atlanta public library.

The house lights dimmed and a familiar hush fell across the audience. The players filed out onto the stage and took their seats under standard applause. My mother crossed the stage with the conductor, and the applause rumbled the walls. This was only her second guest performance, but many were in attendance just to hear her play. She took a bow and placed herself at the front of the orchestra, put on her game face, serious and unwavering as the conductor directed the harps to set the beat. She put her instrument under her chin and for the next forty minutes was a woman possessed.

Rachel's expression was a curious combination of adoration and perplexity as she watched. I tried to imagine what was going through her mind, based on what I had seen over the past month and what I'd read in my mother's Halloween journal entry. Perhaps it wasn't she who'd cast the spell over my mother, but the other way around.

I had seen it happen so often with the men in her profession, the way their eyes followed her through a room, musing over what they'd say to her if given the chance, concocting schemes to place themselves in her line of sight, just for a wave and a grin, or better yet, to happenstantially wander into her personal space for conversation, like Gabe Neale.

I wondered if that had been Rachel's plight as well, so many years ago, a blossoming college girl with a drink in hand at a party somewhere, assembling the courage to invite the beautiful brunette into a dialogue about Puccini or Britten. Perhaps she'd dreamt of her, the way a man would dream, infatuation too precarious to confront during waking hours, no matter who you were.

When it was over, the audience rose for an ovation, and my mother took a final bow and left the stage. Rachel shook her head as she applauded and watched her pass, as if she had somehow underestimated her. What did she think, that Jolán Edmunds would disappoint her, or anyone, for that matter? My mother was a perfectionist about being a perfectionist, the head of her own cult of extremism who crushed the notion of mediocrity under the heel of her boot. Of course her performance was exceptional. She'd have it no other way.

MOM ASKED HER to come inside when we got back to Marietta. They stayed up late, talking in the den over gourmet coffee and cinnamon biscotti. Mom sent me to bed but I couldn't sleep for my own relentless curiosity, and I wondered what Dad would make of all this and if it even mattered anymore.

He never asked much about her, never tried to slip a question about her social life into our conversations, looking for a glimpse into her exclusive new world. He'd set her free per her request, and I imagine he was relieved, now that her needs weren't such a direct reflection upon him, so what was there to wonder, really? Change is perpetual and ruthless, considers no one as it reshapes everything into something unfamiliar. And all you can do is adapt and become someone else, just to stay the pain of having to let go of what was. We had all done it; me, Dad, my mother, even Uncle Cameron.

It was just after midnight when I heard footfalls on the hardwood stairs, then past my door and on down the hall, voices in my mother's bedroom. She was spending the night. Somehow it didn't surprise me the way I thought it would, and I stared at the shadows that stretched across the ceiling, trying to picture the two of them, forbidden images that piqued my senses and raised brand new questions about love and intimacy and female bonding. Was it love or was it base?

My mother had always been so calculating about her image, took risks only when she knew it would rattle the right cages and improve her own standing. This would have to be so closely guarded, as if she didn't have enough to bear, and I couldn't understand why she would attempt to shoulder this, too. Then I thought about Zorna's and the way she melted, if just for a moment, into Rachel Cole's embrace, and it all became clear.

My mother had loved her once. And for whatever it was worth, she was beginning to love her again.

SUNDAY MORNING FOUND her in good spirits. She was heating up the waffle iron for breakfast, stuffing the blender with bananas and strawberries and orange juice while Rachel set the table, freshly showered and smelling of lavender and shea butter, wearing my mother's Penn State t-shirt and a pair of her sweats.

"Hey, sweetie," Mom greeted as I strolled into the kitchen. "Hungry?"

I shrugged, still unsure of how I felt about Rachel in my mother's clothes. Mom had such a tranquil vibe, unusual even when Dad was here. Particularly when he was here. Mom approached me and smoothed my hair and kissed the top of my head. She hadn't done that since I was eight.

"You should eat breakfast," she told me. "You never do, and it's not healthy."

"I eat Pop-Tarts," I mumbled, watching Rachel pilfer through the fridge for the milk, as if she had always lived here.

"Where's your measuring cups, babe?" she asked my mother, and Mom took one down from the cabinet above the sink.

Babe? Was I supposed to just infer that they were dating now? No one had the courage, the decency, the audacity to just sit me down and say so? I wanted my mother to be happy because when she was happy, it made my life easier, and she had gone for so long, living in a prison of her own design. If Rachel Cole had the right words, the perfect face, the heart of a savior, and the persuasion to grant her reprieve, then so be it. But did it all have to be performed in front of me as if I were deaf, mute, and blind?

"I think I'm just gonna go practice," I told them both, and my mother looked vaguely wounded.

"Well, you can practice later. And Pop-Tarts aren't food. We've got eggs, bacon, and waffles, ready in just a few. We were thinking of going to the aquarium today. You've been wanting to go for months." She set a plate of bacon on the dining table and looked to me for a response.

It was nearly perfect payola, the aquarium. A green light on that piezo and preamp would have shut me up until adulthood, but I figured a day with the piranhas and killer whales might get us through the week, at least until my birthday. "I guess."

Mom raised a perfectly sculpted eyebrow and regarded me strangely. "You guess? After all that fuss about Beluga whales and giant spider crabs? I would've thought you'd be racing us out the door. What's with this 'I guess' stuff?"

"Nothing. It's cool," I told her. "Really, I wanna go."

And I did. But I was suspended in a weird kind of limbo, drifting between stilted resentment and curiosity. I certainly didn't want to be a third wheel on another *date*, but then Mom said Uncle Cameron would meet us there, and so I relented and grabbed a strip of bacon to go with the scrambled eggs that Rachel scooped onto my plate.

THEY TALKED ABOUT Rachel's restaurant bar while we ate. She and her best friend Corina found the place for sale online, and Rachel offered her a general management position and a provisional salary if she would agree to move with her from Boston to Atlanta and help run the place, and so Corina accepted. They dumped most of Rachel's windfall into authentic English-pub-style renovations that took close to a year to complete and called it The Canterbury Tavern, after the Chaucer tales.

Mom marveled over how she'd seen the place a dozen times in the past three years, had driven right past it on the way to rehearsals or to the dentist. She and some of the orchestra musicians had even planned to go there for drinks one evening, but then someone suggested a closer place, and they all agreed and went somewhere else instead.

"Everything in its own time," Rachel said to her and smiled.

My mother smiled back. "Guess so."

Rachel poked at the food on her plate, thinking. "I don't know what I'd have done if you had walked in there, out of the blue, after all that time." She laughed a little and tucked her hair behind her ear, like a blushing schoolgirl.

Again, I'd known my mother to have that effect on men. She made them stumble over chairs and over their own words and over themselves, but this was something new, this unspoken provocative impact on a woman. I could suppose there had been others, perhaps some orchestra flautist my mother's age with an absentee husband and a midlife crisis, pining quietly from the far side of the stage, or one of her high school violin students, coming to terms with her own identity, suffering through a secret crush under my mother's weekly instruction. Those were scenarios I could entertain and discard as unlikely, but now there was Rachel Cole, the flourishing entrepreneurial poetess, palpable and vivid, sampling bites from my mother's breakfast plate on this bright Sunday morning at our dining room table.

"You should give me your pants suits," Rachel suggested to Mom through a sip of her smoothie. "I'll take them to the cleaners when I go to the restaurant tomorrow. It's on the way."

Now they were making domestic arrangements. I drowned my dismay in a huge swallow of orange juice.

"That would help me out a lot, actually," Mom told her. "I've got students all day, and I'll need something to wear for Tuesday's show."

She smiled her thanks and held a gaze for just a moment longer than would a friend, sharing another one of those classified notions that drove me crazy, not knowing, knowing only that whatever it was, it made my mother feel contented and settled, comfortable in this precarious new skin. She gave Rachel a wink and went back to her waffles and bacon.

I finished my breakfast without a word, then excused myself to change for our trip into the city.

THE GEORGIA AQUARIUM looked like the bow of a great glass ocean liner as we approached the entrance. Uncle Cam stood waiting for us, tall and husky in his black Falcons jacket, smiling, his hands shoved into the pockets. People stood in line at the doors behind him, couples and small groups of friends and families with kids younger than me, a preschool boy on his father's shoulders with his fingers laced under the man's chin.

Dad had never done that with me, but Uncle Cam would often swoop me up from behind and straddle me over his head, and there I'd ride all day long on outings like this. He was thirty-six and divorced like Mom, no kids, a project manager for Rockwell Automation and the whole reason my mother moved here fifteen years ago. He said she needed a change of scenery, somewhere warm and uncharted, far from the Pennsylvania winters and my grandparents' meddling.

She had been born in Bensalem in 1971. And that's all I'd ever known of her life before me, but for the recent glimpse through the mysterious poet Rachel who hung an arm around my uncle's neck for a hug, as if they'd known each other since grade school. Uncle Cam hugged her waist and kissed my mother's cheek and turned to me.

"Where's your wet suit?" he asked, smirking through a closely trimmed goatee. "How're you gonna go swimming with the sharks in jeans and a sweater? You'll surely drown."

I rolled my eyes and smirked back. "I left my scuba gear back in the garage, with your sense of humor."

He grabbed his chest as if he'd been shot and stumbled backward. "Brutal comedy," he gasped. "What was I thinking, messing with the master?" He gave me a playful slap across the back of the head and I shoved him away, giggling.

I'd long outgrown a perch on his shoulders, and so this was how our relationship had evolved, into an ongoing affectionate battle of banter. He had otherwise become my sole confidante. When my father was too busy with work and while my mother was drifting off into herself, Uncle Cameron would sit with me out on our patio at family barbecues and talk to me as if I mattered, like a colleague, or a neighbor sharing a beer. He'd take swigs from a dripping bottle of Michelob and I'd drink root beer from stout brown bottles made to look like the same thing, and he'd tell me to just ride my mother's wave, let her find her way back to us in her own time and that she loved me more than I would ever know, even if most days I felt like a ghost.

The aquarium floors were gleaming, cream colored and polished to a liquid gloss, purple neon backlights hummed over the exhibit entries and reflected off the tiles. An attendant in black khakis and a polo shirt greeted us with brochures and directions to the rest rooms and gift shops, speaking around a headset mic wired to his belt.

Uncle Cam took three booklets, gave one to me, kept one for himself, and gave the other to my mother and Rachel with the presumption that they would share, the way they had begun to share everything lately. He seemed to know subtle things that I didn't, made privy to their relationship by virtue of being another adult, I supposed.

Mom looked back at me and smiled and opened an arm to hang across my shoulders as we walked, Rachel at her left with the brochure folded out so Mom could see. Everything glowed electric blue, neon green, giant white mushroom tops anchored askew to the ceilings, the smell of seawater and Buffalo wings.

The place was chilly. Mom had assumed so before we left and wrangled into a navy blue hoodie from the living room closet and gave Rachel her WindWall jacket. They were virtually the same size, Mom just a bit taller with a sleeker figure where Rachel had shapelier curves at the hips and breast, but they apparently wore the same shoe size. Mom in the hiking sneakers she'd worn to Zorna's and Rachel in my mother's Trail Runners, still wearing her sweatpants. I thought it safe to suppose last night had been unexpected, an impulsive segue into a Sunday afternoon tour of the manta ray tanks and river otter habitats.

We spent the day wandering through rock-faced entryways and into dark grottos, where sturgeon fish and golden trevallies weaved around bright green sea grass and up under spiny coral limbs. We watched giant, orange jellyfish wave their spaghetti tendrils, heads like parachutes flapping against the brine as they ascended up and up, where the white water plain rippled overhead.

One of the displays had a little orange Nemo clownfish darting through the reefs with a companion blue tang Dory swimming opposite, the two of them making figure eights around the plants. A school of piranhas hovered at the neighboring window, beneath a painted driftwood warning sign. *Flesh-eating, razor-sharp teeth.* They didn't swim like the rest of the fish. They just lingered at the glass, watching us watch them, so still it was eerie, orange-silver wedges suspended in clear jello. Had there not been a foot of tempered starphire laminate between us, they'd have devoured us to the bone and made us chum for the hammerheads.

Uncle Cam tugged at my sleeve and pointed up into the blue distance of the next tank.

"Check that out," he whispered. "Wouldn't wanna come across him down at the Gulf, not without a really big harpoon."

It was a whale shark, and all the other wanting little species dispersed and made way, like dandelion seeds scattered on a breeze. It moved its brown spotted bulk through the water right toward us, then past the glass with a quick turn back the way it had come, a fake charge, then it banked left and glided up along the transom and across the windowed ceiling.

Uncle Cam laughed a little. "What a monster. So, who do you think weighs more, me or him?"

"You," I told him distractedly, watching the thing push off through schools of batfish and potato groupers until it vanished. Cam thumped me on the back of the neck for that one, but he'd left himself wide open. I swatted him back, and we moved along.

Mom and Rachel had walked away to watch the sea horses hovering among feathery plumes of yellow seaweed. They stood close. Sometimes Rachel would hook an arm around my mother's as they browsed the tanks, at ease in each other's company under the hazy blue ocean shimmer, their silhouettes like ink against the red coral reef, unobserved by everyone but me. Mom said something in Rachel's ear that made her grin, and she leaned in close against my mother's shoulder and gazed up into the marine as we moved on to the Ocean Voyager display.

They stole a kiss in the underwater tunnel. Nobody noticed for the giant stingrays that floated over our heads, the black-tip reef sharks and swordfish making criss-cross passes around the exhibit. In the next room, I stopped in front of a penguin enclosure. There were several glass observation pylons built into its floors, just enough for little kids to climb underneath and poke their heads up through, like a Whack-A-Mole game, and they laughed and watched the animals waddling by.

I thought it a strange habitat for penguins, creatures so far out of their element without a single patch of ice or snow on the dusty brown rocks of a manufactured environment, more like the New Mexican desert than the Antarctic Tundra. I looked around for Mom, and she saw me there and wandered over while Rachel and Cam peered in at them on the other side of the room.

She ran a hand over my hair and stood with me at the big bay window. "So, what do you think? Pretty cool, this place. Let me know when you're ready to eat, and we'll get a burger or something."

I nodded. "'Kay."

I glanced at Rachel and Uncle Cam and back to Mom with a counterfeit smile, as though nothing were out of the ordinary, but she knew me too well to pretend I hadn't seen them, in the tunnel, by the red coral reef where the sea horses bobbed and nodded, last night in the Land Cruiser. She gazed into the enclosure, thinking, with that tight-lipped pensive smile she wore when something made her uneasy, her laugh lines like little parentheses around her mouth, the only feature that confessed to her thirty-nine years. She looked back down at me, but I didn't know what she wanted me to say or do, and so I said nothing, stuffed my hands into my coat pockets.

A penguin hobbled to the edge of the sandy rocks and spread its wings and dove into the water. The people watching them with us walked away, and so it was just Mom and me, our reflections like shiny apparitions in the glass.

"She's a good girl," Mom finally said of Rachel, as if looking for my blessing. "Has the heart of a saint. Always did."

I nodded, with that same pensive half smile of hers, my mother's daughter. We couldn't have a real conversation here, not about that, and so I shrugged and told her, "She seems real nice," knowing it was lame, a conditioned response just to forestall the inevitable.

"She wants to get to know you," Mom offered. "She's interested in your music, your hobbies, wants to hear you play someday."

I shrugged a shoulder. "Why?" It wasn't me she dressed up in silk and diamonds for. I had no spells to cast, no mysterious months of moon to string us together like beads on a hemp cord, it wasn't my magic she was after.

Mom made a little sound beneath her breath, something like laughter but not quite. "Well, why not?" she said with a hint of absurdity. "Because you're my kid, that's why." She looked at me, her eyes glistening, even in the muted half light, made greener by the sea shine from the tanks at our backs. "You're a part of me, and that makes you important to her."

"Yeah, well, I'm a part of Dad, too. So, whatever." I probably shouldn't have said that, but it climbed out from under my better thoughts and leapt from my lips out into the chilly exhibit air before I could swallow it.

She wrapped her hands up in her sweatshirt pouch and peered at the Mojave penguins, followed one with her eyes as it sped past the window through the murky water. She wasn't smiling anymore, not even a little, and I waited to be scorned, to be reminded of my place with a quiet forewarning of the boundaries of her patience.

But she surprised me with civility instead. "You're better off," she said, still looking into the glass.

Perhaps my upcoming fourteenth birthday had brought me across some threshold with her, to a place where mothers and their adolescent daughters found themselves kindred between otherwise distant, parallel worlds.

"I just need you to trust me when I tell you that." She kept her hands buried in her sweatshirt and turned her head just enough to look at me. "Nobody'll ever love you more than your dad and me, but we can only do that best by living separate lives." She gazed back at the penguins and breathed a long and heavy sigh. "I know that sounds like the biggest crock of shit. But it's the closest I can bring you to the truth right now. And it's a difficult truth, one you have every right to know, but you're just gonna have to be patient and bear with me while I figure the rest of this out, and then I promise, I *promise* you I'll tell you everything."

She looked down at me, with a sincerity she'd never offered before, like a timer had gone off somewhere to mark the end of my childhood, and I was standing suddenly at the outset of maturity, another one of the De Carlo women in bloom, and so I decided maybe I should rise to that challenge.

"All right," I conceded, and she smiled and placed her hand on my shoulder with a reassuring squeeze.

She needed my trust and patience. I'd never felt so involved in her process, so vital to her psychological wellness, and I wondered how long I would have to wait and what I would have to do, what kinds of bridges I would have to build and cross for her to tell me everything. And what exactly was *everything*?

Uncle Cam came over to join us, and Rachel followed. She came around next to Mom with a little smile and rubbed an affectionate hand across her back, the way Dad used to do, and she asked if we were ready to go eat. We decided on pizza and chicken fingers at the food court and made our way back to the lobby with the cream-colored floors and purple neon.

Mom was still thinking about our conversation. I could see it on her face and in the way she walked, the contemplative stroll of a woman preoccupied, here but not here, and Rachel could sense it, too. They were just a few paces ahead of us, but I could read her lips, asking my mother for her thoughts with a whimsical bump of the hip, looking to bring her back to brighter spirits.

Mom gave her a heartening smile and told her it was nothing, but I suspected it would take the remainder of the day to revive her, because that was just her way, slow to digest the heavy stuff.

"You guys okay?" Uncle Cam finally got involved while in line at the concession stand. He tipped his chin toward Mom as she grabbed a handful of napkins from the condiment station. "You need me to rough 'er up a little? Toss 'er in with the Beluga whales? I got a roll of duct tape in my truck. Might be handy."

I grinned and shook my head. "It's cool. We're fine. We just . . . I dunno . . . started talking about her and Dad, and it got kinda deep. But we're good."

"Ah." He nodded and stared out at the people in the dining room, a familiar subject we'd talked to death over a hundred Michelobs and A&W's.

It took the next three orders in line before I mustered the gall to ask him what he knew about Rachel, where she came from, how he knew her, why Mom had been on her knees with adoration since she'd showed up. He was my liaison, the only common thread between all my insistent curiosity and the elusive truth, and I knew now that I didn't have the patience I'd promised my mother. I should have just let it lie, should have waited for her on my side of The River Trouble and built my own bridge to cross, with solid sturdy bricks of trust so she could meet me halfway when she was ready, like she'd asked, but I needed to know something, anything, everything.

Cam didn't say much for several moments. He took so long to assemble an answer that it was our turn at the counter, and we had to place our orders first, pepperoni for me, and the works for him. Then he gave me the pensive family smile, his mustache stretching over thin lips pressed tight with indecision, brown eyes searching for an appropriate way to phrase his thoughts. Had there been so much confidentiality that even he had been sequestered?

Finally, he threw a glance across the food court to where my mother and Rachel sat saving seats for us. "Your mom's seen some difficult days. And Rachel was there for a lot of it."

"Before I was born?"

"Yep. Long before that."

He took his pizza and handed me my own, and we walked to the condiment station for straws. "It wasn't all bad. Some were good days, *damned* good days, and she was around for those, too. And so was I."

He looked at them again but hesitated, as if stricken by some distant profundity, and so I waited to see what that was. Then he looked at me and said, "Rachel was the best thing that ever happened to your mother. Hands down. In fact," he stabbed a straw through his drink top, "you *could* say she's half the reason you were ever born." He nodded once to punctuate that and smiled at me, then headed over to the table to join them.

I stood watching as he walked away. I couldn't move, stunted there at the straws and napkins and ketchup dispensers. Half the reason I existed? It seemed fantastical, too impossible to make any sense. She had come from nowhere, landed on our lives like space junk, and now she was some divine medium from my mother's mysterious troubled past?

What miracle could she have possibly performed that would've altered the entire landscape of my mother's life? Was that the source of the spell? The questions made me dizzy, and I would have stood there pondering them all afternoon, but the paper pizza box grew suddenly hot in my hand, and that snapped me clear.

I slipped the wrapper from my straw and punched it through the drink lid, spinning. I understood this to be classified knowledge, a minor security breach, a secret only Cam and I could share, and so I collected myself and sat down at the table where I discreetly studied her, like a secret agent mining for data.

Rachel Cole was intriguing to me now. I could no longer dismiss her as a side effect of my mother's bewildering midlife crisis. She had dimension and purpose, a deep dark well filled with story and lore, a link in a very delicate chain that secured me to my mother like a charm around her neck.

I was careful not to gawk while I ate and watched her peripherally, pretending not to listen while the three of them sat talking, telling vacation stories that made Rachel toss her head back and laugh out loud, and I began to realize just how infectious she was, like sunshine in a neighborhood park. She wasn't as complicated as my mother, spoke with a bright and measured cadence, selecting her words the way my mother gleaned the notes of a Paganini solo, a poetic purist who talked with her hands where Mom spoke most effectively with her eyes.

In paying such covert attention, their attraction became clear and natural as rainwater, when I filtered out all my mother's temperamental angst, of course, the moody runoff that had collected from the eaves over the years. Rachel Cole was an open sky, spacious and undemanding, and my mother was stellar constellations in flux. No wonder time and distance couldn't keep them apart. In what other sky would the stars exist?

I began to think of myself, then, as a kind of predetermined accident, an inevitable product of my father's misfortune because I believed he had loved my mother, loved her to pieces, he would always say. Now I realized she had come to him that way, fragmented, torn away from something fixed, something much larger than he. My father was merely a ploy within some romantic paradox, necessary only to complete my mother's picture. Now that picture was complete, and he wasn't in it.

I glanced at Rachel through a bite of pizza, and then at Mom who gazed at her like a sunset and listened to her speak as if sonatas were drifting from her lips. And that was when I knew. She never loved him, not the way she may have wanted and certainly not the way he needed her to; she couldn't. She was only a reflection, for fifteen years, stars he watched gleaming off a lake, shining down from someone else's sky.

AFTER LUNCH WE sat in a dark auditorium and watched dolphins doing back flips and somersaults under royal blue stage lights, set against a huge back screen with accompanying graphics—ocean waves, rainbow pastels, a black star-cluttered sky that turned on an axis. A trainer came out under a bright spotlight, dressed like Errol Flynn in *Captain Blood*, and he sang cheesy Broadway-style tunes for the dolphins to swim to while the other trainers straddled their backs and rode them like jet skis.

Mom and Rachel held hands for most of the show, stole another kiss during the finale, and when it was over Uncle Cam took pictures with one of the dolphins perched between us at the edge of the wading pool.

MOM WRAPPED AN arm around my shoulder as we walked to the car. "We don't do these kinds of things often enough, and we should. I'll make more time from now on. How's that?"

"Mm-kay."

She was quiet for a while. "And I meant what I said in there. About having that talk. We'll sit down and have a heart-to-heart, just you and me. Or if you want Rachel there, then that's fine, too. There are things you need to know, things I've had every intention to tell you when you were old enough, but I just need to get my head around some of it before we do, that's all."

We had come to the Land Cruiser and the alarm chirped as she dug out her keys. I climbed into the backseat and she stood there at the door, waiting for an answer, so I gave her an easy smile.

"I do have some questions. But for the most part," I said, "I pretty much think I get it."

She looked at me as if she wasn't quite sure what I meant by that, but I didn't say anything further. I just gave her another smile and shut the door.

chapter four

MY GRANDPARENTS FLEW down from Bensalem for my birthday. I could've had a party with friends from school, invited the neighborhood kids to play laser tag or watch horror movies in the den all night. Mom and Rachel suggested everything from Hawaiian themes with tiki torches and virgin piña coladas to a traditional party with a cake, ice cream, and a scavenger hunt for Dollar Store prizes. But when Nanna and Pap called and said they would be here for the entire weekend, with Rachel having practically moved in since our day at the aquarium, I thought it might be best if I kept my friends out of it.

So, I asked instead for a family day with crab legs and grilled shrimp skewers, fettuccine Alfredo, and cheese broccoli. Rachel recommended a crab recipe straight from The Canterbury menu, baked in a garlic butter marinade rather than steamed, and so I gave it a shot and watched as she prepared it in the kitchen, wondering what would be my grandparents' reaction to her steadfast new presence in my mother's life.

Mom had no intention to hide her from them, worked her right into the weekend plans as if it were perfectly natural and said Nanna and Pap would just have to adjust, and if they couldn't, they could hop a red-eye back to Pennsylvania and stay there until the Second Coming. I couldn't decide whether I thought that was incredibly courageous or batshit foolish, the kind of foolish that inspires a man to walk a tightrope between skyscrapers without a net.

My grandfather, Dr. Douglas De Carlo, was a retired economics professor from the University of Pennsylvania, and Nanna Sylvia had worked in customer service at PECO for as long as I could remember, but she still moonlighted as a ballroom salsa instructor two nights a week. They'd given us Christmases in the Pennsylvania Poconos and Fourth of July fireworks at Penn's Landing, summer weekends at the Jersey Shore, the Amish countryside where we bought sarsaparilla and hand-dipped candles, Paleozoic fossils from Crystal Cave, New York City, and they never uttered a critical word to Mom until the divorce. Then it seemed a door slammed shut with a sign on the knob that read: *here we go again*, or *same shit different decade*.

I never understood why the divorce had taken them to such a disparaging place except that they regarded Dad like a savior, a redeemer of all my mother's imperfections who had somehow lifted her up to a standard they had set for her long ago. Now she'd cast him back to the world, and so my grandparents sat waiting for some great and tragic fall. They had been waiting for more than a year, yet she had remained on her feet, upright and steady as a mast.

THEY SHOWED UP toting Samsonite wheel bags from a rental car parked behind Rachel's Volvo in the driveway. I could see them from the kitchen, through the dining room window, and Mom and Uncle Cam greeted them at the door with hugs and chatter about the flight. I glanced at Rachel who would have made a very convincing show of composure if her expression hadn't gone suddenly inert, the way it had when Linda Morgan presented her to my mother at Giovanni's.

She must have seen me staring. She flashed a quick smile and pressed five cloves of garlic into slivers with the flat of a butcher knife and scooped them up onto the blade and slid them into a sauté pan. "Keep your heat low. Then add your lime juice and sea salt." She sliced open a fresh lime and squeezed it into the pan.

She went to the refrigerator and took out a small bushel of parsley and brought it to the cutting board, then went to chopping it to a grade finer than beach sand. She was fast. Like a sous-chef from a Food Channel show, and I thought she'd surely nip off a fingertip.

She smiled. "Time passes a lot more quickly in a restaurant kitchen. You gotta get stuff like this done as if your life depended on it sometimes."

Then she showed me the secret to keeping your fingers attached, with the knuckles flat to the blade, fingertips curled underneath.

"Not everyone follows that rule, I'm afraid." She swiped the parsley up with the knife and dumped it into the pan with everything else. "Had an accident or three because of it, which can throw a bit of a wrench into a Saturday night dinner rush."

"Anyone ever cut off their whole finger?" I asked, and she laughed lightly, uneasily.

"No, not yet." She knocked three times on the cutting board, then took it to the sink. "I've got a pretty conscientious kitchen manager, so we try to avoid anything too dramatic. But sometimes things happen."

"What's the worst you've ever seen?"

She hesitated, unsure whether to indulge me with gruesome kitchen tales while preparing my birthday meal, but I didn't care. I was fascinated and I wanted to know. She swirled the garlic mixture in the pan, flipped it twice, set it back on the burner and adjusted the flame.

"We make brick oven pizzas." She looked at me with a tentative grin, her brown eyes cautious and indecisive, and she glanced into the house for Mom who was busy getting my grandparents settled in the downstairs den. "It's not an oven like this one—it's a wood-burning flame oven, so it gets hotter than hell in a heat wave." She took out a large Pyrex baking pan from under the counter and set it by the stove. "I don't know exactly how it happened. I was in my office at the time, doing paperwork or something, and the next thing I know I've got servers at my door, freaking out, panicking, because apparently my pie guy had overturned an entire veggie pizza, straight out of the oven on the paddle, and right onto his bare forearm."

"Whoa."

"Yeah. Whoa is right." Rachel went back to the fridge for the crab legs and unwrapped the paper and placed them in the Pyrex pan. "Needless to say, he was rushed to the ER by another cook and wasn't able to work for several weeks after. Needed skin grafts, crates and crates of pain meds, poor kid. Had to change the uniform shirts for that station after that, of course, something long sleeved, but it's hot back there, and they roll them up, anyway, no matter how much I bitch about it. So, what are you gonna do?"

"That's grisly."

"Yeah. And that's all the grisly you're gonna get for your birthday, before your mom has me flogged."

"So, if you're the owner," I asked, "then why do you do so much work? Isn't that what you hire other people to do? You'd think you could just sit back and chill, just eat and hang out. That's what I'd do."

She laughed and poured the simmering marinade over the legs in the oven pan. "Well, I suppose if I were just an investor, maybe that'd be my thing. But I'm a working owner. That was the arrangement from the beginning, and I enjoy it, really."

"Can you make everything on the menu?"

"Yep. Sure can. Bartend, too, if we get in a pinch, if we're real busy or shorthanded."

"Is it hard?"

"Not once you get the hang of it. Why? You looking for a job?"

I watched her slide the pan into the oven and set the timer for twenty-five minutes. "Nah, just curious."

"I can put you to work, now," she insisted, smiling. "Stick you in the prep kitchen with Miss Gloria, filling béchamel cups, portioning feta cheese for salads. You'd have a blast." She gave me another teasing grin and a little wink. "Couldn't put you on the payroll for another two years, of course, but hey, you can hold out till then, right?"

She was so pretty it was hard not to look at her without smiling, and I could only hope to have that effect on people by the time I got through high school, much less at forty years old. There were only certain subtleties that gave her away, the same little things my mother had acquired, the faint smile lines at the corners of her eyes, her hands, more slender and vascular than mine, declarations to years of earning paychecks that I wouldn't even begin to collect until college. The rest was girl-next-door beauty, sun and open sky, warm, clean, and effortless.

Music drifted from the living room. Uncle Cam had put on my mother's Santana CD, the old one with the live versions of "Black Magic Woman" and "Se a Cabo." He came into the kitchen and gave Rachel a look and rolled his eyes back out into the house, which I presumed had something to do with my grandparents.

"They haven't seen me yet. Do they even know I'm here?" Rachel poured fettuccine noodles into a pot to boil and took the garlic marinade pan to the sink and washed it.

"I think Jolán mentioned it downstairs," he said. "But they haven't put it together yet, no."

Put what together? That she was my mother's not-so-new girlfriend, a resurgence from her youth, come to fill a void that my father never could? It took me all of about twenty-four hours to nail that one, and I was beginning to embrace the idea well enough. But I was a child of the twenty-first century. I wasn't seventy years old with stories of The Great Depression at the tip of my tongue, a devout Catholic who had the same seat at St. Rita's Saturday evening mass for the past thirty years.

Pap was second generation Italian whose grandparents came through Ellis Island, and Nanna had childhood memories of Fidel Castro's revolution in Cuba before they fled to Miami and then on to Philadelphia when she was fourteen. Old world, old country, old-fashioned.

Rachel glanced at me, then said to Cam, "Well, as long as they assume I'm someone recent, then maybe it won't . . . you know . . ." She trailed off into that secret bubble where only she, Cam, and my mother lived, the one made of ballistic nylon, the one I couldn't penetrate with a bunker buster and a S.W.A.T. team.

Uncle Cam went to the fridge and grabbed a beer. He twisted off the cap and tossed it like a basketball free throw into the trash can. "Jo's not taking the highest road where they're concerned. So, I might brace myself if I were you."

"What does that mean?" she asked.

Cam didn't answer that. Instead he said to me, "Hey, kiddo, do me a favor." He gestured into the living room with the beer bottle. "Go load the CD changer with some other stuff. Hell, it's your birthday. Drive us crazy with whatever you want." It would have been an awesome suggestion if it hadn't really been a ploy to get me out of earshot, so he and Rachel could elaborate in private, but I didn't argue.

I made myself scarce and went to the CD rack by the entertainment center, but all my music was on my iPod. I'd have to go upstairs for that, and I wanted to eavesdrop, so I chose things from Mom's collection instead, and I watched them where they stood framed in the kitchen pass through, training my ear on their dialogue, but it was muddled by Santana's guitar solo.

Cam said something that made Rachel prop a hand on her hip and shake her head. She answered with something like, " . . . and she thinks that's going to help the situation how?" And Cam replied with words like "reckless bravado" and "shock value."

I didn't know most of the artists on the rack. I slid one out that had a guy in a Bolero hat, posing with an electric guitar; I liked his hat, so I set him to the side. Then another with a black-and-white burning blimp—she had a few of those, so I picked the one with all the colors, where the blimp wasn't on fire and plummeting to the ground. *Celebration Day*, it read. Sounded suitable enough, and I set that aside as well. There was Itzak Perlman, whom I had no choice but to know. Hilary Hahn and a collection of Bach concertos. The Kronos Quartet. The soundtrack to *Schindler's List*. More Santana.

"My parents know how to push her buttons," I heard Cam say clearly between tracks.

"El Nicoya" pattled through the speakers and drowned them out again. It was just like the music Nanna Sylvia listened to around their house in Bensalem, lots of syncopated percussion and acoustic guitars, the words all in Spanish, and it made me wish our family hadn't crossed into this alien region, that we could go back to the family I recognized, when Nanna played Cuban salsa in her kitchen with the table pushed aside so she could teach me the steps. She called it Casino and said it dated all the way back to the seventeenth century, that Cuban history was born of music and dance. Music was in our blood like platelets, and so it was no wonder my mother couldn't breathe without it playing somewhere nearby, or playing it herself. Me neither, for that matter.

"Jeezus, it was seventeen years ago," I heard Rachel say, and she frowned, perturbed. She was pouring milk into the sauté pan and adding some kind of cheese. "She's done her time, they can't give her a fucking break?"

"To my dad, seventeen years is seventeen minutes." Cam took a swig of beer and wiped his mouth with the same forearm.

Then my grandparents appeared from the den with Mom, and Pap opened his arms wide to me.

"Look at this," he said through a huge embrace.

I hadn't seen them in a year. He stood me out in front of him, his hands on my shoulders. He was tall and broad chested like Uncle Cam with a full head of silver wiry hair and sad brown eyes made larger by thick prescription lenses.

"She's almost as tall as you," he said to Mom, and she smiled. "Fourteen, eh? Sure those numbers aren't backwards, as grown up as you look?"

"Slow down, Dad," Mom said. "You make her forty-one, and that'll make me sixty-four."

"And your mother and I buried in matching plots, that's true," he confessed. "Okay, so fourteen it is. You driving yet? Ya got a job?"

I shook my head. "Mom lets me start the Land Cruiser sometimes but that's it."

Then it was Nanna's turn, and she took my face in her willowy hands and kissed my forehead. "Don't you pay him any attention. Your paps is pulling your leg. Happy, happy birthday, *mija.*"

My mother had inherited most of her features from Nanna Sylvia, and by proxy, so had I, her hazel eyes a shade browner than ours, the soft ringlets gone salt and pepper, her figure still lean and kept, slighter than Mom's but reminiscent of a once fit and sturdy younger woman. She could still kick and twirl around a dance floor, though, to all the merengue and Rueda classics, wearing four-inch heels and her black, single-shoulder ballroom dress with the red ruffled seam. She made me think of Rita Moreno in *West Side Story*, and I loved the way she smelled, like gardenias and sandalwood.

"So, what's cooking?" Pap rubbed his big hands together, searching for the source of the sweet, warm butter and garlic that had begun to seep from the kitchen.

Cam had gone out to the deck to light the grill for the shrimp skewers, and so Mom took Nanna and Pap in to meet Rachel. I followed, kept my mouth shut, and watched the introduction from the doorway. Heavy blues played from the stereo now, slow and driving with a deep droning bass line and a shuffle beat. A man sang a raspy chorus about his girlfriend walking out on him.

Rachel wiped her hands on a dish towel and smiled at my grandparents, shook their hands, and followed my mother's lead.

"Are you a musician as well? Someone from the orchestra?" Nanna asked.

"Oh, no, ma'am." She chuckled foolishly. "They're doing very well without my help, believe me."

"Rachel's a poet," Mom told them. "Has a collection published with a house out of Florida."

"Well, now that's not something you run across every day," Nanna remarked, intrigued.

But Pap said, "Poetry, eh? How's the market for that sorta thing? It was huge in the seventies, I remember, with the war and women's lib and whatnot. They still have a niche for that, these days?"

Rachel gave that a half nod. "It has its place. You'd be surprised, actually. I do it now, mostly for passion's sake, do a reading here and there, a few signings when I can."

"She owns a restaurant in Buckhead as well," Mom added.

That seemed to pique my grandfather's interest a bit more than the blissful musings of a solitary dreamer, scratched down for the benefit of the wind. Now she had practical value, and I think that was my mother's intent.

"It's a pretty nice place, the best Pittsburgh steaks outside of Pittsburgh." Mom gave Rachel a flirtatious little smirk, and I cringed inside because there it was—the prolonged and tender gaze that broadcasted the nature of their friendship like a lighted billboard. Pap didn't catch it, but Nanna did, and she smiled uneasily to herself and looked off in thought, pondering the very same notions that blindsided me three months ago.

The doorbell rang. It was Jackie and she let herself in, carrying a covered sheet cake as she announced herself through the house.

"Sorry I'm late," she called to whoever was listening. "Kroger's was packed, and the bakery had a wait. Popular day for birthdays, I guess."

She came into the dining room and set the cake on the table, and her smile beamed for my grandparents whom she hadn't seen in a year, either.

"Oh my goodness, there they are." She hugged Nanna's neck and kissed Pap's cheek. "You guys look great," she said as she shed her coat. "Retirement's been treating you like royalty, I see." She came over to me and cupped a hand around my head and pulled me to her with a kiss to the temple. "Happy birthday, sweetie." And she handed me a card.

I opened it. Huge music notes in electric green and orange and purple, cartoon '60s flowers and birthday wishes in fat round font. Inside were two twenties and a ten.

"I'd tell you to save that for college, but why be a downer? Spend it how you want, kid," she said.

I looked at Mom for consent, and she smiled with a permissive shrug. "You only turn fourteen once."

I took the bills between my fingers, fresh and crisp and brand new. I knew exactly what I wanted. Dad had taken me to Maple Street Guitars last night to price them for Christmas, but now I wouldn't have to wait that long. He was coming back after work tonight to see Nanna and Pap and to take me to the movies, but maybe I could persuade him to make one last stop before the stores closed.

I thanked Jackie and took the card with the money in it upstairs to my room and stashed it in the nightstand drawer, waiting to be traded for a thirty-dollar Boss AVA preamp. Mom was going to come right out of her skin, but this was my money, not hers, and not Dad's. You only turn fourteen once.

WE ATE OUT on the screened patio, the Georgia weather indifferent to the winter calendar, just twenty days from Christmas and balmy as early spring. Nanna said it rivaled December in San Cristóbal, where she and her sisters spent Christmas Eves tossing firecrackers off their apartment balcony in shorts and flip-flops, the wind across the Caribbean warm and smooth as rum-buttered cider, swishing the tall palms.

After her family moved to the States, she met Pap in 1967 in Philly, at a bakery off Broad Street during the Mummers Parade on New Year's Day. He'd seen her first and followed her for three blocks, threading through crowds and down the alleys all the way to Trimini Pastries, just to introduce himself.

They were married in 1968 and gave birth to my mother on June twelfth, 1971, then Uncle Cam in '74. They'd made their marriage work for forty-six years, never considered separation or divorce, and though Cam had betrayed those ideals eight years ago, they had expected a bit more from Mom.

Pap took a leg from the stack on his plate, snapped it partway, right in the center just so, then the other way, just enough to keep the meat from tearing, and he unsheathed a thick white finger of crab, perfectly intact, and showed it to me with a satisfied smile. He and Mom were the only ones who could do it. The rest of us trawled up into the broken claws with our little seafood forks, making mounds of shredded meat that would get cold before we could clear every shell.

"It might've been nice if Ben could've joined us," Pap said to Mom. "I know you got the house, but I don't think he'd be trespassing on his daughter's birthday, do you?"

"He *relinquished* the house," Mom said lowly. "For school district reasons. And he'll be here later." She glanced at him and tried to smile. "He's taking Myla to a movie. Hardly trespassing. Please don't start, Dad."

Nanna asked what we were going to see, trying to avert the argument that was simmering beneath the small talk, and I told her I hadn't made up my mind yet. I should have thrown any film out for discussion, even if it was R-rated, with sex and gore and assault weapons unloading in strip clubs. Car chases over sidewalks with mothers pushing strollers would have been better conversation than what was brewing between Mom and Pap, and we could all feel it, churning the atmosphere like tornado weather.

"Well, that's big of you," Pap muttered to Mom as he stabbed a forkful of fettuccine. "To open your home so graciously to the father of your child. I don't suppose you've thought about reconciliation, then."

"Come on, Dad." Uncle Cam gave him a look.

"Douglas." Nanna eyed him over the brim of her soda glass, too, and he looked at them both with a blameless shrug.

"What?" he insisted, as if he'd mentioned nothing more than last week's hockey scores. "It's a viable question. It's been more than a year, plenty of time to work things out."

"There's nothing to work out, Dad," Mom told him quietly.

She didn't look up from her plate but I could see her eyes were electric again, gleaming the way they did when Linda Morgan baited her into fights about improv.

She gestured to me with her fork and said to him, "I'm not doing this with you today."

"Doing this," he muttered. "Doing what? She's been through the worst of it already. What's a little conversation about patching things up gonna hurt?"

"It's a nonissue. A done deal. Has been for sixteen months," she snapped, her voice ticked up a notch, and she looked at him straight. "And the sooner we all get in step, the better. Really."

"I'm not so sure a broken home is a nonissue." Pap tossed a shrimp into his mouth and wiped his hands on his napkin. "Sometimes you have to make concessions, compromise. I think Benjamin was more than willing, but you?" And he threw up a hand, shook his head, and went back to his meal. "You, I dunno. Seems like you *wanted* single parenthood, chased after it like some kinda prize. It's not that easy, you know. You can't take the easy way out all the time. I know it's in your nature, always has been, but one day it's gonna catch up to you again, and we can't be there to bail you out, we're too old. And so are *you.*"

Mom just sat there, chewing, glaring, thinking. She was so silent it seemed Pap had called down some inadvertent hex to turn her to stone, right there in her seat, and I thought he didn't know his own daughter very well because Mom never took the easy route. She was more complicated than chaos math, worked very hard for most of my life to design herself according to the standards of her field and, I thought, to the expectations of my grandparents. But he was speaking to her as if she was the only one at the table who hadn't matured past adolescence.

"Dad," Cam said. "Do you really think this is necessary today? You guys haven't been here two hours and already, this crap. Come on. Let's just drop it, okay?"

"He's right, Doug," Nanna said, and she touched his arm. "There's a better time for that. Let's just eat and enjoy ourselves."

I sneaked a glance at Rachel, and she was focused on her plate, silent as my mother but visibly bothered. I wished I had ESP. Some way to telekinetically extract the words and pictures from her head because she looked sad, as if she wanted very much to say something poignant, but it wasn't her place, and so she just poked at her broccoli and listened, her thoughts like flood waters lapping at the levees.

"Did it ever occur to you that I was dreadfully unhappy?" Mom said to Pap. She startled me, she'd been so quiet. "That maybe I was circling the psychological drain and taking my kid with me?"

"And did it have to be all about you? *Your* unhappiness? *Your* mental well being? A marriage is *two*." He held up two fingers, like a peace sign.

"Three, actually." Mom nodded down to me, but I hated being drafted into their seventeen-year war, even in theory, because that was all I really was when it had begun, a concept, my grandmother's daydream. I was as divided then as I was now, a thousand miles between my mother's ovaries and my father's seed, born of constellations and mirrors under a wide open sky. I never asked to be Jolán De Carlo's ironic destiny.

"It *had* to be about me," Mom said to Pap. "If I fell apart, she wouldn't know the first thing about putting me back together." Her eyes were on fire now, scorching my grandfather from the other side of the table. "She shouldn't have to. It was never her job, and it wasn't Ben's. It was mine. And I pulled myself together, just like I did in Bensalem—with the help of *everyone* else but you."

Pap was quiet. She had shut him down. Laser efficiency. Then she looked at me and apologized without words, with just a little motion of her head, disappointment in her eyes.

"So, who wants cake and ice cream?" Jackie began clearing away the dishes. "We've got chocolate and cherry vanilla. Big bowls or little? Who wants what?"

"I'll get the candles." Rachel pushed herself up from the table and took Mom's plate.

They couldn't get off the patio fast enough, leaving me and Mom with my grandparents in a stilted silence, choking off the dialogue like a gushing limb. Uncle Cam leaned way back in his chair, and he laced his fingers behind his head and stared at the tabletop.

After a while, the music revolved back around to Santana, a slow Cha Cha. Dishes clattered in the kitchen, water ran from the faucet, a silverware drawer opened and shut. No one said anything for a very long time.

Mom broke the quiet. "You know what this means?" She looked at me and pointed back into the house toward the music, smiling a little now.

The storm was in a lull, and she had begun to settle under the piano and percussion that seeped from the living room. She sang along, just a few lines, her Spanish natural and pretty, her singing voice a bit raspy for having smoked until I was nine, but she was good. I liked when she sang, though she didn't do it very often anymore, only to certain songs she'd play around the house or if something she liked came on the radio in the car. She translated the lyrics loosely to personalize them as they went along, and I smiled at her.

She had been so wound up and rigid since the divorce, but she was climbing out of that now, trying to connect with the woman she had been when I was little, and I imagined my teens would make that more complicated. Tomorrow she'd wake up and I'd be twenty-seven, or thirty-one. And so today she sang to me as if I were coddled in her lap, my head in the crook of her shoulder where the Omnia Crystalline sweetened the slope of her neck, toying with the golden crucifix that lay glittering against her caramel skin. Who knew when she would ever get that chance again?

Rachel came out onto the patio with a stack of small plates and fresh silverware that she set around the table at everyone's places, and she smiled sweetly at Mom who was singing to her now, and a rush of uneasy butterflies bloomed in my chest because I knew enough Spanish to know those were the "I love you" lines, and she sent them fluttering out to Rachel as if no one else was in the room.

Rachel looked away, snared for only a moment, but in that moment her eyes betrayed any effort to pretend my mother hadn't swept her into a trance with those words, long before today. And I wondered if this was what Cam meant by "reckless bravado," if she was doing it just to spite my grandfather, a telegraphed signal that Benjamin Edmunds had been willfully and eternally replaced.

Nanna sipped her coffee. She had been observing it all, and she gave a fleeting look to my mother and set the cup in its saucer, then watched as Rachel came around the table and filled my glass with soda. Pap was pecking his cell phone screen, oblivious, offended only by my mother's insurmountable stubbornness, which she had inherited directly from him. Rachel went back into the house, and Nanna watched her go. She took another sip of coffee, smoothed the tablecloth, brushed away a crumb.

"When we're done here, you should go upstairs and get ready," Mom said to me. "Your dad'll be here soon."

"'Kay."

"So, how do you two know each other again?" Nanna asked Mom. It was like the sound of glass breaking, abrupt and disquieting. I had so hoped she wouldn't ask because I had the terrible feeling my mother was going to tell her.

"You and Rachel?" Nanna clarified. "She's not a musician, not in the orchestra with you. So I was just curious how you crossed paths, what you would have in common."

Cam took that cue to excuse himself to the rest room, and he got up and walked out. But he didn't go upstairs. I watched as he went to the kitchen where Jackie and Rachel were scooping ice cream. He was going to warn her, to let her know my mother's bravado was about to go into full tilt.

"Well, I do more than just music. I like poetry, good food, and good conversation," Mom told Nanna, as if it were that simple, but she was just stringing her along, luring her through a maze, the sumptuous truth waiting at the other end, irresistible and fragrant. "Music is how I spend most of my time, but I do have a social life outside the orchestra."

Nanna smiled, but it was feigned, pensive, and she half shook her head. "Apparently so," she declared and peered at Mom over another sip of her coffee.

Mom stared back, relaxed, her elbows resting on the arms of her chair, hands folded in her lap. I'd seen hit men in movies sit as comfortably, just before snatching a Beretta from the underside of the tabletop and opening fire.

"So, are you sure that's healthy?" Nanna's eyes shifted to me for the briefest moment, trying to be subtle, but Mom read them like runes.

She cocked her head just a bit. "I'm sorry? What does that mean—healthy? How exactly is it *un*healthy?"

Nanna looked away to the tabletop and shook her head. "I just thought we had put all that behind us, that's all." Now she had Pap's attention, and he glanced up from his phone and looked at Nanna, then at Mom.

"Put what behind us?" he asked.

"I dunno, Dad," Mom said, staring at Nanna. "I'm not sure what she's talking about. And I'm not so sure she knows, either. Because the things I *needed* to put behind me, I *did*. Long time ago."

Pap held up empty palms and looked at Nanna, then back at Mom, bewildered. "What the hell are we talking about? We went from singing and dancing in Cuba to putting unhealthy things in the past. What am I missing?"

"Is *that* why you split with Ben?" Nanna said, suddenly astounded, but she was reaching for too much, grasping at the wrong things, forgetting me entirely now because she thought she was on to something, but even I knew it was a false positive. "Were you having an affair?" The words whispered from her lips the way the afternoon breeze rattled the oaks in the backyard, and Mom laughed. I knew why. She had baited my grandmother through the maze, around the corners, and along the hopeful passages and right into a wall.

"*Who?*" Pap insisted, still trying to catch up.

But Mom did what I was praying she wouldn't, and she handed her the prize, anyway. "No. No, I wasn't. Rachel came later. After everything was settled."

Nanna looked at her as if she'd been robbing liquor stores for the past three months, and Pap said nothing at all. He placed his hands on his thighs and just sat there, trying to piece together all the clues.

The "Happy Birthday" song came from somewhere in the house. It got louder, approaching the patio. Rachel, Cam, and Jackie appeared in the doorway with the white-frosted sheet cake, fourteen candles flickering against their grinning faces as they placed it on the table. When they finished everybody clapped, and the topic of Mom and Rachel's forbidden romance evaporated with the smoke from the spiral candles. But the scent lingered for a long while after.

I HAD AN hour that was only for me. We ate cake and didn't talk about divorce or the past or speculate on extramarital affairs. I opened presents instead, while Uncle Cam recorded videos on his phone. I got clothes from Nanna and Pap—sweaters and pajamas. I got a wooden jewelry tree with six pairs of earrings from Rachel, a new pair of headphones for my iPod from Cam, and Mom got me a new violin bow that I'd been lusting after for months. It fit my hand just right, and the weight was perfect.

I took everything upstairs afterward, changed into something for the movies, and put on a new pair of earrings—the silver Shamballa double hoops with the crystal stones. I liked them, they made me look older without looking tacky. Mom always said there was a line between fashionable and slutty, and the wrong jewelry, the wrong dress, even the wrong posture could make all the difference. When I looked at Rachel, it was clear my mother had very particular standards that she kept like Commandments, and I wanted to be just like that.

I put on a coat of lip gloss, the kiwi flavored, and pulled my hair up in a twist, thought about wearing a low ponytail, the only way Mom ever wore hers if it wasn't down, but mine was longer, and I could do more with it. I held it in the twist and turned to the side, checked it in profile, and decided I liked it.

There was a knock at my doorframe, and Rachel peeked inside. She gave me a huge smile, pleased that I was wearing the earrings. "Wow, kiddo. Those really work for you. I was hoping silver would go with your complexion. It's different than your mom's. She's always done better with gold, so I wasn't sure."

"The hoops aren't too big," I told her, checking the mirror again. "They're just right. I like them. Thanks."

"Well, good."

I wasn't sure where it came from, perhaps out of some blossoming part of my brain lying previously dormant, or from an untapped hereditary well where my mother's bravado had been collecting for fourteen years, but I pinned up my hair, and without missing a stroke, I said, "So, let me guess. You're up here trying to escape that look on my grandmother's face."

Her smile changed from delighted to apprehensive, the sun shrinking behind a cloud, and I could see she was first going to pretend she had no idea what I meant, but she had been here too long for that. And she knew that I knew it. So, she strolled in from the doorway and stood behind me in the mirror.

She pulled at the ringlets around my neck for a while, fixing them just so. "Your mom and I were never very good at laying low. I guess you've probably noticed that by now. We've been putting off a conversation with you about it, only because she has some other things to discuss, and she's been looking for the right time."

"Yeah, she told me."

Rachel nodded and secured my hair clip tighter so it would stay.

"Did you break her heart?" I heard myself ask, again, without a clue where I was getting this courage. "When you guys were young. Is that why Nanna said she thought Mom had put you behind her?"

She looked at me in the mirror, then her eyes fell to the dresser top, a memory, brief as a grace note yet loaded with regret. She cast it off and straightened the collar of my shirt. "Did she say that, your grandmother?"

I nodded. "Did she just not recognize you at first or something?"

"Well, sweetie, I'd never met your grandparents," she said. "Not until today. So, I'm not sure what she meant."

I suspected that to be another shadow, like all the shadows they'd been throwing on their story since October, but I didn't push. My mother said she'd tell me everything in due time, and it seemed unfair to corner Rachel prematurely. She was just a passenger, like me, with my mother at the wheel, promising not to get us lost.

She seemed satisfied with her grooming and grinned at my reflection. "Your dad's gonna be knocked out. He's not even gonna know his own daughter, as beautiful as you look, all grown up and teenagery," she kidded, and it made me laugh.

I could hear him downstairs now, in the living room, chatting with my grandparents and Mom, and so I grabbed my purse and took Jackie's birthday money from the nightstand.

I started for the hallway but stopped and turned to her. "She really loves you." I didn't know why I felt so compelled to say so. And I didn't know what else to say next except, "If she didn't, she wouldn't have sung it to you in front of my grandparents. She doesn't sing much at all, anymore."

I walked away with a smile and left her standing by the mirror.

chapter five

I SAT ON my bed with my new violin preamp, still in the box. It ended up being a Fishman G-II, with four hundred hours of battery life, the package said. It was virtually useless right now, just a hunk of wires and plastic no bigger than a paperback, but with the piezo pickup and the amplifier, I'd be in business. I could play on street corners in Little Five Points for dollars in a mason jar, hire myself out for friends' birthday parties and Bar Mitzvahs, or audition to play accompaniment pieces for performance artists in Piedmont Park. I'd need a guitar amp, though, something small that I could set up in my room, something I could carry around by a handle and plug into a standard socket. I was only a hundred and fifty dollars away, on the low end.

I wasn't sure if Dad was willing to go that steep, and I knew my mother would sooner shave her head with a bush hog machete or take a bath in sulfuric acid than contribute one dime to my latest novelty, so I slid it back under the bed until I gathered the nerve to tell her I'd bought it last week with Jackie's birthday money.

We had to take Rachel to work in an hour. She'd dropped her car off for maintenance that morning, while Mom followed so she could give her a ride back, and it would be there well into the afternoon. We'd meet Jackie at The Canterbury and stay there for lunch, then Mom wanted to do some Christmas shopping at Lenox Mall before her students showed up this afternoon.

I thought about asking her for an advance on my allowance, but I only got fifteen dollars a week. She said anything over that she'd buy for me, and only if it kept me fed, clothed, and protected from the elements. I hoped the approaching holidays might soften her into something I could work with, something pliable, that maybe Rachel's spell could hypnotize her into at least considering the piezo. But I would have to be clever. I'd have to talk fast, speak in Petrarchan sonnets with rose petals dripping from my lips, and I didn't know if I could pull that off.

Mom could spot a swindle from a hundred miles off the coast of Maine, had intuition sharper than the Oracle of Delphi if she thought something was amiss, and I just wasn't that eloquent. I didn't have raindrop diamonds and white doves and glittering stellar ballets to entice her. I had Linzi Stoppard, and Berklee, and a future in a Playboy Bunny outfit playing at the MGM Grand, all the things she feared most for me.

"Speak in sonnets, Myla. Sugar and spice and all that other crap that usually works." I headed downstairs to find them.

JACKIE WAS WAITING in front of The Canterbury Tavern when we got there. The place was crowded, but Rachel swept us right on through to an open bar-top table with a partial view of the kitchen. It was a beautiful place. Behind the long dish shelves you could see the cooks in their crisp white chef coats and black bandanas, hustling between stations like bees in a jar, as if someone sounded an alarm. Jazz music played omnisciently throughout the main dining area, but not my father's jazz. This was something artsy, like you might hear in a basement club in Harlem, lots of string bass and piano and trap-set drums, complicated time signatures and all the right wrong notes.

Rachel flagged down our server. She was a bleach blonde college girl with freckles and a French braid that tapered all the way down her back. She said her name was Lori.

"They're with me," Rachel instructed over the noise. "So, theirs'll be comped. Whatever they want. Just bring me their ticket when they're ready to check out." She leaned in and kissed my mother's cheek. "I gotta get going, honey. Into the breach." She smoothed my hair and pointed to Lori. "She's gonna take good care of you guys, okay? And I'll try to stop by again before you go. If not, just pick me up at nine."

And with a smile and a wave, she was off, calling after someone by the dish racks, slipping right into the action as if entering a rushing freeway. I'd never seen her so occupied. She had always sat at our dining room table, or lay spooning on the couch with Mom, watching movies in the den, savoring all her moments like hard candies. Who knew she had four more gears and a turbo switch?

Lori took our drink order, two Irish coffees for Mom and Jackie, and an iced tea for me, and then she, too, vanished toward the kitchen.

"So, now I see exactly what you've been up to the past couple months. That little spark of something I sensed back in October has a name," Jackie taunted Mom with a wily grin. "I would've mentioned it last weekend at Myla's party, but your parents were already at DEFCON-one, and I didn't wanna stoke the flames." She sipped her ice water and looked at my mother with an expression of sympathy. "Why didn't you say anything all this time?"

"I dunno." Mom shrugged. "It wasn't a sure thing at first, we didn't know where it was going. And I didn't know what you'd think. You've only known me with Ben, and this is . . . well . . . a bit of a departure." She smiled a little and unwrapped her silverware.

Jackie watched her, concerned. "When, in all our ten years, have you ever known me to judge you? I know stories from your darkest hours, for shit's sake. And you were afraid to tell me you found someone like *her?*" She gestured back into the restaurant toward Rachel with a wince. "She's a knockout, first of all. *And* she's got her shit together. Obviously." She held a hand out to the dining area. "She's smart, she's creative, treats your kid like gold, and she's nuts about you. What's to hide? Hell, if I were single and into women, I'd arm wrestle you for her right now. No kiddin."

Mom laughed lightly. She looked around the restaurant for Rachel and found her, focused and busy by the kitchen food window, calling out orders to the cooks, but she might as well have been standing by a Venezuelan waterfall with passion flowers in her hair and pearls around her neck. My mother was so in love she had to snap herself out of a trance just to finish a thought. And I wondered if anyone would ever look at me that way, like a work of art, if I would ever draw some boy's gaze from across a room, make him walk three blocks through suffocating crowds just to know my name.

"How'd you know? At Giovanni's that night," Jackie asked. "That's the only thing I'll never comprehend, how you can just . . . *know.* Forgive my ignorance, but she doesn't exactly . . . Well, shit. You know what I mean."

"Well, we're not entirely new to each other," Mom said. "Rachel and I go back a ways, met in '92, actually, dated then."

Jackie put two fingers to her lips and looked across at Mom, probably thinking about the night at Rachel's reading because it suddenly occurred to her, and she touched my mother's arm. "That's right. You did say that. Linda almost fell over a folding chair with delight, I remember it now." But then she frowned again; the wheels of her memory had come to a halt. "Wait, *ninety-two?*" she said as if my mother had somehow bungled her own chronology. "Well, wasn't that . . . ?" She left the rest behind the ballistic nylon, a fourth member of the loop I had been waiting so patiently to enter.

Mom glanced at me with a thin smile. Not today. "Yeah. It was."

Listening to their conversation was like reading a soiled newspaper with the ink running, holes worn through and perforating the paragraphs, the story pausing at a hyphen with no continuation page. Lori returned with our drinks and set them on the table, but no one had bothered to look at their menu except me, so Mom sent her away with a pleasant apology.

Mom and Jackie suspended their talk to browse the Reuben sandwiches and goat cheese burgers, spinach strawberry salads, and Thai shrimp tacos. I had already decided on a mushroom Swiss burger and sat watching all the bustle, servers snaking around bar tops, balancing impossibly loaded trays on their palms and shoulders. A female bartender twirled a bottle opener up from her back pocket like a gunslinger, popped open a Guinness and whirled it back into her pocket again and poured the beer foaming into a frosted mug. She no sooner she set that down that she grabbed a bottle of Amaretto with one hand, a jug of juice with the other, and splashed together three more drinks, and she didn't stop, except to turn an ear to a customer, nod, then grab another glass, another bottle, spin the opener.

At the end of the bar was a small display rack with Rachel's poetry books for sale, and there were a few at the register counter where we came in. Classic jazz sizzled the room, a woman singing something sultry about the wind, warming the oak hardwood and bounding off the walls, patches of brick lying under deliberately unfinished plaster, like countries on a medieval map. Exposed white ducts ran along the ceiling where multi-national flags hung between gothic chandeliers fixed to the rafters, and two huge ceiling fans swiveled lazily at either end.

Jackie stopped reading. She looked at Mom, something stirring in her brain. "She wasn't . . . ?" She gestured discreetly to where Rachel stood reviewing an order ticket with a server.

Mom looked up at Jackie, then across the room to Rachel, then back at Jackie, silently filling in another smudge in the story print. She shook her head. "No. Not at all. It was just me."

Jackie nodded and went back to the menu.

Lori came back with a ticket book open, a pen poised to take our order. Mom got the fried Brie with a Tanya salad—spring mix tossed in cranberries, pumpkin seeds, white cheddar, and couscous with a light balsamic, and Jackie ordered the shrimp bruschetta and a Caesar salad dry, dressing on the side. Lori promised it would all be out in fifteen minutes, then left us to our conversation.

"So, tell me everything," Jackie said to Mom, but I knew it wasn't the "everything" I'd been waiting for, so I didn't get excited. "You met again at Giovanni's. And then?" She was grinning, her hands tucked between her knees like a giddy teenager, and I wondered if that was how I needed to approach my mother about that preamp, as if we shared some girlish bond over subharmonics and sidewalk performances for tips. "Was it love all over again, fireworks and moonlight? Come on, dish it, lady."

I had a feeling not, because Mom's expression faded into that hesitant family smile.

She shrugged a shoulder. "I dunno about fireworks. There were definitely sparks. But more like the ones from a bad socket. We had some things to work through first, some old," and she thought for a moment and glanced across the room at Rachel, "discrepancies. Seventeen years can muddy the picture a bit, and we had a lot to clean up."

Jackie waved her on. "Okay, so you scrubbed away all the mud. And then?"

Mom smiled. "And *then,* we did dinner at Holeman and Finch, talked a lot about marriage and divorce, mine *and* hers."

Jackie sipped her coffee. She looked bewildered, and I'm sure I did, too. Another divorce? Did this happen to everyone born after 1970? Was no one safe from the crumbling edifice of modern matrimony?

Jackie knitted her brow, narrowed her eyes. "Wait, *she* was married, too?"

Mom nodded. She rested her arms on the table edge, glanced at me. "Yup. Four years. To a woman. Some chick named Michelle, up in Boston. It's legal there, has been for a while, and they don't kid around when it comes to the paperwork. You want out, you get yourself an attorney to split everything down the middle, then draw up the papers and hope they sign them with no contest. Same bullshit, same nightmare. The only thing she couldn't get her hands on was Rachel's inheritance. Good thing, too." She swept her eyes around a very successful restaurant, then rested them on Jackie's fascinated face.

"Yeah, really." Jackie sighed. "None of this is any of my business, I know. But when you said that, I couldn't help but ask."

"No, it's fine," Mom said. "It's nothing she wouldn't tell you herself, it's not classified. Rachel ended the marriage four years ago, infidelity reasons, from what I understand, then moved down here not long after."

"What are infidelity reasons?" I heard myself ask. I was no less enthralled in the scandalous new details of Rachel's marital issues than Jackie.

Mom searched for an appropriate reply in the last swallow of her coffee, but then Jackie said, "It means a very foolish woman in Boston didn't know what she had, apparently. Michelle from hell cheated on her. What an oblivious bitch," she muttered. She shrugged and turned to Mom. "Well, you know what they say—pearls at the feet of swine are still pearls; you dust yourself off and keep on truckin."

Mom smirked. "Is that what they say?"

"In a matter of speaking. Hell, I'm not Confucius. You know what I mean."

IT DIDN'T TAKE fifteen minutes. Our server showed up with our food, but it took two trays, the other carried by a tall, skinny guy with a name tag that said, "Russell."

I could see Rachel at the kitchen door. Someone else was calling orders to the cooks now, and she seemed to have a moment to breathe. She wore a pair of snug-fitting green khakis with a white Bridgette blouse, unbuttoned just enough to be tasteful with a gold charm necklace catching the overhead light, and she stood with her hands in her back pockets, observing the dining room for efficiency. Her eyes fell on our table, and she watched as Lori and Russell made the final touches on our service. She saw me, smiled, and waved her fingers.

I wondered if she was a good boss, a good wife. Everyone called her Rache, even Mom, so I imagined she made them feel comfortable, appreciated, needed. I knew I would never meet this Michelle From Hell but decided I didn't like her just the same, and I was glad she lived in Boston, fourteen hundred miles from demolishing anything else.

Halfway through our meal, Rachel had a moment to check on us. She stood by Mom's chair with her arm resting across the back and she seemed pleased, like a doting mother basking in the nourishment of her family.

"Which do you like better, doing this or writing poetry?" I asked.

She thought about it at length, then shook her head. "You know, I'm really not sure. I get great satisfaction from both, though poetry does come with a lot less stress."

"But the stress is the adrenaline rush," Jackie pointed out. "I bet you like to skydive, too. And rock climb. Maybe get behind the wheel of a race car, if somebody tossed you the keys." She wiped her mouth and raised an eyebrow. "Am I wrong?"

"Race cars don't have keys," Mom noted, smirking into her salad.

"Will you get your nose outa my personality test? Mind your business. Eat." Jackie pointed at Mom's plate, and my mother chuckled, sipped her water.

"I've never been skydiving," Rachel said, "but I have done some rock climbing in Yosemite, actually, so yeah, I'm an adrenaline junkie. Guilty as charged."

"You went rock climbing?" Mom said. "You never told me that."

Rachel smiled and stroked my mother's hair, toyed with a ringlet. "Well, now you've got the rest of your life to unravel all the mysteries of me, babe."

"Will it really take that long? How many are there?"

"Way too many to mention while I'm working, I'm afraid. And I gotta get back to it. I'm sorry. I just wanted to check in with you guys, make sure everything was right." She kissed Mom's cheek again, then came around and hugged my shoulder.

"Everything's perfect," Jackie assured, kissing her fingertips. "Absolutely delicious, thank you."

"Well, then I'll see you two at nine." She pointed to Mom and me and left us to our meal, waving as she headed through the dining room and disappeared into the kitchen.

We finished our food and parted ways with Jackie. We didn't see Rachel again before we left. She had been absorbed by all the clinking glasses and fry pan sizzle, fifty conversations competing at once, string bass and piano and cash registers, her life outside my mother's gaze.

AT THE MALL, my mother bought her a John Hardy sapphire bracelet from Neiman Marcus. She had it gift wrapped for Christmas in a white leather box with a black velour cushion and said if I told her she'd put me up for adoption. We ate walnut brownies from the food court and window-shopped the trendy clothes stores for outfits she thought looked too revealing, or unkempt, too beachy for school, overpriced, too snug around the hips. She bought me one of each and handed the cashier her credit card, shaking her head.

"You're not wearing any of this until after Christmas break," she said, ambling past the fountains with her arm across my shoulders, bags rustling at our legs. "You got it? It's supposed to be a gift. No pleading, no lobbying for exceptions 'cause Breanna next door's wearing hers, none of that crap. Deal?"

"Deal." That was when I saw my piezo begin to crumble and break apart. She was shutting the door on reasonability, and I needed to stick my foot in the space before it locked, and so I said, "I had a really nice time today, Mom. I know you work hard all week, with rehearsals and lessons and whatnot, and I just wanted to say thanks."

I smiled up at her, a genuine smile because I meant it, but I also had to warm the clay in my hands so I could knead it how I wanted. But not too much. It wouldn't hold its shape, and she'd see me coming.

She smiled back, pulled me closer with a hug. "Well, good. You've been doing pretty well, lately, with your grades, your music. You've been very mature about Rachel coming into our lives, too, and I really do appreciate that, and so does she. I know it's been an adjustment, something none of us expected, but you've handled it like an adult, and I want you to know I'm proud of you for that." She squeezed me again and kissed my hair. "You're a good kid."

No, I wasn't. I was an imposter looking to manipulate her, a trickster carrying the good daughter's clothing, and I felt suddenly reluctant to pursue this plot to buck her system. I thought maybe I should just ask for what I wanted, no schemes, no false gratitude, no more compliments to mold her into submission. But when I opened my mouth, all that came out was, "I think Rachel's awesome, now that I've gotten to know her a little. She has really good taste in earrings."

Mom grinned. "Yeah, well, she's always had a good eye for stuff like that."

It was off my intended topic, but I decided to just go with it. "Even when you guys dated before?" I asked, feeling for the boundaries.

She looked down at me as we walked as if considering whether to indulge me or keep the subject simmering a while longer. Finally she nodded.

"Yeah. Even then." And a distant smile crossed her face as a memory came to mind. "She used to like to make her own jewelry. Seashells on cotton twine. Indian beads. Polished stones. Anything she could find, no matter where we were. I might even still have some of it, somewhere in the attic, maybe." She laughed a little to herself. "Man, I haven't thought about that in years."

She seemed so rapt in the musings of their past, I thought perhaps she'd tell me the rest if I was delicate, and now I wasn't sure which I wanted more, a piezo or the truth, something or everything.

"Did you love her as much back then?" I asked, careful with specifics, one bread crumb at a time.

"Yes, I did." She stared out into the glaring storefronts, but she was really watching pictures of her youth, playing across the screen in her head. "Most of the time I couldn't believe she was mine, she was so pretty, such a light all the time. Everybody could see it. For miles they could see it."

It sounded strange, such an open admission of insecurity coming from my mother, almost impossible, natural as a talking mailbox, or a singing cat.

"Well, you're pretty," I said. "I'm sure she must've thought so, too."

Mom chuckled lightly and shrugged. "Well, she thought I was stubborn as a rock in concrete, I know that. But the rest, who knows? You'll have to ask her, I guess."

I wasn't sure what else to ask, which questions would keep her following the trail and what would spook her off into the shadows again, and so I laid out a few more crumbs.

"You said she made jewelry no matter where you guys were. Did you travel a lot or something? I thought you guys met in college." But then I realized that couldn't have been so. Curtis and USC were on opposite coasts. I started to append that with another question, but I could see her expression darken again, the pictures on her memory screen beginning to melt, burning at the edges, the film catching fire and slapping at the reel. "I'm sorry," I said quickly. "You wanted to wait for that talk, and I shouldn't have said anything."

"It's all right." She tried to smile, but it wasn't real. "We missed a lot of time, Rachel and I. And I just wish we hadn't."

Then she shut the door. I could hear the dead bolts clacking into place, one by one, and the subject was dropped until further notice.

"We need to be getting home," she said, shifting back into the Jolán Edmunds I recognized. "I've got a student at four, and you need to practice as well." And so we headed for the exit and left the past lingering at the mall, sitting with the pennies at the bottoms of the fountains.

THAT EVENING, AFTER the students had gone, and the dinner dishes were washed and put away, after The Canterbury night shift had long turned the chairs over onto the bar tops, I saw them. In the den. I was looking for fresh batteries for my television remote and got halfway down the stairs when I saw them on the couch through the wrought iron railing, Rachel in a white tank top and her plaid flannel pajama bottoms, lying beneath my mother in her blue sweats and sports bra, twined together like moonflower vines, kissing, laughing, speaking in hushed tones, like the lovers in the movies they thought I never watched.

They had always been so discreet about their affection, careful not to display more than I needed to see, and I thought about turning back, checking the kitchen drawers again, but I'd never seen my mother smile that way, not even on the patio singing "I love you" in Spanish, her face in Rachel's hands, foreheads touching, my mother's palm smoothing the bare skin above Rachel's flannel waistband, sliding up under her tank top, then around to the small of her back through another kiss so warm and deep I wondered if everyone kissed that way, or just two people who'd been waiting seventeen years to fall in love again.

They spoke softly, so much that I had to read Rachel's lips when she told my mother she loved her, brushing the curls from her eyes, fingertips tracing the arch of my mother's cinnamon shoulders. I had no idea this kind of thing was real; I'd never seen it before, not without a symphony scoring something moving and minor, with a fade to black and credits at the end. But this was my mother's life now, a Saturday evening moment in December under the light of a Tiffany lamp, smiling into the eyes of her beautiful blonde poet.

They hadn't seen me, and I thought it better that way. I left them to each other and crept quietly back to my room.

WHEN I CAME home from school on Monday, Mom had her Santana CDs on again, and the drums rattled the house like a nightclub, electric guitars and trumpets dueling for attention, the bass line vibrating the hardwood floor. The Christmas tree was up, in the corner by the fireplace, naked and unfinished, some of the branches still strewn about the base. A tangle of lights lay bunched on the couch.

I found her in the spare bedroom, pulling ornaments down from the closet shelf, tattered boxes with transparent lids flaunting metallic red, gold, and silver balls, twisted wire hooks scattered in between.

She saw me, grinned. "Hey." She took out a sheet of silver garland, still wound around the cardboard, and tossed it to the bed with everything else. "You see the tree? I thought it was about time we put it up. Christmas is only, what? Twelve days away?"

"Your music is blasting." I winced. "Since when did '70s Latin rock become Christmas music? It's not exactly 'Jingle Bells.'"

She shrugged, smirked at that. She was in a good mood. "You're the one who always says Christmas music is *corny.*" And she made little quotes with her fingers, then threw me the star for the top of the tree. "So, I thought I'd switch it up, for a change. And there *are* bells, they're called cowbells. That should suffice, no?" She smiled at me again.

"I guess."

She pointed to the boxes and garland on the bed. "Grab some of those."

And so I did, and I followed her out to the living room where "Para los Rumberos" pummeled the walls at a lightning tempo. Mom went over to the tree and hung the missing branches in their respective slots, did a little salsa stutter step, bent the plastic pine limbs into shape.

"Where's Rachel?" I asked over the music.

"She worked the morning shift today," she said. She went to the stereo and turned it down a notch. "Left before you were even up for school, something about a supply shipment coming in, inventory stuff. She'll be here in a little while." She pointed to the knotted wad of Christmas lights on the couch. "You can untangle those, or you can put the hooks on the ornaments. Pick your poison."

I chose the lights. I liked the challenge. I sat with them in my lap and watched my mother unravel the garland, singing the Spanish lyrics to herself as she draped silver ropes over the armchair, ready to be strung when we got the ornaments on. She loved Christmas. No matter how chilly the air might have gotten between her and Dad, she never let it spoil the holidays, dragged out the tree and the lights and the stockings with the enchantment of an overgrown kid, and I imagine it held a particular magic now, with Rachel on her way home. She wanted to share that with me, didn't want me to outgrow it.

She found the door wreath in a box by the fireplace, straightened the little red bows sewn into the fake pine, and set it on the couch. Then our stockings—Myla, Jolán, and Cam in rainbow glitter glue across the cuffs. There was one for Dad, and she set it with the others. She said he was still my father, which made him part of the family, and if I wanted to fill it with aftershave or cuff links or a new business organizer she'd take me back to the stores to find something. There was a new one now, too, waiting for "Rachel" to be scrawled in cursive with the same glitter.

As I watched her, I realized the door that had slammed on our conversation at the mall was now standing wide open, propped in place with pine-scented Yule logs and the six-foot inflatable snowman she'd eventually set up on the lawn. From across the threshold she smiled at me, danced a salsa shuffle, talked of making sugar cookies with candy cane cutouts and the red-and-green sprinkles. If I was going to ask for that piezo and tell her about the preamp under my bed, I now had a first-class invitation. I didn't need to sculpt the clay and mold her to my will; I had Santa Claus and mistletoe and the Baby Jesus on my side. I'd wait until after dinner, though, when the house was twinkling red, yellow, and blue, sweet with the smell of baking, after she had a while to melt under Rachel's warm chocolate gaze, maybe a glass or two of brandy.

I worked on the lights for a long while, threading and unbraiding and shaking them out until I finally had three individual chains. We strung them top to bottom. We staggered the ornaments on every other limb and draped the garland and spread the red-and-white felt at the bottom to cover the stand. Mom was in a hurry to get the stockings hung; she wanted everything to be ready when Rachel showed up so it would be a surprise. She went to the den and rummaged through her desk drawers for the glitter glue and found it, brought it upstairs, and let me dribble Rachel's name across the stocking top. We set it aside to dry, and I put the empty boxes back in the spare room while Mom got a good fire going.

We heard keys in the front door just as Mom was standing up the fireplace screen, and Rachel came inside and stopped, stared around at the living room transformed. She set her purse down with her mouth drawn in astonishment. Mom had dimmed the overhead light so that all the colors glowed and moved across the walls, so the silver ribbons would reflect the firelight, and the Christmas Star of Bethlehem would radiate from the top of the tree.

"Oh my goodness." She laughed. "You two have been busy, this is beautiful."

She came across the room to Mom and cupped a hand to her cheek and kissed her, a longer, sweeter kiss than usual. She wrapped her arms around me, too, marveling at the twinkling tree through a hug that smelled of Eternity and The Canterbury, a little hops and liqueur, she must've been bartending today. She pulled off her coat and laid it on the couch, still grinning at our surprise.

"I can't believe you guys did all this. I would've helped you," she insisted, slapping at Mom's shoulder.

"Well, we left a little something for you to do." Mom handed her the stocking. "You're gonna have to hang this yourself 'cause we're beat."

She took it, smiling, admiring it like a newborn, and she looked at Mom and me, shaking her head. "I don't know what I'm gonna do with you two."

She kissed my mother again, then hung the stocking over the fire, on the new nail Mom added next to her own. Now my mother's family was complete, and she rested an arm across Rachel's shoulder, the other over mine. The last time I'd seen her this content was in a beach chair at the Jersey shore, watching the sun break the Atlantic plane with a steaming cup of Kona and her legs swaddled in a qiviut throw. I was about seven then. And I was beginning to think my uncle was right when he said Rachel Cole was the best thing that had ever happened to her. I didn't know what she had done for my mother seventeen years ago, but it had only taken her three months to do it all over again.

MOM MADE A pan of lasagna for dinner, my great-grandmother's recipe on Pap's side, and we talked about Mom's upcoming Christmas performance at the Catholic Shrine. They only had four more rehearsals and would perform on Christmas Eve and the evening before that. She and the conductor had decided on Ralph Vaughan Williams's *Fantasia On Greensleeves* and *Carol of the Bells* and Corelli's *Christmas Concerto in G Minor*.

I had a solo for a school recital coming up on the last day before holiday break. We wouldn't play anything terribly complicated—"Little Drummer Boy," "We Three Kings," "Jingle Bell Rock," but I wondered how my solo would sound played in the haunting style of Mari Kimura, plugged into a pickup with a few special effects like Linzi. I'd be a celebrity at North Springs, land first chair before the end of the school year and have all the cutest boys follow me through the halls and into the cafeteria, begging to pay for my lunch. One of them might even rest his palm against my cheek, kiss me sweetly on the lips and whisper, "I love you" while brushing the curls from my eyes. And twenty years from now we'd find each other again, in a coffee shop in the East Village somewhere, and he'd invite me into a chat about Paganini, ask me to marry him within a year and stay with me until I'm seventy.

I finished my lasagna and took the plate to the kitchen where Rachel was loading the dishwasher. Mom had gotten out the Merlot and two glasses, set them on the counter. It was now or never.

I gathered my courage. "Hey, Mom?"

"That's my name," she said, popping the cork.

I couldn't say anything, hadn't rehearsed the words.

She looked at me, waited. "What's up?"

There was a dish towel on the counter where I stood leaning. I grabbed it, folded it for no reason, collected my thoughts. "You know how you said I'd been doing real well, lately, with my homework and all?"

She poured herself a glass of wine. "Yeah. Why? You have something to tell me? Miss an assignment or something? Let me know now so I can help you make it up, 'cause I don't want your teachers calling me over the holidays, telling me you're behind. I don't have time for that, Myla. I've got too much going on."

"No, no." I stopped her. "It's nothing like that. I'm caught up just fine."

She looked at me again, her green eyes suspicious now. "Okay, so what is it?"

"Well," I stuttered. "You know when you said you'd find some rewards for me doing so well and all?"

She waited, didn't say anything.

"Well, I was just wondering what kind of stuff you had in mind. Because I thought if I could get that piezo for Christmas, then Dad could get the guitar amp 'cause I'll need one of those, too. I didn't know that at first, but I looked it up, and you have to have one for it to work, and since I already have the preamp, nobody would have to spend any money on that, so it wouldn't cost as much, and I could just keep it in my room and use it in there. You'd never even know I had it."

She frowned, took a small sip from her glass. From the corner of my eye, I could see Rachel rinsing a bowl. She glanced at us but stayed out of it. She was family now, but she hadn't been here long enough, had no stake in my mother's decisions for my future yet. Mom didn't say anything for a long moment, and I thought maybe I had her, that maybe Rachel's aura had ballooned out across the kitchen and enveloped her in a tender place of kindness, that the Christmas lights and all the talk of *Greensleeves* and blushing poinsettias had held open the door so I could reach in, grab my piezo and amplifier, and be on my merry way. I crossed my fingers in my pockets.

Mom looked down at her shoes, thinking, her arm folded across her waist, propping up the hand that held the Merlot. But then she shook her head. "Myla, you know how I hate those things. The answer is no."

"But, Mom—"

"But mom nothing. You asked me, and I'm telling you no. We've talked about this before, and I told you no then. So, let's just drop it. Come on, don't turn this into an argument tonight, all right?"

"But I thought you said I was doing really well," I begged. I couldn't believe she was pulling this chameleon act, Saint Mom all afternoon and while we shopped at the mall, and then with the one thing I wanted most, she completely pulled the plug. "I thought you said I was so mature and that you appreciated my patience with you and Rachel. You thanked me and said how proud you were. What was all that about? Just a bunch of crap to make it seem like everything was cool? I'm just asking for this *one* damn thing, Mom. I don't get what the problem is, why you're being such a tyrant about this, it's not a big deal. It's just a piezo, one little piece of equipment. But you act like I'm asking for a freaking machine gun or something, and it's totally not fair!" I knew I was dancing the merengue through a minefield, but I didn't care. I didn't care that her hazel glare was so piercing right now, she could have straightened my hair from across the kitchen. I felt betrayed, unfairly dismissed, like a prisoner at a parole hearing, watching the panel stamp "denied" onto my case file. And the more I thought about it, the angrier I got.

"You were acting mature until about thirty seconds ago," she said, glaring, pointing at my nose.

I wanted to slap her hand away, send the Merlot shattering into the wall, but I knew much better. I wouldn't wake up from that until *I* was thirty-nine.

She said, still pointing at me, "As long as I am your instructor—never mind your *mother*—you will follow my standards. You will use the methods that I've taught you, and you'll respect them. The answer is no, Myla Christine, and that is the end of the discussion."

I could feel my jaws tighten. I could feel Rachel's eyes on us and all of Jackie's profanity doing cartwheels on my tongue. I wanted to call her a bitch, tell her she was a closed-minded fucking music Nazi on a power trip, just because she had all the orchestra *sheeple* throwing roses at her feet as if she was God's anointed prodigy, that she could shove that Joseph Curtin so far up her ass I hoped she choked on the strings.

But she lowered her hand and walked away from me. "When you're an adult and living out on your own, you can buy all the gimmicks you want, get yourself an electric violin and play it hanging upside down from a disco ball, for all I care. But under my roof, under my instruction, you follow my rules."

"So, then what am I supposed to do with the preamp?" I said, fuming. "Without the other stuff it's worthless."

She knitted her brow and turned to me. "What preamp?" She must not have heard me in my earlier desperation, but she put it together quickly and raised an eyebrow. "Is that what you spent your birthday money on?"

I didn't say anything. I gave her a look instead, a defiant shrug.

"Take it back," she demanded flatly, gesturing toward my room with the wine in her hand. "Do you have the receipt?"

Take it back? That made absolutely no sense. "Mom. Why do I have to take it back if I can find a way to get the other stuff?"

"There *is* no other stuff, Myla." She was getting rattled now, her voice dialed up a degree. "What language do I need to say it in? *No hay otras cosas. Intiendes?* Huh? That better?"

I rolled my eyes.

Rachel shut the dishwasher and turned it on, and she wiped her hands dry. "Hey, guys. Why don't we take a break for a minute? Talk about something else for a while, maybe sleep on it, come back to it when everybody's cooled off, huh?" She rubbed a hand across Mom's back. "Come on, honey."

But Mom wasn't finished with me yet. She looked at me straight and said, "You're taking that thing back, and you're gonna get your money back and spend it on something useful. Hell, Myla, even if I did let you keep it, you'd be eighteen before you could tell me to screw off and go buy the other stuff yourself. Do you have any idea how quickly music equipment depreciates? How fast technology evolves? That thing'll be a dinosaur within five years. Trust me."

She was either deaf or stupid. Maybe even crazy, because she was acting as if she hadn't heard a word I'd said. And she didn't care. She just wanted to win, to show Rachel that she had a handle on her kid, that she could snuff out my dreams with a wag of her finger and a little *Español*, and I couldn't have despised her more right now.

"I swear to God, this house *sucks,*" I muttered and headed for the living room, telling Rachel over my shoulder, "Welcome to the freakin family. Hope you know what the hell you're getting yourself into."

Mom was on my heels. I could almost feel her climbing up my back, like a specter, looming up from the shadows as I stomped up the stairs, making sure my shoes slapped the hardwood like firecrackers.

"Jo!" Rachel called after her, but neither of us stopped.

We got to my bedroom doorway, and she reached a hand through it. "Give it to me. Give it to me, so I can give it to your father and have him take it back."

"Do you even care about what I want?" I shouted, tears beginning to muddle her image as she stood in my doorway, her hand outstretched, waiting for me to submit. "No! You don't! All you care about is that I follow in *your* footsteps, do everything *you* want me to do, go to the college *you* choose, play the music *you* want me to play, and I'm freaking *sick* of it!"

"I'm not gonna get into a shouting match," she told me, her hand still extended. "Let me have it. And if you have the receipt, I'll take that, too, thank you very much."

"I'm not you!"

She was ignoring me now. I was disappearing where I stood, shrinking under her indifference, and soon I'd be smaller than a period, a speck on her mirror to be flicked into oblivion. Well, I'd be damned. She was going to hear me, see that I existed beyond the relentless daily music lessons and mandatory recitals and string camps in Pine Mountain with kids I didn't even like. I jumped up onto my bed, made taller than her by a head and a half now, and I let her have it with both lungs.

"I'm not you, and I never wanted to be! Don't you get it? I don't wanna

be anything like you! I *hate* you, and I wish you would just drop *dead!"*
I hopped down from the bed, dug out the Fishman G-II and slammed it
onto the dresser top by the door. "Here. *Take* it."

I went back to the bed and dropped onto the mattress, arms folded at
my chest, tarrying between fury and regret because I knew what I had
done. And so I sat there and waited to see what came next, to see what she
would do. I waited for something awful, to be excommunicated from the
sanctuary of my home, to be relieved of the De Carlo name, but she was
so silent I thought someone turned the sound off on the world, hit pause
and froze the frame on this bitter, terrible evening. I glanced up at her.

She'd lowered her arm and stood propped against the doorframe,
looking at me in a way that made my stomach hurt, but I'd said it and
now it was out there, a fine silt of disappointment that covered everything
in the room.

She turned from the doorway, and she was gone. She didn't even
take the box, left it sitting where I'd slammed it on the dresser. I heard
Rachel say, "She didn't mean that," from somewhere down the hall.
Their footsteps on the stairs. Then nothing. So much nothing I could have
wrapped myself up in it like cellophane and suffocated.

I wasn't exactly sure why I was crying anymore. It was the worst fight
we'd ever had, I knew that. All the winds had gone and everything was
still, and now I sat looking through eyes wet with remorse, my room and
all its stuff, the computer desk, the flat screen TV, the vanity table and
chest of drawers, the portable stereo, my violin packed away on the floor,
the cottage-style sleigh bed I was sitting on, mounded with pillows and
stuffed animals.

I took one and sat cross-legged and hugged it in my lap. None of it
felt like it belonged to me anymore, as if I were a trespasser here, in some
other girl's room who'd never wished her mother dead, never imagined
slapping a wine glass from her hand so it smashed against the wall, who
hadn't silently called her a stupid fucking Nazi bitch. I didn't want her to
hate me. I just wanted to be acknowledged, to be given a choice now and
then, to paint my own pictures where the colors didn't run every time she
opened her mouth. It seemed so simple, yet everything would be different
now, I knew it. I looked at the Fishman box on the dresser, and I wanted
to throw it through the window, crush it under foot so there'd be nothing
left of this horrible night.

I sat for as long as I could stand it. I went to the dresser, grabbed the
preamp, and made my way downstairs. I couldn't just let things stay this
way. I had to do something.

I heard their voices on the patio. The worst thing I could do now
was interrupt, barge into their conversation uninvited, so I waited in the
darkness of the living room where the tree lights shifted and blinked, the

fireplace waning, and I tried not to listen, but the quiet made their voices carry, anyway. I could just about see them on the settee, Mom with her elbows on her knees, hands clasped between them, Rachel sitting close, hugging my mother's arm with her chin resting on Mom's shoulder.

"She's at a difficult age," Rachel said into her ear. "Were you or I any different at fourteen? I know I wasn't. You'd have thought my mom and I lived on either side of the 38th Parallel, we fought so much."

Mom nodded, stared at the carpet. Rachel combed her fingers through my mother's hair, tucked a ringlet behind her ear so she could see her face. "She loves you like crazy, sweetie. These disagreements'll happen, but it never changes that."

Mom didn't say anything, and I didn't know why except that she probably didn't believe it anymore. Could I blame her? Love doesn't say the things I said, and love can't take them back, either. Words like that carry their own immunity, untouched and isolated as planets.

"Is it really so bad to be like me?" she then said, and she looked at Rachel for an answer because she honestly wasn't sure. I couldn't believe I had shaken her confidence. I had gotten into her head like a tiny parasite, burrowing into her self-esteem, feeding on her doubt, and I wanted to climb into the fireplace and turn myself to ashes, let it shoot me up the flue and scatter me into the night. "Have I been such a terrible example? Maybe I'm a shitty mother, and I've just been deluded all this time, maybe she's right." She shrugged. "Maybe I don't listen."

"Baby, you know that's not true, come on." Rachel kissed my mother's shoulder and gave her a little smile. "You're stubborn, and you're passionate, and so is she. You see so much of yourselves in each other, it's a wonder you can tell yourselves apart sometimes." She kissed her again. "I think she's damned proud of that, if you ask me. She just won't say it until she's about thirty." And she wrinkled her nose and nodded, and it made my mother laugh a little.

They didn't say anything else. They just sat huddled on the settee while my mother decided whether she had been a failure and if I'd ever really loved her, and so I rose from the couch and went to the patio door, knocked on the jamb as if I'd just gotten there. They both looked up. Rachel smiled, but Mom's face was illegible, hesitant, still reeling from the war.

"You know what, I'm gonna go run some bathwater and get ready for bed. I've got another early day tomorrow." Rachel left my mother with another kiss and slipped me a reassuring wink and a little nod as she passed into the living room and on up the stairs.

I stood in the doorway, holding the preamp at my side. Mom and I just looked at each other, everything replaying in both our heads. She glanced at the box but didn't say anything, and I didn't like that she was looking at

me like a stranger, like someone from a concert audience whose approach
had caught her off guard, as if waiting civilly for me to state my business.

I stepped onto the patio, wandered a little closer. I set the preamp down
on the glass coffee table in front of the settee. She leaned back against the
cushions, crossed a leg over the other and sat looking at it with her hands
folded in her lap. She looked back up at me. The mildly intrusive guest
who might want their program signed or to take a picture while she was
trying to gather her music and put away her instrument.

"I'm sorry I said all that." It came out of my mouth as if I had strep
throat, pinched off and croaky. But that was because the tears were
creeping back again, making my nose burn and run, and I sniffed and
caught the first ones on the shoulder of my sleeve. "I really didn't mean
it. I didn't mean any of it."

Mom just kept nodding, staring out at some thoughtful spot on the
far side of the patio, but she still didn't say anything. After a very long
while she finally looked at me again, this time as though she recognized
me somewhat, and so I stood there hoping she believed me. I felt naked,
couldn't look at her anymore. I had snot in my nose and I didn't know
what to do with my hands and so I shoved them into my pockets but
couldn't keep them there because I had to keep swiping tears off my chin.

"Apology accepted."

It was like the sound of search-and-rescue, calling from a breach in a
collapsed mine shaft after days in the dark.

But then she said, "I think you meant some of it."

I started to refute that, but she stopped me and said, "It's all right. I
know which parts came from the heart and which were . . . well . . ." She
didn't finish that thought and instead patted the cushion seat beside her.
"Come on. We don't go to bed angry in this house. Sit."

I did, and she adjusted herself to look at me, stretched an arm across
the back of the couch.

"Neither one of your grandparents are musicians." She thought for
another moment. "But when I was growing up, learning to play, they both
stayed on my case like heavyweight boxing coaches. Never let me go a
day without practicing, never let me miss a performance, paid through the
nose for years to get me the best instructors they could find."

These were the precious details in a fourteen-year mystery, tiny jewels
embedded in the volcanic rock that had been my mother's past for so long,
so I kept quiet and let her continue.

"I loved to play, don't get me wrong, but at times it was relentless. The
monitoring. The nagging, Jeezus. But after I got much older, I realized
they were trying to give me a good future, doing something I loved but
enough to make it lucrative, you know? Pay the bills, so it wouldn't just
be a waste of time. Now, I don't know if music is what you wanna do for a

lifetime. Maybe not. And it doesn't have to be. I want you to do whatever makes you happy, and if it seems like I've been steering too hard, well, then maybe I have, and I'm sorry for that."

I wasn't sure what I was hearing. An apology? To me? After everything that took place tonight, it was almost ludicrous. I was the aggressor, here. It was me who had busted open a bag of manure and stood slinging it to the walls like a certifiable nut, stinking up the house with all my passion and spite.

And so I said, "I don't mind being like you. Everybody admires you. Sometimes people even brag about knowing you. I hear them, at the parties and backstage after your shows. It'd be awesome for people to see me the way they see you." I looked into my lap, fidgeted with my shirttail while I put together my thoughts. "But I don't know if I'm as talented as you, and I don't think I am, actually. So, sometimes it seems like I'm trying for something I could never achieve. I *look* like you, but I don't *play* like you, I can't hear it the way you do, and it frustrates me so much sometimes. And I just thought if I had something unique, some cool special effects or whatever, maybe I could still be a good musician, just in my own way. But I guess that's stupid. I should just stick to the right way and practice."

"First of all, you're fourteen, and I'm thirty-nine. You've been playing for *five* years, and I've been playing for *thirty-three*. If you had my skills at your age, I'd have you on every late night talk show I could find. You'd be out making your mother rich," she said with a smirk, and I laughed a little. "I didn't put a violin in your hands until you were nine, and that was for a reason. I wanted to see if it was what you wanted to do, if maybe you'd be destined for the math club or the NASA space camp instead. Maybe you'd wanna run track or be a painter. I wanted to let you come to me for music, and you did, remember?" And she smiled. "I was downstairs in the den, practicing for my first concert with the Atlanta Symphony, and you came down and asked if you could hold my violin."

"I thought you'd laugh in my face," I said, thinking back. "You never let me touch that thing, 'cause you said it was expensive and I might drop it or break a string."

"I did say that, and for good reason. That instrument cost more than I plan to spend on your first car, so yeah. But you were careful, and you looked good with it. Like a little pro. Knew how to hold it, had pretty good posture." She resituated so she could look at me straight. "I know I've been tough since then. I've had a dozen opportunities to send you to other teachers, and maybe Linda's right. Maybe you would be better off with someone else, but you know what? I see you getting older, growing up, becoming a teenager now, and I know you want your independence—you should. You wouldn't be normal if you wanted to hang out with me all the time. And I guess I've held on to the lessons because . . ." She hesitated and ran a finger along the couch seam, thinking. "Well, because it's time I know I'll get to spend with you. At some point, it might be the only time I'll ever get. Soon you'll be dating and staying out with your friends. Driving, God forbid. But it's not because I don't think anyone else can teach you. I'm not quite *that* arrogant. I guess I've just been afraid to let you go 'cause I know what's out there, when you let go of a kid's hand, and it scares the living shit outa me."

"Why?"

She looked at me in that way again, like she did at the aquarium, that hesitant De Carlo smile. "Because I know what's out there," was all she said about that. "And since I know I'm gonna have to be brave and cut the cord sometime before you're fifty, I'm gonna give you a choice. You can continue playing, learning from me. I can send you to Dr. Bernadeaux or someone like that. Or you can put the violin down altogether and try something else, another hobby, see what else you might be good at. What do you think?" I started to respond, but she held up her hand. "Don't answer that now. I want you to give it some thought, sleep on it. Then you can let me know what you've decided within a couple days or so. I want you to be sure."

I nodded. "All right."

"Okay." And she extended her hand. "Friends?"

I smiled and shook on it. "Friends." She pulled me to her for a hug. "I am really sorry for saying those things."

"I know." She gave me a forgiving smile, told me that she loved me, then waved me off to bed. "You've got school tomorrow, so get your stuff together and get some sleep. Go."

I started for the living room, but I still had one last question, so I turned back, hoping our talk might have gotten me closer to an answer. "Mom, what happened in 1992?"

She gave me that smile again. "A lot of things. Let's get through the holidays first. Then we'll talk, and I'll tell you all about it."

I was disappointed, but what could I do? I let out a sigh and nodded. "'Kay." And I headed upstairs to bed.

chapter six

WHAT CAN I say about Tuesday, December the fourteenth? What will I ever be able to say? I remember it was raining, just a little. I was home from school before lunchtime. I sat holding my backpack in the living room. The Christmas lights were off because nobody had been there all day. Dad showed up by one p.m., his phone kept ringing. Jackie showed up not long after. Uncle Cam left, no one else knew to tell Rachel, he didn't want to do it over the phone. My grandparents were on the next flight down. Someone called Patterson & Son Chapel, made an appointment, I think it was Dad. Jackie knelt on the floor in front of me and held my hands, she'd been crying.

Dad sat next to me when he got off the phone, hugged my shoulder, kept saying, "We're gonna get through it. We're gonna get through this, pumpkin, we can do this."

Someone called Jackie, and she took it to the patio but I could still hear her. Myocardial infarction. Endocarditis. She was crying again, sitting on the settee with her palm to her forehead, the phone to her ear. Linda was on her way now, with others from the orchestra, some had been at the hospital, waiting with Uncle Cam. They all found out together at 10:46 a.m. It took Dad too long from Adamsville, too far away, and he wasn't her next of kin anymore.

I was.

IT RAINED FOR four more days, but on the fifth day it stopped. We went casket shopping—the Star Legacy Sienna Bronze with the gold latches and trim. Jackie picked out flower arrangements, said we should use the orchestra head shot. You could blow it up to the size of a painting, put it on an easel. Dad and Nanna provided all the details for the obituary. It was in Friday's paper. Someone had to write a eulogy, so Jackie volunteered for that, too. We had to pick out a plot, choose a caterer, arrange for musicians to play—the whole orchestra volunteered, but we only needed a quartet. We had plenty of time because they had to do an autopsy. When your heart stops at thirty-nine years old, with no history of heart disease and no genetic predisposition, they want to know why, but I could've saved them the trouble. I knew exactly why.

IT TOOK RACHEL a week to pull herself together. She showed up at the funeral with Uncle Cam, dressed like a movie star but looking as though she hadn't seen a bed since November. He had her ride to the cemetery in the limousine with us. When we got there she started to sit in the middle rows with Jackie and everyone else, but Cam got her and brought her to the front and sat her between me and Pap. It made a lot of people sit and wonder, but no one said what they were thinking. They wouldn't dare. They all put their roses on the coffin as they passed, hugged my dad, my grandparents, my uncle, and me, and they nodded their respects to Rachel just the same.

Afterward, our house was filled with people dressed in church clothes. Everyone was mumbling, standing in every corner with drinks and plates, and the Christmas lights were still off. I'd spent the week at Dad's, and my grandparents stayed at the Marriot, so no one had been here until today. I figured it would probably be cancelled, Christmas. Nobody was really in the mood now, anyway. Out on the patio, the quartet was playing an arrangement of "Sheep may safely graze" from Bach's *Cantata No. 208.*

I sat on the couch with a Styrofoam plate of potato salad and egg rolls. Nanna Sylvia was going to cook mostaccioli and make a pan of empanadas, but she had only slept two days all week. Pap didn't want her puttering around the kitchen like that.

"You'll catch your hair on fire," he said, "burn the place down. Let the caterers do it."

People I didn't know, or whom I only knew by face, approached me from time to time, sympathetic brows knitted to the occasion, touching my knee, my shoulder, my cheek. Some of them had been crying, others maybe not. They all said what a ray of inspiration my mother was, how gifted, an irreplaceable loss to the classical music community. They promised prayers. They asked for my name, wanted to know how old I was. They had no idea. My name was Matricide. Electra. I was Ptolemy X in a minidress. It was why I couldn't cry, why strangers had shed more tears than I did. Monsters don't have them, they just watch everyone else weeping for their deeds.

I could see Rachel through the beveled oval window of the front door, sitting alone out on the porch step. She was inside for a short while, but she couldn't stand it, the music, the quaint refreshments lined along the counters, the murmuring, my mother's family still hanging from the darkened fireplace mantle. Stay or go, she must have been thinking. How long was long enough?

Last week I heard Uncle Cam telling Jackie that she'd collapsed into his arms when he gave her the news; her knees couldn't bear the sorrow of losing a soulmate. He said she'd spent twenty minutes rocking, holding herself, doubled over on the couch in her office, that he didn't know how to make it easier except to let her cry. Cry until she caught her breath again. Cry until Corina could drive her home, where I imagine she cried all night.

She'd held my hand at the funeral, and her hand was unusually cold, but I knew why. She had died that day, too. And now she sat out on the steps, hugging herself at the waist, overcast as the afternoon, a shell that I had picked clean with a forked tongue.

THE PLAN WAS that I would stay with Jackie. She lived outside my school district, but it was closer than Dad's, and the school would make an exception under the circumstances. He was trapped in a condo lease that he couldn't dissolve for another year. So, I would finish out the school year at Jackie's, and by next fall Dad will have relocated back to Marietta, and I would come back home with him, graduate high school, go to college, get married, have a daughter, and pray she never wished me dead. But first we had to get through Christmas.

We spent it at Jackie's. She surprised us and went all out, baked a ham and two pies, cherry and rhubarb, Mom's favorites. There were dinner rolls and corn pudding and a green bean casserole, eggnog spiked with Captain Morgan rum and a separate pitcher for me, and Cam and Jackie's husband Bryan made a bonfire in the backyard. All their Christmas lights were on, and she had us bring our gifts and stockings and place them under their tree.

At the table she made a toast. She said we'd done our grieving while it was time for us to grieve, and now we would celebrate the holidays as Jolán De Carlo Edmunds would have wanted. She'd loved Christmas too much for anything less. "To tradition."

So, I made an effort—I owed her infinitely more than that, but it was a start.

After dinner, Nanna Sylvia helped Jackie clear the table, and Dad and Pap found a football game in the living room and sat talking, sipping glasses of Samuel Adams. Even Rachel had cast off her melancholy enough to sit with me out on the deck, bundled in our coats and scarves under the security lights, watching Cam and Bryan drag the downed oak branches across the yard for the fire.

"She would have liked this," she said, gazing out into the night, nursing a wine cooler. "The food, the decorations, everyone together." And she nodded quite assuredly. "Yeah, this would have been just right." She tried to smile, but it was brief and strained, like everyone's smile over the past two weeks. Then she looked at me for a moment, thinking, studying me, the warmth trying to find its way back to her soft brown eyes. "You doing okay? Been a long week."

I nodded, shrugged. It made me uneasy, that question coming from her. I had no business being okay. I had made her sit up nights and cry until her beautiful eyes carried black bags of grief. It was me who had stolen her joy. I had burned out all the stars in her wide-open gorgeous sky.

"It never feels the way you think it will, losing someone. I only met my dad twice in my life before he died. I was twenty-five then, and you'd think it would've just come and gone, and that would be that. Just information, an update." She stared out into the yard again, leaning on the deck rail. "But it hit me like a bus. I cried for two days, and I still don't really know why." She was quiet for a moment. "Our parents are part of us, and we're a part of them. You lose something. There's just no way around that."

I suppose she was waiting for me to say something. But I hadn't said anything at all in eleven days. Nobody had noticed, not even me, not until now. There were too many visitors, neighbors with potted lilies and cards and plates of cookies. Everyone's cell phones ringing, all day long, vibrating the dining table, the coffee table, the car console. Nanna needed a prescription to sleep, so we made trips to CVS and to the bank. Everyone knew I was there, but no one had seen me. Too much to be done; the adults were talking. I was in a box of two-way mirrors.

"You're the only one who knows." I heard it in the dark, wrapped in a bonfire, slipping up into the sky with the embers.

"Knows what, sweetie?" Rachel said.

It startled me. I didn't know who she was talking to at first, and she asked again, gently. "What do you mean? Knows what?"

Now I realized it was me, that they had been my words, at last, my voice in the vacuum. Bryan and Cam stood chatting by the fire, beer bottles in hand, kicking at the edges of the circle with the toes of their boots to keep the kindling from lighting the dry grass. A precautionary measure. A ring of stones just might not be enough. You had to tend a fire that big, contain the cinders, or before you knew it the whole house would be ablaze, and then the next one, and the one after that, until the entire neighborhood went up in flames and everyone's lives were reduced to ash and memory. From a single unruly spark.

I decided to speak, this time with the awareness that I was doing so. "You know what I've done, that it was me who did this. You don't have to pretend to be nice. And you don't have to forgive me. You shouldn't, really. I don't deserve it from anyone, not even myself."

Rachel didn't say anything for a very long moment, and so I glanced at her. She wore an expression as if I'd spoken in tongues, and her eyes searched the hardwood deck for the English translation.

She shook her head and looked at me again. "What on earth are you talking about, Myla? Did what? Forgive you for what?" She made a little preposterous sound and thought about it some more. Then it seemed she found my meaning, clear as plate glass, and she raised an eyebrow. "Wait, you think this is *your* fault?" There was urgency in her voice now, and the look in her eyes changed to something like fear. She set her bottle on the bench and stared at me.

"Of course it is. I said it that night. You heard me. I know you did. You were coming down the hall when it happened." I swallowed back fresh tears, wouldn't let them get far enough to fall. "I wished her dead," I confessed flatly. "And now she's gone. It's really not that hard to put together."

Rachel took a very deep breath and looked at me as if I'd just drunk a bottle of Drāno. Then she took me by the shoulders and peered at me straight. "I want you to listen to me, Myla. Listen to me very closely. Your mother's death had *nothing* to do with you. *Nothing.*" She said the words with explicit enunciation, her eyes still bright with alarm.

"But I said—"

"No. That had nothing to do with it. I know what you said, and people say things when they're angry, but words, honey . . ." She shook her head at the floor, then looked out into the yard for Cam, her hands still gripping my shoulders. She looked back at me. "Your mother had a heart attack, sweetie. And there were factors for that, causes that go back years and years. It wasn't you, or anything you said or did. Jeezus," she whispered, looking for Uncle Cam again. She didn't call him over, though. Instead she turned back to me. "There are things you need to understand, things about your mom that . . ." She stopped to collect her phrasing. "Things she was gonna tell you. About her life, about herself, about *you.*"

"Yeah, I know. She'd been promising that forever," I mumbled. "But now she can't. Because she's dead. I said what I said, and she died the next day. Don't you get it?"

"Yes, I get it, Myla." She was growing frustrated now. "I get that it was going to happen whether you had a fight or not. She could've bought you three of everything you asked for and spent the night dancing on the rooftops, and she would have *still* died the next day." She paused because the tears were trying to strangle her again, and she blinked them away and took a steady breath. "It was her time, honey. The damage to her heart had given her exactly thirty-nine years, five months, and twenty-four days. And then it gave out. And no amount of CPR or defibrillation was going to change that. Do you understand? She wasn't angry with you that night, sweetie. I know because we talked about it. She was happy when she came to bed. You guys had worked everything out, and she felt *good* about it, I promise you."

I didn't say anything. I still didn't buy it, not entirely. The coincidence was just too startling, too uncanny not to have been the work of my hatred, a momentary spark of rage that had turned a dozen lives to smoldering ruin.

She let go of my shoulders and stood looking at me, trying to decide what to do, what to say next. She wasn't getting through, and she knew it, and so did I, so she backed off and made me a proposition. "All right, listen. You do me one favor, okay?"

I peered at her sideways, waiting.

"You put that thought on hold, put it aside, just for a few days, and then I have some things I want to show you. Things I can tell you. Stories, accounts of her life that I know firsthand because I was *there*. Everything she was going to tell you herself." She looked at me, pleading behind desperate brown eyes, hoping I'd give, just a little. "You can't shoulder this, Myla. It's not your fault. There's a whole other explanation for why this happened, and I can prove it if you'll give me just a few days to get things together. Then I'll tell you all of it."

It sounded tempting, though I'd been given that promise before, and I'd been waiting for "all of it" since October. If she could swear not to drop dead, too, maybe I'd feel more inclined, but I didn't say that. Instead I nodded. "All right. I guess."

She let out a breath of relief and wrapped me in one of her Eternity hugs, strong and warm, relishing one of the only living pieces of my mother she had left.

"Thank you," she whispered. "I promise it will explain this."

I COULDN'T IMAGINE when we'd have the time. I thought about all the errands and plans Dad had made through New Year's. He and Cam had to move my bedroom suite into Jackie's downstairs office, convert it into a place of my own. The mail had to be forwarded to his house in Adamsville. We'd have to hire a landscaping crew to keep up the property for the next year. Nanna and I would have to go through my mother's things, decide what was what, which clothes could go to Goodwill, or to friends, or neighbors.

That was the task I dreaded most, it seemed too sudden, but Nanna said there might be things of hers that I'd want to keep. She said she didn't want to do it, either, but it had to be done. It was morbid to leave it all there for a year, with no one in the house, everything in suspended animation, but maybe that's where I wanted to be, hanging in midair between my bedroom floor and the bed, Mom's hand outstretched through the doorway, frozen in those precious moments before it all went up in flames.

THE DAY AFTER New Year's Nanna Sylvia and I stood at my mother's bedroom doorway, brown boxes broken down and folded under our arms, a roll of Hefty bags. It seemed like such an intrusion, and we hadn't even crossed the threshold, peering in from the hall like a room in a museum display, our reticence a velvet rope across the entrance. The black Maribel platform bed and matching chests filled with her things glared back at us, the floor-to-ceiling windows drawn shut with beige Grommet curtain panels. There was an issue of *The New Yorker* on the nightstand with a half-empty water glass beside my picture, two additional paperbacks on the opposite stand that must've been Rachel's. So many things, yet it looked so empty, so still, the space where I had probably been conceived, where I had spent school mornings sick with fever and chills, tucked under the black-and-tan comforter, miserable but content to lie there with my head on her stomach, the rise and fall of her breathing like waves on a raft.

"Well, her things aren't going to pack themselves," Nanna finally said with a sigh.

I had butterflies in my legs, strange place for them to gather, but I wished their wings would lift me out of there altogether.

They didn't. We started with the walk-in closet, her pants suits, jeans, and button-downs on padded hangers, dress shoes and sneakers, winter boots, summer sandals. All of it went into the first boxes. We taped them shut. We labeled them accordingly. We set them aside for someone else to browse, to hold up against their figure in a mirror somewhere, slipping into my mother's life for $5.99 and a coupon. *Your receipt's in the bag, thank you for shopping.*

The tape dispenser ran out, so Nanna went downstairs to look for another roll, and I pulled the step stool up to check the closet shelves. I found winter scarves I didn't know she had, a baseball cap and a pair of Ray Ban sunglasses, a pile of old issues of *Classical* magazine and *The Strad*, random photographs of me when I was in the fifth and first grades, and one picture of her. It had been taken last summer at an outdoor restaurant in Panama City Beach, her auburn curls pulled into a loose ponytail baked with amber highlights, grinning in her sunglasses and a blue tank top, her swimmer's shoulders the color of honey—I put it in my pocket.

On the very back of the shelf was another box, but it was out of my reach. I stepped down and moved the stool closer and climbed back up and tried to pull it to me, but it was heavier than it looked. It was the type they used for printer paper, with a lid that I could get my fingertips under, and I dragged it across the plywood and hugged it to my chest, wondering if she collected rocks in her secret spare time. I brought it to the floor and opened it.

Notebooks. The wire spines all laid opposite to fit squarely, a full stack of three-subject Meads in every color, the covers faded and cracking at the edges. There must have been at least a dozen, maybe more. I took one off the top and flipped through it, the pages gone yellow with a faint waft of patchouli and nicotine and the pulp of an old library book. It was filled front to back in my mother's handwriting, some in pencil, the rest of it in black and blue ink, and I paused at a page toward the front.

> *One month into this new life, and already the pressure is like barotrauma. I should scuba dive, become a marine biologist. After four weeks of Curtis' grueling demands, it'd be a breeze. I could discover all those hidden species five miles down without ever coming up for air, and when they asked me how I did it, I'd give them Dr. Colianni's fall semester syllabus. I had forgotten in all my many days of freedom that music is work, knowledge is work, success is work. Well, it works if you work it, so I've been told. I just wish I knew which month I get to sleep.*

They were journals, dated from 1991 to 1994. Handwritten accounts of . . . *everything.* She would have been in her early twenties at this time, I thought, perusing the pages like a secret find in a Middle Eastern cave, so much to read, too much to ingest, the Holy Grail. I laughed to myself, incredulously, marveling at the stack a foot high, the dates doodled onto the covers in huge superhero letters, "Jolán De Carlo" scrawled in shadowed black cursive, the ink so heavy and deliberate it raised up through the other side like braille, or scar tissue.

I heard Nanna on the steps, so I put it away and replaced the lid and shoved the box to the side, far from the others, in an area I would designate for things to keep. I would take them with me to Jackie's and shut myself away with them until *I* was in my twenties if that's what it took to read them all, and I would learn her like geometry, study the words as if they were Kafka's, make her real again if only in my mind. It was as good a place as any now.

IT TOOK THREE more hours to pack the rest for storage. I kept the black-and-tan comforter and her pillow, still sweet with traces of Omnia Crystalline and fabric softener and shea butter body wash. I kept her hairbrush, her green kimono bathrobe with the gold stitching, and the near-empty bottle of perfume from the dresser. I kept necklaces and bracelets and an emerald ring she'd bought during a trip to London to hear the Philharmonic perform Mahler's *Symphony No. 8* when I was a baby.

She had several, but this one had always been my favorite, the stones inlaid in a crisscross pattern around the silver band. I kept her sheet music, CDs from her collection, and a coffee mug that read: *Never look at the conductor. It only encourages them.*

When I got back to Jackie's I surrounded myself with my mother, sat in my new room among the bags and boxes, the comforter spread across the bed, her pillow in my lap, propping up the 1994 journal I had started reading that afternoon. It was her college years at The Curtis Institute in Philly. I thought it was the year she'd met Dad, but she hadn't gotten to that part yet. Only one semester left to graduate. She was exhausted, suffering from something physical that made the credit hours in music instruction, orchestra performance, and string quartet participation like "swimming in wet cement." On top of it all she had to practice for a final solo recital to be performed in front of the entire music board for her Masters of Music degree.

She was lonely. I could hear it between the words like ghost notes. She was living with Nanna and Pap, she said, driving Pap's old Honda to school and back, and she was tempted, on occasion, to just hit the Pennsylvania Turnpike west and keep going, but she never did, never said why. So far she hadn't mentioned Rachel at all, and I wondered about that. But then, as if conjured from the very thought itself, Jackie knocked on my door with her phone in hand.

"Someone wants to talk to you," she sang. She looked around my room at all the boxes as she handed me the phone. "If you need any help with this stuff, let me know, hon'."

I threw her an "okay" sign and took the call to the living room.

It was Rachel. She had spent the week since Christmas digging in her closets and basement. She said she'd found as much nostalgia as she could and that Uncle Cam had done the same after she told him of our conversation. I had four more vacation days left, and so we agreed to spend Thursday afternoon rummaging through it together. I told her of the box of journals I'd found in Mom's closet, that I'd started reading one of them, but she made me promise to wait because she said there were many explanations necessary for much of it, things she needed to tell me first, prefaces to my mother's past like a concordance to a holy book. I can't say that didn't pique my interest further, like telling someone not to think about the color blue, or to sit in front of a television and ignore it. But she insisted that I promise, and so I did.

And for the rest of the night, there they sat—green, red, blue, and yellow covers, some of them so weathered the colors had white cracks across the front, like nations divided on a map. They sat under the glow of the desk lamp, spread out on the carpet, waiting for me to ignore them while I read vampire love stories instead. Everything forbidden, still.

I had stuck the Panama City Beach photo into the mirror border on my dresser, and I took it down and dropped back onto the bed and lay looking at it for the hundredth time, wishing she didn't have her sunglasses on because I wanted to see her eyes, but I could imagine them behind the black lenses, striking and vibrant. The last time I'd actually seen them was on the patio the night before I'd cursed her into oblivion. I thought about that night, about our talk and how she'd asked me to decide my future.

The girls' basketball team had tryouts after Christmas break, and I was tall enough, had a pretty decent free throw average, thanks to Dad and Uncle Cam. And the boy who played first chair viola said Dr. Bernadeaux wasn't as decrepit as Jackie had described. He said he'd been studying under him for four years and that he was patient and thorough, even a little funny. I stared into my mother's picture, held it to the light so all the colors brightened.

"I picked you," I said to her, looking futilely for the golden-green behind the Ray Bans. "So, what am I supposed to do now?" Her image grinned back at me, silent as a galaxy. I set it back on the dresser.

It was after midnight now. I turned out the light and balled myself up in the comforter, hugging her scented pillow, and I wondered if there was an afterlife like the one I'd heard people describe, where all the greatest singers and musicians gathered to play forever, an eternal concert like nothing you could imagine. I hoped it was true because that's where she would be. I pictured her, waking on the other side of life to Beethoven and Stradivari himself, Janis and Stevie Ray, John Lennon and Jimi, all those she admired most. She would take a seat next to Nicolò Paganini, adjust her violin beneath her chin, put on her game face, and jump right in at the first line. I decided I would try to dream about that, and I shut my eyes and listened to their music until it lulled me to sleep.

RACHEL LIVED IN Brookwood, closer to our house than I thought. It was a brick bungalow on Alden Ave, smaller than I would have expected, and we pulled up into the gated driveway and parked in front of the garage. The backyard had an in-ground Jacuzzi and an outdoor stone fireplace with a gas barbecue grill and a glass umbrella table. Potted ferns hung from either side of the back door, and a lush patch of Virginia Creeper climbed the brick and stretched around the corner.

"If it's a little cluttered," she said as we entered the kitchen, "you'll have to forgive me. I haven't been home much this week. Kinda been living at the restaurant, lately. Keeps my mind off things."

I never understood why people with beautiful, immaculate homes felt the need to apologize for a mess that wasn't there. The place reflected her warmth, hardwood floors all the way through. The kitchen had white-painted window cupboards displaying neat stacks of bowls and saucers, a set of blue coffee mugs and various wine glasses. Two red candles in bronze holders sat in the middle of the kitchen island, and on the counter was a small stack of unopened mail and a few framed photographs, one of an older woman whom she resembled as closely as I resembled Mom. She saw me looking at it and smiled.

"That's my mother," she said. She hung her car keys on a hook by the door and dropped her purse into the chair beneath it. "She lives in Ohio, but I've been trying to convince her to come south. I think she'd like Atlanta, but she's much too independent to relocate just yet."

"She's pretty. You look like her, same mouth, the full lips. The eyes, too." I smiled and put it back on the counter.

She thanked me and said, "It's an older picture. I think she was close to forty in that one, not much older than me. She'll be fifty-seven this spring, but don't tell her that. She still likes to think she's thirty."

I did the math in my head and looked at her funny. "Wow. She had you really young. Seventeen. That must've been hard."

She took two glasses down from the cupboard and went to the fridge. "It wasn't a walk through the park, no. My father was young, too, only eighteen when I was born, and he split to Las Vegas, didn't want the responsibility. There were no DNA tests to prove paternity then, so there wasn't much she could do." She held up a bottle of orange juice and a can of Coke for selection. I chose the Coke. "She raised me by herself, worked at the tire plant for years while I was in school." She poured my drink and slid it across the island. "The plant shut down when I was a junior in high school, and so she started her own house cleaning business, did pretty well. Akron, Ohio has just as much dust as any other place."

I sipped my soda. "I guess she had to save up a lot to put you through college." I was going to say that Mom had opened a special account when I was born, just for my college tuition, but the thought was still too troubling, so I kept it to myself.

Rachel motioned me into the living room, and so I followed. "My only ticket to college was a scholarship and a student loan. When she got laid off, we went through her savings to stay afloat for two years until she got her business started. I got into USC and Syracuse but chose USC because it was farther away. I'd never been out of Ohio, so I couldn't wait to cross the California line."

We sat on the couch, and she thought back to that era and smiled and sipped her drink. "Man, she was fit to be tied when I chose California. I'll tell you what. Not that she didn't want me to go. She was just scared. I was eighteen, inexperienced, and all alone in LA. But you figure it out. You learn what's where and who's who. Didn't take long. I had enough studying and classes to keep me from getting into anything *too* crazy, partied a little but that was it." She gazed at the coffee table, thinking. A wide grin stretched across her face. "And then I met your mother."

I regarded her strangely. "What's that mean? Why do you say it like that?"

"Well, let that be a segue into why I brought you here." She rose from the couch and held up a finger. "Sit tight. I'll be right back." And she disappeared into the next room.

The living room was small but comfortable, decorated with earth tones and autumn colors, and it smelled faintly of her perfume lingering and some sort of spice I assumed was from another candle on the end table.

The fireplace mantle had a collection of knickknacks from all parts of the world, a Greek burgundy urn and an African fertility mask, an antique maritime sextant, two more photographs of herself with friends, and an hourglass that looked as if it dated back to the Middle Ages, but I doubted that. On one of the walls was a large painting in a mahogany frame, arched corridors in what may have been a medieval castle, diminishing to infinity. Warmth and culture. That was the theme, and I liked it.

There were poetry books on the coffee table. I picked up the one closest to me and thumbed through it, opened it to the middle. This poet wrote about stars and the force of God in the wind, humanity's future as virtual as a hologram. I found most of it confusing but hypnotic to read, nonetheless. I put it back, sipped my drink, and waited.

Finally, she returned with a large shoebox. It looked as though it had seen some years, and she sat next to me and set the lid on the table. She also brought two pocket-sized leather-bound diaries and a few home-burned CDs. I took one and looked at it more closely to find it was actually a DVD. There were three of those.

Rachel nodded at the DVDs and CDs. "Those are from your uncle. This stuff was all he had, but I think you might be pretty intrigued. We just need to talk about some of the content first, not sure what's age appropriate and what's not. The DVDs were burned professionally this past week; the original footage was on Hi8 tapes that are obsolete now. There'd be no practical way to watch them." She smiled guiltily. "Yes, technology that was cool when we were in college is now ready for the Smithsonian. It'll happen to you, too, so don't laugh." She handed me the box. "I've had this stuff since I was twenty-one. Took it with me to Ohio, then on to Boston, and now here. I could never bring myself to throw it away or leave it behind, and now I'm so glad that I didn't."

I sat with the box in my lap, with the discs and the diaries. I didn't quite know what to make of it all. I thought I was here to listen to stories, maybe cop a few old pictures for a scrapbook, and I just looked at her, bewildered.

"We promised you everything," she said with a shrug. "We've got the journals now, too, so I think between this stuff and as many stories as your uncle and I can recall, it oughta cover it."

"And these?" I asked of the diaries.

"Those are mine," she said. "I wasn't as diligent as she about keeping daily entries, so they're probably a little sparse. Your mother—now, *she* was detailed, wanted to write a book about her life one day, and so she wrote down as much as she could so she wouldn't forget anything. But I was doing poetry, mostly, and I kept all that in a separate binder. You can keep those as long as you like." She pointed to the diaries. "Take your time, I'm not going anywhere."

"Okay."

The box was a hodgepodge of old photographs, stacked and strewn every which way, the edges curling, some of them cracking through the middles like Mom's notebook covers. Others were collected neatly in thick yellow-and-white Kodak packets. There were random bar coasters, a hemp bracelet knotted with pink seashells, a few memento beer caps, and a laminated dollar bill—*999,999 more to go* scribbled with a black Sharpie across the plastic.

Rachel was quiet, watching as I took the first picture and studied it, then turned it to the back for a date: *August, 1992* in faded ink. I recognized them both, Rachel and Mom at a table in a bar or a nightclub somewhere, sitting close, Mom with her arm across the back of Rachel's chair, and there was a young black guy with dreadlocks and glasses sitting next to Mom. Several bottles of Heineken and Budweiser cluttered the tabletop with a full ashtray and a pack of Marlboro Lights within reach, my mother's brand for years. Nobody was looking into the camera, a candid shot of Mom in mid-sentence, talking to someone outside the frame with Rachel focused on her, listening.

I smiled, laughed a little at how young they were, fresh-faced versions of their current selves, a time lapse backward. I chuckled at Mom's hair, so much longer than she'd ever worn it in my lifetime, the auburn spirals falling way down past her shoulders, like the cover of the Carole King *Tapestry* CD that Jackie liked to play in the car. She was a bit more slender during this time but still fit and healthy, her free arm tanned and resting on the table edge, a beer in her hand, and even at this distance her green eyes were the jewels I'd grown to love and fear, you couldn't miss them. Rachel's features hadn't quite matured yet, either; she looked more petite than she was now, and she had a baby face, the lines softer around her cheeks and mouth, but her lips and eyes were exactly the same, her golden blonde waves tied up into a loose twist, much the way she liked to wear it now.

I took out another small stack and shuffled through them. Rachel leaned over to look at them with me. Poses with friends in restaurants and apartment living rooms and college campuses. Another candid of Rachel, lounging on a plaid sofa with my mother, leaning back into her arms, her expression drowsy and relaxed, content to stay right there forever. I found a close-up of Mom in the next stack, resting against the passenger's side door of what might have been a truck, the world rushing by behind her, blowing a head full of ringlets in the open window breeze, those eyebrows jackknifed in a devilish grin. She looked as though she had just sneaked a handful of tacks onto your chair seat, and I grinned with her. I'd never seen her with such a smile in my life. The closest she had ever gotten to a smile like that was during her last months with Rachel, laughing and teasing her in the kitchen or in the front seat of the Land Cruiser. But even then it paled against the vibrancy captured in these photos of her youth.

Rachel took that one and looked at it as well. She smiled dreamily. "She was somethin else, your mother." She touched a fingertip to the photo and traced the lines of my mother's face, and she laughed a little. "I was so in love with this girl, it wasn't even funny. She could've asked me to go with her to Neptune, and I'd have my bags packed in an hour. I don't know what it was." She shook her head at herself. "But she would look at me with that smile and those eyes, and I'd feel my stomach soar like a roller coaster ride. Never failed. And she knew it, too." Then she said, mostly to herself, "But I had her locked onto me, just the same. I made sure of that, I had to. There was just too much competition, everybody loved her, men, women, you name it. She was one of those who pulled people in, like the moon to the tide."

She didn't say anything else for a long moment. She just sat there, gazing at my mother, and I was beginning to wonder if she'd forgotten about me.

She chuckled at Mom's mischievous grin. "Nut," she said to the picture, then put it aside with the others.

I grabbed one of the Kodak packs and opened it. The first was of the three young men in the other pictures, and Rachel pointed to each. "That's Dominick, Matt, and Evan. Dom's married now, lives in Michigan, works for Maxell doing some kind of music marketing. He came down for the funeral, actually, but he wasn't able to stay, or I would've introduced you. Evan, I'm not sure, haven't kept up with him in years, but last I knew, he was teaching at the University of Connecticut." Then her voice softened a bit, and a slight pall came over her. "Matt's no longer with us. He passed away pretty young." She nodded with a regretful smile but didn't elaborate.

Matt was taller than the other two, slim and lanky, with dark brown, cropped, shaggy hair and huge brown eyes. I wondered how he died, but it didn't seem my business to ask, so I left that alone. Dominick had a stocky build, the shortest of the three, with just a shadow of a beard and reddish curly hair, like a mini afro. He was amusing to look at and wore a silly smile that suggested he probably knew that. Evan was the guy in the bar picture with Mom and Rachel. He was handsome and smart looking with a goatee like Uncle Cam, and I really liked his dreadlocks. The three of them stood arm-over-shoulder in front of a bar café, a nighttime photo.

I flipped through the others and then stopped on one of Mom, sitting on a couch with the most hideous upholstery I'd ever seen in what appeared to be some kind of motor home. There was a long bay window at her back, a stainless steel sink to her right, and beyond that a narrow hallway leading into a makeshift bedroom. She glanced up into the camera, an eyebrow raised with a crooked smile, and she was holding a beautiful acoustic twelve-string guitar. It must have belonged to one of the guys.

I shuffled through the rest of the package, and soon the photos fell into a kind of series, several of them taken at one particular event—it was some sort of performance, a show or concert, but it wasn't at Symphony Hall. The place was a bar called Montego's, according to the banner on the back wall. I looked closer into the picture details, then realized it was Dominick at left stage, and he had a bass guitar. Matt sat opposite at a Fender keyboard, and Evan was in the back, shirtless and in mid-solo on the drums. And at the lead mic, with a black-and-burgundy Stratocaster guitar strapped across her shoulder, was my mother; she was the frontwoman.

I almost laughed out loud. It might have passed for a joke, but as I studied the photo more closely, I could see their postures were deliberate and professional, confident, at home behind their instruments. This was no lip sync contest, nothing close to a karaoke stunt for charity or door prizes. It was the real thing, and I looked up at Rachel, confused, trying to reconcile the Jolán De Carlo Edmunds who'd raised me with the girl in the pictures, the girl whose alien mothership had apparently come for her sometime around 1994 and replaced her with my mom.

Rachel smiled and let it simmer for a moment. She could have said something as soon as we had sat down, but now I realized she wanted me to discover it on my own, to have it naturally unfold there in my lap, develop right under my fingertips. I frowned, shuffled the pack, puzzled and dizzy with questions. My mother, illuminated under red-and-blue stage lights. My mother, standing at the mic in a swirl of equipment cords. My mother, soaked in sweat, auburn curls pasted to her neck and face, her Stradivarius hands around an electric Fender. My mother, beamed down from Planet Whatthefuck.

Rachel smiled at my astonishment, watching me stretch my brain around it like spandex shorts around a station wagon. But *how?* I sat holding the picture pack, searching the coffee table for what I thought of this.

"The guitar was your mother's second instrument," Rachel finally explained. She took one of the photos and smiled into it. "They were called Portland Downs. A roadhouse rock band, did mostly covers, requests. But God Almighty they were good," she muttered distantly.

She was quiet as she stared into the picture, caught between sweet nostalgia and lingering grief, and I could see her eyes growing shiny with fresh tears, but she blinked them away and smiled instead.

I didn't know what to say to that except, "But what about the violin? I thought . . ." And the notion trailed off into a great black hole that had just swallowed up everything I thought I knew about my mother.

"Oh, she still played," Rachel assured. She took up another picture and looked at it for a moment. "But Jolán De Carlo had a whole other gift." She shook her head, thinking on my mother's secret talent, lost in 1992. "So, she took this era to focus exclusively on that, took a break from the violin, I guess you could say. Traveled around the country for close to a year, doing gigs everywhere from Portland to Denver."

"But how come she never said anything?" I asked. It still made no sense. It wasn't a big deal, now that I was settling into the idea, so why the secrecy? "She never once picked up a guitar or gave any hints that she knew how to play one. I don't get it."

Rachel thought about that for a moment. "There were reasons for that. Some of them I understand now, but not all of them. It was her life, her choices, so what could I do?"

"What reasons?"

She looked at me and sipped her drink. "Well, I've been thinking on that for several weeks, actually. And I know I could just tell you outright, lay it on the table as is. But I think it'd be best if you understood what happened in context, in the scheme of everything that was going on at the time. I know your dad wants to talk to you about some things, too. But in the meantime, I'll tell you my version, my experiences with her as I remember them. Then you can take these videos and CDs with you, check them out on your own time, at your own pace, and when we get to your mother's journals and look through those, you'll have a better understanding of what you're reading. How about that?"

"I guess so." I shrugged, nodded. "If you think it's better that way."

"I do."

AND SO WE spent the rest of the afternoon together, a good portion of it on the couch with the photos and memorabilia. She started from the first night she'd ever seen my mother, at a bar in Hollywood called The Regal Blue. She was a cocktail server then, working the night Portland Downs was booked to play.

We decided to make dinner while she told me the rest, and by the time we finished eating, she had only gotten to their second date, but it was fascinating. I was learning a version of my mother so contrary to what she'd shown me over the years that sometimes I forgot whom Rachel was describing. She said seventeen years changes a person, reshapes your temperament and seasons your viewpoints on everything from politics to spiritual beliefs, and now, at twenty-one years old, I can say that she was right. I've only had seven years since that evening to evolve, but I can see my own very complicated and subtle process, the shape-shifting metamorphosis from a bemused and displaced ninth grader to a young woman in my senior year in college, trying to plan a future in music education.

I took those videos, CDs, and diaries, the pictures and mementos home with me, and I spent the next weeks, months, and years immersed in the storm that was Jolán De Carlo. I watched her living and laughing, eating and sleeping, playing her music and loving Rachel Cole so much it was nearly overwhelming, free as oxygen, and as Pap would say, full of piss and vinegar. She was confident to a fault. Invincible at twenty-two. I poured over her journals in their proper chronology, seventeen in all. I read them over and over for years, and in them I saw the transformation like climate change—gradual, understated, disbelieved until the waters rose and swept her under, but I can say her perseverance was impressive. She'd never lost that trait. It was the one familiar thread that connected her youth to the woman who drove me to school every day and tucked me into bed at night.

I'm not so sure I see change as ruthless as I once did, but I also don't know if it will be any kinder to me than it was to my mother. Decisions make all the difference, Rachel said that night over dinner. They quantify everything that is to come, and they tallied up Jolán De Carlo like quadratics and, in the end, left her with but one legacy—me, hoping now to do her justice by telling her story as she would have wanted, with no illusions and without pretense. I owe her infinitely more and nothing less.

And so this is where I must begin . . .

Part II

chapter seven

THE NAME PORTLAND Downs was an amalgamation of the two major horse tracks in Portland, Oregon—Emerald Downs and Portland Meadows. It had come from Matt's Uncle Rick who lived in surrounding Aloha and who had a compulsive gambling affliction. When Uncle Rick won a thirty-thousand-dollar windfall on "Campaign Daddy" in 1983, he took his winnings and purchased a thirty-five-foot Class-A Fleetwood Pace Arrow motor home, fully loaded with all the bells and whistles, a microwave, working kitchen and bath, a single bedroom, a television, and a large-capacity storage area beneath the coach.

In 1985, Uncle Rick was diagnosed with chronic sciatica, and his dream to visit every major landmark in the country crumbled and left the Fleetwood sitting in the front yard for six years while he endured two surgeries and searched futilely for a cure. Finally, in 1991, he conceded to his lower back problems and put the Fleetwood up for sale. Nobody wanted it. The vehicle sat for another year until his nephew, Matt Frantz, a twenty-one-year-old pianist at Berklee College in Boston, and Matt's schoolmates—Dominick Keller, Evan Mahan, and my mother, Jolán De Carlo—made him a thousand-dollar proposition to take it off his hands. There was only one condition.

"You'll have to come and get it," Uncle Rick told Matt over the phone after he agreed to the price. "I'll have my mechanic give it a once-over, make sure she runs. But I'm not coming to you. And I doubt you're willing to pay to have it towed across the whole United States."

Rick had sent them a picture of the Fleetwood the previous week, just the outside. It was as long as a school bus, a three-tone brown-and-tan metal box on wheels, but the body was in good shape. It was perfect. And who else would go that low on the price but a relative?

A relative who lived three thousand miles from the Berklee campus.

"ARE YOU *SHITTIN* me?" Dominick looked at Matt and my mother as if they'd suggested a mission to Saturn, land on the rings, do laps.

"We can take Evan's 4Runner," Mom said. "Three days, max. We get through finals, graduation, and by the end of the next week we're on the road." She was seated on the couch next to Matt in his apartment, the two of them peering up at Dom, hopeful, the future a vast, empty frontier.

"We can stay with Rick and Aunt Lenni," Matt said, rolling a joint as he spoke, and he licked the paper, lit it, and took a drag. "Lenni said she knows people in Portland, she can get us gigs. We do a few shows, use the money to move on down to Frisco, Sacramento, and by the end of the summer, we'll have a fan base all over the west coast."

"Voilà!" Dom tossed up his hands and let them drop. He regarded them both incredulously. "And by the end of *next* summer, we'll make back the money it cost to get to *Portland*. Brilliant business strategy. Remind me to give you my retirement portfolio when we get back."

"I thought you wanted to do this," Mom said with a sigh.

"I *do*. But why can't we find something *here?* No one has an RV in Massachusetts? No one camps? Maybe it's the climate."

Matt handed the joint to my mother and got up and went to the kitchen table and grabbed that week's *Boston Globe*. It was open to the classifieds, the local prospects circled in black ink, and he brought it into the living room, reading aloud. "1985 thirty-two-foot Winnebago Class B, fifteen thousand bucks or best offer. '82 Airstream, thirty-foot, remodeled interior, ten thousand dollars. Well, that's much better. Oh, here's one; Dodge Sportsman, 1987, fifty-five-thousand miles, only nine thousand bucks. You're right, dude. They're giving these things away." And he tossed the paper onto the coffee table.

Dominick stared down at the classifieds. He ran a hand through his wiry hair, massaged his bearded chin, and shook his head.

"So, we start the tour on the west coast instead," Mom said through a toke of the joint. "Big deal. They've probably got better clientele there, anyway, not so many hicks when you get too far south. Out there, California *is* the south. We won't end up tied to a tree in our underwear somewhere, squealing like a pig." She raised an eyebrow and grinned, blew a stream of smoke out between them. "Unless that's your thing, of course. Your business is your own."

"That's real nice," Dom mumbled, staring at her. "That's wonderful imagery."

"Thank you. It's not mine."

"Yeah, I know."

She looked at Matt. "What about our gear? There's no way it'll fit in Evan's car with the rest of us, too. We've been caravanning to gigs around here, but we can't do that for three thousand miles. Hence, the need for the RV, no?"

Matt thought on it, shrugged a little, thought some more. "We're gonna have to ship it. Just the big stuff, the PA's, guitar amps, mostly."

Mom sucked the air through a grimace, half shook her head, and flicked the ashes into the ashtray. "Uh, yikes. Are you serious?"

Matt tapped his pen on his chin and stared at her, contemplating a cheaper alternative, but there was none. "It won't be so bad, split four ways. About a bill each."

"Yeah, and for the record," Dom said. "A bill would mean one hundred of *these.*" And he pulled a dollar from his jeans pocket and flapped it in their faces.

"Listen, it's doable," Matt said to him. "Your investment in this venture would be exactly $427. If you didn't eat."

"And, of course, I don't." Dom pursed his lips. He stood thinking it all over, his hands on his hips. Mom and Matt waited. After a very long while, he finally nodded, begrudgingly. "All right. Screw it. Let's go. If it turns into a disaster, I'll just take you both out of my will."

Matt made a sad face, pouting his lower lip. "Aw, you mean I won't get your Zippo collection and the keys to the Datsun?"

Dom pointed at him. "That truck has classic tags. It's a *cherry.* Asshole," he muttered and walked away to the kitchen, and he grabbed a Budweiser from the fridge.

Mom and Matt slapped a high five.

Mom took another hit, then checked her watch. "Shit, I got a class in twenty minutes. Gotta go, gotta go." She handed the joint to Matt, then called to Dom as she grabbed her bag and went to the door. "You're a damned good man, Dominick Keller. It'll all be worth it, we promise."

Dom waved her off and grumbled something through a swig of beer, and she hurried out into the late April afternoon, backpack over her shoulder.

She met Evan in the building breezeway on her way downstairs. He nodded a greeting on his way up. "What's goin on? You gone already?"

"We're gonna need your car," she told him as she passed.

He stopped. "Uh, okay. Where we goin?"

"Portland."

"Maine?"

"Oregon."

"What?" He turned and followed her.

"Matt's got all the details. I gotta go, I'm late." She unlocked her mountain bike from the railing, slung the pack onto her back and hopped on. She nodded up to the second floor window. "Just make sure Dom doesn't talk himself out of it again. I'll be back tonight."

Evan stood at the edge of grass, watching her go. "Out of it. Out of *what?* Jo!"

Mom wheeled off toward the main road, waving, auburn curls blowing like tendrils as she vanished around the corner.

AND THAT WAS how "everything" started. My mother had done her undergraduate studies at Berklee, the very school she snubbed when I'd chosen it for myself, and I was perplexed by this. Through the first ten journals, I couldn't figure it out. She'd gotten a scholarship, a full ride through violin performance. She was a stellar academic, a gifted musician, at one of the most prestigious music schools in the country, and she never mentioned a word of it to me. It took years of research into all the chronicles of her life to uncover the elusive reasons, hours and hours of home video shot by Uncle Cam during a month he'd spent with Portland Downs after his high school graduation, a gift of sorts from Mom, and the bane of my grandparents who despised this new alternative music venture as a roadhouse blues guitarist.

Cam explained her shift in aspirations while at an outdoor music festival in Little Five Points, during the spring after she passed away. He said the guitar had originally been his instrument, that he'd gotten a Johnson acoustic for his eleventh birthday and began lessons a month later. He was poorly apt, hadn't the musical affinity my mother had shown since kindergarten, and he struggled through the weekly instruction.

My mother was fourteen at the time, and she would hear him practicing in his bedroom or in the family room, plucking half-muted scales and strumming botched chords until he was red in the face with frustration. His fingertips had become swollen and blistered, so much that he'd be forced to put the instrument down for an entire week to let them heal, which only dragged him right back to lesson one for lack of practice.

It was a relentless cycle for weeks, and she began to feel sorry for him, tried to explain the theoretical concepts behind the chord structures and the tonal intervals that built their corresponding scales, but it was nuclear fission, calculus wrapped in black hole thermodynamics, and the mechanical application of it all was just too physically painful. But not for my mother. She'd had eleven years, my uncle's entire lifetime, to develop calluses on her left-hand fingers from the violin, and once she figured out the tuning differences between the two instruments and transposed what she knew from four strings to a six-string, everything else augmented rather quickly. Too quickly. By her senior year in high school, she was hooked and she was *good*, dividing her time between the violin and guitar now, enough to sit in with a neighborhood band that played their school prom and did birthday parties.

My grandparents frowned upon it and insisted she concentrate on the violin; you could teach at a university, or earn a steady living with the Pops or the Philadelphia Symphony, stay out of trouble, meet yourself a nice man and live out their dreams.

She'd gotten halfway there when she found herself at Berklee College, a senior poised to begin graduate school in the fall of '92 as one-fourth of Portland Downs, its lead guitarist and frontwoman who'd just made the three-thousand-mile trip to Aloha, looking to go in on the purchase of "Betty," the thirty-five-foot motor home, compliments of Campaign Daddy.

"SO, WHO'S GONNA drive it?" Evan asked the others on the day of their arrival.

They all stood in the yard, looking at it, arms folded across their chests, the Oregon springtime chirping from the meadow at the edge of Uncle Rick's property, a sweet breeze perfumed with English lavender and blue fortune. Rick got in and started it up. Betty coughed and rumbled and sent a diesel cloud drifting past their heads.

Dom looked at him grimly, fanned away the fumes. "Well, we thought since you have a sport utility vehicle that you would drive it."

Evan lifted his eyebrows and peered over his glasses. "And you have a truck. Why can't you drive it?"

Dom shook his head. "The Datsun has lower suspension, it's not the same."

"And this is the same as a Toyota?" Evan held a hand out to Betty. Uncle Rick revved the engine, and it roared and sputtered. "I drove from Boston to Des Moines, dude. I forfeit." He waved him away. "You got us all the way from the Big Boy in Omaha, Nebraska, to the Shell station in Lincoln . . . *Nebraska.*"

"All right, guys. Shut up." Mom sighed. "We rotate. That's what we should've done on the way out here, but we're here now. Is he gonna let us see the inside?" she asked Matt, and so he waved an arm for Uncle Rick's attention. Rick shut the engine off and climbed down into the yard.

"She's got a new battery now," he said, adjusting his pants at the waistband, pulling them up over a beer gut. "The damn thing sat for so long, the other one looked like it had barnacles on it, there was so much corrosion. But no worries." He smiled. "They replaced all the wires, new distributor cap, rebuilt the carburetor, replaced a couple blown fuses. Your generator's good for a hundred-and-eighty-five hours, not much, but it'll get you through if you're conservative. And you've got towing capability, plenty of pulling power for that." He clapped his hands and rubbed them together. "So, you ready for the grand tour?"

He showed them to the side door, demonstrated the retractable awning, and pointed out the basement storage along the hull. He brought them inside. The first thing to assault the eye was the upholstery. Dirt brown, camel tan, burnt orange, and flat black triangles packed into kaleidoscope patterns so disorienting it made you dizzy. On the sofa. Around the driver's and passenger's seats. Up the curtains. Along the cushioned Formica table benches. Mom looked at Evan, and Evan looked at Matt, and Matt looked at Uncle Rick who proceeded to show them that the microwave worked like new. The only one who liked it was Dominick.

He saw their faces and shrugged. "What? It's retro. Vintage. And so are we. It's totally us."

"No," Mom muttered. "No, it is *not* us. It's *A Clockwork Orange*, and I don't mean the color."

"Yeah, well, we're stuck with it now," Evan said beneath his breath as Uncle Rick opened up the refrigerator and cabinets, explained the features of the stereo system and where you could control the air conditioning units. "I'm gonna need a new prescription when I get out of here," he mumbled and took off his glasses, polished them on his shirttail, and put them back on again, blinking.

"Probably why he couldn't sell it for six years," Mom whispered with a smirk, and he nodded.

"She's only got ten thousand miles on her. We took a couple trips to Yellowstone and back in '84 and '85, and then, ya know . . ." Uncle Rick gestured to his back. "My wife's scared to drive the thing, wouldn't get behind the wheel if she was being chased by a T-Rex. So," he shrugged, "here she sat. I started her up a few times, drove her into town on occasion, but if you're not on vacation, who the hell wants to maneuver this boat around a grocery lot?"

He showed them the bathroom, the extra closet space, and the bedroom with the island bed and the overhead lamps built into the headboard. He stepped outside to give them time to settle in and left them with an invitation for dinner in an hour.

"So, who gets this?" Dom asked the others about the sleeper.

"We draw straws," Evan suggested.

"Rocks-paper-scissors. It's better," Matt said.

Mom rolled her eyes. "We *rotate*. None of that worked for the drive out here, did it?"

"It's not our fault if Evan's unlucky," Matt told her.

"I'm not unlucky, you prick. You cheated."

"How can you *cheat* at rocks-paper-scissors? Are you serious?" Matt said.

"Oh, my God," my mother breathed, exasperated. "Knock it off. Christ. We'll work it out, okay? We'll figure out a schedule for driving, sleeping, pissing, bitching. All of it. Just quit with the bickering. You're like a couple of old women, for shit's sake."

THEY TOOK DINNER in the house with Aunt Lenni and Uncle Rick—pot roast piled with new potatoes and carrots, mushrooms and peas, tall glasses of iced tea, and lemon meringue pie. Comfort food,

Lenni called it. She was a petite woman, silver hair wrapped in a pre-tied headband, pretty for her age, as attractive as Nanna Sylvia. She said she had friends from the bowling league who spent a lot of time at the bars and taverns around Portland. She would make a few calls, try to arrange for my mother's band to meet with the right people, but it might take a few days.

"I imagine it's rock 'n' roll, you guys play," she said to Mom while she and Matt helped with the dinner dishes.

"It's not that stuff they're doing now, is it?" Uncle Rick asked from the living room recliner. "That gangster crap, shoot 'em up bang bang, your mother's a whore stuff?"

Matt rolled his eyes and dried a plate. "No, Uncle Rick. Nobody gets killed. We're a cover band right now, till we can get some originals together."

"Mostly older stuff. Clapton, Hendrix, stuff like that. We had a percussionist for a few months in Boston, did some Santana for a while. But he graduated, moved to New York." Mom rinsed a handful of silverware and set it on Matt's side of the sink. "If we can find a replacement someday, we'll put that back on the set list, but for now it's mostly classic rock, blues."

Lenni gave that a nostalgic smile. "Hendrix, huh? Which tunes? You know I was at Woodstock, right? I was nineteen, covered in mud, and high as a robin in a Redwood."

"You were at Woodstock?" Evan marveled from the living room. "That is beyond cool. If I had a time machine, that's where I'd go, 1969 Woodstock, New York. And maybe to fourth century ancient Greece, watch the Spartans kick the hell out the Persians, but definitely Woodstock."

Dom snorted and sipped his beer. "You would totally get your ass kicked. The Spartans?"

"I didn't say participate." Evan winced at him. "I said *watch*. From a cliff. Or a mountain or something. What the hell is the matter with you?"

Dom tossed up a hand. "With me? You're the one who wants to take on Xerxes. Or was it Achilles? Either one, you'd get your skull smashed. You *and* your time machine."

"Neither," Evan told him. "Neither one was a Spartan. Read a book. And I didn't say that. You took it completely out of context."

"Whatever," Dom mumbled. "You. Spartan. Brain. Pudding. That's all I'm sayin."

Mom ignored them and said to Lenni, "We've got 'Voodoo Chile' and 'Are You Experienced' down pretty well, 'Little Wing.' I can't bring myself to set my guitar on fire, though, as much as my folks would probably like that."

Lenni grinned. "Uh oh. They must disapprove." She nodded to Matt. "His mother's my sister, and Matthew is a very lucky boy. He's had a lot of support, which is why we let you guys have the RV at such a steal. We know how it is. You have a dream and wanna make it a reality. Betty's a good idea." And she glanced out the window, to where the RV was parked in the front yard. "She'll get you where you need to go, that's for sure."

"Jo's a violinist, too," Matt told her. "Virtuoso type, a scholarship jockey. Just got accepted into grad school."

"Double major?" Lenni asked her, and Mom shook her head, handed Matt a glass to dry.

"Nah. Guitar's a hobby. I just love it too much not to play. Can't really explain it."

"She's Stevie Ray incarnate," Dominick said. "He crossed over and then crossed right back the minute we counted off 'Cold Shot' the first time at practice. I kid you not. The voice and everything, just a female version."

Mom raised an eyebrow and looked at him sideways. "I would call that blasphemy, and so would about a million of his fans. Have you lost your mind?" She shook her head at Lenni. "That's not true. I do okay. I hold my own, but that's it."

"Three people said the exact same thing within a week, completely unrelated to each other," he said. "Take a compliment, for Christ's sake. Be encouraged. You think I'd be here, three thousand miles from the original plan and five hundred bucks in the hole if that *wasn't* true?"

Mom shook her head again and told Lenni, "We work really hard to get the songs right, do them justice. We're a cover band. We imitate. We just do it well, that's all. It's where the money is. You suck, you don't get gigs. No gigs, no money. Pretty simple."

Lenni smiled. She handed her a mixing bowl to rinse. "Looks like your band really believes in you. They'll follow you anywhere, it sounds."

Mom looked around at her band mates—Dom on the couch with a Budweiser bottle, watching the local news with Uncle Rick, Evan in the other recliner, doing the same, and Matt, working next to her with a kitchen towel and a dripping Pyrex pan. She breathed a deep sigh. "Yeah, well, either that, or they're all completely nuts."

THE REST OF the equipment showed up the next afternoon. Two big black power amps, Mom's guitar amp, Dom's bass amp, three monitor speakers, two rolling console racks, and Evan's drum kit, packed in soft black travel cases. He had a ten-piece burgundy set with gleaming brass cymbals. He inventoried everything meticulously when it arrived, looking for scratches and dents, divots in the drumheads, accounting for every wing nut and cymbal pad, the double bass drum pedals, the cymbal stands, the drum seat. It was all there, undamaged and ready to go.

The plan was to load the drum kit and the smaller amps into the 4Runner, which could be towed behind Betty as an equipment trailer, and then haul the instruments and power amps in the RV, because in two days they were to play their first west coast gig. It was a private party that Aunt Lenni found through a neighbor lady who'd taken the band's demo tape to the function's organizer, a man named Martin Reed who'd called them back within an hour after he'd listened to it. They were willing to pay eight hundred dollars.

"Why?" Matt asked Lenni after he hung up the phone with Mr. Reed.

"Well, it's at the Ellington Club, hon. It's a country club in Portland. I really don't think they're all that concerned about the pay. If they wanna give you eight hundred bucks, kid, don't balk. Take it. Jeezus."

"Yeah, it nearly covers Betty in one show. Are you kidding?" Mom told him. "What kind of function is this, anyway?"

Matt shrugged. "I dunno. He just said it was a private banquet. Not black tie or anything, just a closed event. Might be a birthday party or something. Anniversary? Class reunion, maybe? He heard our demo, he knows what we play, so whatever. What difference does it make? Get money, *chica*." He grinned and patted her shoulder, then went out to the RV to tell the others.

THEY SET UP in Uncle Rick's garage and rehearsed for the next two days. That was when they decided to change the original band name from The Infamous They, which was already taken by a punk metal band out of Jersey and with whom they were much too often confused, to Portland Downs, after Uncle Rick's 1983 windfall. They slept in the Fleetwood to stay out of Rick and Lenni's way and to familiarize themselves with the new mobile living arrangements. It took another round of rocks-paper-scissors to decide who would start the rotation for the master sleeper. Mom won. Then they went alphabetically to determine the driving shifts and the rest of the bedroom order, which put Dominick at the wheel, two days later, as they loaded Betty up and towed the Toyota along Interstate 5 toward the Ellington Club.

"This thing handles like a fucking skateboard," he grumbled, gripping the wheel as if it were trying to escape. He kept checking the side views, glancing at the dashboard display, wrestling Betty into submission. "How do we know if the 4Runner's okay? I can't even see it," he muttered.

He changed lanes, heading for the Dalles exit. Someone blew a horn. He swerved and Betty rocked, knocking Matt's soda off the table.

"If you kill us before our first show out here, I swear to God," Matt snapped. He found a t-shirt from the clothes pile on the sofa, checked to make sure it was his, then dropped it to the floor and soaked up the Sprite with his foot.

"Had to go in alphabetical order for the driving," Dom said. "Not the bed, of course. But the driving."

"Stop whining," Mom said to him. She was in the passenger's seat, a foot propped on the dash. "That was two nights ago. Tonight's your night, so just relax and get us to this place in one piece, please." She took a cigarette from her pack, lit it, and gave it to him. "Here. Chill out." Then she lit one for herself and cracked the window.

"So, what's the set list for this shit, anyway?" he asked her.

"The same as we did in Hartford at The Hidden Door." She blew smoke out the window. "Everything we rehearsed. 'Fool in the Rain,' 'Dear Mr. Fantasy,' 'Don't Fear the Reaper,' that list. And whatever's on the demo, since they liked that. What is it? 'Stairway to Heaven'?" She shook her head. "But we can't do that one right; we don't have Gwen on flute, so skip it. What else?"

"We can do it. Just replace it with the keyboard."

"Yeah, but it sounds like shit that way; we need Gwen. We've got 'Little Wing' on there. 'Crazy On You,' but I wanna take the key down another step, it's still too high. I can hit it, but my voice'll be shot before we get through the first set."

"What about 'Ramble On'?" Matt suggested from the couch. "I can play rhythm guitar, you on acoustic. I got the chords and licks for the break. You showed me last semester, and I still know it. Plus, you and Evan sing the hell outa that song. People love it."

Mom half shrugged, took a long drag, flicked the ashes into the breeze. "That's too much Zeppelin, though. Just stick with the Hidden Door list, the Hendrix stuff, Stevie and Clapton, and the demo tracks. That oughta be eight-hundred-bucks worth. This gig came up quick, so they'll get what we know." She watched the Portland cityscape rise up out of the traffic and sat thinking. "We gotta put some more originals together, seriously. We're too qualified to keep spittin out other people's shit every weekend. We've got degrees, for Christ's sake. Or damn near, anyway."

"That's what I keep saying," Evan agreed. "We did that one, the real progressive one with the crazy time signature. Dom was killin the bass till it fell apart at the end. Just gotta work out an ending, and it'll be straight. And give it a name."

"I think we should call it 'I Got My Ass Kicked by the Spartans,'" Dom suggested. "You can get full production credit, come out wearing a red cape and a little kilt, the helmet with the Mohawk brush thing across the top. Chicks'll go crazy."

Mom laughed and coughed through a hit of her cigarette. "Yeah, trying to get *away.* " She slapped fives with Dom.

Evan shook his head. "Dick," he muttered. "And kilts were for the Scottish, idiot. Can't believe you're still on that shit, anyway." He watched the cars pass. "What was that? Like a week ago?"

Dom steered Betty to the exit ramp and glanced over his shoulder, grinning around the cigarette between his lips.

"Okay, and so 'Spartans' is one," Matt said. "What about the other two-hours-and-fifty minutes?"

"It's not about the fucking Spartans," Evan insisted and cut his eyes back to window. "Let it die, for Christ's sake. What the hell?"

"We have others," Mom said, smirking at Evan. "Everything's unfinished. Instead of working on another Hendrix song, we need to work on those. They take longer to learn, but it'll be worth it. Just gotta do it. Do it until we do it, right?"

THE ELLINGTON CLUB sat right in the middle of a rolling emerald golf course, a thick line of pines and sycamores like a wall around the edge of the green. They pulled Betty around the circular drive and up in front of the clubhouse, parked, and went inside and asked for Martin Reed. He came out of the back office, a middle-aged man, smiling with his hand extended. He wore a white polo shirt and a pair of crisp brown Dickies and penny loafers, no pennies.

He shook my mother's hand. "Thanks for doing this on such short notice." He led them back out the front door and across the lawn toward an adjacent building where the event would take place. "We had a local group scheduled a month ago, but their drummer broke his ankle playing softball last week, so that was the end of that. I hope the pay is fair. It's what we'd planned on giving the other outfit, so it's all the same to me. I'll give you cash at the end of the night. Just come find me." He turned and smiled at them as they walked. "So, you're friends of Mona, then? A relative, one of you?"

"She's my aunt's neighbor," Matt said. "She's the one who gave you our tape. No relation."

"I see. It's all about who you know in your line of work, isn't it? Great demo, by the way. Perfect for this, the classic stuff. Great renditions." He gestured to Mom. "And a female up front, at that. Can't go wrong, there. That you I heard on the guitar?"

"It is," she said.

He grinned. "Not many girls play like that. You're certainly not timid with that instrument, that's for sure."

"Plays the same, no matter which gender has a hold of it," she said. "Same strings, same notes."

They had come to the main ballroom, and he showed them where to set up. The late-day sun came through the floor-to-ceiling windows and cast wide columns onto the polished parquet floors. Ten banquet tables were arranged around the room with maroon tablecloths and pink carnation bouquets in the center of each, tucked into tall glass vases. Banquet servers were laying out silverware, folding napkins into pyramids at each table, scooping ice into silver serving pitchers. There was a kitchen in the back, and the chefs came and went through the swinging metal door. They lit little blue flames under long stainless steel food warmers and brought out stacks of glass salad plates, sharpened their carving knives.

Matt looked for the closest electrical outlets and found two along the wall behind the stage, which wasn't really a stage but rather an open side of the room where they would have to lay a set of oriental rugs to keep the amps from scuffing the floors. It was all routine.

"So, is this some kind of class reunion or something?" he asked Mr. Reed. "That why you went with us, with the retro sound?"

Martin clasped his hands behind his back and smiled. "Well, it is a reunion of sorts. Mona didn't tell you?"

Matt shook his head, glanced at Mom. "She just took our demo, told my aunt you might call if you were interested, but nothing else."

Mr. Reed gestured to the opposite side of the room, where two attendants were hanging a big plastic banner between the windows. *1992 Annual Cancer Survivors' Banquet.*

"We do this every year," he told them. "Been doing it since '85, and it's always been a wonderful success. We've gained a few attendees over the years, lost a few."

Dom turned away from him and took the cigarette pack from his shirt pocket and stuffed it into his jeans.

"But we should have a great turnout tonight, and I think they'll love you." Mr. Reed pointed to the food table, where the Bunsen burners simmered. "Help yourselves to anything you want. It's our pleasure to share. Life's too short to be stingy, right?" He left them with the start time and headed out onto the grounds toward the golf shack.

Dom looked at Matt as if he'd brought them to a funeral. Matt shrugged him off. "What? How was I supposed to know it was a cancer thing? She didn't tell me that."

"I *asked* you," Mom said. "Two *days* ago. That was your cue to maybe find the fuck out."

"I don't see what the big deal is," Evan said. "They're just gonna eat. And talk about . . . hell, I dunno . . . medication or whatever, and they wanna hear music, dance or somethin. So, we play. Play and get paid. That's what we do, right? Who cares what it's for. It's eight hundred bucks."

Mom thought on it and nodded. "You're right, you're right. It's just a show. Just would've been nice to be prepared, but we can do this. We're professionals." She took another look around the performance area, sized it up for space. "All right. Well, come on. Let's bring Betty around so we can load in."

IT TOOK THIRTY minutes to set everything up, and by that time a few of the guests had begun to arrive. The dress was casual, which was a small relief to the band in their tattered jeans and cardigans and t-shirts. Most of them were Mr. Reed's age, the oldest maybe sixty-something, still young enough to appreciate the song selections, another minor comfort.

The band did a quick sound check with "Voodoo Chile," tested the acoustics, refined their instrument tuning. Mom stepped out in front while they played, listening for quirks in the EQing, training her canine hearing on the monitor speakers, making corrections on the sound mixer until all the tonal shades were perfect. When they finished, the handful of early goers gave a pleasant round of applause while Martin Reed stood watching from the ballroom doorway. He shot them another big smile and a thumbs-up.

After a while, the rest of the guests straggled in and found seats, about a hundred or so, and they filled the room with chatter, sipped their iced teas and bottled beer and white wine while the banquet servers went around with the ice water pitchers. Mom and the rest of the band took advantage of the open bar and got themselves bottles of Bud Light and stood around waiting for things to begin. They didn't know when they were supposed to go on. There were program flyers at each table on which Portland Downs was listed individually at the top as "music performed by . . ." but nothing more. Mom took one and folded it up into her jeans pocket for a keepsake. She did that with every show, as I found many of them tucked into the pages of her journals between the corresponding entries.

Soon Mr. Reed came to the stage. He tapped Mom's mic to be sure it was on, introduced himself, and went through a monologue about the history of the function, the money raised for research since the last event, the medical advancements over the years, all of which got healthy applause, deservedly so. Then he handed the show over to a gentleman in the back at a movie projector, and the place grew very quiet. The staff went to the windows and drew the curtains to dim the daylight, and a mechanical movie screen unrolled at the front of the room. A video presentation began. No one had said anything about that, but the band watched patiently with everyone else.

It was snippets of a home movie, one of the reunion attendees with her children at the beach in Santa Cruz, waving to the camera in big white sunglasses, the Pacific surf rushing over the sand as "Don't Let the Sun Go Down On Me" played through the PA system. The clip then faded into a head shot of the same woman. It was tagged with her birth and death dates in white French script; she had passed away six months ago. Mom and the guys shared an uncomfortable glance but kept watching.

The theme music continued, and so did the film, another candid clip of another reunion guest, washing his car and laughing and flicking suds at the camera lens. Then he was riding a horse along a wooded trail with friends and family, and then a still shot of him and his wife, his name, birth, and death dates fading away as Elton serenaded them along.

The next was a series of photographs of another guest, a woman not much older than the band members themselves; the music changed; "Someone Saved My Life Tonight." Pictures of her college graduation, her wedding, shots of her various hospital stays.

Sobs and sniffles began to move around the room. Some of the guests held hands at the tables. Others watched with brows furrowed, hands folded sorrowfully at their chins as the images passed across the screen in languid, sentimental frames, timed to the music. This went on for ten minutes, and it still wasn't over. "Goodbye Yellow Brick Road," "Landslide," vacation footage and holiday candids and tears, birthdates, death dates.

"You have got to be kidding me," Dom leaned in and uttered to Mom, looking around at the tables, at the people holding one another, tissues and handkerchiefs out, dabbing their eyes, some of them at prayer.

Everyone in the band looked at Matt; he pretended not to notice until he couldn't anymore.

"What?" he hissed and gave them a desperate shrug, frowning. "How was I supposed to know they'd do this? He didn't say anything about a freakin . . ." And he held a hand out to the movie screen, then folded his arms tight across his chest. "This is so not my fault. I am not taking the heat for this. Fuck that."

"The entire audience is in *tears*. We are a *rock* band. We play high energy and blues. *Blues,"* she reiterated, glaring at him while the music serenaded a hundred guests into mourning. "Does it look like we're prepared to entertain these people with the list we rehearsed?"

"So much for opening with 'Don't Fear the Reaper,'" Dom mumbled, watching the crowd weep for their friends.

"Yeah, cross that shit off your set lists. Christ," Mom instructed frantically. "We're not starting with that. And get rid of 'Stairway to Heaven,' too. I didn't wanna do that one, anyway, so it's just as well."

"So, now what do we open with?" Evan asked. "If we don't turn this crowd around, we're not gonna see eight hundred *cents."*

"I'd dig up anything we can find with the word 'alive' in the title," Dom said. "I'll play the freakin Bee Gees right now, if I have to."

Mom shook her head, watching as the memorial film finally faded to a close. "I dunno. I'll figure something out. When it's time, just follow my lead."

The curtains were thrown open again, and the late afternoon sun beamed into the room. The guests blew their noses and murmured remembrances, some still embracing, speaking comfort to one another while Mr. Reed strolled back to the microphone.

"This is always the most bittersweet of our gatherings," he said, peering around the room with a solemn countenance. "But we must never forget those who fought so courageously to remain with us for as long as possible. They were our friends, our loved ones, and they will be dearly missed."

Dom glared at Matt again. "Don't let me forget to put my foot up your ass when we get back to your uncle's."

Mr. Reed gestured to the band. "We'll go ahead and help ourselves to dinner in just a few, but first may I introduce our entertainment for tonight, straight from Boston Massachusetts, here to give us a night of classic tunes from the some of the best years of our lives . . . Portland Downs."

And the audience crackled with applause.

"You and me." Dom pointed at Matt as they took their places. "I'm your new proctologist. You just call me Dr. Dom."

Matt gave him a glower but otherwise ignored him and took a seat behind the keyboard.

The place was silent as a desert. They all sat waiting, drying their eyes, composing themselves for whatever came next. My mother had a twelve-string acoustic and the Fender both leaning in A-frame stands beside Matt's keyboard, and she grabbed the acoustic, shouldered it, and stood at the mic. She cleared her throat, looked around the room, gave everyone a discomfited smile. They all waited.

After a long moment, she finally said, "My grandmother on my dad's side, she uh, she wasn't one to hold her tongue. She was from Italy, and uh, she was diagnosed with stomach cancer when she was fifty-seven. It was a pretty long battle, six years, and she fought like a champ, wasn't afraid one bit. Way too feisty for that." The audience chuckled a little, and so she continued. "Well, when the time came, my dad asked her how she wanted her, uh, her final arrangements, and she said she wanted to be cremated. So, he asked if there was anything special she wanted done with the ashes, and she said no, and she told him, 'just put them in an envelope and mail them to the IRS, with a little note attached that says: *there, now you have everything.*'"

It was a blind leap, a gut call, and she prayed to the entertainment gods that it wouldn't go over like an iron kite. And it didn't. The crowd laughed and applauded, and the mournful faces turned to grins.

Mom exhaled. "I thought we might spend tonight celebrating the lives of those who've passed on after fighting like hell with this disease, your friends and family, and my grandmother, Elena De Carlo. I know Nanni Lena wouldn't have it any other way. She might prefer Sinatra to the classic rock we're gonna play for you tonight, but she's just gonna have to let us have this one. My name is Jolán De Carlo, and we are Portland Downs." She turned to the band and gestured to Matt to grab the Stratocaster, then counted off "Over the Hills and Far Away."

AT THE TIME of reading her journals, I had no idea who most of the artists were to whom my mother's band paid such homage. I had to look most of them up online. And I knew nothing about my great-grandmother's bout with stomach cancer, either. I knew her name and that she had been an accomplished pianist, but nothing else. I'd once seen a picture in one of Nanna Sylvia's photo albums; my mother was seated in Elena's lap as a toddler, at a dining table scattered with leftover dinner dishes.

We looked nothing like her, but I remember Pap saying my mother had inherited not only her musical talent but also her candor, her fearlessness, the way she could spin a dicey situation to her benefit and talk her way out of most anything. I imagine she would have been proud of her granddaughter, that night at the Ellington Club, for calling upon her gifts as comfort to a roomful of strangers.

THE BAND SPENT that evening taking requests. People asked for everything from folk rock to psychedelica, and their first show as Portland Downs earned them another at a downtown bar called The Taproom the following weekend. They took that week to mail out newly revised press kits and demos to several west coast clubs that Evan contacted first by phone, under the guise of Demetrius Booth, Portland Downs' hypothetical booking agent. The bars rarely booked unsolicited acts; you needed representation, and it was a strategy they'd used to get gigs across the northeast until they could find someone trustworthy to do the job for them. Evan had the most professional telephone voice and knew exactly what to say and how to sell them to skeptical, overworked bar managers with short attention spans and long booking lists.

Within a month at Uncle Rick's they had played The Taproom twice and had shows lined up in Eugene, Sacramento, San Francisco, Palo Alto, Fresno, and Los Angeles, a schedule that would take them past Spencer

Butte and across the Tower Bridge, into the Castro District and onto the Stanford University campus, and by July, it would bring Portland Downs to Hollywood Boulevard and introduce my mother to the best thing that would ever happen to us both.

chapter eight

I'VE BEEN TRAVELING the east and west coasts for the past two years with three straight men. Need I say much more? We move through a heterosexual world and play straight bars where the women are beautiful and salacious and who don't quite know what to make of me because I won't change the pronouns in the lyrics, most of which were written by straight men who played straight bars and who sang straight to them, used their instruments as foreplay, crawled right up their skirts before they ever stepped off stage.

Dom is a master pig, as much as I love him, thus we typically have to budget for motel rooms for the sake of privacy. Betty is not so accommodating that way, although Matt doesn't seem to mind. I've heard enough utterings to Christ and pleas to God Almighty to call this a traveling revival, seen more big-nippled tits and thongs and stilettos coming and going through that sleeper curtain than backstage at a strip club. They stroll right past me as if I'm somehow not the same because I'm a woman, as if their wasted friends haven't already propositioned me for threesomes with Evan, which I respectfully decline, every time. "I don't swing, but thanks." Silly, oblivious girls, bumming cigarettes from me, or a toke of my weed pipe while I'm reclined on the camper sofa, most of them bra-less in their open blouses from the night before, snakes and roses tatted to their midriffs still silted with coke residue, presumptuous and cool, too drunk to remember I never changed the pronouns in the songs that spread their thighs for him, there in the sleeper last night. "What'd you say your name was? Chrissy? Jolán—nice to meet you, too." Or, you two. Breasts hanging in my face as she leans down for a light. Matt and I share a grin as he escorts her out to the Sunset Boulevard curb when she's ready to forget him, to where her Celica's parked three blocks away on Las Palmas.

SHE WAS, BY self-proclamation, a lesbian, which made my existence and a fifteen-year marriage to my father that much more bewildering. She was fairly active as well, kept her dance card full enough to have mentioned a girl named Sarah whom she dated during her second year at Berklee, and another she met at a show in Newtown a year later named Nadia. Allison came somewhere in between, but it was unclear where she'd found her or if it was even serious. She'd loved Nadia the most, a music composition major from Covington, Virginia and spoke of her as having beautiful hands and eyes like sapphire. It must've been quite a visual, the two of them side by side, all that sapphire and golden emerald, like the ocean personified, staring back as you wondered how colors like that found their way into the human figure.

They'd lived together for a short time, inseparable until my mother's band gained local traction and their popularity drew a dozen other women every week to my mother's feet, throwing themselves into her hypothetical bedroom from three feet off the stage. Nadia found the attention unnerving and bombastic, and my mother was too much of a showman to push them away; she knew her job was not only to perform but to invite fantasy, to lead the band and lead the willing women along, because no, she never changed the lyric pronouns and sung to them in that raspy, soulful voice, promising that together they'd be able to fly, and that everything's better when wet.

Nadia came to feel that a Fender Stratocaster in the hands of a woman like Jolán De Carlo attracted home wreckers in every style of minidress and four-inch pump and sweet-smelling perfume on the market. They hung on my mother's shoulder at the bar tops between sets, bought her drinks with fake IDs, gave her free dime bags of pot, toyed with her auburn ringlets and took pictures with her in front of the stage amps. Mom's argument was that she never touched them, no more than to drape an arm around a waist for a picture, or to shake hands upon introduction, that she came home to Nadia after every show because she loved her. Girls in bars who fell over musicians were like roaches—they had their purpose but were otherwise a nuisance and usually scattered once the house lights came on. Those who stuck around for more found themselves ignored while my mother busied herself, loading the equipment out to the cars for the ride back to Boston.

It took four successful shows as The Infamous They, teaming with under- and over-aged groupies who latched onto the band like wood ticks, and Nadia had had about all she could stand. Mom came back to their apartment at three a.m., one December morning, to find it half empty. She thought they'd been robbed until she found, *"If I wanted to be one of your whores, I would've had you leaving cash on the nightstand from day one,"* scribbled in black eyeliner on the bedroom mirror, then on the bathroom mirror, and on the living room wall over the couch, and on the inside of the front door, on the kitchen cabinet above the sink, and across the television screen. She sat on the couch, in the middle of Nadia's scrawling tantrum for a very long while, trying to decide between the two loves of her life. It took about an hour, and she finally called her old dorm roommate to let her know she'd be moving back in the next day. It was closer to Matt's and just a block from the campus rehearsal rooms.

She had since kept her romantic relations at arm's length, gave most women no allusions one way or the other for fear she'd find herself in the arms of the Chrissies of the scene, perhaps sharing them with Dom if they were booked for more than one night, a notion more unappealing than "Chrissy" herself.

The bi-curious girls who frequented the west coast bars weren't much different from those in Boston. They came around after the show and sat in her lap and stretched their legs out across Evan sitting next to her, some of them so high on sherm they'd have run through the whole band at just a nod toward the door. Most of the interested men seemed to hesitate, a bit daunted by Mom's button-fly Levi's and Converse chucks, the Pink Floyd t-shirts and tank tops under unbuttoned Oxfords that usually came off midway through the first sweltering set, revealing those athletic trapeziuses and deltoids. They weren't sure what to make of the six-string aggression that growled and wailed through 1400-watt stage amps, the fearless vocals singing "she" and "her" and the fuming cigarettes tucked into the strings at the Stratocaster headstock, Clapton style.

They loved her face, her eyes, her hair, the way her lower lip was succulently fuller than the top, her olive skin and arched eyebrows. But the rest of her scared the shit out them, and she knew it, and she preferred it that way because they rarely approached her with anything but compliments on her playing. As far as she saw it they, too, had paid the cover charge, from which she often took a decent cut, then moved on to the next town, forgetting their middling names and flushed drunken faces. It was the perfect racket.

THEIR FIRST GIG at The Regal Blue in LA gave no indication that it would be any different from the ones they'd done throughout California, aside from a generous thousand bucks, plus ten percent of the bar. It was a holiday weekend, and Hollywood Boulevard was jammed with local cruisers and tourists, moviegoers to the Galaxy theatre and those headed to all the other clubs hidden along the side streets off the Walk of Fame.

The band had to double park the RV between Vine Street and Cahuenga Boulevard to load in, as there was no rear lot and no accessible side entrance. They didn't go on until eleven, with a sound check at eight, and so the summer sun still burned a hole in the city smog, hovering between the tallest palms at the west end of Santa Monica. They met with a fellow by the name of Steven Zhare whom Demetrius Booth had conned into giving them the gig more than a month ago, but he was impressed with their demo package, and all the gushing east coast press was authentic, so Steve never asked of Mr. Booth's whereabouts when they showed up for sound check. If he had, the answer would always be the same; Demetrius was in the city just ahead of them, wrapping up negotiations with another club owner for the next show.

Evan was particularly excited about the timing of this gig because it coincided with a professional drum clinic at the LA Musicians Institute, which would run for three days during the upcoming week, just blocks from where they parked Betty after loading all the gear into The Regal Blue. He didn't care if it cost him his entire cut; he planned on spending every moment of Wednesday, Thursday, and Friday immersed in the wisdom of his idols, and so the rest of the band would have to entertain themselves from Sunday morning to Saturday afternoon, when they'd pull out for a gig at The Diesel Lounge in San Diego.

The club's soundman was stocky and ruddy faced with a blonde mustache and a Gap cap turned around backward. His real name was Gene, but he told them to call him Boomer. He rounded up a handful of in-house technicians who went right to work unraveling all the equipment cords while he himself inspected the output gear and what it would take to patch the band into the house system. The stage was a twenty-foot by fifteen-foot riser, black painted plywood that dipped in certain spots when you walked across it, but it was otherwise standard issue. Evan set up his drum kit while my mother connected the Fender effects pedal and unpacked their microphones.

The place was a basement bar, located beneath one of the office buildings along Hollywood Boulevard. There was a network of water pipes running across the ceiling, draped with clear white string lights, and they had a pool table in the very back. The room smelled of stale alcohol and fryer grease and nicotine, but then a cocktail server brought out a pack of incense sticks and lit several at once, fanned out the flames and placed them fuming around the club in inconspicuous nooks in the brick walls. Soon the room filled with the scent of patchouli, Mom's favorite, that and a scent called passion fruit, which had lingered on her journal pages for decades. She said the smell released creative chemicals in her brain that would otherwise go untapped, even under the influence of Jim Beam and marijuana and the occasional line of coke shared with new acquaintances in back room lounge areas.

Another handful of workers ambled in, more cocktail servers in tight black jeans and black blouses unbuttoned to the cleavage, barbacks, security staff, and kitchen cooks. The sound techs soon had everything wired up and routed to the main mixing board, and Boomer brought the band to the stage and directed them from his perch in the sound booth.

They ran through the first couple verses of "A New Day Yesterday," a bluesy Jethro Tull cover they would open with and which gave Mom ample time for soloing and Boomer a good read on the guitar EQ. The song was a slow-chugging pile driver that my mother sang in that rasping voice of hers, made for Dominick to rumble the walls with an outro at double speed so Evan could run crackling solos to rival all the fourth of July fireworks scheduled for that Monday.

Mom was in mid solo when she saw her. Four bars of lightning arpeggios on the upper guitar frets tumbled into feedback. Then silence. The rest of the band kept going. Boomer frowned, checked for a short in the connection; maybe he'd accidentally muted the guitar track.

She'd walked past the stage, lighting the tea candles on the bar tops with a little orange Bic, the first thing in fifteen years to break my mother's musical concentration. Boomer held up empty palms from the booth; nothing was amiss on his end. Mom glanced back at the band, suddenly aware that she had stopped playing, and Dom frowned at her because it was an oddity that none of them had ever seen before—Jolán De Carlo had choked on stage.

She shook it off, turned to Evan with a signal to jump to the outro, and resumed the solo at double speed, watching the petite blonde server move about the bar, taking chairs down from the tabletops and standing them upright, lighting the little candles in the centers as she went. The song came to a close, and the staff gave them a round of applause, which drew the girl's attention to my mother whose focus was now divided between watching her and adjusting the mic stand to a suitable height.

The girl smiled at her. Mom looked away, down at the effects pedals, and she tapped them each with the toe of her sneaker, testing them arbitrarily so she could appear indifferent while digging for the proper interpretation of that smile. This was another straight bar, and as stereotypes go, the girl *looked* as though she might've had a six-foot boyfriend somewhere, some college jock or Navy sailor who'd show up around ten p.m. to shoot pool and monitor how close the customers' hands came to her ass, so he could turn some drunken admirer into a head kabob with his cue stick. And my mother wouldn't have blamed him; she was the prettiest girl she'd seen across sixteen states and five thousand miles.

"Hey. Rip Van Winkle," Dom barked at Mom. He unshouldered his bass and leaned it in the stand. "Welcome back. The sound check went great, not a single fucking glitch. We were beasts, you shoulda heard us."

Mom shook her head foolishly. "Sorry about that. I got a little sidetracked. My bad."

The girl was at the bar now, spraying it down with cleaner and wiping it dry with a rag. Mom watched her. She slid her guitar pick up under the Fender strings, took out the set list sheets from a folder in her backpack, handed one to Dom, and laid the others on everyone's instruments. She glanced back at the server.

Dom did the same and saw her at the bar, with her dishwater ponytail and black hiphuggers, and he looked back at Mom. "Are you serious? *That's* what blew out your pilot light in the middle of a solo? I didn't even know that was possible."

Mom frowned, looked at the blonde, shrugged at Dom. "Huh? No. I was trying to remember if I brought the set lists in from the RV, lost focus."

"Yeah, okay." He put his hands on his hips and watched the girl cleaning. Then he smiled at Mom. "She looks mighty tasty, actually." He leered at her a little longer. "Look at those lips. Mary Mother of God. Didn't see *those* till she turned around. I bet she could suck the paint right off the Fleetwood."

"You have got to be crudest man I have ever met."

He nodded. "That is rightly possible." The house jukebox came on to pass the time before the show, playing "Suck My Kiss," and Dom pointed to it. "See? Anthony knows all about those lips. A man of good taste. As am I. And since this isn't the Cockblock Club in San Francisco where *you* have the advantage, I'll be right back." Mom laughed at him, and he walked away backward, playing air bass with Flea and singing the chorus aloud. He descended upon the ponytail blonde, moving into her personal space as if to place her under citizen's arrest.

Mom went over to the table where Evan and Matt sat with dripping bottles of Bud Light, their first of an open tab, and she took a seat and watched Dom flirting with the server. He was leaning on the bar rail, trying his wit against the girl's interest, and he made her smile, briefly, but she kept polishing the counter, inching him along the bar and around the chairs as she worked her way down.

Mom pointed it all out to Matt and Evan. "He's gonna make her spray him in the face with that shit. Mark my words."

Evan laughed. "He'll do the whole show smelling like bleach, or ammonia."

"He already smells like ammonia," Mom said. "Have you spent more than ten minutes in his hotel room in any given city? Piss and some kind of cheese. If she knows what's good for her, she'll crawl over that bar to get away. And do it *now.*"

"You're more sadistic than I realized, putting him through that." Matt took a swig of his beer and shook his head, tapping his cigarette ashes. "Are we supposed to be placing bets or what?"

"What are you talking about?" Mom flagged down a passing cocktail server and ordered a Jack and Coke. "He walked into that all on his own. I had nothing to do with it." She shrugged. "Give him a chance. He's a funny guy. A furry, funny guy, in a beat-up teddy bear sorta way. Girls like it. She just might give him some rhythm. She hasn't sprayed him in the face yet, so he's got that much going for him."

Matt half shook his head and looked at Dominick. "If I were a bettin man like my uncle, I'd put half of tonight's cut on you over him."

Mom lit a cigarette and gave him a peculiar smirk, blew smoke into the air above his head.

"She was checkin you out long before you got your fingers tangled in your strings, or whatever you did up there," Matt said, tipping his chin toward the stage.

"What the hell ever." Mom handed the server a five dollar tip as she placed her drink on the table. "I was making a lot of noise. The whole staff was listening to us. They always do that wherever we go. People stop and listen. That's the idea." She took the little stirrers out of her cocktail and set them on the napkin and sipped straight from the glass.

"That's not what I mean," Matt said. "You forget. I have the best seat in the house, the perfect vantage point. I see everything. She bumped into a table, staring at you, before you even knew she was in the room."

"How do you know it wasn't Dom?" she asked.

Matt gestured to the bar. The girl was sending Dominick on his way, shaking her head at all his propositions, and then she disappeared through the back kitchen door with the rag and spray bottle.

"She has cataracts," Dom told them as he came back to the table. He pointed to his own eyes and made a face. "It was unpleasant, actually, a little sad." He took a seat next to Evan. "I didn't wanna just walk away, ya know. But it's good they hire the impaired here. Says a lot."

"I think it's you with the impairment," Evan said. "Sexually challenged. Socially stunted. 'Cause I saw her when she came in, and she looked fine to me. Hellaciously fine, as a matter of fact. Probably why it only took her five minutes to make a run for the kitchen. Good job, dude." He slapped him on the back. "Good work."

"Kiss my ass. There was a language barrier, if you *must* know."

Evan sipped his beer. "And what language was that?"

Dom thought on it, shook his head, looked at him sideways. "Not sure. Swedish, I think. Maybe Italian. Or Turkish. It was difficult to place."

"I know what was difficult to place," Matt mumbled. "Your dick in her pants. Swedish." He rolled his eyes.

THE CLUB WAS nearly full by ten-thirty. They had spent an hour in the RV after sound check. Mom liked to smoke a bowl of weed before a show because she became nervous and feared she might get tongue tied or miss a break in the music, an irrational idea that had never come to pass until tonight. Now she knew it was possible to go completely dark, for the breakers in her brain to flip and shut off all the lights, and so she held her lighter to the ceramic pipe as the contents glowed and sizzled under the flame. She passed it to Evan and got up from the couch and grabbed her cigarettes from the RV console, checking her watch.

"Twenty minutes, guys."

She didn't like the lingering marijuana smell on her clothes; it staled too easily, and so she rummaged through her bags for a bottle of Bucheron and misted herself, dusted a bit through her hair, then headed out into the club with the others.

Many in the audience had seen Portland Downs the previous night at a tavern on Sunset called Pascoe's and followed them to The Regal Blue tonight, and so the reception was quite enthusiastic when the band took the stage. They began as rehearsed, with "A New Day Yesterday" cranked up to twice the volume to compensate for three hundred bodies now altering the sound check acoustics. The place rumbled to life, and the crowd whistled and hollered as if at a Raiders' game. The stage lights flashed red and yellow and blue and strobed in time with the music through a gray veil of manufactured fog, floating up from the smoke machines at the base of the stage.

My mother was not at all the proverbial metal-band-style soloist, throwing herself into wide dramatic stances, swinging her hair and sliding onto her knees for screaming shreds. I watched Uncle Cam's videos of her performances like a detective searching for crime scene evidence, studied at least a dozen individual song clips and two full-length shows, and she played with a sense of composure, no matter the complexity of a riff or lick, with a steadiness I imagine came from years of classical training.

She let the instrument do most of the work and let the Fender be the star; her hands moved around a lot more than she did, but she liked to make deliberate eye contact with anyone close to the stage. She would sing to them, play just for them, if only for a few lines, and she smiled a lot, a sly crooked grin as if sharing a private joke between herself and the crowd; she took herself a lot less seriously than they did. She drew energy from Dom and Evan and turned to them often throughout the show for improvised duets and extended jam sessions, and they had a blast making things up as they went along. She could solo for eight minutes straight, and the people loved it, and so did I. Sometimes she would even work the first few lines of Bach into a solo as lighthearted homage to her classical abilities, and then fuse it all back into thundering blues.

She had approached the violin with similar passion. It was just as much an extension of her own hands as the guitar, but the genre was structured and conservative by tradition, and now I understood why she stepped outside the lines of classical convention so boldly. She couldn't help herself. She had always existed within a very precarious space between two alternate worlds, both in music and in her personal life, and each ego had been fighting against the other like a virus and a vaccine. Which was which? I'm not sure she herself ever came to any conclusions, but I have my theories.

They closed a thirty-minute set with "Cold Shot," which segued into an original song they had been working on called "Comfort Zone." They had an entire set's worth of originals now and incorporated those between the more well-known cover songs. This was a crucial strategy, as they were still an unknown act, and unless an audience was avidly familiar with a band's exclusive material, people just didn't want to hear it all night long.

Mom had already shed her button-down Oxford under the blistering stage lights, threw it onto the closest power amp between songs and did the remainder of the set in her signature form-fitting tank top. She occasionally found her ponytailed server while she played, following her with her eyes as she made trips from the bar to the tables, leaning an ear in to a customer to catch their order over Portland Downs' bass-driven rumble, Evan's crash cymbals, and the flanging wail of the Stratocaster under my mother's intrepid hands. Twice she glanced up to the stage and caught Mom staring. She gave her a sweet smile and kept moving, a drink tray balanced on her palm as she delivered white Russians and martinis and hot wings to the bar tops and booths.

AFTER THE FIRST set, it took my mother ten minutes to get back to their table; everyone stopped her along the way, shook her hand, pulled her aside to chat, patted her on the shoulder, and handed out business cards for local photographers and music management. It was always like that. She took the cards and indulged a picture or two, lingered for conversation, waited for phone numbers written on napkins and drink coasters. She smiled, thanked them, gave them what they wanted, and eventually found a seat with the guys. They all shared high fives for a successful Regal Blue debut, then searched around for the server who'd handled them at sound check. The jukebox started up again, preset to Top 40s, and "Two Princes" came through the house system. Mom took the hair band she wore around her wrist and tied her curls into a low ponytail, and she fanned herself with a cocktail napkin and wiped the perspiration from her neck and face.

"What does it take to get a drink around here?" Dom mumbled, looking for service. "We just rattled the mortar loose and probably sold about five hundred bucks of liquor for this place. You'd think we could get a beer."

She came from the opposite side of the bar, an empty tray tucked under her arm from dropping off the last order, and she approached with an apologetic grin.

"Hey, you guys," she greeted, swiping the hair from her eyes. "Sorry. We're just really busy tonight. You guys brought a lot of business." She smiled, a bit winded. "A lot of people said they saw you at Pascoe's last night. So, what can I get for you?" The jukebox volume was a lot lower than that of the band, so she didn't have to shout or strain for the orders now, and she glanced shyly at my mother. "Hi."

"Hi." Mom smiled back, the same one they'd been sharing all night, from the tables to the stage. She ordered another Jack and Coke. Dom and Matt got Bud Lights, and Evan took a Seagram's and 7-Up.

"All right. Well, my name's Rachel, and I'll be back with those in just a few. Sorry again for the wait." She gave the guys a quick smile but saved a special, prettier one for Mom as she disappeared into the crowd.

Mom smirked at her band mates, amused and triumphant. She slipped a cigarette from the box and looked around for Rachel.

"That has got to be a freak of nature," Dom said. "Do they grow these girls on farms somewhere? They were all over the place at that Cockblocker lesbian bar we played in Frisco. Are they genetically engineered in laboratories or some shit? Scientifically designed for unbearable hotness, just to frustrate the heterosexual male population?"

"It's a conspiracy, that's for sure." Matt chuckled, then said to Mom, "If you leave LA without taking her straight to the sleeper, I will shove that Stratocaster up your ass."

Mom pursed her lips, flicked her ashes. "Not without dragging that mattress into the parking lot and setting it on fire, as many skanks as you've been screwing on it."

"Okay, so what's one more? She's obviously got her panties all moist for you, so go for it."

Mom frowned. "Come on, now. Don't be a prick. Watch your mouth, Matty, huh?"

"Uh oh. That's the first nail in the coffin," Dom said. "She's defending her honor already, and she hasn't even brought our drinks yet."

"I'm not defending her honor. He's as disgusting as you sometimes, and maybe she's a nice girl. Ever consider that?" She gestured around the crowded club. "She's out here, working her ass off, trying to make a living just like us. You think she deserves a couple douche bags calling her a skank while she's off getting their drinks? Their *free* drinks?"

"Wow," Matt said, staring at her. "You've really got that Italian mother guilt thing down pat, don't you? Now I feel like a total dick. Thank you for that."

"You're welcome. Any time."

Rachel returned after a short while, her tray filled with drinks for Mom's table and another one nearby. She came over to Dom's side first, set his beer on a napkin, then Evan's Seagram's.

"You guys have an open tab. Your drinks from earlier were on the house, so this round'll start your tab, and I'll tally everything up at the end of the night." She went around to Mom and smiled at her again, and Mom smiled back, making direct eye contact, fully aware of the startling pull of that hazel gaze.

Rachel grabbed Matt's beer from the edge of the tray, lured by my mother's implicit flirting, oblivious to the fact that she was taking their drinks from the right, the side closest to herself, with the rest of the orders, making the tray suddenly left heavy, and a Long Island Iced Tea, two Fuzzy Navels, and Mom's Jack and Coke went toppling onto the table and into my mother's lap.

Mom tossed up her hands and stared slack jawed at all the ice and Coke and orange juice and liquor soaking a huge wet blotch into her jeans, so stunned by the chill she couldn't speak.

"Oh my God." Rachel was no less mortified, her brown eyes wide as saucers, and she made little motions to clean it up, but she had nothing to use, no towel, not enough napkins, just an empty dripping tray and Dominick, laughing like a donkey on the other side of the table. "Oh my God, I'm so sorry." She plucked a glass from my mother's lap, set it on the table, then another. "I'm so sorry." She snatched up another glass from the floor so no one would fall over it, and the people at the next table watched, not sure whether to laugh or try to help. Rachel looked at Mom. "Let me get you a towel. I'm sorry. Just . . ." And she held up a finger. "I'll be *right* back. Just one second."

Evan and Dom clapped and cackled as if at a comedy show. Matt smiled and shook his head, peering down at my mother's alcohol-drenched crotch. She finally stood up and pulled at the icy denim to peel it from her skin.

"You have got to be kidding me," she mumbled. "Holy Christ, that's cold. *Wow.*"

"That's probably the coolest thing I've seen all summer," Dom said. "Pun intended."

He slapped fives with Evan who said to Mom, "Maybe she was trying to send you a hint. Hell, it works on guys. I dunno about women. How's it feel? Still got the hots for her?"

"I'd say not right now," Matt said over the brim of his glass.

"Shut up," Mom muttered. The bottom half of her tank top was wet, too, and she pinched it between her fingers and shook it out away from herself.

Rachel weaved back through the tables with a handful of clean kitchen rags and gave one to Mom, and she attempted to help her but realized that would look awkward, inappropriate, so she went about wiping down the ladder-back chair and the tabletop, apologizing.

"Everything okay over here? What's goin on?" Steve Zhare showed up and looked my mother over and let out a noisy sigh. He gave Rachel a look and said to Mom, "Man, I apologize for this, Jeezus. Really, I'm sorry. We'll get you guys another round on the house, and these'll all be comped as well." He turned to Rachel. "Nice going. This is all coming outa your tips, so say 'you're welcome.' Help her get cleaned up, and then I wanna see you before you cash out tonight."

"Steve, it was an accident, I swear." She handed my mother another rag. "The tray just . . . slipped. I dunno what happened."

"Yeah, it always just slips." He waved her off. "Just clean this shit up and get back to work. There's four other tables waiting for drinks."

Rachel glanced at him guiltily. "Five. Table 12's drinks were on the tray, too. I'll get it straightened out, I promise."

"Hey, man, it's fine. Just an accident." Mom smiled at Steve. "I was hot as hell from the stage, anyway, so her timing was perfect. A little unexpected, but right on time." She shrugged. "It was my fault, really. I distracted her when she was trying to pass them around. Shoulda kept my mouth shut, it's no big deal. I can just go change."

"Well, still. The next round's on the house, whatever you guys want." Steve looked at Rachel again and pointed out into the crowd. "Five tables waiting. Go! *Now!*"

Rachel held her tongue but gave my mother another guilty glance before she walked away. "I'm sorry." And she squeezed past the bodies and vanished toward the bar, empty tray and wet towels in hand.

"You sure you're all right?" Steve asked my mother again, pursing his lips at the mess.

Mom looked around the club for Rachel, but she was gone. She nodded to Steve. "Yeah, I'm good." He patted her shoulder, flagged down another server, and assigned her to their table for the night. Then he headed away toward the bar, calling after someone in the kitchen.

"Okay, then. So, welcome to Prickville," Dom said, glancing back at Steve. "It was funny. It wasn't a federal offense, what a fucktard."

"Power trips can make dickheads of otherwise decent men," Evan said through a swallow of his drink. "He was cool as hell on the phone. Guess not so much when the doors open."

Mom didn't say anything. She checked around again for Rachel and saw her busy with another table in the back of the club. "I'm gonna go to the RV and change. I'll be back. Don't go on without me." She gave the guys a wink, then made her way through the crowd toward the exit.

THEY TOOK THE stage again at midnight, played two more sets, and by one-thirty, my mother was sweat drenched, hoarse, and a bit tipsy from three Jack and Cokes and a shot of bourbon, bought by a couple of Chrissies, one of whom was now in Dom's lap with her lips brushing his ear lobe. The other girl was sizing my mother up for experimentation, perhaps to coax her into a room at the Best Inn around the corner, see if she performed as well without a guitar in her hands.

"I've never done this before, but," she whispered into my mother's ear, smelling of Tequila and cigarettes and remnants of stale Obsession.

She didn't know how to ask and so she just simpered coyly, leaning an arm across the back of Mom's chair, and she swung herself around to the opposite side, waiting for my mother to catch her meaning. She was pretty, very tempting, but looked like she'd seen more of the far west end of Hollywood Boulevard than the holes along the Regal Blue stretch.

"You're into that, right?" she conferred lowly. She looked my mother over, smoothed a hand across her shoulders, and ran her fingers up into my mother's hair, asking again with her eyes this time.

Mom took the last swallow of her cocktail, set the glass on the table, and turned to her. She gave her a simple smile. "Would it really make any difference to you if I wasn't?"

The place was beginning to empty, and she rose from her chair, looked around the thinning crowd for Rachel but didn't see her. Servers were making trips into the kitchen, going to and from an office at the back of the bar while others cleared the ashtrays from the tables and helped the barbacks with the spent bottles and tumblers.

"I gotta go get paid, settle my bar tab," she told the girl. "Thanks for the offer, though, babe."

"Melanie," the girl corrected her as she walked away. "My name's Melanie, actually."

Mom glanced over her shoulder, waved good-night, forgot her.

Steve paid them what he'd promised plus an extra two hundred from the bar. She took a hundred dollar bill from the stack and handed it back to him for the drinks, but he wouldn't take it. He said everything was comped and asked if they could come back in the fall for another weekend. She and Matt were due back in school by the end of August, as Matt had to finish his senior year, and she was to begin grad school. She suffered to turn down a good-paying gig, but there was always next summer. Steve gave that a desultory shrug and said he'd keep them in mind, never a good way to close a conversation about employment, but what could she do?

Evan was already tearing down his drum kit when she came back out to the bar. Matt and Dom had loaded the PAs into Betty, and all that was left now were the monitor speakers, the racks, and Mom's guitars and amps.

She counted out three hundred dollars from the cash in her hand and gave it to Evan. "Here. Have fun at your convention. Good show, buddy."

He pushed his glasses up onto his nose and unscrewed the wing nuts on the bass drum pedal. "Clinic. It's a clinic, not a convention. Do I look like a Trekkie to you?"

She smiled down at him. "Yeah, actually. You kinda do."

"Fuck off."

"That's real nice." She laughed a little, then went around breaking down her gear.

SHE WAS CARRYING the Fender in one hand and the twelve-string in the other when she came outside and saw her, leaning against the wall just a few paces from the entrance. She looked as though she were waiting for someone, arms folded at her waist, her purse slung over her shoulder. She was staring down at the sidewalk, tracing the cracks in the concrete with the toe of her shoe.

Mom stopped and watched her for a moment, unsure of what to say. "Hey, I really meant what I said; your timing was perfect. Gets hotter than the devil's sauna up there sometimes."

Rachel looked up. Mom shrugged, smiled.

"Oh, God." Rachel stared out across the Boulevard. "Just what I need to top off the night. Talk about timing." She looked at Mom. "I really am sorry. For the twentieth time, okay? I'm sorry."

"The seventh time, actually," Mom said. Rachel looked a bit confused. "You apologized," she pointed back into the bar, "seven times. Well, nine now."

My mother came closer, amused, but Rachel was not. Mom set her guitars down on the pavement, took out a cigarette and cupped a hand around the lighter flame.

"Well, it's not so bad," she tried again, blowing smoke into the California air. "There's always tomorrow. Start over, have a better night, right?"

Rachel rolled her eyes out to the passing traffic. "Probably not. Not here, anyway, seeing as I just got fired about a half hour ago." She must've seen my mother's face run pale because she said, "It was bound to happen sooner or later. I'm not very good at this, apparently."

Mom came closer. "I *told* Steve it was an accident. You want me to go talk to him? I just came from his office. Maybe I can get him to change his mind. That is total bullshit."

Rachel shook her head, defeated. "No, it's okay. It won't make any difference, trust me. He's had it in for me for months. Tonight was just the perfect excuse."

"Well, I feel like shit now."

"Why? It wasn't your fault. There's a right way to serve drinks, so you don't throw the tray off balance and spill forty bucks of liquor on the lead singer of the band. It's not astrophysics."

Mom shrugged a shoulder. "Probably just regular physics."

Rachel tried to resist, but she couldn't help but laugh, just a little. She looked sideways at her, eyeing the cigarette in her hand. "You got another one of those?"

Mom took one out and gave it to her, held the flame to the tip, and stood watching her. "You smoke anything else?" She gestured to the RV parked on the corner of Vine Street. "We've got some bud in the Fleetwood if you wanted to unwind."

"I do," Rachel said. "From time to time. But my ride's almost done with her side work. I gotta be out here when she's ready to go. USC's already out of her way, so she won't be too happy if she has to come looking for me."

Mom nodded and flicked her ashes to the concrete. "Is that where you go to school? USC?"

"Yep. Senior year next year. Then I can get a real job and leave these shithole dives alone for good."

"Gotcha." Mom glanced around to the RV, where Dom and Evan were loading the drums into the 4Runner, and she watched them for a moment. It gave her an idea, and she looked back at Rachel. "Well, I know of a pretty good job for you, actually. Just came up."

Rachel dragged on her cigarette. "Is that so? And what kind of job would that be?"

"Tour guide," Mom said with a little smile.

Rachel looked at her, bewildered. "A tour guide? For who and touring what, exactly?"

Mom exhaled a long stream of smoke overhead. "For me. Show me LA. I've been here for two days, and all I've seen are barrooms and the hideous upholstery in that RV over there. There's gotta be more to this place than that. Maybe not." She propped a foot on the acoustic guitar case and gave Rachel a moment to think about it.

Rachel toked her cigarette and stared out at the amber-lighted streets, at the Capitol Records building, a glowing twenty-story cylinder against the Hollywood Hills. A sparkling '78 Cutlass rode by, blasting Mariachi music as if it were Hip-Hop or Dancehall, and it faded away toward the tourist end where two huge spotlights from the Chinese Theatre cast whirling white beams into a starless sky.

"I don't have a car," she finally confessed. "We'd have to take the bus, or the Metrorail, depending on where you wanna go."

"Anywhere you're going." Mom smiled, and Rachel looked at her.

After a moment, she smiled back, the one she'd offered inside when she was lighting all the little tea candles, the real pretty one.

The club door opened, and a dark-haired girl with Gothic makeup and Japanese calligraphy tattooed onto her neck came outside, wearing a server outfit like Rachel's. She was stuffing tips into her front jeans pocket, car keys dangling in the other hand. She saw my mother and stopped.

"Oh . . . my God. You guys were the *shit* tonight, girl. You rocked the *hell* outa that place. One of the best shows we've had yet. Nice job." And she shook my mother's hand. "You sound like Amy Ray. The Indigo Girls chick. I guess people tell you that a lot, not the most original compliment, but hey."

Mom felt a bit self-conscious, but she said, "Yeah, they do. She's awesome, though, so it's always a good compliment, thanks."

"No problem." The girl turned to Rachel, dropped her shoulders pitifully, and went to her with an arm around her neck. "I'm so sorry, sweetie. Steve's an asshole. Screw him. We'll find you something else, okay? Something better." She looked into her face with a sad smile. "You ready to go?"

Rachel nodded and started away with her, then turned around to Mom, walking backward toward Argyle Avenue. "So, how am I supposed to find you tomorrow, anyway?"

Mom motioned over her shoulder to Betty. "I don't think they'll tow it with us sleeping in the camper. Just knock on the door. *Mi casa es su casa.*"

Rachel rolled her eyes, then she nodded. "See you tomorrow, Jolán De Carlo."

And she disappeared around the corner with her friend. Then she reappeared and poked her head back around the building.

"How do I know you're not a serial killer?" she called out to my mother.

"Are you serious?"

Rachel lifted her brows, waiting for an answer.

Mom gazed out at the cars going by and shook her head. She looked at Rachel and tossed up her hands. "All right. You got me. That's what I really carry around in these cases." She nodded down to the guitars. "All my murdering tools. It was the perfect cover. Until now, anyway. Case closed. Good work."

"This *is* LA, you know."

"Yes, it is. And I'm stuck here for a week. I promise not to do away with you. At least until I've seen the La Brea Tar Pits," she said. "So, I might save that for last, if I were you."

Rachel stared at her, thinking. She looked her up and down, glanced at the guitar cases on the sidewalk, then gave her a coy little smirk. "I'll be here at noon, so be awake."

Mom checked her watch. "Well, it's after three now, and I've had a bit to drink, so I'll do my best."

Rachel smiled and vanished around the building, leaving my mother standing with a grin at the corner of Hollywood and Vine.

chapter nine

SHE DIDN'T KNOW what she was doing there. The late morning was hot as most afternoons, the sun a pale muted version of itself behind the brown Los Angeles perma-haze, still low in the sky and shining at her back, baking her shoulders in the white spaghetti strap top she wore with a short pair of denim cutoffs and grey hiking sandals. She thought maybe she should turn around, get back on the 210 east to Vermont Avenue and go right back to USC where she was safe, look for a new job, clean her side of the dorm room. But all she could see was my mother's eyes and that smile. She could still hear the beautifully aggressive wail of the Stratocaster from the night before, and she felt her feet moving her toward the RV as if on an autowalk at LAX.

The Fleetwood looked dormant as she approached, but as she came to the side door she could hear music coming from inside, sounded like Alice In Chains. It took her a full minute before she decided to knock on the door, standing there with her hands in her back pockets, contemplating the irrational curiosity and reckless fascination that had awakened her at nine a.m., pushed her into the shower, and out to the bus stop by ten-thirty.

It took another full minute before it opened to the keyboard player. He looked at her as if she'd fallen from the stars, then glanced back into the camper, presumably for my mother.

He had a bowl of food in his hand and stood there chewing for another moment before he said, "Hey. What's goin on?"

She felt foolish, but she said, "I'm here for Jolán. She should be expecting me. If she remembered." She let out a sigh and silently scolded herself because it was probably the dumbest thing she'd ever done, showing up at some traveling musician's motor home whom she'd just met less than twelve hours ago. Looking for what? She couldn't say.

"Jo!" Matt called back into the camper. "Hey, yo! You got company, you slick motherfucker, you." He invited her in.

She, too, was arrested by the complicated color scheme exploding from the furniture, so much that Matt saw her expression and smiled.

"Yeah, it takes a little getting used to. It's all original, though. We like to think of it as vintage." He looked toward the back of the camper again. "Hey, Jo, get your ass out here, *chica!* You're one hell of a host!" He dropped into a seat at the Formica table with his bowl in hand and scooped a spoonful into his mouth. "Heard you got fired last night. That sucks. We would've talked to Steve if we thought he was gonna do that."

She smiled thinly. "He wouldn't have cared, but thanks, anyway."

Matt gestured to the couch, and so she took the offer and sat down. Across from her on the opposite pullout was Evan, sprawled on his stomach beneath a blue-striped bed sheet, one leg hanging off the edge, arms tucked under his face, hidden by a fan of dreadlocks.

Matt gestured with his spoon to his sleeping band mate. "He's sleeps like a coma victim, so don't feel like you have to be quiet. He could sleep through a hurricane, wake up in a tree somewhere, wondering what the hell happened." He looked into the back of the camper then, and he shouted for Mom again. "Jolán, come on, Jeezus!"

"Yeah," she finally answered. "Yeah, yeah, yeah. I heard you the first eight times."

After a moment, she came out from behind the sleeper curtain, barefoot in a white v-neck t-shirt and a pair of pale blue boxers, rubbing her face, running a hand through her hair, wild reddish curls untamed from sleep. She looked at Rachel and grinned apologetically, squinting at the daylight from the side bay windows, drowsy and a little embarrassed.

"You did say noon, didn't you. Sorry. Kinda thought you might stand me up, actually." She looked her over and smiled. "You look nice."

"Thanks," Rachel said. "You look . . . sleepy. But nice, still."

Matt went to the stereo and turned it up. It was the only thing to make Evan stir, and he groaned and turned onto his side, opened an eye to my mother and then to their guest.

He rolled back onto his pillow. "Damn, Jo. Was I that wasted? Or were you really afraid of Matty shoving your guitar up your ass?"

Mom took a seat at the table across from Matt and cracked the side window. "She just got here, dude. It didn't go down like that. Go back to sleep." She gave Rachel a guilty smile and searched around for her cigarettes. She found them in the table seat, took one out, and lit it. "I should probably go ahead and get ready so I can get you as far away from these guys as possible. Before you decide you don't want anything to do with me."

Rachel waved them off. "I'm fine. Take your time. Don't forget I've spent the past year working in bars. There's probably not much I haven't seen or heard."

Matt laughed into his cereal bowl. "Well, you've only been around us for five minutes. Give it time. We can probably break that streak by tonight."

"And on that note." Mom got up from the table, cigarette dangling from her lips. "I'll get a shower and be ready in a few, before he proves himself right." She held a finger up to Rachel. "Don't go anywhere. Just give me ten." And she disappeared behind the curtain again.

Evan was bobbing his head to the music, still lying prone on the pull out, trying to wake up.

"We're really not that bad once you get to know us. You just need thick skin," Matt said. "Jo's been around us for two years, and she's . . . well . . . not your average girl. She's kind of a Renaissance woman, you might say. Dabbles in things, here and there, dabbled in us in '89, and now she's our fearless leader, much to her credit. It takes a unique woman to tour the country in a rolling tin can with a bunch of rock musician dudes and not jump out at the first red light." He shoveled the last of his cereal into his mouth and smiled.

"It takes a unique anyone not to jump out at the first red light," Evan mumbled into the sheets.

Rachel grinned. "Well, I guess I'll see what you're talking about by the end of today."

Matt got up and took his bowl to the sink. "Oh, she'll be on her best behavior, no doubt. She's pretty taken by you, so she won't wanna fuck it up."

"Is that right? Well, she doesn't even know me . . . yet. And I've only got, what? Five days? So I guess she'll have to get the abridged version."

Matt dropped back into his seat and lit a Marlboro. "The Rachel Cliff's notes."

"Exactly."

The side door opened to Dominick and a blonde in a pair of tight blue jeans and a dressy black blouse. Her hair was pulled up into a careless morning twist, and her mascara was smudged from sleep, or the lack of it. Dom was still in his clothes from the night before, and he stopped when he saw Rachel, then laughed out loud and clapped his hands.

"You are a *beast*, Jolán De Carlo!" he called into the camper. "I *knew* it. Where the hell are you so I can shake your fucking hand!"

"Hey, asswipe." Matt winced at him. "She's only been here five minutes. Relax. You're the only one who's at nine hundred decibels *and* without a hangover, which I didn't know was possible, but so go the mysteries of Dominick Keller."

"I pace myself," he said. "Quantity always does best in moderation."

"And so do you," Matt muttered. He gestured to Rachel. "You know that thick skin I was telling you about? He's why it's so important."

"Yeah, I got some experience with that yesterday. And no," she said to Dom, "they don't 'grow us' on farms or in laboratory Petri dishes. But thanks for the left-handed compliment, anyway."

"You heard that?"

She smiled and nodded. "It's a skill you learn as a cocktail server, just in case someone adds to their drink order as you're walking away. Or if some guy has something asinine to say."

Dom drew back, impressed, and he looked at Matt and pointed at her. "Jo's gonna like her. 'Cause I like her already." He went to the fridge and took out a beer and gave one to his date, then offered one to Rachel, but she shook her head. He regarded her strangely and looked at his watch, raised one eyebrow. "It's after twelve. It'd be a completely moral decision."

"I'm fine, thanks."

"Suit yourself." He twisted off the top and took a seat at the table and had his girl sit next to him.

"Weren't you the chick that spilled that tray of drinks last night?" the blonde asked Rachel, taking one of Dom's cigarettes from the box.

Rachel gave that a little sigh. "Yep. That'd be me."

The blonde blew a stream of nicotine out the cracked bay window. "You'd think they wouldn't put those tables so close together so you guys could get through without assholes bumping into you, with their legs all stretched out for people to trip over them. Not hard to figure out." She leaned back against Dom's chest and propped a foot up on the seat.

"Well, that's not how it happened, but you're right," Rachel said. Finally she took out a cigarette of her own from her saddle bag, and Matt gave her a light.

"Damn, you guys," Evan grumbled from the pullout. "I don't even have to smoke to get as much tar and formaldehyde in my lungs as you do. Open a window or something, shit." He rolled over onto his back and glared at them all with one eye.

"Stop being such a pussy." Dom pulled the side window open wider. "You've been rollin with us in this thing for three months. You'd think you'd develop some kinda tolerance by now."

Evan stared at him, then counted heads and burning cherries. "There's four fucking cigarettes going, and when Jo gets out here, there's gonna be five. This is a thirty-four by ten-foot space, you jackass. Why not toss a can of tear gas in here while you're at it, too?" He sat up and searched around for his glasses. He found them on the shelf beside the bed and slipped them on and tied his hair back into a ponytail. "And good morning to you, too." He hauled himself to his feet, wearing nothing but a pair of boxer briefs; he looked down at himself. "Sorry. Jo's kinda used to it. We don't usually get much company around here, none that stays for very long, anyway." He snatched up a pair of sweatpants from the clothes pile and pulled them on.

"Hey, don't get dressed on my account, hon. I wasn't one bit offended." The blonde smirked at him and cuddled close to Dom. She was still a bit tipsy from the night before, and she giggled and ran a high-heeled shoe up the back of Evan's thigh as he passed toward the front of the camper, but he ignored her. He was looking for his weed pipe and found it in the console with a tiny plastic baggie, half full of pot, and he poured a dab into the bowl and lit it.

"Oh, and that's much better," Dom said from the table. "Smokeless herb. Of course. What was I thinking?"

"It's better than that shit," Evan said through a stifled breath. "Smells a hell of a lot better, and this won't kill you." He offered the pipe to Matt. "So, is Jolán still in the shower? I gotta piss. And you know we're gonna have to dump those tanks again." He turned to Dom. "We should be able to wait to refill the fresh water tank in San Diego. We still have enough if we don't go nuts with it. There's an RV park in La Mesa, just outside the city." He rubbed the sleep from his eyes with the back of his hand.

"Yeah, well, you can keep that shit," Dom said. "Last time I did that, I had to burn my clothes and take seven showers just to get back to normal."

"It's not that bad if you do it right," Evan told him. "I showed you back in Fresno. It's not my fault if you can't follow instructions. You have to hook up the hose *before* you turn on the pump, genius. It's Matt's turn, anyway, so you can go on smelling the way you always do until we get to Tucson."

"Oh, no the hell it's not," Matt protested. He flicked his cigarette butt out the window and took a toke from the weed pipe. "Nice alphabet skills, bookworm. J comes before M, remember?"

"Yeah, but Jo took your turn twice, dude. You were too hungover in Bakersfield and cried like a girl, said it'd make you puke until you dehydrated or some stupid shit like that. She's more of a man than you are, apparently."

"I'm still not doing it." Matt offered the pipe and the lighter to Rachel, and she took it, held the flame to the bowl and sat listening.

"Me, either," Dom said.

Evan shrugged, leaned against the back of the passenger's seat, and folded his arms at his chest. "Fine. She's not gonna do it three times in row, I'll tell you that right now. So, you can all catch scabies and E. coli and whatever else germinates under there. Have fun with that. Me and Jo'll take the bus to Tucson. You guys ride around in the sludgemobile."

"Matt." Mom appeared through the sleeper curtain, her ringlets wet and shiny as Christmas ribbons. She wore a green Bob Marley t-shirt, faded jeans, and a pair of leather Topsiders sandals, and she held a bath towel to her hair, scrunching it dry as she came into the coach.

"See, now you've awakened the dragon," Dom mumbled to his band mates. "You got her started."

"It's *your* fucking turn," she told Matt sternly. "I'm not screwing around with you. And I'm not doing it again. That's bullshit. We go in order, like everything else. I took your turn last time 'cause I felt sorry for your drunk ass, but I'm not doing it again. We get to La Mesa, and you do the tanks." She pointed at Dominick. "If they need it again in Tucson, it's your go. Everybody got it? Christ," she muttered, aggravated. "It's like preschool. What do we gotta do? Make out a chart where everybody gets a gold star and a cookie? Just do the shit like we arranged."

"How about a gold star and a blunt?" Dom suggested, and the blonde in his lap laughed out loud. "That might motivate people a little more. Then the cookie *after* the blunt."

Mom smiled a little and took a seat next to Rachel. "You know what? If that gets it done, I swear to God I'll do it. We'll work out a reward system, so all the little boys get their chores done." She looked at Rachel with a rueful grin. "You have to excuse us. This is just how it goes around here sometimes."

Rachel handed her the pipe. "No need to apologize. It's entertaining, actually."

"Yeah, well, it's entertaining until you have to live with it."

"Hey, nice show last night, by the way. You make really great sex faces," the blonde said to Mom and chuckled and dragged on her cigarette. Dom almost choked on a swig of beer.

Mom raised an eyebrow and gave Rachel an uncomfortable glance.

The girl saw that and waved it all off. "Oh, honey, don't worry. You can have her. I was talking about her playing, that's all. Trust me, I'm more than comfortable right here." She winked, then patted Dom's leg and snuggled in closer.

"She's a free woman." Rachel shrugged. "I have no claims whatsoever. I'm just here to hang out and be . . . What did you call it?" she asked Mom. "A tour guide?"

"Yeah. Tour guide. And how about we start with you guiding me out of here, far from here, very far." She stood up and stuffed her cigarettes into her pocket and tossed the bath towel into the laundry bag. She ran her fingers up into her hair and shook it out and let it fall past her shoulders, then went to the side door and motioned for Rachel to follow.

"Hey, I expect you to have her back here by ten . . . tomorrow." Dom tipped his beer to Rachel and nodded once. "You got it?"

She laughed as she went to the door. "We'll see about that. No promises."

"SO, WHERE WE headed?" Mom asked as they made their way across the lot.

"Well, I thought we might start small, start with the obvious." Rachel pointed up to the Hollywood Boulevard street sign at the corner. "We can walk everywhere we wanna go, if that's okay with you."

"A walking tour." Mom nodded. "Works for me. I'll let you lead the way then."

"Yeah, that'd probably be a good idea." Rachel grinned, and they turned west down the Boulevard toward Cahuenga.

But then a parking lot attendant emerged from the booth and flagged them down, calling after them as he trotted out to the sidewalk.

"Hey, how long you parking here, this thing?" he asked, pointing to the Fleetwood. He was Latino, short as Rachel, brown skinned, round faced, and chubby. "No dumping. *No dejar.*"

Mom looked at him, a little confused. "Dumping?" Then she caught his meaning and shook her head. "No, no dumping. *Intiendo. Cuantos seis días? Uno semana. Desde hoy hasta Sabado.*"

He looked around the lot and he put his hands on his hips and looked back at Mom. *"Es diez dólares por día,* but you gonna stay *en la noche tambien.* Is more, six days, six nights. *Es mucho."* He regarded her as if willing to strike some sort of deal and he checked around himself again and looked back up at her, so she took out her wallet.

"Un cien." She offered him a crisp one hundred dollar bill, held it out low as to keep the transaction discreet. *"Un cien y no problemos.* Nobody tows us, *sí?"* She gestured to the Fleetwood, then pulled the bill away, waiting for him to commit. *"Quiero un recibo, un billete,* proves we've paid."

He eyed the money in her hand, which he would pocket for himself if he agreed. He held up a finger and jogged off toward the ticket booth. *"Uno momento."* After a few minutes, he came back with a handwritten receipt and gestured to the hundred. "Is a deal. *Seis días, no mas.* You stay more, you pay."

"Está bien." She held out the money, and they swapped receipt and bill at once, and she nodded to him as he headed away. *"Gracias, señor."*

He waved and trotted across the lot and disappeared back into the booth.

Rachel looked at her sideways as they started back toward Cahuenga. "So, we're bilingual as well. Very interesting."

Mom laughed a little. "Well, my mother's Cuban, came here when she was twelve, so I really had no choice. When she was in a hurry, or if she was pissed off, she didn't take the time to search for English. She spoke to you in Spanish, and if you didn't know what she was saying, you were screwed. My brother and I both speak it. Not as well as she'd like, but enough to get by. Enough to keep from getting towed, anyway."

"So, was all that legal back there," Rachel asked. "Something tells me no."

"Legal and me stopped getting along a while ago." Mom smiled. "He just wanted to line his pockets for the week. We have enough parking issues with Betty, so if I could settle one without any problems, so be it."

"Betty?"

"Betty. We didn't name her. We got her from Matt's uncle a few months ago in Portland. Apparently, that's been her name since '83. We liked it, so we kept it."

"So, you're from Portland."

"Nope. Bensalem, Pennsylvania. Well, that's home, anyway. We're all from Berklee music school in Boston."

Rachel nodded as they walked. "I know of Berklee. Great school." Then the geographical snag seemed to hit her. "So, you guys are out here from Boston, traveling around in Betty the motor home, which you got in Portland." She half shook her head at all that. "Sounds like a lot of driving. Must be expensive. Those things aren't cheap to maintain."

Mom shrugged. "We get by. Can't say we're all that well-off, but we make enough in one city to get to the next, maybe a little extra to piss away."

"On illicit parking deals?"

"Yes. On all sorts of illicit things. You'd be appalled." Mom grinned.

"Okay, so you're a guitar performance major at Berklee, then. You're obviously twenty-one. Or at least you make the right people think you are if you're playing all these bars and clubs everywhere."

"Wrong, and wrong," Mom said.

Rachel gave her a bewildered glance.

"I'm twenty-two, actually. Just turned, twelfth of last month."

"Well, happy belated."

"Thank you."

"And I'm wrong about what else?"

"Not a guitar performance major. Not even close."

Rachel thought about that. "All right. Music education, then."

Mom shook her head. She took out a cigarette from the pack in her pocket and waited while Rachel floundered over all the wrong guesses. "I'll give you a hint. Think Stradivari. Or maybe I shouldn't make it that obscure. Think instead, I dunno, Vivaldi."

"I know them both. The violin. Are you serious?" Rachel looked at my mother as if she'd been sewing quilts in her spare time, and I imagine it had the same bemusing effect the rock concert photos had on me, seventeen years later in Rachel's living room, because she laughed out loud, then apologized. "You just don't look like a violinist to me, not at all. You don't carry yourself in any way that suggests you've even been *close* to an orchestra."

"Stranger things," Mom said. "It's my first instrument, actually. Been playing since I was six. It's all true, I swear."

Rachel gazed out at the Boulevard as they walked. "Wow. Well, I'm gonna need you to prove it, sometime before you leave on Saturday. Or I'll go the rest of my life telling people I met this amazing woman in college who was a rock star but who pulled some line of shit on me about being a classical violinist. So, I sent her packing." She looked up at Mom. "It won't be a good story, not favorable at all for you." She gestured for Mom's cigarette, dragged on it, and handed it back to her.

"Well, then I guess you'll get a free and very personal concert later on. 'Cause I don't want you to send me on my way just yet."

THEY SPENT THE afternoon browsing the tattoo shops and souvenir stands along the Boulevard at Highland Avenue. They watched a mime pretending to climb a ladder in front of the El Capitan Theatre and ate mozzarella sandwiches from the Snow White Café because Rachel insisted they had the best in LA. They went through the Wax Museum and strolled the exhibits of Marilyn Monroe and Freddie Krueger and Michael Jackson, watched his impersonator dance to "Billie Jean" in front of the Grauman's Chinese Theatre and spent a while in Frederick's of Hollywood at Rachel's request, so she could window-shop the lingerie. She did this with delicate intent, hoping subtly to arouse my mother's interest. She shared Mom's fountain sodas and toked from her cigarettes and stood closer as the day wore on because she wanted to kiss her, but she came to figure it was no better than fostering a puppy; you'd only get attached, then be forced to give it away to its real owners at the end of the week.

She found herself in a silent quandary as they browsed a sidewalk newsstand on Las Palmas, struggling between attraction and practicality, for she wasn't a one-night-stand kind of girl. And it seemed almost cruel that the universe would send her someone like Jolán De Carlo, stamped with a six-day expiration date. She could have gotten herself a ticket from the Spanish parking lot attendant and been no better off, paid for it with wishes and daydreams, maybe a kiss before the week was out.

She loved my mother's boyish-but-not demeanor, something I saw most during summertime tennis matches at the park with Uncle Cam. That's when every bit of her femininity stayed home, and an athlete sprang from the bench and usually beat the crap out of my uncle. I can only suppose, from the videos and pictures and Rachel's diary accounts, that the freedom of my mother's early twenties produced a very different young woman than the one I had gotten to know.

And I was fascinated, intrigued by all the enticing little devices meant to lure Rachel Cole into my mother's charms like a hypnotist with a pocket watch. The flirtatious crooked grin. The way she'd find a place to prop an arm and stand salaciously close without ever quite touching her. Fingertips on the curve of Rachel's hip as my mother guided her through the crowded bottlenecks along the Walk of Fame. These things sent electricity through Rachel's thighs and up into her chest until she felt flushed and unsteady, so much that she'd have to move away, or commit a spectacle of lewd conduct right in front of the Kodak Theatre and all its tourists. She took all day to think it through, then decided she would spend every possible moment with my mother for the remainder of the week, even if it was pointless, even if it left her nothing but a handful of winsome memories.

They ended the evening with a movie at the Galaxy Theatre, and they walked all the way back to Vine Street without ever holding hands or sharing a kiss. Rachel wanted to make my mother wait. It gave her a certain amount of control, as Mom seemed naturally to dominate, but my mother didn't push. She stood with her at the bus stop at Hollywood and Vine and waited to see her safely on board.

"So, tomorrow then?" Mom said as the 210 Metro line approached. "It's the fourth, so we were gonna find some place to grill out. Got any ideas?"

Rachel thought about it and nodded. "I do, actually. Might be kinda crowded, but if we get there early, it should be fine. I'll be back by in the morning."

"And I'll be awake, this time," my mother promised with a little smile. "See you then." She touched Rachel's cheek, a little reassurance meant to keep her interest through the night, and she stood watching as Rachel climbed on and found a seat by the window. They shared another smile through the glass, and the bus pulled away down the Boulevard toward Vermont.

"I CANNOT BELIEVE you let her get away like that," Dominick said to Mom the next day at Griffith Park. The two of them stood by the cheap little grill they'd bought from a Wal-Mart in Sacramento. Dom was turning burgers and chicken thighs on the grates, and he glanced at Rachel who sat talking with Evan at a nearby picnic table.

"I didn't let her get away," Mom told him. She was sipping a beer and watching him cook. "I was trying to be a . . . whatever you call it for women . . . a gentlewoman."

"A lentleman," he clarified, poking at the meat. "It's a lady and a gentleman combined." He looked up at her with a silly grin. "Get it?"

"Yeah, I get it. Okay, so I was trying to be a lentleman. She didn't wanna stay or get a room, and she didn't seem like she was ready to be kissed, so I did what most men never think about. I backed off, gave her space." She winked at him, then pointed the tip of her bottle toward the picnic table. "That's why she's sitting over there today, and not at some other get-together with some other chick." She gave him a smile. "See how that works?"

"Whatever," he mumbled. "Even you dykes get caught up in all that sappy, pining, heartrending schmaltz." He lifted a chicken thigh and let it sizzle on the back of the grill, and he fanned the smoke from his face. "Meanwhile, you and the flying nun over there can talk about Mozart and Shakespeare while guys like me are gettin laid. It's pretty basic."

Mom made a deliberate show of looking around the camping area. "And so where's your little blonde again? What was her name? Do you even know?"

"Her *name*," he insisted, "was Trisha. I knew her fucking name, for Christ's sake. I'm not *that* bad."

"Funny, you speak of her in the past tense already, and it's only been twenty-four hours."

"She has a job."

"Okay, she has a job. What kind of job?"

He looked at her. "If you're trying to make me out to be a prick, you're succeeding. 'Cause I don't know. Okay? I didn't ask. There. You satisfied, you feminist witch?"

Mom laughed. "Yes, actually, I am." She patted him on the shoulder and went over to the table and sat with Rachel.

She smiled at Mom. "Hi."

Mom smiled back. "Hi."

Rachel gestured to the beer in Mom's hand. "Do me one favor today. Try not to get smashed 'cause I have something I wanna do later, and you're gonna have to drive."

"Drive? Where're we going? I thought all our escapades would be on buses and subway trains."

Rachel glanced at Evan. "Your drummer, here, has offered us his car to go on a date tonight."

Mom looked at her, surprised and amused. "So, are you asking me out in some cavalier, unorthodox way, Miss Cole?" she asked and sipped her beer. "How do you know I'll say yes?"

"If you don't, you're a blithering idiot," Evan said. "She's pretty cool, this girl. I've been talking to her for a while, and if I were you, I'd just say yes and ask questions later."

Rachel smirked and waited for my mother's reply.

Mom poured her beer into the grass. "Let me go get a Pepsi."

WHEN IT DREW closer to dark, Evan gave Mom the keys to the 4Runner, and they left the guys with Betty and headed away from the campgrounds. The ride out was fairly smooth, as most people were settled in for the show, waiting in lawn chairs and on blankets and truck tailgates for the Observatory fireworks to begin. Mom and Rachel left the park and made a right onto Los Feliz, which became Franklin Avenue where they headed west to Highland toward Mulholland Drive, a dark narrow two lane that wound up and around in serpentine curves and complicated switchbacks through the Hollywood Hills.

"Okay, now this is where it gets tricky," Rachel said.

The Mulholland street lamps were sparse, and there were no sidewalks, only a soft grassy shoulder and the occasional house lights glowing through the brush from a patio or a kitchen window.

"Just be careful. People pull out of their drives along this stretch, and you'll never see them around these bends."

"So, I'm thinking maybe it's you who's the serial killer," Mom said, driving slowly, peering out at the darkened million-dollar spreads, hidden behind flowering walls of jacaranda trees and mountain laurel, growing up and around the tall privacy fences. "Taking me up into some spooky place in the hills where no one can ever find me."

Rachel giggled. "No, silly. It's just a place not a lot of people know about."

"My point exactly."

"I promise I know where we're going."

"I don't doubt that one bit. It's what you're gonna do to me when we get there that I'm worried about."

Rachel checked her watch. "It's the coolest place in LA, trust me. But we need to kinda hurry, or it'll all be for nothing."

Headlights appeared at the next curve. Mom squeezed the wheel, veered right, tried not to hit a mailbox, and straightened the car back onto the road. "It'll all be for nothing if we end up hanging from the Hollywood sign with Evan's car in flames in the canyon below. Nice driving, asshole," she grumbled into the rearview.

"Just be careful." Rachel pointed to a driveway up ahead. "Okay, here. Slow down. I always know it 'cause it's right past the house with all the potted plants in front. Pull up to that drive and just park, but don't turn the car off."

"This is starting to sound like criminal activity," Mom said. "Maybe I should marry you."

Rachel grinned as she opened the door. "After you see this, you just might want to."

Mom watched her in the headlights. It was another private gated drive, but that didn't seem to be much of an obstacle. Rachel slipped through an ample gap between a brick support pillar and the gate itself and jogged down the drive on the opposite side. She was looking for something along the ground. Then she found it, and she jumped up and down, forcing all her one-hundred-and-twenty pounds onto what was apparently the sensor wire that ran across the blacktop. The gate began to creak and bounce, and then it swung open wide, giving Mom full access to the property. Rachel waved her on.

"You have got to be kidding me. I am breaking and entering. This cannot be legal. God, I love this girl already," Mom whispered and threw the 4Runner into drive and rolled down the pathway.

"Okay, now just pull up till you see a dirt road," Rachel said as she hopped back in. "You won't be able to drive it, so we'll have to park and walk the rest of the way." She checked her watch again. "We still have time. Just go ahead and park up there."

Mom's attention was now warily divided between the chaparralled darkness around the headlights and Rachel Cole. She shook her head and pulled up to the dirt. "I underestimated you. I'll tell you that right now. But if you get us kidnapped or thrown off these mountains, no second date for you."

"We're not gonna get kidnapped, I promise. Hell, I've already kidnapped you, if you really wanna get technical." She smiled and got out, and Mom got out with her.

They walked about thirty yards down a ragged trail, and Rachel took Mom's hand and led her along. Soon they came to a clearing, and then it all sprawled out before them.

"Holy shit," Mom marveled. "Whoa."

Rachel gave that a huge grin, and she pulled her in closer. "Come on. It gets better."

She walked her up onto the main ridge where they stood looking out at an endless expanse of orange, white, and yellow city lights that stretched from one end of the horizon to the other, from the foot of the hills all the way out to the southernmost city limits. There was a park-style bench in the middle of the clearing, and Rachel brought my mother over and sat with her.

After a moment, the highlight of her impromptu adventure began. Every fireworks show in Los Angeles, Hollywood, Pasadena, Culver City, Santa Monica, and Long Beach erupted at once. The Hollywood Bowl, the Rose Bowl, Marina Del Rey, Dodgers Stadium, Exposition Park, Redondo Beach, the Queen Mary, and all the other local displays, legal and otherwise.

Mom was thrilled, thoroughly impressed. She glanced at Rachel who was giddy as a child, hugging Mom's arm, swinging her legs from the bench, and smiling as if she'd won something.

"Look at you cheesin," Mom said with a chuckle, and she looked back out at the city scene, shaking her head.

"This is completely over the top with coolness," she said after a long while. "Best date ever. Hands down."

"Really?"

"You should get an award for this. How'd you know about this place, anyway? And how long before the cops get here?" Mom looked around behind her.

Rachel laughed. "There's no cops. My dorm roommate and some friends from school showed it to me the first summer after freshman year. It's sort of what Evan and the guys are seeing from the Observatory, but not quite like this, they don't have this vantage point." She pointed to the mansion up on the hill to their right, a black silhouette against the starless amber gray. "I don't know how true it is, but my friend said that place used to belong to Errol Flynn, the actor, but it's abandoned now, has been forever. Probably haunted or something. I don't know who else knows about this spot, which is what we unofficially call it—The Spot. I've never seen anyone else up here in the few times we've come, so your guess is as good as mine." She looked at Mom with that girlish grin. "So, you like it?"

"I love it. I don't know how you're gonna top this, actually. But you've still got four more days to figure it out, so we'll see." She took Rachel's hand, interlaced their fingers, and held it in her lap and watched the pyrotechnics throwing rainbow glitter to the California sky.

"I've heard on a clear day, when the smog isn't so bad, you can see all the way from downtown out to Catalina Island," Rachel said after a while. "But we've only ever come here at night, so I wouldn't really know."

"Yeah, it might be best to do this under the cover of darkness," Mom said. "Wouldn't want any neighbors watching you shimmy through the security gate."

She smiled at her, Rachel smiled back, and this time she was snared, pulled deep into that hazel gaze, fireworks and city lights sparkling peripherally. That was when my mother leaned in just enough to invite their first kiss, the one Rachel had lain awake each night imagining since Saturday. It was much softer, warmer than she had expected, my mother's hand cool against her cheek, fingertips combing golden blonde from her face as she smiled and kissed her again.

Rachel felt a ripple of butterfly wings that could've lifted her off that hillside and out over the LA cityscape, watching my mother look at her that way, studying her features with an arm relaxed across the back of the bench, the other hand touching her chin, her neck, musician's fingers tracing the lines of her lips, and she kissed her once more.

My mother pulled away, so absorbed in Rachel's pretty details she had almost forgotten about the fireworks still bursting like fountains among the city lights, and she glanced out across the landscape.

"All expectations duly exceeded," she declared lowly. "Best date ever, without question."

Rachel ran a hand through my mother's ringlets and across her cheek. "Yeah." And she kissed her again. "Hands down." She sat thinking for a moment, toying with the beaded hemp choker around my mother's neck. "I think I have an idea for a second date." She looked at her with a little smile. "I'm assuming I get one."

"Oh, yes, ma'am. You get several. As many as you'd like."

"Good." She pulled at the curls that hung down over Mom's shoulders and twined one around her finger. "'Cause you know when I said you can see all the way to Catalina from here?"

Mom nodded, smoothed Rachel's hair as she continued.

"Well, I've never been there, not in the four years I've lived in LA, and I've heard it's very beautiful. But you have to take a ferry to get there. You don't get seasick, do you?"

"I have no idea. I don't think so. I've been on the Staten Island ferry and didn't get sick. Is it any worse than that?"

Rachel laughed lightly. "I've been on the Staten Island ferry, myself, and I did fine. I imagine it's the same for Catalina, just a longer ride." She scooted closer on the bench and took my mother's hand. "I was thinking we could go tomorrow, or Wednesday, maybe."

"I wouldn't care if you wanted to go dumpster diving tomorrow," Mom said. "I'm down to go wherever, as long as I'm going with you."

Rachel smiled. "Well, we'll save the dumpster diving for another time. Meanwhile, I'll check around, see what it'll take to do Catalina instead."

"Sounds like a plan."

All the displays were winding down now, and so they watched the finales, reclined there on the lookout bench, Rachel at home in my mother's arms, and my mother content to keep her there much longer than her Los Angeles stay was going to allow. But she didn't think about that. She took the moments and measured them out in spoonfuls, one at a time, each distinct to the next and untroubled by the last because if she started counting the days, it would have made her crazy with disappointment.

She didn't know if she was falling for this girl, and it seemed preposterous after only sixty-two hours. Who does that? And who lets that happen, knowing the future would arrive at a precipice steeper than the edge of Errol Flynn's abandoned property? She decided she would save those concerns for another day and instead sat watching the fireworks with Rachel Cole wrapped up in her arms. That was all she wanted to know; it was the only moment that mattered.

chapter ten

TO WATCH HER sleeping is better than the full moon out over the Catalina harbor, better than the miraculously clear Pacific when the sun shines off it like glass. This is when I get all the uninterrupted details, except for her eyes, but I've got those memorized now—chestnut brandy in the sunshine, honey russet in the firelight, mahogany when we're making love. Two little freckles on her left cheek just above her chin, the tiny lines in her lips, every eyelash, the faintest scar beneath her left eyebrow from falling off a swing when she was seven, a wisp of blonde baby hair across her ear, two holes pierced at the lobe. She's got one hand tucked under the pillow, the other draped over my waist, the Avalon morning climbing the hotel blinds, throwing a tea rose sunrise into the room and across her bare shoulders, yellow pastel sheets pulled up just to the small of her back so that her stomach, her breasts, the top of a thigh all find pieces of sunlight and shadow. She is a picture ready for canvas, a song I'll write sometime after I've gone from here. This time tomorrow I'll be at the wheel of the Fleetwood, south on Interstate 5, a hundred miles in front of me, and behind me—this wonderful light lying here with me now, sound asleep with a leg stretched across mine. Dreaming, I hope, of the way we fell into these sheets two nights in a row, just a little drunk off the Moscato she ordered from downstairs. Hands everywhere. Passion like a drug you don't remember taking but now you're on it, in it, swept away for the indefinite ride, and what a ride it was.

She smelled like honeysuckle, and tropic tanning oil, tasted like cinnamon, and she felt like pearls, warm as the sand out on that beach beyond the balcony, her legs around my waist with an arm across my back, nails digging into my shoulder, the other between her legs, massaging herself while I kept a good steady rhythm with three fingers, one of those perfect nipples erect between my lips like a bead, making her buck against my hand until she grabbed a fistful of my curls and let everything out as if struck by a beautiful kind of lightning.

And now, she sleeps, naked on her side with a hand tucked under the pillow, sun on her face, her shoulders, her breasts. I grin and brush the backs of my fingers over a nipple to wake her, and she stirs and jumps a little, stirs some more, breathes a delicate sigh and opens her eyes, at last, still mahogany gold from our night before. She looks at me for a long while with a drowsy little smile and touches my face.

"Come with me to San Diego."

IT WAS THE one thing neither of them wanted, the inevitable place in which they'd now found themselves, as if stepping off a cliff somehow wouldn't call down the laws of gravity and crush them both against each other when they hit ground. And so there they were, considering, with all variety of desperation, what it would take to postpone goodbye for just a while longer, something my mother hadn't come to fear until she'd realized how close it was to Saturday morning.

For Rachel, it was sudden, an idea she hadn't even entertained until it drifted from my mother's lips, lying there in bed at the Villa Portofino in Avalon, Catalina.

She adjusted herself on her side and looked at my mother, thinking. Before she could say anything, Mom told her, "It's just a couple hours away, it's not far. We'll be there till Thursday. We have a show Wednesday night, it'll give us five more days."

Rachel was quiet, looking at my mother with temptation whirling around in her head, trying to rationalize it through. Five more days. It would mean tomorrow wouldn't be the last time she'd see Jolán De Carlo after all, and what else did she have to do? For the next five days? What couldn't be put off or reworked or utterly forgotten for those eyes, for that kiss that lifted her to the ceiling every time, for those wonderfully talented hands that played love songs just for her and smoothed the hair at her temple, those sensual hands that had set her skin alight with blazing tremors until she didn't know whether to cry or black out from excess.

But that couldn't be her reasoning, purely carnal, sexual. She was better than that, made of something true and substantial and resolute, and she had already broken a good handful of her own rules, sleeping twice with a ghost. This beautiful ghost who was willing to rattle her chains for just a few more days, lying beside her with that smile, the one she would never forget, she promised herself. She had already broken so many rules.

She wanted to know one thing before she answered. "You'd be going on to Tucson. How would I get back to USC?"

Mom didn't hesitate. "I'll put you on a bus, or a shuttle. I'll pay for it, I'll make sure. I won't leave you stranded, I swear."

"You promise."

"I promise. You have my word."

Rachel weighed it all out for another moment. Then she smiled. "Okay. I'll go. I'll go with you."

"Yeah?" Mom slid close and took her into her arms.

Rachel gave her another pretty smile and kissed her lips, her neck, her chest between the well of her breasts. And she turned her onto her back and climbed on top of her. "Yeah."

They made love again, threw away the notion of goodbye for a little longer, and let the Avalon sun rise past the window shades. They let the morning disappear into the pastel sheets, falling into that perfect space between two kinds of inevitability—an unexpected romance and the unbearable idea of separation.

RACHEL ROAD SHOTGUN in the Fleetwood while Mom drove. They'd stopped by USC so she could grab some clothes, and now they were southbound on the 5 Freeway with perfect driving weather and Evan's Miles Davis tape playing through the system. Mom was in a particularly good mood because not only did she have Rachel Cole by her side, but she had also spoken to Uncle Cameron when she'd called home from LA, and he would be meeting them at the airport in San Diego. He'd gotten three thousand dollars in graduation money that was originally intended for a trip with friends to Miami Beach, but Mom talked him into joining them on the road instead, much to the disapproval of Nanna and Pap. He'd graduated from high school with honors and won a scholarship to Georgia Tech, and he was eighteen now, a consenting adult with a nice wad of cash at his disposal and the summer off, so he pleaded his case to my grandparents on just those merits and was scheduled to land in San Diego within twenty-four hours. He would do two weeks with Portland Downs, then fly out of Tucson when they reached Arizona.

"How're we gonna get him into the bars?" Matt wanted to know when Mom told them of the arrangements. "He's a kid. Does he have ID?"

Dom waved that off. "Give him a mic stand, let him carry my bass, make him a roadie."

"Yeah. Make him a roadie," Mom said with a simple shrug. "If he's with us, he's in. We're up for sound check long before they open, anyway. He'll be fine. The kid's six-one with a full beard. He doesn't look eighteen. No one's gonna stop him, and if they do, oh well. He can hang out in Betty, watch the camper."

And so that was the plan as they cruised Interstate 5 past San Clemente, the sun strobing through the palms along the roadside, Mom in her aviator shades at the wheel with a Marlboro and a twenty-ounce Coke and Rachel her co-pilot, relaxed in the passenger's seat, sandaled feet propped on the dash, sandy blonde blowing freely in the open window breeze.

Evan leaned up onto the console with a map folded out to the San Diego quadrant, and he watched the signs going by. "There's a KOA park not far from downtown. I figure we can hang out there, get showers, dump the tanks, plug in for a while so we can save the generators for practices."

"Sounds good to me." Mom took a sip of her drink and flicked her ashes out the window.

"So, is that what you do to practice?" Rachel asked. "Put on free concerts for people in RV parks? You should at least put out a tip jar, make some extra gas money."

"We dry camp, go park somewhere remote," Evan said, "set up there, keep everything low and play for about an hour or so, just once a week."

"Not everyone at a public campsite's gonna wanna hear an hour of heavy blues rock," Mom told her. "The acoustic stuff is usually cool, but not all plugged in with the guitars and the drum kit going."

Dom handed a weed pipe up to Evan from the back, and he toked it twice until it went out. He held the smoke for a moment, studied the map, and blew a gray cloud up into the windshield.

"Once we get to Oceanside, we're halfway there," he said to Mom and handed her the pipe and a lighter.

She gestured to Rachel. "Let her hit it first. I've got too much shit in my hands. We're about thirty miles from Oceanside now, so we should get into San Diego by two o'clock."

Rachel took her turn and held the pipe to Mom's lips so she could smoke hands free, then gave it back to Evan. "You know once we get to San Diego, we're only twenty minutes from Mexico. You guys ever been to Tijuana?"

They were all quiet, having never considered that.

"We don't have passports," Dom finally said, "and I'm not crossing the Rio Grande and climbing the fence, just for a burrito and a bottle of Tequila. I can get that in San Diego."

Rachel turned around to him and shook her head. "You don't need a passport, not for Mexico."

"Have you been?" Mom asked.

Rachel smiled and nodded. "Last summer. We did Tijuana and Ensenada, rode horses on Rosarita Beach, did the whole driving tour. Everything's cheap there. Cigarettes, liquor, food. American dollars are like gold."

Mom smirked at her sideways, watching the road. "And who'd you do all this with?"

"My ex, yes. But she got violently ill after the first day, and that was that. You can't drink the public water, and the food's hit or miss. She was unlucky."

"So, is that what you do? Take your girlfriends to Mexico and see how tough they are?"

"Actually, it's to see how smart they are. I warned her long before we crossed not to drink the water, and she ignored it and brushed her teeth from the hotel faucet instead of using the bottled water I'd brought with us." Rachel winked, then leaned back against the seat and crossed her ankles on the dash, sipped her soda.

"Point taken." Mom smiled. She glanced around at the others. "Okay, so who's up for Tijuana, then? We park Betty at the campgrounds, pick up my brother tomorrow, and drag him with us. We can take the 4Runner."

"The drinking age is eighteen there," Rachel told her. "We won't have to worry about getting him into the bars, so that'll be good."

"Yeah, he'll like that," Mom said. "A much better vacation than Miami Beach already. So, who's down?"

Dom raised his hand from where he was lying on the couch, and Evan and Matt were up for it as well, and so now that was the new plan. They got to the RV park and the guys spent that night in the RV while Mom and Rachel took one of the campground cabins, as it was Matt's turn for the sleeper. When all the traveling details and chores were complete the following day, they unhitched the 4Runner and headed back out to Interstate 5 toward the airport.

UNCLE CAM HAD his video camera going as soon as they showed up at baggage claim, announcing the commencement of his journey from behind the lens. "And the world famous Portland Downs are now making their way across the terminal. My sister, Jolán De Carlo, looking killer as usual, blues rock guitar legend in the making."

Mom laughed and hugged his neck, and the camera wobbled through her hair and whirled around the terminal, past Rachel, Dom, and Matt.

"Is that the best intro you could come up with? In the 'making'? I'm gonna have to educate you, little brother," she said into his shoulder. She pulled away and grinned into the lens. "Are you planning on putting that thing down at all this trip?"

"Probably not." He turned it on himself and raised one eyebrow like a mad scientist. "Be afraid. Be very, very afraid of a man with a video camera." He spun it back onto his subjects again.

Mom introduced him to everyone, and they made their way to the turnstiles, picked up his bags, and headed out to where Evan waited in the 4Runner.

The camera was in his face now, too, and he smiled and waved at it from the driver's seat.

He reached in and shook Cam's hand. "Hey, how's it goin? Evan. It's good you brought one of those things. We need some live show footage. You mind taping us on Wednesday night at the Diesel Lounge? We'll make you our official videographer if you don't fuck it up."

"Sure," Cam told him as he climbed into the backseat. "I got ID, by the way," he said to Mom and then turned the camera off. "You remember Jimmy Conrad from over on Stanwood? His brother misplaced his wallet, got a new driver's license, then found his wallet three weeks later." And he produced a valid Pennsylvania license from his own wallet with a picture that, in the demure sidewalk club lighting, would pass nicely for a twenty-two-year-old Cameron De Carlo a.k.a. Mark William Conrad, 6'2", 190 lbs., brown hair, brown eyes, no beard, but that was incidental.

Mom took it and looked it over thoroughly, then handed it back to him. "Should be fine. Just don't use it unless you have to. We'll get you in with us whenever we can."

"You won't need it where we're goin, though, kid," Dom said to him from the passenger's seat.

"And that is?"

Dom did a little merengue chair dance and said, "Where the beer's fifty centavos, the Tequila's flowing like Niagara Falls, and the señoritas'll be lifting their skirts at every corner."

"LA?"

Mom winced. "No, bonehead. Tijuana."

"You mean, Mexico?"

"Well, it's not in Oklahoma," Mom told him. "Yeah, Mexico. So, I hope you don't have jet lag, 'cause that's where we're going. Right now. You can thank Rachel. It was her idea. None of us would've thought of it. We all thought you needed a passport, so sue us."

"Well, who's the bonehead now? Even I know you don't need a passport for Mexico." He clapped his hands and rubbed them together. "Hell yes." He picked up the camera, turned it on, and pointed it at himself. "I've only been in Cali for fifteen minutes, and already this dude is heading for the border. Day-fucking-one of the Tijuana excursion begins," and he aimed the lens out the 4Runner window as they pulled back onto Interstate 5, heading south, "now."

HE KEPT THE camera going all the way through the El Ysidro border crossing and into the town itself. He never turned it off. He should have worn it strapped to his forehead or mounted on his shoulder, like the cinematographers for Hollywood stunt men. He kept a running commentary, read aloud all the landmark signs as if his intended viewers were blind. He never stopped talking. He put the thing in everyone's faces as they browsed the vendors along Tijuana's main thoroughfare, but none of them seemed to mind because no one had thought to videotape their travels until now. They'd taken pictures with disposable cameras and still hadn't developed them, and so this was a technological upgrade, a whole other way to be immortalized.

The town's main feature was *Avenida Revolución*, a two lane bustling strip lined with stout palms and graffitied storefronts, oversized murals of Cesar Chavez, bright yellow Aztec suns, and huge white doves, entire buildings painted electric blue, chartreuse, and hot mango. There were pharmacies for *medicina* on almost every corner because the pharmaceutical prices were cheaper than in the States. Red, white, and green balloons bobbed in the breeze, strung from Spanish mission-style hotel balconies, and every so many blocks was a donkey painted like a zebra, led by a local who'd offer photos with the animal for a few dollars. At the end of the avenue, the Tijuana Arch towered over the city with a sign that read *"Bienvenidos Tijuana"* anchored in the center.

Cam and Mom were the only Spanish speakers among the group, and they interpreted negotiations between merchants for the best prices on souvenir key chains and bracelets and t-shirts. Children no older than kindergarten approached them, looking to sell little packages of *chicle* for *diez centavos*, which Mom translated as chewing gum, ten cents a pack. Rachel bought one kid out completely, and so four more came running and followed her through the streets with offers on baseball caps and hand-strung beaded necklaces and Virgin Mary dashboard statuettes. That's when she warned the guys to put their wallets into their front pockets, as the children were no less adept at pickpocketing than they were at marketing their goods. She nevertheless smiled and spoke to them sweetly, pushed her sunglasses up onto her head and stooped down to have a look at their wares while Mom interpreted and Uncle Cam filmed. I could see my mother's gaze falling upon her like a cool rain, watching with her arms crossed at her waist as Rachel tried her hand at my mother's Spanish.

"Tienes rojas?" she asked one boy of the necklaces, then looked up at Mom for approval on the pronunciation. "I want red *and* yellow. How do I say that?"

"Then ask him *tienes rojas y amarillos?* He has more in his bag. Say, *tienes mas en tu bolsa. Puedo ver los otros?* He'll know what you mean."

She shifted her weight to the other heel and looked up at Mom, shading her eyes from the sun. "I'm not gonna remember all that, baby. You have to go slow."

So Mom just asked him herself, and the boy dug into the plastic grocery bag, fished one out, and handed it to Rachel.

"Dos dólares," he said. *"Es muy linda, como usted."*

Cam laughed aloud, and the camera shook. "He's a regular salesman, this kid. Knows how to work the ladies. He's pretty smooth."

Rachel looked up at him, a bewildered grin.

"He's flirting with you, said you were a total fucking hottie. Now you *have* to buy it."

"No, he didn't." She laughed, then looked at Mom.

Mom shrugged. "Yeah, he did. Kinda. He was more respectful than my dipshit brother, though. He said the necklace was as pretty as you. He has good taste."

Rachel smiled at the boy. "Well, *muchas gracias, mijo. Me llevo dos, por favor. Quatro dólares, sí?"* She handed him four dollars and took the trinkets, put one around her neck, and the other in her shorts pocket. She bought two of everything else from the others, and that was when Mom shooed them away.

"Esta bien. No mas. Vete, ya!" She waved a hand out to the streets, and they all scattered, stuffing dollars into their pockets as they disappeared into the crowds.

They walked the blocks again and soon found a restaurant with patio seating where they ordered something called a "whistle shot" that they'd seen at a neighboring table. The waiter wore Tequila bottles in holsters on his hip, and for a dollar he would come around to your table, fit you with a red plastic bib, hold your head back over the chair rest, and as everyone cheered and clap-chanted your name, he'd pour Tequila straight down your throat while blowing a coach's whistle in your ear until you just couldn't take it anymore. Then he wrapped the bib over your face and wrangled your head around as if to unhinge it from your shoulders. When he felt satisfied with your complete disorientation, he let you loose to watch Tijuana spin for twenty minutes.

Dom and Matt got it done twice, and since Evan was designated driver, he held the camera while Cam took his turn. Rachel opted out with just a few beers, but Mom was fearless; she could drink like a sea sponge, and she let the waiter drown her in liquor and rough her up as readily as the guys. Matt and Cam vomited behind a dumpster an hour and two margaritas later, which Evan filmed as well, laughing at them both from behind the lens.

WHEN THE SUN finally set over the Laguna Mountains, they went walking in *Zona Norte*, Tijuana's red light district. Mom was fairly lit by then and steadied herself on Rachel as they strolled past the bars and strip clubs, salsa music and mariachi and Spanish techno all competing between the shoe stores and souvenir *tiendas*. Dark-haired prostitutes leaned along the storefronts under flashing rainbow neon, wearing red-and-black pumps and tight skirts up to the shadows at their crotches, all of them busty in their lacy bustiers and crinkle tube tops, and they nodded to the guys for offers. A few even made gestures to Mom and Rachel when they saw them hand in hand.

Dom grinned at Mom, and he pointed a thumb at the girls in the doorways. "Hey, looks like they don't discriminate, Jo. Your money's good as mine here. You two should go make yourselves a sandwich."

Rachel gave him a sarcastic smirk. "Yeah, okay, just keep walking, dear. And please stop trying to sell the Mexican whores to my wasted girlfriend, thank you very much. Three's a crowd, and I don't share."

"I am not wasted," Mom mumbled. "I am pleasantly buzzed."

"You're pickled as a jar a beets, babe," Rachel said, patting her arm. "No whores, and no more liquor for you for a week."

"That sounds like a threat to me, Jo," Matt said. "You just might have to put her in her place with one of these." He was standing at the lighted window of an adult novelty store, *Diablitas* airbrushed in red and black over the entrance, and he pointed at a leather bondage kit, complete with ceiling tethers and silver spiked handcuffs and a body harness that looked like a complicated black spider web.

Rachel rolled her eyes at him and tried to pull my mother along, but she resisted and moved toward the entrance.

"Are you serious?" Rachel sighed. "You really wanna go in there?" Then she rethought that. "Yes, of course you do. You're drunk."

"It'll be educational," Mom said, urging her inside.

"I have plenty of education, all the education I need," she told her coyly. "I think you know that by now."

"You ladies can stand out here and discuss sex ed all night if you want, but I'm goin in. 'Scuse me." Dom stepped past Mom and pushed open the glass door, and it jingled a tiny bell overhead. Matt, Cam, and Evan followed, but the cashier shook her head and wagged a finger at the video camera, told them to turn it off or leave, so Evan showed her the little red recording light, then switched it off.

"All right, fine." Rachel took Mom's arm. "Come on, horn toad."

They had all the things you might expect and then things you couldn't imagine, all of it sealed in hot pink and glossy black boxes with every type of human nakedness superimposed onto the covers, magazine and video racks that shoved double D's and penises into your face, unwrapped toys on display along the counters for customers to have a closer look at how they functioned. Feather boas, S&M masks, horsewhips, incense and body oil selections in glass cases, plastic life-sized dolls with all the necessary orifices facing front through cellophane packaging.

Dom picked up a dildo the size of a fire log that was standing on end in the corner. "I never told you of my days as a model for these things," he said to the others. "Still haven't gotten my royalties from this one. Guess I'll have to make some calls."

Evan took one the size of his own finger from a hook on the wall. "You mean these things?"

Cam laughed and took it from Evan, waved it in Mom's face. "I don't guess you have much use for any of this. Never did."

"Fuck off," she muttered and batted it away. "If you really want me to buy you one, just ask. Don't be shy."

Cam whacked her on the head with it, and she shoved him and moved on.

Matt was over by the video stand, and he had one turned over to the back, reading the "plot." He kept it with him as he browsed the rest.

"See, these girls are exactly your type," he said to Dom. "You play the hell outa the bass, but if it doesn't work out, hey, there's always other professions. You should think it over."

"Oh, believe me, I have."

Rachel stood close to Mom, an arm linked around hers as they walked the aisles. She watched my mother's face, looking to see where her eyes landed the longest, then took an inventively designed vibrator down from the shelf, which had drawn my mother's glance more than twice. She turned the box in her hands but couldn't read all the Spanish details on the back, and she handed it to Mom.

"I think the pictures are pretty universal," Rachel said. "But if there's something else we should know, maybe it's in the fine print."

Mom looked the thing over and shrugged. "If this works for you, then it works for me. Maybe we should just get a basket." She gestured to the front of the shop.

Rachel laughed and hung it back on the wall. "I actually had something else in mind, now that we're here." She handled another novelty, looked it over, and put it back. "But it's not something we've really discussed, and since I don't know when I'm ever gonna see you after Thursday." She shrugged, didn't finish her thought.

"All that can be worked out. I got my brother here from Bensalem, didn't I? There's still another two months before school starts again."

Rachel didn't say anything. She glanced up at my mother and back to the hanging toys in every shape and color, perfectly molded renderings of male genitalia in various shades of flesh for all races, others that could've belonged to some erotic alien species—Martian green, Neptune blue, Mercury red—inhuman appendages attached for added pleasure, whatever you were into, whatever planet you were from, everything vivid as the *Revolución* murals under white fluorescent lights.

After a while, they went to the counter with their purchases, took them back to the 4Runner, and locked them in. They went back to the strip and wandered into one of the nightclubs with salsa music ringing out into the traffic. Cam kept the camera running inside and panned it over the green whirling lasers and red and yellow spotlights passing through gray clouds of artificial fog, flashing in time to Grupo Niche and Celia Cruz.

The women were beautiful, voluptuous. The men were slick and handsome. Dom did shots from between a cocktail server's cleavage while Cam and Matt explored the shameless girls near the dance floor who bent their asses into the camera for Evan, then reeled around and hung on their necks with umbrella drinks in hand, hauling them each to the center of the crowded checkered floor where Mom was teaching Rachel to rumba.

They were playing "Ay Candela" now, and the whole place sang along and clapped in unison to the downbeat. She had good timing, picked it up rather quickly, and let my mother twirl her like a pro, all the moves Mom had learned from watching Nanna Sylvia rehearse for the Tikoa Club on Saturday nights. Rachel spun way out to the end of my mother's hand, then back into her arms, laughing at herself as Mom planted a kiss on her cheek and wrapped her in a bear hug, and they stayed that way and danced the rest of the song cuddled close. No one gave them a second glance; it was anything goes for the rest of the night under hypnotic conga rhythms and deep bass rumbling the stucco, detuned Spanish guitars and Latin horns playing tag in complex duets, heat and smoke and spinning strobes and my mother's lips locked on Rachel's, freshly tipsy from the empty Coronas sitting on their table in the corner.

BY THREE A.M. they needed to find a hotel. Everyone was spent and tanked, unsteady as they left the club. Matt couldn't light his cigarette; the flame kept going out, and he had it in his mouth with the filter to the wind. Rachel took it from him, lit it properly, and gave it back while my mother sang "Lamento de un Guajiro" in slurred Spanish, propped up with an arm across Rachel's shoulder as they walked.

They came upon the Hotel Caesar right along *Revolución* for two hundred pesos, which came out to about sixteen American dollars at the 1992 exchange rate, and it was the most luxurious hotel on the strip, equivalent to the average Motel 6. But none of them would notice much until morning. They took rooms along the first floor where Mom passed out on the bedspread. Rachel roused her enough to get her undressed and comfortable, and she climbed in beside her.

The city streets whirred beyond the window screen. Some of the clubs were still open, and the music seeped inside. Rachel held my mother's head against her chest in the dark, running her fingers through her curls, thinking about Thursday morning when the band would pack up the Fleetwood and head east toward Tucson while she found a window seat on a northbound Greyhound. She was foggy and dizzy from too many *cervezas*, and she thought that must surely be why the tears came so easily. She kissed my mother's hair, listened to her breathing, and watched the shadows slide across the walls from the passing Tijuana traffic.

chapter eleven

EVERYTHING WAS QUIET when Rachel awoke, the desert waiting beyond the windows, offering just a few slices of sunlight through the vertical blinds above the headboard. My mother was asleep on her stomach, flat on the mattress with the pillow shoved askew, one arm hanging off the bed, the other folded under her chest. Rachel leaned onto an elbow and pulled a handful of ringlets from Mom's sleeping face, kissed her bare shoulder, and reached across for the watch on the nightstand. It was almost three in the afternoon. She set it back on the table, ran a hand through her hair, and looked down at my mother with a distant smile.

"Wake up, superstar," she whispered into her ear. She laid across my mother's back, her lips to her ear, fingertips brushing the curls at her temple. "Baby," she uttered again and waited.

Finally my mother roused a bit and sent a little sound like groaning into the mattress. She opened her eyes and blinked at the daylight.

Rachel kissed her cheek. "Good morning."

Mom lifted a sleep-heavy arm to the nightstand and checked her watch, then turned onto her side and looked over her shoulder at Rachel. She rolled onto her back and gave her a groggy smile, gradually bringing herself around.

"You really are something to wake up to," she rasped, sweeping a honey-blonde strand from Rachel's eyes.

"I guess I'll take that as a compliment," Rachel said. She pushed her hands up under my mother's back and rested her chin on her chest, lying between her legs.

"Do, definitely," Mom said, admiring her details, the shape of her upper lip just slightly fuller at the edges than the lower, her complexion flawless, a shade lighter than my mother's with a rosy strip across the bridge of her nose from the sun.

"We need to be getting on the road soon," Rachel reminded her. "How're you feeling? You drank and did a lot of shit last night. I thought I was gonna need a wheelbarrow to get you into bed."

Mom made a face, as if a pint of liquor, a quarter ounce of weed, and two rails of cocaine were equivalent to a quart of milk, a pack of Oreos, and a Pixie Stix, and she nodded and gave her an "okay" sign. "I'm good. I'm always good. Nothing fazes the invincible Jolán De Carlo. You'll figure that out soon enough."

Rachel wasn't entirely convinced of that, but she let her up to get showered. "Well, Evan's driving, so at least you can rest on the way into the city." She leaned back down and kissed her again. "Come on. Up." She tried to crawl away, but my mother grabbed her hips and pulled her back into bed.

"You don't believe me." Mom kissed her neck and wrapped her arms around her waist to keep her there on top of her. "I can see it on your face."

"I believe you partied like today would never come," Rachel said. "A normal person would be a miserable pile of dog shit, this morning, and I just wanna make sure you're in shape to do what you've gotta do."

"I'm in great shape. In fact, I can prove it." And she rolled her over onto her back in one swift move that made Rachel squeal with laughter, and she smiled down on her, aware that the afternoon sunlight had found its way through the blinds and into her hazel eyes. *"Vamos hacer el amor, querida,"* fluttered over my mother's lips, and that was about all it took.

By now, Rachel understood exactly what that meant, and against it she had no defense, and my mother knew that.

"Besame, mi novia linda." She parted Rachel's thighs with a knee and let herself down between them with a long deep kiss meant to melt her into the sheets.

There was a knock at the door. They ignored it, focused on each other. After a moment, there was another knock.

"Hey, yo! Jo, Rache!" It was Dominick.

"Go away," my mother grumbled, running her tongue along Rachel's ear lobe.

"Come on, get up. We gotta go eat and get on the road." That was Cam.

"Go. *Away.*" Mom grabbed a pillow and threw it at the door and went back to Rachel's neck.

The guys were quiet for a moment.

Then Dominick groaned. "Oh, for shit's sake. Are you serious?" He'd apparently figured out why their presence in the hall was untimely. "We don't have time for a cowgirl ride, Homosabe. We got shit to do. Put your toys away and let's go."

"Are you friggin kidding me?" Mom griped. "What part of 'go the hell away' do they not get?"

Rachel stopped everything, went abruptly cold. "You wanna hold this thought? They're not gonna leave, and they're probably right."

Mom dropped onto her back, perturbed. "I don't see much choice, now. Kind of a mood killer, my goddamned little brother at the door. What's next? A phone call from my mother? Bag of dead kittens under the bed?"

Rachel grinned and sat up. She reached for Mom's watch and checked the time again. "What's next is a shower."

She saw my mother's expression change into something mischievous, those eyebrows raised with a devilish smile.

Rachel hit her with the other pillow. *"No.* Strictly for hygiene purposes. I'm serious. We don't have time; we have other days."

"Hey, do we need to call an ambulance or some shit?" Cam persisted through the door.

"Give us twenty minutes. Go find coffee, smoke a bowl, do whatever. We'll be out in a few."

"Roger that," he said. "And hurry the hell up."

IT TOOK MORE than twenty minutes. It took forty-five minutes because Rachel couldn't decide what shorts to wear, or which earrings to pair, or what shoes went best with the earrings—leather sandals or flip-flops—or whether to blow dry her hair straight or clip it up in a twist. Mom sat ready and waiting on the edge of the unmade bed, watching in a pair of jeans and a Gibson guitars t-shirt, her hair damp and shiny and tied back in a loose ponytail.

Rachel's feminine indecisiveness was bemusing to her. She suggested the silver earrings with the aqua stones. Rachel held them to her lobes, chose the little gold hoops. She stood in just her shorts and a bra and held a pastel green halter top up to her chest, looked to Mom for approval, then offered a plain white baby tee, switched them back and forth. Mom shut her eyes and pointed. Her finger chose the baby tee, and so Rachel put it on. When she had finally coordinated that with the flip-flops and her hair up in a twist, they grabbed their bags, headed through the Frontier Motel lobby to drop off the key, and then out into the blinding Arizona afternoon, the Tucson skyline hazy in the distance. Mom threw on her sunglasses.

"Nice of you ladies to join us," Matt said at the side door of the Fleetwood, beer bottle in hand. "We have sound check in three hours, and we still have to get into Tucson through rush-hour traffic, find parking, load in. You know, all that unimportant shit we've been doing for the past three months."

"Is that your breakfast?" Mom asked of the beer and pushed past him into the camper where Cam accosted her with the video camera.

"The legendary Jolán De Carlo, ladies and gentlemen. A bit under the weather today, it seems. Maybe a little hungover," he announced, walking backward into the Formica table, but he kept rolling. "My guess is those shades won't come off until sometime after midnight." He put the camera down and tapped her shoulder, and she turned to him, frowning.

Mom snatched off her sunglasses. "Jeezus, *what?"* Cam made a discreet little gesture to his nose, shrugged a shoulder. She didn't know what he meant until she tasted blood on her upper lip, and she raised a knuckle to it, saw it on her hand.

"Shit." Rachel snatched a paper towel from the roll by the sink and balled it up and held it to my mother's face, but Mom took it and wiped it away herself.

Rachel looked at her, displeased. "I told you to slow down last night," she muttered, eyeing the bright red on the paper.

"It's no big deal," Mom said, lowly. "Happens sometimes, coke does that, doesn't mean anything."

"I can cut that out," Cam assured, holding up the camera, but he forgot and never did.

Mom stared at Rachel who was staring at her. "I'll leave it alone for a while. Okay? You had your share, too, you know." She turned away and took her bag to the sleeper, holding the towel to her nose.

"Yeah, but I don't do it every weekend, I keep it at a minimum." Rachel followed her. "Just don't go nuts with that shit is all I'm saying. It's supposed to be recreational, occasional, not a full-time hobby."

"Yes, ma'am." Mom wrapped her arms around Rachel's waist and pulled her close for a kiss, but Rachel saw the pale pink swath of blood still under her nose, and so she took the paper towel to the bathroom and wet it and came back.

"Be still." She held Mom's chin steady and faced her to the window light and dabbed her clean. "Better." She gave her the kiss she was looking for. "Slow it down, 'kay?"

"All right."

AND SHE DID. Until she didn't, anymore. They had two nights scheduled in Tucson, Friday at the Guns At Ten tavern on the south side and Saturday at Montego's in the 4th Avenue district of downtown, opening for a band called The Brush, an alternative blues-jazz trio out of Denver who were popular in the southwest and along the west coast. The Brush were in Yuma on Friday and would finish a six-month tour when they got to Tucson, so said the club's promoter during his follow-up phone conversation with "Demetrius" last month. After listening to Portland Downs' demo, he thought they'd be a great fit and promised a piece of the door, and so Evan set it up.

GUNS AT TEN was a little freestanding place in South Tucson off Silverlake Road, the Santa Catalina Mountains towering in the distance beyond a great, vast stretch of tumbleweed wasteland. It was a tawny brown stucco structure with a red Spanish tile roof and wrought iron bars across the entrance, but the outside was deceiving. Somehow, the place seemed twice as large inside, with a dusty mosaic tile floor, red vinyl booth seats, and bruised darkwood bar tops with nicknames and profanity carved into the surfaces. The bar area had a collection of antique license plates tacked to the walls and ceiling under hanging lamps made of old hubcaps, and by ten-thirty what seemed like an obscure, out-of-the-way little dive came to life with a line at the door that stretched around into the parking lot.

"It's probably like one of those mom-and-pop burger stands," Matt said of the sudden popularity as they waited at a booth for show time. "A local icon that you gotta live here to know about or some shit."

"It was listed in the back of a music magazine, a little ad, so I looked it up and sent them a package 'cause they were along the route," Evan said, and he sipped his beer and watched the place fill with college students and middle-aged hippies, bikers, bar sluts, and suburban couples.

It was getting close to show time, and so Mom slid out from her seat and gave Rachel a kiss. "All right. Well, let's give 'em a little Boston blues, shall we?"

She brought a beer to the stage, took a preparatory swig, lit a cigarette for the Stratocaster headstock, and tucked it fuming up into where the strings met the tuning pegs as the others settled in behind their instruments. She nodded once to the soundman and counted off "Cold Shot," no band intro; she liked dropping something hard and heavy and unprefaced onto a cold crowd.

She had a cocky streak and knew most people were skeptical of a frontwoman like herself taking the stage, and it gave her the secret satisfaction of a sucker punch, right in the face. The response was a rush of octane adrenaline that sped through her veins and made eight-minute solos look easy and sound incredible; it made the obscurity and months of being broke worth every microwaved frozen burrito and "Jolán who?" from Boston to San Diego. And now she had Rachel Cole's smile and eager applause from the edge of the stage to dial it all up another notch.

They spent the first thirty minutes rattling the glass racks and vibrating the tabletops with three originals spaced between "Are You Experienced" and a ten-minute rendition of ZZ Top's "Just Got Paid." Mom waited until the end of the set to introduce herself and the rest of Portland Downs, then stepped off into fifteen minutes of handshakes, back slaps, and casual chats while Uncle Cam's Sony Hi8 followed behind. Then someone stopped her with a business card, just as she made it back to the booth.

"Where'd you learn to play like that?" he asked.

She glanced down at the card: *Michael Freiburg. Artist & Repertoire.*

Geffen Records, Santa Monica, CA. She didn't answer and instead eyed him suspiciously.

He was in his thirties, clean shaven and shiny faced, a little sunburned, dressed for a vacation rather than business in an unbuttoned yellow dress shirt over a plain white t-shirt, khaki shorts and a pair of boat shoes. She looked at the card again. Cam had the camera pointed down on it, but she palmed the lens and moved him out of the way.

The man smiled and said, "Well, I know you can sing, but can you *talk?*"

"I learned mostly from Stevie Ray Vaughan," she finally told him and walked away.

"You mean lessons? Rest his soul, by the way. Tragic loss," he noted, following her. "You knew him? As a mentor, I'm guessing?"

Mom stopped and looked at him with a peculiar frown. "No. I *listened.*" She pointed to her ear. "Him and every other blues guitar legend. They were all mentors, if that's what you mean. The rest I taught myself, just trial and error, and a shit-ton of practice."

Michael Freiburg shifted his eyes to Dom, Matt, and Evan who had gathered around while Rachel listened from the booth. "How long you guys been playing together?"

"Two years," Mom said, "three if you count me and Dom in another band together in '88. Why?"

"Pretty damned good chemistry for two years." He pointed to the card that Evan was now reading. "Well, I'm one of the A&R scouts for Geffen Records. Ever hear of a band called Guns N' Roses? Nirvana?"

Mom and Matt shared a peculiar glance, and Matt said, "Who the fuck hasn't?"

"Yeah, well they're with us," Michael told them. "I heard a few originals up there. How many do you have? You did a lot of covers."

"We have six originals right now." Evan handed the card to Matt. "We're working on more, though."

"Hey, listen," Mom said, before Michael could respond. "We've been jerked around enough by assholes with business cards and promises. It's always the same, so you might wanna peddle your bullshit somewhere else 'cause we don't have time for it." And she grabbed the card from Matt and handed it back to Michael, but he wouldn't take it.

He glanced at it with a sigh. "You might wanna get five more originals together. At least. Or Geffen's never gonna give you a second look. You can't sell a CD full of cover songs. People've already bought that shit. They might buy the new stuff I heard tonight, too, but nobody's gonna pay fifteen bucks for a CD with six tracks on it. Ya understand? That'd be an EP, and we don't do EP's."

Mom didn't say anything, and so he told her, "You've got a hell of a voice, and I don't know if you realize it, but there are no female blues guitarists in the limelight right now, none your age, mainstream, with your looks. The guys'll go nuts." He shrugged at that. "Hey, it matters. It sells. What can I say?"

"Does it?" Mom looked at him, eye to eye. The end of "Immigrant Song" played from the jukebox, muddled with bar chatter.

Michael shrugged again, as if to say it wasn't a perfect business, but it never really had been.

"Yeah, well, maybe they're not the ones I'm playing for," Mom told him.

Dominick pulled her aside, and he spoke to her in confidence. "Come on, don't be a bitch, here. This guy sounds . . . I dunno . . . like he might be real," he urged, a cautious endorsement. "Geffen's got two of the biggest bands in the fucking *world* right now. I mean, what's the worst that could happen? We send them a demo, and they tell us to fuck off. So, what else is new? What have we got to lose?"

Mom pursed her lips and looked around the bar, then back at Dom. "Anyone can get a business card made to say whatever they want. Remember that douche bag in Brooklyn? The one who said he was with a subsidiary of Warner Brothers but turned out to be the bus driver for some funk band . . . twenty *years* ago? He had a card, too. And he showed up at the 'meeting' in a rusted out '78 Malibu with no hub caps, lots of promises, and then we never heard from him again." She glanced at Michael who was chatting with Evan now. "He looks like he's been sipping Martinis at a poolside bar all day, with a hooker on each arm." She made a face that said Michael Freiburg was a complete waste of their hopes.

"And if that's the case, then we keep doin what we've been doin, Jo," Dom said. "You won't catch any fish if you don't bait the damned hook. Christ, we drove three thousand miles to do this shit, but what the hell for if we tell every prospect to go get bent. Use your goddamned head for more than a coke depository, huh?"

Mom gave him an ironic eye roll. "Yeah, that's real nice. And you should talk, Blowfly."

"I'm just saying to give it a shot. Nothing bought, nothing sold."

"Yeah, yeah, yeah. Nothing ventured, nothing gained. You only live once. You got any more of those I can jot down in my journals?" But then she nodded and turned to Michael. "We've got two more sets, three more originals you can hear, but there's only one on the demo. We recorded that at Berklee, and we've been on the road since May, so it's not updated."

Michael checked his watch. "I have to be at a club downtown in twenty minutes to hear another act."

Mom looked away and shook her head. "But of course. My mistake," she mumbled. She looked at the business card again. "So, is this where we should send our material when it's ready? Make it attention Michael Freiburg, or is there some other contact?"

Michael smiled at her. "I haven't made much of an impression on you, have I?"

Mom shrugged. "Same as anyone else."

"I'll tell you what," he said. "How many nights do you have here?"

"Just tonight. Tomorrow we're at Montego's on fourth, opening for The Brush. We go on at nine-thirty."

He pointed at her and said, "You promise to work three more original tunes into your show, and I'll be there. Might not be right at nine-thirty, but I'll make it happen. I've got an early flight Sunday morning to Chicago, but if you show me what you've got by eleven tomorrow night, I'll start opening doors at Geffen next week, talk to some people." He looked at her expressionless face and laughed a little. "Don't be such a hard ass. I get the whole jaded, disillusioned thing. Really, I do. But there's a lot that can be done with your act, with the grunge, alternative scene breaking open. You guys fit, but with a whole different kinda twist, which I think can really work if we market it right." He glanced at his watch again. "I gotta split right now, but I'll see you guys tomorrow night." He started to walk away but he turned back. "Listen, if I don't show, then you're free to call me a charlatan and tell me to fuck off. But if I do, then I want your undivided attention so we can have ourselves a little talk." He extended his hand to my mother. "Deal?"

She looked down at it for a moment, then accepted his offer with a half-hearted shake. "Sure thing."

"Good." He smiled at her persistent skepticism. He shook hands with the rest of the band, nodded a good evening to Rachel, and disappeared through the crowd. The band watched him go, and they all stood quiet for a while.

"What just happened there?" Cam finally said. "Did that guy really just—"

"No." Mom leveled him with that hazel glare.

"Well, I'm gonna go get another beer," Evan said. "Anybody want anything?"

Cam was up for that, so he went with him.

"Yeah, I gotta take a piss." Matt looked around the bar for the rest room and found it over by the pool tables. "I'll be back."

"I think I heard my amp cuttin out a little during the last intro, might be the cord." Dom gestured out to the Fleetwood. "I'm gonna go find another one, just in case. Be back in a minute."

Everyone scattered except for Mom who took a seat across from Rachel. She gave her a quick smile, and Rachel glanced around for Mom's suddenly scarce band mates. "Are they okay? They all just bounced. They're not pissed off at something, are they?"

Mom shook her head. She took out a cigarette and lit it, tapped the first ashes into the little red tray between them. What she wouldn't say was that there were three very basic things going on with the members of Portland Downs in the upshot of meeting Mr. Freiburg—the stupefying "oh shit" phenomenon for having possibly just been discovered, the superstitious paranoia that silenced any related conversation for fear of jinxing it, and the inevitable creeping doubt that reminded them how asinine they looked (and felt) for having celebrated prematurely the last three times they'd thought this happened. Everyone just needed a moment alone to gather it all together.

Mom was no less stifled than the guys, and so she smiled and said, "So, next stop's Albuquerque. What are my chances of having you with me there, too? I mean, if you feel like you need to get back to LA, it's cool. Just let me know, so we can get you on a bus before we head out on Monday. It's up to you."

Rachel regarded her strangely. She rested her forearms on the table edge and leaned in to say, "I didn't get out of the 4Runner at the last Greyhound station. What makes you think I'd get out here?" She raised an eyebrow and took Mom's cigarette from between her fingers and dragged on it, exhaled a cloud over her head, and gave it back. "And that's a funny way of asking me to stay, if that's what you're doing."

Mom smiled at the tabletop. "I'm just trying to keep my Catalina promise."

"Well, don't."

Mom looked across at her, tapped her ashes. "You sure about that?"

"I was sure in Tijuana."

The jukebox was playing "Don't Fear the Reaper" now, and Mom grinned and sang along with it. She sang the chorus to Rachel, offered her hand at just the appropriate line, smiling, getting a bit lost in her beauty.

Rachel reached across and took Mom's hand. "How romantic of you."

My mother laughed it off. She looked around at the crowd and up to the stage. "Now we gotta take that off the set list. Nobody's gonna wanna hear it twice. It's redundant." She shrugged. "Guess we'll have to try one of those originals instead."

"Hey, Jo!" Dom approached through the crowd.

He had someone following, a very large man wearing an American flag bandana, a black leather vest over a Molly Hatchet t-shirt, faded jeans, and a pair of black harness riding boots. He had to have been six-five with classic ape handle sideburns that didn't quite meet his thick brown mustache under a red bulbous nose.

"This is Sweet Paul," Dom said. "He's here with the Harley crew, you know, the guys with all the bikes outside."

Sweet Paul reached a huge hand down to my mother, and she shook it. "I ain't never heard a girl play a six-string quite like you," he said in a smooth baritone. "I've seen a few in my travels, no doubt, but you're the best so far. Nice playin."

"Thanks." She nodded.

"Sweet Paul's a musician, too," Dom said. "Plays the shit outa the harmonica. He was just playin outside, you shoulda heard him, he was *killin* it. I told him he could sit in for a song or two, maybe on 'Comfort Zone.' We said we wanted a harmonica on that song, anyway." He pointed to Paul. "Well, now's our chance to see what it'll sound like. Couldn't hurt."

Mom considered that and looked Paul over. "Well, let me hear something. What've you got?"

By then Cam and Evan had returned from the bar, and they stood listening as Sweet Paul fished a little black-and-silver Lee Oskar harmonica from his vest pocket, then went to wailing on it in the old style of Max Geldray. Mom was impressed, and so were Rachel and the guys, so my mother gave him permission to sit in.

He shook her hand again. "It'd be an honor to play with musicians of your caliber. That's why we come here when we're passing through from Amarillo. It's a dinky little shithole, but they've got the best bands around, always have for years. Just let me know when you're ready for me to come on up."

Mom checked her watch. "It's about that time, actually." She tipped her chin to the stage. "How about now? We're gonna open with one of ours. You should fit pretty well."

"You got it."

Mom told Cam to roll the video, and she had Matt set up another mic stand when he got back from the rest room, and they took the stage with an introduction for their impromptu guest performer. Several of Paul's crew came inside and stood among the crowd, eight-inch graying beards and bandana headbands and tatted biceps, black leather everything and wifebeater tank tops. They raised their beer bottles to the rafters and roared for Paul's debut as Portland Downs gave Dom a thundering intro, then shifted into gear with Sweet Paul yowling along as if he'd been rehearsing with them for months. The place lost its collective mind. Mom grinned and gave him the spotlight while his buddies whooped and howled as if at a Lynyrd Skynyrd concert. He played well, had decent improv skills, and the crowd loved the whole ensemble.

What Paul did not seem to understand, however, was that most live song arrangements are structured so that each musician has ample solo time, and when it was my mother's turn to play, Sweet Paul didn't stop. She got about fifteen seconds into her solo, and Paul was still at the edge of the stage, cupping mic and harmonica to his mustache and wailing overtop as if he were the only member of the band. Mom segued out and let him continue. She went back to playing rhythm guitar, a little unnerved, but she forgave it because the audience was having a blast, oblivious to the guy's lack of professional etiquette.

When it came time for her vocals, there was another cluttered competition between them, but she continued through the verse, trying to alter the melody and phrasing into a kind of duet, but it was the Sweet Paul show now, and she glanced back at Dominick with a little shrug and a frown. Paul's gang hollered for more of Paul, and so Paul kept playing. He was so enthralled in his newfound stardom that he stopped paying attention to Evan's tempo and began to fall off beat, running up and down blaring scales meant to be complicated and impressive, but it was only a jumble of noise now.

Mom nodded a signal to Evan to wind it down, and the song came to a crashing, screaming close. The audience was thrilled and clap-chanted Paul's name as he raised a massive fist to the ceiling and thanked them repeatedly.

"What the hell's his problem?" Mom said into Dom's ear over the noise. "He was fine at the table, but now he sounds like shit."

Dom held a hand out to the crowd. "Well, they like it. We told him he could sit in. Maybe he's never done this before. Give 'em a break. He might be nervous."

"*You* told him he could sit in." Evan leaned up from behind the drums and pointed a stick at Dominick. "He's *your* boy now, nervous or not."

"And the rest of you Mozart motherfuckers heard what I heard and gave it a go, too, so don't put this all on me," Dom defended. "Let him do another song and then that'll be it."

Mom shook her head but didn't deny Sweet Paul a second chance. She tugged at his vest and told him, "We're gonna do 'Voodoo Chile' next, so just hang out, and then we'll do 'Fool in the Rain,' and you can jump back in."

"No prob."

Mom stepped back and began Jimi's famous vox wah-wah intro, and it sent the crowd roaring. Evan picked it up on the hi-hat and bass drum, then Dom and Matt chimed in, and the song exploded through the power amps. But Sweet Paul was up at the mic again, and he was playing in the wrong key now, completely unaware that his little harmonica was pretuned to the key of C major. The first song was in that key, but "Voodoo Chile" was played in the key of E minor. Even to an untrained novice, that combination is to the ear what a horseradish and peanut butter sandwich is to the palate, which was why my mother asked him to sit out, and the crowd seemed to fall into a kind of bewilderment that made her cringe with mortification. She glared at Dominick but had to keep playing because the one thing you never do on stage is stop, no matter the melodic train wreck, regardless of the clashing, abrading tones that make all the musical sense of a Times Square traffic jam.

My mother was furious. I could see it on her face, even through Uncle Cam's bobbling, grainy cinematography from ten feet off the stage. Paul was playing over her solo again, playing over her vocals, playing at his own tempo, in his own key; he was a spoonful of mustard dolloped onto a Hershey bar. The band never stopped, but Dom was conferring discreetly with Matt now, leaning over the Rhodes in some kind of underplayed dispute, and Mom kept glancing back at them, gesturing down to the mic cord with the guitar neck as she soloed, a silent suggestion to disconnect Sweet Paul from the show altogether. Dom was the only one who could do it without being noticed, perhaps unplug it with his foot, as all eyes were on my mother and Paul. Dominick stepped up to Mom and said something in her ear as Paul blew contrary melodies into the microphone, and then he moved away as she snapped something like, "Do it *now*, or I will tie you to the tow hitch and *drag* you to Albuquerque!"

It took another minute for Dominick to gather his courage. But then he did, and the deed was done. Sweet Paul vanished from the music as if raptured up into the stratosphere by his tone deaf Creator. He didn't realize it at first. It occurred to him that something was missing, and that something was *him*. He turned and smiled foolishly at the band, and Dom shrugged with a puzzled face and made a show of looking around at the equipment for the "malfunction" while my mother came to the mic for the final verse. Matt feigned a glance up to the sound booth for affected "help," but Paul just stood at the front of the stage, shaking his head at Portland Downs. The song finally rattled to a close, and the audience was merciful and gave them their deserved applause.

Paul looked at my mother and Dom. "That bad, huh?"

"No, no," Dom insisted over the crowd noise, still searching the floor for the fictitious cause. "It was great. I dunno what happened. Must be that bad cable. Thought it was my bass cord, but I guess not."

Paul chuckled and dropped his harmonica into his vest pocket. "It's cool. I get it. Thanks anyway, though. Had a good time while it lasted." And he hopped down from the stage, slapped fives with his friends, and they all shouldered through the crowd toward the exit and left.

THEY PLAYED ANOTHER two sets without Sweet Paul, and the crowd forgot him as quickly as my mother did and re-embraced the Portland Downs that had taken the stage at eleven. By one-thirty they had gone through the rest of the show and ended with a ten-minute rendition of "Pride and Joy," which my mother sang word for word, straight to Rachel. The serenade drew a few sideways glances, but neither of them cared. The guys loved it, and some of the women found themselves in a state of drunken envy, so much that Rachel had to place herself between my mother and a tipsy little brunette who offered a variety of sexual favors after the band left the stage. It was an artful move on Rachel's part, a non-confrontational sidestep into my mother's space with her arms around Mom's waist, sending a very clear message that Jolán De Carlo was not for sale, and the girl wandered away into the thinning crowd.

"If I'd known I'd have so much competition, I would've brought my pepper spray," Rachel said with the kiss to Mom's neck as she disconnected her guitar.

Mom looked at her, a bit wary. "That's never gonna change, you know. It's the nature of this game. An endless stream of liquor, heavy blues rock, and a woman with a guitar all seem to have that effect, even in straight bars."

Rachel waved that away. "Baby, I know that. I've watched security toss more than a few drunks out the door for harassing the band. Don't worry, I know the drill. I promise not to go all psycho girlfriend on you and get myself arrested."

Mom smiled. "Well, good. 'Cause I can't afford bail, so stay outa trouble."

"I'll do my best," Rachel said and kissed her again.

Mom was disassembling the effects pedal and rolling up the cables, and so Rachel broke down the mic stands and helped her carry everything out to Betty. The guys were doing the same, and Mom and Rachel passed Dom and Cam who were on their way back inside to help with Evan's drums while Matt stayed to watch the RV.

There was a sizeable crowd lingering around the entrance outside, chatting amongst themselves, making after-hour plans for breakfast and discussing which parties to crash around the city. Many of them stood talking with the bikers whose Harleys and Yamahas drew a lot of attention, parked in a gleaming row along the curb, immaculate sparkling chrome catching South Tucson's Silverlake streetlights. Mom and Rachel loaded the guitars and the mic stands into the camper and Mom went back inside to collect their cash while Rachel waited in the RV with Matt. She took seven hundred dollars from the bar manager and divvied it out to Dom and Evan, and she offered Cam fifty bucks for his camera and roadie work, but he wouldn't take it.

He pushed the cash back to her and grabbed a stage monitor. "I'm a guest on this venture. Hell, it's my turn to fill the gas tank, and you're giving *me* money? How much Jim Beam have you had tonight?"

"None," she said. "I kept it conservative, nothing but beer."

He hefted the speaker into his arms. "Well, I was gonna blame it on the liquor, but I guess you're just stupid." And he headed for the exit.

She laughed a little and watched him go. "Nice. You do wonders for my confidence."

She separated hers and Matt's cuts from the bills in her hand and stuffed a hundred-and-seventy-five dollars into her pocket as she followed Evan to the door. He was carrying the drum stool and a floor tom, and Dom was going around the stage, gathering up all the remaining lead cords.

"Kinda hate it for ol' what's his name, Mr. Harmonica guy," Evan said to Mom at the back of the 4Runner as he shoved the drum stool into the hatch. "You'd think he would've known he couldn't play that thing to every damn song."

Mom made a face and shifted the drums around so she could fit the last cymbal stand between them. "Well, he obviously didn't." She winced. "Christ, it was like nails on a chalkboard, like a chain saw cutting through sheet metal. My ears are crazy sensitive to pitch, and I thought I was gonna throw up, it was so grating."

Evan chuckled. "Well, it's all good. We got through the rest of the show and still got paid, so it wasn't a complete disaster."

They locked the tailgate and checked all the doors and started for the camper. Then they saw Dominick, rounding the corner into the parking lot. He was breaking for the Fleetwood at a full sprint, equipment cables flailing like octopus arms.

"Go! Go! *Now*!" He waved them on, nearly stumbling over himself as he hurdled a row of parking cones.

Mom and Evan stood stunted at the hatch. They shot each other a peculiar glance, didn't know quite what to do until six bearded behemoths appeared around the corner in Dominick's wake, led by none other than Sweet Paul.

"You little motherfucker!" Paul was lumbering after Dominick, and he had a crowbar in his hand. "Unplugged my goddamned mic! Now I'm gonna unplug your fucking *face*, you little Berklee *faggot*!"

"Drive!" Dom screamed, loping toward the RV, his face flushed with panic. "Start that bitch up and *go*!"

"Oh, shit." Mom and Evan darted for the camper, leaving the side door open for Dominick.

Cam already had the Sony rolling, aiming it out Betty's bay window. He'd seen them coming around the corner and thought he better get it on tape, just in case.

Mom made it in first and swung herself into the driver's seat but she didn't have the keys, Evan did, and he dug them from his pants pocket and tossed them across the camper and over the back of the driver's seat. She snatched them out of the air and jammed the right one into the ignition, and Betty rumbled and coughed as she threw it into drive with Evan and Matt at the open door, reaching hands out to Dominick who ran alongside as they rolled across the lot toward Silverlake Road, a not-so-sweet Paul and his compadres running after them, swinging the tire iron at the back of Dom's head. It missed and clanged into the aluminum hull like a shot.

"I'm gonna kill you, you bass-playin piece a shit!" He growled, tailing them, swinging the iron again.

The others threw empty beer bottles that shattered into the RV and smashed onto the ground around Dom's sneakers. Matt and Evan each had him by a forearm, his feet sputtering over the asphalt as he tried to pull himself inside, and everyone pitched left as Mom made a wild right out onto Silverlake. Cam fell backward into the table, and the camera went wonky and whirled around the ceiling and down over the kaleidoscope upholstery and up past Dom's face, wrenched in terror in the still-open doorway, the road rushing by beneath him. Matt and Evan braced themselves against the frame, trying to haul their band mate into the RV while Rachel grabbed at the back of Dom's t-shirt, trying to help. With one last effort, he burst into the camper and the four of them tumbled into a heap at Cam's feet.

Cam staggered back to the sleeper window, shoved aside the curtain, and pointed the camera out at Sweet Paul and the others, shrinking into the distance as the Fleetwood careened along Silverlake at top speed. Another beer bottle exploded onto the pavement behind the 4Runner, but they were well out of range now. Matt clambered back into the sleeper with Cam and watched them vanish, then he dropped onto the bed, exhausted and traumatized.

No one said anything for a long time. They just drove. Evan climbed into the passenger's seat, checked the side views, peered down the length of the camper and out the back sleeper window. "Think they'll follow us?"

Mom glanced at the side views, too, shook her head. "I dunno." She let off the gas a bit, and Evan looked at her warily. "I gotta slow down. It's Friday night, and there's cops out. We've got enough shit in this RV to put us all away for the next year, we can't get stopped."

Evan nodded, then looked around at Dominick on the couch with his elbows on his knees. His jeans were torn at the leg from where the side door hinge had caught the fabric when he dove inside. Rachel was sitting next to him, rubbing comfort across his shoulders, her expression flat and troubled as she watched the Arizona darkness going by.

Dom saw them all staring, and he laughed a little. "Well, that was a buzzkill."

No one quite saw the humor. They just looked at him, waiting for an explanation, and so he sat back and told them what had happened in an irritated, sing-songy tone.

"Look. I didn't provoke the guy. Okay? He was minding his own business, and so was I. They all had a bunch of chicks around them, lookin at the bikes, and everything was cool, and then I don't fuckin know," he insisted, holding up empty palms. "I was comin out of the bar with the last of the stuff, with the cords and adapters and shit, and the next thing I know he's pointing at me, sayin 'there's that son of a bitch who cut my mic off.' He got up and started through the crowd, and then all his giant fucking friends got up, too, and he was telling me to come here." He made a face with a preposterous snort. "Like I was gonna walk over and get my head caved in. Right. So, I ignored him and kept walking. Guess he didn't like that 'cause he started getting real pissed off and walking faster, bitching about the show and calling me a liar, telling me to bring my 'pussy ass' back there, which was decidedly a very *bad* idea, and so my pussy ass kept going. And then they started fucking chasing me, with every intention of giving me a sidewalk face-lift." He looked at them all. "The rest is kind of a blur, so I'm sorry if I can't provide any further details." He gestured up to the Handycam. "I think it's all been accurately documented, so maybe you can just check the video."

"I don't even know where you found that guy," Matt said. "I was off taking a piss, and then he was on stage with us, so I just went with it. Who said he could come up there, anyway?"

Dom pointed up to the driver's seat, but Mom couldn't see him, so Rachel spoke in her defense.

"It was a *collective* idea," she told Matt, glaring sideways at Dominick. "He sounded fine at first, so everyone was down with it, not just Jo."

"Yeah, but she has final say," Dom insisted, trying to deflect blame.

Mom suddenly frowned and glanced over her shoulder into the camper. "Hey, asshole. She's right. It was *all* our decision, so don't even try that shit."

"And it was your decision to unplug his mic," Dom grumbled, tugging at his torn pant leg. "Which, I might add, almost just got me killed."

"And what the hell else would you have suggested?" Mom questioned. "That we kept him up there, sounding like a fucking goose caught in a goddamned bear trap? He was ruining our show."

"So, you admit, then, that our near brush with death was on account a *your* decision. Thank you," he said. "That's all I wanted to hear."

"You're gonna hear my foot going up your ass in a minute," she grumbled and made a left onto S. Kino Parkway toward the city.

"Oh, that's terrifying," he said. "Compared to cranial reconstruction with a four-way tire iron, yeah, I'm trembling over here."

"Okay, guys, just knock it off," Rachel said. "It's over now. Minimal damage. So, let's keep it that way. Jo, just relax. Let it go. And get us somewhere safe so we can all get some sleep, please."

No one said anything else. They weren't followed, and so they found a desolate but well-lighted stretch off Kino and parked for the night. Mom and Rachel took the sleeper while Matt and Dom collapsed onto the pullouts. Cam and Evan made themselves comfortable on sleeping bags and blanket pallets on the floor between the pullouts.

A cool desert crosswind blew in from the west and rocked the camper while they slept. My mother lay awake on the island bed with Rachel asleep in her arms, thinking about Michael Freiburg, about Geffen Records and all that she'd read about their new artists' unparalleled success. If the guy didn't show, then to hell with him. But if he did?

A PROMISE IS a promise. Until it's not, anymore. I think she always knew that. She doesn't hold on too tight, though she never quite lets go; I can see it on her face. The apprehension, clouding her beautiful eyes for just a moment, but I've got this. I know where the boundaries are, and maybe I've crossed them, but I know my way back like I know my way home. Just follow the bricks. I need this. I need her. I don't want to need anything else, and so I won't because I've got this under control. I know my way home from any place this road sees fit to take me. I always have. I need her . . . to trust me. Can she do that?

THEY GOT A chance to see The Brush early on Saturday afternoon at a Tucson music festival in Reid Park. Evan tried for weeks to get Portland Downs a slot, but he had discovered the event too late, missed the submission deadline by three days, and now only a cancelation would have made it possible for them to play. All the scheduled bands had shown up, and so Portland Downs watched The Brush from inside the fence at stage right, next to the speaker stacks and lighting towers. There were close to a thousand people there, gathered on blankets and beach chairs under a southwestern sun so bright the grass looked almost blue across the lawn. The audience was rabid for The Brush. Some of them wore black t-shirts with the band's logo stenciled in orange Dark Horse font, negatives of the trio's facial profiles pasted white around the logo, and they had bumper stickers in the same style tacked across the vocal monitors.

"Merchandising," Evan thought aloud, watching, bobbing his head to their music with arms folded critically across his chest.

"It's expensive," Mom noted.

The crowd was singing along. They knew the lyrics, all the musical breaks, and places for call-and-response.

"If you wanna do it right, anyway," she added.

"I've been saying it all along," Matt told them. "We need something to sell at our shows besides us. These guys are great, and then they send themselves home with you in a paper bag. And they're not even signed, not that I know of."

The lead singer was a racially ambiguous, olive-skinned fellow with a head full of brown-and-blonde dreadlocks matted all the way down his back, and he was seated in a straight-backed chair, playing a Weissenborn lap guitar. Earlier he'd been playing the regular acoustic and an electric Gibson as well.

My mother marveled at his talent, watched and listened as if at a college seminar, rather than a rock concert, studying what she could from thirty feet off stage right. His bass player was tall and wiry like Matt, with a crew cut and forearms inked with tattoos that disappeared up into his t-shirt sleeves, and the drummer, though difficult to see from their vantage point, wore a long blonde ponytail and a braided goatee.

"They have a nice sound," Cam said.

He wasn't allowed to film them, but he was doing it, anyway, had the camera rolling and tucked into the crook of his arm, the lens aimed up at the stage.

"It's a little different than you guys," he said. "But I think they're gonna be a pretty good act to open for."

Mom thought about that for a moment. "Yeah, either that or they're gonna end up being the competition, if that Freiburg dude shows up, turns out to be what he said he was."

"Took the words right outa my mouth, *chica,*" Matt said and eyed her sideways.

The Brush knew how to play for a large crowd, had obviously done these kinds of festivals before, where my mother's band had mastered the more intimate bar crowds and had only done one large event in Boston the previous summer. They were two very different performance styles, so it was anyone's guess which band Montego's audience would embrace most.

Dominick had wandered away into the crowd, looking for a port-a-john, and he was coming back with a hot dog in one hand and a CD in the other.

He gave my mother a nudge and showed her the CD. "Check this shit out."

She took it with a curious frown, and everyone else craned around to have a look at The Brush's debut album entitled *Forced Entry*. She looked up at Dom. "Did you buy this?"

"*Hell* no," he said through a bite of the hot dog. "The guy at the signing tent gave it to me when I told him I was with Portland Downs. He already knew who we were, knew about the show tonight, so I got a promo. They're ten bucks, though. Tapes are five. And they've got about eight boxes of 'em back there, maybe twenty to a box. When was your last math class?"

"About three years ago," Mom muttered. She took off her sunglasses and turned the disc in her hand to read the back, looking for the label affiliation. "Brushstrokke Records. With two k's," she noted with a little half nod. "Who the hell is that?"

"I'll take a wild guess," Evan said. "I'm thinking it's them. They're doing this themselves, all of it, the merch, the marketing, booking, CDs, and tapes. Everything."

The Brush pounded the amps while the frontman sang in a clear, emotive falsetto, the Weissenborn in his lap, tuned with a heavy fuzz effect that resembled the whine of a NASCAR race. The audience clapped along in unison, a thousand strong in the heat of the afternoon.

"That's gotta be astronomical for them," Rachel said. "I know they have a following out here. They've played in LA a few times, but even the bars and clubs back there don't pay *that* much."

"Yeah, well, they're doing it," Mom said. "And just imagine what they could do with major label backing. They'd be unstoppable."

"The question is, not what a label can do for them, but what they can do for the *label*. Think about it. They've already got a fan base, already have a CD, a trademarked logo, experience in front of crowds like this, and probably sold a few thousand units of these." Evan took the album from Mom and looked it over. "All a label would have to do is stamp their company name on this and book them for a year in Europe. The band's done half the legwork already. Less capital invested, less of a gamble. It's the perfect carrot on a stick, just the other way around. It's brilliant."

"Thank you for that very insightful economics lesson, Evan, but that's really not what I wanted to hear before this gig tonight." Mom patted him on the shoulder as the crowd whistled and screamed for The Brush's finale, and they headed back to the Fleetwood to prepare for Montego's show.

HIS NAME WAS Gavin Graser. He was twenty-six, a Denver native who studied guitar and music theory at the San Francisco Conservatory of Music until 1988; he'd been playing since the age of ten. His drummer was Bryce Pearce, also from Denver, no formal music education, but he did study privately under a local jazz drummer for twelve years; he and Gavin grew up together. Sandro Valentine joined the trio two years prior after moving to Colorado from Tempe, Arizona, and he replaced their previous bassist who'd gotten married and left the band for a "real job" in computer programming. That was the backstory they gave Portland Downs while the nine of them sat around the bar tops, having impressed each other during sound check at Montego's.

They were drinking Heinekens and filling the ashtray with stubbed-out filters as the bar staff went around making ready for the doors to open at eight-thirty. The soundman played a CD by a psychedelic '60s group, "Bring Me Coffee Or Tea" was the track, haunting acoustic and electric guitars in a Middle Eastern key with a Wurlitzer padding under syncopated drum licks. The only one who could correctly identify the artist was Gavin. It was exactly his thing, and the soundman was in awe and offered him a free drink, but he just grinned and waved it off.

"Dude, you don't have to get me drunk, just for knowing some obscure band," he called over to him. "It's unfair. Obscure is all I do." And he smiled across at Mom, shaking his head and laughing a little.

My mother would've liked to have settled into the moment, to just relax there with three new colleagues, with Rachel seated next to her and her own band mates gathered around, discussing instrument techniques and telling tour stories. But she couldn't quite focus tonight. She was having trouble with the jitters, with the anxiety of three lines of cocaine racing through her heart and making her nose run. She ordered a shot of whiskey, but it didn't help, and the bottle of beer sitting in front of her might as well have been an Evian. She wanted to be alert and coherent for this, and so she'd chopped three lines on the back of the Fender case in the sleeper before sound check, much to Rachel's disappointment, but that was a debate my mother quickly squelched with a reminder of the potential stakes for tonight's show.

"You heard them, this afternoon," she told her, sucking back a bitter wad of mucus while her throat went numb. "They're fucking amazing. I have to be, too."

Rachel stood in the sleeper doorway, watching her, trying to decide what to do or not do. "You already are," she finally said, and turned away and walked out.

NOW SHE WAS sitting beside my mother at the bar tops, settling into a kind of resignation, a helpless absolution toward a promise she suspected was bullshit all along, but she was in love with her and had been since Tijuana. And so she assumed the role of the watchful lover, nursemaid to my mother's afflictions, keeping tabs, reassembling her broken parts, and propping her up with devotion, simply because my mother loved her back. The good with the bad, right? That's what true love takes into account.

No need to inventory which was which. It was all relative, anyway, and Rachel had her own demons, so who was she to split hairs, to lecture?

Mom tried to smile. She took Rachel's hand while Gavin spoke about their tour of London last year, how they got gigs just by setting up on the sidewalks with little Peavey amps and a gallon milk jug scissored in half for tips. He said they'd forgotten about the currency difference and had no idea how much they'd made the first afternoon. One hundred quid.

Rachel gave my mother a probing glance, checking her head space.

Mom nodded at first, but then she shook her head, telling her discreetly that she didn't like the way she felt, but what could she do now? Her jaws were tight as tetanus. Her guts were cramped and quivering. Her hands had a jittery tremor. Her eyes shifted from one face to the next, to the bar, to the exit, to the tabletop. She felt like a caricature of herself on cocaine, trying to engage in conversation, but she didn't know if she was making much sense, thought maybe she was talking too much, but no one seemed to notice. She smoked another cigarette and talked with Sandro about his tattoos and got the fleeting idea to have the Stratocaster inked onto her back while they were in Tucson, but he suggested an artist in Denver instead.

Somewhere in their dialogue, the club had opened, and people were filing in now. The soundman turned up the music, but it wasn't the same group anymore. She was pretty sure it was a band from the '80s, but maybe not, she couldn't think. She checked her watch—it was almost nine o'clock. She didn't want to sit there any longer. But if she got up, where would she go? To the bathroom, maybe. And then what? She didn't have to pee. She flagged down the server and ordered another whiskey shot, and the girl brought it and Mom knocked it back. She waited to feel better but didn't.

"Goddammit," she muttered and watched the door for Michael Freiburg.

She looked down at her hands, and they were trembling, and on the inside she was a bag of mice on a vibrating mattress, and she thought, now, that Sandro might be staring at Rachel's cleavage. She put her arm over the back of Rachel's chair and leaned in close, watched his eyes to see where they landed again, but they found another girl at the next table to undress. Good thing, because for a moment she wanted to crack her empty beer bottle across his face, and that certainly wasn't her nature.

Then Bryce smiled at her. "Hey, man, you okay?"

She gave him a blameless stare, nodded, sniffed. "Yeah, I'm good."

He looked at her for a moment, gunmetal blue deducing more than she cared to divulge, and he massaged his braided beard. "You're not nervous, are you? That Geffen guy coming to check you guys out and all."

Gavin took the last swig of his beer and leaned on the edge of the table.

"Fuck him, whether he's genuine or not. The majors'll rob you. Rape you, rob you, appropriate your soul, and leave you rotting on the shelf. It's corporate criminality all dressed up to look like fame and fortune. I mean, you guys do what you want. But if what you want is creative control, to share your music with the masses and keep the hard-earned profits, then independent is the way of the future, man."

Mom tapped her ashes into the overflowing tray. "Sounds a little too utopian to me. The majors have pull. They have the overhead, the capital we'll *never* have unless we win the damn lottery. When's the last time you played the lottery? Did you win? Doubt it, so I rest my case." She checked her watch again, and it was time to start making their way to the stage, but she was a bundle of live wires all shorting out and fizzling like holiday sparklers.

"You sure you're all right, man?" Bryce asked again.

This time she conceded. She stood half in her chair with one foot on the floor, unsure how she would bring herself to a steady place to perform, or run the risk of overplaying and screwing up her own timing, missing important transitions in the music, getting distracted and flubbing a solo like a second-rate amateur.

She shook her head and told him, "I'm just a little geeked up right now, a lot more than I'd like. Unintentional, but fuck it. Gotta do this, so here goes." She started for the stage, but Bryce called her back over.

He got up from his chair, cigarette dangling from his lips, and he reached into his jeans pocket, then motioned for her to follow him, and so she did.

Rachel was uneasy. They'd all just met, and anyone was capable of anything. She pulled at Dom's sleeve and gestured for him to go with her as she followed Mom and Bryce into an adjoining lounge area. The room was empty at this early hour. Bryce had Mom sit with him on the couch. He glanced up at Rachel and Dom but wasn't all that opposed to their presence, figured they were likely interested in what he was offering my mother.

"I know how much this show means to you guys," he told them. "And too much snow can make for a pretty chilly night, jacks up your concentration. But," he revealed a little clear nasal spray bottle with a dark brown liquid, "this'll level you out, rock steady, I promise you."

He glanced at the doorway for security, or management, or narcs. No one appeared, and so he unscrewed the lid, wiped off the tip on his shirttail, and handed the bottle to my mother.

She just sat there, looking sideways at him. She shifted her eyes to the container and then back to Bryce. "And what is this?"

"That's garbage, Jo," Dominick said. "I know exactly what it is. It's heroin, Black Tar heroin, a liquid form, diluted down. I've seen it before, some dude had the same shit at the Diesel Lounge in San Diego. It'll eat you alive. Come on, just have another shot, I'm buying. If you're tweakin that damn hard, it'll wear off. Trust me." And he waved her back into the main room, but she didn't get up.

She looked at Rachel who said nothing and just stood watching, waiting for her to make the choice on her own. She wouldn't make it for her.

"I can't focus. I fucked up," Mom said to Rachel. "I blew too much fucking coke. You were right. But I just might have the show of my life in," she checked her watch, "ten minutes. I mean, if this shit'll help, then why not?"

"You're a moron." Dominick turned for the doorway. "You're on your own with that shit, I'm outa here." He shook his head and walked out.

"Look," Bryce said, "you won't even feel it. How much blow'd you do?"

"Three pretty fat rails," she confessed, sniffling. "About an hour ago."

"Then this'll just even you out. It won't take much. Just a bump, a little spray. It's not gonna be that heavy." Bryce shrugged. "Hey, it's up to you. If you don't want it, then fine. I'm just tryin to help."

Mom took the bottle and sat there, examining it, her knee bouncing as she turned the stuff over in her hand. She looked up at Rachel. "I'll be fine. He just said it's not real strong. I'm too wired to play, baby. Come on, don't look at me like that."

"Then let it wear off. Don't go on. Come down first."

"I *can't*. They have a schedule. We're not the only band tonight, remember?" She held up a placating hand and gave her an assuring nod. "You know me. I'm good. I'm always good. It's just for tonight, I swear to God. After tonight, never again. Okay? I promise."

Rachel made a little sound like laughter, humorless, but she said nothing.

"She won't get crazy high off this, not by snorting it just once," Bryce said to Rachel. "There'll be nothin to chase. She's got too much coke in her system, anyway, and they'll just cancel each other out, bring her down to a good place, and then all will be right with the cosmos."

"So, what are you, a doctor or an astronaut?" Rachel said, glaring at him.

She cut her eyes back to my mother who was already throwing her head back. Mom ran a forearm across her nose and made a sour face, and she swallowed and exhaled heavily. Bryce had her hold her head back again. He said it needed time to absorb. Rachel watched, quiet, crushed but curious just the same. It took a few minutes, but my mother's face gradually went placid, as if someone had drilled a hole in her brain, siphoned out all the anxiety, and replaced it with everything warm and tranquil.

She sat for another long moment, settling into a new woman. Then she looked at Bryce and nodded, sniffed, feeling for herself on the inside. "You just might be a miracle worker." She gave it another few beats, chuckled a little, and let it take hold. "Yeah. I think it's working. Just a little rush, a hella *nice* rush, but that's it. No weirdness, it's good." She looked at the bottle curiously, and she gave it back to Bryce.

"Told ya." He smiled and replaced the cap.

She looked up at Rachel and held her arms out at her sides. "See? I'm still here. I'm fine. Just needed to bring it down a little, that's all. Never again." And she sliced the air with both hands.

Rachel didn't have much to say. "You have to go in five minutes. They're waiting for you."

Mom clapped her hands together once and stood up and sniffed back the Black Tar residue. "All right, then. Let's do this."

She came to Rachel and kissed her lips but got a frigid reception. She sniffed again, didn't seem to notice.

"Let's hit 'em with a little Boston blues," she announced to the guys tuning up on stage, and she climbed on and shouldered the Stratocaster. She introduced Portland Downs to the Montego crowd, then opened up with "Just Got Paid," and the power amps rumbled as if explosives had gone off.

SHE PLAYED THE show of her life that night. The band cranked out four original songs, and my mother's confidence seemed to exceed that of her earlier performances. She made one urgent trip to the rest room where she said she vomited after the second set, but she came right back to the stage, feeling good as new.

Cam got the entire gig on video, even panned across the faces to get Michael Freiburg on film, for proof that he'd shown up and for posterity's sake. The Brush snubbed him after the show, and so he sat and talked with Portland Downs for a half hour in the back lounge. He explained what he could do for them and what they needed to do for him. A demo album. Ten originals, minimum, professionally recorded, which they could do at the Berklee campus studio. He was the real thing. He had the prize wrapped in golden promises, waiting for them in Santa Monica, and topped with a little platinum bow. All they needed now was to keep their end of the bargain. And the only place to do that was back in Boston, putting another three thousand inevitable miles between my mother and Rachel Cole.

chapter twelve

FORGIVENESS. I'VE MASTERED it in just the way the Fender and violin's craftsmanship respond to my touch, a magician of sorts, sleight of hand for the willing eye, sleight of words for her to take at their value, whatever that might be for the moment. She sees me. She doesn't miss a trick. She wishes I were something like an anchor to hold us both fast to the docks so we won't float off into a nightmare. I so very much meant to be. I am in love with a girl who is in love with the woman I am supposed to be, and almost am. I'm not that far from shore, and she knows this as well, and so she is forgiving, loving daily that little pinpoint of light on the horizon, letting her know I'm still here, I'm still me, still close enough to touch, to reach for in the dark, warm and alive and reaching for her. And then all our flaws and demons recede into the empty oblivion behind us, that void we call yesterday, into someone else's music playing on the radio for us to make love to and forget ourselves, knowing only the swelter of our sex that makes the blankets too heavy, too binding, and so we throw them off, and she forgives me some more with arms around my neck, her lips parted and brushing my cheek through little gasps like pain, but I know so much better, pretty legs twined around my waist where our Tijuana toy's strapped tight, the motel headboard knocking on the neighbor's wall, something I am inexplicably good at for a woman, but it's work, and I admit I'm getting a bit tired. So, change positions then, and I slide out and let her turn over onto elbows and knees, breathless, so fucking eager for my faux seven inches she makes me miss the first time in, readjust, and I am forgiven again, absolved of my sins at a nice brisk pace hard enough to make bruises, you'd think, but it never does, and she likes it that way, my way, the only woman she's ever let inside like this, so unlike a man because it's just different, she says, better somehow, because she loves me more than she's ever loved anyone.

She shouts something rapt and desperate into the pillows, twists up a fistful of sheets, and backs herself up against my stomach and stays there pressed into me, trembling until it's all out of her system, then pulls away and drops to the mattress, overheated and spent for a while.

A half dozen candles we bought back in Tucson perfume our tiny corner of Route 66, lighting our room for two here at the Palomino Lodge with a scent they call "fresh linen," which I think is slightly ironic while I lay sweating on my back, the toy unfastened and strewn to the floor so she can lay on top of me, her thighs spread across my shoulders for just a little more, all the different kinds of skins and folds between them at my face, warm and slick from the past hour, and she tastes magnificent to me, music and perfume and fire glow and her mouth making love to me there, hot and full and drawing me up between her lips so that I'll do the same, and so I do, a silent little game we play to give each other precisely what we want, suck right here, just so, lick there, like this, follow me along and I'll follow, too. She is remarkably talented. And I am a lightweight, a helpless sucker for her oral expertise, and I try not to stop doing her just to lay back into my own pleasure, but she makes it almost impossible, hooks her arms around my hips, fingertips spreading me open with her lips pulling at the pearl, her tongue slipping everywhere into all those perfect places at once, and I'm off on a solo flight, anyway, because she's got the most beautiful waves rolling up my thighs and over my stomach and into my chest like cresting a roller coaster hill at a hundred miles an hour, and she knows it, forgiving my selfishness with a flutter of her tongue over that spot she has memorized now, and I couldn't love her more as it all swells and builds, up and up into those stars I'm starting to see, and I release in a single aching breath sent straight to the ceiling where the candlelight throws our intertwining shadows.

I don't want her to touch me. Just give me a moment. It's too much sensation while I'm coming down, but she does it anyway, making me jump and shudder, and she climbs off and turns around grinning, amused by the complete control she has over every single one of my nerve endings as she crawls up for a long deep kiss that says she loves me with all she's got. She's not going anywhere. And neither am I. Forgiven tonight, so says her mahogany gaze. For a while, I've got the anchor resting heavy on the reef, and we'll be fine, because I always find my way home—I am already there.

IT WAS A weekend of phone calls. They had two shows scheduled in Albuquerque, similar to the Tucson itinerary, but everyone needed to check in with family, as it was drawing nearer to the fall school semester. Rachel lay on the motel bed, twining the telephone cord around her finger, examining her blonde highlighted split ends, listening to her mother Sonya prattle on about rising tuition and textbook costs and how Rachel should use her credit card with prudence; it was never intended for summer-long excursions into the southwestern plains.

"What's next? Backpacking across Europe, Rachel?" Sonya Cole admonished. "You are at the most critical point in your education, and that shit isn't cheap, kiddo."

"Kiddo? I'm not a kid, Mom."

"No. You're not. Believe me, I know this all too well. You're a grown woman, for all rights, which is why you should start *thinking* like one. I thought you had a job in LA. What happened to that?"

"I got fired." Rachel propped an ankle across her knee and fidgeted with her sandal strap. "My boss was an asshole. What do you want me to say, Mom? It happened. It is what it is, so now I'm taking some time to see the country with friends, see the Grand Canyon, the mountains. What's so horrifying about that?"

Sonya Cole issued a breath of absurdity into the phone. *"Friends?* A rock band you met in Hollywood two months ago. You're a smart kid, Rache, but sometimes . . ." And she suspended that thought and said instead, "You just make sure you've always got bus money. There are bus stations in almost every town. If those people—"

"Mom. Jolán and I have already talked about this. If I wanna leave, I can leave, and she'll pay for it."

"Jolán, huh?" Sonya was quiet for a long moment. "And so is this something romantic between you two?" she finally asked. "Just tell me the truth so I know what I'm dealing with, here."

Rachel frowned and narrowed her eyes, affronted. "What you're *dealing* with? What does that mean? And yes. You want the truth, so yes. We're together. I don't know for how long, but we're working on that. We've got some options."

Sonya laughed but she wasn't amused. "You have *one* option, Rachel Christine, and that's to get your ass back to USC in three weeks. I worked like a Hebrew slave so that you could have a decent life with no stress, so you could get good grades, and get yourself that scholarship, and by God, if you *fuck* it up over some chick with a guitar and a pretty smile, you will eternally *regret* it. I *promise* you."

Rachel rolled her eyes at the Palomino ceiling. She peered at my mother sitting cross-legged beside her with one of the spiral-bound Meads in her lap, chronicling all the events of the past week. Mom could hear Sonya through the receiver, and she pursed her lips and shook her head at Ms. Cole's melodramatics.

"Tell her thanks for the compliment," she muttered and kept writing.

"Look, Mom," Rachel said. "You're starting to trip, and I can't talk to you when you're like this. So, I'm gonna let you go." Sonya tried to keep her on the phone, but Rachel cut her off again. "I gotta go, Mom. I love you, and I'll call you from Denver." She dropped the receiver into the cradle on the nightstand, exhaled a long heavy breath, and stared at the ceiling.

"Yours was a stroll through a daisy field compared to mine. You know that, right? My dad accused me of contributing to the delinquency of a minor. He doesn't even know how old his own son is, apparently. And the fact that he's staying another week went over like a napalm drop." Mom laughed a little and scribbled that into her journal. "They act like we've got him carousing the floating bordellos of Indonesia."

Rachel twirled a strand of her hair and looked at Mom. "Some of these bars aren't much better. Might as well be brothels, some of them."

"You're supposed to be on my side."

Rachel grinned. She rolled over and took the notebook from my mother and set it aside. "I'm always on your side, baby." She kissed her, pushed her back onto the pillows, and kissed her again. "You'll never find me anywhere else." She lay on top her, brushing the ringlets from my mother's face, studying all her particulars, tracing a fingertip over her lips, the lines of her cheekbones, her nose, sharp and perfectly straight like my grandmother's, long dark lashes framing those eyes she couldn't resist.

The phone rang.

Mom looked at it, then at Rachel. "Might be the call I've been waiting for." She raised her eyebrows with a quick wink, and Rachel let her up to answer it.

It was Gavin Graser, and she swung her legs over the opposite side of the bed and tucked the phone into her shoulder and took out a cigarette, tapped the flat of the filter on the box.

"Ms. De Carlo," he said. "Just got your message, sorry, we were rehearsing. I didn't think you'd call, thought maybe you guys had drunk the poison and took off to Santa Monica after Mr. A&R."

Mom lit her cigarette and blew a cloud into the heavy magenta drapes. "I dunno about any poison punch, but I'll tell you we're interested in your guys' offer. We're interested in his, too, though, so maybe that's gonna be a conflict. You tell me."

"No conflict," Gavin said. "I told you last weekend, you guys do what you think's best for you. Just seems counterproductive to drive all the way back to Boston to record that shit when we've got the resources here in Denver, just a few hours away. Maybe even do a collabo', you and me, like Hendrix and Dylan, a separate project, of course. Imagine that."

"The thing is, I *am* imagining that, and it's a pretty nice freakin picture," Mom said. "Your version of 'Voodoo Chile' at Montego's blew me away, completely, totally different than ours, like funk meets psychedelica meets some kinda heavy jazz, what the hell?"

Gavin laughed aloud, and it crackled through the phone and made Rachel smile as she lay listening. "It's The Brush, baby. That's what. Hey, you held your own up there, Superwoman. Feels nice to sit in with like-minded souls, doesn't it?"

Mom tapped her ashes in the tray on the nightstand. "Sure does," she said, mostly to herself, musing over all the creative possibilities that had sprung from their Tucson show.

She and Gavin had done an impromptu duet on The Brush's finale rendition of "Voodoo Chile," the Stratocaster dueling with the Weissenborn, vocals in unique harmony, Gavin's high tenor and my mother's soulful rasp, like warm honey with a whiskey bite. The musical potential was an overwhelming contemplation, so much that the deal was done before they'd even loaded out at Montego's. The call today was merely to get directions to Gavin's place in Denver where Portland Downs would stay for three months and record Michael Freiburg's demo, a detail both my mother and Rachel had omitted during their phone calls home, a bridge they'd cross when the time was right.

"So, you got the two gigs there in Albuquerque," Gavin confirmed. "Then you'll be heading my way, when? Monday?"

"Yeah." Mom tapped her cigarette, blew a drag into the air. "There's six of us, but my brother's going back to Philly in a week, leaving from there. So then it'll just be my band and my girlfriend. We'll stay out in the RV so we're not in your way."

"That works, however you wanna do it. We've got space, though, two extra rooms we can invent downstairs if we clear out some junk."

"What about rent and shit, food?" Mom asked. "What's gonna be the cost? I've got me and my girl covered, but I need to let the guys know their share."

"Won't be much," he assured. "Kind of a trade-off. You lay a few rhythm tracks on my shit, some background vocals, and we'll get you gigs here, open for us, headline at some of the smaller places we've burned out. It'll all come together. Seren-fuckin-dipity, baby." She could hear him grinning. "The universe is spinning in our direction. And if you're lucky, maybe I can talk you guys down the independent road while you're here."

Mom half shrugged, switched the phone to the other ear so she could jot down the details. "I'll leave that slummin to you, doing it the hard way, I'm telling you."

"Then three the hard way, we are," he said with a chuckle. "So, we'll see you guys in about three days, then you'll be here for three months. Damn, look at all those three's, sign of unity, trinity. Mind, body, and soul. Demonstrates love through creative imagination. It's a good omen."

Mom let out a little breath of amusement. She had never thought much about those things before. "Well, let's hope you're right. We'll see you guys Monday night, so be lookin out for us."

"Right on. We'll be waitin."

They hung up, and Mom turned to Rachel. "All right. It's all set up."

Rachel made a face, a mixture of excitement and apprehension.

"You sure you're down for this?" Mom said. "We can figure something else out."

Rachel nodded. "Yeah. I can take a semester off. It's not gonna ruin my life. You're doing it, and I go where you go. It's where my place is now. With you." She crawled across the bed and wrapped her arms around my mother's waist, rested her head on her shoulder, kissed her t-shirt sleeve, and Mom kissed her hair. "I'm in this for keeps. The good with the bad. If I have to go to Denver to keep that promise, then I will."

"You know, at some point we're gonna have to go back to school," Mom said. "It's not gonna be easy. It's gonna suck. A big plate of elephant shit we're both gonna have to eat."

Rachel cuddled closer. "Not if Geffen likes you. Everything would change for you, for *us*. We could always be together then. You'd be doing your music, and I could write full time, work on my poetry, go with you on tour, *real* tours. Not this roughing it, gig-to-gig, fleabag motel shit. Don't get me wrong, I love this adventure with you, and I'd do it all again a thousand times over. But we have dreams like anyone else, baby. You're a gifted musician, and you deserve more than this." She kissed her cheek. "I'm here now, and I'm staying with you to see it through, regardless how it turns out. If it doesn't work with Geffen, then we'll ride around in that crazy RV with the ridiculous upholstery and be poor and eat box macaroni and bologna sandwiches together until something else comes along."

Mom laughed a little and sat thinking about that. She draped an arm around Rachel's shoulder and kissed her hair again. "All right then. Bologna sandwiches for as long as it takes. Me and you."

THEY PLAYED A little saloon called Quicksilver's that evening for a modest crowd of about fifty, but the owner made good on a five hundred dollar guarantee. They were competing with the last two days of a hot air balloon festival, and then a classic car show along Central Avenue, the historic Route 66 through Albuquerque, and it had been going on since the afternoon. So, they finished early and loaded out in time to catch the last of the '58 Chevy Impalas and '45 Cadillacs, the '37 GMC long bed trucks and '69 Torinos all parked and cruising along the thoroughfare under red, blue, and green buzzing neon.

My mother met a guy there named Knox who was looking at a '59 Ford Skyliner convertible. He'd been in the audience at Quicksilver's, and he was flirting with her at first and trying to impress her, said he owned a successful insurance company there in Albuquerque, but Knox had a side hustle. He knew precisely how to market to out-of-town prospects like my mother and her band and had sold to Dom in the rest room at the bar.

And so Mom stood looking at the Ford with her hands in her jeans pockets, waiting wordlessly for Knox to make her an offer, and then he did. She told the others she was going to find a rest room and excused herself into the Stockland Diner across the street, knowing it was fairly risky, but he'd already proven himself safe, and he followed after her a few minutes later. They met around the corner, out the side entrance, and he offered a teen of coke, a little less than two grams, and she took that for forty dollars, unimpressed because Dom had scored more than that from him at Quicksilver's, but he wasn't finished.

He checked around for passersby, then presented an eightball of Black Tar heroin. He wasn't sure if it was her thing, and she didn't think she was sure, either. Something else spoke for her, a second mind she had no idea was acting on its own, a new brain operating concurrently to the one she had been using since birth, Siamese and Hyde-like. They exchanged bag and fifty dollars at once, and she pocketed her purchases and turned and left him there. She found her way back to the '59 Skyliner where Evan and Matt smoked their cigarettes, admiring the exposed interior, tritone black, white, and red, with the original dashboard and deep-dished steering wheel.

"All better?" Rachel startled her from behind, slipping her arms around Mom's waist.

Mom turned to her and switched on a smile. "Yep."

She kissed Rachel's forehead, and they clasped hands and strolled the rest of the Central Avenue exhibit. My mother wanted to put some distance between herself and Skyliner Knox. She wanted to forget him, and so she did. Most of the classic cars were heading out now, and so they made their way back to the Palomino Lodge where my mother sat for a long while with a pocket full of heroin, watching *Twin Peaks* reruns while Rachel lay beside her with a leather-bound blank book, scratching her thoughts with a motel pen. My mother watched her for a while.

After a moment, Rachel stopped writing. She looked over the words and said to Mom, "I think I've got you captured in poetry."

Mom smiled. "And how so? It must be a haiku, or a limerick."

"No, silly. Stars," she said, her eyes trailing the page. Then she looked at Mom. "Your smile is like stars, stars dancing a ballet." She thought about it some more, crossed something out, scribbled something else. "Your smile commands the stars to dance a glittering ballet," she recited, and she looked at Mom again, decisively. "That's not what really happens, but it should."

Mom laughed lightly. "Well, now you're making me blush."

"I'm immortalizing you." Rachel went back to writing. "From a mountaintop on Venus."

"And you want me to believe you've never done psychedelics?"

Rachel grinned into the page. "I've done shrooms," she confessed, jotting down another idea. "But no time recently. This is all love induced. You should feel very influential."

Mom laughed a little but didn't say anything. She turned her focus back to "the man in the smiling bag," to the cellophane bag shoved deep down into her pocket with such relentless clarity of purpose she could almost feel the outline of it against her thigh. She didn't know whether to be alarmed by that or not, and chose not. It was simple curiosity, normal to want to know. If she did just a chip, just a tiny diluted droplet, the way Bryce had shown her at Montego's, maybe it'd be nothing more than a weed high by itself, and she could sleep on it, sleep nicely without three rails of cocaine setting her nerves alight like powder keg wicks. She needed some good sleep. Sex was always a nice alternative, bliss out until the endorphins flooded the brain with that natural orgasmic sedative.

Rachel finally noticed her staring and gave her a glance and a smile and went back to writing, then grinned because she felt my mother's eyes on her like spotlights. She didn't look up from her journal. "Yes? Can I help you, Miss De Carlo?"

Mom thought about the bag of hammer in her pocket, about the taste of Rachel's skin, the sensual trance of their lovemaking, the scent of it, the sound of her beautiful moaning sighs, and she wondered if it would all be enhanced by this enigma burning a hole in her jeans.

Rachel looked at her, exploring my mother's gaze for what might be going on in her head. "I can read your mind, you know."

Mom knew that to be rhetorical, and she was glad. But then she said, "I have to tell you something." She decided honesty might be the better path.

Rachel waited.

My mother reached into her pocket and produced the bags, one of which drew no adverse reaction, but Rachel frowned at the other. "I talked to Bryce about it on the phone last week, and as long as you don't do it consecutively, you're fine. If you take breaks, dilute it the way he showed me. 'Cause I was worried, you know? I had the shit in my system, and I wanted to know. It lasts longer than herb. Might be cheaper in the long run if at least one of us isn't smokin up the stash."

"Where did you get that?"

"Does it matter?"

Rachel's eyes widened with absurdity. "Uh, *yeah*. It matters, Jo. It fucking *matters.*" She looked at her crossly and said, "I'm no stranger to drugs. I've bought my share, long before I met you, and it matters who you get it from, no matter what it is. You know that, come on. And something new? Are you serious?" She plucked the bag from my mother's palm and held it up to the lamplight. "You don't know what this shit is cut with, if it's dangerous, or even worth what you paid." She peered at her sideways. "How much was this?"

"Fifty. Look, I know it's okay. He sold us the coke, too. Dom copped from the same guy at the bar, and I tasted it, tried a short rail when you were in the shower, and it was fine."

She lifted her brows at such a figure. "Fifty freaking bucks?" She threw the baggie back at her. "That's groceries for Betty for a week, Jolán." She thought about the rest of what my mother had said and winced. "And you blew a line while I was in the shower? What are you, hiding it from me now? When'd that start?"

"No. I wasn't hiding it," Mom insisted with a ridiculous shrug. "You were in the shower. I wanted a bump to make sure it wasn't blanks. Would I have shown you this if I was hiding anything? I'm trying to be honest, here, 'cause I know you have reservations."

Rachel went back to her journal, perturbed. She didn't say anything for a long moment. She finally said, without looking at my mother, "I have reservations because it's trash, Jolán. And because the last time that shit was under your nose, you told me never again." She looked at her then. "You remember that?" She started to wait for an answer but didn't. "What happened to slowing it down? Hell, even I've stopped blowing freakin coke since we had that talk, but you?" She issued a humorless breath. "You honestly think you're indestructible, Jolán."

"No. I don't. Not at all. Which is why I talked to Bryce. He's experienced with it, and as long as I know my limits, it's as harmless as weed. It's all about moderation, rules. Hell, even liquor comes with a disclaimer, Rache. Anything in excess is bad. Look at how many cigarettes we smoke, how much junk food we eat. We're not exactly in Olympic shape, you know." My mother sat up on the bed and pointed at Rachel. "You decided to stop doin coke. You had your fun with it, and now you're done. You put it away. Okay, then tell me what's the difference? I just wanna see if it's worth the money, maybe replace weed with it, alcohol too, shit. It's all Bryce does, nothin else, no weed, and if he drinks it's a beer or two, tops. He's been fine on it for four years, says it's the most economical if you cut out the other stuff. Aren't we trying to stretch our money, here? If it turns out to be the opposite, then I'll do what you did and leave it alone. You have my word on that."

Rachel turned the page, didn't say anything. What was there to say? My mother had already made up her mind or she wouldn't have bought it, and words would only ricochet around the room and come to rest at a stalemate.

My mother was not a stupid young woman. She was remarkably controlled, even at twenty-two, and this trait had not escaped Rachel Cole in the short months they'd spent together. If Jolán De Carlo believed she could make something happen—or not happen—her success rate to date had spoken volumes. But she hadn't yet met her match, and this was what Rachel feared most for her, the moment she found herself in the ring with something bigger, stronger, more determined and willful than she. My mother didn't think there was such a thing, and so she tried soothing

Rachel's apprehensions with a hand cupped to her chin, and she turned her face to look at her straight. She smiled warmly, serenely, met her uneasy brown eyes with golden jade consolation dancing that stellar ballet.

"You're worried for nothing. I'm never gonna let anything happen to us. I'm responsible for too much, here. My band, you, myself. You don't think I know that, baby?" She smiled brighter. "Why would I jeopardize that? If I thought this shit would do that, I'd flush it right now. It'll be fine. I won't let it be anything but fine."

Rachel stared at her, listening, searching for the courage to believe that. My mother had given her no cause for distrust. She was faithful, dependable, had been a somewhat conscientious drug user, and she had always been honest, notwithstanding tonight.

Rachel set the journal down on the bed and turned to face her, and she took her hands. "You said there were rules. Well, then I'm going to add a few of my own."

Mom nodded, smiled. "All right. Rules."

Rachel knitted her brow and held up a stern finger. "I'm not fucking around, here, Jo."

"Okay," Mom insisted, her full cooperation offered up on a placating platter. "I'm listening."

"First off, if you're gonna experiment with that shit, then don't you ever hide it from me. I want to be present, in case something goes wrong, so I can at least . . . I dunno . . . try to help you."

"Understood."

"I don't want you sneaking off to get high, as if I'm some kind of dope tyrant. Don't make an ass out of me that way. I can handle this. I don't *like* it, but I can handle it, okay?"

"All right."

"Secondly, don't ever score from a goddamned stranger again. We get hooked up by local heads with their *own* connections, and you *know* that shit. I know you think you're this superior judge of character, but people are deceptive, and someone's either gonna sell you straight up poison or have your ass in handcuffs, and you won't be able to talk your way out of it, like you do everything else." She looked at her directly. "I need you. I need you here with me, and I need you alive and healthy. So, if you've just got to chase this crazy fascination, then you do it safely and you do it smartly, Jolán."

My mother nodded. "You're right. And I'm sorry. Once we get to Denver, nobody but Bryce. He's proven himself cool, and his product is clean. You have my word."

Rachel didn't respond to my mother's promises. She told her instead, "If that shit starts to fuck with your head, you *drop* it. You drop it before it gets too big. You swear to follow these three simple requests, and

I promise not to nag you till you get this crazy exploration outa your system."

"Done." My mother nudged her closer with a kiss to her lips. "I won't leave us hangin. I swear to you, I won't. Everything'll be fine." She saw the sad complicity in Rachel's eyes, and so she said, "Look, I'm gonna be busy recording for the next few months. I'm not gonna have time to party like we've been doing on the road. Hell, we spend half our time in bars right now, so it's only natural to do a little dope and drink entirely too much. But all that'll stop once we get to Denver.

"You're not familiar with what it takes to record an album, even if it is just a demo. It's time consuming. And it's tedious. It's work all on its own, and that's what I'll be busy with, ten, maybe twelve hours a day. We'll do a few gigs while we're there to earn our keep and pay for the studio time, but that's it." She gave her a gentle smile for persuasion and brushed the hair from her eyes. "Okay? You're getting all worked up for nothing."

Rachel nodded, but it was hesitant and sheepish, barely complicit. "Just stick to our agreement," she said and reclined back onto the pillows with the journal resting on her thighs. She opened it to a clean page and started writing again.

My mother left her to those thoughts for a while, gave her time to let the idea settle, to take its uninvited roots. When she felt certain Rachel had worked it through, she touched her hair, massaged the nape of her neck, and gave her an easy smile, then pulled her closer for a kiss to quell her misgivings, a kiss that dissolved into another, and then another until there was only the two of them, intact and safe there in the dark of the motel room.

My mother made a special kind of love to her that night, unhurried and deliberate so that Rachel might know precisely the depths of my mother's devotion, clear as a rain shower, unsoiled by chemical intrigue, pure and true and extraordinary. It came from a place that would remain forever absolute, and she needed her to know that, to find peace there and to trust in it wholly. When they were finished, Rachel fell asleep, soothed and satiated, secure there in my mother's arms for what was left of the night.

IT WAS A muted topic that vanished into the New Mexican sunshine. It was Sunday afternoon in Balloon Fiesta Park, and the Sandia tramway was cluttered and bustling with last day events. Most of the vendors were gone, but those that remained sold their novelties and snacks at a discount, and so Mom and Rachel strolled hand in hand along the concourse, sharing a basket of nachos with Uncle Cam, whose videography was relentless as ever. Matt, Dom, and Evan opted out and said they'd seen what there was to see over the past two days, the Albuquerque sky a perpetually dotted mass of teardrop globes that floated up over the Sandia Mountains and out across the pueblos along the banks of the Rio Grande.

Out on the tramway, some of the local balloon companies were offering short, last minute rides for half off, looking to make a quick profit from the lingering festival crowd. A pilot waved them over for a closer look while a group of others were stepping on board.

Mom smiled at Rachel. "You wanna go up? They've got room for five more." Then she looked at Cam. "I know *you* wanna go."

"Shit yeah, I do. I thought you had to make reservations, though."

The gondolier shook his head when he heard that. "Not today. This is the only flight, though. Last one. So, if you guys are going, you better take me up on it while you can."

Rachel shielded her eyes from the sun and peered up at the huge swaying bulb, a bit apprehensive. "Are you sure it's not a death trap?"

"It's fine, *mija*. I thought you were supposed to be such a daredevil. What, are you scared of heights now?" Mom nudged her.

"No, not at all. As long as I'm not gonna go plummeting to the earth, then I'm fine." She turned to the pilot. "How does this thing work? How do we know it's safe?"

After an abridged lesson in aerodynamic drag and propane BTU's and Archimedes' lift principle, she seemed fairly convinced of its safety and agreed to a thirty-minute ride out across the desert, and the three of them paid the man and climbed into the basket with the others.

"You sure you're okay?" Mom asked her as the pilot stepped inside and donned his gloves.

Rachel nodded and tried to smile, but Mom could feel her hand around her waist, gripping a belt loop under a fistful of her t-shirt, the other hand planted firm and white-knuckled on the edge of the gondola.

The basket rocked as the burners shot a column of flames up into the billowing canopy, and before they knew it, they were on a horizontal takeoff, a gradual ascent, just ten feet from the grass at first, then up into the air and over the treetops. The tramway and all the strolling onlookers shrank into the fields below. Cars and houses became toys you could almost pluck from the ground and hold between your fingers. It was chilly, windy up there, and Rachel huddled close to Mom who kept an arm around her shoulder. Cam pointed the camera up into the mouth of the balloon and shot the gondolier making adjustments on the burners, the sunlight illuminating the green-and-yellow nylon like stained glass. Then he panned the camera down across Mom and Rachel, and Mom smirked into the lens and kissed Rachel's temple, caramel blonde and dark auburn ringlets fanning and twining in the wind.

Late day sunbeams shot like lasers through low-lying clouds over the

Sandias, celestial and angelic, like the cover of a religious greeting card, and the balloon climbed to nearly three thousand feet, high as any prop plane. Cam pointed the lens directly over the basket and filmed the earth below, then zoomed in on all the horse farms and Spanish adobe homes with their smooth round corners and red tile roofs. Chamisa and swaths of chaparral sage and lavender Apache Plumes passed underneath in a languid slow motion. The pilot took them way down over the winding Rio Grande, so low that the bottom of the basket nearly skimmed the muddy water plain, then back up past the Sandia bluffs where the balloon cast its tall rippling shadow onto the rock-strewn bajada. Then he steered higher, twisted the burner knobs, and pulled at the ventilation ropes, and he took them out across the festival grounds for one more pass.

After a while, they came to rest back where they'd started, and Rachel was thrilled and spent most of the afternoon talking all about it to Dom and Matt, watching the video replay on an adapter for the VCR while my mother and Evan left in the 4Runner for a quick trip to the closest electronics store.

It was an urgent, last minute errand because Evan had a technical problem that needed a solution before that night's show. He and Dominick had come to an impasse on one of the new songs during last week's practice. It was a timing issue between Dom's complicated bass riffs and Evan's drum solo, and so Evan was going to need an electronic metronome, but not just any ordinary time-keeping device. He needed something with a visual indication of the tempo, a device with a blinking light, timed along with the audible click, something he could still follow while the band was blasting away at full volume. But it was a Sunday, and most of the music stores were either closed, didn't have what he needed, or they were out of stock.

"I *need* this fucking visual click," he told Mom, irritated as they made their way across town. "I think I can rig one up with the right stuff; a soldering gun, a single LED light, probably a pack of resisters."

"I have no idea what most of that shit is," Mom said, "so you're speaking Greek to me right now."

"I can show you when we get back. It's not hard. You just have to have all the proper gizmos and a power source, that's all."

And so they bought two rolls of red-and-black electrical wire, a package of tiny LED lights, a trimmer, and a box of 150 ohm resistors, and they found the solder and soldering gun at a nearby hardware store. When they got back to the hotel, Evan dug a pair of scissors and a roll of duct tape from his toolbox and set everything out on the 4Runner tailgate, and he walked my mother through it as she watched.

Dominick came out to join them, a plastic cup of beer in hand, and he peered down at the makeshift lab. "You honestly think you can rig up a visual click track in the middle of a motel parking lot?"

"Yes, actually. I do," Evan told him distractedly as the soldering gun sent a little gray smoke stream up over his project. "Okay, and so now we just need to fuse the negative wire to the negative LED leg . . . like so." He demonstrated and held the thing up for Mom to see.

Dom sipped his beer and nudged my mother's shoulder. "He just might be able to rig up a little somethin for you and Rache. Hey, dude," he said to Evan. "What do you need to make that thing vibrate? Jo's curious."

"Fuck you," Mom mumbled.

"I'm just tryin to get you the hookup. Free toys, courtesy of Louie the Lightning Bug over here. You should jump on it."

"And you should jump on this." And she held up her middle finger, watching as Evan wrapped the exposed wires with electrical tape to prevent them from shorting out against the metal equipment racks.

"Actually, it's good you're out here," Evan said to Dom. "That song is best for you at, what? About seventy-two beats?"

"Yeah, I can't make the transition into the chorus if it's any faster, and I don't wanna drop it out. It's too fucking cool. If you wouldn't get a damn fire under your ass and rush the end of the verse, we'd be fine."

Evan shook his head and smoothed the black tape around the twisted copper threads. "I don't even realize I'm doing it. Doesn't feel like I'm speeding up, but apparently I am, so." He shrugged, with no other solution but the electronics spread out across the tailgate.

When he was finished, he had a neatly wired, flashing red light, about the size of a Christmas tree bulb, timed with a trimmer to precisely seventy-two beats per minute. He had it connected to a 6 volt lantern battery for demonstration and testing purposes, but later he would run it through the amplifier power source, once the band was set up on stage at The Arroyo.

Dom eyed the contraption with a peculiar wince. "That is ugly, man. Looks like you smashed open a transistor radio and ripped apart the guts."

Mom shrugged. "Yeah, but it works." And she laughed a little, watching the gadget blinking in perfect time to the metronome click, and she patted Evan on the shoulder. "You're a regular fucking geek, dude."

Evan smiled at her. "Well, fucking thank you. I'll spruce it up a bit, see what I can find to hide all the weedy wiring and shit, might be something in the Fleetwood I can use. As long as I can mount it where I can see it, we'll be good."

Mom went back to the RV. Rachel was in the sleeper, reclined on the bed with her diary on her lap, recording her thoughts for the day. Mom watched her from the cabin and smiled, but she left her to it and grabbed a beer from the fridge and sat down at the table with Matt.

"So'd Evan get his doohickey thing working, or did he electrocute himself?" he asked.

"Yeah, he made it happen. He'll show it to you later. It needs a few final touches to make it presentable, but it works." She took one of Matt's cigarettes and lit it, then tipped her chin back toward the sleeper. "She's in her zone, I see."

"Oh yeah. She's been goin on all damn afternoon about that balloon ride." He chuckled a little. "That was a major score. She'll drop her panties whenever you want for the rest of her life over that one." Mom gave him a look, and he waved her off. "Come on, I'm kiddin, Jeezus. Don't get a hair up your ass. She's a nice girl." He smirked at her and patted her knee. "Ya done good, Jo-Jo. Found you a keeper. She loves you. That shit's hard to find in our world."

Mom smiled and thought on that. "The world of the traveling blues band. Full of club rats and floozies." She dragged on her cigarette and flicked the ashes into an empty soda can on the table. "Now it's your turn to settle down."

Matt grunted and half shook his head. "I dunno 'bout that. I think I like my floozies just the way they are, thank you. Maybe one of these days I'll let myself get trapped, but until then I'll live vicariously through you guys, if that's all right."

Mom nodded and laughed a little. "So, how do you feel about this Denver situation? Not a bad deal, if you ask me."

"Not at all. Gavin's a little bit of a granola head, all that trippy shit about soul surfing, being one with the cosmos or whatever the hell. But they seem like good enough guys. I just don't know what they're working with as far as equipment. Might get there and find out Boston was a better deal. Berklee's got state of the art."

Mom made a little face and shrugged. "Yeah, maybe. But sometimes the lo-fi sound works better for what we do, gives it a certain rawness, makes it more authentic. I dunno if I want it all polished up and overproduced. Their album sounds pretty nice. If they can get us even halfway there, we'll be in with Geffen, no question."

Matt finished his cigarette and dropped it into the can, and it made a little hiss as it fizzled in the backwash. "Welp." He stood up with a stretch. "You're the boss of this venture. Wherever you go, I go. You want raw and lo-fi, then off to Denver it is. Just make sure we get some gigs up there so we don't starve, and I'm all yours."

"I'll see to it." She smiled. "Starvation is not an option. We'll eat Dominick in a pinch if we have to."

Matt made a sour face. "God only knows what kinds of salmonella and Ebola he'll infect us with. Might as well ladle up some chow from the black water tank under this thing." He went to the side door and opened it to the early evening twilight. "Speaking of chow, I'm gonna go across to the store and get a bag of Combos. You want anything?"

Mom shook her head. "Nah, I'm good. I'll find something that's not Dominick and not black water. And not Combos. Just be ready for sound check by eight. The place is right down the street, so we shouldn't get lost." She winked, and he threw her an "okay" sign and shut the screen door behind him.

THE ARROYO WAS a slick, spacious nightclub with lots of blue lighting and gleaming chrome trim, and the main stage was impressive, a thirty-foot skirted riser that took up most of the back end of the club. The owner was Stu Kenoi, a tall, husky, brown-skinned fellow with salt-and-pepper hair, and he greeted the band with a grin and a handshake.

"So, you're her, eh?" he said to Mom. "The girl on the demo tape, the one in the promo pics."

"Yes, sir. That'd be me." She smiled and introduced the rest of the band, and she presented Uncle Cam as their videographer, since he already had the camcorder running.

Stu showed them to the stage and introduced them to the soundman while the technicians went right to work preparing the in-house system. "We're relatively new. But we've got a big college crowd from the university. Your bio said you guys are Berklee students? Pretty long way from home."

"Me and my piano man, yeah. My bass player and drummer are free men now," Mom told him. "They graduated right before we left for the road."

"Right on," Stu said, nodding. "Well, then you'll go over big with the clientele, the blues rock, the classic stuff. It's a nice change from all the dance and techno. Plenty of that around town, and we wanna offer something different for live entertainment." He raised a hand to the stage. "Well, go ahead and load in, do your thing. Jimmy, my sound guy, he'll get you squared away real nice."

"And the guarantee? We're still set on that, right?" Mom handed him a typed, one-page agreement to sign, and he took it, glanced over the details and nodded.

"Sure thing." He took out a pen from his shirt pocket, leaned down to a nearby table, and scribbled his signature. "A thousand, plus ten percent of the bar. It might be a Sunday, but our Sundays have been pretty jumpin this summer. No classes, so the kids are here from the time the doors open till last call. You should do all right. Just come by my office after the show, and I'll have it for you."

"Good deal," Mom said, and they shook hands again.

She had Rachel save them a bar top close to the stage, and she gave her a quick kiss, then headed out to the Fleetwood to start loading in.

MUCH LIKE THEIR Hollywood shows, Portland Downs had drawn a word-of-mouth crowd from Quicksilver's, and they packed The Arroyo to capacity by ten-thirty. The energy was tremendous, a welcome departure from the subdued little atmosphere of the previous bar. The crowd seemed to like the heavy blues a bit better than the classic rock, so Mom made a quick midshow adjustment on the set list, adding bass-heavy renditions of "Down by the River" and "Born Under a Bad Sign." They tested out five originals as well, including a twelve-string acoustic instrumental called "Rise," which my mother had been working on since their stay at Uncle Rick's, and they ended with their own "Comfort Zone" and an extended version of "Are You Experienced."

Their table was right next to the stage, so all the after-show attention came to them, the small talk and handshakes, pictures and passing kudos from those on their way to the bar. Rachel sat back and took it all in while Cam filmed, but then his battery died, so he went out to the RV for a replacement.

Mom took a seat and ordered a glass of whiskey while Matt, Dom, and Evan found conversations with the local girls at the other tables.

Rachel smiled at my mother, her chin propped in her hands.

"So, what are you all cheesin about?" Mom said.

Rachel shrugged. "Just incredibly proud of you tonight, as if you couldn't tell."

"Well, baby, I'm just doing my job."

"Just another day at the office?"

"Yep." Mom held a hand out to the club. "Nice office, huh? 'Bout time for a raise, though, a good six or seven figures, but that'll come in due time."

"Fingers crossed. You played the one I like, the new one on the acoustic guitar," Rachel said, and she reached across and took my mother's hand.

"Just for you," Mom said with a crooked grin. The house system was playing techno now, and it thumped through the overhead speakers. "They're all for you, really. You're half the reason I'm doing this now."

"So does that make me your muse?"

"It makes you a very important part of my creative process, yes." The server set my mother's drink on the table and reminded her of the open tab. Mom set the little white stirrers aside, swirled the ice in the glass, and took a sip.

"Well, likewise," Rachel said, my mother's hand in hers in the center of the tabletop.

Cam returned from the RV and powered up the Sony again and pointed it into their circle of two, the spotlight glaring off Mom's whiskey tumbler. "I passed Dominick and some dark-haired chick on their way across the street to the Fleetwood." He panned the camera around the club, then turned it off and set it aside. "I guess if Betty's a'rockin, we ought not come knockin for a while."

Mom heaved a noisy sigh and rolled her eyes. "Are you kidding me? The sleeper's supposed to be ours tonight. I'm not sleepin on those sheets after he's been screwin some skank for an hour. What the hell is his problem?"

"Well, it looks like another night at the lodge," Rachel said. "But it's just as well." And she gave my mother a sexy wink. "More privacy."

Mom grinned. "Yes, this is true."

"You know," Cam whined. "I'd tell you guys to get a room, but since it looks like that's already the plan, I'll ask you to refrain from the over sharing, thanks."

"Aw, what's wrong?" Mom bumped him with a shoulder. "Can't find any Albuquerque girls willing to give a Pennsylvania boy a hand job? This is a nightclub. Surely there's a few who'll do it for free. You can save your money, for a change."

"Yeah, you're a real freakin riot. A whole new act if this music shit falls through. The De Carlo comedy hour, comin to you live," he announced.

"Well, then I guess that'd make you my straight man, Mr. De Carlo. Get it? *Straight* man?" And she nudged him again and sipped her drink.

Cam picked up the Hi8 and switched it on. "I gotta get this shit. You're on a roll, here. Your new future as a failed comic begins now. Go ahead. Gimme another one. Hit me."

Mom smacked the camera with a *thwump* that cuffed the microphone, and it swerved around and wheeled through the club. "Not what I meant, but okay." Cam was trying to straighten the lens, fiddling with the focus. "You know I could take you to civil court, sue you for damages to this thing." He swiveled the mounted light back into place and re-adjusted the exposure that had gone completely black.

"See, now *you're* the comedian." Mom lit another cigarette and blew smoke into the lens, and the frame filled with a swirling gray vapor.

"Probably right," he said, zooming in on the orange glowing cigarette cherry. "I'd get what? All of about twenty bucks from your broke ass, as much as you spend on—"

Somebody let out a scream from across the bar. It came from somewhere off the far side of the stage. Mom and Rachel both looked at each other, and Mom turned in her chair to search for the source.

"Some drunken asshole. Real nice," Cam said, sweeping the Sony toward the opposite side of the club where the crowd was beginning to congregate around a barback in a brown leather apron, a dish tub filled with empty glasses and beer bottles in his arms. "And he works here, at that. What a 'tard."

The guy was pointing down at the floor beside the stage, walking backward into a gathering mob. "Dude, no shit!" he shrieked. "It is a fucking *bomb!* Look at this shit!"

The people around him were backing away as well now, and all the club chatter faded to a murmur. Dance music bumped and ticked through the system. Stu Kenoi shouldered through the crowd for a closer look at the thing behind the bar tops.

After a very long moment of critical study, Stu turned and waved everyone toward the exits. "All right, go, go. Everybody outside. Now. Go!" He gestured to one of his managers and made a telephone sign with his hand to his ear and mouthed, *"Call 911."*

"What the hell? Are they serious? They're actually gonna make us leave?" Cam complained, but he started backing out as well, the Sony bobbing and bouncing through a river of baseball caps and hair scrunchies and spaghetti-strapped shoulders and t-shirt sleeves as people shoved and rushed for the fire doors. The camera bumbled past Mom and Rachel. Mom had Rachel by the hand, but she kept glancing over her shoulder for the band's gear, forced to leave it all behind while the cocktail servers pushed against the panic toward the rest rooms to clear them of their occupants. Jimmy the soundman shut the music off and made a last-second announcement for everyone to calmly make their way to the exits. Then he, too, hopped down from the booth and vanished into the melee.

Everything after that happened so fast it was difficult to follow. People streamed out of The Arroyo and onto Route 66 and headed across the road, milling around at the convenient store and moving their cars parked along the curbs, creating a small traffic jam to rival that of the classic car show. Mom, Cam, and Rachel followed everyone out to the other side of Central Avenue where they found a spot to watch and wait.

It wasn't long before sirens approached, howling in the distance. Fire trucks blared at the far intersections and soon a whirlpool of red-and-blue lights swirled and flashed across the building facades, and the sirens crescendoed to a squealing cacophony. Stu and his bar managers warded everyone to the opposite side of the street, directing traffic to make way for all the emergency vehicles the city of Albuquerque could possibly dispatch.

"This is insane." Mom kept an arm around Rachel where they stood at the curb. "So, what? They saw something under a table or some shit?"

"Guess so. I thought the guy was just drunk, lookin to cause a commotion for laughs." Cam moved the camera past all the faces gathered along the sidewalk and around the convenient store lot, then over to the fire trucks that pulled up in the middle of the street.

Cops parked their squad cars askew and jumped out and took over. The yellow tape went up; a female officer went around wrapping the sidewalk trees and street signs to rope off the area while a Channel 4 news crew set up cameras on the southeast corner.

"This is too fucking wild," Cam marveled from behind the Sony. He adjusted the focus and panned over all the twirling police and ambulance lights.

After a while, a helicopter came sputtering overhead, and he tilted the camera to the sky to film that, too. It made wide circular passes around the block with a spotlight swiping across the storefronts and over the lots and then onto the glossy white panel of a bomb squad disposal truck, making its way through the scene with a K-9 unit right behind.

Dom and Evan found my mother and Rachel at the curb, and they all stood together, watching as the other businesses and bars were evacuated. People trotted from the exits, ushered by police to the far side of the block as firefighters tugged at their hoses and dragged them up to the closest hydrants, working around a team of German shepherds on long leashes led by officers in S.W.A.T. gear. That made my mother more nervous than the idea of explosives planted just thirty yards away.

"There's entirely too much law enforcement out here for my taste," she said to the others. "Betty's dirty as hell; you guys know that, right?"

"I don't think they're all that concerned right now," Dom told her. "Ya know, with the whole bomb thing and all." And he gave her a ridiculous glance.

"I don't care," she mumbled. Then she said, "Dom, go get everything we've got in the camper and flush it."

"Hell no." He frowned and crossed his arms over his chest. "It's hard enough gettin hooked up on the friggin road like this, and you want me to just *flush* that shit? Are you psychotic? Screw that."

"Yeah, I got a dub down in the damned console," Evan mumbled, rubbing the back of his neck, trying to look inconspicuous. "Scoring twenty bucks of weed on the road is like a CIA mission for stolen uranium. I'm not flushing that shit, either."

"Dom, Evan," my mother insisted. "I don't give a damn what you do with it. Hide it, eat it, shove it up your *ass*, for all I care. Just get it out of that RV. And be cool about it. Don't draw attention to yourselves."

"Jo, they're not—"

"Dom, just *do* it," she snapped, telling him lowly, "I'm not going to jail 'cause you think you know everything. You don't have to flush it if you can find someplace to hide it. But if those fucking dogs can smell a bomb, they can smell a *bong*. So, just keep that in mind."

He shook his head, planted his hands on his hips, and stared around at all the commotion. "I'll get it out of there, but I'm not flushin it. I'll find someplace to stash it till all this confusion dies down and these cops are gone."

"Thank you. Jeezus." She held a hand out to the crisis and said to Rachel, "It's bad enough all our damn gear is still in that place, waiting to go up in flames, but then they want us all to get a freaking drug charge on top of it? Really?" She turned and called after Dominick, and he came back. "Listen. In the side pocket of my backpack, at the foot of the bed, there's a little black drawstring bag. It's got some extra picks, another capo, some packs of strings. Get that and bring it to me, please."

"If your guitar gets blown to bits, you're not gonna need that shit," he said.

"Just bring it. Okay? Please."

"Yeah, yeah, all right. Got it. Whatever," he muttered and turned back for the Fleetwood.

A hazardous device technician was suiting up beside the bomb squad vehicle now, donning his bulky green protective gear. He strapped on a shielded Kevlar helmet and a pair of thick-padded gloves. He followed one of the dogs into The Arroyo while two more officers took the other K-9's around, sniffing at the cars and into the adjacent breezeways and up under the sidewalk mailboxes.

"So, if all your equipment gets blown to hell," Cam asked Mom. "Does the club have to pay for it, or are you just shit outa luck?"

She shoved her hands into her pockets, disturbed and unnerved. "I don't know."

"They should have insurance," Rachel told him, watching it all with her arms wrapped around her waist, sticking very close to Mom.

"If something happens, they'll be liable. It's on their property," Evan said.

"Sure as hell hope so."

Dom came back from the Fleetwood, and Mom turned to him, asking with her eyes if all had been handled.

"It was already done. Matty and you think alike. He was in there at the first siren, cleaning her up." Dom handed her the black pouch. "Here. Matt didn't know what I was talkin about, so I found it myself. Interesting priorities you've got there. All our gear's at the mercy of some whack job with a bomb, and you're worried about your capo."

Mom didn't say anything. She opened the bag and checked inside for the little ball of heroin she'd bought last night, and it was still there, tucked under the guitar picks and string packs. She rolled up the pouch and shoved it into her jeans pocket. "My priorities are right where they should be," she told him. "Don't you worry about my priorities."

The bomb specialist emerged from The Arroyo, with the dog trotting out to its handlers, and he gave some sort of signal to the crew behind the truck and plodded over to where they stood looking at a blueprint of the entire block. They took a few minutes to discuss their options, and then one of them went over to the rear of the disposal truck and swung open the doors and lowered a ramp onto the blacktop. After a moment, a squat little robot rolled down onto the street, controlled by a S.W.A.T. technician with a remote, and the thing did a wheelie and a one-eighty and headed toward the bar.

"You have got to be kidding me." Cam was following it with the Handycam as the helicopter followed it with the spotlight.

"So, they definitely found something, then," Rachel said.

Mom groaned. "Ten thousand bucks of equipment. Took us three years of starving and begging our parents for loans, and now Johnny Five's gonna go plowing through it, looking for a fucking bomb? You cannot be serious."

"Johnny looks pretty serious to me," Cam said, trailing the robot until it disappeared through the double glass doors. "I wonder if it has guns built into the arms, like the one in the movie. Get too close, and it'll shoot you full a holes."

"They're new," Evan said. "The military used them for incendiary devices during the '70s, for the IRA conflicts in Europe, and now American law enforcement's got improvised models for urban use. Crazy."

Matt weaved through the crowd and found the others at the curb. "So, what's goin on now?" He turned to Mom and spoke into her ear. "The RV's good. So's our shit. I handled it."

"Yeah, Dom said." She gestured out to the club. "They just sent in a robot."

Matt laughed. "Are you fucking kidding? This is some *Die Hard* shit, man. Maybe it's the Palestinians." He folded his arms and watched.

Evan winced at that. "The Palestinians? And what the hell would they want with a nightclub in New Mexico?"

Matt pointed a thumb toward the east. "Roswell, dude. It's just a hundred miles from here. You know, Area 51." And he shrugged as if that was the most obvious deduction. "The large array of satellite dishes? Out there where we camped last week in Socorro? We could see 'em from the RV. There's like fifty of those things, big around as baseball fields, man."

Evan stared at him for a very long time, baffled. "Unrelated," he finally said, shaking his head a little. "All of it. Not *one* of those things has *anything* to do with the other. Where do you get this shit?"

"Unrelated, so you say," Matt mumbled and raised a conspiratorial eyebrow. "That's exactly what they want us to think, dude."

". . . that Hamas is conspiring with the Klingons to rearrange the United States satellites by blowing up all *our* band equipment? Did you just smoke everything we had in the RV? Is that how you got rid of it?"

Now Mom and Rachel were peering sideways at Matt, but then Dom nudged Evan and tipped his chin out to the commotion. The droid had emerged from the bar, whirring and buzzing along the sidewalk and down over the curb, carrying something in its grapnels, and it brought it out to the middle of the street and set it onto the macadam. Dom looked closer, watching as it went to work examining its discovery.

He asked Uncle Cam for the camera. "Lemme see that for a second." And he took it and pointed it at the robot and zoomed in close on the device it was picking apart on the concrete. "Hey, Evan?" he said from behind the lens. "Question."

"All right, shoot."

Dom zoomed in and adjusted the focus. "What exactly did you end up using to hide all those wires for your click track gizmo thingy?" he asked, rather gingerly.

Evan shrugged. "Just a section of piping I found in the Fleetwood, back by the water pumps. Someone replaced it a while back and left a piece, so I took it, used it. Why?"

Dom lowered the camera for a moment, and he stared out across the road, whirling with red-and-blue emergency lights, the white helicopter spot quivering over the bomb disposal droid in the center of all the chaos. He raised the camera back to his face again, aimed it at the scene, zoomed in closer. "Was it a white plastic tube, by chance? About, oh, six inches or so, duct tape around the ends, maybe? Little red blinking light panel taped around the middle?"

Evan looked at him. "Uh . . . yeah. Why?"

Dom didn't say anything. He just handed him the camera.

Evan took it and peered through the lens, and now Mom and Rachel and Matt were looking at Evan, then out at the bomb squad, and then up at the circling police chopper, and around at the fire trucks and ambulances and the German shepherds barking at the robot in the middle of a crowd of five hundred Albuquerqueans gathered along Route 66. Evan lowered the Handycam and gave it back to Dom who gave it to Cameron, and they all stood looking at Evan, silent as Mongolian monks.

Evan shoved his hands deep into his pockets and stood there, thinking. "It's . . . it's not a bomb." He shut his eyes to the melee and shook his head. "It's not a bomb."

"*PVC* piping?" Dom demanded lowly, growling into Evan's ear. "You *duct* taped a flashing *red light* . . . with a network of electrical *wiring* . . . to a piece of *PVC plumbing pipe* . . . and left it *blinking* on the floor of a *nightclub?*"

"Oh, my God." Rachel stared back out at the scene, slack jawed and dumbfounded. But then she looked at Mom with a scowl. "You *watched* him do that. This afternoon. You went with him, Jolán, to get the parts, and you *saw* him. What were you *thinking*?"

"I didn't know he was gonna do that," she insisted. "I walked away; he wasn't done with it, yet."

"She was inside with Matt," Evan confessed, waving that away, so woozy with dread he looked as though he might fall over. "I finished it on my own. Christ, it musta fell off the stage after the last set." He ran a hand through his dreadlocks and cringed. "But I didn't think . . . it wasn't . . . Who *thinks* about that shit? I mean, fucking *really*?"

"Well, they do." Matt held a hand out to the Albuquerque emergency vehicles. "Congratulations, Einstein. You are now officially *the* dumbest mechanical genius I have ever known." He gazed around at all the confounded turmoil wreaked upon the city. "I mean, look at this shit."

"Well, hold on. Maybe it's not that bad." Cam motioned out to the robot. "I mean, if it's not a bomb, then it's not a bomb. Johnny Five'll disassemble it, figure out what it is, and then it'll all be straight. No harm, no foul, right?"

Someone tapped Evan on the shoulder. He jumped, then turned to find two ATF agents at his back. "Are you Evan Charles Mahan?"

"Holy shit, they're already using his middle name." Dom moved away from him.

Evan looked at the others, looked back at the agents, swallowed a rock. "Um, yes. But I can explain—"

"Well, you'll get your chance to do that, son," one of them said. They both flashed their badges, and Cam turned off the camera.

I RIFLED THROUGH my mother's stack of notebooks for the one with the corresponding dates, but they were out of order now. There was no additional video footage of that night, and I had to know what came of it. My mother would've spent hours recounting the details of that experience, and she'd have plenty of time on a four-hundred-mile ride to Denver.

I couldn't find it for a long while, and I began to wonder if they'd all been arrested, and maybe that was another one of the many things she'd hidden from me, from everyone she knew. Perhaps the authorities had searched her person and found the drawstring bag with the dope in the bottom. Maybe they'd brought the dogs to the Fleetwood to nuzzle around in all the secret compartments behind the pullouts, up into the innards of the passenger's seat, back in the shadowed shelf over the black water pump, along the side of the hull where they kept the rubber dish gloves they used for draining the shit tank.

I flipped through the nicotine-scented pages, read the dates, scanned the text, another wrong book. Maybe the black one with the guitar sticker on the front. The pages in that were so densely scrawled, it made me hesitate, as if a madwoman had a grudge against her own thoughts and had taken it all out on the paper. It was the wrong book, anyway. No time to decipher my mother's hieroglyphs; that was going to take scholarly analysis, and so I pillaged through the others and, at last, came upon the Albuquerque entries, fluid and sound, a linear cursive account of that week, dated for *August 1st, 1992,* and I read along to discover that they'd all been questioned by the ATF.

They took Evan first, escorted him down the block and around the corner to an unmarked van where they shut the doors and kept him for two hours, grilling him for terroristic intent. In that time, they separately detained Matt, Dominick, Rachel, Uncle Cam, and my mother, who sat through the entire interview with a little ball of heroin in her pocket. By then, the authorities were aware that it was all a misunderstanding, and so the theatrics were exaggerated as a scare tactic, but my mother wasn't buying it. She nevertheless obliged them and answered all their questions as not to create any unnecessary suspicion.

". . . *AND SO YOU were with him when he purchased the parts for the device?"*

"Yes, I was."

"And you were present while he began to assemble it."

"Yes. But it was supposed to be . . . it was a metronome, a visual . . . he's a drummer, so he needed to be able . . . see, our bass player couldn't . . . it's difficult to explain if you're not a musician."

"Now, you said you walked away while he was still manufacturing the device."

"That's right."

"So, you don't know what his intentions were, at that point. You never saw what he'd ultimately created because you weren't there."

"Correct, but he . . . it was a metronome, strictly for time keeping. All the stores were closed, so—"

"Do you know if Mr. Mahan ever had any anarchist beliefs? Any ill-intent toward the United States government?"

"What?"

"If he may have been affiliated with an extremist group?"

"Uhh . . . just ours. I'm kidding. We're a band. Just a rock band."

"Do you find all this amusing, Miss De Carlo?"
"No, sir, I do not."

BY FOUR A.M. the area was cleared and the band was set free with no search and seizure of Betty's contents, but the visual metronome had been destroyed by Johnny Five as a precaution.

Stu Kenoi gave them access to the club for their equipment, but he didn't want to pay them, yet he'd signed the payment agreement before sound check, which my mother didn't hesitate to produce. He'd asked for a service, and they'd provided it, long before all the unintentional mayhem ensued, and so he handed over the cash guarantee but refused the cut from the bar as restitution for his police-trashed nightclub. Fair enough. Everyone was tired, and everyone was vexed. The band accepted the deal and headed back to the motel where no one slept until the Monday morning daylight broke across the New Mexican desert.

chapter thirteen

MY MOTHER SAT in the sleeper with Rachel as the Fleetwood passed through Trinidad, Colorado, nearly two hundred miles from Denver. She was at the edge of the bed, the curtain drawn shut against her band mates up in the cab, the twelve-string case across her thighs with a small plate resting in the center.

She unwrapped the little ball of Tar she'd purchased in Albuquerque and chipped off a piece about the size of a grain of rice and did exactly what Bryce had explained to her in Tucson. She used a plastic drinking straw she'd cut down to the length of her own pinky to trap a droplet of hot water from the Styrofoam cupful beside her. Then she deposited that onto the obsidian grain in the middle of the plate and stirred it with the razor for a very long while until it finally dissolved into something like black coffee or cola. Such preparation was necessary because this particular grade of opiate could not be snorted on its own, the way you might inhale cocaine; it was too strong, and it was the wrong consistency with too much acetic and it needed to be broken down first, diluted, the way it was in Bryce's little nasal spray bottle. It could also be cut with a crushed Oxycontin or a Benadryl or baking powder, but she didn't have any of that. Only a little water from the RV tap.

Rachel sat leaning against the headboard, critical and wary, watching. Dominick changed lanes along Interstate 25 and the camper rocked a bit and Mom grabbed up the plate to keep twenty-five dollars from dribbling onto the floor, but now the hit was stretched and thinning across the plate, and so she gathered it back into the center with the razor blade and put the straw to it and sucked it back before Dom's driving wasted it altogether.

Rachel sat up and came to her. "Okay, well? Is it all it's cracked up to be, or did you just flush our groceries into the tanks?"

"It's not my first time." Mom was holding her head back, trying to compensate for the drip.

"Yeah, I know. But by itself? The first time was kind of an unplanned speedball, so what about now?"

"I don't know yet." My mother gave it a few moments. "It tastes like shit, like vinegar and some kinda . . . I dunno . . . metallic aspirin. And it burns." She blinked, wincing. "I don't remember any of that from Montego's."

"I freaking *told* you. God only knows what that shit is cut with.

Dammit." Rachel took the plate and set it aside and babysat my mother through this blind leap into an anomalous black hole.

Mom was careful not to let the liquid escape down her throat any more than it already had and sat sniffing ever so gently, flaring her nostrils to let the solution absorb into the nasal membranes, and when it finally did, she went docile, wilted just a little under its treacherous charm.

"No, it's nice," she uttered, feeling for it. "More than nice, actually, it's brilliant. It's warm. Like a cashmere body suit, straight from the dryer on a freezing cold day."

"You don't put cashmere in the dryer."

"Yeah, but just think if you did," she told her and smiled. "And instead of wearing it on the outside, you put it on the *inside*. It tingles a little. Like warm carbonated butterflies made of silk."

"I thought it was cashmere." Rachel grabbed the guitar case and set it upright by the bed, but my mother wanted it back and gestured for it. She started to sneeze but she held that in as not to spray all the dope onto the RV paneling.

She opened the case and took out the twelve-string and hugged it to herself. She twisted the tuning pegs, tested the E string against the others, her immaculate pitch chemically unaffected. "I'll try to play what it feels like. How 'bout that? It's the best way I know to communicate it."

She chose her chords carefully. Then she began with slow arpeggios, E minor and dissonant, and she filled in a pretty melody as she went. She would eventually flesh it out into a song called "All That Remains" that would go on their Geffen demo, a copy of which she sent to Uncle Cam and which later ended up with the CDs I got from Rachel. But in these fetal, impressionistic stages in 1992, the song was meant solely to ease Rachel's concerns over my mother having just inhaled a tenth of a gram of Black Tar heroin she'd bought off a New Mexican stranger.

She felt confident now, worriless and ultra focused on bringing Rachel around to brighter thoughts, and so she tried humor as she played, made up insipid lyrics about chinchilla butterflies dropping tiny little firecrackers into her bloodstream while she skinny-dipped in a pool of warm caramel, but it bombed, and Rachel rolled her eyes instead.

"Is that your version of 'Lucy in the Sky with Diamonds'?" Rachel asked and stretched out on the bed behind her. "Heroin's not supposed to be a hallucinogen, unless I missed that memo."

Mom laughed and kept playing. "I'm trying to describe it, it's the best I can do. I didn't say I *see* that shit. It's what it feels like to me."

"The music is beautiful, I'll give you that."

"This high is beautiful." Mom played another few bars. "I should probably record this. I don't want to forget it."

She dug out a microcassette player from her backpack, rewound it for cueing, then set it to record on the nightstand. To this day, I'd pay a lot of money to have that device and all its little tapes filled with band rehearsals and my mother's spontaneous creative bursts, but they were lost over the years and exist now only within the pages of her journals.

"So, how long does this last?" Rachel asked.

"Not sure. It got me through the show and into the night last time, but I had coke in my system, too, so who knows these things?"

"I feel sorry for your nose."

"And yours?" Mom countered. "You haven't exactly treated your sinuses with kindness, either, my love, and you started that before you ever met me."

Rachel didn't say anything. Mom plucked her pretty scales, strummed sweet chord progressions, and sang a little improvised ditty about throwing stones and glass houses, and Rachel rolled her eyes again.

Mom smiled at her. After a while she said, "I'd love to have sex on this stuff. I bet it's better than weed or coke sex."

"I thought you liked coke sex." Rachel had taken out a collection of Marianne Moore poems and was half reading while carrying on this distracted conversation with my mother.

"I do, but sometimes you want something gentle, not so aggressive, where things don't get broken." She grinned. "Remember that painting in San Diego? On the motel wall? I was trying to catch it and hold you up, too, but that didn't quite go as planned."

Rachel lay reading, thinking about their last night in the San Diego Gaslamp Quarter, at the East Side Motel, the faux Picasso hanging beside the dresser where she clung to my mother with her legs around her waist, her back pressed to the plaster, arms and hands buried in dark auburn ringlets, and she let a tiny smile creep across her lips. "Forty-five extra bucks, that picture cost."

"Might as well have grabbed a couple pillows on our way out, too. At least it didn't shatter. That would've been worse, at least for the housekeepers, anyway."

MOM KEPT PLAYING for a long while. She played until the notes filled the sleeper like a twilight mist across a meadow, Rachel there on the bed, quietly absorbed in her book of poems under the headboard light. Outside, the Colorado landscape was nonexistent but for the highway lamps that lit up the evening in white passing waves. Headlights burned behind them. An eighteen-wheeler pushed passed on the right, the logo stamped in big red letters across the silver trailer, you could just about see the driver in the cab. My mother had fallen into a kind of satisfied haze, her fingers working twelve strings as if her hands belonged to someone else, every note in its own bubble, floating around the sleeper and out into the camper.

There was a little knock at the paneling just outside the drawn curtain, but my mother ignored it, and so Rachel invited them in. It was Matt. He stood leaning against the doorway, listening for a while.

"So, would you put piano with that or maybe some synth pads?" he finally asked.

Mom didn't answer. She just kept playing, her head down, ears trained on the changes.

"You might wanna wait till she comes down, whenever that'll be," Rachel said. "She's been a bit out of touch for the past thirty minutes."

Matt frowned. "I didn't think the New Mexican homegrown was *that* damn good. She must be in a zone." He waved a hand in front of her face, and she glanced up at him, smiled a little, and kept playing.

"It's not weed," Rachel muttered. "And she's in a zone all right. Not sure I'm all that cool with it, but it is what it is."

Matt looked at Rachel, waiting for her to elaborate, but she didn't look up from her book. "And it is . . . ?"

She opened her mouth to answer, but then my mother stopped playing. She was still for a moment, only the whir and rush of the RV wheels along the road. She threw the guitar aside and bolted from the bed and pushed past Matt as she disappeared through the curtains.

They could hear her in the rest room now, retching, and so Rachel got up and went to her. She hadn't made it to the toilet and stood vomiting into the sink. Rachel scooped aside her hair to keep her from vomiting into that, too. Matt was standing behind them in the rest room doorway, and he looked at Rachel with puzzlement while Mom spit and rinsed her dinner down the drain.

Rachel glanced at Matt, annoyed. "Yeah, heroin'll do that to you," she mumbled. "Put that kind of poison in your system, and your system tends to try to get rid of it."

Matt's eyes widened, but he didn't say anything.

"I'm fine," Mom breathed, spitting the last bit of slime off her lower lip. "Just gimme a towel or something, please."

Matt grabbed the paper towels from in on the kitchen sink, and Rachel unraveled a thick handful and gave that to my mother, and she swiped it across her mouth and blew her nose.

"I'm good." She sniffed and straightened herself up. "Totally fine. He said that might happen. It's not a big deal, happens to everyone, so just relax." She pulled another bundle from the toilet paper roll and blew her nose again, then tossed the paper into the toilet and flushed it.

Matt knitted his brow and looked at Rachel, then at Mom. "He who?"

"Bryce." Rachel was twisting my mother's hair into a low, loose bun, tucking her ringlets to make it stay, just in case she had another wave of nausea. "The Brush's drummer. Apparently, he's got the hookup on all sorts of interesting things."

"He sold you smack?" Matt asked Mom. "When was this? At the club?"

"No." Mom leaned back down to the sink, ran the water, and cupped a handful to her mouth, swished it around and spit it out, then went to brushing her teeth.

"He gave her a little free sample," Rachel said, watching her. "Supposedly to bring her down from too much coke that night. Had it in some kind of liquid you snort like nasal spray."

"Yeah, I knew about that," Matt said. "Monkey water; I've heard of it. Never seen it before, though. Dom was kinda pissed about that shit for a while, but he got over it."

Mom rolled her eyes at them both and insisted around her toothbrush, "He saved my ass that night, saved all our asses. I was in no fucking shape to play. Freiburg woulda walked in there and then walked right out again."

She spit a frothy white splotch into the sink and rinsed it, wiped her mouth on her forearm. She took a swig from the mouthwash on the counter, gargled it around, and spewed that into the sink, too.

She looked at Matt and cocked her head to the side. "Don't tell me you're gonna throw a guilt trip now, too. A little dash of snow in your weed pipe from time to time, Mr. Cocoa Puffs?" She stepped past them and went back into the sleeper and stretched out on the bed with her eyes shut, letting her stomach settle.

Matt followed her with a shrug. "Nah, I just wondered how much it was."

"I didn't buy it from him."

"She bought it from some stranger on the street," Rachel said as she came into the sleeper. She took Mom's guitar from the bed and stood it in the corner.

Mom opened one eye and looked up at Rachel. "I thought we put that to rest, baby."

"We did. I'm just telling him where you got it." She looked at Matt. "It was fifty bucks, twenty five of it now swimming in the gray water tank under the Fleetwood, with all the mouthwash and toothpaste spit."

Mom smiled. "I wouldn't say that. I had a pretty nice buzz long before I puked. And now I'm fine, right back where I was." She held her hands open at her sides to indicate no permanent damage.

"You're still high?" Matt questioned.

Mom smiled again and nodded pleasantly as she situated herself against the pillows.

Matt stood in the doorway, watching her for a while. "So, what's it like?" he finally asked.

"Don't *even,*" Rachel warned him. She dropped into a seat on the bed and glared at Mom. "I'm sure as hell not babysitting while you two play Hot Potato with a hand grenade."

"More like an M-80. And don't be such an alarmist. We talked about this."

"Yeah, we did," Rachel said. "Which would mean you don't get another taste of that shit for a week, so you better enjoy it."

"I know my limits," Mom mumbled. "And I *was* enjoying it until you guys penetrated my bubble."

"So, was that before or after you barfed in the sink?" Rachel snipped. "Nice bubble."

Mom laughed.

"So, is it like weed?" Matt asked. "Like, I dunno, Chronic or some shit?"

My mother made an absurd little sound beneath her breath. "No, not like that." She thought about it at length. "Imagine yourself completely naked, out in the cold. It's raining, freezing, you've been stuck out in that shit for hours."

"That sounds un-fucking appealing," he said.

Mom held up a finger; she wasn't finished. "You've been like that for hours, and then finally—*finally*—you come inside where there's a fire going, candles burning and food cooking, where there's someone who loves you almost as much as my beautiful girlfriend loves me, and she brings you a big soft bath towel straight from the dryer and wraps you all up in it. That feeling. Right there—times about ten. That's what it feels like."

"She's been coming up with all sorts of descriptions. That one seems to be the most elaborate so far." Rachel looked down at Mom. "So, what else have you got in this quaint little Hansel and Gretel cottage of yours? Butterflies and . . . honey, was it? Warm honey?"

"Caramel."

"Ah, that's right. Caramel." Then she said to Matt, "And the bath towel's made of cashmere. But now it's ruined from being in the dryer and feels more like a big clump of felt, or wool. Have fun with that." She took up her poetry book and went back to reading.

Mom grinned. "So, I'd venture to say it's nothing like Chronic, nothing at all. Poppies and cannabis are two very different botanical species, I'm coming to find." And she tucked her arms behind her head and sank back into the remainder of her high.

Matt stood looking at her for a long while, then glanced back into the camper at the others—Dom at the wheel and Cam dozing on the sofa and Evan at the table with his headphones on, drum sticks in hand with an ankle propped across his knee, pattering something on the edge of his sneaker sole. Taillights glowed up ahead through the RV windshield, burning little red holes into the Colorado darkness.

Matt turned back to Mom, slapped a hand across her foot to rouse her, and she opened an eye. "Lemme try it, see what the hell you're talkin about." He dug into his back pocket for his wallet and pulled out a ten and offered it. "Not tryin to get high on your dime. I know it's not cheap."

Rachel cocked her head and gave him a look. "Really, Matt?"

"I just wanna see. I'm cool. I'm a big boy, I can handle myself, Mama Rache. Calm down. Jeezus."

Mom waved his money away. "You'll have to snort it with water. Not the most convenient method, but it's Tar, not the Brown or China they get in Boston, the powdered shit. It's just what it sounds like. Black and sticky."

"Just don't kill me with it," he said, joking, but not really. "Same dose you had. I'm a skinny motherfucker, so it's probably not gonna take much."

"Which side of Idiotsburgh did you guys get lost on? I mean, seriously." Rachel looked at my mother who lay looking at her. "Jolán, come on. I don't know if I'd rather watch this or a game of three-bullet Roulette with a fucking revolver."

"So dramatic." Mom shook her head. "That must be what makes you a poet." She got up, kissed Rachel's cheek, and went to her backpack and fished around for the black pouch with the dope at the bottom. She sat down and gestured to the nightstand for the plate and water cup, and she had Matt put the cup in the microwave for thirty seconds to warm it again.

When he brought it back she said, "This is the only way I know how to do it, the only way he explained it, and it takes a minute, so don't get impatient." Mom unwrapped the Tar while Matt sat observing the ritual.

"Only him," Rachel insisted. "In fact, I want you to give that shit to me when you're done."

"Are you rationing it now?" Mom smiled, chipping off another little black grain, like a crumb of licorice in the center of the white porcelain on her lap.

"Yes, actually. That garbage is causing way too much fascination between you guys."

Mom held up the plate, offering a taste, but she put it down for fear it might get slapped into the wall because Rachel was not the least bit amused. So, Mom went about stirring the little grain with a dribble of water for several minutes until it came to an acceptable consistency, then handed Matt the straw.

"Same as coke, but don't rail it too hard, it's liquid, obviously. And it's gonna burn, so be prepared. And don't sneeze. You're probably gonna want to, but don't or you'll waste the hit, and then I'm gonna have to take that ten bucks after all."

He did as instructed, and Mom and Rachel waited for the effects.

"Hold your head back a little." Mom placed her fingers under his chin to tip his head to the proper degree. "Don't let it go down your throat, though, either. That'll waste it, too. Just let it soak into your nose."

He nodded. Then, after a while he, too, fell into a kind of quiescence. He sniffed the stuff back and let himself go languid. He gazed down into the plate, then at my mother, and smiled. He turned to Rachel. "You don't know what you're missing, Mama Rache. You wouldn't be half as ruthless if you just gave this shit a try. I am so not kidding."

"I have my vices, and I'll stick to those, thanks." Rachel held out her hand. "You guys are done. Give it here."

But my mother hesitated. "So, are you saying you don't trust me? Trust us?"

"It's not you I don't trust." Rachel shook her outstretched hand a little, waited.

Matt lay back onto the bed. "She's probably right. This shit is so damn nice, *too* damn nice. I wouldn't want to get too used to it."

"He has a point," Rachel said to my mother, her hand still waiting for what was left of the dope.

Mom laughed a little but she wrapped it back up and handed it over. "I can control myself, but if you insist."

"I do."

MY MOTHER PICKED up the twelve string again and continued to serenade them both while Matt made mental notes on the possible keyboard parts. After an hour, Rachel was asleep, the book laying page down on her chest, and Matt was awake but basking in the warmth of his high at the foot of the bed. My mother had stopped playing, but he was still humming his part, and Mom gave him a little shove.

"Go make a pallet up front," she whispered. "She's out cold, and I'm gonna see if I can sleep on this shit, get a little rest before we get to Denver."

He didn't want to get up, but he did. He wrestled himself into a sitting position and then just sat there, comfortable and hazy.

Mom shoved him again. "Come on, Matty, take it to the couch. We only have a few more hours."

He raised a hand to slap fives with her. "You made my night, *chica*. Absolute best shit ever."

"Yeah, it's good stuff. Nice little treat after being chased by a biker gang and almost getting arrested for domestic terrorism. Kinda made it all worth it."

"Definitely worth it." He rose and gave her a captain's salute, then disappeared behind the sleeper curtain.

My mother woke Rachel to get her into bed, and she climbed in beside her. Rachel cuddled close, then looked up at Mom, groggy, studying her for the lingering heroin effects. "Are you okay?"

Mom smiled through the darkness. "Yeah, I'm fine." Rachel didn't say anything, and so Mom kissed her forehead. "Baby, I'm okay. Really. I promise I am. Go back to sleep." And she kissed her again.

Rachel laid her head on my mother's chest and draped an arm across her stomach. "That stuff scares me," she whispered. "Please be careful." She looked up at her again. "Okay? Please?"

"I will, sweetie. I promise. Now, get some sleep."

IT WAS JUST after daybreak when they pulled up to The Brush's driveway on Fillmore Street. There was a brown '85 Honda Accord and a blue-and-silver 1990 Blazer in the lot, an '83 Mustang at the curb, a faded red convertible with a torn black soft top. The place was a two-story bungalow with a screened-in porch and a chain link fence that wrapped around and connected to a six-foot privacy fence in the back.

The neighborhood was middle class, blue collar, lots of homes like Gavin Graser's tucked between ranch-style spreads and single-story cottages with tricycles and swing sets in the yards. A disassembled Chevy up on blocks two houses down. Lots of white-and-green plastic porch furniture, potted plants dangling in braided macramé hangers, pink-and-orange Day-Glo chalk drawings on the sidewalks. His next door neighbor was an electrician, *Duarte's Electrical Contracting* painted onto the door of a white utility truck parked in the lot. A man came out of the corresponding house, middle-aged, Latino, wearing a tool belt and brown leather work boots, and he glanced at my mother and Dominick as they made their way to Gavin's front door. He nodded a greeting, then got into the work truck and drove off through the neighborhood.

"Early risers around here," Dom said, watching the neighbor drive away. "Something tells me not so much at Casa de Graser, though."

"Yeah, well, we need to let them know we're here," Mom said, and she rang the bell. "Then they can all go back to bed, and so can we."

After a moment, the door opened to a freckle-faced girl with hair black as onyx, cut in a short bob, and she regarded them with surprise, her crystal blue eyes skeptical, searching their unfamiliar faces. She glanced out to the curb and saw the RV and broke into a huge smile.

"Oh, hey!" she sang, and held open the door. She was wearing light blue hospital scrubs and a pair of running shoes. "You guys are the band Gavin was talking about. I'm sorry, we thought you'd be here last night. I didn't mean to look at you like Jehovah's Witnesses." She laughed. "Come on in."

"Yeah, we got a little, uh, detained," Dom said. "Long story."

"Oh, no problem." She offered her hand to them both. "I'm Naomi, Gavin's girlfriend." She glanced back into the house, then bit her lower lip, thinking. "The guys are all still asleep. They were up late recording last night and just went to bed, actually. And I was on my way out to work, or I'd keep you company. But there's still some coffee left." She gestured over her shoulder to the kitchen. "Help yourselves if you want. Make yourselves at home. Gavin'll be so stoked that you're here when he gets up."

"Thanks, but we're all pretty beat," Mom told her. "We've been driving all night, so we're probably gonna take Gavin's cue and get some more sleep."

"Okay, that's cool." Naomi went to the secretary desk by the living room window and took out a pen and scrap paper from the drawer. "I'm sure he'll see your camper out front, but I'll leave him a note to let him know you're here, just in case he goes straight upstairs to the studio when he gets up."

She jotted all that down and took it to the kitchen where she tacked it to the fridge with a Ross Medical Center calendar magnet.

"He'll grab a protein drink before he does, so he'll definitely see this," she called in to them. She grabbed her purse from the counter and came back to where they stood in the living room entry. "My shift starts at seven, so I gotta jet. But I'll be home around four. The guys should be up by then."

"Can't promise we will," Dom muttered with a thin smile. "But I'm sure we'll all catch up eventually."

"Hey, do your thing. No rush. You guys are here till November, at least, so sleep away." She shrugged and laughed a little. Then she looked at her watch. "I really gotta get going. But it was nice to meet you, and we'll all hang out tonight."

"Sounds good," Mom said.

They all left together, and Naomi got into the Accord and backed down the driveway, waving as she headed south along Fillmore.

THAT EVENING, THE ten of them sat around the backyard picnic table, strewn with after dinner dishes and half-empty beer bottles, the grill still smoldering from the rib eyes Gavin and Sandro made for the arrival of their house guests. Gavin had a CD of old rare Hendrix recordings playing in the living room with the windows open, and the music drifted out onto the yard while Naomi and Rachel went around lighting citronella torches to keep the mosquitoes away. She and Rachel were the odd women out of all the music discussions, so they carried on their own conversation about Naomi's job as a nursing assistant at the medical center. She'd been there for three years, she said, but had no interest in becoming an actual nurse because she didn't like the politics.

"Nursing assistants end up doing most of the patient care, anymore," she explained, holding her lighter to the wick of the last torch. "There's so much paperwork placed on the nurses now, that we end up spending the most time with the patients, which is why I'd want to be a nurse in the first place—patient interaction. I get that now, so why change? The pay's pathetic compared to an RN salary, but I guess it's a trade-off I'm willing to make."

"I never saw myself in the medical field," Rachel said. "Not because I don't have what it takes to be a caregiver, but I've always been more of a creative soul, I guess."

Naomi laughed a little. "You sound like Gavin. He's pure artist, through and through. I don't know what he'd do if he didn't have music. Probably crawl under the bed and waste away with the dust bunnies."

"I admire what you do," Rachel said as they found seats in the lounge chairs near the picnic table. "Don't get me wrong. It's a vital job. Probably a lot more than what I plan on doing, but so it goes."

"And that is?"

Rachel smiled abashedly. "I want to write a book of poetry, one day. Have it published and studied in college classrooms, sometime when my grandchildren are in college, I guess. They say most writers and poets aren't truly recognized until they're dead. At least you're appreciated while you're still alive."

Naomi lit a cigarette and looked at her with blue eyes bright and determined. "You shouldn't sell yourself so short. You could do all that in your own lifetime, no problem. You just have to envision it. Master of your own ship. It's the whole reason Gavin and the guys are doing things independently, to create their own destiny. It's totally doable if you've got the right strategy."

"You mean self-published?" Rachel winced. "Do you have any idea what they say about those vanity press publications? It means you couldn't get published by a real publishing house, so you did it yourself. That might work for the music business, but not for writers and poets, I'm afraid. The criticism comes from a completely different place for us, and it's not a nice place, not at all."

Naomi dragged on her cigarette. *"Couldn't* get published by a major, or chose *not* to? It's all about perception, girl, creative control. Just like being a nurse or a nursing assistant. I choose not to be a nurse, and I have my reasons, which are as valid as I need them to be. I get my own sense of accomplishment from what I do. I don't have to justify it to anyone who can't appreciate that, and neither should you, and neither should the bands we're unofficially married to."

Rachel could see her point. She glanced back at the table full of musicians. My mother was much more comfortable than she was the last time they'd all sat talking like this, and Rachel watched her and smiled. "So, how long have you and Gavin been together?"

"Six years, this Christmas."

Rachel lifted her brows, impressed.

"And you and Jolán?"

"Since the fourth of July. Not very long, but it feels like years. In a good way." She gazed back at my mother who sat talking with Gavin about soloing techniques. "We knew after our second date that we were meant for each other. It came as naturally as breathing. And with everything that had to happen for us to meet, it was just too uncanny."

"How so?"

Rachel shrugged and peered out at the neighbor's juniper tree on the opposite side of the privacy fence as "Villanova Junction Blues" drifted through the kitchen window screen. "Gosh, where to begin," she uttered, then turned to watch my mother at the table, a beer and cigarette in the same hand so she could demonstrate air guitar finger placement with the other. "We started out on completely opposite coasts. No way we'd ever cross paths if not for Matt's uncle."

"The one you got the RV from," Naomi said.

Rachel nodded. "But not even so much that. Even *his* circumstances played a part, not being able to just drive the thing out to Boston, deliver it himself. They *had* to come to the West Coast, had to get all the right gigs to get even *more* gigs that brought them to LA. Then they had to get my boss Steve on the phone to confirm, which is nearly impossible, trust me. They took a table that wasn't even in my section that night, but there were regulars at one of my tables who asked for my co-worker Janine, friends of hers, so Steve switched us so she wouldn't be overloaded and I wouldn't get shorted on tips. Janine got my table four, and I got her table ten. And then there she was." She smiled at Naomi, then looked back at Mom. "I didn't know if she was interested in me or not, but I suspected it and certainly hoped I was right. She was staring at me enough to give me reason to think so, anyway. So, I gave her a few smiles to let her know I was available . . . then proceeded to dump an entire tray of drinks right into her lap."

Naomi's eyes went wide with astonishment, and she cupped a hand to her mouth and laughed.

"Yep. Smooth as a rock slide."

"And it all came out of your tips, of course," Naomi grumbled, tapping her ashes. "I did some serving before I got on at Ross, so I know exactly where this is going."

"It came out of my tips, yes. And I got fired," Rachel said.

Naomi's expression went flat, and Rachel waved it all away.

"No need to feel bad about it. That's half the reason I was able to do all this with her. It gave us this time together, to get to know each other, see all these great places, meet people, fall in love. I should thank Steven Zhare, actually. That asshole did me the biggest favor, letting me go that night."

"Well, since you guys'll be around for a few months, I can get you a serving job while you're here. I mean, if you want that. 'Cause I'll tell you what—when they start recording, you'll think it's interesting to watch for a while, but that'll last for, oh, about an hour. Then it gets really, *really* boring if you're not a musician." She crushed her cigarette out in the ashtray on the little table between them. "It's not the perpetual rock concert you might expect. They play the same sections of the same songs over and over and over until it either puts you straight to sleep, or makes you want to pull your fucking hair out."

"Yeah, Jolán explained some of that to me."

"You're really gonna want something else to do, especially since I'll be working most days. You'll be bored outa your mind." Naomi got up and went over to the drink cooler and fished out two beers for herself and Rachel.

"So, what kind of serving job are we talking about? Cocktail serving? Restaurant?" Rachel asked.

"There's a little tavern not far from here called King's Pub. You can hop a bus to and from," Naomi said, and she handed Rachel a bottle opener and dropped back into her seat. "You've got experience working in bars, and I know the general manager. His mother was one of my patients a few months ago, and he was there every day with her for weeks. Plus, you're gonna want something that matches the band's hours so you and Jolán aren't on opposite schedules, or you'll never see her. That's my problem working at the Medical Center right now. My hours have me saying good morning when Gavin's telling me good night. There are no third shifts available, so we're just stuck with it for now. You wanna avoid that if you can, it really sucks."

Rachel thought on it for a moment. "All right. If you can set it up, that'd be great. Don't go out of your way just for me, but if you can work it out without a hassle, that'd be awesome. I'd appreciate it."

"It's no trouble, girl. Gavin's guests are guests of mine." She held up her beer, and they clinked bottles to a new friendship.

Rachel took a sip. "I'm gonna use your rest room, if you don't mind."

"Yeah, sure. Second door, right past the kitchen."

She got up and stopped by the picnic table to kiss my mother's cheek, then went on into the house where a muddled lo-fi recording of "With the Power" filled the living room.

She assumed it was Naomi who kept things so tidy, though most of the furniture was worn and scuffed, a blue-and-cream plaid thrift store couch with a matching love seat, an oval oak coffee table that needed polishing, brown shag carpeting, and a bookshelf cluttered with hardbacks like *The Alchemist* and *The Prophet*. On the rest of the shelves were rows of classic rock CDs and cassettes, and there was a stack of vinyl albums on the floor—Captain Beyond's *Sufficiently Breathless* facing front.

She wandered down the hall past the kitchen, but there was only a single door to the left, the laundry room. Then the hall made a turn to the right, so she tried the first knob, presuming it was the second door, but she was wrong again. She poked her head into a bedroom instead, peered around mistakenly, and started back toward the hall when her glance fell upon the nightstand.

Next to the lamp was a white candlestick, melted down to a lopsided nub, the wax dried in thick runnels over a black pedestal holder. Beside that, a latex medical tourniquet, a tarnished soup spoon, and a small insulin needle case with two packaged needles and one unwrapped beside the candle stand. Rachel shut the door. It was none of her business. It wasn't her house and it wasn't her problem, and as long as it never left that room to find its way out to the RV, she would leave it right there on the other side of the wrong door. My mother seemed to have a preferred route of administration for the drug, anyway, as well as a certain amount of vanity, which she wasn't likely to forego for a telltale string of track marks.

She found the bathroom, one door down—second door on the right, past the kitchen, *minus* the laundry room—got it. It was tiny but well kept, and she couldn't help but wonder how four people, particularly three men and a woman, managed to coexist with but one bathroom. Then she thought about the Fleetwood arrangement.

"Guess you make it work if it's all you got," she muttered, peering around at the counter lined with aftershave and face cream, the curling iron wrapped in its own cord aside the electric razor, a dark green, gender-neutral shower curtain pulled across the tub. She couldn't say why, but she was tempted to take a peek into the medicine cabinet after she peed, but she didn't. She washed her hands and kept to herself instead, then went back out to the yard where Bryce was seated next to Matt at the picnic table, listening with everyone else as Matt and Dom traded versions of The Arroyo bomb squad incident.

Rachel took a seat in my mother's lap, kissed her temple, and draped an arm across Mom's neck, pretending to listen along while doing a discreet examination of Bryce's forearms. He had a tattoo along the inner left arm, not the extensive work that covered Sandro from wrist to shoulder, but rather a single elaborate image of torn skin, revealing what looked like an alien exoskeleton underneath. It was well done, very realistic, and if there were any IV indications, it served as great camouflage.

Dominick laughed. "They wanted to know if I thought Evan was capable of treason." He pointed a thumb at Evan sitting next to him and made a face. "This guy's like a Golden Retriever, he's so fucking loyal, and I told 'em that shit. So, the ATF chick says to me, 'So he's the real devoted type, then. Devoted to whom and to what?' I wanted to say, 'devoted to getting head from chicks like you—you're exactly his type, so why don't you go ask *him?*' But I thought that unwise." He grunted and took a big swig of his beer.

"I am *so* glad you did not say that shit," Evan mumbled. He was preparing a blunt on the tabletop, slicing through the wrapper of a peach-flavored cigar and dumping out the tobacco into a napkin.

"Yeah, be very glad," Dom told him. "I was so fuckin pissed at you that night, I almost told 'em you had a hard-on for Hezbollah, but I politely refrained."

"Thank you for that. Prick." Evan filled the cigar shell with the weed Gavin bought from a dealer they called Quint who'd come by earlier that afternoon. "For two hours, they had me thinking I was off to Leavenworth before the sun came up, then on to the federal penitentiary by the end of the week." He licked the blunt leaves and smoothed them shut, shaking his head. "Scariest shit I've ever been through, thought I was gonna take a dump right there in my pants." He held the lighter flame to the seal and waved it back and forth to dry it, then lit the end and took the first toke.

"They're so full of bullshit, the fucking government," Gavin said. "You shoulda known when they said Leavenworth it was all a smoke screen. Leavenworth's for military criminals, not civilians. They were just testing you to see how far they could push it."

Evan handed him the fuming blunt, and he took his turn with it, filled his cheeks with sweet-smelling smoke, then handed it to Naomi.

"They wanna know where your loyalties lie," Gavin said and exhaled a cloud over my mother's head. "But they're the most corrupt of us all. No conscience, not a care in the world for the struggling man. Follow all these laws that we ourselves break on the daily," he recited from his own world view. "Or we'll cage you like an animal for the rest of your worthless life. Deemed worthless, of course, by the very government that claims to care for you."

Mom took the blunt from Naomi and toked on it. "Wow. Good thing you were in Yuma that night."

Gavin laughed at that. "You know what? You're probably right, my friend. I applaud you guys, 'cause dunno if I coulda held my tongue. Too many opinions they don't like to hear." He reached across and patted Evan's arm. "I mighta spoken too freely and had my man, here, doing a bid in the pen. Over a homemade metronome. Tragic, to say the least."

"To say the very least," Evan grumbled.

"It was pretty brilliant, though," Bryce finally said. "Despite the fact that you made it look like a pipe bomb, of course. But still—an LED, a few fuses, and trimmer? Nice idea. You should talk to the guy next door, the electrician. Maybe he can make you an apprentice while you're here."

Dom took the blunt from Mom and tapped the ashes. "Why? So he can rig somebody's water heater to look like a nuclear missile? That'll make us real popular with the neighborhood watch."

"Yeah, just make sure I'm long gone before you do that shit, dude," Cam said to Evan. "I've only got a few more days with you guys, and I'd like them to be cop free, thanks." He looked at Mom. "And don't you ever tell Mom and Dad I was questioned by the ATF on this trip. I've got more shit on you than you realize." And he charaded a camera rolling, smiled, and winked at her.

"And likewise," she told him. "We've been at that stalemate for, what? Fifteen years? Since you were about four? So, that's a dead horse, deader than dead."

"Which is what we'll both be if they ever found out all the shit that's happened on this trip," he insisted.

Mom shrugged that off. "They've got no say in my life, anymore. Yours, either, really." She passed the weed from Sandro up to Rachel. "But it's a newer phase for you. They're not gonna be too quick to let go, so just humor them. At least until you get through your freshman year. Then you'll have more to negotiate with. Trust me, I had to do the same thing, and they're just now starting to back the hell off."

"Oh, the joys of overprotective parents." Naomi smiled. "Glad those years are behind me. I'm twenty-five now, but while I was in school for nursing assistance, mine were like MI-fucking-6, I swear." She turned to Cam. "But she's right. After a while they'll move on with their lives and eventually be glad you're gone. Just give it time."

"Speaking of," Rachel said to Mom. She handed the blunt to Cam. "I gotta check in, told my mother I'd call her when we got here, which she thinks was yesterday. She's probably already called every hospital and morgue from here to New Mexico." She asked Gavin and Naomi if she could make a long distance call and offered ten dollars, but they both waved that off.

"Our home is your home for as long as you're here. Take all the time you need." Gavin gestured into the house. "There's a cordless in the kitchen, and you can take it up to the studio if you need privacy. It's totally soundproof. Go do your thing."

"I'll be back, babe." She gave Mom a quick peck and went back into the house to the kitchen, found the phone on the counter, and dialed home.

Sonya Cole answered.

"Hey, Mom."

"Rachel, Jeezus, where are you? Are you all right? Christ, I've been on pins and needles all week. You were supposed to call two days ago. I don't have a crystal ball in front of me; I can't know where you are from one minute to the next. You have to call me when you say you're gonna call."

"It was yesterday, Mom, not two days ago. And I'm sorry. We got a late start out of Albuquerque. There was nothing I could do. Everything's fine. We're here."

"Where's 'here'?"

"I *told* you last week. Denver. We're in Denver."

There was silence at the other end. Then a long sigh. "Just how long is this excursion gonna go on, Rache? I mean, really. You can't be there for more than another week, I know that. School starts back on the twenty-sixth."

Rachel took the phone into the living room, but the music was too loud, and so she backtracked down the hall and went into the bathroom, shut the door, and sat on the toilet lid. "Well, that's something I wanted to talk to you about." Sonya didn't say anything, so Rachel continued. "I'll be taking the fall semester off this year. Then I'll start back in January, after Christmas break."

"Absolutely not." Sonya chuckled a little, as if the idea didn't infuriate her in the least, but Rachel knew better.

She let out an aggravated breath, leaned back against the tank, and stared at the spackled ceiling. "Mom, I already talked to financial aid, and my scholarship allows one semester off, as long as I've maintained my GPA for at least four semesters, which I have, and as long as I don't do late registration when I return, which I won't. And besides, my student loan would cover the last year if anything went wrong. I can pay for books myself if I have to. Okay? Everything's not always a freaking crisis. I wouldn't be doing this if I couldn't do it right, so just relax. Jolán's doing the same thing before she starts grad school. We've totally got this covered."

"Oh, is that so?" Sonya said with bittersweet sarcasm. "Jolán's doing it. I see. So, tell me again where you found this woman. In a *bar*? The transient rocker chick who lives out of a *motor home*? That's your inspiration for this crazy idea? I mean, I just wanna be sure I've got all this straight so when you screw up your life over this girl, I know exactly who to *hunt down* and *strangle*, Rachel Christine."

"She's not a transient, Mom. She's touring. Big difference. And there's a reason why we're doing this, if you'd just listen and not go off on your own assumptions all the time."

"There's not a reason on earth for you to be ditching an entire semester of school. I can't think of a single thing that'd be worth it."

"Of course you couldn't," Rachel snapped. "That would take an open mind, a little trust in my judgment, for a change."

Sonya Cole laughed aloud, but she was hardly amused. "So far, your judgment hasn't impressed me, Rache. Not lately, it hasn't. You lose your job, then take up with a group of total strangers who've been dragging you all over the country, where God only knows what can happen. And now you're telling me you won't be going back to school next week. Yeah, your judgment's spot on, darlin."

"Why did I ever think you could possibly understand this?" Rachel uttered, mostly to herself, but her mother took that ammunition and loaded it into the receiver.

"What's to understand?" she insisted. "You're blowing off your senior year in college for a woman you met in *July*. It's *August*, Rache. Do the math!"

"It's not my entire senior year, first off. And secondly, there's a very good reason why I'm doing this, but you haven't even asked. You just assume whatever you want, then proceed to insult Jolán, whom you've never even met, and treat me like I'm a damn teenager. I'm twenty-one years old, Mom, legal on all counts, and I really don't owe you an explanation at *all*, frankly, but I wanted you to know the truth so you'd know where I was and why. But so much for honesty. As usual."

"Oh, well, then do tell, Rachel," Sonya said. "What could you *possibly* be doing in Denver, Colorado, with some woman and her rock band, whom you barely even know? I'm sure it must all be *so* pressing as to keep you from finishing school, so please do fill me in."

Her words were biting and so undignified Rachel couldn't gather the will to respond. She just sat there with the phone to her ear and a boulder in her stomach, toying with the fringe of her cutoffs, wondering how the two of them could've ever been related.

"Come on. I'm at the edge of my seat, here," Sonya persisted. "Don't leave me hangin."

"You know what, Mom? Nevermind. It was supposed to be good news, but screw it. I can't even tell you when something good happens 'cause

I'm afraid it's not gonna measure up to your standards. And I think that's a shame. Really, I do."

"Is that supposed to make me feel guilty? For pointing out the obvious?"

"How can anything about my life be obvious to someone who's two thousand miles away? You're an armchair spectator, Mom, and it's not just with this. You always have been. If not on the other side of the country, then it was the other side of town. I grew up alone. It's just the way it had to be, and so I learned to make that work for me because I knew you had good reasons, and I trusted that. So, can you just do the same for me? Trust that I have my reasons and that maybe they're good ones? For *once*?"

Now Sonya was quiet. Neither of them said anything for a long moment. Jimi Hendrix seeped in from the living room, there in Denver. Traffic from the Innerbelt highway hummed in the Akron distance, a neighbor's dog barked, the phone rustled as Sonja switched ears.

"All right," she relented at last, begrudgingly; it was the best she could do. "Tell me why, then." She sighed. "What's this great news? And it better be good, kiddo. It better be the news of a lifetime, so let's have it. I'm listening."

It took another few beats for Rachel to decide if it was worth telling at all, whether it still carried the same excitement from the show in Tucson, and she decided it didn't now, but she told her, anyway. "Jolán's band got discovered a few weeks ago." It dribbled from her lips like a sip of sour milk. "By a record executive, a talent scout from a major label." She gave it a pointless shrug, all the enthusiasm deflated under the weight of her mother's cynicism. "It's a really huge deal. Geffen Records has two of the biggest bands in the world out right now. They've made millions, and Jolán's just a demo album away from the exact same contract, the same success. That's why we're in Denver. To record a demo, so the label can decide if they wanna sign Portland Downs. We met some other musicians on the road, and they live here, offered us their studio so Jolán's band could get this done without going all the way back to Boston. It's just a business thing. She's got it all worked out with them; she knows what she's doing."

"At twenty-two years old, she knows what she's doing in the music business." Again, Sonya's tone took an abrasive slant. "I'm no expert, but don't most music groups record an album *after* they get a record deal? Are you sure you're not getting duped by this chick, two thousand miles from home and a thousand miles from the college education you plan on ditching? I know you don't like hearing the voice of reason if it's not your own, Rachel, but have you really thought this through? It seems to me you've got stars in your eyes, hon'. You're thinking with your heart and not your head, and maybe you think you're in love with this girl, and that's why you're doing this. But love has blinders, babe. It can be a spinning compass when you need to find your way out of a mess, and frankly, that's what I see this becoming, a clusterfuck of epic proportions. Maybe I'm wrong, but my gut's telling me you need to get yourself to a bus station before you ruin your life, and little miss rock 'n' roller breaks your heart."

She waited through Rachel's silence.

"Now, I wanna ask you something else," she finally said. "And I want you to tell me the truth, don't screw with me." She hesitated, looking for a response, but all she got was muffled Hendrix playing "The Wind Cries Mary." She proceeded, anyway. "I've got enough street smarts to know there's about five rock bands in the history of rock bands who didn't have a steady supply of drugs and liquor coming in. And my guess is your girlfriend's band isn't one of them. Am I right, or am I wrong? Tell me the truth."

Still, Rachel said nothing. But now it was as if she'd been comfortably naked in the privacy of her own room, and her mother had just yanked away the window blinds. She tried to dispel the images of the past couple months, but her mind was quicker than she and flashed them across her memory screen, anyway. Two packaged needles and one used. Coffee-colored liquid pooling on a porcelain saucer. *It's nice, actually, works like a charm.* Flesh torn from an alien exoskeleton.

"Listen, I wouldn't ask if I didn't love you." Her mother's voice startled her, like the sudden blare of a car horn at a red light gone green. "Come on, don't you see that, Rache? You're all I got, kiddo. And even at twenty-one, you've still got a hell of a lot to learn. It's *what* you're learning that scares the christing bejeezus outa me. You can take care of yourself until you can't anymore, and it's my job to figure out when to step in, so I need to know the truth about what's going on out there—is this my cue or not?"

It didn't matter whether it was or it wasn't. There was too much at stake now, too many walls to come toppling down around her.

"No. It's not," Rachel said.

The Ohio traffic whirred on the other end. Sonya Cole was far from convinced, and Rachel knew that, but her mother gave her another moment, another chance to sell her a story she could believe.

"Look, I don't care about a little pot," Sonya said, looking for honesty with a change of tactic. "Hell, your father and I conceived you over a joint, two stolen Millers from his dad's cooler, and a Janis Joplin record, and we were younger than you. Just tell me that's all it is so I can sleep at night, Rache, and then I'll leave it at that."

Rachel took a very deep breath and studied the mint green floor tiles.

There were voices in the living room now—everyone was coming inside. The music stopped, then changed to something she didn't recognize, sounded like Gavin's band. Someone would need to use the bathroom soon, so she got up and went to the door.

"Everything's fine, Mom. You've got nothing to worry about."

"You're sure?"

"Yeah. I'm fine. I gotta go, though. Other people need to make calls, and it's not my phone. I'll be in touch. I love you, and I'll call again soon."

"I love you, too. And please be careful. They're the only words of wisdom I've got left. Be smart, and be careful."

"I will."

chapter fourteen

AUGUST PASSED INTO September, which pressed on through October, when the Colorado weather began to change, when the sycamores and western catalpas littered all the yards and sidewalks with orange and gold, their half-naked limbs clawing the pastel sky. It reminded my mother of home. She'd spent so many months baking under the southwestern sun, roaming the Arizona deserts and Mexican beaches and the smog-heavy summer streets of Los Angeles, she came to welcome Denver's brisk autumn allusion to Pennsylvania.

She and Rachel made shopping trips with Naomi to the vintage stores downtown where they bought hooded sweatshirts and fleece jackets and a thick, navy blue comforter for the RV sleeper. On Saturday afternoons and Monday nights they sat in the downstairs den eating hot wings with the guys, watching NFL and college football, and they all placed their wagers paid in beer and dime bags of chocolate Kush. They bought firewood and cider from the grocery store and made Hot Toddies and drank them in the cool evenings around the fire pit in the backyard, while Gavin and Mom played folk duets on their guitars. You could hardly distinguish the smell of flaming spiced oak from the weed cloud that churned the embers and floated up into the stars.

On the nineteenth of October, it was Rachel's twenty-second birthday, and so she and Mom took the 4Runner up along the winding switchbacks of Mountain Base Road for a weekend in Golden Gate Canyon Park, where the citrine-yellow aspen groves shimmered like lemon jewels among the pines. They rented a cabin with a view of Tremont Mountain and talked of one day buying a house with floor-to-ceiling picture windows and a wraparound porch that overlooked the whole world.

They spent the first day making music, Rachel whispering poetry into my mother's ear while Mom played along on the twelve-string, and they spent the next day making love all over the cabin—in the kitchen, on the sofa, in front of the fireplace while "Rose in the Heather," "Dream of the Archer," and "A Thousand Days of Yesterday" played from the classic station on the portable radio.

My mother could no longer see the future at all unless Rachel Cole saw it with her, and Rachel Cole wanted to climb right into my mother's skin and curl up safe there forever, go with her everywhere, be her oxygen. They even speculated on what their children might look like if it were possible, if nature had allowed such a thing, like little combinations of them both, my mother's eyes and Rachel's smile. My mother wanted to marry her.

By the end of October, Rachel was working full time at King's Pub, Portland Downs had eight promising new songs recorded for Geffen, and my mother was thoroughly addicted to Black Tar heroin. She didn't know it at the time. She'd left all the rules back in Albuquerque and thought now that its daily use was still a conscious choice, a soothing reward for the hours spent shut away in the vocal booth of The Brush's home studio, the outside world reduced to a stream of bass and drums and keyboards funneled into her ears through a pair of battered binaural headphones. Gavin had even convinced her to incorporate the violin on two of Portland Downs' tracks and one of his own, and he mixed it all down into a one-woman rock 'n' roll symphony, like ELO, or The Moody Blues.

The studio was set up in the bungalow's attic space, with a seven-foot ceiling just high enough to keep the taller guys from having to duck under the joists, but it was otherwise spacious and warm through the chilly autumn nights. Eggshell foam covered the east and west walls for soundproofing, from the Oriental rugs to the pine-knotted rafters, and against the rear wall was a ranch-style tweed couch with sunken threadbare cushions and a torn undercarriage that drooped to the floor like a fishing net, its wooden armrests mottled by drink rings and cigarette burns. Hanging over the couch was a black-and-tan Kokopelli tapestry, the hieroglyphic Native American god of music and fertility, dancing with his flute across the desert.

Gavin and Sandro had built the vocal booth the previous summer, nothing more than a padded closet at the top of the stairs with a little window in the door, much too cramped for a guitar or a keyboard, so all the instrument recording was done acoustically in the middle of the room. This made silence critical while laying the instrumental tracks, as the slightest footfalls or whispers could find their way into the feed and ruin an entire take. My mother was particularly fussy about that, so they rigged a garage droplight to hang from the outer door at the base of the attic stairwell to indicate when they were live and in session.

Between takes, Bryce taught my mother to make a substance he called cheese, sometimes with a dab of baking powder but most often with a crushed vitamin B12 that cut Quint's Black Tar into a tawny powder, much easier to inhale than the monkey water she'd started with back in August. It was a bit more time consuming to prepare but eliminated the bacteria factor of the liquid version while leaving the drug itself unadulterated and reasonably pure. She came to prefer this form and kept a small baggie of it in one of the red velvet compartments of the Fender case, doing little match head bumps throughout the night off the corner of a playing card—the Two of Spades.

In the beginning, she and Matt were budgeting about thirty dollars each from their weekly local gigs, just enough to make a few little bags, but by early October it had doubled and was now up to more than a hundred, which made Dom and Evan a bit uneasy.

My mother's playing had become moody as a result, but it was still very innovative, and everybody liked it, even her long-winded super solos that Gavin would have to edit down as not to be too lengthy for radio play. She experimented with all sorts of effects and techniques, including a Frampton-style talk box Gavin borrowed from a guitarist he knew down in Littleton, all of it inspired by a chemical fusion of opiates and raw passion.

And so, while Rachel waited tables five nights a week, my mother sat up in the smoke-filled attic on Fillmore, headphones crackling with the Stratocaster hugged close, whetting her talent on the single edge of a carbon steel razor blade.

BY THE FIRST Friday in November, the demo was only a song away from completion. It was two-thirty in the morning, and Mom sat listening on the tweed couch while Dominick laid the final bass tracks against Evan's drums, an up-tempo pattern that seeped from Dom's headphones and out into the studio silence. Gavin was at the mixing board. It was a secondhand 16-channel console with all the band instruments abbreviated on strips of masking tape tacked alongside the corresponding slide controls.

Gavin sat bobbing his head as he listened, making occasional adjustments to the volume and equalizing while my mother chopped up the last of the Tar she'd purchased from Quint. She liked his dope. It wasn't as sticky as what she'd gotten from Skyliner Knox; it had a crumblier consistency, which was easier to combine with the B12 and a small amount of water. But she was running low now, and no one had been able to get in touch with Quint for two days. Gavin was a strict marijuana connoisseur, and he had a variety of contacts for that, but none of them dealt in anything heavier than Ecstasy or acid, so Bryce had been on a mission to either find another dealer, or get to the bottom of Quint having gone completely off the radar.

"If he got busted, we're fucked," Bryce muttered, the cordless phone in his hand. He sat holding it against his forehead, thinking.

My mother mashed up the mounded concoction on the plate in her lap. She dribbled another drop of water onto it and covered that with a daub of the crushed B12. "If he did, then we'll just smoke weed till he turns up. Or until you find somebody else. It'll be a step down, but no big deal."

Bryce grunted. "Yeah, sure. Let you tell it. It's not gonna be that simple." He dialed another number and rested his head in his palm while he waited for someone to pick up. After a while somebody answered, and he asked a few quick and coded questions. Whomever it was, left him with the promise to call back within a half hour. He hung up and breathed an uneasy sigh.

Mom scraped the dope onto the Two of Spades and offered it over, but he shook his head. "You should take me up on it while I'm willing to share." She grinned and waited a moment, then shrugged a shoulder and sniffed it off the corner of the card.

"I had a dose that'll last me a while tonight, and I've got enough to get me through tomorrow. Maybe," Bryce mumbled. "Snorting it's a fucking waste of money, anyway." He sat back against the cushions and watched Matt do a bump off the tabletop, and he shook his head at that. "And you wonder why you guys are spending more on that shit in a week than I spend on my part of the rent."

"We split it," Matt said, "so the economic burden isn't all on one person. Just like the rent."

"Yeah, well. It's your money," Bryce said. "A hundred bucks a week for a substandard high, if you ask me. I spend half that much for twice the ride." He nodded down to the dope on the coffee table. "You'll go through that by the end of tonight, mark my words. And then you'll be assed out till we score again, which probably—"

The phone rang. Bryce sprang from the couch with the receiver to his ear. Mom and Matt listened, waited.

Dominick dropped into a seat in the folding chair beside the couch, his bass leaning upright against his knees. He glanced at the plate of cheese and shook his head. "You'd be better off railing a pile a dirt from a radioactive landfill. You know that, right?"

"And you'd do well to cut a few Big Macs outa your weekly diet," Matt told him.

"That and a couple packs of Twinkies," Mom added, smiling, and Matt slapped fives with her.

Dom lit a cigarette and blew a thin stream into the air, then a series of smoke rings that Evan poked with his finger as he came over and sat on the couch beside Mom.

"My guess is a little diglyceride and some Yellow Number 5 don't even run a close second to all the anesthetics and coenzymes in that shit," Dom said. "You could set an entire pharmacy on fire, snort the ashes, and have nearly the same damn thing."

"And the fact that they cut it with a vitamin is pretty ironic, too,

I think." Evan gave my mother a strange glance and sat twirling his drumstick like a baton trick.

"Better than a sleeping pill or an Oxycontin," Matt said. "Kill yourself quick like that, way too much depressant if you don't measure it out right. What's a B12 gonna do? Nothin."

"The equivalent of a protein shake with one of my double bacon burgers," Dom said. "Keep shoving that shit up your noses, and see what happens."

"She plays like a beast on it, though," Sandro finally added. "Both of 'em do." He was kneeling on the floor, restringing his bass, pulling the steel cords through the eyelets in the bridge and snipping the ends with a wire cutter. "Not my drug of choice, but whatever works, whatever enhances your creative process."

"I won't argue that," Evan said. "If it gets the job done, then cool. It's just hella risky is all. But so's sword swallowing, paragliding. Do your thing, just know the hazards of the hobby's all I'm saying."

"And you've been saying that since August," Mom mumbled. "You, Dom, Rachel, all of you a bunch of mother hens. You'd all do well to mind your own habits."

"Hey, it's all done outa love," Gavin said from the mixing board. He rolled to the end of the console in the captain's chair and adjusted the levels on Evan's drums. "One man's peril is another woman's Godsend, so we plead our cases with caution and leave the rest up to fate." He gestured over his shoulder to Bryce, who was still on the phone. "I stopped riding his ass about that shit three years ago. He's his own man. I've got no say in how he gets his kicks, so long as it never conflicts with the band, and it never has." He lifted his shoulders and held up empty palms in resignation. "Simple as that. Do what you do, until what you do becomes a problem for the heads around you. I've got no judgment otherwise, 'cause who the hell am I? Just a man with his own problems."

Dom tapped his ashes and eyed my mother sideways as she dumped the last of the hammer into a little one-ounce zip-lock. "Well, you're a better man than me," he muttered and turned to Mom. "I'm taking his stance on this—do what you want, but if it interferes with the band, I'm putting my size eleven up both your asses."

Mom smiled at that, and she laughed a little as she sealed the baggie. "You should know better than to flirt with me. I'm not nearly your type."

"It was nonsexual, believe me."

"As if that's even possible for you." She looked at him with a grin, but he wasn't smiling, and so she rolled her eyes. "Okay, okay. A colonoscopy with a size eleven Wallabee. Got it."

Bryce got off the phone, and my mother and Matt gave him an inquiring glance, and he shook his head.

"Nothin. This kid up in Northfield said he heard Quint was at Denver County, couldn't get around a roadblock out on Colfax and got popped by the po-po's, so that's just beautiful." He thought on it some more with a heavy sigh. "I'm really not trying to go sniffing around for some crackhead homeless fucker to hook me up. They always want a bag, too. Goddamned vultures."

"So, you don't know anybody else?" Matt relaxed back against the sofa and told him, "Looks like we'll be going on a field trip tomorrow, then. I've done open-air cops for coke and weed. Boston's got lots of little spots to score, and sometimes you just gotta do what you gotta do. The hookers are usually pretty wise and don't tend to rip you off. I dunno how they are out here. Might have to wait a while for her to score, probably share a little, but it's better than bein all dry and pissed off."

Mom lit a cigarette and fanned away the smoke. "You guys make that trip if you want, but I'm out. Rache would have my head on a spike if she found out I was cruising the Denver whores for H. I'll put in for mine, give you guys some gas money, and you can get me an eightball or something. But other than that, it's a no go for me. I'll smoke blunts with Evan and Dom in the meantime. I'll be fine."

There was a knock at the stairwell door, and Rachel called up into the studio. She stepped lightly up the stairs and peeked around at everyone.

"Hi. The droplight was off, so I figured it was okay to come on up." She was still wearing her black server apron with the order book stuffed into the pocket. She shed her jacket and sat in my mother's lap, smelling of beer and fries and the stale nicotine of a long night waiting bar top tables for two dollars an hour, but she'd made eighty bucks in tips and slipped them from the flap of the order pad and put them in her pocket.

She kissed Mom's lips, smiled, and ran a hand through her ringlets. That's when she saw my mother's pupils reduced to the size of pencil leads, and her smile wilted into something pensive, disenchanted. She made a casual search around the coffee table, at the cigar guts and pot seeds and empty Budweiser cans, the cigarette lighters and two overflowing ashtrays. Then her eyes fell upon the heroin-silted dessert plate, the razor blade, and vitamin B container, Bryce's blue rubber tourniquet band and charred silver teaspoon with the 29 gauge hypodermic needle lying beside it, the tip snapped over as confession to its earlier use.

"So, how was work?" Mom asked, pulling her close.

Rachel forced another smile. She took Mom's cigarette and dragged on it. "Work was fine."

She looked around again at Bryce's rigs on the table and tried not to glance at my mother's arms, but concern and curiosity drew her eyes like compass needles to the North Pole. They looked unscathed, smooth, and tanned and intact, but for the reddish streaks where she'd been scratching them.

"How's the tape coming?"

"Almost there." Mom plucked the cigarette from between Rachel's fingers and took a hit, gave it back. "We should be ready to mix everything down by tomorrow, might take a few nights. Then we'll ship it to Freiburg on Monday, hopefully hear something back by the end of next week, see what he says." She lifted her brows and smiled, bounced her on her knees a little. "It's gettin close." Giant picture windows and laughing children and shopping sprees glinted in her eyes.

Rachel said nothing. She kissed my mother's forehead and listened to the latest track punching the studio monitors on the shelf above the mixing board, where Gavin sat twisting the channel knobs and adjusting the release envelope on Evan's snare drum.

He motioned to my mother. "All right, you're up, superstar. I wanna lay the rest of your tracks now 'cause they're the most complicated."

Rachel let her up and Mom navigated around Evan's drum kit and came to the mic. "Are you trying to say I'm an EQ nightmare? *Me?*" She took the guitar from the stand and held it up by the neck. "With *this* thing?" She threw the strap over a head full of curls. "Can't be any worse than Jimi was for his engineer."

Gavin pointed at her and laughed. "I'm sure *you* are a pleasure in comparison. You got the right instrument, 'cept yours is tuned. All you need now is a shitty ground, smoke yourself a spliff, and have at it. Oh, and don't forget to stand right in front of the amp, but lemme bust a few holes in it first, and you'll be golden." He gave her a big smile and a wink. "I can see you've got a nice buzz going, so we're halfway there already."

"Oh, I'm all the way there, Mr. Soundman," she said with a flirtatious grin, but it was just the dope pooling around the pleasure centers of her brain, creative anticipation like the smell of a chocolate bar, just before it melts on the palate.

Gavin laughed and played along with the kind of look he might normally save for Naomi, but he and my mother were very comfortable with each other now, and it was all just an enticing platonic game of artistic encouragement. The others were chatting amongst themselves in the background, and so he held up a hand to silence everyone as my mother donned the headphones.

He gave her a nod. "So, you ready?"

"Hell, that's my line. Are *you* ready?"

"Ready for you to blow my mind, baby girl, do all them beautiful thangs I like." He double checked the recording levels and cued up the tape. "And we're rollin."

There was a little digital beat count, and then the music began, but the end of their conversation was inadvertently recorded and left as a candid preface to the song my mother called "Behind Closed Doors," track number six on the CD I'd gotten from Rachel.

THEY RECORDED AND mixed until six a.m. Rachel had fallen asleep on the couch with Evan and Matt. Sandro and Bryce had gone downstairs to bed as well, and Dom followed not long after and headed to the basement den, which had been converted into a makeshift bedroom for the Portland Downs guys, so Mom and Rachel could have the privacy of the Fleetwood.

The studio was stale and stuffy with eight hours of lingering cigarette and pot smoke, quiet, only the hum of the equipment fans and the final song chugging lowly through the monitor speakers. My mother and Gavin conferred at the mixing console, digging in for the last stretch as the morning sun crept through the single attic window, making all the dust sparkle.

"If we clean up the low end of the Strat," Mom suggested as Gavin adjusted the reverb, "then we should have enough sound space for the bass and kick drum, and the guitar won't be so thin."

"Takes a minute to find that sweet spot. Be patient. We've been at this since yesterday, so a little while longer to get it in the pocket's not gonna kill us." He listened for another moment, tweaked the mid-range knob on the guitar track and chuckled at what he heard. "You and those classical chord inversions. You can take the woman away from the orchestra, but you'll never get Vivaldi out of her system."

"Creates more space, fills out the sound, I think. Nice and wide and full." She smiled at him. "I like space, if you hadn't noticed, lots of room to improvise freely."

"And that, you do. I dunno how your fingers don't get cramped, doin all that shit for ten, fifteen minutes straight. Three-and-four-step bends around all that finger stretching? Hell, even I gotta take a break and drop back into rhythm guitar for a while, or I'll start gettin sloppy."

My mother shrugged that off. "I cheat a lot, do lots of tricks to make it sound more complicated than it really is. Smoke and mirrors, babe. That's all it is." She trained her ear on the mix and frowned. "Are you sure my B string isn't outa tune? Keeps sounding flat to me, but I'm tired and high, so it might just be my imagination."

He switched on a hi-pass filter, which would give the guitar more clarity among the percussion sounds and listened, then muted the rest of the instruments to isolate the Fender altogether and listened some more. He shook his head. "Sounds all right to me, but you could hear a dog whistle in a windstorm, so you decide. If it is, no one else on earth'll hear it, nobody normal, anyway."

Mom thought about that, then waved it away. "If it's not glaring, then whatever. I'm not redoing that shit. Twenty hours of recording, just for the guitar? There's no time to fix it now, so I'll just have to leave it between me and God. Carry on, maestro."

The stairwell door opened, and Naomi came upstairs, dressed in her hospital scrubs.

"Damn. All work and no play, you guys." She laughed, then noticed Evan, Matt, and Rachel asleep on the couch, and she cringed with a guilty wince. "Sorry," she whispered and walked gingerly to the console to give Gavin a kiss. "I just wanted to stop in before I left for work."

"I dunno how you do it," Mom said to her. "Sleep so soundly with the floors rumbling all night, then wake up all chipper and sunny. You must sleep like Evan. As soon as his eyes close, he goes completely deaf. It's remarkable." And she gestured back to the couch where he slept sitting up, openmouthed and snoring with Rachel curled in a ball at the end of the cushions, sock feet tucked under his thigh. "See? Comatose."

"Believe me, it took seven years to adjust. Now it's like living next to a fire station or the train tracks. After a while you just don't hear it, anymore." She turned to Gavin. "Tell Bryce I'll have some new rigs for him tonight. The charge nurse, the one who hates me, has been lurking around the med room a lot lately, but she's on vacation this week, so I can probably get a hundred-count box. Just tell him it'll be fifty, and he can pay me tonight." She gave him another kiss. "I'll see you around five. And don't burn yourselves out up here. Take a break, get some sleep. It's flu season," she reminded them. "If you get run down, you'll be leaving yourselves wide open."

"Yes, ma'am," Gavin said. "We'll wrap it up in a minute. Have a good day, and be careful with that shit, baby. Watch your back. You know how those fourth floor bitches can be, smile in your face and slice you open at the same time. Just cover your ass. Fifty bucks ain't worth your job. Bryce'll figure things out for himself if he has to, find his own damn needles."

"I know what I'm doing," she told him from the top of the stairs and left them to finish their work, but they were both exhausted, and so they agreed to pick it back up after dinner and get a few hours sleep in the meantime.

Gavin headed downstairs, and Mom went over to the couch and shook Rachel's shoulder. "Come on, baby. Let's go to the camper," she whispered.

Rachel groaned and stretched and opened a sleepy brown eye that caught the sunlight through the attic window. "What time is it?"

"Almost six. Come on."

"In the morning?" Rachel rubbed her face and blinked at the daylight. "Jeezus, you guys."

"Yeah, I know. But we're almost done." Mom slipped an arm under Rachel's neck and lifted her upright, then slapped at Evan's leg and shoved Matt to rouse him as well. "Dudes. Go to bed. We're done up here." She shoved them both again. "Let's go. Unless you two wanna spoon here on the couch. Not my place to judge."

Matt gave her the finger.

Evan yawned, then swallowed uncomfortably and rubbed his throat. "Smoked entirely too much Buddha last night. Damned Colorado weed is harsh as shit."

"Might be the heat up here, too," Mom told him. "My head's startin to hurt, guess I'm just sleepy." She helped Rachel to her feet and kissed her temple, and they headed downstairs and out through the chilly morning to the warmth of the Fleetwood.

MY MOTHER SLEPT restlessly that day. She couldn't get comfortable, and she itched all over as if lying in a patch of poison oak, so much that it woke Rachel twice, once to find her stretched out horizontally across the bed with an arm contorted in an impossible position behind her own neck. Rachel helped her back to the proper side of the bed and nuzzled up next to her. The second time, my mother was talking nonsense in her sleep; she never did that.

When Rachel woke her, she was disoriented and confused. She thought she was still up in the studio and didn't know how she'd gotten to the sleeper until Rachel jogged her memory and tucked her back in again. And that was how the hours passed, disrupted and poorly slept, waking each other until exhaustion finally prevailed, but by then it was nearly lunchtime.

BRYCE HAD GONE into the city after he woke up at noon. He went alone. He couldn't take my mother or Matt because they were unfamiliar faces, which would only hinder his search and create unnecessary suspicion among the street dealers downtown. He came back three hours later with bad news, said he wasn't able to score. "Fucking dry as hell out there," was all he offered as consolation. He gave their money back, then wandered off to his room to wait by the phone.

Rachel had the night off, and she wanted to go grocery shopping for something to make for dinner. Gavin and Naomi had been good hosts. They'd fed Portland Downs on their own dime too often for Rachel to ignore, and she wanted to return the favor with a shrimp pasta recipe she'd found in the back of a food magazine, so she and my mother made a midafternoon trip to Safeway.

Mom sat in the 4Runner's passenger seat, shuffling through the last of their food money, and she shoved it into her coat pocket and tried to focus on the rush hour traffic along Colorado Boulevard, suffering through a dreadful headache that had started last night and was steadily progressing into something worse. Evan had complained of fatigue the previous day, and he said his throat still hurt that afternoon, so now everyone was popping Ibuprofen and Vitamin C and trying to stay away from one another as the winter pathogens came calling.

Mom rested her head on the SUV window, crossed her arms at her chest, and knitted her brow against the pounding in her skull. She sneezed and cringed at the pain, then sank back into the seat with a miserable frown.

Rachel gave her a glance at the next red light. "While we're there, we'll get you some flu medicine or something. You had a pretty bad night last night."

Mom nodded, didn't say anything.

"Naomi jinxed everyone, talked it up." Rachel tried to laugh a little, hoping to draw my mother out of a funk.

Mom just scowled at the late gray afternoon, the Denver sky like a dirty bedsheet stretched and darkening over the city, everything rigid and cold and monochrome. They might as well have been living on the moon.

"I think Matt might be catching it, too," Rachel said. "He feels as shitty as you, hasn't come up from the den all day since Bryce got back. Damn weather." The light changed, and they pulled off toward the grocery store, just a few blocks ahead. "So far I've been okay, but I'm still probably infecting everyone at King's. Customers, too."

Mom was quiet. She cracked the passenger window, checked the heater setting on the dash, and pushed the temperature slide into the blue. "Fucking hot in here."

Rachel reached a hand across to Mom's forehead, then down under her hair to the back of her neck. "Dammit," she muttered. "You've got a fever, babe. We'll make this quick." She made a left and turned into the lot. "Looks like it'll be chicken soup and crackers for you tonight, no milk products, they sour in your stomach when you have a fever and make you nauseated, so my mother always said."

She found a spot by the cart return port and shut off the engine, then peered at Mom again who just sat there, recoiled into herself, brow furrowed in an uncomfortable knot, her arms folded tight with her head against the window. She sneezed again.

"You wanna just wait out here?" Rachel asked. "I won't be long, I promise."

My mother mulled it over. Now that the heat was off, she felt suddenly cold and was beginning to shiver, so she wrangled herself into a slouch and dropped a hand onto the door latch. "I'll go. Gonna freeze to death out here if I don't."

"You sure? You were just hot a minute ago."

"Yeah, come on."

"You don't look good, baby."

"I'm okay. Let's just go, get it over with. Please." Mom opened the door and climbed out.

The late autumn breeze was like a volley of carpenter nails. It was coming on quick now, after nothing but a jackhammer headache and some mild nausea all afternoon. She found herself thinking back to when she was a teenager, lying on the living room couch in Bensalem, plagued by the same symptoms, Nanna Sylvia sitting at the edge of the cushions with a cold rag and a box of tissues in her hand, waiting for the thermometer to register. And for the first time in almost a year, my mother was beginning to miss her.

INSIDE, THEY WERE ambushed by fluorescent lights and crying children and Muzak. Shopping carts crashed and clattered like animals rattling cages, and no one was paying attention to where they walked or stopped or reached. Couples called out grocery items to each other from across the aisles while they checked their scribbled lists, bumping into my mother who stood propped on the mini-cart Rachel had grabbed from the entrance.

"We'll check the medicine aisle first," Rachel said. "Get you guys something for that crud."

Mom followed her through the store, past the canned goods and pet foods, the endcap displays with Rubbermaid sets on sale, around the flower racks and down onto the row where all the antihistamines and laxatives and arthritis remedies lined the shelves, a dozen choices for every ailment. An anonymous and terrible rendition of "I Love You Just the Way You Are" played from the intercom speaker overhead, all saxes and flutes replacing the vocals. My mother leaned on the cart and laid her head in the crook of her arm.

Rachel smoothed a hand across her back. "Hang in there, sweetie. We'll get you fixed up."

She was reading over the back of a Theraflu box, and she tossed it into the cart. Then she stopped and looked at Mom and frowned. She felt up under Mom's jacket again. Her thermal shirt was damp and clammy, and she pulled the curls from Mom's face, glistening with sweat.

"I'm getting a thermometer while we're here," Rachel said. "You're drenched. Why didn't you tell me you were feeling this bad, baby? I wouldn't have dragged you out here with me."

"I wasn't," Mom mumbled into her sleeve with a sniffle, and she sneezed again. "It crept up on me. Are we almost done? I'm freezing." She straightened up and buried her hands in her coat pockets and stood scowling at all the noise, the obnoxious lighting, the cashiers' echoing announcements for price checks, interrupting the bad music that made her head ring like a bell.

"Yeah." Rachel chose a bottle of Tylenol, some Pepto-Bismol for nausea, and a digital thermometer from the end of the aisle. Mom pushed the cart.

Things were beginning to lose their shapes, the colors bleeding and fuzzy; someone turned up the air conditioning to rival the Antarctic tundra while at the same time following her with a heat lamp bearing down like a spotlight.

Rachel threw two cans of chicken noodle soup into the cart. A woman pushed past them, chasing a small boy, didn't apologize. Rachel scanned the shelves, then headed to the produce section, talked about antibiotics and ginger root tea and dropped a netted bag of oranges next to the soup cans. She found a box of penne noodles, three aisles over. Two jars of mushroom Alfredo, way down next to the spice racks.

My mother's head throbbed. She tried to focus, to deal with her sudden misery like a trooper. But the more Rachel walked and talked and made selections and promised relief, the more my mother thought about Bryce, and Quint, and Matt. Rachel said something about Lysol, and Mom could've sworn she smelled vinegar, tasted it, even, in the back of her throat.

She was growing despondent as they moved on to the frozen food section, where Rachel grabbed a bag of peeled shrimp from the freezer, and it hit the metal basket with a crunch that sounded like bones breaking. My mother hated this, whatever it was, the aching, the chills, the incessant sneezing, her stomach sour and swimmy. She wanted to be back at the bungalow, warm and snug and comfortable again, relaxing in the studio on the pleasantly scratchy tweed sofa, their amazing new music swirling around the rafters while she laughed and talked with Gavin about pentatonic scales and beautiful women, a joint in one hand, the Two of Spades in the other. It was starting to be all she could think about.

" . . . so, did you wanna just do that, or do you wanna wait and see if the tea works first?"

"What?" Mom looked at Rachel, vacant and bewildered; it was as if she'd just appeared there from some other life entirely.

Rachel held up the box of Theraflu. "The medicine, baby. Did you want this before your soup, or a cup of ginger root first?" She shifted her weight and gave my mother a very long and critical stare. "Do we need to take you to the ER?" she finally asked. "I don't like this. You are totally out of it. I should've left you at the house."

"No," Mom grunted. "No emergency rooms. I'm okay. Just sick. Ready to go. Can we go? Please?"

"Come on." She took my mother's arm and guided her to the checkout stand.

WHEN THEY GOT back to Fillmore, Rachel quarantined my mother to the Fleetwood where she took her temperature, 101.8. She tucked Mom into bed and turned the heat on through the RV generator, then prepared a bowl of chicken soup and a steaming cup of Theraflu. She brought it all to the sleeper on a lap table and placed it straddling Mom's thighs where she lay sweating and shivering under the new comforter.

"I'm not hungry," Mom grumbled, hugging herself.

"Then drink the tea. I'll get you some orange juice, too. You have to stay hydrated if you're not gonna eat."

Mom heaved a deep and miserable sigh and shook her head, but she took the mug to her lips with a little sip and made a face, twisted and bitter. "Christ, this shit is awful." She glared sourly into the cup and set it on the table. She snatched a tissue from the box on the bed, sneezed into it, blew her nose.

"Probably means it works," Rachel said and combed a damp wayward ringlet from my mother's eyes, then went to the refrigerator and filled a Styrofoam cup with orange juice, and she brought it back to the bed. "Drink this with it. It'll kill the taste, but drink all of that, too." She pointed to the medicine. "You're not gonna get any better just riding this out. You know that." She took a cool rag she had put on the nightstand and ran it down and around my mother's face and neck. "I'll check your temperature in another hour, see if the Tylenol helped."

"You are so lucky you don't feel like this," Mom said through a stuffy nose, settling back into the blankets with a shudder. "I say, give it twenty-four hours, and you'll be right here next to me. Just how long can you stay immune with this shit going around?"

"As long as I'm okay to see about you, then that's what I'm gonna do." Rachel took the cup of medicine from the table and held it to my mother's lips again. "Come on. Drink up. It tastes worse when it's cold." Mom waved it away and turned onto her side. "Baby, don't be like this. I know you feel like shit, but—"

"I just want this to *stop*."

"It will if you do something about it."

Mom was quiet for a long moment, lying on her side with her back to Rachel, rocking herself under the comforter. Then she threw it off, mumbled something about being hot, and the downy fabric fell over the lap table and into the soup, nearly knocking the orange juice into the bed with her, but Rachel grabbed it up before it toppled.

"Okay," she announced. "We're not getting anywhere with this." And she lifted the lap tray from the blankets and set it on the floor at her feet.

"I've got shit I need to do," Mom growled into the pillows. "I don't have time for this fucking bullshit. *Why?*" she begged the stars. "Why am I sick *now*? Of all the fucking times. Two weeks left before Freiburg writes us off for good, and I'm on my ass like a goddamned invalid."

"Gavin and Evan can finish the music. You need to take care of you right now."

"Gavin doesn't know what I want. You don't understand. Mixing involves subtleties, nuances, effects. And Evan's not gonna make those decisions without me, neither is Dom. The whole shit's on hold while I'm out here freezing and sweating my ass off, my skull splitting like it's in a motherfucking *vice*!" she rumbled with her arms up at her temples, and she sent a furious, desperate roar into the mattress. "*¡Maldición, chingao!*" Rachel rubbed her back. Mom squirmed away from that. "Please don't do that, baby. Feels like sandpaper. Like some kinda . . . friggin . . . prickly shit."

Rachel rested her hands in her lap and sat there at the edge of the bed, watching her, pitiful and powerless. She shook her head and peered around at the camper, thinking of what she could do to alleviate my mother's suffering, but there was nothing, so she said, "Just give it some time, honey. The first day's the worst."

The camper door opened; it was Dominick. He came in with his sweatshirt pulled up over his mouth and nose, and he frowned at my mother and Rachel. "Just came to get some batteries for my tuner," he said through the fabric. "I'm gonna redo the chorus on 'Comfort Zone.'" He looked at Rachel and tipped his chin to where Mom lay shivering. "She's pretty sick, I see."

"Yep." Rachel blew a noisy, hopeless sigh.

"Why are you redoing 'Comfort Zone'?" Mom questioned wearily, and she twisted around and winced over her shoulder. "What's wrong with the chorus? It was fine."

"I'm clipping at the end of the fourth bar, every time, peaking out. Doesn't sound distorted to me, but Gavin wants it out of the red, so we're redoing it." He rummaged through the gym bag he kept stored in the RV closet, dug out a pack of AA's, and slapped them against his palm. "Won't take long."

But Mom was already wrestling up out of bed. "I need to be up there," she muttered. "Too much going on without me, and I don't like it."

"Jo, it's cool. We got it covered. Just keep your germ-infested ass away from everybody else. I'm already gettin a scratchy throat from Evan, who now has a full-blown head cold full a snot. Sounds like a damn coffee percolator. Lay the hell back down, you look like shit. We got this." He held up a hand, and his sweatshirt collar slipped off his chin. He put it back.

"Yeah, you're not going anywhere," Rachel told my mother, but Mom was on the edge of the bed now, putting her sneakers on. Rachel stood up and watched her, irritated. "Jolán."

"What?"

"What do you mean, what? You're sick as a dog."

"And I need to be in the studio."

"No, you don't. You need to be in *bed*. You need to be drinking fluids and taking medicine and waiting for that fever to break."

Mom tied the other shoe. She stood up wearily. "One day you'll appreciate why this is so important. Our whole future's riding on this album." She lumbered toward the door. *"All of it."*

A car pulled up in front of the RV, a brand new sedan, midnight blue, maybe black; it was difficult to tell in the dark, idling under the streetlight that glared off Betty's windshield. A girl got out. She had a long brown ponytail, wore a bomber jacket and baggy jeans, and the three of them glanced out after her as she headed for the house.

"The demo's gonna be great, don't worry about it," Dominick said to Mom, "just needs some tweaking. Hell, it's already great."

"By whose standards? Gavin's? Sandro's? Naomi's?" Mom snatched up her coat from the table bench and threw it on. "It all comes down to me. I'm supposed to have the ultimate say, not Gavin. He's got a great ear, but this is Portland Downs' project, not his." She sneezed again and held a hand to her pounding forehead, then stepped past him and out into the chilly Denver evening.

Dominick gave Rachel a desultory shrug and headed out after Mom.

INSIDE, THE GIRL with the ponytail stood with Bryce in the kitchen, and she threw a cagey glance to my mother and Dom. She was a white girl, pretty, with a slight olive complexion, maybe mixed with Latino, her lips traced with black liner, eyebrows drawn on thin, like half moons meant to look perpetually happy, but the muscles in her brow creased against them as my mother and Dominick walked through the living room.

Bryce waved them off. "They're cool." Then he said to Mom, "Hey, I fronted you. Just give it to me upstairs, it's fifty." He did a double take as she passed toward the attic stairwell, and he laughed a little. "Yeah, you're gonna thank me."

My mother didn't know what he meant by that. She said nothing as she passed and climbed the attic stairs behind Dominick, drained to the core, the pain in her head pulsing under each heavy step.

In the studio, Gavin was at the console with "Comfort Zone" playing through the monitors, the orange channel lights on the ADAT recorder flashing and zipping up and down to the music. He turned in his chair when Dominick and Mom came upstairs, and he regarded my mother as if she'd been pulled up from the city sewers with a dragnet.

"You should probably take it easy, superstar," he said. "I got your back till you're on your feet again."

She wrapped herself up in her jacket and came to the mixing board. "What's up with the bass track on this?" She gestured to the ADAT machine. "It was fine last week."

"Not really." Gavin pointed to the machine's meter display, a visual screen on the front panel where all the instruments and vocals were separated into their respective channels, much like the EQ monitor on a home stereo. Dom's part was jumping along with everything else, like the puck on a carnival High Striker game, but every so many seconds the orange line flew up past the others and clipped into the red.

"Told you," Dom mumbled as he sank into the couch. He popped open the back of his tuning device, whacked it against his wrist, and dumped out the old batteries.

Mom gazed around at the mixing board for the corresponding channel, thinking perhaps it was a simple fix, that maybe Gavin had the mixer volume too high, but that wasn't it. All the slide controls were well within their proper ranges. She frowned at the board and at the chilly aching shivers beading her brow like condensation on a drinking glass.

"Well, why didn't we see this before? When we were recording? We're wasting time now, redoing his parts." She pressed the button that soloed the bass track and listened to it by itself, and now she could hear the little distorted pops and crackles that had escaped her two weeks ago. "Dammit." She shook her head. "I don't know why I didn't catch this."

"Everything sounds beautiful when you're high, baby girl," Gavin told her, grinning. Bryce was coming up the stairs now, and he pointed over his shoulder at him. "Especially on that shit. It's my bad, too. It got by me, but we're fixing it now, so all is not lost. It's the kinda shit you miss when you get in a hurry." He tied his thick sandy dreads back with a loose hair band and scooted the swivel chair up close to the board, then went to work adjusting the levels for a new take.

Bryce came to the couch and he beckoned my mother over, and so she weaved around the trap set and took a seat. He handed her a cellophane ball, black and shiny as its namesake, about the size of a dime. "Fifty a gram. Took me a minute to get in touch with that chick, but she came through, drove all the way up from Meridian, so be thankful. Quint's gonna be outa pocket for a hot minute, but Lecia's pretty reliable if we make it worth her while." Mom just looked at him. He seemed to be aware of something she was not, and he unwrapped his own piece of dope, looked at her sideways, and gave her a shrug.

"It's not your birthday, is it? You didn't spend the money I gave back this afternoon, did you? When I came back from the city? I mean, you're cool and all, but hey." Mom shook her head, and so he held out his hand. "Okay, then. Fifty bones. I got Matt's, too, so you might wanna get him up here from the den." He gave her a second look and mumbled, "Nevermind, fuck that. I'll get him. You're in a lot worse shape than me." He gestured down to the Tar in her hand. "Theraflu ain't gonna help shit when you're hurtin. Not when you're dope sick." He saw her empty puzzled expression, and so he explained. "Where do you think all that sneezin and chills and body aches are comin from? It's withdrawals, babe. Your last hit was like a day ago; those are the first signs." He pointed down to the dope again. "You best get to choppin that shit up if you wanna feel any better at all."

Mom glanced at Dominick who sat listening. He saw her looking at him from the corner of his eye, but he said nothing and wouldn't acknowledge her now. He just kept twisting the tuning pegs on his instrument, thumbing the strings, watching the little tuner light blip from red to green. His silence was a punch in the gut, the "I told you so" that needed no words.

Mom nevertheless pulled her wallet from her coat pocket and handed over two twenties and a ten that Bryce shoved into his jeans.

"I'll be back," he said and trotted downstairs to get Matt.

My mother just sat there, sniffing, shivering, rolling the little ball of hammer in her palm. She hesitated only because Bryce's words were flying around in her head like bats in a cave, startling and nonsensical, because it couldn't possibly have been so. She had gone days on end in the past without touching it, without even thinking about it, soaring over the desert in hot air balloons and going to the movies and making love every day until noon, satisfied with her own endorphins sedating her in the afterglow.

She'd kept a half gram of it unopened in her guitar case for over a week, for Christ's sake, she knew her limits, but somehow the boundaries had shifted and slipped so much closer to the quick. She'd blinked, and now her own free will was straggling behind her on the other side of some threshold she didn't even know she'd crossed.

She stared at the dope and held it between her fingers, something so small, demanding access to the neurotransmitters in her brain, begging for a ride on those receptor cells, looking to surf the reward pathways right up into everything good and contented again. Her headache was already beginning to subside just gazing at the stuff, one mind subduing the other, unequally matched from the start, like that boy and the looming biblical giant, only in this version Goliath lifts his massive foot and stomps the boy into the ground before he can even think about a slingshot.

Dominick stood in the center of the room, headphones on, his bass shouldered and tuned. My mother was quiet about crushing up the B12, did it on the coffee tabletop and scooped it onto the plate with the edge of her palm, dabbled it with a splash of water she fished out with her fingertips from yesterday's glass.

Dom was about to begin, but the downstairs door opened, and they waited for Bryce, Matt, and Evan to come up. Matt looked like an afflicted hostage, hair greasy and pasted to his flushed and glossy forehead, mouth drawn in awe of how wretched he felt, and he eased himself down into the cushions beside her. They shared a glance that said more than they'd ever anticipated when they started this venture back in Boston, sitting together like this on his apartment sofa at Berklee, sharing a joint with the classifieds spread open and Dominick bitching about travel costs. Neither of them said a word. What was there to say now?

Matt went to work on his own purchase while Evan plugged in the droplight. Bryce took a seat and began cooking up a dose with a lighter and a clean spoon from the kitchen.

"All right, folks, we're live," Gavin said from the captain's chair.

Dom kept his back to everything, focused on the music buzzing through the headphones, his bass plunking along under the gentle hiss of Bryce's Bic lighter while Mom and Matt worked quietly on their dope with the focus of explosive technicians disarming a time bomb.

Mom chipped off a bit more than a tenth, more than she normally did, because she needed it to work; she had no choice, as the symptoms would only worsen and leave her writhing in a very dark and treacherous place. She had hers ready first, and she gathered the improvised powder into a tiny mound, slipped it onto the corner of the card, leaned down and railed it up into the left nostril. Relief was on its way. The chills had even begun to wane, or at least she thought so, but it was likely psychosomatic, not enough time for the real remedy, but it was remedy enough, and she sat back and waited and watched Matt chop and slice and scoop and dribble until he had the same perfect blend.

That was when the waves began. The sun on her face again, at last. The sun glowing inside, warming away the shudders that had rattled her jaws from the produce section to the RV sleeper. The punishing headache had vanished and the nausea was draining away, as if she had only dreamt about all that, and she could breathe easily again. She laid her head back against the tweed cushions and settled in, dismissing the notions of her better mind that told her what a fool she'd been for making this pact, this blood contract with Mexican poison, that the only escape clause now was written in braille because she'd entered into it with her eyes wide open and still didn't see this coming.

Bryce was seated at the end of the couch beside Evan, and Mom could smell the tart caustic solution steaming in the spoon now, and so she sat up with her elbows on her knees and watched him. He had a little pea-sized ball of cotton on the table, and he dropped that onto the spoon, then placed the needle tip into the cotton and drew the dope up into the barrel, a translucent amber, like cream soda or cider. He tied himself off at the biceps with the blue medical band, felt around a while for an ideal spot, eased the needle into his forearm, deliberate and steady, right between the metallic alien tendons, and a bright burgundy plume whirled up into the barrel. He exhaled a little, relaxed and pushed the plunger and sent it all back into the vein, then released the rubber tourniquet, and it jumped off his arm and fell away into the couch cushions.

My mother had half seen him do this on occasion, but until now she had always been distracted with recording and producing Portland Downs' new material. She took a cigarette from the pack in her pocket and lit it, watched Bryce closely for the effects while Dominick slapped at the bass strings and Matt snuggled into his corner of the couch with his feet propped on the table edge, comfortable as she now.

The middling rush she'd gotten from her own hit had already begun to plateau, but she was still worlds away from the cruelty of that afternoon, so disappointment seemed a bit like ingratitude. Bryce's eyes fell shut with just enough time to pull the needle from his arm, toss it to the coffee table, and wipe away the blood that started a tiny runnel over his tattoo. He sat back and went utterly flaccid, arms heavy at his sides, his cobalt blue eyes shut and shifting behind the lids. It looked orgasmic, but she knew enough now to let her imagination expound greatly upon that. She thought about the best sex she and Rachel had ever had, in the Fleetwood, right there in the driveway out front. She was high on smack that night, too, and Rachel knew it and seemed to be competing with it, eager to surpass its brilliance in a race for my mother's pleasure centers, and she came quite close, a photo finish loss to the dopamine spike that would eventually become my mother's insatiable, barefaced mistress.

After a long while Bryce opened his eyes, heavy lidded and glassy. He saw my mother looking at him, and he smiled a little. "Feelin better?"

Mom nodded.

"You're welcome," he muttered and sat listening to Dominick's bass licks.

Mom puffed her cigarette and wondered where Bryce's head was at, if he was somewhere happy to be disconnected and drifting around between sedation and reality. His chin dropped to his chest as the dope pounded him into blissful submission all over again. That was when my mother began to realize that the race car she thought she'd been driving all this time was really just the Pole Position cockpit at a fifty-cent arcade. And she'd been paying twenty bucks a ride. Just how long could she keep that up? And why would she?

Now she had a hundred different things to consider. She had gotten herself into this addicted predicament, but it was too late and too pointless for reprimands, so what to do? The thought was killing her buzz, and she considered waiting until she was sober to figure it all out, but that was the complicated catch—she understood now that complete sobriety was something at the far end of a minefield, something way out at the clear and sunny edge of a hurricane, something locked away in a glass booby-trapped case; reach for it at your own risk, or lose a hand to the swinging blade.

FOR THE NEXT couple of hours Bryce went in and out of touch, then eventually grew bored with the studio and excused himself to his room. Dominick had finished recording and found conversation with Evan, and he ignored my mother and Matt who were both quite content with that and listened instead to the fresh new version of "Comfort Zone" bumping the monitors.

To Mom, Dominick's cold shoulder didn't seem to matter much now, and she liked that. She enjoyed the patience of being high, a smooth and level kind of apathy that left her thoroughly at peace with herself. Like a sieve that filtered out all the external irritations and kept her from telling Dominick what a condescending, self-righteous prick she thought he was, that she could buy an island with the money he'd spent on blow in the time she'd known him. She wasn't at all inspired to point out his hypocrisies, had no desire to tell him that if it weren't for her and Matt lobbying to make this trip in the first place, he'd still be gazing at his dorm room rock posters and nowhere near a meeting with executives from Geffen Records. She left all criticism and angst behind the black sticky veil between herself and the world of shit she was in, now that the dope had begun to taper off, cracking the door to reality again and forcing her to re-dose.

She unsealed the single-ounce baggie she'd prepared earlier and poured out a bigger hit than last time, but then she hesitated. She did a quick calculation of the gear she had left against the rate at which she'd been using it, and the math was suddenly preposterous at fifty bucks a day, three hundred dollars a week. And the high seemed to have incredibly short legs, only an hour, maybe two before it waned and sputtered out. She could up the amount, but that would only deplete her supply, and by morning she'd be rattling all over again, sweating and fiending in a fetal ball until Lecia got around to making another trip up from Meridian, then re-up, chop another rail, rinse, and repeat.

Portland Downs had a gig in two days at a place in Aurora called The Sound Station for a thousand dollar guarantee, and she made a mental budget of her expenses. A hundred for her part of the rent and studio time, one-fifty for Black. They had food covered through Rachel's tips, but they needed a new generator for Betty, a five hundred dollar investment for which Mom agreed to go half, since she and Rachel were using it most. She had a credit card in Pap's name, a two thousand dollar limit, but she hadn't used it yet for fear he'd be tracking her around the country along a paper trail; if she wanted my grandparents to know where she was, she'd call them herself. Rachel wouldn't go in on a micro-crumb of heroin, wouldn't put up a single wooden nickel for the stuff, and so my mother had to make an economic decision to stretch this new habit into something she alone could afford. It wasn't going to be popular, but no one was putting it to a vote, either.

She nudged Matt's knee to rouse him from a pleasant doze, and he opened an eye.

"I'll be back," she said, and he scooted aside to let her through.

DOWNSTAIRS, THE HOUSE was quiet. She could hear the TV in Naomi and Gavin's room as she passed, the Late Night monologue, something about the presidential election, the audience laughed and applauded. My mother went down the hall, then knocked on Bryce's door. There was music playing on the other side, but she couldn't place the artist until he opened up.

"What's up?" Bryce left the door standing open with an unspoken invitation and dropped back onto the unmade bed, a cigarette dangling from his lips. He'd been thumbing through a music magazine, and he grabbed it back up from the rumpled covers. "You guys done up there already?"

Mom shook her head, stood in the doorway. Sonic Youth's *Evol* album drummed lowly through the detachable stereo speakers. "Nah. Still a lot to do yet."

Bryce flipped through the pages, nodded, took a drag from his Newport, and flicked the ashes into an empty drink can on the nightstand. He looked up at her again. "Demo's almost done. You gotta be pretty stoked. Maybe a bit overwhelmed? Needed to get outa there for a minute?"

Mom smiled a little. "Yeah, guess so."

Neither of them said anything for a long moment. My mother just stood in the doorway while Bryce glanced through his magazine. The song changed to "Shadow of a Doubt," metallic and haunting with a heartbeat drum track. Mom came inside and shut the door behind her. Bryce gave her a peculiar look, and so she thought she'd better state her business, get to it before he got the wrong idea.

"I want you to dose me up," she said.

Bryce didn't respond to that. He just looked at her, and so she gestured to the IV rig on the nightstand to make herself clear. Bryce went back to his magazine, toked his cigarette, and blew a nicotine cloud up into the spackled ceiling. He dropped the butt into the soda can and perused the pages, quietly turning that over in his head.

"I wouldn't ask if I hadn't thought it through," my mother said. "Been thinking on it all night."

"Is that so?"

"I can handle it. I'm sure I can."

"You'll kill yourself."

"That's why I came to you. I want you to do it, show me how."

Bryce still hadn't looked up from the magazine. He turned another page. "You're on a slippery slope, Jo, askin for that," he said after a moment. "It'll redefine everything you thought you knew about smack. It's a giant fucking leap from just snorting that shit."

"Well, it's a leap I need to take. I'm already screwed, as you probably figured out, so it's not like I can get outa this now. Not without a time machine, anyway. I don't guess you've got one of those?"

Bryce smiled, laughed a little. "Nope. Sure as hell wish I did, though, and so will you."

"This is hard enough, dude, asking like this," she said. "Don't make me feel like a dumbass."

"Hell, I won't have to. Lady Black'll do that well enough on her own if you give her your blood, let her under your skin. She's a beautiful two-timing bitch, take you to a place you'll love, and hate, and love to hate, and hate that you love it so fucking much. Round and round we go. And where it stops . . ." He shrugged, turned another page.

"Okay, and so what about you? You function. You work, hold down a job at Sam Goody's, keep up with your band, pay your bills." Mom wandered further into the room and stood leaning against the dresser. "How bad can it really be?"

"Pretty damned bad. It's a delicate balance, precarious as fuck, actually. Imagine walking a tightrope over the Grand Canyon on a string of dental floss, carrying a bag of cinder blocks. One good glorious binge, and all stability is gone." And he made a little whistling sound, like a bomb dropping, and twirled a finger spiraling downward into the blankets. "It takes a herd of elephants to keep it at bay some days. So far, so good . . . so far." He looked up at her. "You've been pussying around snorting it for only two months, you *and* Matt, and just twenty-four hours dry and you're both hurtin like hell. IVing is a whole other scary ball of shit. You'll regret it. I promise you."

"You said so yourself, railing it's a waste of money. My tolerance is getting higher than I am. I'll need my own Brinks truck parked out front to stay ahead of it, at this rate."

"Well, maybe you'll have just that if Geffen signs you," Bryce said into the magazine pages. "If they don't shelf you, first, let you record an entire album they never intended to release, just to keep up their roster, then write the whole investment off in taxes while you're trapped in a five-year contract."

"Look, I didn't come down here for business tips." Mom sighed. "Are you gonna help me out or not? If not, then just say so, and I'll figure it out myself."

"Jeezus, relax. I didn't say I wouldn't do it. I'm just trying to make sure you know what you're getting yourself into. The shit is complicated, and it's risky. You gotta think about everything from needle gauges to abscesses." He looked up at her and said, "You know, infected injection sites that take huge chunks of your arm before they're done with you. You fuck up—you fuck up *big*. The biggest, of course, being that permanent nod, the one you never wake up from. Short of that, you can blow a shot, miss a vein entirely and all your dope's wasted, not to mention the money you spent. You can jack up your veins for life, catch hepatitis, MRSA, staph, clog your rigs with blood so they're useless at the most critical dope sick moments, all sorts of junkie mishaps."

"You've been lucky then?" Mom tipped her chin to his tattoo. "No tracks, no sores, no diseases. What makes you so invincible? And if snorting it's such a waste, then what was up with the monkey water at Montego's, the first night we met?"

"Slamming in a night club bathroom's inconvenient. And it's ridiculously unsanitary, if you haven't noticed. I keep a bottle with me for gigs on the road, just a bump, a little taste to keep from getting sick between shots before a show, but that's it. The liquid's easier to pass off than powder, and that's what I gave you, a cookie for a toddler." He sat up and rolled back the cuff of his cargo shorts to mid thigh. There was a quarter-sized scar on the inside of his left leg, looked like a bullet wound. "I started mainlining when I was your age, three years ago after a year of just snorting and smoking it. But I didn't want tracks on my arms 'cause I knew I didn't know shit about what I was doing. So, I figured I could hide it better if I used the leg veins. It was fine for the first, I dunno, six or seven shots. But I didn't know I was supposed to rotate injection sites, so one day I skin-popped a hit, missed the vein completely and shot all my gear into the skin instead, and low and behold—a fucking abscess." He smiled and presented the wound with a little hand gesture, like a game show host. "Took a week to get it seen about 'cause I was fucking embarrassed, and two months for it to stop draining and finally scab over. Now, if I wanna impress some chick after a gig, make her think I'm all hard-core and shit, I just tell her I got shot running from the po-po's during a raid." He smirked at that and unrolled his shorts.

"That's the lamest shit I think I've ever heard," my mother said with a huff. "And girls believe that bullshit? That a cop would shoot a suspect who's running away, first off, and then manage to hit him in the inner thigh from behind. Brilliant."

"I'm trying to tell you nobody's immune to the worst. I got lucky. I live with a nursing assistant who hooked me up with free antibiotics, so the shit never progressed to, hell I dunno, amputation? Staph? I learned a lesson and got some help. But you don't live here," he said. "I can show you what to do, tell you everything about harm reduction and safety and all that, but once you leave here, you're on your own. My advice? Try smoking it, freebasing first. You'll save yourself a whole lotta trouble."

"I need to save myself a whole lotta money. You said you get twice the ride for half the cost. I'm stuck with this shit now, apparently, so if I'm gonna do dope, then I wanna do dope, no half steps. Tell me what I need to know to make it safe and worth my while."

"IVing isn't always the most economical answer, Jo-Jo. There's a thousand factors."

There was a knock at his door, and he motioned for Mom to see who it was. She went over and cracked it just a bit, and a flutter of apprehension quivered in her chest.

"Hey." Rachel stood looking in at her from the hall, tentative and concerned. She flitted a quick glimpse around at what she could see of Bryce's room. Black curtains on the windows. A swirling vintage lava lamp. Two broken drum heads propped against the scuffed wooden dresser. Electric blue carpet.

"And, of course, there's always your friends and loved ones to consider," he announced and went back to the magazine.

Mom didn't say anything.

"You left the RV hours ago," Rachel said through the crack. "I figured you needed space so you could work, but I started getting worried. Are you okay? How're you feeling?"

My mother let her in. "Yeah, I'm fine, feel a lot better."

Rachel and Bryce shared a wordless greeting, and she came inside and stood in an awkward spot by the door, arms crossed at her waist, uncomfortable and guarded. She looked my mother over and frowned at what she saw, bewildered by her astounding recovery, her color bright and full again, the perspiration gone. Mom leaned against the dresser, relaxed and steady, as if none of it had even happened.

"So, are you guys still recording?" Rachel asked.

"No, we're done," Mom said. "We're just mixing now."

Rachel nodded. It was all inordinately strange, the vibe was off, too much tension in the stuffy bedroom air, and she wasn't sure how to read it until she looked into my mother's eyes and found the abysmal answer, constricted and glassy and unconcealed. She stared at my mother for several beats, assembling all the clues, reconfiguring the illness of the past twenty-four hours, and the conclusions were at once bleak and devastating.

Rachel took my mother by the chin and looked at her more closely, and her expression drained into a pall of regret. "Jolán, you have got to be fucking kidding me."

Mom pulled away from her. "What?"

"Do not say 'what.'" She stood back with her hands on her hips, then glared at Bryce who said nothing. He kept reading, smoking, flipping through the pages. Rachel looked back at my mother, crushed and afraid for her. "It wasn't the goddamned flu," she mused aloud as it all came clear, and she spewed a disgusted breath through pursed lips. "Not even close."

"Yeah, and I really don't need a lecture right now, either." Mom walked away from her and went to the bed and dropped into a seat at the foot. She took out a cigarette.

"Really? Uh, well, I would say you *do.*"

"And what's it gonna change, Rache?" Mom held the flame to the tip and blew a noisy cloud into the air. She looked up at Rachel. "It is what it is, and now you know, it's out there, so please just back off and don't make me feel any worse. I didn't mean . . . you know? It wasn't supposed to . . . " She shook her head at herself and tossed up a hand. "Shit, I dunno. I'm sorry. Okay? What else can I say now? I'm fucking sorry."

Bryce sat up and climbed off the bed, and he grabbed his gear from the night table. "You know what, I'm gonna get a beer and go back upstairs. You guys chill in here as long as you want. This business is none of mine."

"How convenient," Rachel muttered as he came to the door, but he didn't say anything.

He left them to each other and disappeared down the hall.

"It's not his fault," Mom said through a drag of her cigarette. She searched around for the soda can by the bed and took it to her lap, tapped the ashes. "I made my own choices." She sat staring into the can, and she pried away the pull ring and dropped it into the hole, thinking.

"You lied to me."

"How so?"

"You broke a promise, it's the same thing. You didn't even try."

"I didn't realize it had gotten to this point. What do you want me to do, Rachel?" My mother looked up at her then, frank and defeated.

"You're supposed to be so much smarter than this. You *swore* to me. And now *look* at you. Look at the shit-fucked boat you're in now, that *we're* in now."

"This is my problem, not yours," my mother muttered, rolling the orange cherry across the soda top and sweeping the ashes into the opening. "You've had one of your own, don't forget."

Rachel scowled at her and took a step closer. "Don't even think about putting that shit on me, Jolán. I *stopped*." She pointed to herself. "I knew where the boundaries were, and I never crossed them. I put *us* first. And you promised to do the same, to get out before it got too big, yet here you sit, three months into a *smack* habit you swore would never happen."

"And stating the obvious does what, exactly?" My mother looked up at her. She waited for a response, but Rachel didn't have one. "I fucked up. Is that what you want me to say? Well, all right. I screwed the whole thing off royally, which means the game's changed, and now I gotta figure out a whole new set of rules. I've got no goddamned choice because I let the shit get away from me. Fine. I deliver myself up for your condemnation, Rachel." And she held her arms out in front of her, as if waiting to be shackled. "But while you're doing that, I'm the one whose gotta decide how to cope, how to deal with this shit so we don't go fucking broke."

"Broke?" That got Rachel's attention, the cost beyond the cost, and she narrowed her eyes. "What exactly does that mean, broke? How much? What've you been spending on that shit since we've been here?"

Mom hesitated. She peered down into the can, took another drag, tapped her ashes, and swirled it around.

"Jolán, how *much?*"

My mother looked at her straight. "One-fifty."

"A month?"

My mother considered the truth and its consequences. Everything was stripped down and exposed now, nowhere to hide, nowhere to stash the evidence, and so she shook her head.

Rachel read that for what she could and stood thinking, then raised her eyebrows. "A *week*? Oh, for Christ's sake." She shut her eyes and dropped back against the wall, arms folded tight at her chest.

She stared down at her shoes, wondering where it had all derailed, so quickly, how she'd missed a complete washout approaching at a hundred miles an hour. She hadn't been around enough, five miles away for thirty-five hours a week over the past two months while a sink hole formed beneath everything they'd been building since July, slumming it on bar tips and Ramen Noodles, folding tens and twenties away under the sleeper mattress for a decent life, a life *without* a recording contract because that was never promised, a dream worth dreaming but a fantasy just the same. Reality came in the sturdy cardboard boxes you kept to pack your things when you woke up and realized the fantasy never happened.

"It doesn't have to increase," my mother said. "Okay? In fact, I can bring it down, maybe fifty, seventy-five at the most. I can cut it in half, no more than we ever spent on weed, and we can cut weed out altogether. It doesn't have to be a financial burden at all."

Rachel stood staring at her sneaker laces for a very long time, shaking her head. "I'm not stupid, Jo," she finally muttered. She gazed down into Bryce's electric blue carpeting, specked with lint and dirt tracked in from the chilly world outside. "If you're getting dope sick, it means your tolerance has gone up. Tolerance and money are links in a chain—you pull on one, and the other follows, it's common sense. Please don't bullshit me with addicted rationale, Jolán. It doesn't convince me of a damned thing and only makes you sound desperate."

"I'm telling you I can rein this in."

"How?" Rachel glared at her. "How are you gonna do that now? Cut down? Quit? You could barely handle day-one withdrawals, Jolán. What do you think day three or four would be like? This is *exactly* what I feared for you, this trap. I *begged* you to be careful, to monitor what you were doing. But now you . . ." Then it seemed Matt's predicament dawned on her as well, and she huffed, laughed a little, but she wasn't at all amused. "Now you *and* Matt, I'm assuming, are wandering around a whole new fucking frontier. I take it he didn't have the flu, either."

My mother didn't respond, which was all the response Rachel needed, and she shook her head at the floor.

"Well, congratulations, you guys. Not such a party anymore, is it? So much for recreation. Did you touch the money we've been saving?"

"No."

"Not a cent of it?"

"What do you think I am, Rache?"

"A heroin addict, Jo. It's a viable question. We've been saving that for months, and it's off limits, so I don't know what you're gonna do. Get a job? Can you hold down a job? Do you even have time?"

"I won't have to. That's what I'm trying to tell you."

"We have a shit-ton of other expenses coming, the trip back to LA if Geffen wants to meet with you, rent for this place, repairs for the RV. You've got musicians union dues next month. And our credit cards are no option, they're for emergencies and my textbooks next semester."

"And none of it'll be a problem if I switch up how I use. It's cheaper, more practical."

Rachel squinted at that. She stood with her arms still wrapped around her waist, leaning against the door, and she crossed an ankle over the other. "What's cheaper? Switching up to what?"

It took my mother a moment, but she finally glanced around at the hypodermic needle on Bryce's nightstand, gesturing to it with her eyes, and she looked back at Rachel and made a little motion to her own forearm.

It was as if my mother had told her a bad joke, and Rachel scoffed beneath her breath. "That's the stupidest shit you've ever suggested, Jolán. Have you lost your mind?"

"Bryce can show me the safest method. No tracks. No disasters. It's more, I dunno, concentrated that way, costs less. It'll fix this." My mother peered up into Rachel's dreadful expression, looking for a glint of cooperation. She wanted her support, but the decision had already been made, and so my mother said, "Naomi can get clean needles, they're not much."

"Fuck Naomi."

"Why are you being like this? Don't you understand I've got no other options now? Either that or it's twelve hundred dollars a month and counting. Or quit altogether. Is that what you want?"

"Is that what *you* want?" Rachel waited. It took my mother entirely too many breaths to answer that. "This was never about me. This was *your* experiment gone wrong, so very, *very* wrong, Jolán. *So* wrong that you don't even hear yourself right now, looking for my approval so you can be a full blown smackhead, but I'm gonna tell you something—you start IVing that shit, and I walk."

Mom said nothing. The silence in the room was as if a switch had flipped. Even the music stopped; the CD ended, spun in the player, slowed, then clicked off. Silence so heavy it was an entity all its own, but even so, my mother didn't believe her. She lit another cigarette, sitting at the edge of Bryce's bed with her elbows on her knees.

"Look, I'm trying to make this work. I don't know what else to say to you. I've apologized. I've spent all night looking for a solution. And when I tell you I've found one, you threaten to leave me." She blew a little breath of irony through her lips and tapped her ashes. "Well, that's just fucking perfect." That was when she felt the pull of escape, tasted the bittersweet promise of apathy in the back of her throat, just a little dose of patience to guide her through this sudden disarray. "As if I don't have enough on my mind," she mumbled. "Three months a shut-in to the goddamn studio so we can have something better."

Rachel just stood watching her, trying to decide what to do or say next.

"I did keep one promise, and that was never to hide anything from you," Mom said. "You should give me some credit for that."

"You want a pat on the back?"

"I want the benefit of the doubt, Rache. I want you to trust me."

"I did. And you became a junkie. Anything else?"

My mother breathed a gentle sigh. "Not sure what else there is." She looked back up at Rachel. "If you don't trust me, then how on earth can you possibly love me?"

The bedroom door opened. Bryce came halfway in, glanced around at his poor timing, and turned back toward the hall again, but my mother called after him.

"You're cool. It's your room, anyway, shit." She looked at Rachel who stared back at her.

"So, what'd you decide? What are we doin?" Bryce asked my mother. "Sandro wants me to make a beer run, so lemme know what you're gonna do."

Rachel was quiet. She and Mom just looked at each other, eons passing through a miserable and familiar standoff. It was Montego's all over again as Rachel waited for my mother's answer. Mom looked away and dragged on her cigarette, scraped the ashes into the aluminum opening, and studied the hot orange cherry, anxiety blooming in her chest, too much confrontation, more turmoil than she had anticipated, and she wanted out, needed comfort, to go back to oblivion again where the filter would sift this all out and cast it aside to be forgotten.

She looked up at Bryce and nodded. "I'm down, I'm ready."

Rachel let out a long and shuddering sigh. She stared down at the carpet and shoved her hands into her pockets and fought back tears.

Bryce stepped past her and came inside, and he stood looking down at Mom. "You sure about this?" He shot a quick glance to Rachel. "If everybody's not on board, you might wanna rethink this, take the advice I gave you before. I can teach you that, too."

"She's not the only one who's gonna be pissed off, but so it goes." Mom looked up at Rachel and told Bryce, "It's the best option I've got right now."

"All right. If you say so." Bryce went over to the nightstand and opened the drawer. "Let's go ahead and get this party underway then, I got shit to do." He rummaged around for a clean new rig, the rubber tourniquet, a packet of gauze pads.

Mom stared up at Rachel who refused to look at her now, but she didn't move, she just stood by the door, eyes on the blue carpet, pondering whether to walk out, or burst into tears, or slap my mother's face and break it all off for good.

Rachel watched herself doing all those things in that exact order, imagined following through, storming out of the house and throwing open Betty's side door and stuffing her gym bag with all the clothes she could carry. She'd pluck her toothbrush from the cup in the bathroom, grab her shampoo off the shower ledge, pull her knapsack full of summer clothes from the closet and pack it with books and journals and souvenirs and photos, then call a cab to the downtown bus station, buy a one-way ticket to LA and spend the twenty-two-hour ride falling out of love, trying forget Jolán De Carlo forever. That's what any sensible woman would do, she would wake up from this, snap herself into action. If she could just get her back off that goddamned bedroom wall.

Bryce went out to the kitchen. They heard the refrigerator door open and close. A drawer slid out, silverware rattled, the drawer slid shut. Water from the faucet. My mother had nothing else to say. She finished her cigarette and dropped it into the can and waited for Rachel to do something, say something else, declare it a catastrophe and walk away, but she made no such moves and stood with her hands in her pockets instead, scowling at the floor, suspended at the verge of making good on a solid threat, yet nothing happened.

Bryce went past the bedroom doorway, down the hall to the bathroom, the medicine cabinet creaked open, clicked shut. He came back to the bedroom with a teaspoon, a bottle of distilled water, some rubbing alcohol, a bag of cotton balls, and another beer. He set it all on the nightstand and popped the can and took a sip. He took one of the wrapped needles from the night table drawer, sat on the edge of the bed and pulled back the plastic packaging, set the needle on the table.

My mother watched him, and Rachel watched my mother. Mom's knee was bouncing, anxious and edgy. The dope from three hours ago was wearing off now, opening a brief window of clarity, like a lens twisting her decision into proper focus.

"You know how much to give me, right?" she asked. "I've still got some in my system from earlier, maybe two tenths, one and a half. Everything's clean? I'm not gonna get some kind of infection from this shit, am I?"

"Calm down," he mumbled, drawing about thirty units of water from the container up into the syringe. "You get all tense and jittery, and it makes for problems finding a vein, keeping the shot steady." He glanced over his shoulder at her jumping knee. "You're really gonna have to stop that shit, seriously."

My mother tried to settle down.

He went back to work, bending the spoon flat and level, and he placed a chip of Tar in the center and squirted the distilled water in with it, then took up the lighter from the table and held the flame to the spoon, waving it back and forth underneath as not to boil the dope to a sticky, useless sludge; the idea was to heat it just enough to dissolve, and every few seconds he stopped to stir it with the needle plunger, applied the flame again, stirred and heated and checked it until a sweet, pungent vapor streamed up into the air at his face. Then he took a tuft of torn cotton and rolled it into a little ball between his fingers and set that into the spoonful of smack to filter out the impurities and any other tiny matter that might clog the needle, or worse—get injected into the bloodstream for a dirty hit, creating a variety of health complications.

My mother's eyes were riveted on the ritual, hypnotized and awestruck by her own courage, if she could call it that. It was desperation in disguise, really, drawing her to the Good Doctor's snake oil to soothe her imagined afflictions, a woman with a Golden Hammer and now everything was a nail.

Bryce came around to where she sat at the foot of the bed. He pulled up a ladderback chair from the other side of the room and took a seat in front of her. He looked into her eyes, the needle loaded and ready.

"I don't wanna waste this shit," he said. "You sure this is what you want before we go any further? Speak now, so I can keep it for myself, if I have to."

My mother was surprised at how quickly she nodded. She thought she would've hesitated, reconsidered the drawbacks, shied at the possibility of death, but death didn't seem to have the urgency of dope sickness, the crush of financial ruin, and so she pushed back her thermal shirtsleeve and offered up her left arm. From the corner of her eye she could see Rachel by the door, watching, but my mother wouldn't look at her, she couldn't; the guilt and disapproval that would pass between them would only shatter my mother's focus, make her twitch or fidget or shift in her seat while someone stuck a 29 guage needle in her arm.

Bryce tied the blue rubber tourniquet around her biceps. It pinched her skin, pulled at it tightly and forced the circulation down into the forearm where her twenty-two-year-old athletic blue veins rose beneath the caramel surface like a complex road map. "Jeezus, you got some ropes," he muttered, holding her by the wrist with one hand, feeling around the inner arm with the other. "You don't wanna blow these babies, that's for sure." He spoke lowly, thinking aloud with laser concentration as he tapped two fingers at the space just below the elbow crease. "You wanna take very, very good care of these. Some people aren't so lucky, have to dig and dig to register a hit." He swiped at the area with a cold square of alcohol-soaked gauze, threw it into the trash can. "You let your veins go to shit, and you'll find yourself diggin around in a damned corner for hours, covered in blood and tears, rattlin like crazy and gettin sicker by the minute. Not a way to spend an afternoon, believe me." He held up the loaded rig, flicked the needle three times with a fingertip, like any physician or phlebotomist, and he laid it against my mother's skin.

"Wait." Mom looked up at him, apologized. "I just wanna make sure it's not too much. You didn't cook too much, did you? 'Cause seriously, I still got a mild buzz from the bump I did upstairs. You sure this is cool?"

Bryce stopped and breathed a long, thoughtful sigh. "I'm not gonna kill you," he promised. "I know how much you did upstairs, I watched you. This is just a taste, baby steps. I'll go a little at a time, see how you do. I'm not gonna just slam you with it all at once. All right?"

There was honesty and confidence in his eyes, an addict's empathy for the fear of getting your cherry popped, the sky diving instructor at fifteen thousand feet, talking you down as you backpedaled at the open door with the sudden realization that parachutes malfunction, cords and cables intertwine in midair, planes crash, death is real. What if?

"The rush is different than what you're familiar with, though. This is not the same, just be aware of that."

Mom nodded, and he gave her a moment to settle, then pressed the beveled tip to the inner cubital vein.

"What you wanna do is keep the needle pointed towards the heart, at a fifteen to thirty-degree angle. Don't jab it straight in from the top, it's not supposed to be intramuscular, you'll rip your shit apart like that. And go slow, you don't wanna hit a nerve. And you'll know it if you do, trust me, the shit friggin hurts, like a lightning strike. If that happens, you *pull out*. Ya understand?" He glanced up at her, and she nodded. "You can do some serious permanent damage to your arm, your hand, lose feeling for life. Just be patient. Be nice to your vascular walls, they're delicate, they can tear. Just ease it in, nice and slow." And then he did.

My mother winced, frowned at the sting, but it faded, not much different than the saline IV she'd gotten during her senior year in high school, a locker room treatment for dehydration after a brutal, late spring tennis match.

"There's a big damn difference between a vein and an artery, too," he continued, pulling on the plunger now. "The best way to eyeball it is to check the blood that draws up into the barrel. If it shoots back with a lot of force, a light frothy red, that's probably an artery, and you wanna pull out, get your rig the hell outa there. But . . ." He pulled the plunger just a bit more as a tiny maroon swirl floated back into the cider-colored solution. "When you see that, you got yourself a good superficial vein, you know you registered. Doesn't always happen on the first try, most times you gotta re-inject, feel around again for a better spot, try again and again, but you're an IV virgin." He grinned. "You got great, untouched veins, so you shouldn't have much trouble if you take good care of yourself." He looked at her straight, twin engines rumbling over a cold, noisy wind, the cabin door standing wide open, a mile up from the earth below. "So, you ready?"

My mother took a deep breath, then nodded. "Ready as I'll ever be."

From the edge of her eye she could still see Rachel, one arm propped on the other with a hand cupped to her mouth, observing from her stunted spot by the bedroom door. Bryce pushed the plunger, measuring each unit with the steadiness of an endovascular surgeon.

A hot current traveled up into my mother's biceps. And the rest was all bliss and rockets, a euphoric shock so stunning and brilliant she thought her chest would explode, a corporeal supernova that struck her at the core, a cessation of breath, like standing upwind of a tornadic gust; she couldn't exhale, and it was beautiful, a thousand climaxes riding the downswing of a giant pendulum, angular momentum soaring up from within, and it kept climbing, flooding up into her head and steeping her brain in a celestial kind of ecstasy, unimaginably warm, ethereal, exquisite beyond reason with a ringing in her ears she placed at a quintuple-high B flat.

She could taste it now, saturating her palate, sharp and sweet as it seeped from her bloodstream and mingled with her own saliva, and she felt her eyes roll back in their sockets and flutter shut. Every limb, every digit, every cell and pore and follicle succumbed to gravity, tilting her toward the bed covers where she sat tranquilized and leaning, a broken marionette abandoned by its master, gliding away into a glorious, transcendental stupor.

My mother thought she understood this drug. She thought she had imagined its potential, that she had thoroughly conceived of all it had to offer.

She had no idea.

chapter fifteen

SUN AND SAND and sea and sky, blues so unbearably blue, unlike any natural thing I've ever known. Does the ocean truly lie so still, like cerulean glass? Warmth beneath me like a sun-soaked blanket, sand so soft it might not be sand at all but rather a quadrillion grains of spun silk. She approaches through the surf in a peach-mango bikini, pretty hips wrapped in a beaded chiffon seaside shawl, caramel blonde damp and blowing across that smile, ocean foam spilling over her bare feet. My goddess. My immeasurable heart. My beautiful open sky to climb up into and glitter there forever. She stands over where I lay, her hand extended and reaching for me, the sun blazing behind her like something sacred.

"We need to find Gunnar." I don't know who that is. "Come on, baby. Gunnar's waiting. We have to go." I open my mouth to ask why, and then the tide rushes in and sweeps her off into the ultramarine and she is gone.

I should have reached for her hand.

"I DON'T KNOW who that is." My mother stared at Bryce. He was standing in front of where she slumped at the foot of his bed. "Where's the ocean?" She sat with an arm extended and reaching for nothing.

He chuckled and shook his head at her, shuffled through a short stack of cassettes in his hands. "About a thousand miles from here, babe." He went over to the boom box and slipped a tape into the deck, clicked it shut. "You *and* the ocean, long friggin way from here."

"I don't understand, I was there. I felt it, the water, the sand." The words were flimsy and slurred, her mouth wasn't working very well. "We're supposed to find some guy. Do you know him?" She looked around, the bedroom dim and smoky, a clothes pile in the corner, red glowing lava slugging up and down in its cylindrical glass lamp on the card table. The heat came on, a draft from the central air vent billowed the window curtains. Music played from the stereo, something psychedelic, dated, she didn't recognize it. "Where's Rachel?"

Bryce tossed the tapes onto the dresser, grabbed his drumsticks, and dropped onto the bed. "She left," he said, drumming along to the music on the thick of his thigh. "About an hour ago."

Mom lifted her brows. "An hour? How is that? And who's Gunnar?"

"My guess—he's a construct of your imagination. Probably represents something buried in your subconscious. You'd be surprised what you've got stored away in there. It all gets unpacked and strewn around when you're on opiates. Lucid dreaming. That's all it is."

"Did she say where she was going?" There was something pulling my mother to investigate Rachel's departure, but it didn't have quite enough draw to get her up off the bed, so she just sat and listened to the music. She pointed at the boom box. "Who is this?"

"You sure have a lot of questions. To answer the first, no. You were nodding; as soon as your chin hit your chest, she walked out." Then he gestured to the radio with a drum stick. "And this is a band called Suck, classic band from '71-ish, maybe. A group out of South Africa."

"Well, they don't."

"Don't what?"

"Suck."

Bryce laughed a little, used the mattress and the other thigh as trap set toms and pattled the next drum fill. "I found it at a garage sale three blocks over, on vinyl if you can believe that, made the cassette upstairs in the studio by running it through the board so I could play it in the car." He smiled at her. "It's one of my favorites when I'm high. It's all covers, but they did a nice freakin job."

"I like the flute on this one. So, you said it was an hour ago?"

He waved it off. "She's probably out in the RV."

"She was pretty pissed." My mother felt a deep, dull aching in her left arm, and she looked for the source and found a burgundy-blue blotch in the elbow crease, just below the cuff of her shirtsleeve, and she rubbed at it with a thumb.

"Leave it alone," Bryce told her. "We'll see how it does by tomorrow. You might need a smaller gauge, maybe thirty or thirty-one. The secret is to rotate injection sites, rotate veins so the last one has a chance to heal before you go pokin at it again. And you're gonna have to learn to ration your dope. You can't just binge whenever you want, like you been doin the past few weeks. That'll get just as expensive, and you're gonna run outa money and veins and find yourself strung out fast, stealin from your best friends, offering some dealer a fuck with your girlfriend just for a little credit. It's a wonderful life."

"She'd never go for that."

"Yeah, I'm thinkin not, too," he said. "You gotta plan it out, set yourself on a schedule, be smart. My advice—never dose up first thing in the morning. Your threshold might be four hours, maybe eight before you start rattling. Nothin worse than waking up at nine and having to wait for a dealer who might not get to you till, shit, maybe four or five in the afternoon, and you've only got a four-hour threshold."

"That's a lot of information." My mother sat thinking, content there at the edge of the rumpled blankets. "You got me remarkably fucked up." She examined the needle bruise on her arm again. "Extraordinary. Nothing at all like what I was doing." She turned to him then. "How long does it last? I got blurry eyes, kinda nauseated but not too much. You look crazy outa focus to me."

"Depends. I didn't shoot you up with much, about ten milligrams, and you still hit the ceiling, so maybe a couple more hours. Your IV tolerance is kinda low. You wanna keep it that way. Don't binge, ration your shit, and you'll get high almost every time and spend less, provided you don't get something cut with a bunch of trash. Lecia's spot on, about sixty percent pure, good as Quint's, but once you leave here, you're gonna have to shop around." He waited for a response to that, but my mother was out again.

She slid down to the floor, this time, and sat slouched against the bed frame, head down and drifting back into serenity. She was drooling onto the front of her thermal shirt.

"Or you could just say fuck it and nod out."

IF THE SUN wasn't so damned lethal, I'd carry a piece of it around in my pocket. God, I love it. She is its host, the place where it resides, and I love her, too, infinitely so. I am the stars, she says. Sun and stars, and the sun is a star, so she and I are one. Without the other, neither is. I've come to a place where I can see so clearly, to the edge of the earth, I can see the planetary curve from here. Stellar dust, that's what we're made of, so said Mr. Del Veccio, eleventh grade biology, the universe manifested, so it only makes sense she and I collided, burst into flames, disintegrated into one another, and found ourselves in love like this. A wondrous thing, love. Makes everything good again, it's all you need. The Beatles knew that all too well, and hell I know that riff. E to the B, G7, D, a little bend on the G. I should play it. I should play it from these rooftops over Boston, bring her here to meet my friends, see the campus, make her my wife someday. Church bells ringing like gongs over Salem Street, the Old North steeple framed in American elms, and I can smell autumn in the wind, the breath of God. They say God is love, but even He knows nothing of what I feel for her, it's out of His league. He can only aspire to be what lives within me now. He'll come around. He'll get there. All He has to do is lay eyes on hers, chestnut brandy with little flecks of honey, and He will be complete . . . the universe manifested, with a little bend on the G.

"WE MAKE A pretty ridiculous pair." Bryce spun his drum stick between his fingers. The music was different now, much more mellow, gentle female vocals, another dated tune from the '60s, flutes and strings in 6/8 time. "You and your air guitar, me and my body drums. I don't think you're in the right key, though."

My mother lifted her chin from the wet patch on her chest, swiped her mouth with the back of her hand, the other still out at her side, holding the invisible neck of the Stratocaster, fingering an Em7 chord. She glanced around at Bryce. "What happened to the Beatles?"

"They broke up, and Lennon's dead."

"Isn't that what we were listening to?"

Bryce toked his Newport, tapped the ashes into the soda can. "Sounds like you were dreamin again, girl. Don't take that for granted. Won't be long before that's a memory, and your high's just a high. It's pretty common your first few times IVing, but after a while it just doesn't happen anymore. You like to write; you should write 'em down while you still remember them."

Mom rubbed her face, scratched at her chest and shoulders. "Christ, it seems so real, unbelievably vivid. The music, the Boston streets, Berklee campus. I was so there." She turned to him and said through a drowsy mush mouth, "So, she left an hour ago? You think she's still pissed off? Maybe she's cool now. She might come back."

"That'd be another thirty minutes now, babe." He laughed a little and dropped the cigarette into the can, so filled with soda-pickled filters it didn't even make a sound. "You don't even realize how long you're gone, it's funny. I thought I hated safe-sitting, babysitting some other junkie so they don't OD, but I forgot how entertaining a newbie can be. All confused and bewildered and shit."

"I could hear you playing. Thought it was people, walking through Berklee, Massachusetts Ave. I don't understand how so much time passes. I go under, and it's like a minute becomes an hour." She scratched at her chest again, sat there itching on the bedroom floor, relaxed against the bedframe, arms resting on her knees, thinking about nothing in particular.

It involved a bit too much effort because she couldn't feel her head, almost everything was going numb now. She held her hand out in front of her and spread her fingers, made a fist, opened it again, watching the muscles move, anticipating the electrical signals from brain to extremity, and somewhere in there she knew that she herself was doing it, but it was as if watching some other woman's hand. The disengagement was surreal and lovely and intriguing, and she sat in it for a very long while, letting it take over.

She should have been frightened. To be simultaneously inside and outside the physical body like this. She would do well to find a way to surface again, but sailing through this vacuum was peaceful in a way that surpassed what she thought she knew about death. She smiled then, couldn't imagine what she'd been so afraid of when Bryce had the pin poised above her forearm, and she imagined death was probably a lot like this, ebbing across that indiscernible boundary into the ultimate, alternate state of being; she believed in the life after; she believed in God.

She thought now that it was foolish of anyone not to. There was so much more. All she ever had to do was look within. There lies the infinite soul, stardust and matter in their simplest forms, while we make everything else so complicated, too many explanations, too much story. Love without conditions—that was the sun on her face, that radiance she felt inside now, and even if all hell collapsed and buried her in a shit-ton of stinking misery, she could always count on love to dig her out.

She didn't know how much time had passed, but she thought she should try to stand, walk, endure the cold Denver evening long enough to cross the yard to the Fleetwood and see about Rachel. She was unsteady at first, like a whiskey stagger. Bryce asked where she was going, and she told him she had to see a man about a mule, something Pap would always say when he thought the answer was insignificant, or unimportant, but my mother was on an impromptu mission to bring Rachel Cole around to her latest self-discovery.

The euphoria was beginning to level off as a stiff November wind blew right through the fabric of her shirt. She should've put her jacket on, but she didn't remember where it was. It didn't matter. The light from Betty's sleeper was on, a soft golden square at the end of the camper like a beacon. My mother opened the door and climbed inside, smiling, warm again. The sleeper curtain was drawn. She went down the little hall and pulled the curtain aside just enough to poke her head into the room.

Rachel was sitting at the edge of the bed; she'd been crying, she was still crying. She glanced up at my mother and looked back into her lap, fingering a wad of tissues. On the bed beside her was a gym bag, chubby and overstuffed, and a backpack, a pair of her sneakers tied around the shoulder strap by the laces. She'd spent the hours packing, cramming the past four months into side compartments and zipping it all shut for travel.

My mother didn't know what to do with the sudden flight of panic that swirled in the hollow of her chest; it contradicted all she'd been marinating in for the past three hours, sunshine darkening away behind a black storm cloud. She looked at the bags, looked at Rachel, and stood like stone in the doorway.

"I gave you a choice, and you made it." Rachel dabbed her nose with the tissues but wouldn't look up from her lap.

Mom pushed the curtains open, didn't know what to say. It wasn't the first time a lover had left her, so she tried to draw some familiarity from that, to ease the blow, but she had never been in love before, not this way, a redefinition of her future, a purpose that reached far beyond herself, solid and tethered to something strong and beautiful and worth building upon. That was all very new, and the swell of trepidation in her gut as she stood at the edge of losing it was boggling and left her dumfounded, with no words in her own defense except, "I never made a choice. How could I? You asked me to choose between air and water. Who does that?"

Rachel gazed down at the tissues. She didn't use them to dry a new stream of tears and caught them on her shirtsleeve instead. "Well, that is a very interesting analogy, Jolán, but it's bullshit." She nodded at her own statement and sat fidgeting with the Kleenex. "I asked you to choose between us and yourself, and guess who won, as usual. I thought I fell in love with a very different woman."

My mother came into the sleeper. She knelt down at Rachel's feet and lifted her chin to look at her straight. "I swear to you I haven't gone anywhere. I'm still here. I *am* that woman. And I know you're scared of what we'll become, but—"

"What *you'll* become. I'm only afraid of what I'd become if I stayed."

"Which is?"

"Jeez, I dunno, Jolán. An enabler, a crutch, co-dependent, addicted to your addiction?" Her eyes were growing dark and angry now. "There are psychology books filled with scenarios like that. You should crack one open—you just might see our pathetic future, like a crystal fucking ball."

"Why do you have to say things like that? So hurtful?"

"I guess the truth just has a way of doing that." She sighed and dabbed at her nose.

"I'm trying to build something here, Rachel, to become something great, and I just need—"

"The dope-slamming rock guitarist? Heroin *chic?*" she mocked, making little semi-quotes with her fingers. "Really?" She tossed the tissues into the waste basket by the nightstand. "You're becoming a cliché, Jolán. Nothing more. Way to dream big. But you can count me out. Hell, what am I saying? You already have."

"I've done no such thing. And I don't think you really wanna leave." My mother looked around at the bags on the bed. "I think it's killing you to go, but it makes it easier if you're pissed off at me, and so you bare these fangs and snarl at me like a fucking Doberman to make yourself feel better."

Rachel didn't say anything. She propped her hands back behind her, crossed her ankles, and stared out at the floor.

My mother leaned down and cocked her head to look directly up into her face. "I came out here to tell you that I love you."

She waited for Rachel to respond, but she just blinked and pursed her lips. After a moment, her eyes met my mother's, but she still said nothing.

My mother smiled faintly, remembering the first night she'd ever seen her, dishwater ponytail and black hiphugger jeans, a tray full of drinks in hand, smiling across the bar top tea lights, a reverie spawned from the pleasure centers still sparking off the last bit of dope in her system.

She touched Rachel's cheek with the backs of her fingers. "And every day, when I think I couldn't love you more, another day comes and makes a liar outa me." She gave her a brief smile and traced her lips with a fingertip. "Isn't that what matters most?"

Rachel thought on it for a while, let herself nuzzle slightly against my mother's touch, but she still had no answer. It was all supposed to be a romantic, impulsive adventure, and for a time it had been. Bonfires and fireworks and beach blankets under so many stars she thought the Milky Way had somehow erupted. So much music and passion, my mother's finest gifts. A hundred-and-seventeen perfect days. And then everything came unraveled and left them here, on opposite sides of a terrible dilemma, lines drawn, ultimatums raised and flapping against the wind like battle flags. She loved my mother too much to leave, and maybe that was the problem—she loved her more than my mother loved herself.

Headlights appeared through the RV windshield, making a left onto Fillmore a block over. They approached and stopped at the driveway. It was a Yellow cab; the horn blew. My mother peered down the length of the camper and out at the glossy hood under the street lamp, then looked back at Rachel, begging wordlessly for her to reconsider.

For a moment, she thought she might have gotten through because Rachel finally touched her. She smoothed the dark auburn curls from her eyes, leaned down, and kissed my mother's forehead. Then she reached around for the knapsack, pulled it to her shoulder, grabbed her gym bag, and rose from the edge of the bed.

"It was never love that made a liar out of you, Jolán," she said as she headed for the screen door. "I think you and I both know that."

"Baby, come on." My mother turned where she sat kneeling and reached for the bag but couldn't get a hold of it to stop her. "Rachel."

The side door opened and the chilly evening wafted in. The cab driver blew the horn again. My mother sat stunned and reeling, sat there for too many moments, then scrambled to her feet as the screen clicked shut and the outer door followed.

"Rachel, please," she pleaded after her, throwing the doors open again, and she jogged around to the front of the Fleetwood, held up a finger to the cabbie and came to the rear window, knocked on it. "Don't do this, baby, come on."

She tried to sound rational and clear, to keep herself composed because a part of her wanted to put a fist through the glass, tear the curbside mailbox out of the concrete and hurl it into the windshield, turn the entire vehicle onto its side in one adrenaline-spiked thrust, but she just stood knocking at the window instead, begging Rachel Cole not to leave her there alone with herself.

But Rachel wouldn't look at her. She sat behind the window, her face twisted and tear streaked. The driver turned and said something, and she nodded. He faced front, pulled at the shifter on the steering column, and the car lurched around the RV and sped off down Fillmore, nearly spinning my mother into a sprawling heap.

"Rache!"

KEYS. SHE NEEDED keys. The 4Runner. Could she drive? She was still a little fuzzy, everything dreamlike, and she wanted nothing more than to be trapped in a terrible lucidity from which she would snap back into Bryce's room with the lava lamp oozing on the table, music on the boom box, drum sticks pattering the mattress while she sat with an unlit cigarette stuck to her lower lip because she'd nodded out into this nightmare before she could get her lighter to work.

She stood in the middle of the road and watched the taillights shrinking toward Colfax. She waited, blinked, felt the cold through her shirt, watched the cab make a right and vanish. She shut her eyes and opened them again and prayed for the bedroom. But there was only the quiet evening, traffic in the distance, a dog barking in the neighbor's yard.

What to do? Her breath steamed like vapors from a hot spring. She planted her hands on her hips and stared at the macadam, paced in a tight pensive circle and then stopped and gazed back down the empty street again. It wouldn't go away. The cold numbed her in a way she didn't like. This was reality. *Her* reality. Fractured and sliding down onto everything else, a shit pile of epic failure, and love hadn't offered a thing except "goodbye."

She sat down right there, where the cab had been, knees drawn up so she could rest her arms on them, and she clasped her hands and just sat thinking, coming down. She hated being so cold but didn't care enough to do much about it, seemed a small price, a rightful discomfort. She should be frozen over and packed solid like the woolly mammoth, left there for some distant era to find and examine and put behind a roped-off display—a twentieth century artifact: Woman, Suspended in Defeat.

The lights in the house across the street came on. Someone parted the window blinds and looked out. The lights went off again. At the end of the block a street lamp blinked and went dark for no reason at all. Someone appeared out of the darkness of the same block, walking a small dog, and he let it pee on a signpost, turned north up the next street, and then they, too, were gone.

SHE WOULD TRY to quit. Cold turkey. Just suffer it through until it was out of her system. She wouldn't be the first to brave withdrawals, to set out through a roaring typhoon on a slapdash timber raft in search of familiar shores. She knew her way home, back to the woman she was supposed to be, the one buried and suffocating under this rock slide she'd brought down upon herself.

She would endure. She would prevail. She would beat this back with a white-knuckled fistful of willpower and grit her teeth against temptation until she was whole again, then head west toward Los Angeles, with or without Geffen Records, and reclaim her place in Rachel Cole's life before some other, cleaner, much more functional woman took her place. She would make everything good again. Buy a house.

Christmas was coming—her sobriety would sparkle in the tree lights and silver tinsel strings, stability like picket fence posts planted at the four corners of a decorated lawn; she would get herself together; she would make it manifest, change her stars so they glittered like they once did. She would find her way through this unprecedented nausea, bear the crushing weight of this vice around her skull and sweat it all out into the sheets until they were soaked with blood and poison. She could do this . . . she could do this . . . she could do this . . .

"Good fucking luck, *chica.*" Matt stood over her at the edge of the bed, hands on his hips, peering down at her pathetic shuddering form, drenched and rocking in a tussle of twisted blankets. "I spent a half day touring this layer of hell, and from what they say, it doesn't get any better anytime soon. You might wanna rethink this."

"Just leave me alone."

"Another bad idea."

My mother kicked at the covers and curled herself into a ball and lay whimpering. It was nearly four in the afternoon, nineteen hours since her last dose, fourteen hours and twenty-seven minutes since she watched Rachel's cab disappear into the Colorado darkness.

"If you're doing this to punish yourself," Matt said, "it's not gonna change anything. You're just gonna put yourself through unnecessary torture, and she'll still be gone, and you'll still be a smackhead. And so will I."

My mother rolled over and vomited into the wastebasket.

Matt offered a wash rag to wipe her mouth and nose, but she didn't take it; she just lay hanging off the edge of the bed, retching up nothing but air now; she hadn't eaten in two days; Theraflu and crackers didn't count.

"*Please* shut up," she finally spewed between breaths.

She turned back flat on the bed but couldn't stay like that, it made her dizzy, and so she rolled onto her side again with her back to Matt and the camper and all the things she despised about herself for falling head first into this hole in her life. Her mind was a spinning collage, pictures of the past tumbling in a dryer. She saw herself at age eleven, in the dress Nanna used to make her wear to St. Rita's Saturday evening mass, a red plaid mini-knit with a white sleeveless top and plaid collar—she hated it. She hated mass. She didn't believe in purgatory. She didn't understand the Trinity.

She saw Father Reyes through the confessional screen; she wasn't supposed to know it was him, but she recognized his voice, soothing tenor with a heavy Spanish accent calling her "child" and prescribing penance for stealing quarters from Pap's money jar on his office mantle, for wrecking Cam's bike and busting the chain trying to jump it off the playground picnic table, for lying to Nanna about a ninth grade algebra test she'd failed because she was really reading *Rolling Stone* magazine when she should have been studying.

She'd done a lot of lying and stealing. She'd destroyed things she'd taken without permission and lied about how they ended up that way. Her eyes ran with blinding tears. Her stomach turned on itself and devoured her from the inside out. Her bones trembled and tried to break apart at the joints. Matt tried to comfort her like a brother, pet her like a fucking dog, but his touch was like talons on gooseflesh and she elbowed him back and called him a *pinche verga* and wrapped her head in a sweat-soaked pillow.

"I don't care what language you say it in," he told her. "Call me a dick if it makes you feel better, but rattling through withdrawals isn't gonna bring her back. We need you in the studio, *mamasita*. This shit'll take days to run its course, and we don't have days."

"It's something I just need to do," she growled through the pillow fluff.

"It's shitty timing."

"Yeah, well." She didn't want to talk, she could hardly get her mouth to form the words through chattering teeth, but Matt kept at her.

"And when you get past this, there's still gonna be me and Bryce. I've got no plans to quit, and neither does he, so then what? You think you can resist temptation twenty-four-seven?"

He was digging into her doubts, his words like fingers on the keys in her brain, playing concertos of uncertainty. He had an agenda he thought worth the harassment. She was vital to the project, and they needed her input, her pristine pitch, her leadership during the most critical engineering hours, and if a rail of heroin made that possible, then so be it. She could detox on her own time, after the recording masters were burned and Geffen's package was in the mail. Then, of course, there was the photo shoot tomorrow, which he tossed in as well.

"What do you think you're gonna look like in West Highlands at nine a.m., doubled over with a string of puke hangin off your lip? Clawing gashes into your own face, drippin with sweat." He shrugged. "Hell, who knows? Maybe it'll pass as some kinda new gimmick. We'll stuff a dead bat into your mouth and just go with it."

He made little camera noises and laughed, but she wanted to cave his head into Betty's bay window because he was right. She hadn't thought about that, hadn't been keeping track of time beyond the hours between intravenous seduction and the taxi cab taillights down Fillmore.

She lifted the pillow from her face. "That can't be tomorrow. What day is it?"

"It's Wednesday, *chica.* Thursday morning shoot with Erin Hayes, Highlands Square, remember? We set it up last week, new promo pics for the labels, the pictures Freiburg requested with the demo."

My mother groaned and twisted herself into a knot again and pounded on the mattress. *"¡Tú me estás jodiendo!* What the fuck!"

She let out another hopeless cry and moaned into the blankets, begging in Spanish for the universe to undo it all, but the universe did not respond. There was only Matt, and Erin Hayes's FM2 shutter lens clicking off three frames per second in Denver's trendiest neighborhood, and the dope cravings like saw-toothed razors, whispering for her surrender as they hacked into her brain space.

"Like I said, your timing's a disaster. And so are you." Matt pulled a little bag of cheese from his jeans pocket and tossed it onto the bed where it landed at her face, and she stared at it, a starving POW with a mid-well sirloin, sizzling under her nose on a bone china platter. "You wanna dry out, do it some other time, when we don't have so much to lose. That day'll come if you still want it, but it can't be today. And it sure as hell can't be tomorrow."

The bag of hammer lay in the wet rumpled sheets, eclipsing her field of vision, a velvet curtain drawn shut against the final act. It insisted she was inadequate, frail, much too under prepared for this fight and that all the agonizing, the head trips, the physical torment had always been avoidable if only she hadn't tried to resist, to slip from its grasp and run for the bolted door, knowing a sociopathic monster was on her heels. It made all the promises she wanted. It was a confidante in her time of grief. It offered a feast to satisfy her self-inflicted famine. She needed it to maneuver the days ahead and make herself presentable again. So what was she waiting for?

She took it from the blankets and held it between her fingers and tried to answer that. She heard Erin Hayes's camera snapping in repetition. She heard the twelve-string through the studio monitors, saw herself seated across from Michael Freiburg in a booth at Roscoe's Chicken and Waffles on Sunset Boulevard, the unlikely place where some of the most historic music deals had been stricken. She envisioned platinum records in glass frames on the walls of Geffen's offices, imagined herself shaking hands with Portland Downs' new entertainment lawyer, her signature on the bottom line. Music award VJs stood with microphones to her mouth. Stadium crowds chanted her name.

Matt was right. Now was not the time. There was always the future. There would be better days to do this. What was she thinking, setting out on this impossible quest, right in the middle of another? Her brain slammed against the walls of her cranium. Her muscles twitched and shuddered. Bile sloshed and soured in her gut. She could put an end to it all within minutes, get back to work, focus, be creative again. After all, who was she if she wasn't making music? She didn't want to be this broken shell, teeming with rot and vomit, hopelessness and gloom, it wasn't her, and she missed herself terribly already. She missed Rachel, but how could she provide for her on a traveling musician's pay? What would she have to bargain with if she didn't pull herself together and get out of the trenches and do something about it?

"Okay," she finally heard herself say. "Just until we find out what's up with Freiburg." And that was all it took to spin the situation toward a brighter light. She sat up then. Her chest tightened with breathtaking anticipation. "But I need Bryce." She sat there hugging herself, clutching the little one-ounce baggie of dope in her fist. "I gotta get to Bryce."

Matt gave her a fickle shrug. "What for? Just rail a bump off the nightstand."

"Screw that." She wrestled herself out of bed, stood up, and steadied a hand on the wood paneling. She tossed the baggie back to him. "There are much better methods."

"Yeah, well, Bryce is at work."

"Now?"

"It's four in the afternoon, Jo-Jo. He closes tonight. You're not gonna find him for another six hours. What do you need him for, anyway?"

"Dammit." She looked around the sleeper, thinking, motivated now, the dope sickness falling away behind a flurry of new and desperate ideas. Then she remembered her jacket, out in the cabin on the table bench, and she pushed past Matt and staggered on into the camper and found the blue fleece and dug through the pockets for what she hoped wasn't just the product of another waking dream, and she grinned as her fingers brushed the crinkled cellophane, the stiff paper backing. She exhaled relief and withdrew a brand new hypodermic needle from the front pocket, a gift meant for a much later date, after she'd had time to practice with a few ampoules of sterile water first, when she knew what she was doing.

Matt's eyes widened. "Holy Christ. Are you serious?"

"Where's the first aid kit?" She sat on the bench and fished out the ball of Tar from her jeans.

"Do you even know how to do that shit?"

"Yeah. I need the first aid kit. There's alcohol wipes and cotton in it. And get me . . ." She searched around for a makeshift tourniquet. "Just get me a belt from the sleeper, there should be one in my gym bag, in the bottom, the braided leather one. Should be good enough."

She was trembling when he finally brought it. She knew that ran counter to Bryce's instructions, so she swiped the tears from her face with her sleeve and swallowed back a wave of nausea that made her swoon. She blinked and tried to focus through fractured brain matter, breathed in through her nose, out through her mouth, an athlete's remedy for anxiety and exhaustion.

Matt rummaged around the cabinets until he found the first aid kit, and she asked for a clean spoon, the razor blade from his wallet, a cup of tap water.

"He had some other bottled shit. But I don't have time to raid the fridge for that. Water's water, screw it."

"This is nuts, Jo." Matt set the Styrofoam cup on the Formica table, flipped open his billfold, and handed her the blade.

She sliced off a chip of the Black Tar and scooped it with the razor onto the spoon, then drew thirty units of water into the needle barrel, just as she remembered.

"This is primo, that's what it is. Now, just chill out. He showed me how to do it last night." She settled her bouncing knee, in through her nose, out through her mouth. "I just gotta bring it down a little, stop this shaking. Dammit," she wheezed, rubbing her injecting hand back and forth along her thigh, trying to still herself, to chase away the jitters.

When her concentration returned, she held her lighter to the spoon and cooked the dose to a fuming caramel extract that bubbled at the edges. She balled up a pinch of the cotton, placed it in the middle of the solution, then pulled it all up into the barrel as Matt watched, slack jawed and mesmerized.

She was still shaking when she cleaned the injection area, but most of her mental energy was trained on remembering the steps now, and it helped. She set the needle on the table and looped the belt at her biceps, stretched it taut and held it in place with her teeth. She had reason to be nervous. She was rigging her own parachute, this time. No instructor to piggy back and pull the emergency ripcord. Just Matt, along for the ride, a passenger strapped in and hugging a flotation device, the plane cruising on autopilot at ten thousand feet with no one in the cockpit. She could do this . . . she could do this . . .

"Point it toward the heart," she recited lowly around a mouthful of leather.

Radial and cephalic and basilic veins rose like tree roots from elbow to wrist as she rested her left arm on the inside of her thigh, her eyes darting between all the wishbones and rolling cords beneath her skin.

"Rotate. Be nice to your vascular walls." She could see a tiny red dot in the middle of the original bruise. "Okay, so not there. Then how 'bout," and she laid the needle to the vein just to the right of it, "here?" She was speaking under her breath, talking herself through it, but the chills were threatening to betray a steady hand, and so she inhaled slow and deep and thought about the high, a magnificent paradise just seconds away, when everything would be fine. No more sickness. No more mental agony. Just the warm and coddling sun shining on her soul again.

"Maybe you should just wait for Bryce, Jo. This is some dead-scary shit."

"Shut up. Please. I gotta get this right, Matty, so please just let me focus." She looked up at him and said around the belt, "If I nod out, if I go down too far for too long, you *wake* me up. Do *not* let me sleep. You understand?"

He nodded, and so she nodded, too. They held an indecisive gaze, my mother reiterating with her eyes that he not let her die there in the Fleetwood, and he assured her again, without words, that she was the sister he'd never had and that nothing would stand between him and a round of rescue breathing, if it came to that. My mother turned her attention back to the needle.

He said she'd feel a slight pop when she penetrated a vein, a torrent of pain for an artery. She didn't feel the stick, the topical pinch of injection, her brain was wired around other things instead, and pain had assumed a very different nature over the past few days. Thirty degrees. Nice and slow, steady as she goes. No pop, though, and she wondered now if she'd done it right.

Check the barrel, then. She pulled at the plunger with the same hand, it was awkward, palming the rig while trying to draw up and register with her thumb and forefinger—aspiration; definitely a skill worth mastering under better circumstances. Still no pain, no lightning shock from stainless steel against the pronator teres, none of the inexplicable swelling Bryce had spoken about in her hand or fingers. The blood pluming in the syringe was the color of Floribunda roses, the ones Nanna used to plant around the shrubs in the backyard garden, but my mother tried not to think about her, or Bensalem, or Berklee, only the fact that she'd registered on the very first try. It was the miracle she needed.

She let loose the belt and pushed the plunger while Matt held his breath. Then she did the inevitable swan dive out the open Cessna door and left him behind to watch her free fall.

SHE LANDED ON my grandparents porch steps. Inside, Afro-Cuban rhythms played from the stereo, the *Afro Roots* album Nanna Sylvia played when Mom was a child. It belonged to Nanna's father, Angel Cordoza. My great-grandfather Cordoza died when Mom was only five, but Nanna kept his record collection and played them often in the summer afternoons while she fried plantains and stuffed *boliche* with chorizo sausage and hard-boiled eggs. My mother could smell it through the front door. She went into the house, and all was as she remembered it from her youth, the emerald green Davenport sofa, the Danish step end tables, the upright Steinway piano that used to belong to Nanni Lena, standing next to the turntable floor console. Mom's eighth and ninth grade school portraits were framed on the wall over the stereo, and Cam's stood propped on the fireplace mantle with Nanna and Pap's wedding photos.

Nanna Sylvia then spoke to her in Spanish from the kitchen, and Mom went on through the house. Nanna was in a hurry to get dinner ready, and it was Mom's turn to set the table, so she prodded her along with a silver spatula, poking her in the shoulder with it. *"¡Espabilate ya!* Dinner's almost ready. *¿Dónde está Cameron?"*

"I dunno. Probably in his room," Mom said, a little unsure how she'd gotten there except for the remarkable way in which heroin could bend space and time. She stayed out of Nanna's way and took forks from the kitchen drawer and set them on the pearl laminate tabletop.

"Your father will have to take you to your violin lesson tonight," Nanna told her. She banged a big serving spoon on the edge of a two-gallon pot of yellow rice and turned down the flame. "I've got dance rehearsal at eight. And make sure he writes a check, this time. It's embarrassing when they think we can't pay. *Él es tan olvidadizo*; he'd leave his head somewhere if it wasn't attached."

"He's forgetful when he wants to be. He thinks a hundred bucks a month is too much. He says it all the time."

"Well, then he should have gotten a Cocker Spaniel and a goldfish instead of having children. His daughter is gifted. She needs guidance, and proper guidance for gifted children isn't cheap. And where is your brother? *Ay Dios mío. Ese chico va a ser la muerta mí."* She went to the kitchen doorway. *"Cameron! Ven acá!"* she called up into the house and hurried back to the stove.

"Meta Rumba" played from the living room. There were scratches in the vinyl, so it hissed and crackled under the turntable needle, syncopating the already complicated conga and woodblock rhythms while the singers harmonized in sparse major fifths. *Tú cantas, tú bailas . . . Oye mi tambor, oye mi tambor . . .*

Cam came into the kitchen and ignored my mother who was sitting at the table. He was ten, maybe eleven, stocky with a face full of peach fuzz, and she couldn't help but smile at him. He went to the fridge and took out a soda, then caught her smirking, and he raised an eyebrow and looked at her sideways. "What are you smilin at? Last time I checked, I wasn't a Bensalem basketball cheerleader."

"Cameron," Nanna scolded. *"*Don't say such things about your sister, it's vulgar, and it's insulting. *Dile que lo sientes."*

"Why say I'm sorry if it's true?" He popped open the can and grinned at Mom. "Everybody knows she's a switch-hitter."

"Wrong term, jackoff," Mom said. "That's for the ones who go both ways, but maybe it's a little over your head. Everything else is."

"Everything else is," he mocked sourly, but Nanna wouldn't have it.

She was at the sink, rinsing a mixing bowl, and she said over her shoulder, *"Callate,* both of you. This talk is no good in the kitchen before dinner. We don't say things like that in this house. Cameron, your sister is a good girl. And Jolán, you watch your mouth with your brother. Now go wash your hands before your father gets home. Let's go. *¡Apúrate!"*

She shooed them away, spritzing dishwater with wet hands, and it sprinkled my mother's face. Cam swatted her across the head as he took off into the house.

There was another splash of cold water, and someone slapped her again, and she frowned, confused; Nanna was still at the sink, and Cameron was gone; she could hear him jogging up the living room stairs.

Somebody took her by the shoulders, shook her hard. "Jolán! Hey! Come on, don't do this. Come on, come on, come *on.* Ssshit. I knew this was a bullshit idea, *damn* you stupid motherfucker, you."

My mother sucked back a deep and desperate gasp. The music stopped. Silence in the Fleetwood. Matt was on his knees in front of where she sat slouched at the table bench, a full glass of water in his hand, poised to dump it over her head if she hadn't opened her eyes.

My mother winced. She brought a heavy hand up to wipe her face, wet and clammy, the curls at her temples dripping onto the orange Formica. She pulled up her shirt enough to dry herself off.

"What the hell are you doing? What is your problem?" she mumbled, trying to bring him into focus through blurred vision.

Matt set the glass on the table and watched her, the panic draining from his eyes now. He exhaled with a breathy little whistle.

"Holy shit. You were gone for, like, I dunno. Maybe a half hour?" He stood up and ran his fingers through his hair and leaned against the opposite counter, glaring at her as if she were hexed. "I was making a couple burritos in the microwave. I turned around for just a minute, and when I turned back to check on you again, you were *not* breathing, dude. Just sat there with your head hangin like a friggin dead woman. Scared the goddamned shit outa me! How much of that shit did you do, man?" He tipped his chin to the works and paraphernalia on the table, then reached down for the dope spoon, swiped it up and threw it clattering into the sink. "Hell, even Bryce doesn't nod out that damn hard. What the hell?"

My mother sat there, putting it all together, the smell of food, Nanna Sylvia creeping into her subconscious moments before she'd pushed off, all the vivid components for another dream. She felt the ache of a new bruise on her arm, and she looked at it, a two-inch bloody streamlet going brown and dripping from the injection site, like a paint spatter.

She didn't remember withdrawing the needle, went deep under after an explosion of pleasure not quite like the flight she took in Bryce's room, but it was satisfying enough. She shook her woozy head and mumbled, "Hell if I know. It shoulda been the same dose I had last time. I thought it was, anyway. Looked right. It's the same dope, same cut, so I dunno." She gave him a quick and guilty smile and tried to sit up straighter. "Sorry 'bout that." She gestured to the paper towels by the sink, then to the blood on her forearm. "You mind?"

He unrolled a wad and wet it at the faucet and handed it over, scowling.

Mom could see him from the edge of her eye, felt the judgment like heat radiating from the backyard firepit. She glanced up at him as she cleaned away the last of the dried blood.

"It was an economic decision," she muttered.

He didn't say anything, just nodded and sat staring at her arm and at the soiled rig on the tabletop.

"I don't expect people to get it," she said after a long silence, the words a bit slurred and soggy. "I don't need them to. Dope is dope, anyway. How you do it is a personal choice, and we all have our preferences, don't we?" She eyed him, her hazel glare critical and challenging. She tossed the wet towels into the trash can and sat back against the bench.

"The shit was freaky," he insisted. "You were talking to yourself, or to someone else, but it sure as hell wasn't me. And your hands were doing things, I dunno what. Like a mime, performing some kind of invisible task, your eyes half closed the whole time, then *bam*—out." He sliced the air between them like a karate chop. "Down for the fucking count. I never seen Bryce do that shit. *Ever.*"

Mom trawled through her jacket for her cigarettes, slid one from the box, and lit it. She offered one to Matt, and he took it. "Well, it's sorta hard to describe." She was getting drowsy again, but she fought it so she could explain. She blew a long cloud of smoke into Betty's ceiling. "IVing seems to have its own effects. Not sure why. It makes you see shit, takes you to places in your head, in your life, people, locations, images. Happened last night, too. All of it's so damned clear, real, as if you were there, you can reach out and touch someone's face, hear them talking. Bryce calls it lucid dreaming, but he says it doesn't happen to him, anymore." She took a hit from her cigarette. "Sorry if I scared you. But, to me, it didn't seem like anything was wrong. I mean, I felt fine, just time traveling, nodding out."

"You stopped breathing, dude."

"Okay, and so you did what I asked. You woke me up, didn't let me sleep." She apologized again and thanked him. "Welcome to safe-sitting." She gave him a groggy smile. "Not really all that necessary when you snort the shit. The high's way less intense, smoother, but inferior in comparison, I'll tell you that."

"Yeah. Learn somethin new every day," he told her, but it was dipped in sarcasm. "I'll stick with what I know, thanks."

She didn't argue, didn't have the energy, really, and instead found herself drifting back to a contented place of indifference. Just like before, the wretched withdrawal symptoms were gone, wiped away by the merciful hand of Lady Black, and so she sat thinking for a long while, she and Matt sharing space and a semi-comfortable silence. She stared into Betty's kaleidoscope curtains, thankful to be feeling a whole lot of nothing again, and she liked that the orange triangles were brightened by the late afternoon sunshine, seeping through the tattered fabric.

Finally, she looked at Matt. "Do you ever miss your family? Your mom and your brother? We've been out here for months, gone for so damn long." She tapped her ashes into the water glass beside the spent needle and leaned back against the bench.

Matt shrugged. "Sure. Of course. But this is something we gotta do, ya know? Gotta see it through. We'll get home again, after we hear from the labels, one way or the other." He studied her for another moment, toked on his cigarette, and flicked the ashes into the glass. "You sure you're okay?"

"Yeah, I'm good." My mother sat thinking for a while. "It's November. Christmas is coming, Thanksgiving." She smiled a little at a memory finding its way through the high. "My mom, she used to make empanadas for the whole block, gave them away for the holidays. We were the only Latinos—or half Latino, anyway—the only ones in the neighborhood, so it was like a novelty." She dragged on her cigarette, exhaled quietly, chuckled to herself. "All our Irish and Jewish and Anglo neighbors, waiting all year for those things." She stared into the water glass, then turned it in her hand to watch the ashes sink and float around the bottom. "I haven't thought about that in a long time."

Her lids were growing heavy again, and it was getting harder to bring the cigarette to her mouth; it took a few attempts before she could gather enough waning strength for another drag.

"Kinda miss it," she muttered, letting the smoke drift thick and languid from her lips, her body going slack under another crushing nod. She resisted, forced her eyes open, and tried to hold her head up, to keep the cigarette from melting a hole in the vinyl bench seat, but she was losing the fight.

Matt watched as she did what she could to defy gravity. "You know, I'm real sorry about Rache. Really, I am."

"Yeah, me too." It was all my mother could put together, the only syllables her lips would allow as she wilted over the table again and slipped into that empty forsaken crack between consciousness and sleep.

Matt reached around and took the fuming cigarette from between her fingers, and he dropped it into the glass where it hit the water with a gentle hiss.

chapter sixteen

SHE THOUGHT SHE should be more mindful of Bryce's advice, and so she cut back on the dosage the following morning before their shoot with Erin Hayes, just enough to chase off an early round of mild sickness that had crept up on her while she slept.

Bryce guided her through it, pointed her toward a fresh and useable vein, but he was perturbed when he'd gotten home from work the previous night to find she had gone it alone. It was her life, her dope, her veins, but he had assumed a kind of mentorship over this new phase of her addiction and thought she should have waited for him, done a couple snaps of cheese off the Two of Spades in the meantime.

He empathized with her frantic need to medicate after suffering withdrawals, with the despondency of Rachel having gone back to LA, but if Matt hadn't been there to slap her back from the edge of death, what would he and Gavin do with a deceased out-of-town junkie going stiff in the cabin of a dope-infested motor home, parked in the middle of their driveway?

He lectured her for an hour about user accountability and all the other critical liabilities of addiction, that you have to consider those around you, smackheads and straights alike—when you forget the rules, it threatens people's livelihoods, everyone's freedom, puts your friends on the spot and compromises their trust and safety. It was hard enough being an addict, trying to navigate through society with its collective eye passing judgment at every turn.

"The world is unkind to the likes of us," he told her. "The least we can do is be kind to ourselves and to each other. So, keep your head outa your ass from now on, ya got it?"

She got it. She hadn't been thinking much about those things, only that tight little space between sickness and ecstasy, the trap door through which Rachel had vanished thirty-six hours ago. In that time, she and the band had met with Erin Hayes. They walked the shops on Pearl Street in Platt Park while Erin kept an undisruptive distance, camera bag slung across her shoulder, walking backward and snapping off a roll of black-and-white candids, the proofs for which I'd found during the fall after Mom died, packed away in an attic trunk in Marietta. Dad took me to have them re-developed into a variety of print sizes, the better shots framed for display and the rest converted to digital discs for Internet use.

There were others, color shots of the band sitting on the front steps of an historic Brownstone in Stoneman's Row, a moody stoic series that none of them smiled for, the images intentionally granulized for a vintage effect. Erin took a roll of individual shots of Mom at the famous 32nd and Lowell, and I found the negatives for those as well.

My favorite was a low-angled closeup in semi-profile, the sun bursting in a blue sky behind her, the curls blowing from her face through a crisp November breeze. I thought it ironic. She couldn't possibly have imagined, then, that she would one day have a twenty-one-year-old daughter who would keep that photo, enlarge it to a ten by twelve, and hang it under glass on her own living room wall.

There were long shots and mid shots with the Gibson six-string strapped across her back, a local drum circle playing in the background, her hands stuffed into her jeans pockets in mid-stride across the frame. Another set featured the whole band, talking amongst themselves at the bar in Gaetano's historic Italian restaurant, smoldering cigarettes and lowball cocktails in their hands, lots of saturated reds and smooth stainless steel, the glossy laminate wood grains of a 1940's décor, slick and vivid. The best shot was a reflection of the band in the liquor mirror, the four of them dressed fashionably out of epoch, with a row of studded leather sofas in Bing Cherry burgundy, captured in the low-lighted background. It almost made you want to search the dining room faces for the Rat Pack or Nick Gambino or Marilyn herself.

I thought my mother's composure throughout the shoot was impressive. She left no illusions whatsoever to having picked up a drug habit, her constricted pupils in the closeups easily explained by the early morning sun in her eyes, the bruising pin pricks on her arm hidden under a full-length lambskin coat she'd found while vintage shopping with Naomi. She had a model's assurance, natural and competent, effortlessly photogenic— who would ever suspect it to all come unstitched and fall apart without a 10mg shot of Black Tar heroin?

THEY HAD A show that night at The Sound Station in Aurora. Erin met them there as well and took a roll of live publicity pics for the new press kit, in the event that Geffen's business trail went cold. I never saw those, but my mother's corresponding journal entry was dismal in regard to that evening. It was her first show since July without Rachel listening from a bar top, throwing my mother that proud little wink with a pretty smile whenever their eyes would meet.

Mom knew the hours on stage would be difficult, terribly distracted, and so she cooked up a quick dose in the Fleetwood before show time to fill the gushing hole in her heart, careful with the shot, slow and steady, then a deep flush of satisfaction as the tourniquet sprang loose. It wasn't quite enough to send her sliding to the floor, yet the afterglow had a warm and heavy hand that pressed down on her like a lid, but that was all right. She could still think, just not about her. If apathy was the opposite of love, then heroin was its soothing counterpart, and she appreciated the reprieve, the emotional novocaine.

She had business to attend, money to make, a job to do; no use wasting a night of good creative energy, crying over broken sentiments. She wiped the blood runnel from her forearm and dabbed it clean. Bryce was right, she thought. Rotating was good camouflage. The other two injection sites were all but healed now, tiny pinprick freckles vanishing under faint yellow stains so subtle on her olive skin, you might take them for shadows if the light was right.

She took the dope spoon to the sink and rinsed it, then gathered her works from the table and put them away, safe in the nightstand drawer beside the bed. Dom had been adamant about that; he didn't want to see them, didn't want to know, and Evan just thought it was eerie. Even Bryce's rigs left sullied on the studio coffee table gave him a quiver, so it was the least she could do to prevent any unnecessary disputes. Follow the rules. Show some consideration. Keep the peace.

THE SOUND STATION was located upstairs over a restaurant bar called O'Brien's. It was a bitch for the guys to carry the amps and monitors up forty-seven steps, but the pay was worth it at fifteen hundred bucks, plus five percent of the door and whatever tips they could collect from the crowd. Everyone sat around cocktail tables in front of the stage and stood waiting for drinks at the bar in the back; the place was packed. Mom and Evan wandered out to a space-heated balcony that overlooked Havana Street, crowded with college students standing at the railing, dripping Heinekens and wine glasses and cigarettes in hand, shouting down at friends on the sidewalk.

"So, you gonna be all right tonight?" Evan asked as they leaned on the rail, watching the Havana Street traffic.

"I wanna do 'Cold Shot' first." Mom had no interest in the topic of her broken heart.

She'd had about all the lamenting she could bear, and though she knew he meant well, there was only one thing that mattered tonight, and that was a cash guarantee at two a.m.

"We'll keep the rest of the show as rehearsed, but I don't wanna open with 'Pride and Joy.'" She dragged on her cigarette, sipped her beer. "No fucking point now," she muttered. "In fact, scratch that from the rest of our gigs, too."

Evan didn't say anything. He just nodded and gazed down at the busy sidewalk. Inside, the soundman was playing house music for the awaiting crowd, a repetitive, endless bass drum, thumping the walls like an apartment neighbor hanging picture nails. My mother hated it. She would've had something snide and critical to say about drum machines and electronic sequencers replacing human skill, programmed by talentless dolts for more money than the law should allow, but it seemed a useless objection.

She didn't particularly care, anymore, who made their money how. It was anyone's prize; if you could figure a way to cheat the business before it swindled you, then go for it, get yours. As far as she saw it, the music industry had become a certifiable disaster zone, artists clambering for royalty checks like refugees fighting over sacks of rice thrown from a relief truck. And now that Portland Downs' demo package was nearly complete for Michael Freiburg, she herself was no different, just another displaced survivor at the tailgate, climbing over the wounded for a piece of fortune and fame.

She checked her watch, crushed out her cigarette in the nearest ashtray. "'Bout that time."

They went inside and took the stage where Dom and Matt were tuning up and double checking the monitor connections.

Dom gave her a disgruntled glance and kept tuning. That was how it had been for days, quiet bitter exchanges when they passed each other in the house, ignoring each other through that morning's photo shoot. Mom shouldered the Stratocaster and played a few practice licks to test the amp volume. She waited for Evan to climb behind the drums, then nodded up to the sound booth, and the dance music faded.

She called back to Dom and Matt with the set list change, and Dom pursed his lips, annoyed because it wasn't what they'd rehearsed, but he went along with it as she took a vanguard at the mic. The crowd was already stoked and rowdy, clap-chanting her name, three hundred strong, and so she counted off the opener and gave them what they'd all paid for, and Portland Downs went to rumbling power amps for the next two hours with Erin's camera flashing like strobes against the stage lights.

BY MIDNIGHT, ERIN'S job was finished, and she left, as most of the audience was becoming tipsy and obnoxious. Testosterone and liquor had begun to upstage the band, as it often did on nights like this, when drunken resentment found its way into the wrong territories, moving in on someone's date or slopping a drink onto a new pair of Adidas. Too many people and not enough seats, too many personal spaces overlapping, the wrong eyes on the wrong cleavage or crotch while the band fueled it along with Grand Funk Railroad and Zeppelin covers.

A shoving match broke out in the back by the pool tables. The band was vaguely aware of it as security muscled through the crowd and broke it up—Portland Downs kept playing. After a while, another standoff erupted, closer to the bar area this time, and my mother wondered if it was a full moon.

Two females stood snapping at each other, nose to nose, one of them pointing to a chair she'd been sitting in before the other apparently stole it while she was off waiting in line for the bathroom. The boyfriend of the second girl edged himself between them, trying to separate the two, but the other girl's date seemed to take offense to that, and now the guys were bumping chests, arms out at their sides, inviting the other to make a move.

The band kept playing.

The guys shouted in each other's face while the girls tried to decide whether to push them apart or keep barking at one another, and now all their friends were getting involved. Then there was the sound of glass breaking. A beer bottle shattered against the forehead of the boyfriend closest to the stage, and he dropped. Chunks and shards went flying and the crowd dilated, then fell back together again in an all-out raging brawl.

The band had seen this kind of thing before, and so they still didn't stop. They segued instead into an ultra-slow blues tune, Zeppelin's "Cryin' Like Rain," a subliminal tactic meant to settle the mood and make it easier for the bouncers to get a handle on things. But tonight it didn't seem to be working.

The scuffle was gaining momentum, a pandemic snowball expanding across the club, arms and fists and elbows bulldozing over cocktail tables, a furious mass of inebriation pushing toward the sound booth. It flailed on that side the room for a while, overturned the chairs and upended a bar top as security in bright yellow jackets dragged away whomever they could wrestle into a choke hold or a wristlock. My mother watched while she soloed, safe there on a two-foot riser, flanked by a set of 1400 watt power amps nearly as tall as she.

After a long while, it seemed like the chaos might temper down. The shouting stopped, and people had begun to walk away. Bar managers stood pointing customers toward the exits, and the mob was dispersing and splintering off into smaller cliques. But then a guy in a Broncos jersey turned back from the doorway and puffed up his chest and stalked after another guy who was still running his mouth, and the pandemonium started all over again. This time there was a bit more room to box, and so people made weapons of the beer bottles and glass ashtrays, the porcelain dinner platters smeared with ketchup and chicken bones, the hurricane drink glasses, the bar stools.

My mother turned to Evan, and she sliced a hand at her throat with a signal to wind it down; they were only a few songs shy of the final set, anyway. She was about to face the crowd again when she saw his expression go suddenly flat and change into something like panic. His mouth opened to say something and he started up from his seat, and the rest all seemed to unfurl in a peculiar slow motion, with an explosion of pain in my mother's left side.

She went to a knee. She managed to unshoulder the guitar and get the strap from around her neck before she dropped—equipment cables and Dominick's Wallabies at her face now, the foot of a mic stand, plywood grainy against her cheek. Drumsticks bounced off the toms and clattered to the floor, and the music fell apart. Feedback squealed from the monitors over a hundred people still arguing. She saw Matt's jeans and sneakers run past, heard him shouting, calling someone a cocksucker, a piece of fucking shit, fisticuffs and shoving at the edge of the stage again.

"Jo." Dominick was in her ear now, hands on her shoulders. "Evan, get him the fuck outa there!" He leaned back down to her. "Come on, Jo-Jo. You all right? Can you get up?"

My mother shut her eyes tight against an unending, excruciating chain of spasms in her lower rib cage. Too painful to breathe in. Too painful to breathe out. She wondered if she'd been stabbed.

"Matt! Knock it off! Get *off* him, *let* 'em go! Christ," Dom mumbled, his attention back to my mother again. "Where's it hurt, Jo? Can you sit up?"

My mother shook her head, pressed to the plywood, and she growled through gritted teeth; it wouldn't stop, wouldn't let up, an unseen hand around a single rib, trying to snap it in two, or rip it from her side, or crush it from within. She took shallow breaths. She wondered how long she could do that before passing out altogether.

"Yeah, and see if I don't fuck *you* up like I fucked up your boy!" Matt snapped from somewhere off the stage. "Little bitch."

"Just shut up." Evan shoved him away from the scuffle. "They've got cops coming, asshole. Calm the hell down. Just let it go." He pushed him again and walked him toward the stage where my mother lay among the lead cords and toppled mic stands, with a blurry slanted view of all the disarray around the sound booth.

"Yeah, help me get her ass up," Dominick said to him. "I dunno what's wrong yet, but she's holdin her side. Jo-Jo. We're gonna try to sit you up, all right?"

"Where's my guitar?" she finally wheezed. "Is it broken?"

"You get hit with a ninety-mile-an-hour bar stool," Dom said, "and you're worried about your fucking Fender. Figures."

"I think the vibrato bar's busted," Evan told her. "That's an easy fix, though. And it's probably got some scratches. Might be able to buff those out, we'll see."

My mother groaned, unsure which was more painful now, a fractured rib or the idea of her prized possession bashed and mangled by a ferocious drunken mob. The guys each took an arm and carefully leaned her into a sitting position, good side first, but that mattered very little because the pain was explosive, a lightning strike, and she cried out and felt the tears begin to burn. The stage lights were still flashing red, blue, and yellow. A nicotine haze. People were milling about, some of them still arguing, others laughing, recounting their own versions of what happened while servers and barbacks went around ushering people toward the exits and sweeping up the glass.

A bar manager weaved through the mess and came to them. They knew him only as Larry, and he assessed my mother's condition with the fear of a lawsuit in his eyes. "Jeezus, I'm so sorry about this. We've never had things get outa hand quite like that before. You all right? I can call for another ambulance. There's one on the way now, but I can get another one here; you just say the word."

My mother shook her head.

"Jo, we don't know what's wrong," Evan said. "You mighta fucked up something internally. You gotta go get this seen about it, seriously."

Mom shook her head again, wincing, doubled over with an arm folded tight against her side, tucked between her ribs and thigh, like a brace of sorts. She thought if she let it loose she might split in half. "No. No ambulance," she breathed. "Can't afford that shit. Just take me there. In the 4Runner. No ambulance. And no cops, please. Matt." She glanced up at him, and he knew exactly what that meant.

"I got it. I'm on it now. Just let them get you down to the car, and I'll meet you guys out there. Just wait for me." And he jogged away and disappeared through the bar.

She tried to stand and walk, but it was impossible, too many lightning bolts stealing her breath and forcing her knees to the floor, and so Dominick hoisted her into his arms and carried her down two flights of stairs with Evan and Larry spotting him, waving people out of the way.

They loaded her into the Toyota's empty hatch, and Dom climbed in with her. Police lights whirled around the storefronts. The guy who'd gotten his head cracked with the Guinness stout sat in the open doors of a nearby EMS vehicle, blood on his face and sweatshirt, red emergency lights flickering against the crowd. Larry stood waiting at the 4Runner, peering in at my mother who was leaning against the backseats, waiting for Matt to clear out the Fleetwood, an arm still braced against herself to keep the bones from snapping. After a while he left them with his business card and went to see about the others.

"You have anything on you?" Dom asked when Larry was gone. "In your pockets? Tell me you don't have a baggie of that shit in your guitar case. This place is crawlin with po-po's."

Mom shook her head. "Matty's got it handled. He knows what to do."

He was back at the 4Runner within minutes, the designated Cleaner, and he climbed into the passenger seat as Evan threw it into drive and navigated through the commotion toward the closest Aurora hospital.

SHE WAS ABLE to get her legs under her when they got there, but she walked doubled over, as if searching the concrete for a lost contact lens, Matt and Evan on either side with a hand around each biceps. They led her into the waiting room, fluorescent lights and Pine-Sol, a baby crying, Miss Cleo prescribing fortunes on the mounted TV while an intercom voice summoned physicians to their departments. A dozen patients sat around in scuffed plastic chairs, bundled in blankets and heavy coats, miserable and quiet, clutching their swollen sprains, their lacerated appendages wrapped in dishcloths, tissues wadded at their flu-ridden noses. My mother sat among them, hunched in her chair, tear streaked and light headed.

Dom went to the admissions window and explained what happened, and within moments an ER nurse appeared through the double doors with a wheelchair, calling her name ahead of all the others, and the guys followed as he took her straight back to the examination area.

He had her remove her jacket, which was a daunting task, but she winced and wheezed until it slipped away into Matt's keeping. He suggested she climb up onto the gurney and have a seat there so he could get her vital signs, but that was impossible, so she just sat in the wheelchair at the foot of the bed and rested her head on the mattress while he took her blood pressure, pulse, and temperature.

"Can never be too cautious with a broken rib, if that's what it turns out to be," he said, adjusting the blood pressure cuff. He was handsome and well built, even in scrubs, wore a pair of wire rimmed glasses with a military high-and-tight crew cut, maybe a transplant from Ft. Carson. His photo-tag said, *Keith Arrington, RN.* "We'll get you to X-ray in just a little while, wanna make sure it hasn't punctured anything. You having trouble breathing?"

My mother nodded. "Hurts like hell. Hard to talk, hard to breathe."

He held two fingers to her wrist, checked his watch. He asked how it happened, and so Evan told the story so my mother wouldn't have to, and Keith pressed his lips tight with empathy, shook his head.

"Only takes one bonehead to ruin a good time," he muttered.

He made more small talk about the band while he took my mother's temperature, asked about the music they played and where their travels had taken them, what had brought them all the way to Denver.

He released the blood pressure cuff and made notations on a clipboard, and then he sat studying the numbers for a long moment. "Are you an athlete?" he asked her.

"Used to be," Mom muttered.

"What'd you play?"

"Tennis. 'Bout five years ago."

"Not recently, though?"

She shook her head.

He gave that a little half nod and sat thinking. "So, is low blood pressure normal for you, then? Maybe genetic?"

"Dunno. Never really paid much attention."

He shrugged, turned down the corners of his mouth, scribbled something onto his medical sheet. "Just kind of unusual when you're injured like this. Typically it raises the blood pressure a bit, pulse goes up. Yours is 56, blood pressure's 94/50, and I know you're in some serious pain, so . . .." He didn't elaborate any further, but his demeanor seemed to harden a bit.

He looked at her straight, looked into her eyes, then down at the bruise on the arm on which he'd taken her pulse, and she was starting to get the feeling he might be conducting his own investigation into her medical anomalies.

He smiled a little and patted her knee. "Well, just sit tight for a while, and I'll be back." And he took his paperwork and instruments and disappeared behind the curtain.

Evan was sitting on the gurney, looking at her with concern. "They must think it's pretty serious. They sure didn't waste any time getting you back here, so that's good, anyway."

"Yeah, well, there go the next few gigs," Dom said. He glanced down at her side and shook his head. "My dad broke a rib movin furniture when I was a kid, couldn't do shit for at least a month. There's no way in hell you can play if that's what it is. At least the demo's done now."

"Makes me glad I popped that dickhead in his face," Matt said. He strolled around to the other side of the bed and toyed with a tongue depressor from the shelf along the wall. "Hope I broke his fucking nose."

"Hope he doesn't press charges," Dominick grumbled. "We need that about as much as we need this shit."

"If anyone should press charges," Matt said, "it should be *her.* He threw a goddamned chair, for Christ's sake, and it busted her ribs, fucked up a mic stand, and took out one of our monitors. He presses charges, and we're suing his ass. Believe that."

"They're gonna do a drug test." My mother rested her head in the crook of her arm, braced the other against her midsection.

The guys were quiet.

"I could see it on his face," Mom said into her sleeve. "He knows."

"Well, they can't have you arrested, locked up," Matt said. "You've got nothing on you, and your medical records are confidential, so screw them. You're here to get your ribs looked at, and that's all they should be worried about."

Evan seemed to put together the chemical complications, and he folded his arms at his chest. "But they're eventually gonna have to give her something for pain, no? How's that gonna work if she's already got dope in her system?"

"It's not," Dom mumbled and cut his eyes down to my mother. "You know you're gonna have to tell 'em, right? They load you up with a shot a morphine or Demerol or a couple Oxycontins, and you're gonna need a stretcher for real. They'll be wheelin your ass over to the trauma side with shock paddles on your chest and a tube down your throat. Nice way to spend a Friday night."

My mother didn't know what to say to that. She wasn't sure if the legalities would have her in handcuffs by daylight, and she hadn't considered the potentially lethal cocktail from a three-hour-old shot of hammer and 100mgs of Demerol. She'd never been high in the emergency room before, not even on weed or coke. The last time she'd found herself waiting for X-rays, she was thirteen. Pap was holding a plastic bag of ice cubes wrapped in a dishtowel against a bloody goose egg on the back of her head. She'd gotten inspired by Mary Lou Retton's Olympic gold medal vault and tried to do a backflip off the front porch—seven stitches and a mild concussion.

She buried her face in the fold of her arm and waited at the foot of the gurney for the worst.

The curtains opened, and the nurse Keith presented a clear plastic cup. "If you need a female to go in with you, I can grab someone, get a tech to help you. Is there any possibility that you could be pregnant?"

Even with the invisible bolt cutters clamping down on her ribs, my mother found it within herself to chuckle. "No. No possibility at all." She gestured to the cup. "So, do I still need that?"

"Well, we just wanna be sure."

"Yeah, I bet you do," she muttered.

She twisted herself out of the wheelchair and stood, bent over at the waist with a terrible scowl. She felt like she'd been hit with a major league fastball. Keith called after a girl whose tag identified her as a nursing assistant like Naomi. Her name was Bethany; it was all my mother could see of the girl in her current posture, baby blue scrub top, a little emerald clover pendant sparkling in the v-neck, a photo-tag like Keith's with a picture of a blonde about Mom's age.

Bethany walked her to a nearby rest room and shut the door behind them. My mother was mildly humiliated but grateful for the help, just the same. Her left side was useless, and even the slightest jolt brought spasms that stole her breath and squeezed the tears from her eyes all over again. Bethany stood close to keep her from losing her balance and pissing all over her own hand and onto the floor, and when it was done, the girl took my mother back to the gurney with the promise that someone from radiology would be around soon.

AFTER THE FIRST hour passed, Evan thought it best to go back to the club and see about getting paid, and so he and Dominick left Matt to wait with Mom for the doctor. They made the five-mile trip along Colfax to Havana Street, found the manager Larry who not only made good on the guarantee but offered an extra three hundred for the damaged equipment. He had them send my mother's hospital bills to The Sound Station for payment as well.

He felt so bad that he helped them break down and load the rest of the gear into the 4Runner, and by then it was close to five a.m. They hauled everything back to the Medical Center and went inside, looking for Mom and Matt in the waiting area, but they were still in the back, Matt stretched out on the gurney and my mother crouched and groaning in the wheelchair where they'd left her two hours ago.

"So, what'd they find?" Dom asked. "Is it broke? She gonna be outa commission for the next month or what?"

"Nobody's come for her yet," Matt grumbled at the acoustic tiles and fluorescent tubes overhead. "Not a single fucking soul." He checked his watch and blew an absurd little breath through pursed lips. "It's been almost four hours since we walked in. Four goddamned *hours*, dude."

Evan glanced around at the other curtains partially drawn around bronchitis and food poisoning patients, a whining toddler in his mother's arms, a woman with a knee swollen to the size of her own head, nurses and respiratory personnel strolling from one to the next, to the nurse's station where two RN's sat grinning and laughing in a personal chat with a janitor propped up on his mop handle. "I guess they're just busy tonight."

"If that's the case, then how come the bed next to us is on its third patient since we got here?" Matt tipped his chin across the room. "That one's had two people come and go already, too. They haven't even given her anything for pain, for Christ's sake. They did their dope test, they know what's in her system, okay, so fine. Then give her somethin appropriate that'll help without killin her. Is it really that hard?"

"I'm startin to feel like shit," my mother muttered, and she looked up at Matt. He knew what that meant, but he wasn't sure what to do about it.

"Jo, all I got is a little cheese." He glanced around the emergency room and told her discreetly, "This isn't exactly an ideal spot, you know."

"Just give 'em some time, Jo," Dom said. "They'll do your X-rays and then give you some codeine or some shit."

Mom shook her head. "That's not gonna help. They make me sit here for one more hour, and I'm gonna start getting sick. Matty." She nodded to his pants pocket. "I can just go to that bathroom. I'll give it back to you when we get outa here."

"Dude, you can hardly walk," Evan said. "You're like the second figure in the human evolution pictures. If your arms were longer, your knuckles would be dragging the floor. Just stay here and wait for them to come get you."

"I can walk. In a few minutes, I'm not gonna have any choice. I'll just tell 'em I gotta piss."

A woman in a white physician's coat pulled aside the curtain. She scanned all their faces and stopped on my mother. Mom asked if she was a doctor, and she said her name was Colleen and that she was from the lab. She was there to draw blood, and she laid two empty vials on the bed and pulled a tourniquet from her coat pocket.

"Have you ever been exposed to HIV or hepatitis that you know of?"

Mom shrugged. "Not unless it was on that bar stool that hit me."

"And you're sure you couldn't be pregnant?" she asked, slipping into a pair of latex gloves from the box on the wall.

"You guys shoulda known the answer to that about four hours ago," Mom mumbled and rested her head back on the foot of the gurney, fending off a wave of nausea.

"Well, they wanna do a few tests while you're here. Just to be on the safe side." She tore open the needle package and asked my mother if she had a preference for which arm, and Mom held out the right one; the less anyone poked around at the left one, the better.

"The safe side, huh? The safe side of what?" Mom asked as Colleen swiped the area clean with an alcohol swab, but the phlebotomist didn't answer.

She took the vials she needed, applied a cotton ball tacked with a little strip of gauze to the injection site, and disappeared through the curtains. Mom looked up at Matt again, asking with her eyes for the baggie of dope in his pocket.

"Just wheel me over there, and I can do the rest myself," she said.

"If they catch you, you're fucked," Dom grumbled.

"They won't," she insisted.

Matt sat up and swung his long legs around the side of the gurney and hopped down. He pushed her across to the same rest room where Bethany watched her pee four hours ago, and he palmed the baggie into her hand as he helped her out of the chair.

Inside, she shuffled to a seat on the toilet and was able to dig her wallet from her back pocket and slip a business card from the fold. She unsealed the ziplock and scooped a quick bump onto the corner, then flushed the toilet to mask the sound as she sniffed it back with a wince.

Then someone knocked, and it made her jump, jamming a butcher knife between the bolt cutters, and that sent the open bag of dope flapping to the bathroom floor. And now there it lay, in a silt of brown powder on the bone-white tiles at her feet. She stood staring at it with an arm wrapped around herself to keep from bursting open.

"Jo, come on. They're here to take your X-ray, fucking finally," Matt called through the crack. "Hurry it up, before they make you wait *another* four hours."

She peered down at the dope on the floor, Matt's dope, spilled out around the base of the toilet bowl. If she were in better shape, she would get on her hands and knees and scrape it up with the card and dump it back into the baggie where it belonged. What to do?

Matt knocked again. "Come on, *chica.* It's now or never, let's go. You decent? You need me to help?"

"No, just open the door," she wheezed, and so he did, just enough to peek inside to where she sat doubled over, gesturing down to the pile of heroin between her shoes.

He started to make a bitter face, to berate her for his wasted cheese, but he didn't. Instead he said, for the sake of all medical personnel, "Oh, man, you dropped your wallet. Well, don't worry about that. I got it. Just go with them, and I'll hold onto it for you. Yeah, I see all the stuff fell out, okay. No prob. Got it." And he slipped into the bathroom, guided her back out to the wheelchair, and shut the door.

The technician rolled her back to radiology. It took a long and creative effort to get the proper pictures, as she was unable to stand up straight, place her hands behind her head, take a deep breath and hold it. So, the technician lowered the target board to the height of a six year old, had her stand as close to it as she could, and clicked off four images that took another hour to be reviewed.

By seven a.m. they determined that my mother had a posterior hairline fracture of the tenth vertebral rib. She was HIV negative and hepatitis free. She was indeed not pregnant, but it was clear through all their testing and observations that she had an IV drug habit. They gave her nothing for pain, not even a prescription for Motrin. They wrapped her ribs with an ACE bandage, sent her on her way with the suggestion to purchase an over-the-counter pain reliever, and took a one hundred dollar down payment for services rendered.

SHE SPENT THE next two days in the RV, self-medicating at three times the previous dosage. A 30mg shot of Black Tar every eight hours kept her in a pleasant, semi-conscious state of disengagement, which melted away the bolt cutters and turned the lightning strikes to a dull throb. Matt slept on the pullout and safe-sat until the fracture settled into something she could finally tolerate with less dope, which seemed to fall right in line with the ER staff's throwaway remedy. She could still recall overhearing the nurse Keith telling Bethany the assistant that he wasn't about to provide an opiate substitute for some junkie whose injuries probably could've been avoided if she wasn't wasted on heroin. "Damned drug seekers. Who doesn't see a bar stool come flying across the room? Ever hear of the term 'duck'? Probably nodded right off the stage and did it to herself. Serves her right. She's still got enough of that crap in her system to sedate a small elephant, anyway, so she can hang for a while. I've got other stuff to do."

That was at three a.m., an hour after they'd wheeled her in from the waiting room. She was in too much pain to make an issue of it then and thought perhaps the doctor might see it another way, see it for what it was. But it seemed the only steps the staff had taken were to cover themselves, and so now here she lay, three days later in the RV sleeper, with an aching black-and-purple bruise the size of a grapefruit, causing opiate nightmares of mutilated demons come to snatch her up for the torture chambers of hell.

She felt a presence while she half slept, lying with her back to the camper. The mattress sunk with the weight of another, someone sitting at the edge. Matt had been checking on her every morning to make sure she was still breathing, that her lips hadn't gone blue sometime during the night, and she felt bad for him having been put on death watch like this, but Naomi hadn't any access to the hospital pharmacy and didn't know its technicians well enough to strike a deal for Lortab or Percocet.

The only medication afforded my mother now came from the Mexican poppy fields of El Salto, Durango. It traveled up through Tempe and on into Phoenix, across the Colorado plains until it reached Meridian, where Lecia sorted it into eightballs and grams on her dining room table, then delivered it to my mother's doorstep in her little cellophane wrappers.

Mom felt a hand on her shoulder, as she did each morning since Friday. "I'm good, Matty, thanks," she muttered into the sheets. "Just tired. Feelin better, though. You can go inside, I'll be okay."

He didn't say anything.

"Hey, when you go in there," she told him, "see if Bryce can make a call today. I got a hundred, and I'll get yours, too, for the shit I spilled in the bathroom."

He still didn't respond.

She thought it strange and wondered if he'd gotten into her works while she slept, perhaps made the blind leap into mainlining and now had no idea where his own head was at. She got an elbow underneath her good side and pushed herself halfway around to have a look at him, and she froze. She lay propped on an elbow, peering dumbly over her shoulder with her lips parted and ready to say something, but nothing came.

"I've been doing some research into your condition."

My mother blinked, half shook her head. "Um . . . okay. Which—which one?" She motioned down to her rib cage, swaddled in crepe bandaging.

"The one you've been using to alleviate that one." Rachel scooted closer, lifted my mother's t-shirt to see the extent of the damage, and she made a pitiful face. Dark purple and yellow peeked out from under the ACE wrap, an angry blemish making its way down her side and around to the small of her back.

My mother watched as she examined the wound, unsure of what to do with her sudden presence at the edge of the bed. It had been four hours since her last dose, a bit too long for lucid dreaming, but she glanced around the Fleetwood, anyway, for things amiss, for a leprechaun in drag swinging from the kaleidoscope curtains, or Nanna Sylvia in the sleeper doorway, wagging a silver spatula with Spanish admonishments fluttering off her tongue. Rachel touched a fingertip to the injury, and it drove a rod of hot rebar through my mother's side that made her jump, and she growled with a wretched grimace. So much for pinching herself.

Rachel pulled away, apologized. "They should have given you some instructions on how to care for this. Do you still have them? How often do you have to put ice on it?"

"They weren't really all that accommodating," was all my mother could think to say as she tried to resituate. Rachel gave that a peculiar frown, so Mom told her, "As soon as they did a drug test, I pretty much went to the bottom of the list. All I got was a receipt for the co-pay."

Rachel glared at that and looked off into the Fillmore neighborhood through Betty's rear window, thinking. A light snowfall had begun, and the black macadam was going gray under the November flurries.

She looked down at Mom's injuries again and breathed a very deep sigh of discontent. "If *I* had been there . . . " she started to say but kept the rest hidden behind whatever mystery had brought her back to my mother's bedside. She seemed to shift into a new train of thought, and she lowered Mom's shirt and folded her hands in her lap. "Things are gonna have to change. Everything's gotta be different. But before we talk about that, I'm gonna ask you, one last time—do you want to quit? Get some help while this is still a new habit? And your answer won't affect whether I stay or go, only how we're gonna live our lives from here on out."

My mother was confused. She winced and pushed herself up against the pillows so she could look at Rachel straight. "Did Matt call you? Or Evan? Did you, like, fly back out here or something?"

"Jolán, I never left."

Mom knitted her brow and searched the blankets for some way to make sense of that. "But you did." She could still see the Yellow cab taillights shrinking toward Colfax. "Six days ago. Well, five days, six hours and . . ." She reached gingerly for her watch on the nightstand. "Seventeen minutes ago." She looked back at Rachel with a shrug.

"You still haven't answered my question."

"You haven't answered mine."

"I came so close, I could almost smell the ocean," Rachel confessed. "How 'bout that? I sat in that bus station all night long, trying to figure out how to hate you enough to buy a ticket."

"Well, that's not very safe," my mother said.

"And you should talk about what's safe?" Rachel gestured with her eyes to the fresh injection bruise on my mother's forearm.

Mom didn't have anything to say to that.

"For every reason I could think of to stay, I had one really great reason to leave. I asked myself a hundred times, a hundred different ways, if being in love with you was enough."

"And?"

"And I still don't know." She stared down into her lap, contemplating that. Then she looked at my mother. "I know I spent a week at the 11th Street Hostel, playing solitaire and eating fast food and day-old donuts. And then it finally occurred to me. You and this addiction, they're two separate things. And though I am angry with your decisions that led to it, leaving you doesn't change the drug—heroin knows nothing, one way or the other. And since you've chosen to answer my question by *not* answering it." She reached into the backpack at her feet. "I've got some things I want to show you."

She withdrew a manila folder, thick as one of my mother's spiral-bound journals, and she laid it open on the bed between them.

"It took a while to find everything," she said. "The Denver public library isn't exactly a stockpile for books on drug addiction, particularly yours. Not for what I was looking for, anyway."

There were photocopied pages from medical books and psychology journals, pamphlets for Al-Anon, leaflets and articles from the FDA, scholarly papers penned by professors from the University of Oregon and Johns Hopkins, health and wellness magazine clippings, entire paragraphs from each highlighted in yellow with little notations jotted in the margins. She had stacks of loose-leaf sheets as well, filled with her own handwritten notes and data.

"But once I figured out what the chemical compounds of

diacetylmorphine actually *are* and then cross-referenced that with the effects on the human brain, the nervous system, the digestive tract." She looked at my mother and nodded. "I realized what we need to be doing."

My mother had no reply. She just gazed around at all the scientific deductions and sociological theories on the bedspread, then looked emptily at the little poet who'd gathered it all together.

" . . . to keep this from killing you," Rachel reiterated.

Mom took up a photocopied page from the American Medical Association's journal on neurology but still wasn't sure how to respond, and so Rachel said, "Because there are things you can do, see?" And she thumbed through the folder and produced a copy of *Prevention* magazine, then flipped through that to a page bookmarked with a yellow Post-It. "You need proteins; brown rice, peanut butter, eggs. This drug is notorious for suppressing the appetite, and that'll just compromise your immune system. It's bonding with the dopamine receptors in your brain, creating a false sense of well-being; all the while it's really just sucking up the natural chemicals and replacing them with itself. So, you've got to be aware of that. Food stimulates those same pleasure centers, but if they've already been soaking in smack, then food's not gonna matter. You have to find a balance, or you'll waste away and leave yourself open to every illness on the planet." She shut the magazine and sat with it in her lap. "It can also decrease your sex drive, but so far that hasn't been a problem for you."

My mother took the book from Rachel and browsed the articles. "10 Ways to Strengthen Your Core." "Keeping Up with Calcium." "How to Trick Your Family into Eating Better."

She'd gone for days, agonizing over a two-thousand-mile strip of mountains and desert she thought had finally separated them for good. She'd brought herself to a place of resignation, made ready for a life of regret—girl loses girl because girl was too stupid to cast aside her own demons, to keep the doors and windows locked when they came calling, whispering through the cracks for custody of her mind, her body, her soul.

Mom set the magazine down, then looked at Rachel in bewilderment. "So, this is what you've been doing all week? Hanging out in the library, compiling all this . . . this research? There's like a shitload of stuff here," she said, fanning through all the documents and periodicals on the bed.

"It was good practice." Rachel shrugged, smiling a little. "For next year, when I have to do my Master's thesis. Who knows? Maybe I'll find some connection between you and Edgar Allan Poe." She took my mother's hand and leaned in close to look at her directly. "Months ago, I made you a promise. I told you my place was with you and that I'd stay, no matter what, no matter where all these roads and highways led. Now, I don't like where we've ended up; I hate it, in fact. I hate this drug, I hate this addiction. But I love *you*. And I just need you to meet me halfway with this, let me help you. However that needs to be. You can function with this addiction. We can see to that. We can keep you healthy until you're ready to leave it behind. It's possible, you just have to—"

"I tried." My mother pushed herself up against the headboard, pulled a pillow around behind her back.

Rachel was quiet, and she looked to my mother for clarity.

"The day after you left," Mom said, and she thought about it for a long moment, nodding at her own good intentions. "I was gonna take this shit by the horns, you know? Cold turkey. Just suffer through it till I had it beat. I hadn't been at it that long—how hard could it be, right?"

She swept her eyes around the paperwork on the bed and thought back on that moment of failure, the smell of dope fuming in the spoon, blood in the syringe.

"And man, I meant it, too," she said with a little breath of irony. "I was gonna go find you. Ride all the way back to LA and show you I was still worth loving, that I was stronger than we ever thought."

She made a little disappointed motion with her head, fidgeted with the blanket seam as she lay thinking.

"But no such luck. Obviously. It was all too scary. Losing you. Being so fucking sick I thought I'd die, anyway, dope or no dope, 'cause I'll tell you, Bryce sure wasn't screwin around when he said you'll wish you had a time machine," she muttered, mostly to herself, picking at the lint pills on the comforter. "Go back and start over. Be a better woman. Duck." She nodded down to her bandaged ribs and looked at Rachel with a crooked smile, vulnerable there in the center of her own honesty.

Rachel smiled back. She shifted closer, took my mother's face in her hands, and she kissed her lips. "You were never not worth loving, Jolán De Carlo. If that were the case, I'd be at 37th and Vermont right now, sitting in a Medieval Lit class with a cup of stale coffee and no sleep."

My mother chuckled lightly. "So, you opted for a rusted out motor home and a banged up mess of a dope fiend for company?"

"So to speak." Rachel moved away and peered down at my mother's injury again, and she lifted her shirt for another look. "We'll get you back in shape, in due time."

The side door opened, and Evan came inside, dusting snow from his sleeves and dreadlocks; he had the cordless phone in his hand, but then he stopped and stared at Rachel, there at the edge of the bed with Mom.

"Holy shit." He grinned, amused and a little puzzled but relieved for my mother's sake. He approached and Rachel rose for a hug. "Where the hell'd you come from?"

"Downtown," she confessed as they stepped away, and she slid her hands into her back pockets, smiling. "Just needed to figure some things out for a while."

"Right on." He nodded. "Nothing wrong with that." He looked in at my mother and held up the phone. "It's for you. It's Freiberg."

Mom made a face, a silent query into what Geffen's label scout might have to say, but Evan didn't know.

"He just asked to speak to you," he said with his palm over the receiver, and he brought it to the bed. "The package got there yesterday morning, so I guess we'll find out."

The door opened again, and now Matt and Dom were climbing into the camper. Rachel must have sneaked into the neighborhood while they were all inside because there was a lot of chatter and jokes and questions into her whereabouts; everyone was glad to have her back. Mom held up a hand and waved it around to silence them, and so they all settled and stood around waiting.

"Miss De Carlo," Michael Freiberg hailed from Santa Monica. "Heard there's a storm coming your way."

"Well, I've been a little out of that loop for a while," she told him, glancing out at the snow-silted rooftops. "But you might be right. So, what've you got for us? Anything?"

"I've got lots of things," he said. "Actually, I've got good news and bad news. Which do you guys want first?"

Mom didn't say anything. She glanced at the band, at everyone waiting in the sleeper doorway and around the foot of the bed. She resituated against the pillows. "Well, how 'bout I let you decide. Just don't bullshit us. Let us know either way, so we know what we're doing."

"Fair enough," he said. "Then the bad news, it is."

chapter seventeen

SOMETIMES I CAN see them, peripheral glimpses like shooting stars—there and gone before you catch them there, then gone. I wish I knew what they were, who they might be, where they go when they vanish like that and where they come from. Shadows. Of what? Little slivers of darkness, slices of shade like broken shafts of something much larger. Larger than me, larger than this dark and distant moon on which I've become stranded, watching her watch me from the tangible world. I made a stellar effort, didn't I? But the reptilian brain is an entity all its own and carries on with or without you. Keep feeding it, you stupid motherfucker. Give it a life of its own, nurture it until it eats you alive, bites the hand you thrust into its serrated jaws, dripping and drooling that venom into your pitiful gaping wounds. You have created a monster, and the monster is you. Snare that leviathan with a fishhook if you think you can, superstar. Better batten down and seek shelter, if there is such a thing on that far-flung planet of yours. Wide open and caught in a narcomatic downpour. No quarter for the bold and shiftless of your kind, seekers of isolation, doers of dumb shit, the unthankful. You've got the world at your feet and a needle in your arm. And to think she loves you as is. She should have her head examined, and so should you. And so it goes, and so it goes.

CROSSING THE STATE lines from Colorado to California in the dead of winter was a bit surreal. For two hundred miles they were chased by a blizzard that dissolved into a balmy thunderstorm through southern Utah, then evaporated under the scorched and desiccated basins of Death Valley. It was a week before Thanksgiving, and they camped in the Mojave outside a little town called Yermo, just off Interstate 15, and even in the evening it was warm as the Pennsylvania springtime. They got to Los Angeles the following day and pulled into the Hollywood Travel Lodge on Vermont Avenue by noon, took long naps and hot showers, then headed in the 4Runner over to Miceli's Italian restaurant on Las Palmas to discuss the uncertain future of Portland Downs.

Centriole Entertainment was a brand new independent record label, a subsidiary of MGM Music. It had nothing at all to do with Geffen Records, but when Michael Freiberg was unsuccessful in pitching the band's profitability to Geffen's executives, he passed their demo on to a friend and colleague, Neale Roman, Centriole's founder and CEO. Neale was a studio musician, a bass player like Dominick, and he had toured for years with Grammy-winning artists from all over the world. He'd done session work for platinum acts out of Europe and Japan and had invested millions into his burgeoning music enterprise, there in LA, with no less hope for success than the members of Portland Downs. They were all fairly new to their aspirations, but Neale had bona fide connections, experience, and after listening to their demo, he saw it as an opportunity for them to build something lucrative together.

"There's nothing wrong with going independent," he explained, sitting across from Mom, Rachel, and Dominick at a mezzanine table, overlooking Miceli's main dining room, where hundreds of autographed straw Chianti fiascos hung from the ceilings and dangled from the glass racks over the bar. "Where the problem lies is with distribution." He glanced at Matt and Evan sitting beside him and relaxed against the back of his chair. "Without major distribution, you might as well be selling Girl Scout cookies."

He gave that a concessive shrug and a smile, took a sip of draft beer from a thick frosted mug. He was in his early forties, dark haired, blue eyed and rugged, slender like Matt with angular features and the casual bearing of a man who'd seen and done things they'd only read about in *Rolling Stone*.

"I have a shitload of respect and admiration for bands that try to go it alone, like your friends in Denver. It takes balls, a hell of a lot of faith in your following, but word of mouth only works best with accessibility." He tossed up a hand, searched the red-and-white checkered tablecloth for an example. "I can tell my cousin Jimmy in Hoboken all about this killer new band I saw in Phoenix, but if Jimmy can't run down to his local Tower Records and cop their CD, then what the hell's the point, you know?"

"That's what I've been saying all along," my mother agreed. She sliced through the last of the veal Marengo on her plate. "Most struggling bands have no capital. Ambition costs money. And the bigger the dream, the bigger the price tag."

Neale looked at her and smiled, lifted his mug in agreement. "A realist," he said with a little chuckle. "Don't ever lose that quality. You're gonna need it where we're headed." He nodded down to her injured side. "How you feelin? Doin all right so far, or do we need to cut this short?"

She shrugged that off. "I'm cool. I'd have been here in a body cast, if I had to. Curiosity and all. So, where exactly are we *headed*?" She took a sip from a glass of Sangiovese and looked across at him coolly, still a bit skeptical of his commitment to their success and what that might entail.

Neale sat up and folded his arms on the edge of the table, posturing for business talk. "I wanna do three albums with you guys, minimum.

I'll give you as much creative control as you'd like. However, I've got a phenomenal in-house producer, worked on some movie soundtracks, done some stuff with Foghat, Jeff Healey. He's got a great résumé, nice pedigree. You'll like him."

"And what if we don't?" my mother questioned.

Dom shifted in the seat. "Jo, seriously?" he muttered. He held a hand out to Neale and told her, "Can you let the guy finish before you cut his nuts off?"

"What?" Mom shrugged, a forkful of white truffles suspended at her lips. "It's a possibility. I just wanna know Plan B if we're not on the same page as this guy."

"Then he'll find the right page, get there, and make it work. Vic's a professional. He's versatile and he's flexible," Neale assured. "Listen. At the end of the day, everything gets run past me as executive producer. If things don't mesh creatively, it'll be loud and clear. I know what you're looking for. I know right where your sound is, and I like it. With a little refinement, a little polishing and a decent mix, we should have something radio-ready by spring, something you're happy with, and you won't have to sacrifice a thing except all your time and sleep," he told them with a wink.

"Hell, we've been doing that for months already," Evan said. "Nothin new for us."

"And so we'll get all this in writing then?" Matt asked. "My guess is you don't do business on a handshake, so I'm sure there'll be a contract, at some point."

"At some point," Neale said. "That's pretty much up to you guys. No rush, though I'd like to get things rolling at the first of the year if I could, at least get a single recorded so we can start shopping it for airplay. Gives people something to chew on while they wait for the album to drop."

"That'd give you time to heal," Rachel said to Mom. "Get yourself back in shape to record, perform." She took a bite of Manicotti, dabbed her mouth with a napkin from her lap, nodding hopefully at Neale, then she looked to my mother for response.

Mom sat staring into her plate as she ate, thinking for a long while. Centriole Entertainment was not Geffen Records; it wasn't even close. It was one man's independent castle in the clouds, a man whose sharp blue eyes were going greener than my mother's with dollar signs.

Los Angeles was teeming with new bands like theirs, talented, dedicated, marketable cash cows yet to be milked. Who was Portland Downs among them? Better yet—who was Neale Roman among all the slick-talking Hollywood headhunters with business cards and glittering gold? My mother knew only one way to find out. She stabbed a forkful of salad and stuffed it into her mouth.

"Well, we're gonna have expenses in the meantime. We'd normally just nail down a few gigs to get by, but . . ." Mom gestured down to her ribs and looked at Neale, relaxed and expectant. "We can all look for jobs, I suppose, but a thirty-five-foot motor home's gonna be kinda pricey to park between now and April, if you know what I mean."

No one in the band uttered a word; she had said exactly what they were all thinking, and so everyone sat waiting for an answer to that.

Neale smiled at her, a thin knowing smirk, and he sipped his beer and set it on the table. "All right," he said into the dinner dishes. He pointed a finger at my mother and laughed a little. "You're young, but you're pretty savvy, Miss De Carlo. So, make you an offer, eh?" He nodded once. "Fair enough."

Mom shrugged. "You offered to pay for dinner. You're obviously courting us, so court. Isn't that how it's done? I'm just making us available, turning on the 'open for business' sign." She sipped her wine and pointed back at him. "Your turn."

Neale Roman folded his hands on the table and leaned in closer. "Okay. I'll tell you what; you sign with Centriole by the middle of next month," he proposed across the red votive candlelight, "and I'll throw in a two hundred thousand dollar advance. Can't be a bonus." He held up both hands. "I gotta recoup that, gotta get it back in sales. I'm not Verve, sure as hell not Polygram. But I think that's pretty damned good faith. Truth be told, I wouldn't offer you a single red cent if I didn't think I could turn it into a hundred bucks."

Mom didn't say anything. She just sat looking at him, taking it all into quiet, critical consideration, two hundred thousand dollars more than they had ever seen. She could feel Rachel's nails digging into her thigh beneath the table. Dominick flagged down a server, asked her for a pen.

"My suggestion—think it over, sleep on it for a while, then get yourselves an entertainment lawyer. This is LA. You could play spin the bottle at the corner of Sunset and La Brea and find one. But you could also try *The Hollywood Reporter*. They sell 'em right over there." Neale pointed a thumb out toward the newsstand across the street.

And so there it was—the bottom line. It was all speculative, of course, amid the restaurant chatter and jazz piano, the marinara-smeared plates between them, the sweating pitcher of beer and Matt's freshly lit cigarette fuming through his fingers.

Mom looked at him. They were very good at these wordless dialogues, their own private telepathy. He wanted to kiss Neale Roman, dry hump him till he came in his boxers, but his better mind told my mother to let the offer simmer, be adults, go into this like professionals or get screwed for their own impulsiveness. Only the entertainment gods knew what might lie between the lines in a fifteen-page deal full of legal jargon and other Greek.

Evan's expression said something similar, but he set his thoughts free and said to Mom, "I can make some calls tomorrow, see who might be willing to take us on." He left it there and refilled his mug from the pitcher of beer.

Dominick just gave her a shrug to suggest she had no reason whatsoever to doubt his interest.

So, my mother reached across the table and extended her hand to Neale Roman. "A handshake for now. We'll see where the rest of this goes next week."

"I'll have the contract drawn up and ready by Wednesday." He smiled and shook on that. "Welcome to Centriole Entertainment."

NEALE'S OFFICE WAS on the fourth floor of a ten-story glass building in the 9000 block of Santa Monica Boulevard, Hollywood's west end, where the palms were taller than the street lamps and everyone had a car phone and carried a SkyPager on their hip. He had an executive assistant named Victoria, a petite redhead who sat at a cherry wood desk in the front lobby, which was still being remodeled. Electricians on stepladders threaded stereo wires through the acoustic ceiling tiles while a painter touched up the trim around the doorjambs with Million Dollar Red.

There were big potted plants in the corners and cardboard boxes sitting partly rummaged on the hardwood floor, a two-hundred-gallon aquarium bubbling on a black stand with African cichlids swimming among the anubias, a fresh pot of espresso brewing on Victoria's work station. There was abstract artwork in frames yet to be hung, leaning along the hallway and sealed in bubble wrap; the only thing he hadn't wasted any time displaying were two gold records and one platinum album, sparkling under glass on the foyer walls. One of the gold records was his, for co-production on a soundtrack single in '86. The others were complimentary reminders of his indenture to the MGM/Polygram/Verve conglomerate.

He sat behind an ebony pedestal desk in jeans and a t-shirt that looked unassuming but likely cost ten times more than they were worth. He had a corner office with white carpeting and black leather couches, entertainment law and motivational marketing books on the shelves behind him. He presented his contract, twenty pages of royalty and copyright stipulations and Portland Downs hereafter referred to as "Artist" who would hereunder be obligated to all terms and conditions, commencing with the completion of three master recordings, consisting of songs written and performed by Artist, the projects for which shall hereafter be referred to as "Recordings," and so on, until they were unsure whether it was a record deal or a work of William Shakespeare. Legal counsel would definitely be in order. So, their next goal was to find someone competent who might be willing to represent an unsolicited new act out of Boston.

HER NAME WAS Toni Carroway, and she had an office above a souvenir shop at the corner of Hollywood and Orange. She was slender and birdlike, an over-caffeinated transplant from Chicago with sleek black hair and dark eyes like pieces of pressed coal. The consultation was free for new clients, but Toni wanted five percent of Portland Downs advance, to which they reluctantly agreed.

"I thought they got paid by the hour," Dominick grumbled after Toni stepped out of her office for privacy on an urgent call. "I'm no mathematician, but that's gonna turn my beautiful new '93 Maxima to an '88 Geo Metro."

"No, it won't," Evan assured. "It's only ten thousand bucks from the whole thing, still leaves us each with," and he gazed up into the ceiling fan whirling over Toni's desk, calculating, "forty-seven-fifty. It's customary for entertainment lawyers to take a percentage over an hourly rate. It'll take her all of about two hours to look that thing over, trust me. Six, maybe eight hundred bucks versus ten thousand? It's a no-fucking-brainer."

"It's a racket," my mother muttered. She resituated in the uncomfortable oak chair made more irritating by the healing fracture in her side. "She gets hers off the top, don't forget."

"Well, wouldn't you?" Matt sat in the matching oak armchair with a sneakered foot relaxed across his knee. "Four twenty-something rock musicians living on peanut butter and Hot Pockets for the past three years, now cruising the LA bar scene with a giant wad of cheddar in their wallets." He gave that an absurd little grunt. "I can just hear it. 'Sure, just get me the fee whenever you can.' I'm sure that'd go over great. 'We'll just set you up on a payment plan. I'm sure you guys are good for it, right?'"

"Yeah, well, for ten thousand bucks," Mom said, "she should be able to translate that thing into seven different languages and sing it to us in each, like Madam fucking Butterfly."

"Hell, I'd settle for a ten-thousand-dollar lap dance," Dominick said with a stretch and threw an impatient glance out into the hall. "She can do that in whatever language she wants."

Toni came back into the office and laid the phone back in the charger with a casual apology. She took a seat behind the desk, took up Centriole's contract again, flipped through it to the last page and sat reading to herself.

Then she pointed at something in the print. "Okay, good. This is your 'out,' this paragraph right here." She turned the document around on the desktop so they could see. "The first thing I look for in any contract is an escape clause, a way out, something we can use for leverage if you ever decide to move on." She glanced up at them and said, "Sometimes it becomes necessary to sever ties, and you don't wanna be trapped, never wanna sign anything that contains the phrase 'in perpetuity.' That means 'forever.' And forever is *bad* when you're under contract." She gave that a quick little smile, then nodded down to my mother's ribs. "You walked in here a little worse for wear. Mind if I ask what happened?"

"Bar fight," Mom said. "In Denver."

Toni narrowed her eyes and nodded suspiciously.

"I didn't start it," Mom said. "Or finish it. Just kinda got caught in the middle. They started throwing chairs, and I took one in the ribs."

"Can you play?" Toni questioned.

"Not for very long."

"How long?"

"It'll be another month or so before I'm back where I was. Right now—maybe about twenty minutes. Then I gotta put it down for the day."

"The reason I'm asking is you don't wanna give Centriole any cause to find you in breach of contract. If you sign saying you can play, that you can fulfill your obligations and you can't, it could give them an excuse to withhold your advance, which would include my fee, so we need to find our way around that."

She went back to the document and turned a page, then turned and scanned another page.

"Okay, so this is what we call a six point deal," she explained into the desk, then looked up at the members of Portland Downs. "One point is equal to eight cents, so what they're offering as far as royalties go is forty-eight cents per album sold." She shrugged one shoulder. "But let's see if we can bump that up to seven. It wouldn't be unheard of for a new artist. You're marketable, and Centriole's got major label backing; they can tap that resource for a decent promotional budget, and they know it, so let's see how eager they are to spend someone else's money in order to make their own."

"Do you really think Neale'd do that?" Dom said. "Screw us on the advance just 'cause Jo's got a busted rib? I mean, he seemed like a pretty cool guy when we met him last week."

Toni looked at Dominick straight, and she laid her hands flat on the desktop. "'Seemed' is a hazardous word in this business," she said. "Vagary breeds contempt and shit-poor record deals. All you and I have is what's in black and white, the print on these twenty pages. A record executive will do and say whatever it takes to woo an act into signing away their firstborn child if it'll make them enough money. They know their artists are generally right brained, creative, aesthetic types, and they'll appeal to that, paint you a nice glitzy picture, take you to dinner at expensive places, be your pal. But that's their job, not mine. You hired me to hold them to their word and tell you when it's time to put your bullshit boots on. So, that said—yes, I think Mr. Roman would love to keep a quarter million dollars for himself, rather than gamble it away on a brand new rock band with no track record."

"But we've got a track record," Matt insisted. "We've been playing gigs from here to Boston for the past three years. We have a fan base on both coasts. People come to see us 'cause they know who we are and they like what they hear. How's that a gamble?"

Toni put her pen down and rolled herself up close to the desk. "Let me ask you something," she said to Matt. "How many records has Portland Downs sold in the past three years?"

Matt had no answer for that; none of them did.

"You gave me some background when you came in here, and from what you've said, you spent most of that time doing other people's music, for which I'm sure their labels are eternally grateful. By no means am I suggesting you don't have your own uniqueness, a brand worth selling. In fact, I know you do. I listened to the demo you dropped off last week, and if I didn't think you had value, I wouldn't have called, Centriole or not." She pointed to my mother and said to the others, "This is who's gonna sell your music, your *original* music—*that* voice, and *that* face. No offense to you males, but would I be wrong if I didn't think she's your frontwoman for a reason?"

She grinned and looked at each of them, letting that sink in while my mother shifted in her chair again, trying discreetly to get comfortable. She'd shot a half bag in the hotel room before they'd left for this meeting, but she wasn't sure it was enough. There was a fine line between pain relief and being wasted, and she needed to be coherent for this, couldn't look too stoned, but Toni's uncompromising office furniture was making another dose sound more appealing by the minute.

"You've got a world of potential, a beautiful lead singer, a ton of musicianship," Toni said. "You're all young and in touch with what your following wants to hear, but potential is another one of those dicey words. You're gonna have to prove yourselves, and we're gonna make sure Centriole Entertainment does its part in helping you do that." She gestured to Mom again. "You need to get yourself back in shape. The holidays are coming, and you have that going for you, but I would suggest you find yourself a doctor in the meantime, make sure there won't be any complications to prevent you from recording. That'd be all it would take to scrap this deal completely." She stood up and extended her hand across the desk, and everybody rose with her. "Give me another week or so, and I'll have things ready for us to meet with the label. I'll call you when I do."

CENTRIOLE'S ATTORNEYS REDRAFTED their contract three more times before Toni Carroway was satisfied, and on December fourteenth Portland Downs signed their names to a three-year, three-album deal at seven points with a three million dollar budget which, as indie recording budgets go, wasn't really all that much. It would just about cover the studio costs for all three projects, and if the band was successful with the first, then renegotiations would always be an option.

There was money allotted for touring, for music videos, for merchandising and promotion and for greasing the right palms at the radio stations to get their first single into regular rotation, hopefully by spring. Radio payola was an illegal practice thought to have been abandoned in the '50s, Neale explained, but the only thing that had really changed over the decades was the approach. Thousands of Centriole Entertainment dollars were allocated so that caller number seven in WXYZ's next sweepstakes giveaway might enjoy that all-expense paid trip to Hawaii, while the station got their money right back from Uncle Sam, warm and clean and smelling of fabric softener and dryer sheets.

Portland Downs now had professional management as well, a spokesperson to replace "Demetrius Booth" so that Evan could focus solely on the music. Rafe Williams of Intersolar Media Group came to them with a two-year agreement of his own at a twelve percent fee, which Toni finagled down to ten, with a "sunset clause" to prevent Mr. Williams from leeching off any retroactive monies the band might earn after their agreement was dissolved, because that happened from time to time, and he went right to work becoming the band's best friend and watchdog. He saw to the improvements in their housing and transportation. He contacted graphic artists and photographers for the design of their upcoming album cover. He took them to dinner and paid for their meals. He made calls to his own private connections for fifty dollar bags of LA's finest Indica weed because he smoked, too, and even put my mother in touch with a doctor who specialized in orthopedics so that her recuperation could be monitored and possibly expedited.

She never made the first appointment. The Denver ER had left a bitter taste in her mouth for the healthcare profession, and so she kept to her own methods with 20mgs of heroin in the morning and another ten, complimented by a relaxing bowl of Rafe's Indica, in the evenings before bed. When they'd left Colorado, Naomi had given Rachel a medical supply catalogue for a company out of Minnesota. It was a parting gift of sorts, and after two weeks in LA, a one-hundred-count box of 30 gauge hypodermic needles arrived on the doorstep of their new apartment in Hollywood—my mother had already twice re-used the four needles she'd gotten from Bryce, an imprudent last resort that Rachel wanted to nip before it created any irreparable vascular damage.

Their new home was a townhouse loft with hardwood floors and a non-working fireplace in the living room. There were two bedrooms upstairs with ceiling fans in each, and a small single bath down the hall. It was the only unit with a balcony that overlooked N. Kingsley Drive, which Rachel found particularly charming.

The building was well kept and the neighborhood was quiet, shaded by pepper trees and Mediterranean fan palms, just a short stroll from Hollywood Boulevard and four city blocks east of the Walk of Fame. They paid the rent in advance for one year but still hadn't the time for furniture shopping. So they slept on the RV sleeper mattress, which Evan and Matt lugged up the building's front steps, into the elevator, and down the third story hallway to Apartment 328 where they plopped it onto the living room floor in front of the fireplace. It was stylishly Bohemian and perfect for the time being, but Rachel spent the first weekend paging through furniture catalogues for the rest, circling ideas for my mother's approval while they sat around listening to college radio and eating breakfast cereal and Japanese takeout.

They were more in love now than ever and laughed over the night they'd met, just a mile away on Vine Street. Who'd have thought that a tray full of liquor dumped into my mother's lap and a trip to Tijuana would have brought them right back here, full circle, an easy forty thousand dollars in the bank and a veritable fortune dangling just inches from their fingertips? This time next year, they could be in Madrid, or London, Rachel standing proudly aside while my mother signed autographs on Carnaby Street.

The possibilities. The prospects. It was all so overwhelming, they couldn't stop making plans. Their fantasies took them to sidewalk cafés in Venice and down across the Mediterranean Sea to shop the Moroccan Kasbahs in Ben Haddou. They would fly first class from there to Cairo and take a hundred pictures of the pyramids, riding camels across the Gizeh Plateau, then on to Greece for a walk through the Diakopto villages, maybe spend a weekend sunbathing in the lagoons of Kissamos.

"If we budget our money right," Rachel said, cradled in my mother's arms where they sat drinking Moscato on the building's flat gravel rooftop, the LA skyline shimmering in the nighttime distance. "We can take a couple thousand and invest it. You know, put it into something that'll grow."

"Well, we'd probably need an ultraviolet lamp and an extra closet if you wanna do that," Mom said, and Rachel slapped at her and giggled.

"That's not what I mean, silly." Rachel turned in my mother's arms to look at her. "I'm talking about stocks, or real estate, or . . . I dunno . . . buy shares in one of these new computer companies. Nobody ever really does that at our age, and maybe we should be smart. Set ourselves up, just in case, don't you think?"

"I think it's a great idea." Mom brushed the hair from Rachel's face. "I just got some budgeting of my own to do, too. Rafe has a contact, somebody safe that he can trust, and I gotta re-up soon. What I got from Lecia before we left's running low, and I don't wanna be caught hurtin, you know? I can't get sick, I got too much to do."

She saw the hope drain from Rachel's face and vanish, like a candle flame dissolving at the bottom of the wax.

"Don't look like that, baby, come on." She touched Rachel's cheek with a fingertip, kissed her forehead. "You knew this coming back to me in Denver. It'll all be easier now. Not so risky. Not like before."

"How much are we talking?" Rachel asked lowly.

Mom did some quick figures in her head, taking her pain management into account for the next month or so. "Maybe a thousand, a couple ounces. But I can stretch that once my rib's healed."

"Jo, that's a shit load of money for dope, you know that, right? And it's a shit load of dope. You get caught with that, and you won't stand a chance. That's a distribution charge, right outa the gate. Toni Carroway wouldn't be able to do a thing to help you, and I doubt she'd even try."

"I'll buy a safe," Mom said. "A combination safe and keep it upstairs. I'll be the only one with the combination, you won't have anything to do with it."

"I'll have everything to do with it, I live with you. And how is this harebrained idea not so risky again? You lost me at the felony amount of heroin in the John Gotti wall safe behind the dresser. I mean, Jeezus, we just moved in here."

My mother kissed Rachel's hair, wrapped her up in reassuring arms, and gazed out at the downtown lights. "I won't let anything happen. I've been thinking this through from the moment we got here, how I'm gonna manage in an unfamiliar city, cop what I need and do it safely. Rafe's the best way to go, I'll never have to lift a finger to score, never have to show my face." And she kissed her again. "We'll be fine. You'll see. Everything's looking up now, so don't worry so much."

AND SHE WASN'T entirely wrong. The following week, my mother bought a '92 Nissan 240-SX, EVO silver with black-tinted windows and gleaming chrome rims, and she had an Alpine CD player installed, with a detachable face and a set of 250 watt 4-way amplified speakers; you could hear her coming from a block away. By Christmas, they'd furnished the apartment with three thousand dollars of Ikea's Scandinavian selections—an egg-cream sectional sofa and black veneer coffee table, an entertainment center with a new stereo, a 35" TV, and two soft-glowing cylindrical tower lamps in the adjacent living room corners. They bought lush potted ferns to hang on the balcony, a new set of stoneware dishes, all the latest kitchen appliances and a queen-sized, caramelized platform bed with a matching dresser and chifforobe. They turned the guest bedroom into an office so that Rachel could study for school and work on her poetry, and in the hall closet my mother put a fireproof combination gun safe. Inside were their passports and a hundred thousand dollar life insurance policy, benefited to Rachel, in the event that the twelve hundred dollar brick of El Chiva Tar, bundled in tin foil beside it, became my mother's untimely demise.

They spent Christmas in Hollywood. Dominick, Evan, and Matt went back east for the week, and my mother would've liked to have done the same, but there were preventative factors. She hadn't yet gathered the courage to smuggle five bags of dope through the LAX and Philadelphia airports, and after a call to Bensalem to wish my grandparents well for the holidays, she wouldn't have felt welcome there, anyway, million dollar record deal or not. Pap said she was wasting her talent, pissing away all the money they'd spent on music lessons for a life touring the underbelly of a subculture.

"This is not success, Jolán," he told her on Christmas Eve. "It's a travesty. You think you're gonna be rich? Then I should send you a bill for what we've spent investing in your future. A few years out of our sight, and you become nothing but a disappointment to us both. A rock star," he scoffed. "Is that what I'm supposed to tell the neighbors, my colleagues? That my only daughter blew her best shot at a respectable career and flushed her education down the drain over an electric guitar, a toy? Maybe doing things right was just too much work for you. That's always been your downfall. I guess it'll never change."

Nanna wouldn't even come to the phone. But Mom could still hear her in the background, Spanglish disapproval like noxious vapors through the receiver, a weapon so effective she could've bottled it up for biological warfare.

Mom hung up and sat there steeping in it for a long while. Then she went straight upstairs to the bathroom and cooked up the antidote, and within a half an hour, she had no parents to speak of, and everything was good again.

BY THE END of January, my mother's injury had finally begun to heal, but it had taken copious amounts of dope to sustain her through endless hours of guitar and violin practice. Proficiency in both had become imperative for the new album because Neale wanted to showcase every aspect of her talent and thought her classical training would show a softer, more sophisticated side. He said it set her apart from all the other young female rockers and that it would enhance her credibility in certain circles where a formal education had artistic value; the industry critics would take her more seriously and open new doors for solo projects, broadening her creative appeal.

He liked her Bohemian vintage look as well, and he wanted to keep that, so he had Victoria recommend a hair stylist and a few secondhand clothing stores, there on the west end. The only part of her budding public persona that needed revising now . . . was Rachel.

"YOU WANNA CREATE mystique, make people wonder," Neale proposed one rainy evening in early February.

He and Rafe had called my mother in to the studio for a private meeting, said they had something pressing to discuss, some ideas they wanted to run past her while the album was still in its fetal stages.

Neale leaned way back in the engineer's chair. "It's all an illusion, creating a marketable image. The alternative college rock audience is male dominated. It's just the way things are. I'm not saying you have to take any of these lunkheads home with you, but you gotta make them think you might. They're consumers, and they're buying a fantasy, the fantasy of Jolán De Carlo." And he held out his hands, presenting her to his hypothetical world for approval.

"People really just wanna hear your music. They're not interested in your personal business, babe." Rafe was seated on the couch across from the mixing board, dressed down from his usual Tom James herringbone suits, wearing a pair of faded baggy jeans instead, a Hilfiger polo, and a brand new pair of Timberland boots. He held up blameless palms and told her, "Me, I'm completely cool with it. Different strokes. Hell, you know I'm the last guy to judge what somebody chooses to do, but at the end of the day, it's a business decision. It's all about what sells."

My mother took a long time to process that and sat staring at them both, Neale with his unshaven shadow, vampire pale, even under the warm studio track lighting, wearing a sympathetic smile as he folded his hands in his lap, waiting for her to respond. And Rafe, a black Puerto Rican opportunist who'd come to LA from Baltimore ten years ago as a law student at Pepperdine, but he found he had a greater gift for making friends, for developing all the right industry rapports that led him into music management. Now he sat here, at Santa Monica and La Jolla, deliberating over her sexuality in Centriole's state-of-the-art studio with an ankle propped on his knee and his arms stretched across the back of the suede couch, a cigarette tucked behind his ear, waiting with Neale for her consent toward silence.

"Esto es pura mierda," my mother said to him because she knew he was fluent and because she felt a bit betrayed by him.

He had spent the last couple months proving his worth at the band's beck and call, establishing a very vital sense of trust with every drug run, every evening spent in her living room, alone with Rachel while my mother was en route from the studio or away at a photo shoot. He'd taken the band to high profile CD release parties at The Pantages and The Roxy, introduced them to Steven Tyler and even talked them up to the Hughes Brothers for soundtrack consideration. He'd been loyal and valuable thus far and never once overstepped his professional boundaries. Until now.

"You know that, right?" my mother reiterated. "It's bullshit, through and through. No matter which way you turn it or how you dress it up."

"I think you're getting bent outa shape over nothing," Neale said. "Nobody's saying you have to change your lifestyle. We're not sending you to some cockamamie Exodus program, Jeezus. Just tone it down a little, that's all, keep it under wraps. Your personal and professional lives'll just be separate. It's better that way in the long run."

"You know, 'cause there's a shit load of money tied up in this, Jo," Rafe urged from his seat on the couch, trying a more familiar approach, the down-to-earth sidekick only a few years older than she. "You guys have been busting your asses, recording, investing your hopes in all this. Everybody just wants it to pay off. Am I wrong?"

"So, I guess we call it hush money now," my mother said.

The guys shook their heads and glanced at each other with hopeless grins.

"Because that's what it is, really," she said. "You're paying me to make my girlfriend into a dirty secret, when all the while it's been *her* support, *her* dedication to my success that helped me get this far. She's put up with more shit from me than she ever expected, I'm sure, and now you're telling me I gotta throw her under the bus to turn a profit?"

Rafe breathed a deep sigh and rubbed his face. *"No seas tan burra,"* he muttered into his hands for my mother's unyielding stubbornness. He leaned forward with his elbows on his knees. "You're looking at this all wrong, *mija*. It's no slight against Rachel. She's a great girl, and we all think so. This is about public opinion, not anyone's personal feelings, not yours and not ours."

"The world's just not ready for it," Neale insisted. "You go out there, flaunting a female partner for the cameras, singing 'she' and 'her' in the lyrics, and Portland Downs' sales'll take a nosedive, I promise you. And that's just not something I'm willing to risk. It all goes back to that illusion, giving people what they want, even if it isn't real. What they don't know won't hurt 'em." He steepled his fingers under his chin with a knowing smile.

"So, it's okay if some other artist flaunts *their* partner, advertises their *heterosexuality* with engagement announcements and babies on the way, divorce scandals, prenup battles for the tabloids. Just so long as it fits the societal mold."

"Now's not the time to be an activist, Jo," Neale cautioned. "You're in the wrong arena. This is a business, and there's no place for political culture jamming. The industry'll eat you for lunch, and you're too talented to fall into that hole. 'Cause there's no climbing out of it, once you do." He was swiveling back and forth in the captain's chair, peering at her with unfortunate candor, his fingers still pointed up into his stubbled chin. "And let's not forget, you've got three other people whose dreams are riding on this project as well. My guess is a vote probably wouldn't pan out in your favor. Make this easy, Jolán. And just trust me when I say I've got the band's best interest at heart. Once you're established, when you've sold a few million records and earned some status as an artist, you can do whatever you want, and I'll get behind you one thousand percent."

"We just wanna make sure we get you there," Rafe said. "I got shit to do to make that happen, Neale's gotta do his thing, and we're just asking you to help us help you, help the band. Everybody's gotta make concessions. *La plata llama la plata." Money goes where money is; silver calls for silver.*

My mother wanted to fire him on the spot. Concessions. In other words, conform to a lie and crawl back into the closet so that Centriole could recoup its investment and then some. So Rafe Williams could have a larger chunk from which to take his percentage. So my mother could get rich by proxy because, yes, money follows money.

"Well, isn't that just perfect," she uttered beneath her breath, fidgeting with a hangnail, thinking now that she'd do well with another dose of Black to make this decision less complicated.

If only she didn't care so much about compromising her values, about pushing the woman she loved off into the shadows and bending over for the music business and all its pompous suits to run a train right up her ass with no Vaseline. She laughed a little then. Gavin was right, and so was Bryce—she had sold herself and Rachel out for a wad of cash on the nightstand, pawned away her dignity with a ballpoint pen.

"There's not much we need to change," Neale said. "Just some tweaking of the lyrics. It's only the one song so far. Maybe just say 'you' instead of 'she,' make it ambiguous, non-gender specific so anybody can relate to it."

"I don't care about the lyrics," she said to him. "You wanna change those, then fine, we can play the pronoun game. But publicly denying my girlfriend wades into waters I really do not like. What's next? You want me to say I'm dating Matt? Or maybe me and Dom would make a better couple. You know, the opposites attract angle. I don't think you could get Evan to stop laughing long enough to play it off, so he's out." She pointed at him and feigned a brighter idea. "I know—Vic. It'd be perfect. Girl rock musician falls for her producer. It's classic."

Rafe shook his head at the floor with a huge grin. "Now you're just being ridiculous. Nobody's asking you to do that shit, Jo, come on. This is not a big deal," he insisted. "There's plenty of ways to dodge any questions about your personal life without creating suspicion. Artists do it all the time."

"And until now, I always thought it was by choice," Mom said. "Silly me."

Neale just shrugged, as if to say blackballing her wasn't his first preference, but measures were measures; he'd preserve this investment however he had to.

My mother stood up. There was a flutter in her chest, a surge of something desperate in her gut that needed tending, and she started for the studio door.

"So, we're all on the same page then?" Neale asked.

"I gotta do some thinking. Just call me tomorrow." And she flung open the door and hurried into the hall toward the elevators.

SHE DROVE HOME in the rain with the stereo off. The quiet seemed to complement the blankness in her head. Only one thing rattled around in there now, like an empty can rolling across a parking lot. After a while, if the circumstances were stressful enough and if she waited too long, it became a steel door that shut down tight until she could crack the lock with a little hammer. Or a lot of hammer, depending.

When she got to the apartment, Rachel was lying on the couch with the TV remote, flipping channels. She was there but she wasn't. Mom was rain soaked and dripping, and she shed her jacket and took off her shoes, didn't answer when Rachel asked how it went, didn't say anything at all as she climbed the stairs to the bedroom and grabbed her works from the nightstand drawer. One mind. A singular desire spinning the combination dial, don't forget the numbers, two away from Cam's birthday. Slice, blend, stir, cook until golden brown.

Rachel appeared in the bathroom doorway, but my mother had no girlfriend for the moment, only a map of veins from which to choose, find the ones that wouldn't roll, the big thick one running down the side toward the wrist—that one had a reliable register almost every time. She tied off. Rachel said something. My mother needed to focus, so she shushed her, flicked the needle shaft three times, steady as she goes—nothing—try another one, then a rush of those toasty cashmere butterflies bearing the gift of comfort, lifting the steel barrier between my mother and everything else.

" . . . and I don't know how I'm supposed to do that if you don't tell me what's going on," Rachel continued from the doorway.

My mother was on the edge of the tub, high and fumbling with the syringe, trying to set it over on the toilet tank with a heavy hand. Rachel took it from her and unscrewed the needle from the barrel and tossed the sharp into the toilet and flushed it.

"Are you listening to me, or do I need a bullhorn?" she said, wetting a ball of toilet paper at the sink. She wiped all the blood from my mother's arm and threw it into the trash.

"I'm listening."

Mom got up and steadied herself, then went out into the hallway. Rachel followed her downstairs where she dropped onto the couch and lit a cigarette. Mom sat there for a while, scratching her nose and smoking, not quite wasted enough for a nod, but she would've welcomed that. Rachel sat down next to her, waiting for her to explain herself. The Sci-Fi Channel was playing an old episode of *Night Gallery* that filled a long silence between them.

"I think I fucked up," my mother finally said.

"What are you talking about?"

Mom shook her head and tapped her ashes, thinking.

"Jolán."

"Three years is a long ass time."

"In the scope of what? You're not making sense. You come in here, don't say a word to me, and then slam yourself full of dope after a meeting with Neale. What the hell is going on?"

My mother looked at her and cupped a hand to Rachel's face and smoothed her hair. "You know I'd never sell us out intentionally, right? You know I'm proud to be with you."

"Of course I know that. Where's this coming from all of a sudden?"

"Good. Good." Mom smiled a little, went back to her cigarette.

The dope was making her itch, her nose, a shoulder, the back of her neck. It was an irritating side effect that she could've done without, one more aggravation in a long list of things since they'd been back in LA. She didn't like the parking along Kingsley, too many apartment buildings with too many tenants, and everyone had a car; she'd walked in the rain for a half a block to get home tonight. She wished their neighbor's Boston terrier didn't have such separation anxiety at seven in the morning, that the laundry machines in the basement weren't always full, and that the corner store down on Hollywood gave out change for a twenty without making you spend three dollars. All that, and then there were the lies she would have to start telling, as if she hadn't told enough of them in her lifetime.

"How exactly would you be selling us out?" Rachel asked. "I don't even think I know what that means."

"Centriole's got me by the pubes, got 'em right in the zipper, ready to rip them out by the root if I don't keep my ass in the closet." She sat with her elbows on her knees, and she looked at Rachel. "That's what they wanted to see me about."

"They who? I thought it was just Neale."

"Him and Rafe," Mom said through a drag of her cigarette. "Rafe's in agreement with the whole thing. He's supposed to be on my side. That's where I pay him to be, but I can't fire him 'cause it's not my call, and I need him. It has to be unanimous, anyway, all four of us, and the guys don't have this problem, you see. They got it easy, but it seems I am the wrong gender."

"You're not the wrong anything." Rachel rubbed my mother's back. "So, are you saying we have to keep things on the low, keep our relationship discreet? Is that what they want?"

"Or scrap the contract altogether," my mother said.

She scratched at her chest and felt a heavy wave of indolence press her into the couch cushions. She blinked lazily at the television, at a blind Joan Crawford stealing the sight of a witless bookie in *Night Gallery*'s pilot episode.

"Neale didn't come right out and say that, of course. But I'm not stupid. He sees it as a liability, so he'll cut us loose and never look back. He's already filling his roster with other acts, just signed some girl group outa Pomona. They do rap-rock, whatever the fuck that is."

"Well, if that's what it takes to make this happen, then that's what we do." Rachel took one of Mom's cigarettes for herself and lit it, and she half watched the TV as she sat thinking.

"It's bullshit, and I told them that. It was the first thing that came out of my mouth, actually."

"Don't be an asshole to this guy, Jo. He's dangling a carrot, and we haven't eaten for months. And might never eat again if he loses interest in you. Just play their game, baby. It's politics," she conceded with a sigh. "Let them have this. You guys have worked too hard to get this close, just to blow it over me and some stupid ego trip. You were working toward this long before we met; I can live with the longtime companion title if I have to. Be whoever they want out there, just make sure you always come home to me." She kissed my mother's shoulder, bowing out gracefully into the shadows.

Mom turned her head to look at her, their faces so close she had to kiss her, she couldn't resist. The warmth of those lips still the only thing to compete with Lady Black. "I'm sorry," she whispered.

"There's nothing to be sorry for." Rachel took my mother's arm and examined it with a frown. She ran the backs of her fingers lightly over the marks. "All you had to do was tell me this when you came in, and we could've talked about it. You get yourself all worked up and stressed out over stuff that isn't necessary, you know? I get it. It's a business. I don't like it any more than you, but we'll deal. That's all we can do." My mother nodded, and Rachel kissed her again, then looked at the clock on the mantle. "You need to eat something before bed. I'll make you a protein shake and a sandwich." She put her cigarette out and got up and disappeared into the kitchen.

Mom took the last hit of her own cigarette and stubbed it in the ashtray and sat listening to the ice tumble from the freezer tray, the silverware drawer open and shut, the refrigerator door, and then the whir of the blender, all the sounds of a woman who loved her more than she ever deserved. And for the first time, my mother was beginning to feel the dichotomy of addiction, the unadulterated love for the drug and the disdain for her own love of it, the wisdom that said she should lay it down forever and the frightening despair at the very thought.

She knew better, but now it knew her better than she knew herself, and she knew that, too. She knew a lot of things. She just didn't know how to jump this train while it raced past a hundred-foot ravine in the dark, and she might never know that.

chapter eighteen

BETWEEN FEBRUARY AND May, Portland Downs had recorded two-thirds of a debut album, tentatively entitled *Ignition* and tentatively scheduled for release in October, with a handful of radio-ready singles up for deliberation over which would be the band's most effective introduction. Rafe had gotten them a few high-paying gigs, opening for acts at prominent nightclubs like the House of Blues and the Troubadour and, though he refused to discuss the details until it was confirmed, a tentative slot touring across Canada with Pearl Jam. Everything was tentative at this stage; it all hinged on the right timing and the proper negotiations, the weather, the direction of the wind, luck and chance and the power of money.

They were still relatively unknown yet gaining local traction with two feature articles in the *LA Weekly* and *Urb* magazine, and so their faces had become familiar throughout the underground music scene. My mother and Matt signed their first autographs while shopping at The Record Collector on Melrose Avenue, and Evan and Dom now had steady girlfriends because they could finally afford them. They could all get into The Viper Room and Dragonfly for free, rarely had to pay for their own drinks, and got high on the complimentary dimes of the fans who'd come to their shows.

"Just a little taste of celebrity status," Rafe said to my mother, one evening at the after party for the *Point of No Return* movie premiere.

He handed her a glass of Scotch from the open bar and gestured around to all the music and film stars, mingling about the House of Blues while Blind Melon performed on the main stage.

"It's okay to get used to this," he tempted. "We've got a lot of things in the works for you guys, and by next Christmas, this'll just be a way of life. *Your* life." And he held up his Heineken for a toast to the tentative new future of Portland Downs.

My mother had been managing her addiction throughout. Rachel had gone back to school, but she still kept very close tabs on Mom's diet and exercise. She made cheese omelets and oatmeal with sliced bananas in the mornings, bought bags of unsalted peanuts and made power shakes for snacks. She prepared whole grain pasta dishes and chicken salads and left them in the fridge for lunches while she spent the afternoons in class, and for dinner she made steaks and vegetable medleys and turkey casseroles, everything served with skim milk or bottled water. They went to the gym and ran the treadmills on rainy days and did 5k trail runs in Griffith Park when the weather was nice. She monitored Mom's sleeping schedule, replenished her clean needle supply with orders from Naomi's Minnesota catalogue, and even kept her on a vitamin regimen with extra iron because by mid-March, my mother's period had stopped.

They thought it might be the exercise, or perhaps the stress of a burgeoning new music career, but they were wrong on both counts. It was a side effect of IV heroin use, a physiological phenomenon that affected many female addicts in their early to late twenties. It took two appointments and a significant level of trust in a Hollywood OB/GYN for that diagnosis, and the only remedy now was for my mother to get treatment and quit the drug altogether, which she was unwilling to do. There were too many professional deadlines and shows and meetings to attend. Their first single was slated for debut in two weeks on a popular radio show called *Five Minutes of Fame*, which included a candid on-air interview that would give the band invaluable mainstream exposure. There was no time to get clean, not now, not with her entire future propped up on a three million dollar investment.

And so she and Rachel continued as they were. They went back to the gym and to the jogging trails, shopped at holistic food stores and explored the benefits of yoga and meditation, and when the album was finally finished, they celebrated with a weekend of romantic quality time on Catalina Island, strolling the surf on Descanso Beach and making love by firelight in a suite at Hamilton Cove, their one-year anniversary just two months away.

THEN CAME THE day when everything changed. A day in early May when it seemed a switch had been flipped, triggering some sort of enormous vacuum, the roaring nozzle poised above my mother's life, above everyone's lives.

Mom was still in bed at noon when the phone rang. Rachel was already gone to school for a literature class, so Mom slid across to the empty side and fumbled with the receiver on the nightstand, bobbled it into the sheets, pressed it to her face.

"Yeah." She rolled onto her back, eyes shut, suspended between sleep and the consciousness of another Thursday afternoon.

It was Evan. My mother listened. He sounded like he had a cold, his voice thick and breathy, and he was stumbling over his words; she couldn't understand him at all at first. Then she understood him perfectly, and her eyes flashed open to the spackled ceiling.

There'd been an accident, the worst kind of accident, the kind you don't initially accept because it wasn't supposed to happen to you or to anyone you knew or loved; it was surely a mistake, a misunderstanding; Evan had gotten bad information, that's all. Death was simply too remote, it was someone else's allegory, something distant and removed that took place in the pages of a newspaper, or behind the glass of a television screen.

She sat up and pawed through the sheets for the TV clicker and turned on the twelve o'clock news. Yellow police tape, strung from the fence around an apartment building, detectives in shirts and ties, going to and from, carrying Glock pistols in shoulder holsters while a commentator narrated the inconclusive details, ruling out foul play.

Evan garbled something tearful through the phone. He sounded like he had a spear through his chest.

"I'll be right there." My mother hung up, but it rang again, and now it was Toni Carroway. Mom threw on a pair of jeans and a tank top, switching hands to keep the phone to her ear as Toni spoke to her with professional and deliberate haste.

It was all too much. The sudden detonation of explosives in her head. The Iron Maiden had slammed shut with my mother inside, poking her full of holes that bled with sorrow and panic. She had to shut it off, pry it open, stop up the wounds, get to some place warm and isolated.

She kept a pre-loaded syringe in the nightstand drawer, just enough for an emergency dose, and she fished it out, grabbed a rubber tourniquet, didn't bother disinfecting. She tied off, tucked the receiver into her shoulder, and sat at the edge of the bed to begin the vascular search while Toni delivered legal commands.

"Do *not* say a word to the media," she counseled. "If you have anything in your possession, on your person, in your vehicle, in your fucking house that could incriminate you in any way, I want you to flush it. Burn it. Make it vanish. And do it *now*. I am not a defense attorney, and I *cannot* help you if you screw this up."

"I don't understand." Mom ran her fingertips along the inner forearm, so few to choose from now, but then one appeared at the wrist, and she resituated so she could reach it.

"What's not to understand, Jo? Birds of a feather. They found dope at the scene, and they've got your background information, the whole band; they've already shown the promo poster from the Troubadour on Channel 7. They're gonna want to question you, investigate. That's how it's done, kiddo. I don't know where this is going, so you need to get yourself together and be ready to talk."

My mother plunged 20mgs into the median vein and let the phone drop to the mattress. She exhaled into the ceiling and felt a mediocre rush that drained away after a few anesthetizing seconds. Then she went into the bathroom and rinsed the blood that trickled into her palm. She pressed a wad of tissue to the site until the bleeding stopped and covered the area with a braided leather watchband. She'd forgotten all about Toni Carroway whose voice still crackled through the receiver on the bed, calling her name. Mom snatched her car keys from the dresser, trotted downstairs, and headed out to where she'd parked a half a block from the Boulevard.

SHE COULD HAVE walked to New Hampshire Avenue and often did, only two blocks east of Kingsley. But not today, a wise decision. There were local TV news vans, an EMS vehicle and a fire truck, four police cruisers and two unmarked sedans in front of the apartments where Matt, Dominick, and Evan had been sharing a three bedroom flat since December. Mom rolled past the scene, eerily quiet—the only vehicle with its lights still whirling was a single police car; everyone else seemed to know the real emergency was over, nothing urgent happening here, anymore.

Neighbors stood watching and waiting from across the street, arms folded at their waists, some still in bathrobes and bedroom slippers to suggest they'd been there for a while. A white coroner's van was double parked in front of the building's entrance.

My mother felt nauseated, suddenly hot and flushed. She pulled along the street and found a parking spot, three complexes up, and she walked back with a peculiar detachment, as if she were just another reporter, come to see if she could siphon any information from all the apprehensive strangers gathered around the sidewalks. It was the dope blurring the boundary between standard-issue grief and that comfortable indifference she'd grown to rely on over the past year. A police chopper made low passes overhead, and the whole scene made her think of Albuquerque, and that made her want to vomit now.

She stopped and turned toward a landscaped patch of primrose and threw up onto the petals and branches and into the dirt. She couldn't blame that on the dope. It'd been months since smack had made her sick, so it must've been nerves, or guilt, or terror trying to find its way into the proper neural receptors. People eyed her sideways as she wiped her mouth with the back of her hand and kept moving.

A microphone appeared in her face. A Latino woman she recognized from the Channel 5 News stepped into her path, asked if she was Jolán De Carlo, band mate, friend of the deceased.

"No." She shouldered past the woman, ducked under the camera, and tried to go into the apartment lobby but a cop waved her back toward the street. She pulled out her wallet and handed him her ID, explained who she was while the reporter listened in from behind, and then the cop let her through as the Channel 5 News team called questions at her back until she vanished through the halls.

She showed her ID once more to get into Apartment 208 where Evan was sitting on the living room couch, elbows on his knees, hands folded beneath his chin, his face hidden by a wall of dreadlocks. When he saw her, he stood up with lingering tears in his eyes. She'd never seen him cry before, had never seen any of them cry and honestly didn't think it was possible, not for these confident swaggering clowns she'd come to love like brothers.

She could hear Dom in the kitchen on the phone as Evan hung an arm around her neck for a hug. He stood back, nodding, trying to appear composed, unable to articulate just how much this was crushing him. She was glad she couldn't really feel it, grateful for the opiated barrier that kept her steady and emotionally disengaged. She couldn't have imagined walking into this sober, particularly when Evan pointed her to the living room window that overlooked the swimming pool.

"They've been out there with him all morning," Evan said, taking a seat on the sofa again as she pulled aside the vertical blinds to have a look. "Why don't they just take him? I mean, Christ, they've been down there since seven."

More yellow tape and plainclothes officers, a forensic photographer, evidence exhibit tags perched on an umbrella table and along the ground by a lawn chair. Matt lay poolside on the concrete. He had on Navy blue swim trunks. Cops milled around his body and stepped over it, red as a picnic cup from forehead to big toe, as if he'd been slow roasted and turned on a spit, and my mother asked about that.

"Why's he all burned up?" she wondered. "Maybe it was sun poisoning."

She couldn't take her eyes off him, stretched out and barefoot with his puffy, sun-blistered arms at his sides, baking deeper in the midday glare that reflected off the water like a magnifying glass. A long blue pool float was on the concrete next to him, numbered like all the other little clues. He looked bloated, not like the Matt she recognized but rather an inflatable version meant to look lifelike, his hair already dry after hours of investigation. There was a black body bag, lying beside the pool float, unzipped and waiting.

Dominick came out of the kitchen then. She turned to look at him and thought he might approach for an embrace, but his expression was unlike anything she'd ever seen before. He didn't speak to her and went into the living room instead, carrying the phone in his hand. He paced with it for a long moment, from the dining room into the kitchen and out into the living room again. He hurled it into the wall where it shattered, plastic and wires and the battery twirling and splintering off in all directions, and Evan shot from his seat on the couch. "Hey! What the fuck, man!"

Dom turned and pointed at my mother, fuming. "I *told* you, you stupid *fucking idiot*. I told you *months* ago to leave that shit alone, and yet you *still*!"

My mother frowned. She didn't know what he was talking about. Well, she did, but she didn't know why or how it would apply to this, to Matt having apparently drowned in the apartment pool; he never was much of a swimmer.

"Dom, come on, just relax." Evan came to him with his hands up and warded him back toward the dining area. "Everybody's upset right now. Just calm down. Losing your mind on Jo's not gonna help. It's not her fault. It's Matty's fault, it's his own fault."

Dom pointed at my mother again and said to Evan, "She *knew* that shit was trash, and *she* got him hooked." Then he looked at her, his eyes wide and bright and livid. "If you were a guy, I would cave your fuckin skull in right now. *Believe* that!"

"Knock it off. Go get a beer. Relax." Evan turned him around and pushed him back into the kitchen.

"And yeah, she looks real upset," Dominick snapped from behind the partition. "Probably high as fuck. Ain't that right, Jo-Jo? Pickled in smack right about now, it's the only way you can cope with anything, anymore. Fuckin junkie," he muttered, popping a Budweiser bottle top with the edge of the counter. "Can't even play worth a shit anymore. Seven takes for one goddamned chorus. I thought Vic was gonna bash his own head into the mixing board, he was so frustrated."

"Just chill out," Evan insisted. "Matt's folks are gonna be here from Long Island in a few hours. What are we gonna look like, at each other's throats like a bunch a psychos?"

Finally my mother came away from the window. She went to the kitchen doorway where Evan stood between them, and she looked past him and said to Dominick, "It was seven takes because I busted a string on the third one, and then Vic changed the melody. Maybe if you didn't smoke a pound of weed every day, you might remember that shit. Asshole."

"And maybe if you weren't pouring a gallon a heroin into your veins every four hours, one of my best friends wouldn't be a fucking corpse right now!" Dom hollered, pointing into his own chest.

Evan tried to diffuse it, but they ignored him and stood snapping like dingoes over his shoulder and around his outstretched arms.

"And how is this my fault again?" Mom insisted.

"He idolized you! You fucking walked on water in his eyes—he'd have drank a pitcher a *gasoline* if you said it was cool!"

" . . . which still does not answer my question," she said. "I don't even know what happened here! I get a call from Evan, telling me Matty's gone, he's dead, he died this morning, and so now I'm here, and the whole thing's suddenly *my* fault? What the *hell?*"

"He OD'd, Jo!" Dominick announced, then winced at Evan. "You didn't tell her that shit?"

"I was upset. We'd just found out, I couldn't think, I just dialed. I don't even remember what I said." Then he told my mother what'd happened. "He went out to the pool yesterday afternoon. Me and Dom left. Dom went to Denise's for the night, and me and Tracey went out to eat and saw a movie at the Beverly Center. I took her home and didn't get back till after midnight. Matty wasn't up here. I figured he was with you. He's a grown man, I'm not his fucking keeper, so I went to bed."

He stopped, but there was more, unspoken details flickering in his eyes, something bizarre and so beyond the realm of a brother's keeper that my mother was beginning to piece it together on her own now, and she took a step back into the dining room, dumfounded.

"He was out there all night?" she asked beneath her breath. Even the dope couldn't diminish the incredulity of that, and she sank into a dining chair and tried not to get her head too far around it, but now the view from the window made a whole different kind of sense.

"They're not sure, but they think maybe . . ." Evan started, then hesitated under a fresh wave of grief. "That maybe he was, uh . . . that he was probably gone within the first hour. They don't know anything for certain, yet, but . . ." And he just shrugged because it truly didn't take a medical examiner to figure it out—that would just be a formality for legal subsequence.

"And the first hour woulda been around, oh, about two o'clock in the afternoon . . . *yesterday*," Dominick said. "Lovely image, huh? Your dead junkie friend floating around for hours in a pool full of kids. They all thought he was asleep." He swigged his beer. "So, yeah. Pat yourself on the back, Jo. How's it feel to be such a great fucking influence?"

He pushed past them and crossed the living room, then disappeared down the hall to his bedroom, slamming the door so hard it knocked a picture off the wall.

Evan glanced down the hall and then back at my mother. "He's just trying to deal with this. Probably easier to be pissed off at somebody."

My mother didn't say anything. She sat staring into the carpet, retracing her steps over the past forty-eight hours. She'd been there on Tuesday afternoon, around one-thirty, two days ago. She arrived after dropping Rachel off at school.

Matt was asleep when she showed up. He came to the door in his boxers, semi-conscious. He let her in, turned on the stereo, went into the kitchen and made coffee. He was out of cigarettes, so he bummed one from Mom, smoked it while he washed two mugs from the dirty dishes in the sink. He said Dominick was at his girlfriend Denise's place in Pasadena. Evan was still in his room, asleep with Tracey.

Mom and Matt talked about the upcoming studio session scheduled for that night at six. They talked about Vic Lamaire, Centriole's appointed producer *extraordinaire*, and whether she and Matt were satisfied with his contributions to the album—they were undecided, as all the creative control Neale had promised back in November was turning out to be hypothetical, and they didn't like that.

Then Matt said he had something to show her, and he disappeared to his room for a few minutes and returned with a pack of photos from his trip back east to see his family in Long Island, the previous week. She remembered shots of Matt and his younger brother Jake at the beach. His grandparents. Pictures of his mother at home in the back yard, others sitting around in lawn chairs, men standing with drinks by a barbecue grill. He said he'd gone into the city with his cousin Timothy that Friday night, to Queens where Timothy had a connection for weed and where Matt could buy a half bundle of smack, five stamps; it was cheaper in the boroughs than out on Long Island, he said.

He hadn't tried it yet, but he went back to his room and brought it out to show her, a completely different variety than what they would ever find out west. She remembered the packaging, a small wax paper baggie, a graphic of two intertwined dragons, red lettering, but she couldn't recall what it said. It was supposedly from Thailand, a No. 4 grade powder, top of the line and exceptionally pure, and he offered to share, but she didn't know how to cut it for IV use and neither did he.

Matt hadn't any interest in shooting, but he had begun smoking it from time to time, and he was still trying to decide which method he preferred. He wouldn't have smoked it on the first try. He knew best how to measure it for snorting, and he certainly wouldn't have been smoking it out at the pool.

She got up and went back to the window and parted the blinds. They were lifting him into the bag now. He seemed oddly rigid, his arms wouldn't bend. On the umbrella table was a black leather wallet lying on an unfolded blue bath towel, and beside the wallet was something very small and off white; she couldn't make it out from two floors up, but it was all numbered. If she had to guess, she'd say the wallet was likely his, and the item tagged beside it a bit of the souvenir he'd smuggled back from Queens. The LAPD had the right idea, sniffing around in the right places, but the facts wouldn't surface for another several days, after an autopsy and a toxicology report proclaimed Matthew Gregory Franz "1993 Dumbass of the Year," and my mother first runner-up.

When the detectives came knocking again, they sat with her on the couch and asked a lot of questions, a black female and a white male, both in their late thirties but otherwise faceless. The male was homicide, and the female was with the narcotics division. She didn't remember their names.

My mother told them what they needed to know, that Matt had a heroin habit, just like her. They had the dragon stamp in a plastic ziplock, sealed up for evidence, and they showed it to her, asked if she'd ever seen it before, and she nodded and identified it as the dope he'd purchased back east. They seemed to be aware that it wasn't local, and then they asked if he might've had any more stashed around the apartment.

She knew Matt very well, and he was careful, and so she told them no, not to her knowledge. They wanted to know if she herself was in possession, and she denied that, too. They had no legal grounds to search the apartment or her person, so they just took her name and contact information, and left it at that. It was all rather mundane, hardly the sensationalized drug sting that Toni Carroway had prepared her for on the phone. But over the next couple weeks, the fallout was devastating.

It happened so swiftly and thoroughly that it was done before Matt's remains had even landed in New York, a systematic deconstruction of everything Portland Downs had built from the moment they'd counted off their first rehearsal in 1989. Matt died on Wednesday, May 5th. Neale Roman cancelled their contract the following Monday, two hours after the five o'clock news confirmed it as a heroin overdose and plastered the band's picture onto every television screen from Los Angeles to Malibu. Tuesday morning at ten-seventeen, they got a call from Toni Carroway who suspended her services indefinitely. By eight o'clock Tuesday evening, Rafe Williams and Intersolar Media had reneged as well, leaving Portland Downs devoid of all representation, futureless, and fractured from the bottom up.

Matt was buried in Oakwood Cemetery, Islip, New York the subsequent Thursday, but my mother never made the trip. When Mr. and Mrs. Franz learned of the details behind their son's death, they wanted nothing to do with her and asked her not to come, and so she honored their wishes and remained in LA while Evan and Dom flew back for the services. Uncle Rick came down from Aloha with a neighbor friend and took the Fleetwood back to Oregon, which none of the surviving band members disputed—what good would the RV do any of them now?

When Dom and Evan returned the following week, Dominick said they'd done some talking while in New York and Boston. He said they'd gone back to visit the Berklee campus and ran into some old friends who'd been wondering what had become of them all. He couldn't bring himself to tell them the truth, so he said Matt's death was an accidental drowning and that Mom had fallen in love and moved in with a California college girl.

He kept the explanations sterile and pristine, but it wasn't for my mother's sake. He and Evan had come to a decision while they were gone, and so the night after their return from New York, they sat with Mom and Rachel in the living room on Kingsley, sipping Budweisers and passing around a honey blunt.

"I think after the events of the past couple weeks. We can pretty much call this a wrap." Dominick rolled the blunt cherry against the bottom of the ashtray, thinking. Then he looked at my mother who was curled up on the adjacent love seat. "I'm not interested in replacing Matty, and neither is Evan, and even if we were assholic enough to do that, there's not a label in LA that'll give us a thimbleful of piss after what happened. Nobody'll touch us now. The liability alone's ten times what we're worth as a new act, so I think it's safe to say that Portland Downs has seen its best days."

My mother had no response for that. She just sat listening at the end of the cushions, her feet tucked beneath her, a Marlboro fuming in her hand.

"We've all got options, you know? This wasn't the only path we had. Hell, I'm thinking of going back for my Masters. I mean, why not? Maybe in composition, broaden my scope a little, right?" Evan held out a hand to my mother. "You've always had the violin. Or you could stick with the guitar, maybe teach or something."

Dominick grumbled under his breath, and he pursed his lips, and that made my mother sit up a little.

She tapped her ashes and gave him that piercing hazel glare. "What?" she pressed. "Speak your mind, Dom. That's why we're all here, isn't it? That's what you said on the phone, that we were gonna air it all out, be adults? So, let's be adults then, don't mumble. Say what you have to say."

"You know, I would if I thought you were willing to hear it. 'Cause you sure as hell weren't listening back in Tucson. Or Denver."

"And so what does that mean?" she insisted.

"Come on, Jo." Dom gestured to Evan seated next to him. "He means well, but *teach? Really?* You honestly think you could do that now, in the shape you're in? I'm thinkin probably not. Not without some serious soul searching and a twelve-step program, just for starters."

My mother crushed her cigarette out and chain it another one right behind it. "All right, fine. Then you make the call and set it up, and we'll both go." She pointed to the blunt burning between his fingers. "And don't babysit that shit, dude. Come on, you know the rules. Puff-puff-pass. So, what is that, your third one today? It's all good, though. Been a hell of a week. Funerals can be kinda rough without a little chemical help, so do your thing." And she sniffed and dabbed at her nose with a knuckle to imply she hadn't forgotten about his other pastimes, either.

"I really don't think this is why we're here, to point fingers," Rachel said to them both, but Dominick disputed that.

"Well, of course *you* don't," he said, his voice dialed up a notch. "You've been holding her hand through a fucking heroin addiction for almost a year, now, Rache. I think you did the right thing, leaving her ass in Denver. But then you caved and came crawling back for reasons I will *never* understand, and ever since then, she's been worse off than ever."

"You know, I'm sittin right here, Dom," my mother snapped. "Your issue's with me, not her, so I'm gonna need you to watch your mouth and lay off, just leave her out of it."

"That is a low blow." Rachel pointed at Dominick. She moved to the edge of her seat and leveled him with dark brown defiance. "You are the *last* person to take inventory of everyone else's decisions, Dominick Keller. You spent the first six months of that trip, fucking everything with a twat and a pulse, shoving more coke up your nose than Jo and me put together, so save all the holier than thou bullshit for somebody else."

"She *swore,*" Dominick extended a finger toward my mother, "that she would *not* let that shit get in the way, that it would never affect the band, yet here we are, Rache! A three million dollar record deal flushed down the shitter and one of our best friends dead and buried in Long Island 'cause *she* refused to listen when *I* told her to leave that shit alone. I mean, I know the hell I'm not crazy. You were *there*! You stood right there at Montego's when Bryce was offering it up, and you heard me tell her it was garbage, and you *agreed* with me then! Yet suddenly this is all about *my* habits, which, I can say with absolute confidence, have never . . . *ever* . . . had a negative impact on this band. So please, tell me again how the amount of *pussy* I got from last summer to now has any fucking bearing on the breakup of this band *or* Matt's death. I am all ears, babe."

"She never put a gun to Matty's head," Evan said to Dominick. "He made his own choices, took the same gamble she did, and he lost. He got a hold of some bad dope. The shit was cut with poison, and it killed him. It's a chance he took on his own. You can't put that on Jo."

"Thank you," Rachel announced, gesturing across to Evan.

"Oh, really? So who then?" Dominick questioned. "Bryce? Maybe we should make a detour on our way back to Boston, show up on his goddamned doorstep for a first-class, beat-down compliments of Matt Franz. Maybe that's what needs to happen."

"Nothin needs to happen, dude. Everything's *already* happened. It happened, and it's over, it's done." Evan looked at him. "You can be as pissed off as you want, blame whoever you want, and it still doesn't change anything. Everybody has their vices, and everybody made their choices, so just chill out with all the goddamned hostility."

"And you think I shouldn't be a little hostile over the fact that we had a good thing here? A *good thing* going with Centriole." Dom counted off their prospects on his fingers as he spoke. "Million dollar budgets. People with clout to back us up. State-of-the-art recording. Worldwide distribution. A chance to tour with fucking Pearl Jam. *Pearl Jam!* And now it's gone. Now I gotta drag my ass back to Boston and update my résumé for a job in data processing in some cubicle somewhere 'cause my dipshit friends got hooked on smack! Yeah, I'm a little hostile, these days, Evan. *Just* a little." He snatched a cigarette from the box in his shirt pocket, lit one, and blew a noisy cloud into the living room.

My mother did the same with the one in her hand. "And you think you're the only one that lost out?"

"Every one of us lost that chance," Evan said. "Not just you."

"So, we've all gotta look to our Plan Bs now," Rachel said. "It's a shitty reality, but that's just how it is. You guys seem to have some ideas for yourselves, so me and Jolán'll have to figure things out as well. Turn the page, new chapter. And deflecting blame sure as hell doesn't change that."

"And I don't think Matt would want us at odds over this, either," Evan said.

"Yeah, well he doesn't get much of a vote, anymore, now does he?" Dominick flicked his ashes into the ashtray and stared at the hardwood floor between his shoes. It seemed he realized his own poor taste, and he shook his head at himself, yet he still didn't apologize, and that pissed my mother off.

She sat up at the corner of the couch and postured as if she might come across the room for Dom's throat, but she stayed put. "You really know how to be a prick sometimes, I swear to God. You wanna rub my face in this pile of shit? Fine. But you are not the only one who lost a friend, here." She pointed to herself and said, "I gotta live with my own responsibility for this. And if you really wanna know, I was just a dose away from joining him; he offered me a taste, but I didn't try it. The shit just didn't play out that way, and so here I am—with one less friend and no idea where to go next. So yeah, I still got mine. Karma's a real motherfucker, right? Is that what you wanted to hear tonight, Dom? That make you feel better, you self-righteous dick?"

"You never told me that," Rachel said, but my mother and Dominick were talking over each other now, leaning up in their seats, ready to leap into collision, condemnation like bullets from the tips of their tongues that spiraled into a cacophony of accusations and broken trust until Rachel finally shouted the loudest and brought it to a halt.

The room fell silent.

"Just stop! Let it go! *Both* of you, for Christ's sake!" She held her hands up between them, scowling and flustered. She pointed at Dominick. *"You* have said enough here tonight. We get it. We know where you stand." She looked at my mother and said, "You and I have things we need to talk about, and all this bickering and blame shifting's just a waste of time."

Dominick stood up and grabbed his cigarettes from the table. "Yeah, and so were the last three years, apparently."

He started for the door, and Evan got up and followed him.

"You have yourself a good life, Jo. And get her some fucking help," Dom said to Rachel. "Since you're the only one willing to stick around, it's the least you could do."

He didn't shut the door on his way out. Evan shrugged his apologies and closed it behind him as he followed Dom out into the hall, leaving my mother and Rachel in a strained and loaded silence.

They sat reflecting for a long while. The neighbor's stereo drove a low humming bass line through the walls. Mom finished her cigarette and crushed it in the ashtray on the coffee table. She got up and headed for the stairs.

"Where are you going?" Rachel asked.

"Bathroom."

Rachel watched her from over a shoulder until she disappeared to the second floor. She wanted to give her space, let her process these inevitable new changes and find her own way through them, but Rachel knew better. My mother no longer used temperance to navigate these storms. She threw herself overboard instead, bobbing in the angry waters while Rachel tossed a life ring from topside to keep her from going under.

So much devastation in such a short time, evaporated dreams, like a cruel joke. A mirage for a lost and shipwrecked pack of drifters, running toward a waterfall of sand. My mother was content to bury her head in it; you're not lost if you can't see the circular tracks; better to make Lost your destination and set up camp, call yourself a survivor there, basking in the artificial sunshine in a thunderclouded sky. And if it opened up and poured down a torrent of acid rain, my mother wouldn't have cared less, she probably wouldn't have even noticed.

WHEN RACHEL CAME upstairs to the bathroom, Mom was sitting slumped on the floor mat, her back against the tub. A hypodermic needle lay partly injected in the crease of her right arm—she'd been having trouble finding a vein in the left for more than a month, now, and she hadn't quite mastered the art of ambidexterity. Her forearm was bruised and bloody from searching and piercing and probing for a decent register, drawing so much blood you could almost smell it, and the tourniquet was too tight.

Rachel knelt down and took my mother by the chin and lifted her face. "Jolán."

My mother tried to open her eyes but couldn't. She muttered something indistinct, something random—at least she was breathing.

Rachel tried to withdraw the needle, but when she did, a fine burgundy thread spurted from the pinhole and sprayed the shower curtain and dotted the cabinet door.

"Ssshit. Good one, Rache," she scolded herself and untied the tourniquet, which she probably should have done first. She took a wash rag down from the towel rung, wet it at the sink, and wiped down the cabinet and cleaned the blood from my mother's arm, limp as the rag itself, and now she could see Mom hadn't been quite so conscientious about rotating veins. There was an inch-long perforated track just below the elbow line, signaling a dreadful turn in a year-long addiction, a superficial trail of defeat.

Rachel sat kneeling, the bloodstained rag in hand, and she let out a long and brooding sigh. She shook my mother's shoulder to rouse her again.

"Jolán. Come on. You can't stay in here, baby, and I can't lift you."

My mother raised her head, opened her eyes for a moment, but she wasn't seeing, everything smeared and indistinguishable, and she whispered an apology.

"It's all right," Rachel said, trying to get a hand under my mother's arm. But it wasn't all right; it wasn't even in the neighborhood of all right, it was disparaging, the collapse of a gifted life going to pieces on the bathroom floor.

Rachel tugged at my mother's weight, a hundred-and-twenty-five pounds of disillusionment crumpling against the toilet bowl, the bath mat twisted up beneath her.

"Dammit." Rachel shook my mother hard, grabbed her by the jaw, and turned her face toward the overhead light. "Jo! You gotta get up. Walk. Get to the bedroom. I can't do this with you tonight. It's late, and I've got finals in the morning. Now, let's go. Up."

Mom's head lolled out of Rachel's grasp, and she muttered into her chest. "The bedroom's in the hall, just . . . we don't have any more so the, maybe. Maybe wait so . . . What are we doing?" She snapped out of her stupor and looked up, eyes clear for a microsecond.

Rachel seized that moment to get her upright, but three breaths later she was under again. Heavy lids at three-quarter mast. One arm limp in her lap, her head leaning toward the toilet tank with an elbow on the seat, her hand to the ceiling as if raising it for roll call, her fingers working vaguely at an invisible keypad, or plucking the strings of a guitar, perhaps. She could have been anywhere in that head, doing anything with anyone, an astral projection to regions elsewhere, so long as it wasn't 1993 Los Angeles, where dead and angry friends laid their useless dreams at her feet, then cursed her into the past so they, too, could disappear for good.

Rachel pushed herself to her feet. She didn't know what to do. She breathed another heavy sigh and stood looking down at Mom who was fighting against her own lack of willpower, trying to lift her chin from her chest.

Rachel picked the syringe off the edge of the tub and unscrewed the needle, tossed it into the toilet and watched it come to rest at the bottom. Mom said something about the bedroom again. Rachel held the barrel up to the light, and she could see slightly where the dope residue stopped at thirty units, maybe a little more, certainly more than my mother's usual dose. She dropped it into the wastebasket and searched around for the spoon, found it under my mother's leg, the lighter at the base of the toilet. She put the lighter in her shorts pocket and the spoon in the basin and ran the hot water while she went to the bedroom for two pillows, a blanket, and the cordless phone.

She came back and shut the water off, then fluffed the pillows against the wall of the tub and joined my mother there on the bathroom floor.

"Come on," she whispered, pulling her from where she lay wedged between the tub and the toilet, a much easier task from down there. She covered them both with the comforter, laid the phone within reach, and held my mother against her stomach for another night of half sleep, safe-sitting, listening for every breath with a hand lain across my mother's neck so she could monitor her pulse.

The neighbor's music droned through the walls, drowned out just a little by the bathroom fan. A police siren in the Hollywood distance whined and came closer from the east and then crescendoed down Kingsley and faded off toward Franklin Avenue.

My mother shifted in Rachel's arms, uttered something in Spanish but it was swallowed up by the comforter. Rachel pulled the blanket over Mom's shoulders and brushed the ringlets from her face.

"We're gonna get through this," she said into her hair, a faint and staggered heartbeat pulsing beneath her fingers at my mother's neck. "What other choice do we have?"

chapter nineteen

DODGED A BULLET, or so it seems. Probably should've stepped into its path, we'd all be in a better place. I love the fact that I'm not afraid of it because I could be, I used to be. There's something about that disconnection. To triumph over death through thought and mere disposition, although I do desperately wish this fly would leave me be. Goddamned thing's more of a nuisance than those looks she gives me, lately. She wakes me up at night, shaking me, calling my name. Even in the dark, I can see the color rush back to her face when I open my eyes—she's never quite sure that's gonna happen anymore, and she is rightly terrified, because I've figured it out. I know what they are now, those pinpoints of gloom. Indeed fragments of something larger, a thing that rises up from the shadows in the corner of any given room in which I might be sitting. The all-encompassing sadness. A specter come to pay me a visit. Made of darkness. A black cloud of despair for me to pretend I cannot see or feel, but the air in the room is transformed by it, a heavy dew-like unbreathable composite of death and mistake and consequence. My liquid oxygen. What a brilliantly impossible existence I've created here. On the outside of something inside, watching, feeling nothing and very much better off that way. I should apologize profoundly for having this hand in your demise, Matty Greg, but that would throw open too many doors and windows from which horrendous things might come flying out, like vampire bats from an undiscovered cave. I loved you, never said it, should have, didn't, then you died on your little raft at 1 o'clock on a Wednesday and nearly took me with you. Imagine that. Everything kept moving, in case you were wondering. Thursday, the sun came up; I slept through that. People went to work, went to school, went on with this whole business of living as if you'd never been. Wind blew through trees and supermarkets opened and The LA Times *landed on the front steps to my apartment—you were on the second page of the Local section, and that ended up on someone's kitchen floor with dog piss on it. Someone left it in a seat on the Metrorail, lined the bottom of a birdcage, made a paper hat. Impermanence at its finest. Fleeting lives and tragic endings and those left behind here to wait for similarly tragic finales to their equally momentary lives, and I am one of them. She doesn't like me to come up to the roof, anymore. She's afraid I'll fall (or jump?) over the edge, become brain matter and broken bones marinating in a pool of gore between the buildings, something for my parents to identify by the birthmark on my left ankle, or through dental records they'll bring from Bensalem. Shadow figures tell me to take flight, they say it's better for everyone involved, make them suffer, pay for this in my stead. I could pump their lives full of so much pain at any given moment, spread my arms open to this California sky and let the concrete do the dirty work. I've got power like that. But I don't have to make that declaration just yet. I've got plenty of sweet insulation left, that perfect buffer between remorse and unconcern, where the devil does his business and speaks to me through shadows at the corners of the room.*

"I NEED YOUR keys."

Mom looked up from where she sat leaning against the three-foot wall around the apartment rooftop, a notebook open in her lap. She shielded her eyes from the sun, but it was high and bright at two in the afternoon, turning Rachel to a silhouette against a blue pastel sky. "For what?"

"I need to go to Von's. We have nothing in that apartment to eat. And I need cigarettes." Rachel held out her hand and stood waiting. She shifted her weight, and her sandals crunched the gravel. "You should come inside, it's like an oven up here."

"Not to me." Mom dug into her shorts pocket and pulled out the keys to the Nissan and handed them over. She slipped back into her bubble.

Rachel watched her, sun-streaked ringlets pulled back in a ponytail, slender caramel shoulders bent over the journal on her thighs, lean and bronze against the crushed slate gravel. She was losing weight, or maybe it was just the light.

"Did Tower Records ever call you?" Rachel finally asked.

Mom shook her head.

"Did you call *them?* You know, follow up?"

"Haven't had a chance."

Rachel hesitated, wincing up into the late July sunshine. She gazed back down at my mother, stretched out and comfortable on her folded beach blanket, scribbling her melancholy thoughts into the red spiral-bound Mead. "Are you serious, or are you being sarcastic for some reason?"

Mom cocked her head to look back up at Rachel. "I'll call them. I just put my application in three days ago. Relax."

"What about that other band?" Rachel persisted, standing over with the car keys dangling from her finger. "The one you auditioned for last week. What's going on with that?"

Mom shook her head, jotted something onto the page. "I didn't like their music. I don't do punk rock."

"You didn't know that before you went?"

My mother snapped her head up to Rachel's silhouette and stopped writing. "Are you gonna . . . I dunno . . . go get cigarettes, or did you come up here just to badger me?"

Rachel didn't reply to that. Instead she said, "I need some money, too. I'm not gonna argue with you today. I just wanna go get these groceries and get back, so we can eat something besides week-old leftovers."

"My wallet's on the dresser." Mom went back to writing. But then she stopped. "And for someone so obsessed with everyone else's job applications, I haven't seen you filling any out. Or am I the only one who lives here?"

Rachel shifted her weight again and planted the hand with the car keys on her hip, and she scowled down at my mother. "For somebody who can't make it to an interview, Jolán, you sure as hell find time for Wade next door."

"So, what? Are you jealous?"

"You're an asshole."

Mom chuckled humorlessly but didn't look up from the notebook. "So, now I'm an asshole," she muttered. "We went from car keys and grocery stores to Jolán's a fucking piece a shit asshole. In less than thirty seconds. Amazing." Then she looked up at Rachel. "Did you ever think about the fact that he's the only contact I've got now? All Rafe's connects rode off into the sunset with Rafe, I never even knew who they were. It's remarkable I even found Wade. And in the building right next door, at that. Are you kidding me?"

"Yeah, you're a real miracle worker, Jo. You can pull a half ounce of Black Tar outa your ass with no hands, but you can't land a part-time job selling CD's and tote bags." Rachel turned away and started for the stairwell, but then she stopped and turned back. "And by the way, I'll need your car tonight, too. The Regal Blue's under new management now, and my shift starts at eight. One of us had to do *something*." And she cut her eyes at her and walked away.

Rachel yanked open the rooftop door, and slammed it shut behind her. She went down to the apartment and found Mom's wallet, empty, so she took the ATM card instead and headed out to the Nissan, bitter and disgusted as she got in and threw it into reverse, spinning the tires. Neighbors offered peculiar glances, but she ignored them and sped away toward the Boulevard.

These were the days when she wondered what she was doing there. She and my mother were on separate continents now, all the romance extinguished by daily necessity, eclipsed by my mother's addicted tunnel vision. Rachel was once the object of that vision, the only thing my mother could see; she didn't even have to be in the same room, or on the same street. She was the constant. She had my mother's undivided, unlimited focus, carried her gaze around like a locket on a chain, but now it was beginning to tarnish, as does anything without proper care.

She tried. How she tried to have her cake, eat her cake, bake it, decorate it with pink roses made of sugar and devotion, and serve it to my mother with kisses in the bedroom. But now even the sex was preposterous. They made love when—and only if—my mother hadn't dosed up more than a half bag beforehand, and even then, the passion was somehow artificial, substandard. My mother couldn't climax anymore, and Rachel couldn't look at herself in the mirror afterward for the puzzling inadequacy that framed her reflection like a bad aura.

She used to feel so beautiful. My mother made certain of that, with an affectionate whisper just because, the brush of my mother's lips across an ear lobe at the kitchen sink, the warmth of her hand in the small of Rachel's back. Bouquets of flowers and date nights. A kiss to the temple. My mother's arm finding the curve of Rachel's waist in the middle of the night, pulling her close against smooth bare skin. Sleep without sex had its own magic then.

Now they slept back to back, and they woke up alone, even when they woke up together. Depression greeted my mother most mornings, a sad and hopeless nausea churning in her gut before she even opened her eyes, and it only heightened when she did. For Rachel, that had been the hardest part, worse than all the empty, unsuccessful lovemaking. This was a kind of impenetrable darkness that made no sense, had no rules, gave no forewarning and bore no shape or substance. It just was.

And every morning it locked my mother away in an unreachable windowless room, shutting Rachel out behind a door without a knob. My mother would emerge an hour later in better spirits and with a fresh new hole in her arm, a remedy so far beyond the light of love, the distance it placed between them now could've spanned a universe.

Someone blew a horn at a red light gone green on Sunset and Normandie Avenue, jolting Rachel from her thoughts, and she made a right turn and pulled up to the ATM at Bank of America. She took my mother's card from her purse, slid it into the machine, punched in the pin. She needed fifty dollars, so she punched that in as well and waited. The money shuffled down into the dispenser, and the receipt rolled out, and she took it with a glance and started to fold it into her purse but looked at it again because she thought she saw a four hundred dollar balance, which would've been absurd.

They'd started with forty thousand dollars just six months ago, less the rent for one year, the furniture and household supplies, the down payment for the 240-SX. Mom had done five shows since January, each with a ten thousand dollar guarantee, split four ways, which gave my mother two thousand dollars after Rafe deducted his cut from the top. And that brought the figure right back to ten thousand dollars again, added to the twelve thousand dollars they had left from Centriole's advance, give or take a gym membership, six months of utilities and groceries, Christmas gifts, and a trip to Catalina.

Rachel stared into the blue-purple ink—$467.23. She slid the card back into the reader. "You cannot be serious," she muttered, pecking the buttons for balances on both the checking and savings accounts now, and she got receipts for each and sat looking at them as if they were printed in Japanese. The Nissan engine idled lowly. "Justify My Love" was playing from the radio—Rachel turned it down. Their savings had only $1575 left, down four thousand from April's balance.

"What the hell happened to nine thousand bucks?" she begged the stars, calculating the rough total in her head, though she feared she might already know the answer.

It may very well have gone to their neighbor Wade's new stereo system, the one he was showing off last weekend, Rage Against The Machine blasting from his apartment window. Or the three hundred dollar Air Jordans he'd just bought. Maybe it had even gone toward those pricey Lollapalooza concert tickets for himself, his cousin, and his brother—he'd come by to boast about those, too, wearing his new kicks.

"Goddammit, Jo." She crumbled the receipts in her hand and rested her forehead on the steering wheel. "You promised me, damn you, *fucking liar*," she hissed into the dashboard, eyes shut tight against her own foolish oblivion, a hapless repeat of Denver. She'd been so immersed in school, in trying to resolve my mother's deteriorating diet and sleeping patterns, in the chaos around Matt's death and Portland Downs' disbandment—she'd never looked up from any of it long enough to see this coming.

She sat back and peered out at the passing traffic along Sunset. What to do? Her head was whirling with indecision. Groceries or confrontation? Which to remedy first? Frankly, who could eat, knowing you had a siphon plugged into your bank account, funneling thousands into your drug-dealing neighbor's wallet? She shoved the Nissan into first gear and pulled out onto the boulevard in the direction of home.

Friday afternoon traffic was heavy and sluggish as rush hour approached, and so that gave her time to think, to do some constructive evaluation, temper it down before she stormed into the apartment and collided with my mother like volcanic rock and magma. She didn't know whether to be angry or distraught, pin my mother to a wall with every expletive she could muster, or wrap her in a healing embrace and try to reason with her.

But then she remembered—it wasn't my mother she was dealing with, it was the drug, and she had come to realize there was very little difference between addiction and the theory behind demon possession, between herself and Father Karras, carrying on a hostile conversation with an entity more powerful than its host, and she was no exorcist. She had nothing sacred to sprinkle over my mother's marked-and-punctured flesh that might free her from herself.

All she had was words. Words that made threats, words that promised to love, words that offered solutions and made excuses and set boundaries that she never really kept. Maybe this was her own fault. She should have been more firm, more observant, should have gotten on that two a.m. bus in Central Station last November and never looked back. Maybe Dominick was right all along.

She pulled in to the grocery lot and parked and sat there in silence, watching mothers pushing overloaded carts with toddlers swaying in the seats, couples holding hands on their way inside, chatting and squinting from the afternoon sun as they checked their wallets and pocketbooks, a businessman in the Porsche beside her, locking The Club into place around the steering wheel. So much normalcy, the comfortable monotony she would do anything to recapture, but she and my mother had never truly lived within that picture, had they? Everything was erratic and unanticipated, by the drunken seats of their fashionably tattered pants, one good thing always hinging on the outcome of another, with barrooms and motels and rehearsal spaces for backdrops.

Some women's lives were cluttered with preschool toys, report cards and permission slips, art projects made of Popsicle sticks, lawn mowing and landscaping chores to make ready for birthday parties and barbecues. She and my mother had Peavey amplifiers and backstage dressing rooms and guitar parts—tortoiseshell picks, lead cables, steel strings and capos lying around on the coffee tables and bookshelves, sheet music on the floor, contractual agreements in manila folders in the filing cabinets, my mother's music sizzling through headphones while she sat composing on the couch, the Fender in her arms and a cigarette burning in the ashtray.

It was the life Rachel had signed up for when they'd met, a life she wouldn't dream of trading for suburbia's manicured lawns and swimming pool slides, but now that life was in peril, waiting to be obliterated if they didn't do something drastic, but what? Rehab? Rachel scoffed, crossed her arms at her chest and thought about that impossibility.

My mother would shut down like a nightclub in a power outage, just at the mere suggestion; she had too much to do now, a floundering career to resuscitate, new music to write, and time was money. And money was evaporating as if it were made of moonshine, but she could make it all back within months if people just left her alone, got on board with a little support and stopped nagging, throwing stones, demonizing. The litany was always the same.

"Never your fault, is it, Jo? Always so persecuted," she whispered into the windshield. "When the hell did you become such a victim?"

Rachel pulled the keys from the ignition and got out. She grabbed a cart from the return port and rolled it inside, thinking the air conditioning might clear her head, that maybe she might find answers in something as commonplace as grocery shopping.

She bought wheat pastas and fresh fruits—nectarines and seedless grapes and sweet, ashy, Seneca plums. She browsed the meat section for boneless chicken breasts, packs of ground turkey and chose two pink slabs of Alaskan salmon from the seafood section. She picked out another bottle of iron-packed multi-vitamins, hoping to jump start my mother's monthly cycle, which was sporadic at best, but at least she had one again, for now. She went to the produce section and bagged up heads of raw broccoli and fresh cabbage, three big Beefsteak tomatoes, a soft ripe avocado, as if any of it mattered; my mother had the appetite of a canary now and could take up to two days to finish a meal, picking at the leftovers without ever taking the plate from the refrigerator.

She went down the medicine isle and got another bottle of rubbing alcohol, a bag of cotton balls, and a box of gauze pads. She chose a pack of caffeine tablets for herself and stood reading the ingredients; she was exhausted all the time and couldn't afford to be. Too much half sleep disrupted by my mother's night terrors, the restless kicking and tossing, hyperventilation that exploded into wide-eyed panic, slapping and tearing at herself because she didn't know the rats gnawing at her legs and stomach weren't real, that the eyeless, mouthless woman cinching a tire chain around her throat was all just illusion and vapor.

Rachel would sit up, holding my mother to her breast, rocking, uttering comfort into the darkness until she settled. She'd have her sit in the armchair by the closet while she stripped the blankets and changed the sweat-soaked sheets again, then bring her back to bed for the last couple hours before dawn. Three nights a week, she endured this, and so she dropped the caffeine pills into the cart, the least hypocritical alternative to a gram of cocaine tucked into a lipstick lid at the bottom of her purse.

On the way home, she prepared her side of the conversation. No more justifying this outlandish life. Back to the basics—proper nutrition, three days a week of free weights at Bally's, seven a.m. jogging trails, prudent and conservative dope rationing, and no more Wade, because fuck him— he was a candy factory, and my mother was a full-blown diabetic.

When she got to the apartment, she used the intercom at the front gate to ring the house phone for help with the groceries, but my mother didn't answer.

"Figures," she snipped at the speaker and hung up.

She toted the first load into the elevator, which she hated because it was rickety and clunky and took too long to open when it reached an assigned floor, and that always gave her a momentary flutter, the startling notion that it might not open at all, or open between stories, cobwebs and dusty brick and cables hauling black grimy steel, the last thing she might ever see before plummeting to the basement, every bone shattered from shin to clavicle. If only my mother had answered, she would've carried the heavy bags onto this God forsaken contraption, and Rachel could've taken the lighter ones up the stairs, but so it went. The thing stopped, hesitated, made a *thunk* as if to set her free but, as expected, nothing happened.

She poked at the button. "Come on, you stupid thing. I so do not need this today." And she stabbed the "open door" button several times until it finally slid aside at the third floor, and she scurried out into the hall, bags crinkling at her sides, house keys in hand.

Inside, my mother was on the couch, eyes shut, headphones jacked into the stereo, the volume so loud Rachel could hear Jimi calling after "Joe"—*where you goin with that gun in your hand?* She dropped the groceries onto the hardwood floor with a tumbling *clunk*, but my mother was oblivious.

Rachel went over and snatched the headphones from Mom's ears and dropped them onto her chest. *"Hello?* I called you from the gate ten minutes ago. Can you please go get the rest of the bags?"

"Okay, I didn't hear you, Jeezus," she grumbled, sitting up.

"Yeah, no shit." Rachel lugged the groceries into the kitchen. "And you and I need to talk when you get back up here."

Mom sat on the edge of the sofa, putting her sneakers on. "About what?"

"About stuff. Just please go get those bags before someone else does."

Mom didn't say anything. She breathed an exasperated sigh and shut the door behind her. After a while, she returned and brought everything into the kitchen and helped put it all away, but the resentment Rachel had brought home with her was heavy in the air.

She put away a box of pasta and slammed a cabinet door, ripped open the refrigerator, dropped the lettuce and broccoli into the drawers and slapped them shut. My mother's presence in the room was infuriating, and Rachel knew my mother had no idea why, so she decided it was time to air it all out.

Rachel stopped and turned to her. "I just wanna know something. How much have you been budgeting for dope over the past couple months?"

"Why?"

"Just wondering, trying to move some money around, and I'm curious." Rachel stood waiting with affected patience.

My mother leaned against the counter and folded her arms at her chest. "Enough to keep from getting sick, same as always. Why? What difference does it make?"

"Well, give me a figure."

Mom winced and shrugged. "Shit, I dunno," she said and threw out something she thought might sound reasonable. "About fifty a week, seventy-five, maybe. Nothin crazy."

Rachel just stood there, a hand propped on the edge of the counter, and she nodded. "So, seventy-five, then . . . a week . . . on the high end."

"Right."

"You sure about that?"

Again, my mother gave her a casual shrug with a cool air of nonchalance. "Yeah." And she looked her directly in the eye with a lie on her tongue. "I'm sure. What's this about, anyway? Why are you hawking me like this all of a sudden?"

"Is it sudden? You think so?" Rachel watched my mother try to interpret that, to read it for some indication as to which lie she should choose next.

"Well, you've been pissed off at me for weeks," Mom said, "but yeah, all this about money's kind of out of the blue. But you're asking me, and so I'm telling you. Seventy-five a week. Which is no big deal, it's what it's always been."

"So, nothing more. You haven't been, oh, I dunno, dipping into our accounts now and then? Making an extra trip to the bank while you're out?"

"No." Mom laughed, as if Rachel had suggested she were hiding illegal military weapons in the basement.

"Uh huh. Okay. Well, then what the fuck do you call *this,* Jo?" Rachel dug into her purse and fished out the crumpled ATM receipts and threw them into my mother's face.

Mom caught them both against her chest and frowned, bewildered until she unraveled the first one.

"There *was* no cash in your wallet, Jolán. *Big* surprise." Rachel rolled her eyes to the ceiling. "I had to take your bank card. And *this* is what I find?"

Rachel stepped into her space and snatched the slip from her hand and threw it at her again, and it flittered to the floor at their feet. Mom reached down and picked it up.

"How long have you been doing this shit, Jolán? I mean, Christ, it's nine thousand fucking bucks! Everything we had left! Are you crazy?"

No, she wasn't—she was addicted, and so she mumbled, "It's not everything we have left, so just relax, we'll be fine."

She tossed the receipt onto the counter and went to the fridge for a soda, as if none of this was happening, because it couldn't be happening, it was the worst possible scenario, a financial crisis unfolding there in the kitchen with herself as the catalyst. Better to downplay the whole thing and not stoke the flames, open a window and throw a towel over the blaring, squealing smoke alarm. She went into the living room, and Rachel followed after her.

"We'll be fine? So, let me guess, you've got another forty-thousand bucks stashed in the gun safe," Rachel quipped at Mom's back. "Or hell, maybe we can just get a fucking loan from Wade! God knows he's rollin in cash, now that *you* moved in next door!"

"You don't even know what you're talking about," my mother muttered. She dropped onto the couch, set the drink on the coffee table, and lit a cigarette. "You wanna piss all over Wade but what about Rafe? Or Lecia? You never bagged on them. But now all of a sudden you've got a fucking scapegoat, just 'cause you don't like the guy. That's all this is about. You can't stand the fact that I've got a friend, someone I can hang with besides you. Possessive much?" She looked up at Rachel and blew a deliberate cloud of smoke into the air between them, the uninvited dope demon awake and snarling and gearing up for conflict.

"This is not about me, Jolán, so save it. In fact, it's not even about Wade. This is about *you*. It's about you shooting nine thousand bucks of our money into your arm in less than two months. Do you have any idea how fucking scary that is? How much dope that is? 'Cause *I* do." Rachel pointed at herself. "I'm the one who gets the shit end of it every other night. For Christ's sake, I haven't slept in weeks!"

"That is not where it went," Mom scoffed. "I wouldn't even be sitting here if that were true, I'd be a goddamned corpse right now, hangin out in hell with Matt." Then she thought about that and chuckled humorlessly. "Doesn't sound so bad, actually. Sure as shit better than here."

"Oh, poor you," Rachel moaned. "Poor little persecuted Jolán. And yes, that *is* where it went, right into Wade's fat-ass pockets, I'm not stupid. I fucking *live* here, Jolán, I'm not the goddamned mailman."

My mother set her cigarette into the ashtray so she could talk with both hands, and she scooted to the edge of the sofa cushions. "First of all," she began, itemizing each excuse with animated gestures as she went. "There was the rent for this place. There were payments on the Nissan. Food since December. My new guitar amps, three of those. Season tickets to the Atlanta fucking Braves for my brother for Christmas. Your mom's diamond tennis bracelet for Mother's Day, her plane ticket to come see you next summer—first class, mind you—'cause, you know, I gotta make an impression and all. So, unless Wade owns Continental airlines, a Major League Baseball team, and Tiffany Jewelry Company, he never saw a fucking dime of that money. Okay? So, can we just cease with the paranoid accusations 'cause it's pissing me off, if you really want the truth."

Rachel strolled up to the coffee table with her hands on her hips. "The truth? Jolán, you and the truth parted ways last summer, when you started railing heroin up your nose, and you haven't been honest with me *or* yourself since. Because I already deducted those things from what we had left. I sat in that car for fifteen minutes, racking my brain for where nine fucking grand could've possibly gone, and the only thing I didn't account for, because I forgot, was my mom's bracelet. So, fine. You're off the hook for a thousand bucks. Care to do an inventory of where the *other* eight thousand went, or should we just get a statement from the bank in the morning? You know, help jog your memory a little, 'cause I'd sure hate for you to be in the dark over this."

"That's bullshit," Mom said around a drag of her cigarette, but now she wouldn't look at her.

She kept her eyes on the ashtray, the coffee table, out at the hardwood floor beneath the window, beyond where Rachel stood. Anywhere but where responsibility met reality. She was unarmed and naked now, running through a battlefield and caught in her own cross hairs with her girlfriend at the trigger.

"Well, I'll tell you what—that's some pretty expensive bullshit."

"Yeah, well," Mom mumbled. "And even if it *was* true, it's *my* money." Finally she looked at Rachel. "I sure as hell didn't see *you* up on stage working for it. Oh, but you reaped the fucking benefits, though, didn't you. Nice apartment full of furniture. New car to drive. T-bone steaks and Dom Pérignon every week, brand new clothes, partying with celebrities. You didn't mind that shit one bit. Hell, that's probably why you came back in Denver. Didn't wanna miss out on that winning lottery ticket. Too bad it was one number off, though, right? Tough break." And she feigned her disappointment with a derisive little shrug and a wink.

Rachel glared at her. "Oh, wow. Are you really gonna play it that way? As if I should, what? Be *grateful* to you? Are you sure you wanna take it there, Jolán, because I'm gonna tell you something—I couldn't give a shit less about those things. I came back for *you*; it was never to ride your so-called coattails like some gold digging trophy girl, and you damn well *know* that shit, you delirious fucking single-minded dope fiend."

"Oh yeah, that's real nice," Mom muttered, tapping her ashes. "We're name-calling now. That's effective."

"Oh, I've got plenty of things to call you. And they'd all be right on point. How about selfish, for starters? Inconsiderate. Thoughtless. Oblivious. *Addicted*, Jolán! You are a *disaster* that happens *every* other night, and *I'm* the one who has to put you back together! The woman you are today is so far removed from the woman I met last summer, I'm wondering if there's two of you!"

"No shit? Really?" My mother toked her cigarette to the filter and crushed it out with a sarcastic grunt.

"Yeah, no shit, Jolán. I fell in love with a confident, gifted, beautiful woman with healthy ambitions, someone who woke up every morning with a plan to better herself because she loved her life, she loved her music, and she *said* she loved me. But now, twelve months down the road, I've got *this.*" And she held a disgusted hand out to where my mother sat listening on the couch. "A helpless drug addict whose *so* unaware of how helpless she is, she thinks *I'm* the one with the problem! Well, you know what, Jo?" Rachel threw her hands up in exaggerated surrender. "Maybe you're right. Maybe I'm the dumbest chick you've had yet. In fact, I must be, for thinking you had anywhere *near* enough courage to get yourself together, you lost, *pathetic* little girl." And she turned from her and headed up the stairs.

My mother blew a cocky breath through pursed lips. "Little girl," she muttered, then called after Rachel, "Well, if that's how you feel, then why the hell are you even here?"

"Good question, Jo. Shit, I'm surprised you could stay conscious long enough to ask!"

"Okay, yeah. Whatever. You know what—*fuck* you!"

"Been a hell of a long time since you did *that!*" Rachel slammed the bedroom door and left my mother in the unforgiving silence, alone with herself in the middle of the couch.

UPSTAIRS, RACHEL SNATCHED her work jeans from the hanger in the closet, and it sprung from the rod and twirled to the hardwood. She ripped open the dresser drawer for a pair of socks, shimmied out of her shorts and kicked them into the corner, pulled on her jeans. Then she went into the bathroom and locked herself in, washed her face, touched up her eyeliner and retied her ponytail, scowling at herself in the mirror, her pathetic doormat of a reflection, the girl without a backbone. It was a wonder she could even stand upright.

She should have been packing. She should be on the phone with her old roommate, looking for a way to move back in. She still had a Visa card with a fifteen hundred dollar balance, maybe find another apartment in Silverlake somewhere, or south of Wilshire Boulevard where the rent was cheaper.

There was a knock at the bathroom door, an attempt at the knob.

"What." Rachel grabbed her deodorant and swiped it under her arms, sprayed herself with a mist of perfume.

"How long are you gonna be?"

"Why? Your fucking dope's in the bedroom."

"Yeah, but my needles are under the sink. And why do I smell perfume? Where are you going?" Mom questioned through the door.

"I *told* you. I have to work tonight. Maybe if you pulled your head outa your ass you could hear better. Or are you shootin that shit into your ears now? And you want your needles?" Rachel challenged. "Maybe I should just flush 'em all, and that'd be the end of that."

"You wouldn't even."

Rachel brushed a bit of blush onto her cheeks. "You wanna try me?"

"I will break this door down."

"No you won't."

Mom tried the handle again, pounded the door with the flat of her palm. "Rache! Do *not* touch my works, I swear to *God."*

Rachel put her makeup away and stood re-fixing her hair, framing her face just so with honey-blonde strands. "Or what? You'll barf all over yourself? All over me? Not like you haven't done that before."

There was silence in the hall for a long moment, but Rachel could still see my mother's feet shadowed in the space beneath the door.

"All right, Rache, look," my mother said, a change of tactic. "I'm sorry. Okay? I'm sorry for what I said. You're right. I'm an asshole, and I shouldn't have come at you the way I did downstairs, so—"

"Is that you groveling?" Rachel unrolled a wad of toilet paper and used it to blend the blusher into her complexion. "Let me guess—if your needles were *not* on the other side of this locked bathroom door, you'd be in the bedroom right now, calling me a bitch under your breath, just before falling into a heroin stupor. Nice try, Jo." Rachel opened the door and said into my mother's face, "But apologies only matter when they're genuine."

She stepped around her and went into the bedroom for her purse. Then she came back out into the hall, where my mother still stood by the bathroom door. She shouldered past her and headed downstairs, and my mother followed her down and watched as she dug through her purse for the keys to the Nissan.

"These are yours," Rachel muttered and dropped them onto the coffee table on her way to the door.

"How are you getting to work?"

"Walk."

"That's ludicrous. It's daylight now, but not at three a.m. You're gonna walk the Boulevard in the middle of the fucking night? Or wait an hour for a bus full of nut bags?" Mom handed the keys back to her. "Here. Just take the car."

Rachel was in the open doorway, and she turned and shrugged. "Nah, you're right, Jo. I never put one cent toward that thing, never contributed a dime to any of this. So, you just keep those, keep all of it. I'll find my own way home."

She shut the door and took the stairs to the lobby, but Mom was right behind her.

"Rache!" she called out to the sidewalk, trotting to catch up with her. She tried giving her the keys again. "Just take the fucking car. I don't want you walking home at three in the morning."

"What do you care?" Rachel snapped as they walked along Kingsley. "I'm a big girl. I got this. Just go hang out with Wade, go tie off in the bathroom or something, zone out up on the fucking roof. You know, all that junkie shit you do best."

Mom kept up with her. "Dammit. Okay, well then I'm picking you up. I'll be there at two. Just be out front."

"Don't bother. My ride from last summer still works there—Miranda can bring me home. Wouldn't wanna put you out."

"I'm telling you, I'll be there."

"And I'm telling you to fuck off!" Rachel stopped and leveled her with a furious glare.

The Boulevard traffic droned at the end of the block. An inbound flight to LAX roared across the Hollywood sky and faded southward as the neighborhood homeless man played "Yesterday" on the harmonica from where he sat on a nearby curb.

My mother stood with her hands on her hips and gazed around at the apartments and palm trees and the cars all parked along the street, and she nodded. " 'Kay. Fine."

"Fine."

Mom started back toward home. "Jolán De Carlo—officially fucking off," she called over her shoulder and kept walking. "See you when I see you." She waved a hand above her head and jogged up the apartment steps and disappeared inside.

IT WAS A mile hike to Hollywood and Vine, and when Rachel reached The Regal Blue, she stood against the wall by the entrance and tried to collect herself. Fifteen minutes, hoofing it in the heat, brooding over my mother's hopeless spite, words that spit in your face, punched you in the stomach with regret.

She felt nauseated, the heavy-chested sadness that made it difficult to breathe, her throat tightening with the threat of tears. She couldn't cry, not now, she had a shift in ten minutes. She'd look ridiculous. Everyone would feel awkward, and no one would know what to say to the sniffling new chick with the red nose and streaking mascara.

But she just couldn't believe how unhappy it made her to be standing there tonight, in the very spot in which my mother had charmed her into their first date last summer, a foot propped on her guitar case, offering a cigarette as consolation for getting fired. A sweet memory gone so miserably bad. How could that be? What could've possibly wrecked it all, though she knew the answer to that, and she despised it—the enemy to their hopes.

They'd since had their one-year anniversary, and Rachel thought maybe they would've taken another drive up Mulholland for the fireworks that night, if it wasn't redundant, or unoriginal. She was willing to celebrate doing anything, really, but my mother had gotten high over at Wade's that afternoon and had to be safe-sat through a seventy dollar fix, and by the time she came down, it was already the fifth, and the fireworks were over. Flowers a day late and eight thousand dollars short.

She blinked back tears that blurred her vision, sniffed, and took a long deep breath to clear her head.

"Leave your troubles at the door, Rache. Nobody tips a server with a frown." And she shouldered her purse and went inside to clock in.

"WOMEN ARE LIKE car alarms. They serve a great purpose, until they go off for no reason at all, and then you can't get them to shut the fuck up." Wade Tyson sat in his apartment living room, separating the seeds from a hundred dollar bag of weed on the coffee table. He stopped to take a swig of beer and a drag from his cigarette and went back to flicking pot seeds from the sticky green buds he was bagging up for sale.

My mother was in the armchair across from him, tied off at the right biceps, searching ambidextrously for a vein, and she tapped her forearm with two fingers. "You do realize you're talking to one, right?" She glanced at him with a crooked smirk and raised an eyebrow.

"Yeah, but you're not normal."

Mom made a little sound beneath her breath and turned her arm toward the lamplight. "What's that supposed to mean?"

"It means what it means. We're battin for the same team is all. I know you know what I'm talkin about. Rache, she's like . . . I dunno . . . the *girl*, all sensitive and dramatic, and you—you're more laid back, all about your music and shit, just wanna keep a nice buzz goin and enjoy life." And he gave her a thin, pleasant smile. "Like me."

"She never used to be like that," Mom said with a note of wonderment. She stopped hunting long enough to think about it in depth. "But ever since my band fell apart, it's like she's been waiting for a reason to tear me a new asshole."

"And she found it," Wade announced, grinning. He poured a scoopful of Chronic onto the scale and added another pinch until the weight was right. "I'm sure I'm on her shittiest shit list as of today."

"You've been on it."

"Well, I'm honored then. How many shit lists is that now? Maybe a dozen? She can hate me if she wants, but she'll have to get in line."

"You've been a life saver to me. She's just paranoid. She quit everything except beer and cigarettes about eight months ago, so now she's all on that reformed cokehead, 'I don't even smoke weed anymore' trip. So, me doin H is her new pet peeve." Mom held her arm out straight and peered down the length of it. "There you are, you elusive little bitch. Gotcha."

She took the loaded syringe from the end table and aimed it into the left side of her arm, down close to the wrist, and she prayed for a register.

Then she jumped as a bolt of electricity sucked the feeling right out of her thumb. "Goddammit! *¡Pinche cabron!* You mother*fucker*, you." She shook out her hand and drew an excruciating breath through clenched teeth, worked her fingers for a moment, waiting for the pain and tingling to subside. She'd hit a nerve.

"That's the shit that happens when you shove a needle into your arm," Wade noted.

He was the only drug-free drug dealer my mother had ever met. He fancied himself as a businessman, however inconsequential to the dope game he actually was, but he took it seriously. As far as Wade Tyson was concerned, he might as well have been selling stock options, or real estate. He'd taken a marketing degree and organized his knowledge around the fastest cash he could accumulate without having to do much of anything except stay sober, monitor his sources, and provide the best quality product north of Pico Boulevard.

He was a marijuana specialist, but he dealt in everything from cocaine to Xanax because he was trying to save money to buy land in the San Joaquin Valley on which he would build his own home and three climate-controlled, even-span glasshouses, designed strictly for cannabis crops. At the moment, it was all vision. The actual undertaking would cost as much as my mother's now defunct record deal, and Wade was a bit of a spendthrift, so his international enterprise would remain local for now, a one-man petty operation, run out of his apartment, there on Kingsley Drive.

He weighed out another ten dollar portion and watched my mother shake the feeling back into her hand. "You ever consider getting an anatomy book? You know, find out where the nerves actually *are* instead of playing Operation every time you hit up?"

Mom shrugged a little, looked around for something other than her t-shirt tail to wipe the blood runnel, but there was nothing, so she just licked it clean. "You might have a point. Never really thought about it."

"Apparently not," Wade said and he winced, watching her do that. "You do know human saliva's the most contaminated shit on the planet, right?"

"I'll live."

"To the ripe old age of what? Twenty-five?"

"You're a shitty salesman, you know that?" My mother stretched her fingers, made a tight fist, and opened her hand again. She went back to work on the same vein, rested her arm on the inside of her thigh, careful this time. "Nagging your clients right out of their purchases. Where'd you get that marketing degree again? Seminary school?"

"Funny. I'm just lookin out for you," he said, then nodded his chin toward the bookcase behind her. "Hey, toss me those ziplocks from over there, will you?"

Mom glanced over her shoulder and half shook her head. "Can't. Hold on a second. Let me get a register on this fucking thing, do this shot before my head explodes. I'm really not tryin to clog this rig."

"Wouldn't want that," Wade muttered and got up. He came around to the bookcase and reached across her, deliberately penetrating her space so that his crotch brushed against her shoulder, and she leaned away and glowered up at him.

"You mind?" She held up the syringe like a weapon. "I can put this thing anywhere, you know."

Wade grinned and sank back into the couch and spread the extra baggies out on the coffee table. "That's supposed to be my line." He smiled up at her, his thin mustache stretching over full boyish lips.

He was twenty-four, a handsome wavy-haired brunette, slight of build but it worked for him. He was clean cut for his occupation, could've been the guy from down the street who'd mow your lawn or re-paint your porch railing for a few beers on a Sunday afternoon. And despite the obvious emotional impediments, Wade Tyson had an impossible crush on my mother. She tolerated the attention only because he was the dope man, her lifeline, the keeper of the treats just thirty-seven steps from her own front door, and his unrequited advances had been getting worse over the past couple months.

"Your line is as follows: 'Yeah, I got that eightball for you, Jo. Come on by, and I'll give you a discount.' All other conversation is incidental."

"That's friendly," he grunted, pretending to pout but his lopsided smirk gave him away. He gathered all the pot seeds into a neat pile with the edge of his palm and scooped them into a bag of their own. "Only hot chicks get discounts, though, you know that right?"

Mom let her arm hang down to the floor, and she shook it out so the circulation might reveal another vein. "Well, I am genuinely flattered, dude, but you put your dick on my shoulder like that again, and I will set you on fire."

"My kinda woman."

"Not that kinda fire." And she grabbed up her lighter and flicked it once for a little orange flame. She smiled and winked at him and went back to her search.

"Gotcha." Wade sealed the baggie with the seeds in it, took a drag from his cigarette and set it back in the ashtray. After a moment he said, "Well, what if we're meant to have more than one soulmate? I was reading this book, like some Hindu-Gnostic-Buddhism type shit, and it said the soul has no gender and that monogamy is spiritually unnatural. What if they're right?"

"Then you've got a really nice guy out there somewhere, waiting for you," my mother said distractedly, pulling at the needle plunger for a futile attempt at another register. "Maybe even a few of them." She looked at him for a quick second, preoccupied by her own collapsed and rolling vascular system.

"Uh, that would be a negative, babe. I'd rather be a celibate monk, trapped in a monastery on a Tibetan mountaintop, than a faggot." He gave my mother a foolish glance. "Sorry. But you know what I mean."

"No offense taken. I've come to expect that sorta thing from you, actually."

"I'm just saying, what if Rachel's not the one for you? Or not the only one? I just think you should keep your options on the table is all, see beyond a person's gender, give yourself a choice in the matter."

"See beyond *your* gender is what you mean. This kind of begging is a lot more effective when you're honest."

"So, I've been ineffective, then," he pondered aloud. "As in—there's a *more* effective approach that I *should* be taking, and if I *did*, then . . . maybe?"

"Then I'd tell you precisely what I've been telling you, Wade." My mother looked at him directly, the needle pressed to her skin so she wouldn't lose that spot. "I'm gay. I've always been gay. I like the fact that I'm gay. I don't do boys, tried it once in high school, wasn't for me and it's never gonna be. I love my girlfriend, as frustrating as she may be these days. I'm never *not* gonna love her. And I'm never gonna cheat on her, not with you, not with Halle Berry or Jodie Foster or any of my other fantasies. She doesn't deserve that; I put her through enough shit, as it is, and she stays because she loves me back." My mother looked back down at her arm and turned it toward the light. "We're just going through a thing right now. Growing pains. People are ever changing, and we just have to find our groove again, that's all."

"So, you're saying I'm one of your fantasies," Wade announced with a wide smile. "That's enough to hold me over. I'll take it."

"Huh? No."

"Yes. You listed me," he said.

"Listed you? I never listed you, what the fuck are you talking about?"

"Just now. In the category with your celebrity girl crushes, self-entitled fantasies. It's all about semantics, Jo, even if it's subconscious." He shook his finger at her and went back to his work.

"Okay, well you enjoy your pseudo-psychological deductions because that's what they're gonna stay—fantasies—*your* fantasies, not mine."

Wade smiled at her.

They sat in a comfortable silence for a long while. Soundgarden's *Badmotorfinger* album played from the stereo while Wade put together the day's orders—five dime bags, three nickel bags, and a dub sack worth twenty bucks—and my mother concentrated on registering the shot she missed the last three times. Finally, she found a place to draw enough blood for a hit, and she injected 30mgs into her system as if it were sugar water, twenty more than what she'd done only an hour ago. She had just enough time to pull out before it crushed her, and the syringe dropped soundlessly to the carpet.

"You know, you say you love her, that it's all about growth and readjustments, blah, blah, blah. But you're obviously not happy," Wade said. "You've been through a shitty time, but where's the support? Lost your friend, lost your band, record deal tanked. And yet every day it's a new fight. That book I read said a relationship's supposed to be tranquil, easygoing, stress free. I just think that's what you and I already have, and if you could just get past the physical issue, then hell, who knows?"

He looked to her for response, but she was so far under she sat leaning halfway over the arm of the chair, chin on her chest, ringlets dangling into her lap. She was snoring, a heavy ragged gurgling sound from somewhere deep in her chest.

Wade sighed pitiably and watched her. "Jo."

My mother didn't move.

He waited, shook his head, and took the last drag from his smoldering cigarette. "Jo, you're gonna fall outa your chair like that, ya dumbass." When she still didn't respond, he breathed another sigh, took a swallow of his beer, and went to her. "Jolán, come on. This shit's gettin old, babe. You wanna take a dope nap, do it on your own time, not when you're supposed to be hangin out with me, it's fuckin rude."

He took her by the shoulders and pushed her upright against the chair, her eyes half open, staring out at nothing, and he gave her a hard shake.

"Jo, let's *go.*"

No sound came from her at all now, and so he shook her again and waited.

Nothing.

"Jo?"

THE REGAL BLUE was slow on Tuesday nights. It always had been, but Rachel needed to regain her bearings and learn the new menu, so it was just as well. She dropped off two bourbon shots, a White Russian, and an order of Teriyaki wings for a party of three and collected twenty-five dollars from the next table on a fifteen dollar ticket they left under the ashtray. She pocketed the extra ten and cleared the dirty plates and glasses and took them to the kitchen where she met Miranda on her way in, her former ride to and from USC.

Miranda draped an arm over Rachel's shoulder and said to one of the cooks, "The last time I worked with this girl, she was getting canned for giving the band a liquor bath, and I thought I'd never see her again, so you guys give her a break while she gets her shit together. She's a quick study, I swear."

The cook threw a hand towel over his shoulder and slid a plate of nachos into the food window. He snatched the ticket from the order wheel, balled it up, and tossed it into the trash with a quick smile and thumbs-up, then spun the wheel for the next order. "Will do."

Miranda walked with Rachel to the dishwashing station and helped unload the tray. "That's Kevin. He's a man of few words, but he'll get your food out fast and he'll get it right, been here since November. Tommy Novak took over for Steve Zhare about a month after you left last summer. He's a good manager, all about second chances, never dwells on your screwups. Just be real with him, don't try to bullshit the guy, and he'll always have your back. You know, that whole open door policy thing."

"Well, I need all the hours I can get," Rachel said.

She had Miranda follow her to the register so she could ring up her tickets.

"What are my chances there?" Rachel asked. "Does he have any favorites? And if so, how inclined are they to giving away their shifts for a night off?" She let the register drawer spring open and fed it with cash and credit card slips. "I really need to pick up as much as possible."

The two of them went into the dining area and took a seat at a bar top from which they could watch their tables. '80s music played from the jukebox.

Miranda lit a cigarette and said over the chatter, "You know, those kinds of questions usually mean one of two things—somebody's stacking funds for a major expense, or somebody doesn't wanna go home. So, which is it?"

Rachel tried to smile, but it faded into something sad and pensive as she studied the crushed filters in the ashtray between them. "Might be a bit of both. Not sure yet, really."

Miranda waited for her to continue, but she didn't. "Vague much? Care to specify, or are we playing information detective?"

Rachel smiled lightly and apologized. "I've just got some shit going on at home, but I haven't made any decisions on what I'm gonna do about it. Maybe nothing. Either way, I need to make a living 'cause she's sure as hell not gonna do it." She gazed around the bar at her tables, looking for eyes that might be looking for her, and she watched for empty beer glasses or someone pulling cash from their wallet. Everyone seemed comfortable and engaged, and so she asked, "Have you ever felt like the only one in your relationship?"

"I am the only one in my relationship," Miranda confessed with a wince. "I've been single for months, girl, you've been gone too long, you missed everything. Patricia and I broke up in February. Didn't even make it to Valentine's Day. I threw her out on the eleventh and haven't seen her since."

"I'm so sorry."

"Don't be. It was the best thing I ever did, and I imagine she's a happy little clam, now that she can be with her high-maintenance cunt of a girlfriend. The one she was sneaking around with in *December*," she divulged, raising an eyebrow at the wisdom that'd come too late.

Rachel gave that a sympathetic sigh, and though her friend was referring to infidelity, it still sounded all too familiar. My mother had been maintaining an affair of her own since August, a daily tryst with a serial killer who lived in the same house, a kind of Black Widow who struck without malice or forethought and with no respect of person. She was a fixture in my mother's life now, and she wasn't going anywhere and dared Rachel to try and break them up—it would never happen. Lady Black had called shotgun, so take the backseat or take a fucking walk.

"These questions of yours are painting a bit of a shitty picture," Miranda said.

Rachel nodded, watched her customers, but didn't say anything.

"Okay, so . . . ?" Miranda persisted. "I told you my not-so-secret secret. So, who is it you don't wanna go home to? What's goin on?"

Rachel took a moment to gather all the details into something appropriate. She didn't want to bash my mother's reputation, but she needed an open ear, a sounding board, someone with a list of options that she might not have considered. "You remember the night I got fired?"

"You were in tears in the bathroom," Miranda recalled. "I wanted to quit my damn self, I was so pissed at Steve, and I would have if I didn't need this job so much."

"You know the band that was here that night? The whole reason Steve let me go?"

Miranda nodded.

"Well, I've been dating the lead singer ever since."

Miranda's mouth dropped open, and she slapped both hands on the tabletop and laughed. "Holy shit, are you serious? The hot one with the electric eyes and the sexy voice? You slick little player, you!" And she gave Rachel a high five across the table. Then she eyed her slyly. "I shoulda known when I came outside that night, and you guys were out there talking. I thought maybe she was giving you a bill for the liquor stains on her clothes. But, as it turns out, you were gettin your little mack on."

"Well, she was doing most of that. I was just listening to see if she was full of shit. But she was charming," Rachel admitted, thinking back on that evening, when the Hollywood spotlights did figure eights across the western sky while my mother persuaded her to take a chance on a girl with a guitar underfoot and a tipsy sense of humor. "We hung out while she was here that week, and that was pretty much all it took. She was touring around the southwest, and we decided we couldn't stand the idea of being apart, so I packed some clothes, told my roommate I'd stay in touch, and off we went."

"Just like that," Miranda said with a snap of her fingers, in awe of Rachel's adventurousness.

"Just like that."

"You are my new hero, a goddess," Miranda said. "I am now a disciple of Rache."

"Not so fast. Remember, this is the one I'm struggling to go home to now."

Miranda rested her chin in her palm and wrinkled her upper lip with empathy. She dragged on her cigarette and blew a stream out over Rachel's head. "Okay, so then how did Hotness the Rock Star become the source of all your sadness? Tell me she didn't cheat on you, 'cause that just sucks. I'm telling you firsthand." She flicked ashes into the little black ashtray between them. "If she's jerking you around, screwing some other chick while you're here, working your ass off—I say dump her. Dump her while it still hurts. 'Cause if you wait around, thinking maybe she'll lose interest in the bitch and settle back into you, it'll just be harder to leave her the next time. And there will be a next time. Because she got away with it the first time. Know what I mean?"

Rachel thought about that and shrugged one shoulder. "Yeah, but that's not really it. She's not cheating on me. Hell, she doesn't even leave the house long enough to make a grocery trip, and now that the band broke up, no one ever calls, so that's really not the problem."

Miranda frowned, a bit confused. "Portland Downs broke up? But they were amazing. Steve was ready to give them every Wednesday night, but they weren't local. How the hell'd that happen?"

"The keyboard player died last May. And then everything after that just . . . collapsed," she said, her eyes searching the barroom faces for a clean and simple way to explain it.

Miranda threw both hands to her face in sudden recollection, her cigarette smoke fuming up into her ink-black hair. "Wait . . . I remember that now! It was on the news, and I thought about you, about that night when they were here, but I had no idea you still had anything to do with them." She reached over and touched Rachel's hand. "Honey, I'm so sorry. You must've been friends if you spent all that time with them." Then her expression changed into something critical, distasteful, and she glanced around for uninvited ears and said beneath her breath, "They said it was a drug overdose, coke or some shit?"

"Heroin," Rachel confirmed. "He got something . . . I dunno . . . tainted, something from back east."

Miranda rolled her eyes. "Well, ya know, when you mess with the heavy shit, you get what's comin to you. I tell these idiots around here, some of these servers and cooks who wanna play with fire and call it a goddamned game—you end up dead from that shit, and nobody's gonna give a damn 'cause it was a dumbass move in the first place." She held a hand up to Rachel. "No disrespect to your friend, but I mean, seriously. Who feels sorry for the guy who gets mauled by a bear under a sign that says 'do not feed the fucking bears,' right? He *had* to know that shit."

And so there went her confidante, off into the land of judgment with everybody else. She no longer had the will to seek Miranda's advice, and so she just smiled and shrugged. "Yep. You got that right. What goes around comes right on back around."

Someone tapped her on the shoulder. It was the bartender, and he handed her the cordless phone. "It's for you. You're Rachel Cole, right? New girl?"

Rachel knitted her brow and stared at the phone in his hand. "Uh, yeah. That'd be me." She took it and covered the receiver and mouthed, "who is it?" but he just shook his head and left it with her.

"Some guy," he said over his shoulder as he headed back to the bar. "Chad or Wayne or something like that, couldn't hear 'em. He said he's your neighbor?" he offered from across the room, then went back to taking orders and filling frosted mugs with Budweiser on tap.

Miranda raised an eyebrow and glanced down at the cordless. "The guy next door, eh? So, is there something you failed to mention, or am I just being nosy?"

Rachel eyed her strangely and waved that off. She took the phone into the kitchen and found a quiet spot by the glass racks. "Hello?"

"Rache. Hey, it's Wade, your favorite person. Listen, I know it's never good to preface something like this with 'do not freak out,' but do not freak out."

"Wade, what the hell do you want? I'm working. Where's Jolán?"

"Uhh, she's here," he said, almost as if it were a question. "But there's a problem."

"Put her on the phone."

"Can't do that. But you can talk to one of the EMTs if you want. Maybe in a minute. When they're free."

Something spun her where she stood. She went cold and hollow inside as a chilly tingle pricked the hairs on the back of her neck and raised goose bumps across her arms. "Wade, what is going on? *What* EMTs? What the hell happened? And tell me the truth, or I will come through this phone and strangle the *life* outa you, do you understand me?"

He was talking to someone else now, everything muffled through a palm over the receiver. "Hold on a sec." He went back to whomever it was, muddled voices, three of them, she only recognized his.

"Wade!"

"Okay, they're taking her to St. Thomas. You know where that is? The hospital over on Figueroa, downtown?"

"Taking her. Taking her *why?* Wade *please* tell me what's going on. Oh, Christ, I don't have the car," she suddenly remembered. And now the tears had begun to pool as she imagined a long list of terrible possibilities—my mother, covered in blood from a fall off the apartment rooftop. My mother, shot through the chest with a stray bullet from a corner store robbery. My mother, beaten unrecognizably by muggers along the Boulevard.

"I don't have the car," she told him again and turned away into the corner of the kitchen, trying to hide the tears from the cooks half watching as they worked. "I don't have the car. Oh, God, I left her the car."

She put a hand to her forehead and squeezed her eyes shut tight, all her foolish hindsight running down her cheeks and dripping onto the greasy tile floor.

"Rache. Calm down. I've got a car, too, ya know. I can come get you, or I can ride with them, so speak now if you've got another way. But I need to know 'cause they're taking her out."

She nodded, then realized he couldn't see that. "Yes."

"Yes what?"

"Yes, come and get me," she wheezed. She despised him, yet she needed him now more than anyone.

"I'll be there in five. Just be outside." And he hung up, leaving her sobbing in the kitchen corner, holding the phone to her chest, just two hours into a new job with a crisis already and the neighborhood drug dealer coming to her rescue.

chapter twenty

"YOU'VE GOT TO stop this. You can't just take things that don't belong to you."

"Everything belongs to me."

"Well, I don't."

"Oh, but you do. Don't you see the fallacy in what you say? Your flawed, tiny logic? Everything means everything. And so here you are."

"This isn't what I meant. So fuck you, and fuck everything."

"That's the idea. That's perfect."

"Not what I meant."

"You have trouble with that, don't you? You don't know what you mean. Ever. Good intentions, bad ones. It's all relative, shapeless, without boundaries, without thought. Just do, and wonder why, and not know, and do some more. How's that working for you?"

"This was supposed to be different."

"She's never going to forgive you for it. She'll carry it with her like a terminal illness, these images. You should see yourself, a calamity in repose, something like a cyborg with all these machines to keep you simultaneously here and there. Calamity Jo, that's what we'll call you, Calamity Jo. Such a fearless rider for a girl your age, no?"

"Wouldn't have taken the devil for a poet, if that's who you are."

"Shouldn't have taken me for anything, at all, but now that's irrelevant. Too late for sorrys, too late to toddle off into los brazos de su madre, you're all but dead to her."

"Just leave my mother out of this."

"Yes, per her request. Your father, too. The disappointment keeps him up nights, staring at the reflection of the streetlights off the ceiling fan going round and round, the struggle of a man who cannot forgive himself your shortcomings, though he tried so very hard, wanted it so badly, and you gave him nothing to hold onto but disgrace and indignity. Mission accomplished. If only they could see you now."

"But they won't."

"Don't be so sure. You're a frightening debacle of poor choices manifested, death personified, clinging to life out at the edges of her nightmares, so she's certainly considering it."

"She knows better. She knows what that would do to us, to me, she won't even try it, so just shut the fuck up and leave me alone."

"No can do, Calamity Jo. I'm in this now, invested in your future, brief as that may be."

"You came to me. I didn't seek you out."

"Funny how that happens."

"Yeah, a real fucking riot."

"When was the last time you laughed at anything?"

"You wouldn't know if I did or didn't."

"May 3ʳᵈ, 12:17 p.m. Matt told you the first piano piece he could play by memory was 'I Write the Songs' by Barry Manilow. He sang a bit of it for you. You thought it was hilarious. He sends his regards, by the way."

"Who, Matt or Barry?"

"He was thinking of you when we crossed paths. He never had a sister. You were as close as he had ever gotten. If he had it to do again, he would've died just that way, the peace, the undisturbed tranquility, drifting away into all that nothing."

"Must've been a short conversation."

"About a very short life indeed."

"You don't get to have mine."

"But you see, I already do. What you resist, persists, and so it is. There is no you, only me. So quickly you forget, Jolán—I am you."

IT WAS THE second day in ICU, and Rachel would have called my grandparents if my mother hadn't opened her eyes at precisely 7:04 a.m. She was fortunate they let her stay; she wasn't immediate family and not a legal spouse, but when the staff saw her sitting alone, panicking and tear streaked in the ICU lobby, they brought her back into the Unit and hadn't batted an eye since, and for that she was grateful.

Rachel sat with the phone in her lap, a hand on the receiver, waiting, listening to the ventilator sigh and press, watching my mother's chest heave and fall in artificial rhythm. They'd given her something called Narcan to reverse the opioid effects of respiratory depression, so said the night nurse, an RN named Virginia Phelts whose shift was nearly over when my mother finally awoke. She was a conscientious, attentive black woman with beautiful skin the color of butterscotch and huge, vigilant brown eyes that had absorbed every bit of my mother's disastrous condition over the past couple days.

She even stayed an extra hour when she could've gone home to her own family, just to see my mother through to full consciousness because she'd taken a sympathetic liking to her, which she couldn't really explain and didn't try. Maybe it was the tragedy of a promising young life slipping in and out of her grasp for two uneasy nights, or the fascination with what a floundering heroin addict will do to save themselves after coming so close to unintentional suicide. Virginia was the charge nurse, a twenty-year veteran at St. Thomas, and she had a daughter in college at Grambling State, just a year younger than my mother, so maybe that was part of it, too.

They were very careful when they removed the breathing tube because the IV had to be placed into my mother's jugular; they couldn't find a reliable injection site in either arm. The whole process triggered her gag reflex, and she vomited into the sheets, into her own hair and onto the floor, but Virginia had seen that before and thought it a good sign, actually, a compulsory bodily function thrusting my mother back onto the grid. What they hadn't quite taken into account were the opiate withdrawals, brought on by two days of a steady Narcan drip, and so my mother's cooperation took a nosedive by the third evening, when Rachel had gone back to the apartment for a shower and a change of clothes, leaving my mother in the clutches of a frightening and unsolicited detox.

She'd been hooked up to three different types of machines, so at the first sound of the electronic bed alarm, Virginia Phelts hustled into my mother's room to find blood on the pillows, blood spattered across the headboard, a heavy trail of crimson on the blankets and along the floor and up my mother's baby blue gown where it smeared her chest and coated her throat as if she'd been slashed by a monster. She was up and steadying herself by the windowsill, trying to pull her jeans on.

"Whoa, there, darlin! What are we doing? Uh uh! No, no, no, ma'am." Virginia slipped into a pair of gloves from the box on the wall, and she came across the room, took my mother by the shoulders, and stood her upright to assess the source of all the gore—she'd pulled the IV out of her own neck and was now delivering a raspy demand to be self-discharged.

Virginia called for the other nurse.

"Not like this, you're not," she told my mother quite pointedly and guided her toward the recliner, the one Rachel had been sleeping in for the past two nights. "Come on. We've gotta get this fixed, honey, I don't want you to bleed out."

"You don't understand, I can't stay here," my mother insisted, the words barely a whisper through vocal cords ragged from two days of intubation, and she struggled away from Virginia's grip, nearly stumbling over her own woozy feet.

"You can't go pulling IVs outa your jugular vein any old kinda way, either, sweetie," Virginia said sternly, trying to keep her from toppling over. "There's a very particular way that has to be done, and I'm thinkin your last nursing class was never."

The other nurse came in then, a ruddy faced, stocky blonde named Melinda, and together they urged my mother into the chair so they could pull the bloody sheets and remake the bed. When they finally got her settled, Virginia leaned down and looked at my mother straight. "Now, listen. I'm gonna put some gauze on that neck of yours to patch this up, but I can't get that done if you're gonna fight me. So, I need you to be real still and just bear with me for two minutes, can you do that?"

"I have to go. I can't be here. *Please,*" my mother begged, but she stopped resisting long enough for Virginia to clean her up and apply the fresh bandage.

"You are free to go whenever you like, Miss De Carlo," Virginia said as she worked, smoothing the tape so it wouldn't stick to the curls at the nape of my mother's neck. "But if you do, it will be against medical advice, and you're gonna have to sign to that, and I'm not so sure how the doctor's gonna feel about it." She stood up, and she placed her hands on her hips and looked my mother over. "You are by no means a prisoner here, but I am personally asking you to stay because I'm trying to help you, and this is the only place where I can do that. I can't help you out there." She pointed out into the world beyond the hospital. "Once you leave this facility, we are no longer responsible, and there's nothing I can do for you. All my resources are here, sweetie, so this is the best place for you to be right now, you understand?"

My mother was shaking, damp and chilly with the onslaught of dope sickness. "And all mine are out there," she said and tipped her chin toward Hollywood Boulevard.

"Yes, I know. I'm well aware of that," Virginia said. "I know exactly why you're here, and I'm gonna tell you somethin—if you wanna go right back out into those circumstances that brought you here, then so be it. That is your choice. But there are alternatives, ways to get you clean and healthy again, programs we can recommend so that—"

"I wanna go home!" my mother tried to holler, but she sounded like Vito Corleone with strep throat. Then a wave of nausea hit her, as if someone turned on a space heater above her head and tossed her into a rowboat, and she threw up onto the floor between her bare feet.

Virginia pursed her lips and folded her arms across her chest. "I'll have housekeeping come see about this floor, and I'll get you another gown and a blanket. And then we're gonna take your blood pressure. I'll bring you an AMA form as well, but we'll have to see what the doctor has to say when he gets here." And she left her with Melinda and disappeared out to the nurse's station.

That was when Rachel showed up, a gym bag slung over her shoulder full of clothes for my mother's pending release, and she stopped in the doorway and gazed around at the blood on the headboard, the blood-soiled linens and vomit on the floor beside the red dotted trail that led up and across the window sill, and she rested her eyes on my mother, sitting tear streaked and bandaged in the pullout recliner.

"It looks a lot worse than it was," Melinda said, stuffing a pillow into a clean cover. "We had a bit of a meltdown just before you got here, but she's all right now."

"She doesn't look all right," Rachel mumbled and set the bag by the door, then came to my mother and examined her dreadful appearance. "What on earth did you do?"

"Baby, I gotta get outa here," Mom wheezed through chattering jaws, eyes panicked and glassy with tears. She was sweating, and she had her arms tucked into the sleeves of her gown, freezing, all the symptoms Rachel remembered from the Fleetwood, back in Denver. "I need my gear, baby, I don't wanna go through this. You *know* I can't do this, *please.*"

Rachel pressed her forehead to my mother's and took her face into her hands and shushed her. "It's all right, honey," she whispered. "Sssshhh, I'm here, I'm here now, it's okay. But we have to wait for the doctor, just a little while, so he can clear you to go home, and maybe they'll give you something in the meantime, something that'll help."

"No," my mother whimpered. "We don't need that. I can sign a paper, they said, just sign it and I can go. *Please,* let's just go. Everything hurts and I'm sick, I just wanna go *home.*"

"A paper? What paper?" Rachel winced, confused, and she looked up at Melinda to clarify.

Melinda was turning the clean blankets down and adjusting the bed height. "It's an AMA form—against medical advice—if she signs, it means she'll leave against doctor's orders, and the hospital won't be liable for anything that happens, once she's off the premises. Virginia's gonna bring one for her, but if she needs any prescriptions or aftercare, she won't be able to get that, either."

"Oh." Rachel frowned, shaking her head at that. She looked at my mother again, reached into her gown and took both her hands. "Honey, that's not a good idea. You don't wanna do that. The doctor'll be by this afternoon, so let's just—"

Vomit spewed the front of Rachel's t-shirt and ran down the leg of her shorts, and she froze, kneeling on one knee, arms out at her sides as she gaped around at the dripping mess. My mother spit what was left onto the floor and wiped her face with the hospital gown. Then she groaned and sniffled and curled up into a shivering ball in the middle of the recliner.

"Yeah, she's been doing that for a while, started before you got back," Melinda said. "Let me get her into bed and get these monitors back on, and I'll have a tech clean all this up. Do you need a scrub top? I can probably get you one if you wanted to wash out your shirt."

Rachel pulled at the wet sticky fabric, shaking it out away from herself. "Nah, I'm fine. I've got some extra clothes in my bag, but thanks."

Melinda handed her a clean bath towel from the cabinet.

"Okay. One extra blanket, one handy housekeeper coming right behind me, and one AMA form for a Ms. Jolán Elena De Carlo," Virginia announced as she came back into the room, and she set the form aside on the counter.

There was a squeaky metallic rattling outside in the hall as the housekeeper pulled an equipment cart up to the doorway, and the woman knocked and checked around for the requested cleanup. Virginia took my mother by the arm and helped her to her feet, and she and Melinda put her back into bed and reconnected the heart and oxygen monitors while the housekeeper mopped up the floor.

"I need a pen," my mother rasped. "I'm signing myself out of this shithole, goddammit."

Rachel came to the bedside and ran a hand across my mother's forehead, brushing the damp curls from her eyes. "Baby, please just tough this out, just for a few more hours until we can see Dr. Rybeck. Do you remember? He's the one who came to see you yesterday."

"Sweetie, he's gonna make his rounds before dinner, I promise you." Virginia unwrapped another IV cannula, and there was a fresh fluid bag on the edge of the sink. "If you can hold out till then, I'd recommend it. But that is totally your decision. Let me know what you wanna do, though, before I go stickin you again."

My mother moaned and blinked at the ceiling. Tears ran down into the baby hairs at her temples. She didn't answer. She just lay thinking, twisting up the sheets with white knuckles.

Rachel took that window to further convince her. "I'm gonna be here, honey, I'm not going anywhere. I'll stay with you until he comes. We just need to do this right, in case anything happens, you know?" she whispered, fingertips touching my mother's cheek. She wiped the tears and sweat from Mom's face and kissed her forehead. "'Kay? He'll let you go home if you show him you can handle this. I bet he will."

Virginia wrapped a blood pressure cuff around my mother's biceps, plugged her ears with a stethoscope. The housekeeper wrung the mop at her equipment cart, watching the scene with one eye, but she stayed out of it. Melinda stood pressing buttons on the monitors, then replaced the adhesive electrode leads around my mother's chest and rib cage. The room smelled like Pine-Sol now, and Melinda handed my mother an emesis bag in case she had to throw up again, and she did, nothing but air this time, dry heaves that felt like welterweight jabs.

Rachel tried again. "I know you're miserable, baby, but this is nothing new, you've been through this before. When Dr. Rybeck comes, he'll see how much better you are, and then we'll go, and . . ." She hesitated because she hated what she was about to say, a plea bargain that would circle them right back around to the same dysfunction, but what could she do? "And then you can have whatever you want, whatever you need to make it better. We just need to be more careful is all, I need to be with you from now on. What do you say?"

Water trickled into the mop bucket. Visitors knocked at the room next door and went inside with laughter and happy chatter, and then the intercom behind my mother's headboard crackled, the unit secretary paging a nursing assistant, someone named Kelly. Melinda thanked the housekeeper, and the woman gathered her things and rolled the cart away down the hall.

Finally, my mother shrugged, nodded. She turned away toward the window with a scowl. "I just wanna be left the fuck alone. This is such bullshit. But *fine!*" She decided to berate them all. *"Keep* me in here, knowing I'm going *fucking crazy*, but everybody else gets to have it *their way*! Just make sure Jolán does whatever the fuck you want! Can't put my clothes on, can't go get my gear, can't go two *goddamned minutes* without puking my—" She leaned up and vomited into the bag again.

Rachel glanced at Virginia who cocked her head with a half nod.

"I'll take all that as a 'yes' if you will," she said to Rachel and released the blood pressure cuff, like the air being let out of a tire, and she draped the stethoscope around her neck and notated the numbers. "141/92. A little high, but it's a whole lot better than that 50/34 you came in here with. You're distressed right now, though, so we'll keep an eye on it until the doctor gets here." She grabbed a hand towel from the cabinet and wiped my mother's mouth and chin.

"Whatever," Mom grumbled into the pillows, casting her off and tossing aside the extra blanket, her tanned fragile body peeking out from the gap in the baby blue gown.

Rachel gave Virginia a brief smile. "Thanks."

She watched them work for a while, but then it seemed the room was shrinking, growing stuffy and dark with all my mother's hopeless, despicable indignation.

She needed to get some air, and so she excused herself and went out to the ICU waiting area where she took a seat on the couch and buried her face in her hands and cried. She cried for a long time, tears she'd been holding back for two days, trying to stay strong for my mother, but now she was just grieving, grieving for the things they'd said to each other as she stormed off down Kingsley—what if those had been their last words? She cried for a year she'd all but wasted, for the job she probably lost just by being there, for all my mother's addicted resentment, for the mountain of money they'd never get back and for two friends who were no longer their friends, with another one dead because she herself hadn't the foresight to put a stop to this before everything imploded.

She had seen their lives playing out so much differently last summer. She'd imagined herself and my mother in a home of their own, on the trendy, cultured side of somewhere else, my mother immersed in her own success, no inconsiderate neighbors with their yipping terriers at seven in the morning, their fights and arguments seeping through the walls, no landlord nagging for the rent a week before it was due, and no one coming around with an endless supply of poison, living off my mother's self-destruction. She thought everything was going to be fine; it's what my mother had always promised. Everything was supposed to be okay. Even when it wasn't. They loved each other, and that was supposed to carry them through, but if this was what it meant to be in love, then she wondered how anyone ever survived it.

"Miss Cole?" Virginia poked her head around the doorway.

Rachel sat up, made a quick attempt to compose herself, and she smiled. "Yeah. Sorry. I just wanted to give you guys some room to do your thing. Thought maybe I was in the way."

"If you were in the way, believe me, we'd let you know," Virginia said and laughed a little. She gestured around into the Unit. "She was askin for you, wanted to know if you'd left, so I thought I'd try to find you."

Rachel nodded, but she didn't get up. "All right, thanks."

She thought she'd stopped crying, but apparently she hadn't, and she was embarrassed now. She dabbed a stray tear with her shoulder and sat fidgeting with the hem of the shirt she still hadn't changed. She'd forgotten all about it and felt ridiculous, and humiliated, and defeated, Little Girl Fool, the sufferer who drew everyone's pitiful gaze, like the one Virginia was giving her now.

After a moment, Virginia came into the room and took a seat on the arm of the couch across from Rachel, and she folded her arms at her waist. "You mind if I ask you something?"

Rachel shrugged, sniffed, stared at the tile floor.

"How old are you?" Virginia questioned.

Rachel swiped another tear from her cheek. "Twenty-two."

There was a box of tissues on the end table, and Virginia handed it to Rachel. "Twenty-two." Her voice carried a note of amazement as she sat thinking about that. "This is some pretty heavy stuff for a girl your age to be dealing with."

"She wasn't like that when we met," Rachel told her, gesturing into the ICU with her eyes. She wanted to make it clear, even to a perfect stranger, that she didn't ask for this, wouldn't have given my mother so much as a glance if she'd come to her with a head full of nightmares and a needle in her arm.

"How long has she been using?" Virginia asked.

Rachel sighed and stared into the tissues in her hand. "About ten months, the worst of it . . . I dunno . . . started back in May, I guess, when a close friend of ours died, OD'd."

Virginia nodded, resituated herself on the arm of the couch. "And you've been helping her with this, how? I'm guessing you yourself aren't using—I've treated more IV drug users than I care to count, and you're not one of 'em," she said with qualified confidence, looking Rachel over from ponytail to leather sandals. "So, I guess what I wanna know is what you're doing all caught up in a mess like this." She was trying to keep her tone as delicate as possible, but there was a frustration in her voice that she couldn't quite conceal, and she tossed a finger toward my mother's room. "She needs a special kind of care, the kind that you are simply not equipped to give, as much as you might disagree. But I'm gonna tell you, without professional treatment, all that goin on in there does *not* get any better."

Her words and their gentle frankness brought another rindle of tears that gathered under Rachel's chin, and she wiped her face with the tissues but didn't say anything; there was nothing to say. Virginia was right, and Rachel's better mind had been screaming for her to surrender to her own intellect since the night Bryce Pearce sent my mother reeling with her very first shot.

"I know. But I just thought maybe if I stayed," she heard herself say, unsure whether it was in her own head until Virginia stopped her right there.

"And so you did . . . and?" Virginia gestured around to the hospital, at the other nurses going to and from the Unit, doctors in lab coats carrying metal chart boards, some of them surgeons in mint green scrubs, white masks still tied at the neck and pulled down around their collars as they passed the waiting area, stopping to check a pager or to talk to a family member.

"Her situation right now—that addiction—is bigger than you, and it will pull you under like a riptide, and you will drown trying to save her. Take it from someone whose had a lotta years to learn which battles to pick, and which ones to hand off to the experts," she said with a thin, patient smile. "And believe me, I've seen you, sleepin in that recliner every night, holding her hand and watchin those machines like they're gonna get up and do a dance or sprout wings and fly out the window. But there's not enough love in the world, sweetheart. Without some kinda program, a treatment plan designed specifically for her condition, you can love her till the cows come home, and all you'll have to show for it is a herd of cattle and a whole lotta bullshit. It might sound heavy-handed, but sometimes the tough love has to start with the one whose doin the enabling. Because that's what it is, fear and excuses dressed up like a savior. And I have a feeling you're a whole lot smarter than that."

Rachel still had no answer. She just sat with the tissues in her hand and stared out the waiting room window at the downtown skyline, the green cylindrical lights atop the 777 Tower just coming on against an orange-lavender sky. It was a clear enough day to see the San Gabriel Mountains in the northern distance, snowcaps painted pink under a setting sun, and she thought it a much too beautiful picture to be framed in so much strife. The city below indifferent to their two little lives in chaos, directionless, like moths flittering around a porch light, looking for some place to land. An ultimatum was definitely in order. And she knew she was going to have to present it to my mother before any of this went much further.

She stood up and smiled at Virginia. "I should go check on her. She doesn't do well with this sort of thing."

"They rarely do," Virginia agreed, watching her as she started for the hall.

Rachel stopped before she walked away. "Thanks for the chat. Thanks for everything."

"Anytime."

THE DOCTOR SHOWED up within the hour, an hour spent listening to my mother wheeze and groan and wretch into the wastebasket, watching her writhe in the sweat-drenched linens, calling hoarsely in Spanish for someone to make it all stop. They tried to get another IV started in her foot but couldn't get her to stop kicking, because she thought it was more Narcan. It took Virginia a full five minutes to convince her it was only fluids, concentrated vitamins and nutrients to replace the ones she was losing through dehydration, and when my mother finally accepted that, they put the new IV line into her neck again, so it wouldn't get tangled in the blankets.

Dr. Rybeck stood observing it all. He was a blue-eyed older man with a graying goatee and high prominent cheekbones. He checked her chart and assessed her deteriorating mental state over a pair of rimless glasses.

Then he came around to the side of the bed. "Miss De Carlo, I know you wanna go home tonight, and I certainly wish I could do that for you, but I think the best thing is to let you get through this first."

"No." My mother glowered at him, panting, doubled into a fetal position among a half-dozen pillows Melinda had placed around to keep her from whacking herself on the bed rails. "I'm not staying here . . . not another day . . . So *please* just let me go, and I *promise* . . . *please*. I just need my medicine. I just gotta get home."

Dr. Rybeck pushed his glasses up onto his nose and stood with his hands folded in front of him, peering down at my mother's desperation. "Yeah, well that substance you call medicine is the furthest thing from it.

In fact, it's gonna kill you, and it's gonna do it sooner than later. It nearly killed you three days ago. When they brought you in here, you were as blue as my necktie." And he flipped up his cornflower tie for her to see. "Your heart rate was down to twenty-seven beats. The young man that called 911 saved your life that night, 'cause if you had been alone when it happened . . ." And he just shrugged because the rest was understood by everyone in the room. Except for my mother.

"No, *you* did this to me," she insisted huskily. "I was *fine*. I was minding my own goddamned business," she gasped for a gulp of air, "and now I'm in this living hell because *you* gave me some kinda shit to make me *miserable!*"

And she moaned and rolled onto her back and winced at the ceiling, holding her midsection as if to keep from splitting in two. She vomited again, and Melinda came over and turned her onto her side again so she wouldn't choke on it.

"Look, Miss De Carlo, this is all temporary, all part of withdrawals," Dr. Rybeck said. "Let's just get you through this over the next day or two, we'll monitor you, keep some fluids in you, and then we'll see where you stand. I can't send you out there in this condition—how am I gonna do that? You're a mess. Everything about you is compromised right now." He patted her ankle at the foot of the bed. "We'll make you as comfortable as possible, I promise. Just hang in there for a couple more days, and let this pass."

"Fuck you," she breathed and kicked away from him.

He gave the nurses a look and shook his head. He had Virginia follow him out into the hallway, and they shut the door, leaving Rachel to watch my mother suffer under Melinda's unwearied care.

After a while, Dr. Rybeck opened the door again and asked for Rachel. She came out into the hall, and glanced at Virginia who was making notations at the nurse's station now.

"So, are you a relative of hers? A sister, maybe?" the doctor asked.

"No, her family's all in Pennsylvania," she said. "I'm just a friend, I'm her girlfriend."

"Do you have any way to contact her family?"

She shook her head. "I mean, she does, but they don't speak."

"Because of her drug use?"

"No, they aren't aware of that. They've got other . . . I dunno . . . issues. Things from before she and I met, things I don't really understand, but . . ." She didn't finish that thought. Instead she told him, "She doesn't want them to know about any of this. And if you think she's gonna be okay, then I'd really rather not contact them. It'll just make things a whole lot worse."

The doctor nodded. "Well, I think she'll be okay while she's here. But she's got herself a pretty serious problem, and once she leaves here, she's got about a ninety-five percent chance of going right back to it. So, do I think she's gonna be okay in the long run? No. I don't. Not without a program. I dunno how much influence you've got over her decision making, but if I were you, I'd spend some time trying to talk her into getting treatment. Otherwise, the next time she finds herself in the ER," he slapped her chart against his palm and half shook his head, "it might be the last. Just something to think about." He put a hand on her shoulder as he walked away.

Melinda came out of the room and gave her another one of those smiles, the ones that said, "better you than me. Picked yourself a real winner with this one, didn't you?" and she disappeared into a side room that had to be accessed with her badge.

Rachel stood against the wall beside my mother's door, hands in her pockets, thinking. She didn't want to go back inside, and that made her feel guilty, but the past couple days had taken the kind of toll she thought she'd never have to pay, and it was exhausting. She watched Virginia who was on the phone now, talking to someone about Mom, but she was too far out of earshot to eavesdrop for any details. Virginia hung up and typed something into the computer, then got up and pulled a file from the cabinet behind her, flipped it open on the desk, and added more paperwork to it. She sat looking at it for a moment and shook her head with a sigh and then put it back in the filing cabinet. Rachel wondered if it had something to do with Mom or if maybe some other poor soul had gotten bad news.

Something banged and shattered in my mother's room, and Rachel jumped. She turned to find the observation window splintered into a spider web, the blinds inside cocked askew.

An alarm went off, a screaming mechanical whistle, and Virginia bolted from her chair behind the counter and rushed past Rachel and pushed through the door. A piece of medical equipment lay broken, there on the floor, the stand thrown across the room with it.

Inside, my mother was up again, green eyes wide and livid as she stumbled back into the corner, all legs and unruly curls in her baby blue gown; she had the IV pole by the shaft like a baseball bat, rasping wildly to be set free. Several of the heart monitor leads were unfastened now and dangling from her chest, and she'd pulled her IV out again, but this time she separated the tubing at the connector point, the rest of it still inserted into her jugular and leaking like a garden hose, dripping blood onto the floor and slinging it across the windows as she moved.

"Oh, my God." Rachel stood dumbstruck in the doorway. She didn't know whether to go to her or stay out of her way. She chose the latter and took steps backward until she bumped into the nurse's station.

"Melinda!" Virginia hollered, keeping her eyes on my mother, hands up in defense, ready to deflect that IV pole if my mother saw fit to swing it at her skull.

"You're gonna let me go *home!*" Mom roared huskily. "Or I swear to *God* I will tear this place apart!"

Virginia backed off but only to grab a random wad of latex gloves from the supply on the wall mount, her eyes fixed on my mother as she slipped into a mismatched pair. "I have had just about *enough* of this outa you for one day, Miss De Carlo. I know you're hurtin right now, baby girl, but this is *not* the way you wanna test me, I promise you that. Now, just calm your little butt down and get yourself back into that bed so I don't have to do it *for* you. 'Cause you are not gonna like me very much if I do."

"I'm not staying here another fucking day. Are you people deaf?" my mother hissed and she clanged the pole against the wall. "I don't care if I gotta throw myself out the goddamned *window*—I'm *leaving*! I am getting my *shit* and walking the fuck *out* of here!"

"And you will be doing *that* with half my staff on your back," Virginia assured, pointing to the blood-dappled floor. "Now, *put* that thing down and let us do our jobs so we can *help you through this*."

Melinda came running from the med room, and when she saw what was happening she called down the hall for help, for someone to bring the restraints. Then she crept into the room, pulled her gloves on, and flanked my mother at the left, trying to talk her down while she looked for a way to move in and subdue her. That was when she got too close.

Mom took a swipe at her with the IV rod but it missed and crashed into the headboard, sending chunks of plastic twirling in all directions. She swung it the other way and the bay window overlooking the parking lot burst into a spider web to match the one by the door. Virginia stepped in and grabbed her arm and wrung it into a knot, and my mother dropped the pole and twisted away from her and started for the halls, the loose IV slinging an arc of fresh blood across the ceiling and around the walls and onto Melinda who wrapped her in a bear tackle, and they all hit the tiles before my mother could escape to the lobby.

"I need restraints in here!" Melinda shouted out into the Unit again while Virginia pressed a knee between my mother's shoulder blades and tried to pin her arms to the floor, but she was so slippery with her own blood, it was like wrestling an eel into a rabbit hole, and she slithered free again, flipped onto her back, and kicked Melinda in the chest.

Melinda toppled aside but was otherwise undeterred and she rushed right back and wrapped an arm around my mother's shin, using her own weight to keep that leg immobile while two additional nurses came sprinting through the double doors down the hall. One of them was a male, well built and athletic, and he slid into the commotion like a runner at home plate with a set of four-point leather cuffs in his hands as my mother wriggled and pulled and kicked and scratched.

She was unbelievably strong, fight and flight all happening at once, and she flailed against his grip, growling through gritted teeth about cruel and unusual punishment, about being held captive against her will, and then she got an arm free and tried to elbow the fourth nurse in the face but to no avail; she had finally spent the last burst of energy she would have for a while, and they all hefted her onto the bed where Virginia secured her wrists and ankles in the padded cuffs while Melinda went around and strapped them to the underside of the frame.

Rachel just stood there, stupefied, an arm wrapped around her waist, propping up the hand she held cupped to her mouth, watching as they worked to reconnect the IV and EKG leads.

The room looked as though there'd been a hog killing, blood streaked to the ceiling, strewn across the cracked window glass, smeared around the bone-white floor tiles. Everyone was sprayed and stained with it, winded and chattering amongst themselves, pulling things out of plastic packaging and tossing the wrappers to the floor. Then one of them closed the door and twisted the blinds shut.

Rachel could still hear her, frantic and wailing on the other side, yanking at the restraints—she wanted to die in there, wanted them to euthanize her, send a bubble through the IV line and put an end to it, the pain was just too much. She was crying out for my grandmother.

THEY MOVED HER to another room, one that hadn't been thrashed and desecrated, and they were much more strict about the visiting hours now. Virginia would be off for the next four days, and so an older heavyset woman named Gloria took her place, and Gloria had nothing invested in my mother's mental well-being, not like Virginia. Gloria administered meds, changed the bandage on my mother's neck, and kept the restraints secured and buckled down tight—"ICU bed-3" was a danger to herself and others, a combative troublemaker interfering with her own care, and Gloria wasn't taking any chances with the likes of Ms. De Carlo.

They'd given her Ativan to edge her through the rest of withdrawals and put her in an adult diaper that the nursing assistant, Yvette, came around to change every few hours. She called them briefs, not diapers, because it was less humiliating, but they were still a sad necessity for a twenty-three-year-old Berklee graduate, regardless of what you called them.

Yvette was Rachel's age, a nursing student at LACC, the community college down on Vermont. She was Latina like my mother, a petite, light-complexioned girl with a scar on her forearm from where she had a gang tattoo removed, and she spoke to my mother in gentle Spanish whenever she'd open her eyes, which wasn't often during the first day in her new room.

"Soló se necesita un buen descanso," she'd say while adjusting the pillows under the restraint belts. "Just a good rest is all. Be back on your feet before you know it, *mujer,* change your life around, make a big comeback. Just gotta rest for now."

"When are they gonna take those things off?" Rachel asked Yvette of the medical restraints, still affixed to the bed frame. "She's obviously not a risk, anymore; she can barely stay alert. They can't possibly be necessary now."

Yvette was only privy to certain things regarding each patient, but she told Rachel before she left the room, "Not real sure, but they'll probably leave them on until she's transferred. That's what they usually do."

Rachel frowned. "Transferred? Transferred where? To another floor? She should be released from here, no?"

"Down to Norwalk," Yvette said from the doorway. "To La Casa."

"I'm goin home?" my mother muttered through the oxygen mask.

Yvette chuckled a little. "No, *mija,* not that *casa.* La Casa, the psychiatric center in Norwalk, off Rosecrans. We don't have a psych ward here, and they were the only one with an available bed, so." She shrugged. "I'll go get you that other blanket; you said you were cold earlier." And she disappeared out into the Unit, shutting the door behind her.

My mother pulled at the restraints. She was too weak and fuzzy to make much of a show of her displeasure, but Rachel was not. She came to the bedside and smoothed a hand across my mother's forehead. "I'm gonna go find out what she's talking about. I'm sure it's a mistake, probably just looked at the wrong chart or something, 'kay? Just relax, and I'll be right back." And she kissed her and went out to the nurse's station to find Gloria.

She was just coming out of another room, two doors down, and Rachel met her at the counter and asked about my mother's fate.

Gloria didn't look up from her paperwork. She jotted something into the file in front of her and stapled another form to that one. "Blasted techs," she mumbled for Yvette having spoken above her pay grade. "That's something Dr. Rybeck will discuss with you further when he makes his rounds today, but what I can say is that your friend is a suicide risk." She stopped working and looked up from the desk. "She threatened to jump out a hospital window and took a swing at the charge nurse with an IV pole, fashioned as a weapon. Her behavior has been erratic, and she's shown signs of emotional instability. What would you have us do under the circumstances?"

Rachel narrowed her eyes and gave Gloria a cautious stare. "She was withdrawing from a heroin overdose. You guys sent her into a medically-induced detox that she wasn't expecting, and she was confused and terrified. Why, exactly, does that warrant going to a psychiatric center?" She glanced into my mother's room and back to Gloria. "And you've had her in those restraints since yesterday. She's obviously calmed down. Is it really necessary to keep treating her like Hannibal Lector?"

Gloria looked at Rachel overtop her reading glasses and crossed her arms on the edge of the desk. "She's compliant now because she's sedated. The restraints will come off if and when the doctor orders it. I don't make these decisions, Miss Cole, and I don't write hospital policies. She's being transferred to a psych unit because she's combative and self-destructive. Illegal drugs are notorious for inciting that kind of behavior."

"Yeah, and so are the legal ones, apparently. Whatever you people gave her on Tuesday turned her into something I've never even seen before, and now you're penalizing *her* for the side effects. Wonderful," she muttered. She didn't know what else to say. "All right. Thanks for your help, I guess, if that's what you call it." She patted the countertop once and started away, but she turned back and said to Gloria, "She might have some piss-poor judgment, getting herself hooked on that garbage. I'll give you that. But she's not crazy. And the fact that you people are treating her like a *nut*, I think is disgraceful."

"Well, you're entitled to your opinion, dear," Gloria said without discretion. "But we're not here to make excuses for patients like Ms. De Carlo—we leave that to the friends and family." And she went back to her paperwork, tuning her out as if an iron door had slammed shut between them.

Yvette was in the room when Rachel returned. She was taking my mother's vital signs and measuring the urine in the catheter bag that hung from under the bed. The Ativan was wearing off a bit now, and so Mom was more alert as Rachel came to the bedside, wearing an expression that made my mother very uneasy.

Rachel ran her fingers through Mom's curls and tried to smile, but it was brief and artificial, and my mother knew it, but she didn't say anything. She just lay there and listened.

"They just wanna be sure you don't have any other issues going on besides the addiction. And we both know you don't, so—"

My mother shifted in the blankets and yanked at the leather cuffs, her eyes bright with alarm; it was all she needed to hear, and she tried turning her head and twisting her mouth to maneuver the oxygen mask from her face so she could say her peace, but it wasn't working; it was making her more frustrated, so she just spoke through the plastic.

"I'm not going to a fucking nut house. You gotta stop them, I don't need that."

"I know you don't." Rachel didn't want her getting agitated again, didn't want to provoke any more anxiety that might defeat my mother's purpose, and so she said, "It's just a precaution, a step they wanna take 'cause they think it'll help you. They do it in every situation like yours, it's not you, honey, okay? I don't agree with it, either, but it's just protocol, that's all."

My mother made a groaning sound and gazed up at the ceiling, eyes brimming, and she blinked and let fresh tears roll down into her hair as she lay thinking, her breath ragged and heavy and fogging up the mask. The heart monitor sped up, and Yvette shook her head at that.

"You gotta relax, *mija,*" she said from the bathroom where she was dumping the catheter bag. "You get yourself all jazzed up again, and they'll increase your dose." She flushed the toilet and came out into the room. "You don't want them to section her in. Trust me, I've seen it before, and going 5150's the worst way." She glanced out into the Unit, then went over and shut the door. She came back to the bed and looked down at my mother. "You wanna go voluntarily, *mujer.* Sign yourself in. A lotta people don't know that the first time, but if you sign for yourself, you get out sooner, sometimes after just a few days." She reconnected the urine bag and added, "If you fight them, refuse treatment and all that, they'll section you in themselves, you know, have you committed. And then you'll never get out. At least not for a long-ass time, anyway. Longer than you'd ever think."

"Well, they are gonna see that they've made a goddamned mistake, that she's obviously not unstable and certainly not dangerous," Rachel said. "The whole thing was situational, not some kinda mental break. *They're* the ones who are crazy."

"Maybe so," Yvette shrugged, then said to my mother, "The worst thing you coulda done, *chica*, was threaten to kill yourself. Hell, even taking a swing at the nurse carries less weight than a suicide threat. That's what did you in, whether you meant it or not."

"I don't even remember that," my mother moaned. "Oh, Christ, how is this happening? My whole fucking body hurts, and now this shit. *Why?*" Tears ran down her face again.

Rachel took her shackled hand and leaned down and kissed her fingers. "We're gonna get it straightened out, baby. They can't keep you—there's nothing wrong with you. And I'm gonna be there. I'll go with you, and I'll be there every step, so just stay calm, ride this out, and we'll get through it, I promise."

IT WAS A promise she wasn't able to keep. Dr. Rybeck showed up just before dinner and went over the nurse's notes for the past twenty-four hours. The entire incident had been thoroughly documented, and there was nothing at all favorable for my mother's release. She was deemed mentally unstable, a doctor's assessment made lawfully binding as a court order, or an arrest warrant. The following afternoon they came for her by ambulance, no friends or family members allowed. Visitation would be subject to counselor's discretion, as my mother would have to be processed and psychologically evaluated first.

"It's not gonna be so bad, *mujer,*" Yvette confided, just before they took her down for transport. "La Casa's like a freakin resort compared to some. It's just a small place, private rooms, good food, lots of amenities. My cousin had to go last year; she's a cutter. And they were good to her. If you gotta go to a psych center, it's the one you wanna go to, it's nice." She held my mother's trembling hand and gave it a reassuring squeeze as they strapped her onto the ambulance gurney. "Just keep your head up, *chica.*"

"Do *not* call my parents," was the last thing my mother said to Rachel as they rolled her out into the hall. "No matter what comes of this," she made her promise. "No matter *what.*"

IT WAS SUPPOSED to be a twenty-minute ride down Intertate 5 to Norwalk, but it seemed to be taking much longer. They still hadn't removed the restraints but they were downgraded from the padded leather cuffs to a set of stretchable mesh straps that gave her more mobility and comfort. She fell asleep under the last dose of Ativan that Gloria had given her before they left, but she didn't know for how long. She woke up groggy and spent the rest of the ride in silence, staring up at the interior lights and glancing out the rear windows, listening to the EMTs talk about dinner plans and shift changes.

They were a young black male and a white female, the female looked like a lesbian, something about her, but my mother couldn't be sure. The guy had a military bearing, thick in the chest and shoulders, a crew cut, clean shaven. She felt detached from it all, dope cravings a constant maddening tug, ever present like the dull pain in her left knee from where Melinda had tackled her to the floor—it was just a bruise, but it hurt like hell when she had to stand and climb onto the gurney.

A twenty milligram shot of Black would melt that away just fine, but she tried not to think about that, yet thought about it, anyway. She could taste it, smell the phantom aroma cooking in the spoon, relief and regret and desire all bubbling into a single unrequited elixir she wished she'd never touched and needed to get home to.

The ambulance slowed and made turns and stopped at what she imagined were the traffic lights and stop signs she could see fading behind them. Soon there were only foothills and desert as they continued away from civilization again. The suspected lesbian said something to the driver through the back window, confirming their destination, and my mother thought she heard snatches about La Casa being full, an emergency admission the previous night for a failed Metrorail jumper that their co-workers had handled, but she was hazy from the sedative, and her head wasn't processing things properly.

They finally came to another stop, and after a moment she heard a tinny, mechanical rolling sound, a gate perhaps, voices at the front of the vehicle, then they moved forward again. She saw lush green lawns and dusty mountainsides shrinking away through the window, chain link fencing in the distance, palm trees on the outer perimeter, a long circular drive. There was a landscaped terracotta monument sign at the entryway that she could just about catch as they rolled past, and a cold and sudden rush of butterflies bloomed in her chest as she read the copper-plated script.

WELCOME TO WESTLAKE STATE HOSPITAL

chapter twenty-one

THEY STILL HADN'T removed the restraints. They let her climb down from the gurney on her own accord, bound at the wrists and ankles, and they had her stand and wait with the female while the other paramedics locked up the vehicle and collected her paperwork. The grounds were quite expansive with long rows of ironwood trees and yucca plants scattered around a sprawling campus of mission-style structures with Spanish tile rooftops. The focal point to the entire facility was a steepled bell tower that stood two stories above everything else. It would've all passed for Yvette's palatial resort if it weren't for the bars on the windows, the razor wire coiled atop the chain-link fencing.

They walked her inside as she limped along on a sore knee, and she was taken down a long hall with black-and-white checkered floors, tall ceilings, and arched doorways that stretched on and on as if repeating into infinity; the place had to be a hundred years old. Medical personnel and a few people in civilian clothes came and went through locked steel doors, in and out of side rooms with Venetian blinds twisted shut. Soon they came to a holding area, a large examination room where they left her in the hands of a nurse who finally unstrapped her and told her to strip.

St. Thomas had given her a set of blue paper scrubs and a pair of non-slip socks to wear out, and they had sent the rest of her things home with Rachel, so she had nothing for the lock box except her wallet; no jewelry, no toiletries or street clothes, just her own skin and too many questions for their liking.

"Excuse me, but I think there's been a mistake," my mother said to the nurse, a round-faced, chubby woman in flower-print scrubs and an ID tag that bore the name Birdie. "I was supposed to go to Norwalk, to a center for—"

"Well, you're a long way from Norwalk, dear. You're in Santa Clarita. Now, *off* with 'em. You need to be searched. Let's go." She didn't make eye contact, just spoke as if my mother was in another room and stood waiting for her to comply.

"Santa Clarita? But I signed myself in," my mother tried to explain. "I signed myself over to La Casa. That's where they said I was—"

Birdie took two steps into my mother's space and grabbed the paper scrub top by the collar and tore it down the middle. "First rule of thumb," she barked. "When the staff tells you to do something, you *do* it."

She was my mother's height, but she was twice her weight, and she was agile and quick. She threw the paper shirt to the side and started for the pants, but my mother held up both hands and backed away.

"*Okay.* Christ." She slipped out of the bottoms and kicked them across the tiles and stood naked, staring at Birdie as if she'd stepped off a spaceship, unsure whether this was a medical facility or the state penitentiary.

My mother was relatively flat chested then, so she didn't have to lift her breasts, but all other cavities were explored and examined, rubber-gloved fingers prying into places no one had seen for years except Rachel, and when it was determined she had no contraband, Birdie gave back the socks and handed her a pair of pajamas, which were really just a set of white scrubs. No strings, no belts, no zippers or buttons permitted, particularly in my mother's case—she was on suicide watch, with a propensity toward violence.

"Come with me." Birdie opened the holding room door, shut it, and locked it, and the sound echoed through the halls like a cannon shot.

My mother followed her through the building. She didn't know where they were going. She didn't know why she didn't see anyone else in white pajamas. An orderly accompanied them, a white male in standard blue hospital scrubs and running shoes. He was a balding older man in his late fifties, well built for his age, with a white goatee like Dr. Rybeck and heavy-lidded downturned eyes that had probably seen more than she cared to imagine.

He said nothing as they walked, didn't look at her, just followed at her left rear flank with keys jangling on his hip until they came to an office waiting area with a sign that read: *Intake*. There were three or four adjoining rooms inside, an administrative headquarters, but it was dinnertime, and it seemed everyone had gone home for the day except for whoever was in the back, rustling papers and opening file cabinet drawers. On the far right wall was a corkboard with a calendar of activities for August and some watercolor artwork that looked like it had been painted by children.

"Have a seat here." Birdie pointed her to one of the green plastic chairs and left her under the orderly's watch as she disappeared through the building.

My mother glanced up at the man's nametag—Thomas Somerville—and he saw her staring and gave her a deadpan glare down the bridge of his nose. She looked away and sat thinking about Rachel and Wade and the chunk of Tar in the nightstand drawer with her works, how much easier this would all be with a little chemical assistance. Three days, maximum. That's what she agreed to, and then she could go back to her life. There was no escaping from here, anyway, not with Tommy the Bruiser standing watch amid the barred windows and steel doors and barbed wire fences.

She didn't even know where Santa Clarita was, had no geographic orientation whatsoever, she could've been a half mile from Sacramento for all she knew. And she was still weak and unsteady from the Ativan and the withdrawals, the lack of sleep, an empty stomach and no appetite, and the aching left knee still swollen and purple. She wouldn't make it past the first doorway.

"Jolán De Carlo?" A young woman came out of the back, thirtysomething and dark haired, wearing a pair of over-sized round glasses with the tortoiseshell frames. She was casually dressed in jeans and a simple white blouse, and she swung open the gate at the end of the counter and had my mother follow her back.

The office was small and bright with overhead fluorescent lighting and emerald green curtains drawn shut at the single window, unremarkable, like any college counselor's workspace. The woman took a seat at her desk and offered Mom the wooden armchair in front.

"My name is Laura Koepsell. I'm a psychiatric social worker here at Westlake, and I've got some questions for you and some things for you to sign so we can get you processed." She sorted through the forms in front of her, then stopped to read over what looked like my mother's medical records, the folder sent with the EMTs from St. Thomas. Then she looked across at Mom, thinking, tapping her pen on the desktop, scrutinizing her for a long moment before she said, "Is this the first time you've attempted suicide?"

My mother didn't know whether to laugh or give her a glower, so she chose something in between. "See, that seems to be the problem; I've never attempted suicide. I don't know where they got that from. But what I do know is—"

"It says here that you were brought in to St. Thomas Hospital on July twenty-fourth, five nights ago," Laura scanned the medical notes with an index finger, "having overdosed on heroin." She looked at my mother again. "It was a near-fatal dose. If it weren't for someone having found you, you would've been successful."

Mom knitted her brow and tried to read the paperwork upside down but couldn't.

"Found me," she repeated to herself. "But I wasn't alone when I hit up. I was with a neighbor at his apartment, and it was totally accidental. I just wasn't paying attention to—"

"And then on Thursday evening, July twenty-sixth, you assaulted four hospital staff members with a weaponized piece of medical equipment and, again, threatened to kill yourself by jumping out a hospital window." Laura gazed at my mother, trying to appear concerned, but it was transparent and critical instead. "That's why you were referred to this facility. We're here to help you, but it makes our job much more complicated if you're not willing to accept what's been going on with you." She half shook her head and jotted something into the notes.

"Well, see, that's the thing—I *would* accept it, if that was actually the case, but it *wasn't*," Mom said crossly. "You people are taking this whole thing out of context, and I don't understand why, because I do *not* have any desire to fucking *kill* myself and I never did. I mean, I know my limits with dope, and I just misjudged the dose, that's all. This is a misunderstanding. Nothing more. And I really do *not* remember—"

"I need you to calm down." Laura looked at her straight, the artificial light glaring off her lenses. "We're just talking, here, just trying to get some background so we know how best to treat your condition," she said as if talking my mother off the roof of a parking garage, trying to get her to hand over the sniper rifle.

"What condition? And I *am* calm. I'm just trying to explain what really went down, so I can go home. That's all I've wanted since this whole thing began, was to go home. I don't feel good, and I don't want to be here. I just want my life back."

"Then why did you try to kill yourself? I'm trying to get to the root of your problem, but as long as you're in denial, it's not going to help you here."

She noted something else into the file, and this time my mother watched more closely: *17:01—agitated, manic, possible dissociative tendencies.*

"You've obviously got periods of awareness of your condition, seeing as you came here voluntarily, and that's a good start. We can work with that, but you have to help us as well. Now," she continued and browsed through the rest of the file, "I just want you to tell me a bit about yourself. It's in your records that you are a regular IV drug user. Have you ever taken any other substances, or is heroin your drug of choice?"

"Is this supposed to be a rehab program?"

"Do you have an aversion to getting substance abuse treatment?"

"I have an aversion to dope sickness."

Laura scribbled something else onto the pages: *shows lack of insight and judgment.* "How would you perceive your state of mind to be at this time?"

"Displeased. Tired," my mother told her. "I haven't slept in weeks, not worth a shit, anyway. With the exception of being unconscious for two days. Not sure if that counts. Doesn't feel like it, for all the trouble it's caused."

"Do you feel like this situation has been perpetrated upon you by others?"

"Somewhat."

"Explain that to me."

My mother huffed and sat back against the chair. She was fading again; the adrenaline dump after having seen the facility welcome sign was draining away now, but she tried to focus. She *had* to focus, or she might never convince these people she had no intentions to harm herself.

"Well, let's see," she sighed, blinking back an onset of grogginess, "I was minding my own business last Tuesday, tied off at my neighbor's apartment so I wouldn't get sick, then woke up in hell two days later, with a bunch of strangers telling me hell was gonna be my new residence for a while. 'Tough shit, you wanna go home. We're gonna pump you full of Narcan till your eyes bleed if we have to.' Doesn't seem like my kind of vacation, so yeah—I feel a bit violated by the whole thing." She rubbed her face with both palms, then folded her hands in her lap and sat staring at the desktop.

Paranoid, rate and volume of speech fluctuating, easily disengaged.

"Look, I'm a musician, a professional musician, and I have a career to get back to," my mother said. "I don't have time for all this, so if you'll just let me make a phone call, I can have my girlfriend come get me, and I'll be out of your hair. I'm sure you have plenty of folks in here who need your time and attention a lot more than me."

"Have you found it difficult to achieve your goals in life?"

It was apparent the conversation would continue as long as Ms. Koepsell so desired, and so my mother breathed another weary sigh. "Well, when a three million dollar record deal gets flushed down the pot, and you go from touring with Pearl Jam and partying with Steven Tyler to burying your dead friend and having no band at all, I'd say yeah—that's put my future goals on indefinite hold for a while. Anything else?"

"You tell me," Laura said, jotting down her observations for further review. Then she looked across at my mother. "Tell me about your friend. How did your friend die?"

"He OD'd. Yes, on smack. He got a bad batch, he was essentially poisoned."

"You think he was poisoned? Who do you think poisoned him?"

Mom shook her head and gazed at Laura for a stupefied moment. "Dealers?" She shrugged. "Hell, I dunno. Cartels in Thailand. Whoever cooked the shit. What difference does it make? He's dead, and he didn't deserve that. He was only twenty-two."

"How did it make you feel when you found out about his overdose?"

"It wasn't an overdose, *per se*. I just told you. It was poisoning, bad dope. It happens, a recreational hazard."

"So, you weren't negatively affected by it, then." *Emotional detachment, increasing paranoia—feels endangered by foreign drug cartels, grandiosity—patient believes she is a famous rock musician.*

"I try not to dwell on it," my mother said. "I can't bring him back, so what good does it do to cry myself to sleep every night? I've got enough on my plate as it is."

"With your music career."

"Yes. That and my girlfriend nagging me to make more money. Apparently I've been spending more than I make, so I'm gonna have to do something about that. But I sure as hell can't do it if I'm in here."

Laura listened, nodded. "When you say girlfriend, in what context do you mean? A female who is a friend, or a sexual partner?"

"A little of both. Why? Is that gonna affect my admission status now?" My mother smirked. "'Cause I'd sure hate to be disqualified on the grounds of sexual orientation."

For a microsecond, Laura surrendered to the faintest smile, amused. Then she noted something else, but my mother couldn't make it out. "Do you feel threatened right now? By this interview, by these questions?"

Mom thought about that with a deep sigh. She shook her head. "I wouldn't call it that, no."

"What would you call it?"

"A big clusterfuck of a whole lotta miscommunication." She nodded down to the paperwork. "And all that psychobabble you're scribbling right now is complete bullshit, too. A total misdiagnosis, if that's what it's meant to be."

Laura glanced at her notes and looked back at my mother with a thin, piteous smile. "Well, no," she admitted. "That's not what it's meant to be. I don't make diagnoses. I make observations, nothing more. The diagnoses are for Dr. Shah to make, which he will do when he comes in tomorrow."

"So, does today count toward time served, then? Like jail? I signed up for seventy-two hours; it's Sunday now, so then Tuesday you let me out of here? I talk to him, he sees there's nothing wrong with me, I call my girl, and off I go."

"Miss De Carlo," Laura said, addressing her by name for the first time, which my mother thought curious and a little unsettling. Laura stopped writing. She folded her arms on the edge of her desk. "Psychiatric assessments aren't like car engine tune-ups. You need to understand that. We don't just poke around, make a few adjustments, and then hand you back the keys to your life before closing time. It's a process. You came here for some much-needed help, and our end of the deal is to see that you get that help, and we'll try as many treatment options as necessary until we find one that's custom to your needs."

"Which you'll get done by Tuesday," my mother hoped to confirm.

Laura didn't answer that. She just handed her some more forms to fill out. "This is for your Medicaid." She put a finger on the first document. "This is a state-run facility, so your stay here is covered by Medi-Cal, by the state, but in the event that there are any additional costs— testing, prescriptions, procedures and the like—you'll have the Medicaid coverage to offset those costs." She produced three more applications and forms. "We'll need your initials and signature here," she pointed to the first, "and here, which just gives us consent to your treatment. The others are to list your personal belongings, and there's a privacy statement; everything we've discussed is confidential, as is your stay here. It simply states that we do not have the right to divulge any of your medical or personal information to a third party without your written consent." And she handed my mother a pen, which was affixed to her desk by a beaded metal chain. "You can take as much time as you need. I'll need to make photocopies of your drivers' license and social security card, so if you'll take them out, I'll do that while you fill out these forms." She had my mother's wallet in a St. Thomas patient belongings bag, and she set that on the desk as well.

Mom found herself suddenly overwhelmed. Too much paperwork, too much fine print, too many signatures required for treatment she didn't think she needed, and so she hesitated. "I really would like to talk to someone else before I do all this. I've signed enough record deals and performance agreements to know the power of a signature, and I just don't feel all that comfortable with—"

"If necessary, Dr. Shah will assume conservatorship over you and sign in your stead," Laura told her. "That's a very complicated legal process, and it's one that you probably don't want to challenge; it's the hard way. This," she pointed down to the stack of forms, "is the easy way, believe me. So, if I were you, I'd go for what's behind curtain number two. Because either way, we're going to provide you the care that you've come here for. Might as well just settle in and let us do our jobs."

It was no different than St. Thomas—go by choice or go by force. My mother looked over all the documents, shaking her head, pondering her options. She would be doing seventy-two hours whether she liked it or not because somehow she had presented as being in psychological distress, and now she would have to spend the next three days proving otherwise.

"Crazy until proven sane," she muttered at the pile of forms.

"Your ID, please?"

My mother took the plastic bag into her lap and untied the drawstring. She slipped the identification cards from their folds and handed them over. There was no point in resisting. She was too tired, and she felt nauseated again, and her head was becoming cluttered with too many thoughts she couldn't organize.

Laura had Thomas babysit while she went back up front to the copy machine, and my mother sat filling in the blanks. She became quite ill at ease because she suddenly didn't recognize her own writing, jagged and unsteady, like that of a ninety year old, a manual manifestation of all their ridiculous accusations, and that startled her, but she chalked it up to anxiety and sleep deprivation and kept writing. She was having trouble staying on the lines, finding the right boxes to check, remembering how to spell things like "Kingsley" and "Hollywood" and "musician." The pen felt misshapen and awkward in her hand, and she had to stop several times to regroup.

"Think. Concentrate, you idiot," she muttered, then realized what she had said and glanced back at Thomas standing guard. "I was just thinking out loud, dude. Relax."

She spent the next thirty minutes trying to gather all her scattered thoughts into the ones she needed to get this done, but it was a chore. The pages blurred and cleared. The room grew dim. Her motivation threatened to shut down, but she fought it back and produced five poorly legible forms for Laura's new case file.

Laura looked them over, then peered across at my mother. "How are you feeling right now?"

Mom shrugged, nodded, but she couldn't look at her, too many notions and speculations and misgivings circling in her brain. And the dope cravings were relentless, omnipotent, the elusive solution to all this just hours away in her dresser drawer.

Laura took up the pen, checked her watch, and noted something else in the file: *17:47—patient is now uncommunicative, appears dissociated, cognitive function significantly decreased.*

"When was the last time you've eaten?" she asked.

Mom shrugged again. "Few days ago." Then she rethought that. "No. Wait. I think it was yesterday. My girlfriend fed me broth and some cherry Jell-O. I think that was yesterday." She shook her head. "Fuck, I dunno."

"Let's have them draw some blood so we can get some tests going, and then we'll have a tray brought to your room. Do you have any food allergies we should know about?"

Mom shook her head again. "I don't want anything. I already feel shitty as it is." She slumped in the chair and shut her eyes and rested her head in her palm. "Can we just get all this over with? Whatever you're gonna do. 'Cause I really do not wanna be here."

17:59—patient refuses nourishment, mood and behavior have become despondent.

"We'll have a dinner tray brought to your room," Laura reiterated and checked her watch again. "Everyone's already eating now, so it'll still be hot. You can eat or you don't have to, but be aware that a refusal to eat is perceived as a form of self-harm, and in order to prevent that, we will administer nutrients through a feeding tube if necessary. It's completely up to you."

My mother rolled her eyes in disbelief; the coercion here was ruthless. She sat up a little and pursed her lips and shrugged again.

"Fine. Whatever. This is such bullshit," she whispered in protest. "Just bring me a T-bone then and, uh, some oysters on the half shell, and lemme get a Caesar salad no croutons, and a large Coke, no ice." Then she reconsidered all that and gave Laura a lazy, defiant stare. "Oh, but I guess no bones or shells allowed. I might try to saw my own arm off, or fashion myself a key and run off during the night. Nevermind. I'll just take the broth and Jell-O."

"Miss De Carlo," Laura said with a sigh. "I realize you're feeling rebellious and discontented right now. But you should be mindful of your choice of defensive humor. We take any allusion to self-harm very seriously here, particularly from a patient with your history. Thomas?" she beckoned out into the waiting area, and the orderly appeared in the doorway again. "She's ready." Then she looked at Mom. "Thomas is gonna take you down to get a physical with Dr. Bernard. They'll do some tests over the next couple days, get your dietary needs, prescriptions and so forth, get you settled in. Welcome to Westlake." She gave her a quick smile and turned her attention back to my mother's case file.

"When do I get to make a phone call?" my mother asked.

Laura didn't look up from her work. "That will be decided after Dr. Shah's assessment tomorrow."

Mom just sat there, mulling over that and a hundred other things— feeding tubes, restraints, strip searches, her signature giving consent to it all. Three and out, she thought, just two days and a wake-up. There was a loud buzzer out in the halls then, and it gave her a start. She wondered what it was for, an alarm, perhaps. Maybe someone had jumped the fence.

"Let's go," Thomas said from the doorway, and so she rose and followed him back out into the halls.

PATIENTS WERE OUT and about now, milling and meandering and sitting along the walls in white scrubs like her own. Some of them stared, others ignored her. They all looked ordinary, middle adults and younger people close to her own age; it was all males through this division.

She followed Thomas through two more sections, each separated by heavy steel doors that had to be unlocked and re-locked, and now they'd come to Ward 6, so said the stenciled lettering over the door as they entered. It was a day room, plain brown couches and bookshelves overstuffed with board games and craft supplies, a mounted television playing cartoons—Tom and Jerry, no one was watching it.

This area was all females, and there were a handful of them around a card table playing a game of Uno. They stopped to watch her pass, a redhead, two brunettes, and a black girl. They looked like teenagers.

One of them said, "Oh shit, it's Slash," and the others laughed, referring to her neglected curls, she guessed, which did liken that of the famous Guns N' Roses guitarist when unkempt.

Thomas showed her on through, unlocked and relocked another door that led them down a long checkered hall like all the others, at the end of which was the medical office.

Inside, a nursing assistant named Dianna removed the St. Thomas ID wristband and snapped a Westlake band in its place, which was already there, printed up and waiting for her: *De Carlo, Jolán E. DOB 06-12-71. Ward 27. Patient # 65309. DOI 07-29-93.* They noticed her limping, and so they added another one, a yellow band with "Fall Risk" in bold black print.

Dianna took her weight—117 pounds, her height—five foot, seven inches, her blood pressure—92/56, temperature—97.4, and had her read an eye chart from twenty feet away—20/20. Dianna had her sit while the phlebotomist, Clara, spent several minutes looking for a vein in her forearms.

"You'll probably have to get it from somewhere else," my mother finally said after four or five unsuccessful sticks in each. "I've pretty much trashed all those. Sorry."

Clara got what she needed from my mother's calf so she wouldn't have to disrobe out there in the office. She filled two vials, taped a cotton ball to my mother's leg, and left without a word.

Dianna brought her in to an examination room and gave her a gown, and when she was changed, she climbed onto the examination table and sat waiting for what seemed like an hour. There was no clock on the wall, only a mock Rembrandt watercolor and an informative poster with a cartoonish cross section of the human eyeball, a laminated wall cabinet with locks on the doors.

At last, Dr. Bernard knocked and let himself in, carrying a manila folder. Dianna came in behind him. He was short, olive skinned like Mom, middle aged with a large beak-like nose and brown eyes that were kinder than she was expecting.

He smiled and introduced himself. "So, you are our newest guest," he said, pulling a pair of reading glasses from his shirt pocket and slipping them onto his face. He had a slight regional accent that she tried to place, maybe north Jersey, or New York. He set the folder on the counter and glanced over the records. "De Carlo," he read aloud, then turned to my mother. "Is that Spanish?"

"It's Italian," Mom told him quietly. "My mother's Cuban, though."

Dr. Bernard drew back with a grin. *"Wow.* That's quite a combo. Passionate, I'm willing to bet."

Mom shrugged. He was, by far, the most pleasant person she'd encountered here, but her mind was much too preoccupied with cravings and all the unfamiliar goings-on to appreciate his warmth, so she just nodded and said nothing.

"Well, maybe not so much this evening," Dr. Bernard confessed. "But that's why we're here, to see what ails you, make sure you haven't got anything physically detrimental that needs attention, and try to get you back on track as best we can."

He looked into her ears with a lighted scope, handed it back to Dianna. He had her tilt her head up toward the light and peered down her throat, felt around her neck for swollen nodes. He listened to her chest and back with an ice-cold stethoscope and looked into her eyes with a little flashlight. Then he examined her knee, pressed around the sorest spots, twisted it gently, and had her bend and extend it and push up and down against his hand. All of that hurt like hell, and so he ordered X-rays to rule out a fracture. It took a while, but those came back negative.

Ordinarily, he would've wrapped it with an ACE bandage, but my mother's suicidal status prevented that, as the bandage could be used as a weapon against herself—no belts, no laces, no drawstrings. And no four-foot strips of elastic to unravel and experiment with at one's unsupervised leisure.

"Just stay off it as much as possible for the next few days. It's a deep nasty bruise, but it'll heal on its own if you don't fiddle with it. Now," he looked over her chart, "about this addiction of yours. I'm not a drug counselor, but I am a physician, and your blood work is a mess. When was the last time you used?"

Mom was tired of answering questions about an addiction she couldn't quell, but she obliged him, anyway. "Tuesday night."

"And when was the last time you ate anything substantial?"

She couldn't remember. Broth and Jell-O probably weren't what he was looking for, so she just shrugged, shook her head. "Last week, I think. We had some salmon, broccoli. I don't know what day, though."

"The reason I'm asking is you're borderline malnourished," he told her frankly but without judgment. "You've got vitamin deficiencies left and right, and you're underweight for your height by a good ten pounds. The whites of your eyes are becoming slightly off color as well. These are all telltale symptoms that you may or may not have noticed, and heroin hasn't been helping, not one bit. When was the last time you got a full night's uninterrupted sleep?"

Again, my mother couldn't provide a solid answer. She shook her head. "I dunno. Maybe March."

"That's quite a while ago."

"Guess so."

"Well, your white blood cell count is elevated," he explained. "And that means your body's immune system is in overdrive, trying to compensate for the lack of rest and improper nutrition, so it can fend off the illnesses that are knocking on your door right now. Much of your fatigue and fogginess is coming directly from that, and it's only exacerbating whatever psychiatric issues you might have going on as well. One's feeding off the other, like a little duet, but the music's way outa tune. So, I'm gonna help you get one of the players back on key so that Dr. Shah and the rest of the staff can work on the other player." Then he smiled. "I saw in your file that you like music. Hopefully my analogy will make it easier for you to understand." He tapped her good knee with the medical folder. "You can get dressed now, and Dianna will show you back out to the front."

And that was that. Thomas took her back through the hospital, around a dozen corners and up a flight of stairs and through another day room, the one belonging to her assigned Ward 27. The women in there were quieter than on Ward 6, ranging from Mom's age to those in their forties and fifties. They, too, suspended their conversations and Monopoly games as she passed. They looked up from paperback books and glanced away from *Moonlighting* re-runs; some of them nodded hello, one of them waved, others were unimpressed and went back to reading. She'd just been admitted to an insane asylum, she mused as she limped along, so where were all the insane?

As it stood, she was the closest one to it. Thomas took her to the med station where a nurse in pastel pink scrubs came to the counter. Her nametag was hidden under a cream-colored sweater, but she was tall and blonde and wore so much eyeliner it gave her blue eyes the appearance of a cat.

"Your name?" she asked without looking up from the pharmaceuticals.

"Uh, Jolán."

"Last name. I don't have time to go searching every record for a given name."

"De Carlo." She could have taken a few notes on being personable from Dr. Bernard, but my mother kept that herself and waited.

After a few moments, the woman returned with a small paper cup with three pills in it and a cup of water.

Mom hesitated, tipped the pill cup toward herself for a better look. "And what are these?"

"Haloperidol, Lorazepam, and Naproxen," the Catwoman said.

Mom blinked at her. "Okay. I know the Naproxen, but what do the others do?"

"They do what the doctor needs them to do. One is a mood stabilizer, one's for anxiety, and the other one's an anti-inflammatory. I need you take those in front of me, so I know you took them."

Thomas nudged her. "Come on, kid, let's go. This isn't your last stop tonight." He folded his arms and gave her his heavy-lidded stare.

Mom just stood gazing into the cup, at the little pentagon pill shaped like a house, the blue tablet, and the pink one with a hole through it. She looked back at Thomas and then at Nurse Catwoman. Of all the illegal substances she'd taken in her recent lifetime, it was the legal ones that gave her the most pause.

"And you're sure this—?"

"Are you refusing your medication?" Catwoman asked.

Everyone heard it, and now some of the other patients stopped what they were doing, and they all stood watching to see what came next.

Mom glanced around the room, a myriad of faces observing in a stilted silence, waiting for her response, anticipation like a fine mist floating in the air. She had the creeping feeling her refusal might result in something dramatic and unpleasant.

"No. I'm not. Just wondered what they were for is all." And she knocked them back and washed them down with the lukewarm faucet water. The nurse made her open her mouth wide and lift her tongue for confirmation, then sent her on her way with Thomas.

Last stop—a single windowless room at the end of the next hall with nothing but a low-lying bed, a cot, for all intents. There was a gray bath towel folded on the baby blue thermal spread beside one pillow, no sheets. The bathroom had no privacy, just a stainless steel toilet and a small sink with no knobs, only a single steel button for water. Thomas shut the heavy door, a sound like railroad cars clanking into place, and she could hear the keys jingling as he locked her in, then bid her good night with a two-fingered salute through the little porthole. A suicide's purgatory.

She stood at the window for a while, a rectangle of reinforced glass just big enough to frame the nurse's station across the hall, framing her own face as they glanced up periodically from their work, watching her watch them. Two white females, one in blue scrubs like Thomas's, the other in purple bottoms and a butterfly printed top. She came away from the door and took a seat on the bed and looked around.

Cinder block walls, painted drab canary yellow, some of it peeling. A single, exposed, fluorescent tube overhead for light, but there was no switch on the wall; she imagined that was controlled remotely, perhaps on a timer somewhere. The floor was white linoleum and in need of wax. There was nothing else to see. Stainless steel, drab yellow, baby blue, dingy white. Walls. Floors. Ceiling. Toilet. Glass and metal and concrete.

There was chatter out in the halls, where everything carried an echo—your footsteps, your voice, your life, sweeping off into a black hole until there was no sound at all, and there you drifted, debris floating untethered from the world beyond these cinder blocks and scuffed tiles. It would be nothing to disappear here. A simple swipe of a pen, and you'd vanish from society, forever erased from its census.

She found herself thinking about these things for a very long while.

SHE SNAPPED OUT of that, came crawling back to the present and shook it all off, but now something was very wrong.

"What the hell?"

She rubbed her eyes and forehead, frowning at an unfamiliar sense of despair that was now pressing down as if to pound her into a box. She felt drowsy and distorted now, a high coming on that she didn't welcome, nothing at all like the lovely escape provided by her good friend Lady Black; this was something malevolent, flashes of soul-crushing darkness that spun her into a sticky black web and left her feeling drained of everything meaningful and good.

Mom knitted her brow in protest, blinked and blinked in an effort to clear her muddy vision, and she stood up and tried to walk it off because it was coming at her fast, but she stumbled into the wall instead. Then she didn't know why she'd gotten up, couldn't remember why she'd been sitting or if she'd been sitting at all. It was as if she'd been beamed down into the moment from some other moment in some other life in some other place, but where?

She collected a handful of her wits and stood thinking very hard until it came to her—Catwoman, the pills in the cup.

"Oh, Christ." She slid down the wall into a seat on the floor. "You gotta be kidding me," she moaned, her eyes squeezed shut against the onset of God only knew what.

Could it be antipsychotics? Antipsychotic meds for one who had no psychosis—that was absurd. She had friends in college who'd abused the prescription drug Ritalin, people with no attention deficit issues, who didn't need it and got off on the reverse effects, like speed or cocaine, and she wondered if this was something similar. She wondered what she was just wondering about, had lost her train of thought completely, like someone hitting a "restart" button in her head every thirty seconds.

AFTER A WHILE, it seemed she couldn't see the future anymore; there were no pictures, just a black screen. Where there had always been that hypothetical imagery, those ten thousand variables and visual possibilities we entertain each day, the infinite suppositions to hang onto or fear, strive toward or avoid, there was now just a hole with nothing in it. Thinking forward led only to a huge empty void.

Thinking anything at all was a pointless waste of time. But she couldn't not think about thinking, and she thought if she *were* plagued with some dangerous psychosis, these drugs would certainly be the antidote—remove all desire to desire anything, interrupt neurological signals for cohesive thought, and press "delete." She certainly wouldn't find herself slathered in excrement with a bolo sword in one hand and a human head in the other, now, would she. Very effective.

Cinder blocks. Linoleum. Blue thermal. Stainless steel. Time sucked away into an eternal vacuum.

KEYS IN THE door.

"De Carlo." A man's voice, but it wasn't Thomas. She wasn't sure how long she'd been vacant. "Dig in."

A food tray was left on the sink. Black shoes, shadow, scrub pants. The door swung shut, boxcar couplers clunked into place. Keys again. No more voices in the day room. Then darkness—she didn't know which lights went out, the ones in the building or the ones in her head.

She sat on the hard tile floor for a long time, unsure whether she was awake in the dark or asleep and dreaming of being awake in the dark. Then it occurred to her that she was flat on her back, cold linoleum and the lingering scent of urine, dry dust smell.

Something moved across the floor; she didn't know what. Her eyes were apparently adjusting to the darkness because now the little window in the door cast a minimal amount of light into the room, and she used it to find the source of the sound, faint and grainy, like fingertips moving through gravel. Someone stood up from a seat on the bed.

She recoiled against the wall and scrambled across the floor to the opposite corner and tried to focus, spoke to them through jaws clenched tight against her own doing, the words like pottage through a mouthful of mud. She waited, blinked, got no response. Nobody there. Just yellow painted cinder blocks and blue thermal going gray and ashy in the half light. The phone rang out at the nurse's station. A door clanged shut down the long hall.

She huddled in the corner and drew her knees up close and wrapped her arms around them and spent a long time watching for movement in the shadows. She was familiar with that, although it had always been an internal, figurative experience until now, the uninviting space in which she'd find herself when the dope wore off, her unhappy place. She had no idea it was real. She'd never considered its tangibility, harbored away in a hundred-year-old sanitarium in the middle of the California desert, waiting since October for her to show up.

"Now you've really done it, Jo-Jo. Walked straight on through to the other side," she sang softly in the style of Jim Morrison and just sat there in the dark, singing to herself, hugging her knees, eyes wide and alert.

Or so she thought. When she actually opened them, she was on the bed, no concept of time again, and she was covered with the gray bath towel—the fluorescent tube overhead was still off. Then it flickered, a deep red lightning that made her eyelids flutter, and when she felt something moving on top of the blankets, she startled in an effort to scuttle away, but only to find it was her own hands; they'd taken on a tremor, something like Parkinson's, or perhaps a kind of seizure.

She lay there and held them both up trembling in the hall light that streamed through the porthole. She tried to concentrate, settle herself down, mind over matter to make it stop. But they just shook as if she were sharing a rain puddle with a downed power line.

"Usted es impotente aquí."

She jumped. "Huh?" It was a female, barely a whisper beside the bed.

"¿Quien es usted?"

My mother lay very still and turned only her eyes to search for the source, and she lowered her shuddering hands to the mattress and trained her ears on the darkness.

"Hello?" The overhead light flashed red again, and then it swung just a little in its hanging fixture.

"¿Dónde está?" It came from over by the door now, but there was no figure there to block the window light, which she found peculiar, intriguing, impossible.

"You tell me," my mother decided to respond, this time. "Wherever I am, it wasn't where I'd planned. Are you real? Are you . . . are you a ghost? I'm not afraid, if you are. So, you can quit with the light show. And all the other shit, too."

"¿Quien es usted?" Behind her at the head of the bed.

"Who am I?" My mother took a very long moment to think about that. She shook her head. "I don't even fucking know anymore." She raised her quaking hands to the light again. "I'm someone who doesn't like this shit, I know that." She looked around for the voice again. "Is that you doing this? Making me shake like a leaf in a windstorm? Like some kind of cripple?"

"Que hiciste esto a ti mismo." And then again in English, *"You did this to yourself."*

It came from over the bed now, and my mother peered up into the swinging fluorescent lamp but it wasn't a lamp, it was a guillotine blade, and it stopped cold as if grabbed by an unseen hand, dead center over where she lay.

The sudden silence made her ears ring. My mother didn't breathe.

Then the plaster that held the thing in place began to crack across the ceiling, a splintering roadmap that burst from the rafters with a shower of crumbs and mortar that pelted her face as the blade plunged toward the bed, severing her into two parts at the abdomen so that everything she was made of spilled out onto the blanket and over the edge of the cot and onto the white linoleum.

"Que hiciste esto a ti mismo . . ."

THE NURSE BIRDIE, Thomas Somerville, an orderly named Franklin Parker, and a young nurse training under Birdie named Cherie Navedo responded to her screaming at seven a.m. She was frightened at the sight of them, still hadn't quite disengaged from the night's delirium, and she upended the dinner tray in their direction as they approached, then stumbled over her own feet and toppled into a flailing heap in the corner of the cell.

It was a systematic procedure of gathering her up off the floor, placing her onto the bed, and pinning her down by hand so that Birdie could administer another dose of Haloperidol without breaking the needle off in my mother's hip. Chemical injection was a much faster, more reliable method of restraint under combative circumstances, and within a few minutes, my mother went flaccid, a semi-conscious glob of putty trying now to sit upright on the edge of the mattress. The buzzer alarm she'd heard last night at intake resounded again, and now the institution halls were coming to life, a new day glaring through the porthole. Women prattled on and shouted after one another on their way to breakfast. Heavy doors echoed down the tall, distant corridors.

"What's all this fuss about, Miss De Carlo?" Birdie asked, once my mother was satisfactorily numb. Her voice was dialed up a notch in order to grab my mother's attention. "All that noise you're making just disturbs the other residents, and it only makes it harder for you to adjust. Now, what's the problem?"

She sounded like she was speaking through a shoebox under a down quilt. My mother could only catch certain key words. *De Carlo . . . noise . . . residents . . . harder for you . . . the problem . . .*

"I don't wanna sleep here," she managed to mumble through the drug, but it oozed from her lips in a garble of sounds less like language than she was hoping for.

Birdie was nevertheless fluent in the over-medicated dialect of mush mouth, and she said, "You have to be under supervision so that you don't try to harm yourself. When the staff and Dr. Shah feel confident you're not going to do that, you can be placed in a regular room with a roommate, but not until then. Do you understand?"

... have to be ... harm ... staff ... with a roommate ... understand . . . "She tried to kill me. Somebody was here. And I can't think. Can't—my head doesn't work, you don't understand. Please." My mother began to cry. "Please. Please," she begged between sobs.

"Miss De Carlo." Birdie stooped down to look up through my mother's hair and into her tear-twisted face, a compassionate gesture from the woman who tried to rip the clothes right off her back at intake yesterday. She was squat and troll-like with a deep southern drawl, but her voice carried a note of kindness as she explained. "You have to trust that this is all in your best interest. And the sooner you do that, the easier this is all gonna get. Now, who do you think was in your room last night? The nurses across the hall said you were quiet as a church mouse until this morning. No one came or went from here. Once James dropped off your tray, not a livin soul opened this door until now. I promise you. No one's trying to hurt you. We're only here to help you."

My mother stopped crying. She couldn't quite remember why she'd been crying in the first place, and it suddenly didn't matter.

... here to help you .

"Yeah, well you're not." She said it with all the clarity she could muster and looked Birdie in the eye with callous indifference. Then she rolled away onto the bed with her back to them all and let the medication lull her into a wakeful coma.

She could hear Birdie tutoring the new girl over by the door now— *suicidal aggression ... paranoia ... presents as delusional ... intravenous ... history of violence.*

"By no means do you approach this patient by yourself," Birdie said to the girl. "If she needs something or if she's acting out, you call me or one of the orderlies before you attempt to make any contact whatsoever. Understood?"

"Yes, ma'am," the girl assured her, and then they all left.

Heavy steel banged shut. Keys in the lock. And then the great nothingness.

She couldn't feel hate, as much as she wanted it. She thought about Rachel but felt about as much affection as she did for the sink. She thought about heroin, and that desire was everlasting yet not much different than missing someone who was deceased, which brought Matt to mind, and she envied him. Envy—she still had that one left. But it was fleeting, impermanent as everything else, and soon she was devoid even of a desire for death. Not because she didn't want it; she just couldn't tell the difference, anymore, between living and dying. As it stood, she was a little of both.

She now saw things that weren't there. She heard people talking that didn't exist. She wasn't murdered by an imaginary woman not speaking to her in her mother's native tongue during a night that never happened. Christ Almighty, she belonged here now. She should rage against the injustice. She should get herself a lawyer. She should stand up. Get off this cot. The room whirled and blurred as she sat up on the edge of the mattress and waited for the confusion to pass. Maybe it'll pass. Just give it a minute.

She saw everything as if looking through a tube, the antipsychotic blinder effect, only what's three feet up ahead. No distractions. Yellow paint. The hallway chatter had a wide reverb, up and down the ward. Metallic clanks and latches and keys. She sat staring through her own matted curls for an indefinite spell. Then she thought she should stand up, and so she did. Wobbly on a bad knee. She stretched a hand out to the cinder blocks to get her bearings. The steel door was painted orange—she hadn't noticed that last night. Like dirty sherbet. Orange sherbet made from wintertime gutter slush.

One foot was very cold. She looked down to see why and realized she'd lost a sock. She didn't know where, or when, or how. It just wasn't there anymore, and the linoleum was quite cool to the touch. It hadn't occurred to her until then that there were mashed potatoes and gravy and carrot slices smeared across the floor from when she'd thrown last night's meal at Birdie and Cherie Navedo.

She walked to the orange door, a slow sluggish limp, but when she got there, she thought she ought to turn and go the other way again, and so she did, but she didn't really know why and had no particular impulse to figure that out, and so she turned around and walked back toward the bed again, and when she got to the bed, she felt she should go over to the sink now. None of it had any bearing on any particular goal, just a ceaseless roundabout she felt compelled to do for no apparent reason, back and forth to the door and to the bed and to the sink and back to the door again. And that was the extent of the workings of her brain for most of the morning.

THEY BROUGHT HER a breakfast tray. Two orderlies who weren't Thomas or James or Franklin. One was a black guy, and he handled the keys and watched her pacing while the other one set the food on the sink and took up the spilled dinner tray from where it lay near the door. Neither of them said anything to her.

They locked her in, and she stopped walking long enough to stare at the new food—eggs, oatmeal, toast, served in a cellophane-covered TV dinner container with a single, soft-coated rubber spoon, designed to prevent patients like herself from using it as a weapon of self-destruction. She imagined they'd want that back. There was a half pint of 2% milk in the corner of the tray, lukewarm when she picked it up.

She wondered if she was hungry. She stopped and thought about that for a long while, and in the end, she thought she probably should be, so she sat on the bed with the food in her lap and took a long time to eat the eggs because her hands still had a loose tremor, and the eggs kept falling off the spoon and back into the container and onto her lap. At one point, she stopped and sat looking into the tray, wondering how it got there. She didn't remember sitting down with it, but it was there now, so she ate the rest of the oatmeal and drank the milk.

There was a passage of time she couldn't account for. Or maybe there wasn't. She was sitting on the floor against the wall, pushing a carrot disc around the linoleum with an index finger, listening to the women talk in their circular melodies about nothing, so sure of themselves in the shapeless moment. There'd been a commotion; one of them roared like a banshee and something clattered and there was a struggle, and the woman threatened to burn the place down as she passed by the orange door and on down the hall—steel on steel and then the screaming stopped. My mother thought about cigarettes. She thought she smelled one. She thought a lot of things that turned out not to be things at all.

"Go away."

It just leaped out from somewhere under all the mush.

"Go away."

She wondered if she tried hard enough, she might not feel the need to say it again, because she couldn't quite get her head around why she'd said it at all, but at the same time it carried a significance she thought might be useful.

"Go away."

Then it came to her—she was talking to everyone, to the whole goddamned place. To the hammering doors and nonsensical chatter and the food on the floor. The chipped yellow paint and the fluorescent fixture that wasn't an execution device after all, to the man standing by the sink who kept vanishing whenever she lifted her eyes to catch him there.

"Go away."

And then he was back again, living in the peripheral blur. My mother began to sob.

"Go away."

She gazed around at the cinder blocks, the white ceiling, the metal legs of the cot bolted to the tiles, all of it smudged and glassy. She sucked back tears through gritted teeth and sat sniffling with her hands flat to the floor in brown gravy.

"Go away."

She heard keys in the lock. She didn't know if she should look to see if it was so. The orange door made a hollow *clink* and the hinges squealed as it swung open, but she kept her eyes front because she had no idea if she could process yet another non-event. The weight of the 5mg shot of Haloperidol was lifting now, and in its place was something cold and sharp, a distrust of her surroundings, of herself, and so she thought it better not to move. Just cry and be very still.

Shoes shuffled across the tile. A figure to her right, no, three figures now. She pinched her eyes shut and opened them again, wet with icy tears, but the figures persisted, and she didn't know what to do about that, so she didn't do anything at all.

"Miss De Carlo?"

My mother said nothing. Eyes on the yellow blocks, and they'll go away. Paint peeling in vitiligo patches, white concrete underneath. Some of it in the shape of Russia. She could make out a rabbit if she stared at it right, maybe a teapot, a maple leaf, two halves of an hourglass.

"Miss De Carlo, can you hear me?"

Trick question. A fly landed on Russia, crawled into the tea spout, flittered around in a circle, then it was gone.

The figures moved in closer, all of them men. Then a face appeared in front of her, thick brown mustache, dark hair, balding on top, brown eyes like Dr. Bernard, but it wasn't him. Navy-and-maroon striped necktie, blue sport coat, unbuttoned.

Fingers snapped twice at her nose. She blinked. He tilted his head to one side, elbows on his knees, hands clasped between them. Fluorescent light glinted off his wedding band.

"Miss De Carlo, do you know where you are?"

Still as stone. The only thing that moved was saltwater down her left cheek, and it gathered at the edge of her jaw, then dropped into her lap. If this wasn't real, she'd be damned well sorry, sorrier than she'd ever been in her life of poor choices and misguidance. Better not to indulge it.

"My name is Dr. Shah, and I'm a clinical psychiatrist, here at Westlake State Hospital in Santa Clarita. Do you remember why you're here?"

She couldn't even remember why there was gravy on the floor. Or why she was wearing only one sock. But she decided to shake her head for him, anyway, then dared rest her eyes on his to see if he might vanish by doing so.

He didn't. He nodded instead, a quick little smile. "That's all right." His voice was smooth and even, a middle-range tenor, and he spoke gently but without pretense. "It's a common response to stressful events, our brain's way of filtering out things we don't understand, things we're not yet ready to confront." He shifted his weight to the other heel, another fleeting smile. "I'd like to talk with you for a while. If you're comfortable with that, of course. We can do that here if you prefer." But then he glanced around at the mess and looked back at my mother. "Or, if you'd be willing to take a walk with me, we can have the janitorial staff come clean all this up for you. Would you like that? Are you able to stand?"

So far, it seemed he had no designs on killing her. He carried no needles in his hand. He called himself something consistent with what she understood to be reality, and so she drew her uninjured leg slowly across the tiles and got it underneath herself and stood, keeping her eyes on him for signs of deception, and he stood up with her. The other two men encroached—orderlies, one of them was Thomas, but Dr. Shah held up a hand to ward them back, giving her an equal opportunity for trust.

"You okay? Can you walk?" Dr. Shah didn't touch her, but he extended his arm in the event that she pitched forward or staggered into the wall.

She'd been walking all morning; walking wasn't the problem; it was knowing why and to what end that seemed to escape her.

"Take your time," he said, a non-threatening tone, easy and disarming. "Whenever you feel ready, we're gonna go out into the hallway together. There'll be a lot of activity, maybe a lot of noise that might be a little jarring, some unfamiliar faces. If at any time you start to feel overwhelmed, just try to remember you're in a safe place, and try to relax. If it's too much for you, we'll come right back. You have my word. Do you understand?"

She took issue with his utopian view of such a place full of nightmares, although most of them had been in her own medicine head. Gifts from Birdie and the Catwoman. "Yes." She hoped it had come out the way she heard it in her mind, comprehensible English, a single word with so many variables, so many implications.

"Very good." Dr. Shah stepped past Thomas and the other man and stood out in the hall now, waiting for her, and so she took tentative steps to follow him, and he motioned to the orderlies to let her pass. He held out his arm to her again, as if helping her onto a rocking sailboat tethered to a lakeside dock, and he stood smiling. "It's all right. Brave steps."

Everything to her right was moving, a chaos of banter, and to the left—a long hall, lots of metal doorways, the one she remembered from last night. The nurse's station was sealed off behind glass, the staff busy in their big bright terrarium. She stood in the hall for a long moment, absorbing things, placing sounds into aural categories to identify what might be a threat and what might be figmentations; she really couldn't say which was which, but it was less frightening than she'd thought. White pajamas moved about. They weaved around tables and dropped onto couches and popped up from chairs and swayed back and forth by the barred windows. Then one of them approached her.

"Does *she* have a blue marker?" the girl asked the doctor. Evidently, he was supposed to know what she was talking about, and he did, but he shooed her away.

"Melanie, go on back into the day room," he told her in the same forbearing tone he'd taken with my mother, like a father to a fourth grader; she looked to be about thirty.

"But Dr. Shah, I need it to finish my project," she whined. "I gotta do the letters on top, and I need a marker and nobody's got the blue one, I can't find it."

Dr. Shah pointed back into the lounge. "Melanie, go. We'll find you one later."

"But maybe she has one. Did you bring any markers?" she asked my mother, and Mom blinked at her and drew back a little. Melanie was in her personal space now, harmless yet uninvited, a facility violation, nonetheless. Thomas and his associate moved in.

"She's got nothing you're looking for, Melanie, and I need you to step away from her, please," Dr. Shah scolded, trying to encourage my mother along while the orderlies intervened and guided Melanie back toward the day room. "We don't approach another resident that way, you know that."

"*God.* Sorry," she sassed with a sour face and wandered off to a table of other patients and started asking them for the same thing.

"You okay?" Dr. Shah looked my mother over for signs of mental distress, for indications that she might lose her psychological traction and start coming apart, but she nodded, and he smiled at that. "Good. Melanie means well. She just doesn't understand that new residents need time to get familiarized, so she comes on a little strong." He motioned for her to follow him again, and so she did.

Along the way, he stopped a nurse, an RN whose tag said "Rhonda Samuels—Nursing Services Coordinator."

"Cell 16 needs cleanup, Rhonda, so if you'll get one of the custodians in there, that'd be great." He glanced at his watch. "I'll probably be with this patient for about thirty minutes, should be plenty of time, and then she'll need to be bathed as well, get her into some clean clothes before lunch."

Rhonda nodded. "Lemme see if I can page Charles. What size is she?"

He looked my mother up and down, shrugged. "Give her a medium." He smiled as Mom shuffled along, taking it all in with Thomas and his partner on either side. "If I'm wrong," he told my mother with a smirk, "it'll explain why I never shop for my wife, either."

She had no response to that at all, couldn't process nor appreciate the humor except that it was subjective, but he didn't appear to be offended and kept walking.

HIS OFFICE WAS much larger than Laura Koepsell's. He liked golf. He had two young children framed together on the windowsill, both of them boys. He dismissed the orderlies but left the door open and offered her a seat in a studded leather armchair, and he sat in one to match, about five feet away, and took out a yellow legal pad. A broad oak desk, dark green carpet, a lamp on an end table next to a potted plant, his briefcase open on the couch. He smiled at her again. Behind him in the corner was the peripheral man from her cell who'd followed them there, all shadow and blur, gone when she tried to catch his face. Dr. Shah slipped a pen from inside his lapel and made a note of something.

"Can you tell me how you're feeling right now, Miss De Carlo? And may I call you Jolán, or would you rather I keep it formal?" He had his pen poised above the page, waiting to jot down her preference.

"Two days and a wake-up." She was surprised at her own sudden clarity, tongue untied at last, no more mouth full of sand, but something was still awry. Clarity of speech had found her, but clarity of thought was a problem. She saw mostly pictures; her head was a slide show of all the things she wanted most, and she had no idea how to make any of it graspable, but she thought she ought to try, anyway.

"What does that mean to you?" Dr. Shah asked, seemingly unfazed.

She understood him. Everything coming in was properly inventoried, but all she could arrange for a reply was, "The windows didn't open. You don't know that."

"Which windows, Miss De Carlo? Can you understand what I'm saying to you?"

"Yes." She had that one in the right compartment, and she could even nod to go with it. All was not entirely lost, she supposed. The figure moved from the corner and reappeared over by the end table. Gone.

The doctor watched her eyes for a moment, then wrote something on the legal pad. He propped an ankle across his other knee and reclined back against the chair. "You've been through quite an ordeal over the past week. Is there anything you'd like to share with me about that? Anything you'd like to discuss?"

She nodded, still fuzzy but coming out of that. "Everyone lied to me, and now it's all in pictures," she tried to explain but let out a sigh and rubbed her brow because she wasn't going to get very far like this. A shadow beside her chair rose up tall and stood looming.

"Who do you think lied to you?"

"Welcome to Westlake."

The psychiatrist scratched observations onto the paper. "What kinds of pictures do you see? Are they pictures in your mind, or do you see them in your surroundings as tangible objects?"

My mother shook her head, but it wasn't an answer to his question; it was absurdity, absurdity in its purest form, and today she was its blithering sock puppet. Think . . . think . . . speak . . .

"Yesterday," she began. Memory was a trick. It was a circus of illusions she could no longer trust—this whole damned place was one big box of false positives; Pandora would be stunned.

The doctor was patient and quiet while she gathered the rest of her ideas.

"Yesterday," she tried again, "she made the lights go out. Blood everywhere. Next door was a lot safer, but they took away my gear, said it was my fault. I don't belong in a diaper."

Dr. Shah nodded, pondering important things. "How 'bout if I just ask you some questions for a while, questions that only require a yes or no response. You seem to be having some trouble organizing your thoughts, so perhaps that might make our conversation a little easier for you. Would that be okay?"

"Yes."

He smiled. "Good." He made notations again and flipped the page over to start a fresh one. "Prior to your coming here to Westlake, did you find yourself feeling withdrawn from others? Maybe unwilling to participate in social activities like you once did?"

"There was a blue raft, dragons with poison in the bag, but I told them I didn't know anything."

"Yes or no, sweetheart," he urged, but he wrote all that down. "I think for now it will make it less stressful for you."

How could he expect her to explain herself when she had no self? She watched Matt's face vanish under a black zipper. "Yes."

"Very good. Now, what about your mood, your frame of mind in the past weeks or months? Have you been feeling depressed or uncertain about the future?"

"Yes."

"And what about your environment—have things appeared unreal or strange to you? Threatening in any way?"

"Yes."

"Have you seen, felt, or heard things around you that others are not able to experience or be aware of?"

"Yes."

"Do you feel like you want to harm yourself right now?"

"No. Two hours isn't long enough. We were talking about music, but I forgot."

"Do you hear music playing now?"

"No."

"Do you feel you want to harm anyone else right now?"

"No."

"Do you remember trying to harm the ICU nurses at St. Thomas Hospital?"

"No . . . yes."

"Which is your answer? Yes or no?"

" . . . yes."

"Just a couple more questions, and then I'll do some talking, explain some things to you so you understand—"

"I was angry." It was a single lucid transmission through what'd been nothing but static, the tuner finding a hot spot on the dial, and she rolled it back and forth across her brain, trying to bring it back in again, but it was gone.

Dr. Shah stopped writing and looked up at her, intrigued. "When you tried to hurt the ICU staff?"

"Yes. My girlfriend," she started, but thinking of Rachel took her to some other place in her head, and she lowered her eyes to the floor and stared at the green carpet, trying to feel something; she had the intellectual understanding that she loved her, but love was just something walled in behind a big block of ice now.

"What about your girlfriend? Do you think she wants to harm you?"

"No," she muttered to the floor, defeated by her own involuntary idiocy. "We have to do something."

"Yes, Miss De Carlo," he told her in his gentle, even tone. "Yes, we certainly do." He put the legal pad aside and leaned forward in his chair with his elbows on his knees and looked at her pitiably. "You've been exhibiting some symptoms that concern me."

"No."

He held up a hand. "Now, hold on. I'm gonna explain it to you in simple terms, nothing too clinical or elaborate; I want you to understand because I believe you may be suffering from what we call borderline psychosis. Now, I'd like to do some further testing to rule out anything organic, such as brain injuries or a change in your brain chemistry due to stroke or a tumor, perhaps. But I'm gonna be honest with you, here, and say I don't think the latter is the case; however, we'll do whatever is necessary to rule all that out. Now, I also realize you're an IV drug user, but your blood tests came back negative for narcotics yesterday. Yet, here we are." He shrugged. "So, the culprit isn't heroin, although heroin has definitely exacerbated your condition in the past, perhaps even masked it completely."

"No," she insisted, shaking her head. "No. No. No. I couldn't get out if I wanted to. The windows never—"

"Miss De Carlo, listen to me. Just relax," he soothed. "This is all in your best interest. I need you to try and understand that, all right? And there's some good news to all this. The good news is, I'm going to release you from suicide watch, *provisionally.* At this time, you seem to be in a bit of a better place than when you came in. A little confused," he cautioned. "But not so despondent and self-destructive. So I wanna see how you do among the other residents, give you some privileges, and hopefully it'll encourage you to socialize. *But* . . . if you exhibit any signs whatsoever of wanting to harm yourself or anyone else, I'll have no choice but to recommend solitary confinement again, for your protection and for that of the staff and the other patients. Do you understand?"

She took a very deep breath and thought about that. She felt like maybe the miasma in her head was lifting. It had been several hours since Birdie's injection, and before they made her swallow another dose of Batshit Tablets, she thought she ought to try and plead her case.

"It's bad medicine," she explained, impressed with her own improving cognition. "My head's not right. Thoughts are pictures, puzzle pieces, and there was never a phone call."

Dr. Shah just offered a warm and knowing smile. "Well, we're gonna help you get your head right. And yes. Heroin's not the kind of medicine anyone needs, and now you know that firsthand, don't you?" He spoke as if she were one of his kids. "It almost killed you last week, but the goal is to get you back to a healthy state so you're not tempted to end your own life like that again."

He smiled and took up the legal pad, jotted down his diagnosis and the treatment plan forthcoming.

"And I'm gonna lower your Haldol and Ativan dosage as of today," he said, mostly to himself. "Speaking of medicine. We'll see how well you handle things with a little less, see if some of your confusion clears up as a result. Might even switch you over to Risperdal, depending on what your tests show, but we'll see."

"When do I leave?" There it was, clear consciousness, if just for a millisecond.

Dr. Shah gave her another pitiful smile. He put the notepad back on the desk behind him and turned to her with pacification in his eyes, and she didn't like that.

"Two days and a fucking *wake-up,"* she insisted.

"Miss De Carlo, your condition—if it turns out to be what I suspect—is complex, and it's very involved. You and I will need to meet several times in order for me to assess your improvement or the lack thereof. We need to get you a CAT scan, try out some various medications until we know which works best for you, see how you do in the group sessions with—"

"*When.* How *long.*"

He shrugged and shook his head, searching for a time frame. "Maybe a few more weeks, minimum. Depends. Could be as long as a few months if you're not responsive to treatment."

"No." She sat up straight on the edge of the chair and shook her head. "The medicine in my head makes no sense. It's only pictures. I don't wanna die. I wasn't paying attention to the music . . . no." She shook that off, re-scramble. "The music made me forget, and the windows were *locked.* I was pissed off, they had needles in my neck, puke and shit and blood all over the place. What would *you* do!"

"Miss De Carlo, just relax. That's what I would do." He nodded once and kept both hands up between himself and a possible tirade. He glanced toward the open doorway, then looked back at her. "I want you to have some privileges while you're here, but I can't do that if you're going to act out. All right? Now, I know you don't feel this treatment is necessary, but you have to understand—you nearly died less than a week ago by your *own doing*, you showed dangerously aggressive behavior thereafter, threatened to harm yourself a *second* time, then presented as having some significant mental health concerns upon your admission here to Westlake. And these are all things we can help you with, but you'll only make that more complicated by losing control and acting out. It certainly won't shorten your stay, I can tell you that."

He lowered his hands because she had retreated back into her chair and sat very still, glaring at him for a long moment before the tears began to fall. He reached back to his desk and grabbed a box of tissues and handed it over, but she just shook her head and looked away.

"I wanna see my girlfriend. Never got a phone call," she growled, fuming.

But she had the presence of mind to keep the orderlies and Birdie and Cherie Navedo from sending her back to hell, the hell within hell, her very own level with a suicide's circle all to herself. She'd spent half the day climbing out of that, and she really wasn't looking for another tour.

"Phone privileges are earned like everything else," Dr. Shah explained. "If you haven't gotten any demerits within a twenty-four-hour period, you can make collect calls each night after dinner, and there's a fifteen minute time limit. Is that something you can adhere to?"

"Yes." She still wouldn't look at him. She sniffed, let her face grow sodden and shiny with tears. She would simply have to earn a phone call, then. She would tell Rachel where she was, and Rachel would know what to do. She thought about my grandparents, but that was a fool's request, like asking an enemy to free you from a bear trap. It'd be all the ammunition they'd need, proof of her recklessness; they'd probably leave her there to wallow in her own shit and shame. She'd never be able to handle that rejection right now.

"So, can I trust you not to do anything counterproductive to your care? No outbursts, no self-injury or harm toward the other patients?" Dr. Shah asked.

She nodded.

"I know you're upset right now. It's very understandable. This is an unfamiliar setting to you, and it's probably quite overwhelming, but there are some very capable people on our staff, professionals in every sense of the word. If you need help with something, there's always someone to ask. Just make sure they're wearing a badge," he said with a smile. "Some of the residents like to give out advice, but always get confirmation from one of the counselors or nurses. You'll thank me for it."

He was trying to lighten the air, but she didn't know which she wanted most—to throw her studded leather chair across the room or crawl into a closet somewhere and hide from everyone and everything until they let her out of this godforsaken place.

"I want a phone call," was all she had left to say to him.

He stood up and motioned for her to do the same. "Let's get you settled in first. Rhonda's probably got some clean clothes for you, and either she or Birdie will show you to your new room."

And that would conclude the day's programming. She walked with him back to the nurse's station in a different kind of daze now. Everyone was still out milling around, white scrubs meandering about the day room, and they watched her from afar, throwing curious, skittish glances from their huddles and cliques—the scary new chick with the hair; don't wanna get too close, might lose an eyeball, or a finger, or a spleen. Dr. Shah left her with Birdie who was pairing up a fresh new set of pajamas, and my mother could hear one of the patients asking another why she wasn't on the maximum-security ward.

"Did you see her eyes?" another one whispered. "They're like freaky green, fuckin scary."

"Is that blood?"

"No, it's food, I think . . . I *think.*"

"You should go see if she can talk."

"Nobody's eyes are that damn green. Where the hell'd she come from?"

Birdie handed her the scrubs. "Well, you're finally gonna join the rest, huh?"

My mother didn't answer.

Birdie gestured for her to follow and kept talking as they walked. "You'll be in Room 406. None of the rooms are private, so you will have to share space with another resident. Please be considerate and keep your area clean. Meals are served in the cafeteria downstairs, breakfast at seven, lunch at twelve, and dinner at six. You go as a group, single file, with staff members to accompany you. Lights out is at ten p.m. Between meals, you'll attend group therapy sessions and whatever recreational activities the staff has arranged for that day. You get an hour of free time after dinner at which time you may watch television in the day room and are free to move about the halls. At eight p.m. you are to be in your room for head count, and you will not be permitted in the halls after that point. Your medication is mandatory—no ifs, ands, or buts. It's part of your treatment plan, and a refusal of medication will be noted, and Dr. Shah will be made aware. A continuous refusal of medication will alert the staff to your unwillingness to receive medical care, and believe me, you don't want that. Make sure you attend your group sessions and follow the facility rules at all times; a failure to do so will result in demerits, and we can *and will* revoke privileges such as telephone calls, movie nights, and visitations."

My mother limped along behind her, trying to retain all this.

"Visitations. You may have no more than two visitors at a time, and they must present a valid picture ID at the security gate. Without identification, they will not be allowed to enter the building. No children under eighteen will be given a visitor's badge, so if you've got kids, your best bet is to make very good use of your telephone privileges. There's a canteen downstairs where you can purchase cigarettes if you smoke, candy if you've got no dietary restrictions, and magazines and books approved by the staff, among other personal items. You are a resident on Ward 27, which is a high-functioning ward, meaning you are blessed with certain freedoms not provided on the other, lower-functioning wards. If you smoke, there is a fenced-in smoking cage on the main floor, but you may only go there during personal time and only while accompanied by a staff member."

They finally arrived at her room, but Birdie stopped before showing my mother inside.

"No fighting, no spitting, no arguing," she concluded. "No pulling of hair, no gnashing of teeth, no spells, no incantations, no voodoo dolls. When the staff tells you to do something, you *do* it, no questions and no complaints. Whatever we tell you to do is for your best interest, and we expect you to be just as concerned for your well-being as we are. You understand?"

"Yes."

"Good." Birdie opened the door.

There was a girl about my mother's age, sitting cross-legged on the bed with a notebook in her lap. She was frail and mousey, long brown hair to the middle of her back, and she had arms full of puffy pink scars, like hieroglyphs carved into stone tablets.

She looked at my mother, then at Birdie. "Are you serious?"

"April, when have you ever known me *not* to be serious?" Birdie pointed to the bed by the window and told my mother, "That side's yours."

"But she was just in seclusion this morning," April insisted. "Am I going to be safe?"

"Of course you will." Birdie rolled her eyes. "Dr. Shah just released her a little while ago. I think he's a pretty good judge of character. Jolán, this is April. April, Jolán."

She showed my mother the little bathroom and where to put the belongings she still didn't have.

"All right. Well, you two've got about," Birdie checked her watch, "twenty minutes to get acquainted and then it's downstairs for lunch. April, see that she knows where to go when y'all line up. You'll hear the buzzer. If there's any problems, just call for me or the orderlies, and we'll come a'runnin.'" And she left them to each other and shut the door behind her. No keys, this time. No heavy steel cannon shot.

My mother stood there, haggard and filthy and hugging her clean pajamas. Surely she was dreaming all this, the bars, the locks, Dr. Shah and his psychosis diagnosis. Maybe she was still at St. Thomas in a coma, with Rachel at her bedside, touching her face, holding her hand to her lips, speaking to her softly under the hiss of the ventilator machine. Any time now, she would open her eyes to the acoustic tiles above the bed, to Rachel's beautiful face smiling down at her, smoothing the damp curls from her forehead, telling her it was going to be okay, that everything was all right, to just rest, just rest.

But that wasn't some pleasant fantasy—it was a memory. It had already happened. And she was here now, coming down off a shot of Haldol in Room 406 on Ward 27 of the Westlake State Hospital in someplace called Santa Clarita, tucked away in the middle of the California desert. She had definitely made a very wrong turn at Albuquerque.

"If you have to use the bathroom, wipe the seat three times clockwise with exactly five sheets of toilet paper," April instructed without looking up from her notebook. "It keeps the evil spirits from coming through the vents."

. . . and a wrong turn at Tucson. And Phoenix. And Denver. And Hollywood . . .

chapter twenty-two

RACHEL STOOD IN front of Wade Tyson's apartment door for a long while before she finally knocked. Stone Temple Pilots was blasting inside, and she could hear him singing along and thought it must be nice, to not have to care, to just throw on a few CDs, pop open a beer, and sing "Naked Sunday" at the top of his voice as if nothing had ever happened.

He didn't answer, and so she knocked again, pounded her fist on the oak wood above the peep hole until the music finally stopped and she heard footfalls across the floor.

After a moment, he slid aside the chain, unlocked the deadbolts, and stood looking at her strangely through the crack. "Uhh . . . howdy . . . neighbor."

"I need a phone book. Do you have one?" She wasn't interested in pleasantries, only to get what she came for. She stuffed her hands into her back pockets and tried not to make eye contact as he invited her in.

"Pretty sure I got one around here somewhere. You need the phone?" He grabbed up the cordless from the pot-strewn dining table and offered it.

Rachel shook her head. "Nah, just a phone book, thanks. I thought we had one over there, but I guess not. Can't find it if we do."

She stood in the middle of the living room and waited while he rummaged through the end tables and desk drawers and threw aside a stack of magazines in a rack at the end of the love seat. There was a 9mm handgun on the coffee table, and he took it up and put it away in the desk.

"Kind of a mess. Sorry. Wasn't expecting company," he said and flashed her a rueful little smile.

"Well, I'm not *company*, but, it's fine."

She glanced around the apartment as he continued his search. It was much smaller than theirs, the floors covered with tattered, dusty Persian rugs, his JVC entertainment system against the far wall. He had a red velour Victorian couch that didn't at all match the brown plaid, cottage-style love seat, and a cluttered three-shelf bookcase stood beneath a single living room window—the one that faced the breezeway between their buildings. There was a framed, poster-sized photo above the couch of Johnny Cash giving the finger to the world, and on the opposite wall were autographed concert shots of Iggy Pop and Frank Zappa.

The place smelled of sage and stale cigarettes and traces of his Drakkar Noir, and she felt a sudden, nauseating whirl of butterflies at the thought of my mother, unconscious and dying there on his floor, IV bags and shock paddles and EMTs with their radios squawking on their hips, red-and-white emergency lights flickering outside while the neighbors congregated at the curbs. If she'd had a mind for it, she would've slugged him across the face with the phone book he finally handed over, but things were bad enough. No use adding an assault charge to the mix.

"Thanks. I'll bring it back when I'm done," she muttered and started for the door.

He stopped her. "So, hey." He shrugged a shoulder. "How is she?"

Rachel took a long, deep breath and turned to him, scowling. "She could be a hell of a lot better. But she's okay. She'll live."

"Good." He nodded with an uncomfortable smile. "That's Jo for ya—hard-core." He chuckled, folding his arms at his chest. "Made of steel, right?"

Rachel breathed a gentle sigh. "No, actually. She's not. Not at all, but I appreciate the vote of confidence, misguided as it is." And she started back for the door.

"Rache, look." He stopped her again, took her by the arm this time, and she glared down at his hand around her biceps. He released her. "If I'd known she was gonna slam herself into oblivion like that, I'da *done* something. Okay? I'm not that kinda asshole."

"Maybe not *that* kind, no. But you do fit the bill for all the other varieties. Just my opinion. Do with it what you want." He didn't say anything, so she turned for the door once more but then thought about the St. Thomas ER, the night they'd rushed my mother through the traffic along Wilshire. He'd stayed to wait with her for four hours, sitting quiet in the chair beside her with his elbows on his knees, hands folded thoughtfully under his chin; the worry in his eyes was genuine.

She decided maybe he deserved a bit more credit. "I appreciate what you did for her—for *us*—the other night. You coulda been a coward, coulda thought about yourself and bailed, but you didn't. And I thank you for that. We both do."

He held his hands out at his sides and smiled. "Anybody woulda done the same thing. Just glad she was over here, if it had to go down like that. Good thing I paid the phone bill, last month, eh?" And he laughed lightly.

She didn't welcome the humor. Instead, she turned to face him and looked him in the eye for the first time. "Jo's got a problem, Wade. You do understand that, right? There's nothing cute, or cool, or glamorous about the fact that she could've *died* . . . *here*." And she pointed to the dusty carpet. "In *your* house. On *your* watch. From *your* product."

He stared at her for a moment, then gave that a cautious grin. "Hey.

It wasn't *my product* that fucked her up—it was how *much* of it she did. My product is primo, the cleanest shit in LA. Let's just be clear on that one, okay?"

Rachel regarded him crossly and shook her head. "You really wanna argue that point with me? *Now?* I don't give a *fuck* . . . about the so-called quality of your dope, Wade. I don't care if it was blessed by Christ Himself. My girlfriend is in a Norwalk *psych* center," she stressed, "for the next three days because you've got a twenty-four-hour candy store that she cannot resist. Her addiction's not your fault, no. But your existence in our lives?" She pressed her lips tight with a helpless shrug. "It's a menace. Your apartment is a deathtrap for her. So, I'll tell you again that I'm grateful for the quick thinking last week, but beyond that, I want you to stay away from her. For good. We clear on *that* one, Wade?" She went back to the door and told him over her shoulder, "Thanks for the book. I'll bring it back when I'm done."

He had nothing else to say, and she was glad. She headed down the hall and back to their apartment where she dropped onto the couch, flipped through the Pac Bell pages for the La Casa listing, and dialed the front desk for driving directions.

HALOPERIDOL, EVEN IN a slightly lower dosage, had done my mother no favors, particularly when paired with the Lorazepam. She still felt ambushed, cloaked in befuddlement. Her head still hadn't cleared, and by dinnertime on her first day as a free woman in the state sanitarium, she had developed an inexplicable kind of muscle stiffness in her lower limbs. She'd taken a shower, though, and changed into the fresh pajamas, which smelled faintly of old paint and bleach and hotel soap. She herself smelled similarly blanched.

Her hair was clean now but untamed, no conditioner, as her new roommate had an unbearable aversion to creams and lotions. She no longer had mashed potatoes under her nails, but she knew her facial features were gaunt and off-color; the bathroom mirror was no friend of hers and made a mockery of the woman she used to see. There were bags under her bloodshot eyes, and her lips were chapped. She could account for the bags—she hadn't slept soundly in ages—but the oral dryness was a brand new anomaly.

She couldn't connect with a proper stream of consciousness, try as she might to make any concrete sense of herself. She saw halos around the overhead lights as she shuffled down the checkered hall toward the day room. Shadows might not have been shadows, maybe they were. She still heard the occasional Spanglish whisper, but there was enough noise and chatter to absorb most of that. She had no idea why she was out roaming, but it seemed fear had given way to a kind of curiosity, and there were things to see, people to observe, circumstances to levy.

She drifted into the day room and stood there. A television mumbled lots of things about Somalia and David Koresh and flood waters sucking people into the Mississippi, and that made her anxious on the inside, but she was only eyes, and ears, and dermal sensation now. She wondered if smack had put her into a space like this, would she have still fallen so deeply in love with it or if that even mattered now. Probably not, either way. She needed to make a phone call.

"Where are you going, Jolán?" A woman's voice startled her, off to the left.

A nurse. She looked Filipino or maybe some type of Asian-Hawaiian, shorter than my mother by a good three inches, and she took her gently by the biceps and turned her around to face her.

"You've got Group in just a few minutes," she said, speaking as if my mother might be partially deaf. Glasses like Laura Koepsell, short dark hair, almond eyes narrow with cautious scrutiny. "Were you just out for a walk?"

Go ahead—answer with that scrambled medicine head of yours, see if she can make any sense of who you are. "She doesn't know where I am, she'll never find me here." Perfect.

"Who doesn't know where you are, sweetie?" The nurse, whose nametag said "Ana Garcia," herded my mother in a different direction. "How 'bout we get you over to Group, right now, so you can meet some of the other patients and talk about what's going on with you. It'll be good for you, come on." And she encouraged her along, like a five year old who'd gotten lost in a shopping mall.

"I need to make a phone call," my mother mumbled.

They were headed toward a room just past the day room, lots of glass and yellow plaster, white pajamas inside, chairs in a circle. The TV was louder now. "*. . . of course there's no charge if they've spilled your food at Lenny's!*"

"*Denny's!*"

The theme from *Baywatch*.

"You can make a phone call after dinner," Ana Garcia shouted kindly, her hand flat against my mother's back as they walked. "Do you have phone privileges yet? Let me see what Nurse Birdie says, and then we'll try to get you some telephone time later on, okay?"

"Yes."

Others were filing in. She sat in one of the green plastic Monobloc chairs next to a stocky woman whose head was shaved on one side, asymmetrically stylish, long blonde bangs in the front, swept to the left, arms covered in tattoos—one of them was the universal female gender symbol, filled in with rainbow colors. She was a dyke, it was undeniable even without that, and she propped an ankle across her thigh and folded her arms at her chest, nodded hello. Mom nodded back.

Then the woman extended her hand. "Name's Nan," she said with a thin smile. "Welcome to the rabbit hole."

Mom took the offering tentatively, shook on it. "Hello."

"So, you came in last night, eh? How was the penthouse suite? I keep tellin 'em they need a wet bar in there, maybe a Jacuzzi, but they never listen." Nan looked to my mother for a laugh, but Mom had no idea what she was talking about. "Seclusion." Nan pointed back toward the halls with her thumb. "Solitary. Time out. The Box. They didn't waste any time tossing you in there. Everybody saw it."

Mom nodded once. "Oh. Yes. Yellow paint. Gravy on the floor. That's where the lights went out."

Nan drew back a little, frowned, and crossed her arms again. "Whoa. You're baked. What are they giving you?"

Alas—someone who could see through the spider webs, see her dangling there, wrapped in bemusement. "Bad medicine," she begged lowly. "The story's all in fragments, and the pieces don't fit, but nobody listens." She winced at the fluorescent lights, uncommonly bright, and she tried to blink back the glare, but that only turned them to white lasers across the ceiling.

Nan saw that, and she glanced up at the lights, too, unaffected. "You got stiffness in your legs? Seein halos and shit?"

"Yes."

Nan nodded. "Haldol," she muttered. "Haldol's a bitch to get used to, made me piss my pants the first day. Literally. All kinda weird facial shit. You feel restless? Like you can't sit still, just gotta walk and walk, even if you don't know where to?"

"Yes. Bad medicine. I don't need it, but the whole thing's in pictures, so they never listen. They think I'm crazy, and nobody knows where I am."

"Yep. You're in la-la land. How much are they givin you? Do you know?"

"No. I came from LA. Two days and a wake-up was all bullshit. Now I'm a prisoner of the state, and I told them I wasn't alone. The fucking windows were locked, but they turned my head to oatmeal, anyway, brain's not working anymore. Where the hell am I?" she asked Nan who was taking it all in, listening with an expert ear for disorganized babble.

"You're at Westlake State Mental Hospital," she said.

"I know but where?"

"Santa Clarita, California."

Mom stared at her, blinked, shook her head.

"You said you're from LA? Well, then you're about fifty-five miles northwest of there. Is that what you're asking?"

"Yes." My mother nodded. Finally, a map appeared in her head with a little arrow that said, "You are here." "Thank you."

"No prob. It could be farther if I had my way about it, but I can't get transferred. Tryin to go farther north, up Fresno way. This is still too close, still within range, but I've got my ways." Nan leaned in closer to my mother and whispered, "Sally Jesse Rafael blocks the signal. They can't see my thoughts while she's on, and they don't know that. *Yet.*" She gave a little shrug and leaned away. "The Masons aren't just some pack a retards, there's an army of 'em out there and they blend in. They'll figure it out eventually. I just gotta get under the radar, get outa range. And the medication in this dump sure as hell makes for a complicated mission, you're right about that." She smiled at Mom and nudged her with an elbow. "They just need to lower your dose is all. You're kinda skinny, you got no padding, nothing to soak it up before it goes to your head. You'd think they'd figure that out. Assholes," she muttered.

My mother wasn't sure if Nan had actually said all that, or if it was something only she herself had interpreted. So far, input hadn't been a problem, only the output, but maybe that was changing. She thought she ought not to address it and sat waiting while a young woman in jeans and a brown vest over a pink button-down blouse took a seat among the group with a clipboard in her lap, and she smiled at everyone.

"Wow, we've got a full house here, today. That's so good to see. So, how we all feeling?"

One woman raised her hand but didn't wait to be called on before she spoke. "I need a new pillow. I won't sleep on anything that came from China, I'm not a frikkin communist, I keep telling them that. I'm an *American*, people! How hard is that to understand? I mean, Christ."

The counselor held up a placating hand and nodded. "Okay. That's something we'll have to talk about with the nurses, Marie, and maybe they can get that figured out for you. But right now we're going to talk about our thoughts and feelings on stress, what makes us feel stressful."

"Fuckin commies. What do *you* think?" The woman named Marie dropped back against her chair, a leg crossed over the other, swinging it anxiously at the knee.

She was middle aged with shoulder-length hair, strawberry blonde but dark at the roots, and she had dark eyes that made my mother uneasy because they seemed critical and cold, as if she were calculating ways to hurt you.

"Marie. How 'bout we exercise some self-control," the counselor suggested calmly, "and watch our language. It's disrespectful to the other residents and it isn't productive communication. Remember, we talked about that yesterday, and we all agreed to use positive language to express what we're feeling. Right?"

"Whatever." Marie shrugged and sat picking at her fingernails, pursing her lips. She shook her head a little but kept quiet.

"Okay, well, we'll take that as a 'yes' for now." Then she focused on the others. "We've got a new resident, I see, a new member to the group." She nodded to my mother. "Jolán, would you like to tell us anything about yourself? If not, that's all right. You're welcome to just listen and get to know some of the other residents that way, if it's more comfortable for you. My name is Candace, by the way, and I'm a staff psychologist here at Westlake." She smiled and waited.

"They put her in seclusion last night," one of the girls announced.

"It's her turn to talk, Brielle," Candace said. "Please be respectful, and give her a chance to speak for herself."

Fifteen faces, including her roommate, April, some of them staring, others ignoring her. She'd never been prone to stage fright until now. The words, so precisely assembled in her head: *I don't belong here. I'm an unwitting victim of someone's gross incompetence, and now they've drugged me to the eyeballs with antipsychotics so I look and sound and shuffle along like a nut bag, and you want me to speak for myself? I've done that, and they spun it all into psychosis, so now I fit their tragic little picture. How convenient. Maybe, if you're really lucky, I'll lose it altogether in here, and no one will ever be the wiser. Not even me.*

"No." The words were useless in her current state. What was the fucking point? Even when they made sense, they hadn't helped her, so she climbed back onto the hamster wheel and let it squeak and turn and take her back to Nowhereville.

Candace smiled. "That's completely all right. Listening is a good tool, sometimes the best one in the box." Then she said to the circle, "Would anyone else like to introduce themselves to Jolán? April, you two are rooming together, so I imagine you've had that chance. Anybody else?"

April didn't look up from where she sat with one foot tucked into the seat, an arm resting on her knee as she fidgeted with her flip-flop. "I can't talk to her, she's sitting in a bad chair." She dared glance at Mom, then brushed imaginary dust from each of her shoulders, snapped three times and said, "Apples to apples."

"And a 'bad chair' is something specific only to you, though, right?" Candace reminded her. "That's a belief that stems from *your* condition, and we're not supposed to project those beliefs onto others, remember? If Jolán's comfortable where she's sitting, then that's okay for her."

April nodded but still wouldn't look at Mom. "Mm, hm."

"Good." Candace smiled again.

No one else seemed to have anything else to add, and so she got up and went over to a long table against the wall and lifted a large sheet of white construction paper up in front of herself.

"What we're going to do today is use this to make a poster. And on that poster, you're each going to write one sentence that describes one thing that makes you feel stressful. And then we're going to talk about our answers, so we'll start with Marie, and then one at a time, we'll go around the circle writing down our feelings." Candace laid the poster on the table and opened a box of colored markers as a murmur moved through the room.

Mom leaned in and uttered to Nan, "I need a phone call."

"Be my guest," Nan said. "Gotta wait until personal time, though, or they'll revoke your privileges for days. There's a whole wall full of 'em down the administration hall. I'll show you after we eat, but I can't go down there with you, can't get too close. Neural monitors and telephones do *not* mix," she cautioned under her breath.

"Okay."

THE SESSION WENT on for a long while as my mother listened to their stories, and then it seemed to lose structure after that. They all had things to cope with—psychotic depression, delusions of extraordinary grandeur, inconceivable paranoia. These were things they couldn't escape from, the things that seemed to hunt them down, although my mother thought it ironic. In a world where nothing was infallible, where friends died and other friends blamed you for that, where parents saw your accomplishments as failures and lovers felt unloved by you, the best place to be was in the carnival of your own mental illness.

What a wonderful escape; they'd found the answer, really. And here they were, trying to remove themselves from the riddle, figure it all out, re-engage with the horrors and disappointments of reality. She thought them crazier for that than for the impossible things that had been coming out of their mouths for the past hour. Better to be chased by monsters in your head than the ones you thought were allies, the co-workers who never got behind you, family members who refused to be your biggest fans. Better to fear the Illuminati than the landlord. Better to be floating untethered; you could go wherever you wanted, and no one expected you to find your way back; there were no shores; nobody was waiting for you there. Just take the one-way ticket and enjoy the trip. Nobody will hold you responsible for any of it.

She had the insatiable desire for a cigarette.

THE LA CASA facility was just as Yvette had described, a white stucco, single-story building not much larger than a neighborhood movie theatre; there were private homes in Hollywood Hills that were bigger. Rachel pulled the Nissan around the circular drive, parked, and went inside to the information desk.

A middle-aged Latino woman sat at the computer there, and she looked up from her paperwork and smiled. "Can I help you?"

"Yes, I'm here to see Jolán de Carlo. She's a patient here, came in on Sunday night from St. Thomas Hospital," Rachel explained. "They told me on the phone this was a visitation day, but she's probably not expecting me till Wednesday, when she gets released." She reached into her purse for her wallet. "I have ID. They said I'd need that to sign in."

The woman took her driver's license and looked it over, then clattered something into the computer. "And what's her date of birth?"

"June twelfth, 1971."

The lady clicked on things with her mouse, typed something else, then knitted her brow and sat staring at the screen, thinking. She looked up at Rachel. "Are you immediate family?"

Rachel hesitated. They hadn't asked that over the phone, and she wondered if honesty would make things more difficult. But she didn't know how much my mother had told these people in the past twenty-four hours, so she decided she'd better give the woman the truth. "No, I'm not. I'm a friend. She doesn't have any family here. I'm all she has. Is that—is that still gonna be okay? Is that a problem?"

The receptionist looked back at the computer and shrugged one shoulder. "No, not at all. Not if she was actually a patient here. But I don't have any record whatsoever of a de Carlo. You sure she was brought to La Casa? Sunday evening, you said?"

"Yeah." Rachel frowned and tried to crane around to see the screen, but she couldn't. "I was there when she signed the paperwork. I watched them take her out. Are you sure you're spelling it correctly?"

"De Carlo with a C, right?"

"Yes."

The woman clicked around the screen again, scrolled up and down, stared at it and waited, then she shook her head. "Nope. No admissions under that name at all over the past two weeks." She looked up at Rachel. "You might wanna call St. Thomas, see if they know something. But she wasn't brought to this facility. If she was, she'd definitely be on my roster, no question." She gave her a sympathetic smile. "I'm sorry."

Rachel let out a helpless little breath and gazed out through the double glass doors. So, now what?

"Is that typical?" she asked. "I mean, for the orders to just change like that, out of the blue? Because I just don't understand how *you* folks don't know why she's not here, when this was where she was ordered to go. How can the LA County medical system just *lose* someone like that?"

The woman looked as puzzled as Rachel. "Ma'am, I've been off for the past few days, so all I can tell you is that our beds have been consistently full for the past six weeks. So, why St. Thomas would try and send her here, just twenty-four hours ago, is beyond me. They'd have called first, I'm sure, and they would've known we had no openings, so I don't know."

"This is ridiculous," Rachel whispered and peered around the lobby, aggravated now. "Are there any other psychiatric centers like this around town? Somewhere else she could've gone?"

The lady took up a pen and flipped through her Rolodex. "No, ma'am. Not in the Norwalk area. There's the Gateways center up in Silverlake, but last I knew, their beds have all been full as well." She scribbled something down on an index card and then handed it to Rachel. "This is the case management number to St. Thomas. Just give them a call and ask for Cynthia; she's the director there, and she might have some better information for you. It's probably just a mix-up in her records." And she gave her another placating smile. "I'm sorry. I wish I could be of more help to you, but that's the best I can do."

Rachel read over the index card with another disgruntled sigh. "Okay, thank you." And she shouldered her purse and headed back out to the Nissan.

When she got to the apartment, she made the call to St. Thomas. Cynthia no longer worked there, so her questions were handled by a woman named Arlene who insisted my mother's case file had been transferred out to Kaiser-Permanente, and she provided the number to their records department. Rachel had either written it down wrong, or the woman had recited it incorrectly because when she called, she got Hollywood Wholesale Electric. She thumbed through Wade's phone book until she found Keiser's number, called and left a message for someone named Richard in medical records, but after four hours, he never called her back.

In one last coin-toss attempt, she tracked down the number to the ambulance service that had taken my mother away on Sunday afternoon; she remembered the company distinctly because it was her mother's maiden name—Schaeffer Ambulance Service. The technician who answered was helpful, sympathetic. He reviewed their transport log for July twenty-seventh and radioed the EMT's who'd been working that day while Rachel waited on hold. He came back to the phone with some very puzzling information.

"Santa Clarita?" Rachel closed the phone book and set it aside on the couch. "But that doesn't make any sense. That's almost an hour from here. And you're *sure* about that?"

"Yep. Sure as I'm talkin to you. They were re-routed about ten minutes outside of LA. The folks at La Casa called St. Thomas with the update on their bed space, and St. Thomas got her in at Westlake, last minute. I radioed the driver with the changes. So, our techs went ahead and took her up there. Got to the place around five o'clock or so. If you call on up to Westlake, you'll find your friend, I'm sure of it."

Rachel sat in a state of bewilderment for very a long moment, then snapped herself out of it and thanked him.

"No problem. Sorry for the mix-up," he said to her. "Good luck to you." And he hung up.

When she finally found the proper department in Santa Clarita, they said she needed my mother's social security number. She probably should have known that for situations like these, but she didn't. And so she hung up and scavenged through the desk drawers in the upstairs office until she found an old copy of the Centriole record contract; all the band members' vital particulars were typed onto the last page.

She made another call to the Westlake information desk and gave them what they needed. She was then given driving directions, my mother's patient number, which she would need for access at the main security gate, and a summary of the visitation rules and regulations.

"Okay, now is there anything I should bring for her?" Rachel asked the woman on the other end. "Clothes or books to read or toiletries? It's only for a couple more nights, so maybe not."

"Well, our records indicate this patient was admitted for long-term care," the woman said, "so if you wanna bring some under garments and puzzle books or something like that, it should be fine. There's a hospital canteen where she can purchase any other items, so you'd probably do better just to put money in her patient account when you get here. All the items in the canteen are pre-approved."

Rachel knitted her brow, and she leaned up on the desk, confused. "Wait, you said 'long-term care'? I'm not sure I understand. How is seventy-two hours considered long term? You lost me, there."

"I'm not at liberty to divulge patient medical records or diagnoses over the phone, ma'am," the woman said. "That's something you'll have to ask her doctor when you come."

"And how do I find out who *that* is?"

"You'll have to speak with admissions. They'll have that information."

"Well, do you have that number? Can you transfer me?"

"I'm sorry, there's no one in the office this afternoon. But you're welcome to try back in the morning."

Rachel cast an exasperated glare to the spackled ceiling, and she sat back in her chair and chuckled to herself for the sheer ineptitude of these people; the bureaucracy was maddening. But she had no other option but to ride the LA County merry-go-round until someone in the Westlake admissions department saw fit to let her off.

"All right," she conceded to the woman. "Fine. I'll just come up there myself, see if I can get someone to talk to me in person."

"Visiting hours start at eleven a.m.," the woman reminded her. "And be sure to bring a picture ID and the patient's information for the front gate. We'll see you in the morning."

"Yes, you most certainly will."

THEY TOOK DINNER in the same fashion as they took lunch—stand in line at the cafeteria door, come get your tray when your name is called, take the tray to a table and eat, TV dinner style. Shrimp Lo Mein under shiny cellophane.

My mother finally understood that the deafening buzzer reverberating through the halls was a mealtime signal, like the bell between classes in high school. She took her tray to a table by herself, but Nan found her there and sat down directly across from her.

"So, tell me about yourself. What's your diagnosis?" Nan asked. "They figure you out yet? Me—so they say—paranoid schizophrenic with acute psychosis. But I dunno what's so cute about it." She peeled off the plastic tray cover, stirred the food around, and shoveled a forkful of noodles into her mouth. "It's all a smoke screen, nothin cute about that, not when you've been blackballed from the LA film society for life, just so the Masons can have a bigger cut and give half of it to these hospitals. Who the fuck are they? I mean, seriously? They think we don't know what the hell's goin on?" She looked at Mom. "So, come on. 'Fess up. What'd you do to get tossed in here?" She grinned and pointed at her with her fork. "Hold on . . . lemme guess . . . You tried to *off* yourself. 'Cause I mean, unless you smacked Birdie in the head and kicked Tom in the nuts on your way in, they don't just throw you into seclusion the first night, not unless you're threatening to swallow a packet of picture nails or chew off your own tongue." She half shook her head and poked at her food. "Although I have seen that. Not a pleasant way to make a point, but ya know, takes all kinds." She glanced at Mom again, waiting for her to dish.

My mother watched her eat for a moment. She looked into her own plate and pushed one of the little shrimp around the bottom of the container and sat thinking about her plight, about Dr. Shah and seclusion and the fact that after dinner the staff would pour another cupful of pills down all their throats to keep them skating around the edges of sanity for a few more hours.

"I'm innocent," she finally said. Verbal communication had been trying to arrange itself in her head since lunchtime, and she felt a bit more comfortable talking to Nan in her strange and fragmented puzzle-speak, and so she concentrated and told her, "It was an accident. I shot too much dope. They tied me to the bed, couldn't stop puking. It was hell, and they wouldn't let me out. Now my brain's just word soup, alphabet salad, a scrabble board. Dope *never* did this shit to me." She thought, then, that she should try another way to bond, and so she pointed to the rainbow tattoo on Nan's forearm. "Me, too."

Nan smiled. She took a bite of her meal and nodded. "Yeah, kinda thought maybe. Somethin about you. We can always spot our own. Funny how it works for us, but never for them."

"Them?"

"The patrols," she said, glancing around herself. "You ever hear of MI-5000?"

Mom frowned, narrowed her eyes. She shook her head, still hazy on whether this was all Nan's reality or a new contrivance of the Haldol-Ativan cocktail.

"It's the Masonic Illuminati Global 5000," Nan said. "Five thousand being the handpicked elite. They place them in law enforcement, hospitals, the entertainment industry, you name it, anywhere they can influence outcomes, yours, mine, the fuckin President of the United States, for Christ's sake. They've got patrols everywhere, and when you won't conform . . . *bam.* Into the slammer you go. Toss you away for life, keep you quiet, but I'm gonna tell you somethin—drugs aren't drugs. You think you're gettin smack or weed or a fuckin crack rock, go get high and have yourself a good time?" She turned down the corners of her mouth and shook her head. "Nah, man. It's all part of the plan, my little friend. *This*," she pointed to the floor of the Westlake cafeteria, "is your brain on drugs, dude. Fuck a fried egg. Know what I mean?" She went back to eating, but she was honestly waiting for my mother's input.

The only thing my mother could think to say was, "Bad medicine."

"You got that right, buddy."

"So, where are the phones?" Mom asked. "My girlfriend doesn't know where I am."

"Where'd you come from, again? The cops pick you up or somethin?"

Mom had a very vivid image of blood-spattered walls and the sharp feeling of stainless steel piercing her neck. "St. Thomas. They said I was going to Norwalk, but I woke up in the desert, saw the mountains and shit going by, then welcome to Westlake. I just wasn't paying attention." She stirred the noodles around the cardboard package, red peppers in a brown sauce with three undersized, overcooked shrimp.

"Welcome to the Hotel California," Nan serenaded with a big grin and a chuckle. "So, you got duped, bamboozled, led astray to run amuck in this five-star facility." She shook her head at her plate. "You're not the first, comrade, and you won't be the last. It's an epidemic perpetrated by the almighty dollar bill. Probably the Rockefellers. There's a dozen secret societies, and they're the ones who pump all the drugs into the cities and then call it crime fighting. Now *you're* the bad guy. Fucking scam of the century."

My mother was beginning to find the links between Nan's scattered references, like a code, metaphorical at best, and so she said, "Yes. Duped by everyone. I just wanna go home. I need a phone, and then maybe I can see about that. My girlfriend needs to know about all this, come and get me."

"Can you trust her?"

What kind of a question was that? My mother wrinkled her brow. "Of course. She's got the keys. She was supposed to come along, but they gave her all my stuff instead."

Nan shrugged, sipped her water. "All right. Just makin sure. Never know. She do dope, too?"

My mother didn't look up from the food she wasn't eating. "No. She hates me for it. But I love her. How do you work that out? Christ, I'm tired."

"Tired is the way of things here. We're tired, they're tired, the whole damned place is tired, yet nobody sleeps." Nan gestured to my mother's food. "You gonna eat that?" My mother shook her head, and so Nan glanced around for the orderlies standing watch, then scooped Mom's dinner into her own container when no one was looking. "You gotta make them think you ate, or they'll feed you the hard way. And God only knows if it's food."

IT TURNED OUT she had earned one phone call. She shuffled down the long hall behind the nurse's station and found the wall of phones while Nan waited at the other end. She placed a collect call home and stood waiting while it rang five times. The machine picked up, hers and Rachel's voices sharing the greeting. But the operator wouldn't let her leave a message from a government facility, and then there was a dial tone, and then silence.

She hung up and just stood there, thinking for a very long time, too many questions that had no answers, too much supposition, she didn't know what to make of any of it. Something boiled in her gut, and she felt flushed and dizzy. It was panic. There was always tomorrow, but what the hell was tomorrow when yesterday should've never happened?

She felt herself moving back down the hall toward the day room again, going blind, the kind of sightless desperation that makes you do and say stupid things, so when Birdie saw her staggering along with a tearful scowl, my mother didn't respond to her and just kept going. And when she felt a hand grab her by the arm, she tore herself away from that and kept going, still, enraged on the inside, terrified of disappearing, frustrated by her own patience for having waited like a good girl for twenty-four hours, only to have that bitch on the other end deny her just thirty more seconds to sort this all out.

"Miss De Carlo, I need you to settle down, now. Just relax," Birdie warned. She had my mother by the arm again, thumb and fingers pressing tight into her bicep. "Do *not* do this."

"Fuck you." My mother struggled against her but couldn't break free this time, and that only conjured up a whole different kind of panic, because she knew very well what might happen if she continued to fight. But now she was made of fear, all nerves and white lights and whirling faces trying to collect her up for transport back to seclusion.

The mind is a funny, tricky thing; it can sort through a thousand choices in an instant and present the best ones to remedy a bad situation, then veto them all and sweep them from the table like crumbs on a dishrag. Reason has nothing to do with it. Common sense—an alien concept.

My mother let out a scream that was astonishing, even to herself. Perhaps she was, indeed, losing her mind to this place. That quick. Twenty-four hours, and the deal was sealed. She never even felt the needle jabbing her in the hip. Only the stiff, over-washed thermal against her cheek, mattress springs pressing up from underneath, her own ultrasonic heartbeat scraping at her eardrums. Steel on steel and then the keys in the lock.

"Welcome to the Hotel California," she heard Nan singing, over and over on down the hall until it faded off into the darkness.

ON TUESDAY MORNING Rachel made the trip north along Interstate 5, through Burbank and Sun Valley and a little town called Arleta, and then nothing but dust for another thirty miles into Santa Clarita itself, but she had to go farther yet, due west along Henry Mayo and then north again along an empty two lane called Chiquito Canyon Road until she saw the place, rising up out of the lonesome foothills like something from a lost maudlin era. It had all the features of an institution, disguised poorly behind an attempt at southwestern charm. She pulled up to the guard shack at the automatic gate and gave them my mother's name and patient number, and they let her on through to park.

Inside, they searched her purse and had her empty her pockets. They walked her through a metal detector that went off because of her earrings, and so she had to remove those, too, and put them in a lock box to claim on her way out. They searched the gym bag she'd brought filled with things for my mother's stay and confiscated the deodorant spray, the plastic razors, the ballpoint pens, gave back the sneakers and street clothes, thumbed through the music magazines and gave those back as well.

No spiral bound notebooks—the wire binding could be used for malicious intent. No food items—dietary needs were monitored by the staff. No belts, no laces, no aerosol canisters. No electronic devices, so the Walkman and tapes were useless. They left her with a pair of Topsider flip-flops, a hairbrush, and a week's worth of cotton underwear. The rest went into the lock box with the earrings and Rachel's purse, and she was given a clip-on visitor's badge and escorted with the others to a dining hall on the main floor where she sat waiting for another fifteen minutes.

Soon a few patients straggled in. They found their loved ones and greeted them with embraces and took their seats, then a handful more, a couple of orderlies, a man and a woman wearing street clothes and hospital badges.

Rachel looked right past my mother on the first glance, wouldn't have recognized her at all if it weren't for the hair. She was being led at the elbow by a nurse, and then there was the problem of knowing who my mother belonged to because the nurse scanned the room and then spoke into Mom's ear, trying to grab her attention so she might find her own visitor among the others. My mother raised her eyes from the floor, blinked very slowly and gazed around at the faces, and that's when a kind of devastation began to circulate through Rachel's veins like ground glass.

It frightened her, the deadness, the slumped shoulders and hanging matted ringlets, a string of saliva that the nurse noticed and wiped away with a tissue from her pocket. She wanted to leap from her chair and shelter my mother in her arms and lead her right through the front doors and out to the Nissan, alarms blaring and hospital staff on their heels, do a movie stunt, crash through the security gates and leave them askew in a plume of California dust. But she could barely bring her hand from her side to wave them over. She realized then that she was on her feet and didn't remember standing up.

My mother shuffled barefoot over to the table with the nurse Ana Garcia at her side.

"She's just had her medication, so she might be a little drowsy, but here she is." Ana smiled and showed my mother to her seat. She gestured to the clock on the wall. "You've got one hour, and then I'll be back to take her to the ward. Enjoy your time." She smiled again and walked away. As if it were all so normal.

None of the other patients seemed so bad off, and Rachel couldn't reconcile that. Mom sat slouching in the chair directly across from her, hands in her lap and her eyes on the tabletop, lifting her chin every so often to acknowledge Rachel's presence.

It was the adopted second cousin of a heroin stupor, Lady Black's dim and withering stepchild, familiar yet foreign in a way that did somersaults in Rachel's stomach. She reached a hand across the table and moved the hair from my mother's face to have a look at her. No, this was not the same. This had a thick heavy excess, grimy and opaque in its grip around my mother's brain. Covered in a kind of sewage that you couldn't really see.

"You have the keys," my mother said into the table, the syllables monotone and ventriloquial, and it startled Rachel in a deep, dreadful place she didn't know she had. "They put me in the box, red lightning makes the eggs fall to the floor but only one fly, just the one, and the door's a locomotive locks like hammers on steel so I can't use the phone. Nobody's home. Bitch said nobody's home and it's not a fuckin song it's real, it's real, and now it's just me, me and the yellow paint and the bitch on the other end. Too many tunnels. Nothin gets in, nothin gets out, so just walk, walking to the other side of nowhere, gravy, to the sink, one sock on and off to the doctor. Something following me there and not there, maybe a ghost, and it's my fault, says it in Spanish and then the needle on the bed, carrots—"

"Baby?" Rachel reached around under the table and took my mother's hand, and my mother jumped, and Rachel jumped, too, and so she didn't try to touch her after that. She wanted to cry, but no amount of tears could justify her astoundment.

"The medicine," my mother began again, then hesitated, a bit confused for a moment. Then she started all over. "TV dinners and no answer on the other end. Shrimp in a brown sauce. MI-5000 took it away. Nobody saw and I told her you have the keys. Medicine's no good. I'm sorry. I'm so sorry. Two days and a wake-up's a scam. Nobody's supposed to touch you there, now I only have one sock. Apples to apples all night long, never stopped. I dunno what I did wrong. Maybe a bad chair, wrong color tile, even numbers on my birthday. Lights out at ten p.m."

Rachel sat leaning into the hand that was cupped to her mouth, paralyzed, listening, watching my mother's mouth barely moving through a non-stop babble-rant, the incantations of a mental patient who was fine just two days ago. There was the overdose to consider, and the outburst in ICU, but never this. Never this.

"Jolán," she said softly. "Do you—do you know who I am? Can you even understand what I'm saying?"

"Yes." My mother nodded. "Yes."

"Okay."

"You have the keys."

"I don't know what that means, baby. What the hell have they done to you? *What* medication? What was the nurse talking about?" Rachel kept shaking her head, squinting under the burden of bemusement.

"Bad medicine. Words in a blender, maybe months."

Rachel took several, very long preparatory moments of observation and thought. "Jolán, I think we might need to call your parents. I don't know what's supposed to be happening here, but I think this might be too big for me," she told her with a helpless glance around the facility. "I mean, this place? It's not just some little treatment center, baby. This is a *state fucking hospital*, something that could become a legal issue. I can't just take you home, just take you out of here. There are no AMA forms to sign so you can just walk out. They'd never release you to me; I don't have any say in—"

"No." My mother lifted her eyes to meet Rachel's, a shade of green that she had never seen before, a flat dark olive, pupils dilated to two different sizes, which she didn't even know was possible. "No," my mother insisted again. "Quiet as a church mouse. Understand? No."

"But you obviously don't belong in here. Look at yourself, what they've done to you. They told me on the phone that you were here for long-term care," she pleaded quietly and shrugged. "What happened to sending you to La Casa? And what does that mean? Care for what? Long term, meaning *how long?* This really seems like it might be bigger than just you and me, honey. Don't you understand that?" She shifted her eyes out to the orderlies and around to the staff members, then lowered her voice. "If they try to keep you involuntarily? Christ, you might need, I dunno, a lawyer, an attorney to represent you and get you out, 'cause what the hell did they mean by *long-term?* I don't like how that sounds, Jolán; it's scaring the shit outa me, and you want me to be silent? The hospital, the OD, that was one thing, and I understood your reasons, but this is something very different, baby, and I don't think you're thinking clearly. There's razor wire on the fence, for Christ's sake. They took my fucking earrings, won't let you have pens or magazines or deodorant? What the hell for? A *heroin* overdose? Are they out of their *minds?*"

"The windows didn't open, but now it's all word salad, just what the doctor ordered. Brain's in a frying pan. Mom and Dad'll leave it there. Nobody's listening."

"*I'm* listening," Rachel said. "I'm listening to how fucked up you are. They turned you into someone who belongs here when that's bullshit. I almost didn't know who you were when they brought you in. This was never what you needed. Who *does* this?"

"Welcome to Westlake."

"Yeah, really."

"Bad medicine."

"That, too." Rachel looked around the room for someone of import and rested her eyes on the woman in street clothes, standing by the door and wearing a facility badge. "Listen, I'm gonna go try to talk to somebody, see what your situation is 'cause this is ridiculous. So, just wait here. Do *not* get up. Do *not* go anywhere."

"Okay."

She approached the woman with respectful caution and introduced herself.

The woman extended her hand and did the same. "Laura Koepsell, Director of Admissions and Patient Services. What can I do for you?"

Rachel gestured back to where my mother sat waiting at the table. "Why is she so out if it? I mean, she's not even making any sense when she talks. Is it the medication that's doing that? I mean, it has to be 'cause she's like a zombie. What are you people giving her?"

Laura peered at my mother and nodded. "It's probably the medication that's making her drowsy, yeah. But if she's having a problem with disorganized speech, then that I can't comment on; it would be something her psychiatrist would have to explain. He would have a much better take on her symptoms than I would, honestly." She folded her arms, leaned against the door jamb, and looked at my mother. "What I *can* tell you, though, is upon my initial assessment during admission, she was displaying some disorganized thought patterns even then, some mild paranoia, fear of being murdered by drug dealers, very positive grandiosity about being a multi-millionaire and having celebrity friends. Symptoms that definitely warranted placement for observation. I remember she was very manic, very agitated, refused to eat when offered a meal tray, all of which indicated a need for us to assume responsibility for her care. But, from what I understand, Dr. Shah did have an opportunity to observe and speak with her yesterday. I just saw him around here a few minutes ago, so if you'd like to talk to him before you leave, I'm sure I can make that happen." And she offered a sympathetic smile.

Rachel breathed a deep sigh and thought about all that. She frowned and shook her head. "She said that? 'Cause I mean, that just doesn't sound right. But you're saying she was talking like that when she came *in*. Not making any sense, all this roundabout gibberish? She's talking about socks and gravy and trains, from one thing to the next. I mean, it's scaring me, and I just . . . I dunno . . . I don't understand how she could be fine two days ago, and now she's a vegetable. Something's wrong. *Very* wrong, because that is *not* Jolán." She gestured to the table. "I *know* my girlfriend, and that is *not* her, so yeah, if you could let me talk to somebody else, that'd be good."

"Now, whether her symptoms have worsened over the past forty-eight hours is not something I can clarify, either. I'm a psychiatric social worker here," Laura said with a hand to her own chest. "I do intake assessments. I'm not a psychiatrist. But yes, upon her arrival, she was exhibiting signs of significant mental illness, enough to be kept for observation."

"Worsened." Rachel thought about that as well, and she glanced back at my mother. "So, this is not from medication, then? Is that what you're saying? They gave her something called Ativan at St. Thomas, and she was, as you said, drowsy. She couldn't even stay awake at times, but it never did this, not what I'm seeing today."

"And from what I understand in updating her file," Laura said, "Dr. Shah did keep her on the Ativan, once she got here. I do know that. But as far as any other symptoms or side effects, the most common would be the drowsiness and maybe some unsteadiness, anything that would go hand in hand with that."

"But not the disorganized speech, all the nonsense she keeps talking?"

"No, not that I've ever seen, not with Ativan."

"Okay." Rachel gazed across at Mom, unsure what to think of it all now. She gave Laura a brief smile and thanked her. "If you could let me talk to her doctor before I leave, that'd be great."

"I'll see if I can get him down here." And she went out into the hospital in search of Dr. Shah.

Rachel went back to the table and took her seat across from my mother who hadn't moved. She hadn't even turned around to check on their conversation or investigate Rachel's whereabouts, and Rachel found that as odd and disturbing as her chaotic speech and her drawn and haggard appearance. She was too docile, too compliant, a broken spirit lost in her own unfathomable head.

"Baby?"

My mother looked up from the table, attentive but empty.

"They're gonna let me talk to your doctor when we're done visiting, okay?"

"You have the keys."

Rachel shook her head and looked at my mother with terrible pity. "I don't know what that means, honey. I just don't. The lady said they kept you on the Ativan, the same medication from the hospital in LA, so I don't understand this. Are you *sure* they're not giving you anything else?"

"Catwoman wants my last name, last stop, and all hell broke loose. Cut me in half, but it never really happened, lost in a bad fog, you're not supposed to get that close to a blue marker. One's like a little house, pink circle with a hole in it, can't have an ACE bandage, everything's outa tune."

Rachel could only listen. How many ways could she say that she simply did not understand it? My mother's rambling was incessant, catastrophic, a hodgepodge of uselessness, which only my mother seemed to comprehend. "It seems you can understand me, so how about I just tell you some things, just talk to you for a while, okay?"

"Okay."

"Well, I brought you some underwear, some slippers, and a hair brush. That's all they'd let me give you, they confiscated everything else. But they told me on the phone that there's a store here, a place where you can buy things, so I put fifty dollars in your account when I signed in. You can have pencil and paper, books to read; it just has to be from the canteen, whatever they've already approved, so whenever they let you go buy things—I dunno how that works—but you have fifty dollars to spend on things you want until I come back in a few days. I have to close at the bar for the next few nights, and I won't be able to get up here, but Miranda's gonna cover for me next week so I can make more trips, okay?"

"Yes."

"And maybe by then, you'll be better, and we can just go home." She tried to smile, but it wasn't much. "Or maybe sooner, right?" The tears that had been stifled by her previous dismay began to swell, and she swiped at them with the back of her hand as they dripped onto the table. "You have to get better, Jo. You understand me? You have to show them you don't belong here because I don't know what else to do."

"Yes. Catwoman's gotta go."

Rachel sniffed and wiped another tear and stared at my mother. She shook her head in sheer bewilderment. "Christ, how did you get so fucked up?" She tried to compose herself and said, "You know I can call your parents at any time, Jolán. Maybe they might—"

"No. No. No."

"Okay, okay. All right. I won't. I think it's a mistake, but if you don't want me to, then I won't."

Rachel shifted in her seat and searched the floor for another topic of conversation while they waited for the doctor.

"I asked if you could have your guitar and your violin, but they said no. Seems to be a popular word around here. Wade wanted to give me some books to bring for you, but I don't trust him. That's all I need, get snatched up by security for smuggling Tar in here, and then you'd never get out, and I'd be in jail. He's half the reason this is even happening, although I'm grateful he called an ambulance and came and got me, but still." She looked back at my mother then. "When this is done and over with, when we get you home and get you better—*no more*. I want you to quit, leave that shit alone for good."

My mother didn't respond to that. But then she did. "Okay."

"You promise me?"

She lowered her eyes to the tabletop and let things swim around in her head for a while. "Yes," she finally said. "You have the keys, no more poison."

"Yes. That's right. No more poison. None of this was ever worth it."

"Everything's in pictures again, love is hard to find."

Rachel smiled a little. "Yeah, it is." She reached for my mother's hand. "Is it all right if I touch you?"

"Yes."

She took Mom's hand in hers, warm and feverish, frailer than it should have been. It was shaking.

"If you won't let me go to your parents, then this is all gonna have to be on you," Rachel said. "We don't have any money for a lawyer, and I have no power to make legal decisions for you. And I just don't know how you can vouch for yourself in this . . . this . . . whatever it is, this state of mind you're in right now. I know you're in there somewhere. So please, *please* do not get lost in this place; I don't think I could take it. Seeing you now, I think I would've rather lost you to an overdose. Maybe that makes me weak or selfish, I dunno."

"No." My mother squeezed her hand tighter under the table.

Rachel smiled. "I just miss you," she heard herself saying, and then the tears returned. "I miss *you*. Not the addicted you, but *you*. The Jolán I met last summer. I want you to get better in here and come home so we can have some kind of a life. Everything's been on hold, even when we thought we had this thing handled, things were still on hold, waiting around for some kind of miracle, some break in the clouds where all our plans were waiting to happen." She dabbed at her nose and dried fresh tears on her shoulder. "Sorry, I'm rambling. I guess I'm just not handling this very well. I mean, shit, it's not every day your girlfriend winds up in the state sanitarium, you know? Necessary or not."

"No."

"Miss Cole?" A man approached the table.

He had no nametag, but he was dressed in a shirt and tie, and he offered his hand and introduced himself as Dr. Shah. He smiled down at my mother and placed a hand on her shoulder.

"I'm glad we could get her stable for visitation. I know it meant a lot to her." He pointed over to a corner of the room and asked if Rachel would speak to him in confidence, and so she followed him away from the table.

"I understand you have some questions about her care, and I wanted to take a moment to catch you up on what's been going on with her," he said.

"Now, what about her family? Her parents, any other relatives we should contact, or would you prefer to do that yourself?"

Rachel peered at Mom. "I suggested that, and she doesn't want it. She was very adamant, actually, and the relationship's been pretty distant for a long while, so it's her call, I guess. My thing is—this rambling she's been doing. I don't know if you've heard the way she's talking, but it's just . . . I can't even explain it. Babble. Nonsense. Everything's all mixed up, and I don't know why that is. When I left her two days ago, she was sleepy, but she was coherent. She was making sense. And now today . . ." She shook her head and blinked at my mother's defeated posture at the table, like an old dog tied to a fence post. She looked at Dr. Shah and said, "What's happening to her? She keeps saying bad medicine, but the social worker said she didn't see how that could be possible, so I don't understand."

Dr. Shah seemed to anticipate her concerns, and he nodded and folded his arms across his chest. "Well, I've only had one session with her myself; however, she has complained of visual hallucinations, seeing things in her environment that aren't there. She came in under what I considered to be borderline psychosis, which I did explain to her in our meeting yesterday. So far, she hasn't been very receptive to that, which is not uncommon. Certain symptoms of psychosis can seem very real to the patient, particularly if it's gone untreated, but hopefully we can find the right medication to minimize those symptoms, which will help her to understand that she might possibly be suffering from mental illness."

"Psychosis?" Rachel winced. "You realize that is a very scary word. You're saying she's psychotic. Like, Michael Myers, Jim Jones psychotic, or what? Because I don't understand how that's possible, she was *fine* just a week ago. And now she's . . . what? Some kinda serial killer? I will *never* believe that. I'm sorry, I just won't."

He laughed lightly and shook his head. "No, Miss Cole. I don't believe her to be homicidal. If that were the case, we would have placed her on a maximum security ward, which we did not. She has, however, had two major outbursts, which have each warranted chemical restraint and a period of seclusion, but I believe those incidents to be situational, perhaps just an inability to adjust to her surroundings. I understand there was something about the telephones last night that caused her to get extremely agitated, and she was placed in seclusion for the night to cool off."

"And see, that's just not Jolán," Rachel insisted. "She's the *last* person to go berserk on somebody and need to be restrained. That's ridiculous. She'll walk away first, choose flight over fight, believe me. Even when it happened at the hospital, it was unusual, and it was situational *then*. She was in heroin withdrawal, and she was scared, nothing more. But you're saying now it's part of some underlying mental illness? How can that be?"

"When Jolán sat down with me yesterday," Dr. Shah explained. "I asked her a series of questions, which were specifically designed to identify possible psychotic tendencies, and she answered 'yes' to eight out of ten of those basic questions. And yes, I'm aware of her history of drug abuse, yet she'd been given Narcan at St. Thomas four days prior to her coming here. Her system was well flushed of any narcotics or opiates by the time of our assessment on Sunday, yet she still presented as a possible bipolar-1, mixed depressed with psychotic features. I'd be happier than you to put the blame purely on a heroin-induced episode, Miss Cole. Honestly, I would. But she was clean when she came to us. Her blood tests came back negative for any outside chemical that could've caused this. I'm sorry."

It seemed every source had been explained away, defining my mother's condition by the standards of modern psychiatry. How could it be coming together like this? So systematically. It wasn't supposed to make this kind of sense, yet Rachel couldn't be sure it made the sense she thought it did. She gazed out the barred cafeteria windows, at the tall palms and razor wire, the cars all parked in the lot, the green lawns beyond the chain link fences.

"But she was fine," she muttered to herself, a desperate mantra meant to undo it all, make it not so.

Was it the addiction itself, she wondered. The drug making its own methodical changes in my mother's brain chemistry over the months, weakening her ability to manage the slightest bit of anxiety without it? A stress fracture in her psyche, perhaps, just waiting for the weight of a good friend's death, a shattered dream, financial peril, the emotional crush of their own waning romance. And then the overdose, the final straw, two days in a coma and another three spent battling the nightmare of withdrawals.

"Oh my God," she whispered as everything took alarming shape.

"You certainly wouldn't be the first loved one to feel as though it had happened out of the blue," Dr. Shah said. "I've had patients who, just the previous day, had gone to work or school, to football practice or an important meeting, paid the bills, ate dinner with their families. And then literally, overnight, they find themselves under psychiatric care for anything from schizophrenia to psychotic depression. So, you're not alone on that, Miss Cole. But let me also assure you that Jolán is in very good hands here. In fact, I'll give you my information." He slipped a business card from the fold of his wallet and handed it to her. "You'll have my office, fax, and pager number if you ever need anything or if you have any further questions." He laid a hand on her shoulder and smiled. "The goal is to make her well again and get her home. It may take some time, but with the right treatment plan, hopefully we can make that happen."

She nodded, dumbstruck, gaping at his business card in a wordless stupor not much different from the one holding my mother hostage at the table. "Okay. Thank you," she muttered for lack of anything more relevant to say.

Dr. Shah glanced up at the clock. "Unless there's anything else, I don't wanna take up any more of your visitation time. Just be patient with her confusion for right now. Once we find the appropriate medication, I think we should be able to get that resolved. We'll take good care of her," he promised, then excused himself and headed back out into the halls.

Rachel went back to the table and sat down, this time with a very different perspective on my mother's behavior. Mom was drooling again, and so Rachel wiped it away with her fingers and dabbed them dry on her shorts. She sat looking at her for a long quiet moment, and my mother sat, too, hands in her lap, lips parted in a dull and vapid daze, her dreary olive eyes taking in the counterfeit wood grain of the Formica tabletop.

There were things in her head, Rachel could sense that, a thousand notions and opinions, invaluable information that might explain all this, but the route of communication between the mind and the mouth had been demolished by misfortune. She could see it now. Why she hadn't seen the warning signs along the way, she couldn't figure. Maybe there were none, like the doctor proposed. Maybe it was all too subtle. Maybe it was the dope. Maybe she had been drawn toward drug abuse because it was easier to understand herself on heroin than not. Maybe it was none of that.

So, now what? Rachel sat thinking, taking inventory of her own feelings. Did she love my mother enough to wait this out? Did she love her enough to stay, even if she might never get her back again? Did she love her enough to betray her wishes and contact my grandparents if things started looking bleaker than expected? And did she love her enough not to?

"Two days and a wake-up's all bullshit, puzzles on a merry-go-round, it was the music talkin about us, and I wasn't paying attention, blood everywhere, boys in a picture frame gotta get a CAT scan now, maybe weeks, maybe months, shadows in the corners—"

"Baby, just stop." Rachel dared place her hand against my mother's cheek, and she didn't startle this time, but she stopped talking. Rachel began to cry again. She kept her hand to Mom's face and smoothed away the curls. "Just stop. You don't have to say anything. It's all right. It's gonna be okay. I don't know who broke you, but we're gonna have to fix this, somehow. You have to find your way through this, or I don't know what else we can do. You understand?"

My mother nodded. "Yes. Little houses in the trash stay under the radar 'cause fuck a fried egg."

Rachel lowered her hand and looked away. She wiped the tears from her cheeks and chin and stared out the window for a while, finding the whole thing more difficult to fathom. She was starting to see herself at twenty-five, thirty, fifty years old and sitting right here in this green plastic chair opposite my mother's unreachable disease, and it was scaring her. The travesty. The waste. What if? She decided the least she owed my mother was time, give it time and see how it played out, measure her options by clocks and calendars and then see where they stood.

Some of the nurses were filing in to the dining hall now, and Ana Garcia was with them. Their time today had run out.

Ana came to the table, wearing the same easy smile that she wore when she dropped my mother off. "So, how was your visit?" But it was rhetorical. She called down to Mom to remind her that lunch was in fifteen minutes and then helped her to her feet. "Maybe your friend can come back again on Thursday," she shouted. "Let's get you back upstairs so you can eat, okay?"

"Okay."

Rachel walked with them to the doorway, then turned and faced my mother. "You just remember that I love you. That'll never change, no matter what."

She wrapped her in her arms and hoped my mother might do the same, but she didn't, and Rachel didn't know how to feel about that except to attribute it to my mother's muted and broken sense of self.

She pulled away and smiled at Ana, kissed my mother on the cheek, and then headed out with the others to claim her purse and keys from the lock box.

AT THE CAR, she let herself come apart. She sat in the oven-baked heat of the driver's seat and sobbed until she couldn't see through the blur, foothills and desert and razor wire shimmering in a glassy haze. Her stomach felt cramped and her head was pounding and her nose ran until she had no choice but to wipe it clean on her shirttail. She sat there crying for a very long while, staring out the windshield, unable to move, to do the basic things necessary to just start the car. After some time passed, she was able to settle herself down, and she could see the institution in the rearview, the bell tower and Spanish rooftops, bars and brown stucco and the old-world balconies meant only for cosmetic appeal.

There was a line of cars crawling through the security gate, everyone going back to their lives, and she knew she was no different. She had things to do, a job to get back to, utilities to pay. She started the engine and pulled in behind the rest, then out onto Chiquito Canyon toward home.

chapter twenty-three

ONE OF THE pills had changed. The pink pill was gone, and in its place was a light green oblong tablet, which Nan said was likely Risperdal, the younger sister of Haldol, but the most significant difference in my mother's headspace was an amplified sense of agitation. It had been three days since Rachel's visit and physically she felt about the same—she still shuffled when she walked, but she was faster now, which she attributed to, perhaps, a lower dosage of the new Risperdal. She was thirsty all the time, but the halos were gone. Her thought process no longer felt like scattered puzzle pieces, and she could communicate properly, but now she had to pee every two hours. She'd merely traded one nuisance for another, but she was starting to feel confident that, by the end of the week, she might rectify herself altogether and begin the methodical process of escape.

She thought the inexplicable agitation could become a problem. She wanted to overturn the television and let it smash to the floor in a broken pile of sparks and glass. She thought about ramming her new roommate's head into the wall for bitching about the bathroom light. Just that morning, she fought back a desire to fling her meal tray across the cafeteria like a Frisbee, simply to see where it landed and whom it might clobber along the way. She couldn't justify any of that. She felt very stupid most of the time but didn't want to lose privileges, couldn't give Birdie and the orderlies any cause to turn her brain to spaghetti again, as that was where the stupidity was at its height, the brick wall she would encounter trying to tunnel out of this place.

It was shopping day at the canteen, and my mother had just gotten back. She stood in front of her bed, sorting through all her new purchases—a bag of potato chips, a stick of deodorant, two unsharpened pencils, a bottle of shampoo, a toothbrush and toothpaste, and a black-and-white Tops composition notepad.

April sat watching from the other bed, glaring at Mom from the edge of her eye. She was quiet for a long moment as Mom found places in the nightstand drawers for her toiletries. Then she let out a heavy sigh and got up and began the ritual of purging my mother's bad energy from the air.

Mom stopped and stared at her. "What now?"

"I *told* you," April snipped. She went to the room door and opened it, shut it, tapped it five times with her fingertips. "Eleven and five. Got it? *Eleven* and *five.*" She opened the door and shut the door, tapped it, opened it again, shut it, tapped it. "Shit. Now I have to do it double 'cause *you* didn't do it at *all* when you came in. It's not that damned hard. I explained the consequences for not following the patterns. Maybe shit won't happen to *you*, but try thinking about somebody else besides yourself for a change. You're not the only one in the room."

Mom watched her, perturbed. She felt a flash of rage ignite behind her eyes, somewhere in the middle of her brain, and she envisioned herself with a hand around April's throat, slamming the back of her head into that goddamned door eleven times, five blows to the face, blood and broken teeth and an unconscious roommate going pale on the white linoleum.

She probably should have been alarmed by that, but consolation came when she remembered she now had a notepad—a much safer, more acceptable outlet. She took one of the pencils from the bed and tucked it behind her ear. "Sorry."

She waited while April carried out her complicated liturgy. Then April came away from the door, but she still wasn't finished. It was "apples to apples" now as she crossed the little room to the window and back, brushing off her shoulders and snapping her fingers.

"How long do you have to do that?" Mom asked. "Because I need to go back out again and get this pencil sharpened, in case you . . . I dunno . . . needed to do your door thing again."

"Are you kidding me?" April muttered to the stars. "It depends. Until I feel comforted again, which I don't." She swiped at each shoulder, snapped three times. "So, just go and make sure you do it right, please. There are spirits. Apples to apples. Evil, pissed off demons with their hands in everything that happens to me unless the walls are up. Odd numbers make the walls stronger. There has to be an order, and it has to be consistent or they'll get in. I explained this shit to you yesterday. They weren't even supposed to put anyone in here with me, it makes it too difficult, leaves all kinds of gaps in protection." She was doing the routine faster now, compelled by aggravation. "Just go. I'll do the door. Just leave it open."

Mom stood there, watching her with fury balling up inside. Then she started for the halls but turned back and told her, "I can barely remember yesterday. I've been fucked on medication until today. You're not the only one in the room, either."

"Apples to apples. Whatever."

"Yeah, whatever." Mom flung the door open and let it bang against the wall as she headed out toward the nurse's station, resisting the urge to plant a fist into the yellow plaster as she shambled through the day room. These radical impulses made her think about dope, the smell of it, blood swirling into the syringe, the warm and coddling afterglow, and that only seemed to make things worse, everything unrequited, the desire to erupt and the need to escape the desire to erupt, both of them forbidden. So just be. Just burn. Eat your plate of shit and like it.

She came to the nurse's counter but had forgotten about the red line on the floor and stepped across it into a swift scolding from Birdie, warding her back with a fat little finger pointed into the hallway.

"You know the rules, Jolán," she sang, the words drawn and twangy through a Tennessee accent. "Back it up. That line's there for your safety and ours. Now what can I do for you?"

Mom slipped the pencil from behind her ear and showed it to her. "Thomas said you can sharpen this."

"I can." Birdie took it and went back behind the counter. "You seem like you're feelin a little better today. Not so confused and sluggish. Maybe that Risperdal's the ticket. How's the Ativan doin you? Still makin you dizzy?" The electric sharpener whined and whirred as she spoke. "Sometimes the medication takes a week or so to get used to, so just hang in there. It'll level out."

"I feel like shit," my mother said. She could feel her brow creasing into a frown, but she stayed put on her side of the red line and waited.

"Define 'shit.'" Birdie examined the pencil tip. She inserted it into the sharpener once more for good measure and let it grind and chew until the lead was like a sewing pin. "Physically, mentally, or a little a both?" She came around the desk and held the pencil up in front of her but wouldn't hand it over. "You need to tell me what you mean by that, darlin, before I let you have this. You're not gonna go stickin yourself or anyone else with it, are you? 'Cause that scowl on your face is makin me wanna put this right in my pocket and keep it there until your state of mind improves."

Mom lowered her eyes to the floor, irritated, but there were priceless rewards at stake if she let her mouth get ahead of her brain again, so she just shook her head. "I'm okay. Stomach hurts, that's all."

"Well, it's about lunchtime, so you're probably hungry."

Mom nodded. "Probably."

Birdie studied her for a moment, then handed her the pencil. "Make sure you eat, and eat good. Could be the medication, too, so if your stomach still ain't right after lunch, come find me, and I'll see about some Pepto-Bismol or somethin."

"Okay."

Birdie looked her up and down once more, gauging her disposition for future reference as Mom shuffled away down the hall. "Don't let that pencil be a mistake, Miss De Carlo, I'm tellin you," she called after her. "Do right, and you'll make yourself an easier time here."

"Okay." My mother half turned and waved, even gave her a lopsided smile, but it was phony. *"Puta,"* she grumbled as she passed through the day room again, fighting her own electrical impulses, the desire to upend the card table with Brielle's unfinished jigsaw puzzle—a swan drifting across a countryside lake.

She could have done a lot of things but she didn't. She didn't toss a folding chair into the television screen. She didn't shout obscenities at those sitting around the couches, absorbed in their conversational drivel. She didn't kick the potted fern off its stand or throw the television remote across the room or tear down the bookshelves. She bottled it all up and limped along the hall to her room. She left the door open, this time.

"You shut it," she said to April who was no longer performing "apples to apples" and was now in front of the bathroom mirror, fixing her hair for lunch as if she were attending the Oscars.

"What exactly is your problem?" April winced.

Mom stopped and turned to her. She watched her brush and smooth and comb and fix and brush and smooth. "My problem? *Everything* is my problem. *You're* my problem, this fucking *place* is my problem. I'm twenty-three years old, and I have to ask permission for a fucking pencil. I'm in a fucking mental hospital, and now my girlfriend thinks I fucking *belong* here, and you wanna know my problem?"

"Do you really have to say 'fuck' so much?"

"Yes. I do. Does it bother you? I can say it some more if you want. How 'bout in Spanish? *¡Joder! ¡Vete al la chingada!* So, what? You gonna call for Thomas now? Have them dose me up with psycho juice and throw me back in solitary, you fucking *wack* job?"

April didn't respond to any of that. She ran the brush through her hair and pursed her lips. Finally she said, "Call the kettle black much? Last I checked, you were a patient, too, got a wristband and everything. But maybe you're just here on some school psych project, though, right? I guess that's why your status went from voluntary to *in*voluntary in less than forty-eight hours. Took one damn session with Dr. Shah to get *you* 5150'ed, and you're calling *me* a wack job? That's priceless."

"So, you've been reading my case file or some shit? Your stupid chants and charades not keeping you busy enough?"

"No, asshole." April stopped, and she looked at her straight. "It's obvious they changed your status, or you'd have been gone in three days, it's the law. And they sure as hell don't need much, just one good meltdown and a few talking shadows to get a court order, a court order from the 6th Circuit Probate Court . . . *downstairs*, in this *very* building. You don't even have to be there, especially if they deem you incompetent to testify on your own behalf. You get yourself a nice permanent room and a canteen account, and *voilà*; you're all theirs until they decide to let you out. I'm only twenty-one, and I've been here four times, so believe me—I

don't have to go snooping through anyone's files. I *know* how it works."
She went back to brushing.

"Yeah, well, I guess that explains a lot," Mom said, then went to the
bed and grabbed up her notebook and sat with it in her lap.

She should've felt bad about what she'd said, but she didn't. In fact, it
was the first thing she wrote: *No remorse for this hatred inside—so, how
crazy does that make me really? Here, you're chased by monsters until
you become one. As far as I can tell, that seems to be the idea.*

Her writing was scrawled and chaotic, angry in a way that gouged into
each page as if she had a brick lashed to her wrist.

When I'd first thumbed through that journal I thought perhaps it was
displaced, that maybe it belonged to someone else and had mistakenly
found its way into my mother's things over the years. It didn't even look
like the others, just a black-and-white pad like the ones they'd given us in
the fourth grade. But after reading through the first few entries, the ordeal
at Westlake became very clear, and I realized that my mother never truly
escaped the effects of that place. No wonder she wouldn't take anything
for the depression that kept her bedridden during my first year of junior
high, why she refused professional counseling as if we were asking her to
join the Skinheads.

Jackie tried a dozen different ways to sway her into going but failed
on all counts, and now I understood. Now I knew why she hated canary
yellow and the smell of Pine-Sol, why the class bell ringing from the
Catholic school behind our subdivision made her cringe and why she kept
her bedroom door open most nights, even when Dad was still around. The
experience had seeped into her cells and had become an insufferable part
of her. It was a chapter in her story that could never be untold.

THEY SPENT THE afternoon making flowers from crepe paper and
talking in Candace's Group Therapy circle. Mom and April stayed out of
each other's way until after dinner, when everyone lined up at the med
station and got their little paper pill cups as their names were called.

Nurse Catwoman, whose name she finally learned was Jeanie, handed
her the dosages and a cup of water. My mother tossed the tablets onto her
palate and drank the tap water and opened her mouth wide and lifted her
tongue. Jeanie waved her on. Mom shuffled back to her room and was
relieved to find April gone for therapy, and so she went into the bathroom,
shut the door, and dug a finger up into her gums where all three tablets
were hidden and partially dissolving.

She spit them into her palm, soft and chalky, the green oval, the little
white house, and the naproxen. The little house was the Ativan, and she
kept that but pinched it in half and took it down with a palm full of faucet

water. It was the closest thing to heroin she could get her hands on right now, but the dose was too damned much. She needed to be coherent and focused, to make a convincing show of her "recovery" without breaking anything, or any*one*. She dropped the others into the toilet and flushed it and washed away the residue at the sink.

She felt better already. She'd gotten away with it after lunch, too, and wondered what might have been the penalty if she'd failed—a forced dose, no doubt, Birdie's specialty, served with a syringe on a four-inch dirty mattress in Cell 16. But the trick was easier than she'd thought, just a quick tuck with the left side of her tongue to trap them between cheek and gum, then knock back the water, open up for confirmation, and wander off with everyone else. No problem, so long as Jeanie kept a lazy eye on things, half watching the patients and half watching the clock, pining for the end of her shift.

She climbed onto the bed, grabbed up her journal, and recounted everything onto the pages in retrospect, filling in the blanks of her perforated memory. She remembered Rachel's visit, but it was dreamlike, and she couldn't even be sure it had happened except for the money in her account and the underwear and sandals that had appeared on the bed the following morning, bundled in a plastic belongings bag.

There'd been some dialogue between them; she recalled it vaguely. Rachel said things about Wade and Dr. Shah, about getting an attorney and bringing Mom's guitar. She remembered tears on Rachel's face, wood grain laminate, fingertips touching her lips. She remembered Rachel's hands, her voice. She wore her hair down that day, golden blonde highlights resting on her shoulders, her eyes dark with worry, a kind of fear my mother had never seen in them before, and she never wanted to see it again.

Writing was a good tool for memory. The more she wrote, the more she remembered, details emerging onto the page like images in a Polaroid print, undefined and shapeless at first, then the colors, the faces, the things people were wearing, features in the background, the stories behind the pictures, captions and conversations and the intricate emotions tied to each.

Then there were other recollections, things unrelated to her circumstances but vivid and stirring, just the same. The navy blue comforter. The sleeper mattress on the living room floor. Smooth legs, cool and glossy against clean satin sheets, a sweet floral scent, maybe fabric softener, maybe Rachel's perfume. Late morning sun lit up the empty room and glinted off the Stratocaster propped beside the fireplace as the ceiling fan whirled overhead. My mother was telling very bad jokes with Rachel wrapped in her arms, giggling. It was Thanksgiving Day.

"WHAT DO YOU call a pig that knows karate? . . . a pork chop."

"Just don't tell these on stage, or you'll get hit with another bar stool."

"What did the fish say when it ran into the wall? . . . dam."

"I don't get that one."

"Dam. As in Hoover." Mom smirked and looked at her, tucked into the crook of her arm, her head on Mom's chest.

"Unbelievable." She grinned and kissed my mother's shoulder. "Be glad you have good looks and music on your side. They are your saving grace."

"You're my saving grace."

THE BUZZER-BELL rang. Time for head count, everyone back to their rooms. Keys jingled and steel doors clanged and voices bounced around the hallways. My mother kept writing.

She remembered a red wooden bridge over Echo Park Lake, dark water painted electric green with algae, shapes floating on the surface between the lily pads. She and Rachel carried hot cups of coffee from the *taquería* across the street and stood leaning over the rail. February was cold, overcast, even in LA.

"I SEE ALASKA." Rachel peered down into the lake and stood close to Mom. She was beautiful against the white winter sky.

"That's 'cause it's twelve degrees out."

"Try fifty, wuss. It's not even twelve degrees in Ohio right now. Or Bensalem. Can you see it? The mainland, and those are the little islands."

"I see a cat peeing."

Rachel giggled. "No, it's not."

Mom pointed into the black water. "No, there. Beside the hippo you found . . . which looks more like an elephant now."

Mosquitofish dimpled the water plain. Algae frothed and swirled around a pink floating lotus. Rachel watched until it glided under the bridge and vanished. "Do you ever wonder where we'll be in ten years?"

"I wonder where we'll be in ten months, ten weeks, maybe. Ten years?" Mom warmed her hands on the paper coffee cup, took a sip. "You'd need a telescope to see that far ahead. Let the future take care of itself. We'll be there when we get there."

"Well, that was evasive. How do you do that? Just anchor yourself to the moment like that, with no direction, no foresight."

"I give myself a lot of leeway."

Rachel gazed out across the lake and thought about that. "Well, I just hope it's enough for the both of us."

THE ORDERLY, JAMES, rapped on the open door and stepped inside. April was right behind him. He glanced around the room but didn't say anything, and then he was gone.

April performed the door ritual as he left, then went into the bathroom to brush her teeth. She switched on the overhead light three times, turned the faucet on and let it run while she counted to twenty-five beneath her breath—she couldn't let the water touch her hands until she reached exactly twenty-five or she'd have to start over. My mother watched her peripherally as she wrote, and now that the medication wasn't jabbing holes in her brain, she felt a bit sorry for her.

Her story had come in fragments, some of it from April herself, the rest from other patients who'd gotten to know her over the years, and a wave of guilt made my mother feel like an ass for the way she'd spoken to her before lunch.

According to the collected accounts, April killed her younger sister by pushing her off a swing at the neighborhood schoolyard. April was ten at the time, and her sister was eight.

It was an accident. There had been a race that day to get to the swings, and Leslie had a head start, and she got there first and took April's favorite. Indignant, April chose another one and pouted while Leslie swung higher and higher, feeling smug and laughing about her victory.

That was when April made an irreparable decision. She stood up and gave her sister a hard shove sideways, which twisted the chains around those of the next swing, and then everything was tangled and askew, twining and buckling and throwing Leslie to the macadam where she fractured her skull in two places. She died four days later on August sixteenth in the children's hospital on Sunset.

April's parents blamed her with curses from God Almighty Himself and took her to see the minister of their Pentecostal church to be purged of her demons, an exorcism of sorts, which, after two hours of snake handling and biblical fury, was deemed a success. But as far as April saw it, the specters and ghouls never truly left her to live her life in peace—they were always looming, waiting for her to miscount, to misspeak, to forget.

By the time she was fifteen, she'd lacerated herself with everything from paper clips to sewing needles, a perpetual punishment for her own crimes. She thought if she did it to herself, then maybe nobody else would bother. She could control that. She could manage her own penance, set the rules and boundaries, keep bad things from happening on her own account. By the age of eighteen, she was drowning in rituals and superstitions and reasonless mantras that would weaken friendships and make college impossible.

My mother felt fortunate in comparison, even with a dope habit. She, too, had had a hand in killing someone close to her, and all she did was more dope. She'd lost friends because of it but had never fallen victim to anything but her own shit-poor decisions. Two arms specked with needle tracks were the scars of her self-loathing, so perhaps she and April weren't so different. She watched as she wiped her mouth and turned the bathroom light off five times. She thought maybe she should say something.

"Look, I'm really not the prick you've been seeing the past few days." Mom threw April an apologetic glance and went back to writing. "It's the medicine. Just gotta level out."

April climbed into bed and grabbed a Nora Ephron book from the nightstand. She was on page fifty-six, an even number, so she said "capitol" to reverse the hex. Then she told Mom, "It's cool. I get it. I know how medication can make you a douchebag if you're not used to it. No harm, no foul."

"All right, then."

THEY WERE SETTLING into their books and journals when a scream came from down the hall. Mom and April stopped and looked at each other. Screams on Ward 27 were not uncommon, particularly at the end of the day, after people had time to accumulate a head full of angst and needed to act it all out, but this was different. This came from an authentic place of terror, and so April climbed out of bed to see about it, and my mother followed her to the door.

They opened it and saw James, Thomas, and Vincent running past with the nurse Rhonda jogging after them. A crowd of patients had gathered in front of Nan and Brielle's room, four doors down. Some stood with hands cupped to their mouths while others just watched at the doorway, arms crossed at their chests, everyone mumbling assumptions as to what might've happened.

One of the girls turned away into another's arms and began to cry, and then Brielle emerged from the circle and sat down in the hallway against the wall with Marie crouched in front of her, uttering consolation and wiping tears from Brielle's face. There were three short rings from the buzzer-bell then, a female voice over the facility intercom: "Code-7, room 410. Code-7, room 4-1-0."

"You can't be serious," April uttered as she and my mother wandered down into the commotion. She was doing a discreet version of "apples to apples" as they walked, negotiating the checkered floor tiles as not to step on any of the black ones. "This is the second time since June."

"For what?" Mom asked. "What does it mean?"

"Code-7. It's a suicide attempt," she said, snapping her fingers at her sides.

My mother didn't know what to say to that. She just followed her to where everyone else stood gathered at Room 410. Two more nurses came running through the day room, pushing a crash cart with Dr. Bernard following after, and everyone at the doorway moved aside to let them through.

Marie looked up at Mom and April as they approached. "I told you, didn't I?"

"They don't pay attention," April said. "They always watch the wrong ones."

"I should have come back sooner," Brielle said and dried her face on her sleeve. "If I'd have been here, maybe . . ."

"They don't understand, there has to be some balance," Marie said. "You can't just dope everyone up and expect them to find a fuckin happy place. Talkin all day doesn't always fix everything."

One of the other girls said, "She was too quiet in crafts today. She never even came to music therapy, either, and she never misses that."

"Her mom was supposed to come yesterday," another one said, "and I don't think she showed. She didn't seem like it bothered her much, but shit . . ."

"Did she say anything weird?" someone else wondered. "I mean, maybe we just weren't listening."

"Everything she says is weird," Marie mumbled. "How would anyone know a cry for help from a hole in the ground with *that* one?"

"Did she leave a note?" one of the others asked. "I'd wanna know if she gave any explanation, a reason, maybe. At least then we'd know why."

"How she got all that shit down her own throat is what I wanna know." April stood peering into the room where the medical team was working to extract a ball of plastic wrap, a washrag, and a generous wad of toilet paper from Nan's airway. Her face and throat were swollen and blue, and her eyes were still open, fixed on an indeterminate spot on the upper wall. The nurse Rhonda was just removing the last of the debris with a long pair of forceps so Birdie could start CPR. "The determination that took is . . . just . . . I mean, who *does* that?"

"Somebody who doesn't wanna fuckin be here no more, that's who." Marie stood up and craned around for a look into the room. "You get creative. Make use of the things on hand if you got nothin else. Can't give her any points for style, but she got it done, so three fuckin cheers for her if that's what she wanted."

"I should have checked on her," Brielle said again, mostly to herself. She brushed away fresh tears with her shoulder and sat with her head in her hands. "She always watched *The X Files* with me on Friday nights. Always. I thought maybe she was tired, or reading a book. I never even came to see if maybe she forgot. She'd forget the day sometimes, and I *knew* that, and I still didn't go check on her. Why didn't I check on her?"

"'Cause she's a grown woman who doesn't need a frikkin babysitter," Marie insisted, watching with her arms crossed tight. "We're not each other's keepers, we're goddamned adults, so don't start that shit, Brielle, I swear to God. Nobody knows what the connections are, not you, not the goddamned doctors, not even me. Twenty years of psych training, and I still can't figure you people out."

James came out of the room and waved everyone back to their beds. "Lights out's in ten minutes, go. They'll handle it, just go on back to bed. There's nothing else to see."

The only one exempt was Brielle. He had her go wait in the day room with Candace who sat with her on the couch, smoothing a hand across her shoulders as she spoke softly.

My mother limped back to her room with everyone else and then climbed into bed and lay staring at the ceiling tiles until the room went dark. She thought about what it would take to end yourself like that, to really do it, not the way dope could sneak up and suffocate you in your sleep, framing you for your own murder. But to do so deliberately, plan it out, take all the steps necessary to see it through, and then what?

She'd heard somewhere that most people change their minds, but then it was too late. You're already swinging from the rafters with nowhere to put your feet, the toxins have already infiltrated the liver, the sidewalk's approaching at eighty miles per hour, seven seconds to impact and nothing to grab onto. You die panicking in the bed you made, but not Nan. All she had to do was stop. April was right, the determination was astonishing. No regrets. No take backs. Only the pure and fearless will to keep going until it was accomplished.

"I can't wait to get out of this shit hole," April said through the dark.

My mother had no response. She turned over to face the wall and watched the security lights make shadows of the bars on the windows. She didn't remember falling asleep, but she dreamt that she was wandering the nighttime streets of a strange and abandoned city, sometimes she was riding a bike, other times on foot, always alone, then it was Bensalem and then it was nowhere in particular again, street lamps turning everything a golden amber, and she was lost, yet aware of someone in pursuit, a faceless threat, always just a block behind as the landscape shifted and changed, empty sidewalks and black alleyways and no one in sight, no sound but her own footfalls, watching herself move past the vacant row homes with their wrought iron railings, curtains drawn shut behind big bay windows. In them, her reflection was not her own. She didn't know who that was, and then it vanished, but she herself did not. She had the irrefutable sense that she was too far from home, left to wander, to flee the unknowable, to find her way back. She was entirely too far from home.

"SOMETIMES PEOPLE JUST give up. She thought very highly of you, admired you, in fact." Dr. Shah sat across from my mother, his notepad resting on the leg he had crossed over the other.

His socks matched the mustard gold in his striped tie, and my mother thought them both hideous, his socks and his tie, him and Nan, Nan and herself, all of it.

"It came as a shock to all of us, so if you'd like to talk about it, we can."

"She admired what she thought she knew. She invented everything—people, places, stories to go with them. She knew very little about me."

"Was that by choice? Your choice?"

"That's a dicey word around here," Mom said. "It's a setup. You give us the illusion of choice, free will, all that bullshit, when all the while you're watching to see what we'll choose so you can use it as leverage for another assessment."

"You've developed a very cynical take on things over the past few weeks." Dr. Shah made notations, but the pen was running out of ink. He shook it, jotted what he could, then tossed it into the trash and plucked another one from the cup on his desk. "That has me concerned. Your cognitive function is outstanding, a complete turnaround from our first meeting a few weeks ago, but your ideas, your views . . ." He hadn't looked up from the notepad and sat scribbling afterthoughts as he spoke. "Paranoia besets us all in one way or another. It can appear in small healthy doses as foresight, or a hunch." He looked up at her and shrugged. "Will I get hit by a car if I cross a busy street against the light? Or my spouse might be upset with me if I don't make the mortgage payment on time. Or, maybe I shouldn't eat a burger that's undercooked for fear of bacteria. Self-preservation and conflict avoidance are common, rightful motivators. But when does it cross into something else, something irrational?"

"You're the shrink. You tell me. It's not like you won't, anyway, so knock yourself out. I've got nowhere to be. Well, I do," my mother said with an irritated glance to the ceiling. "But so far that hasn't been a consideration, so do your thing." She folded her hands in her lap and waited.

Dr. Shah smiled and pointed at her with the new pen. "You see? That right there." He chuckled. "What is it you're trying to protect yourself from, Jolán? You're very good at using defensive sarcasm to deflect uncomfortable dialogue. You don't want to participate in this discussion, and that's okay. But until you and I can find some equilibrium here, I'll have no choice but to recommend continued treatment. I cannot assess a blank page, a closed book, an empty plate as anything other than unresponsive. You're giving me nothing else."

"You've dismissed everything I've tried to tell you as denial, or what did you call it? Dissociation?" she said. "I told you the overdose was an accident. I told you the medication was making me nuts—"

"And we rectified that," he insisted kindly. "The Risperdal's done wonders. You're participating in activities, you're socializing, your mood has stabilized. You've had your partner here to see you three times since we took you off the Haldol, and those visits have gone well. There's a lot to be encouraged about. Don't think I haven't seen it. But this bitter refusal to address the underlying issues is a problem, and those issues are what brought you here in the first place. If I were a physician, and you'd come to me with pneumonia, a sprained ankle, and a broken finger, what good would it do to fix your ankle and finger and send you on your way, having done nothing about the pneumonia? Think about it. You're addicted to heroin, but *why?* You've got a history with cocaine as well, with marijuana, alcohol, anything to build a wall between Jolán and herself." He pointed at her with an enthusiastic finger, as if having made some monumental breakthrough. "But beneath all that—the drugs, the drinking—who is Jolán De Carlo? That's what we need to talk about before I can even think about releasing you."

My mother looked away from him and swept her eyes over the golfing photos and trophies on the shelves, the pictures of his sons, the empty wooden coat rack in the corner beside a gold-framed Kandinsky on the east wall—scattered geometry, linear intersections and perfect circles and checkered triangles all trying to coexist, too many acute angles, the muted colors didn't know what to do with themselves.

"What do you wanna know?" she asked. "Where I grew up? How I grew up? When I shot my first dose? My favorite flavor ice cream?"

"We can discuss whatever you like. Ice cream's not a bad place to start." He was trying to be lighthearted and smiled at that, but my mother felt like an insect in a jar, and she glanced at the digital clock on his desk; thirty-six more minutes, at least.

She had to be careful with her wording. So much had been misconstrued upon admission to this place, and now it was all a precarious game of semantics. "Butter Brickle."

"Come again?" He turned an ear to her, puzzled.

"My favorite ice cream," she said. "Haven't had any in a long time, though, could never find it out here. Must be an east coast thing. Now you know something you didn't."

"You miss home?" he asked. "Sounds nostalgic, the ice cream."

Mom lowered her eyes to the green carpet and thought about that. He found ways to pull her into loaded conversations, whether she wanted it or not, and so she told him, "Home is a memory, no more nostalgic than any other. My home is Hollywood now. Rachel is my home."

"That's quite a lot of stock to put in one person."

"Maybe. But she earned it. She's the only one who even tried."

"Between the two of you?"

Mom flinched her brow, a quick little frown. She rested her arms on the chair and crossed an ankle over her knee and said, "What would *you* know about it? I give my share in the relationship, I do my part."

"I guess that's where I'm a bit hazy—your part. You told me last session that she's never used."

"I told you she never used dope, heroin. She's had her fun with everything else, no different than me."

"I don't know, Jolán." Dr. Shah sighed and made himself comfortable where he sat gazing down into his notes. He looked up at her. "She seems very different from you. Not that that's a bad thing. But in the context of addiction and the costs it's had against your relationships, *your part* seems to have been . . . well . . . the least cost effective, don't you think?"

"I don't even know what you just said. Speak English."

Dr. Shah smiled. "Your choices have taken a toll on your relationships, and you've taxed everyone to death with the consequences. Overdoses, hospitals, financial problems. You spend freely, indulge in whatever drugs you want at any cost, and those around you pick up the tab in pain and heartache. There's certainly some narcissism to be addressed there, some definite manic behavior. What about the depression? When did that start?"

"I feel fine now. Isn't that what matters?"

"It matters to me that you're honest with yourself. It's the only way you can be honest with me. You said you've had trouble achieving your goals in the past. Depression certainly doesn't help that."

"I don't know where it came from. Okay? I was fine, handled things as they came, but then it just fell apart."

"What fell apart?"

"Everything, shit. Matty died, and the whole damned picture burst into flames. There was nothin left after that. Just me and Rache. No music, no band, no money, just the money we had left from the advance, and yeah, I spent it. I shot most of it up my arms, but it helped."

"How so? How did it seem to be helping you at the time?"

"The guilt wasn't guilt anymore. It wasn't anything. I was insulated very nicely, and I liked it that way."

"So, you no longer feel that your friend was deliberately poisoned."

"I never said that."

"But you did." He reached back to his desk for a manila folder, my mother's case file, and he flipped it open in his lap and read aloud from the intake interview. " 'Patient is exhibiting paranoid tendencies, fears she will be poisoned by foreign drug cartels.' " He shut the folder and peered across at her expectantly.

"I was speaking metaphorically," my mother said.

"Which is common in schizophrenia, you do realize."

"Yeah, I got a crash course from Nan. I'm not paranoid and I'm not schizophrenic, just because I use a figure of speech. I remember that conversation, and by poisoned I meant the dope he got was cut with something deadly, something he wasn't familiar with, and it killed him. I don't believe in MI-5000 or neural transmitters routed to the CIA, so can we please move on to another subject?"

Dr. Shah wrote things down. Then he put the case folder back on the desk. "Why do you feel guilty about your friend's overdose? I'm assuming he made his own decision to use, so where does this guilt stem from?"

"I turned him on to smack in August of last year," she said. "And the only smack I should've given him was across the face. He was one of my best friends, and we thought we were having fun, just playin a game, but I might as well have pushed him in front of a train and called it Mother-May-I. Does that explain it for you?"

"Yet, you continued to use heroin yourself, never sought treatment, even after a crisis that cost you everything, as you say. His death seemed to be the catalyst for a series of misadventures thereafter. But what about prior to then? You've been very obstinate about not contacting your parents since you've been at Westlake. Where did they fit into the picture, say, a year ago? Two years ago?"

"They didn't."

"Was that your choice or theirs?"

"It's been a mutual decision. We have different ideas about who I'm supposed to be. They don't get to define me, anymore, and until I change my mind about that, they want no part of my life."

"And how does that make you feel?"

"How does it make *you* feel?"

"It makes me very concerned about your coping methods."

Mom let out a little humorless breath and looked past him into the sun-kindled window, a thick screen meshed behind the bars; she thought it ironic that even his windows were locked from the outside.

"It gives me cause to think that some of the psychiatric issues you came here with have roots in your familial relations," Dr. Shah said. "I think it's why you turned to drugs and alcohol in the first place, classic self-medication, and I think it's why you ultimately chose the career path you chose; it was the ideal cover, the perfect genre. No one would expect the rock musician to be anything *but* troubled, it sells, particularly now. Plenty of escape mechanisms to choose from; they're everywhere in that scene, and you found them. What would have been available to you in the classical world? Maybe the very same drugs, but I'm thinking the addicted virtuoso would've been a much harder sell, too much work to keep up appearances and expectations; it demanded conformity, too much self-discipline. And so did your parents. I can see, just from your stay here at Westlake, that boundaries make you defiant, rebellious, but it's only within certain boundaries that you'll ever find your parents' approval, their love and acceptance. It's quite an emotional quandary, seeing as now your significant other has set some boundaries as well, and it seems she's been trying to establish them for quite a while. So how, then, can Jolán have it both ways? To enjoy the love and approval of those closest to her while still living freely out on the fringe? It just isn't possible. And so all that turmoil and internal conflict continues to grind and churn and deepen your depression, which, in turn, triggers the psychiatric illnesses that you've been alleviating through substance abuse. It's a formula I've seen a hundred times."

My mother stared at him for a long moment, then rolled her eyes away from him and shook her head, thinking. "Well, at least you believe I'm an actual musician now," she finally said. "You're making some progress, and that's good." She smiled a little at her own irony, knowing it made her sound arrogant, but she didn't care; it was true. "I think your analysis is kind of a reach, but you gotta do your job, draw your parallels and all that, paint by numbers and make everything fit, right?"

"Yeah, well they're your colors, your numbers." He smiled back. "I'm just the guy with the brush. And now that we're clear that you're not a member of Pearl Jam, I think we might make even more progress."

Mom grinned and chuckled at that. "See, again—I never said that. I never once believed that. Your admissions chick put that together. I had opportunities, yes. Unbelievable opportunities, once in a lifetime shot. And if things had gone differently, I'd be in Calgary right now, setting up for sound check at the Saddledome, not here, trying to convince some shrink in a mental hospital that I know I'm not Eddie Vedder."

"But you *are* here," he said. "Things went the way they went, and though the medication has been a tremendous help in grounding your ideations, in curbing some of that grandiosity, there's still work to do."

"The medication, huh?" Mom half shook her head, thinking the secret thought that she hadn't actually taken it for the past ten days. "You might think it helps, but I'll tell you, your medication leaves a hell of a lot to be desired."

"That's an interesting statement." Dr. Shah wrote that down. "What do you desire most from this treatment, exactly? What do you hope to achieve here?"

"Freedom."

"From?"

"Westlake."

"That would be a shared goal," he agreed. "Anything else?"

"What else is there?"

He shrugged, tapped the pen against his chin as he searched for a response. "Well, there's always your future. Not just the immediate future; I mean, the person you'll be able to call yourself in fifteen, twenty years from now. She's certainly worth devoting some time to, don't you think?"

"She'll look back on this conversation and cringe. That, I can promise you. She'll look back on this entire experience and pretend it never even happened."

"And you think you'll benefit from that how?"

Mom laughed lightly. "Hell if I know. But I'm sure it'll be in everyone's best interest whenever the time comes." She was going to append to that and say "if that time comes," a morbid reference just to be sardonic, but her better mind said to hold her tongue.

"Tell me about your goals," Dr. Shah said. "When you're released from here, what do you plan to do with yourself? How do you plan to stay mentally healthy if nobody's there to monitor that?"

"Rachel will make sure. She'll see it as a new project, work up a regimen, make a chart, and tack it to the refrigerator, drag me outa bed every day at six a.m. She likes that kind of thing."

"And do you think that's fair?"

Mom frowned, shrugged. "What's that mean, fair? How is it *unfair?*"

Dr. Shah shifted in his seat and thought about it at length. "Well, it just seems to me you're very co-dependent upon Rachel and how *Rachel* is going to keep you stable. Already, your plan to stay healthy is to let her do most of the legwork, and I don't see how that can be beneficial. It makes me question your commitment entirely."

It seemed she might do better to play this by Westlake standards, and so she walked all that back and told him instead, "I just meant she'll like being a part of the process. I can handle my own aftercare, if that's what you're asking. I gotta get a job, start practicing again, maybe find a new band, see if I can transfer my credits from Berklee to USC and get my Masters. She starts back to school in a couple weeks, too; it's her last semester, so I'll have to be my own best friend most of the time, but that's nothing new for us."

"It all sounds very optimistic," he said. "It's the 'nothing new' part that gives me pause. It'll be very new. You'll have weekly out-patient therapy to keep up with, prescriptions to take, group therapy once a month. Any of that goes to the wayside and, at best, you'll be setting yourself up for another trip back here to Santa Clarita. Worst case? Well, I think you have a very good idea what that could be. I think you have something to offer, a hopeful future. Bipolar Disorder doesn't have to be crippling as long as you take the medication. I think we've got the psychotic features pretty well isolated with the Risperdal, and the dissociation can be managed with therapy, but only if you do the work. Now, I'm not an addiction specialist, but I'll give you some advice—leave it alone. You can call yourself seventeen days clean, at this point, so don't screw that up. Your CT scans came back normal, so whatever psychiatric issues you'd developed over time were worsened by heroin use. Stay away from it. Stay away from coke, psychedelics, opiates, and alcohol. Booze and beer will not mix with antipsychotics, it's an easy way to do yourself in, and I wanna believe we're past all that."

She had so much to say in response but thought it would be best to keep her mouth shut, and so she just sat listening and nodding, letting him form his flawed diagnosis while he talked himself into a release date and, at last, jotted down a post-Westlake treatment plan.

IT WAS A ninety-degree Monday, three days later, when she packed up her things, signed her discharge papers, and met Rachel out in the hospital parking lot. My mother kept her back to the Westlake entrance, never gave so much as a parting glance as she slung her gym bag onto her shoulder and headed across the lot. Rachel stood waiting by the Nissan, smiling in her denim cut-offs and tie-dyed t-shirt, the August sun golden and radiant on her face, and in that moment, she was the most beautiful thing my mother had ever seen.

WHEN THEY GOT back to the apartment, they couldn't undress each other fast enough and spent the remainder of the day making love the way they did in Catalina, sweet honeysuckle incense dwindling on the dresser top, dusk falling beyond the bedroom blinds. Sobriety was a first-rate aphrodisiac, the open floodgate for all the sensations and sentiments my mother had forgotten over the months, and she wondered how she had ever forsaken such an extraordinary feeling.

Deep kisses and fingers interlaced, the smooth bare skin of a thigh pressed against another, my mother's arm curled under Rachel's waist, pulling her in close, golden green and mahogany getting acquainted all over again as Santana played "Samba Pa Ti" on the bedroom stereo. It was the first time my mother had truly smiled since May.

Rachel pressed her lips tight to my mother's cheek where she lay beneath her, fingers buried in my mother's curls. "Don't you ever leave me like that again," she whispered. "I'll never forgive you."

Mom rested her head on Rachel's chest. Then she leaned down and kissed her stomach. "I'll be on my best behavior. I promise."

"Don't promise," Rachel said, twining a ringlet around her finger. "Just do. There's so much to fix now. The money, your career, us. I need you to be present, to be in this *with* me."

"I can see if they're hiring at Guitar Center, check the ads in the *LA Weekly*, maybe find some studio work." Mom traced a finger around the edge of Rachel's navel, kissed her there. "We'll be fine."

"How are you feeling?"

"In what sense?" Mom rolled onto her side so she could look at Rachel directly.

"In every sense. Physically, mentally. Just two weeks ago you were speaking in riddles, and a week before that you spent two days on a ventilator. I don't want you to push yourself. Tell me if it's too soon, if you need more time to recuperate, and I'll pick up more shifts at the bar."

"I'm good." My mother smiled at her and propped her head in her hand. "I've been through the worst of it. As long as I'm home, here with you, I'm invincible."

"I swear that word has gotten you into the worst trouble. But you should be pretty well hobbled now," Rachel noted. "I threw everything out when I knew you were coming home, just so you know. The needles, what was left of your dope, that rubber tourniquet thing, all of it. Trashed, flushed forever."

It was for the best, but the thought still made something tremble in my mother's stomach, a little flutter of panic, but she dismissed it because what else could she do? Love would always have her by the throat, and addiction was no less ruthless. She shrugged a shoulder and said, "Let the sewer have it, then. It was all for shit, anyway, right?"

"I know this is gonna be hard, Jo. I'm not that naïve. But I want this to work, this fresh start we have now. No more dope, and no more fights."

My mother leaned over and kissed her lips. "No more."

AUGUST FADED INTO September, and Rachel had started back to USC. She took morning classes and worked at the Regal Blue four nights a week. My mother never filled the Risperdal or the Ativan prescriptions and ignored the appointments with Dr. Canady, the outpatient psychiatrist recommended by Westlake. She kept her own head together and managed to land a job at Amoeba Records in West Hollywood. It was an enormous, two-story, independent record store with graffiti murals, thousands of titles, and a small stage on the main floor for free live music.

Management liked her immediately, recognized her from her days with Portland Downs, and they appreciated her extensive knowledge of everything from Paganini to Muddy Waters. My mother liked the fact that the dress code was flexible; she could wear whatever she wanted, and that made it easier to hide the track marks on her arms, which were slowly vanishing but noticeable, still.

By the middle of September, she had forty days clean to her credit, and though she was surrounded by dope triggers of all varieties, she kept herself busy and found ways to ignore the pangs of addiction by thinking about Rachel, and Dr. Shah, and the yellow-painted cinder blocks of Cell 16.

She faced a daily barrage of the most obscure reminders. The smell of wet paint when the apartment maintenance men had gone around touching up the outer doorjambs and hallway railings. Grand Funk Railroad's *Closer to Home* album that her co-worker Deliah liked to play in the mornings before the store opened. The most frustrating was the taste of peanut butter; she had to eliminate that from her diet altogether and could only attribute it to all the peanut butter and jelly sandwiches they'd eaten while touring in the RV last summer.

There were the things she wouldn't give up and probably should have—the cigarettes and the occasional cold Guinness after work. She'd sworn off hard liquor but made a proposition to Rachel that, as long as she didn't buy it from Wade, she'd like to smoke an occasional bowl of weed when the heroin cravings made her crazy with anxiety.

Rachel reluctantly agreed and went about finding her own connections at work. It wasn't Rafe's spiced velvet Indigo or Wade's powerful Chronic, just some kitchen cook's homegrown shwag, but he packed his dime bags fat and full and he was discreet, just a quick little hand off between the two of them at his truck after closing.

Wade's appearances had been sparse and usually from a friendly distance, a wave on the way to his car if my mother happened to be out front at the time, the sound of his music coming from the open window between the buildings. After his and Rachel's encounter back in July, he was more than compliant and kept to himself.

ON THE LAST Friday in September, Rachel organized a get together to celebrate my mother's first eight weeks heroin free. It was a small gathering, just a few select friends from Amoeba and the Regal Blue, the ones who had been trustworthy and supportive, and at seven that evening everyone showed up. Miranda from the bar baked a batch of little coin-sized sugar cookies, dyed in the various colors of sobriety chips with the number fifty-six drawn in sprinkles on each, and Mom's co-worker Deliah brought a bottle of non-alcoholic champagne, to which my mother responded with a case of Budweiser.

"One vice at time," she told her with a wily smirk and a wink. "I've parted ways with dope, but me and Anheuser-Busch are still pretty good friends."

Then there was Kyle, another record store co-worker, and Kyle had four years clean from cocaine. He'd gone to treatment, there in LA. Kyle Nolen saw my mother coming from a thousand miles away, knew the moment she walked through Amoeba's doors that she was a smackhead, likely trying to make an awkward go at sobriety; he'd seen it too many times, the distracted uneasiness, the loneliness and preoccupation that hovered around a struggling addict as if they were in some kind of mourning.

He and my mother bonded within the first week, and after a few lunch hours spent talking at Jack in the Box across the street, their conversations eventually evolved into shared stories of addiction. She told him about Bryce and Denver and Matt's death in May. She told him she herself had overdosed, but she left out the St. Thomas drama and the ordeal at Westlake. He was a nice guy, and she liked him. She didn't want to scare him off with stories of antipsychotics and four-point restraints, even if it was all just a comedy of errors.

She told him of her previous attempts to quit using, that they were halfhearted and unsuccessful, but this time she had more to hope for, to strive for; she had finally hit bottom and had no other choice but to start scaling the walls back to the surface again.

"Well, you're in for a hell of a fight without a program," Kyle advised after hearing that. "It's a deep dark trek through a million-mile forest without a map or a compass. You get lucky—maybe you find your way out by following your nose. Have fun with that; it's a long shot."

"I know what I gotta do," she told him. "I know my own weaknesses, and I'll just have to steer clear. Common sense and willpower. That's all it takes."

"If you say so." He pulled his wallet from his pocket and fingered through the compartments until he produced a tattered business card, and he handed it across the restaurant table: *Noreen Palomar, Program Director. The Cedarbrook Center for Substance Abuse and Family Support Services. 3618 Los Feliz Blvd., Glendale, CA.* "Just in case you lose your way."

Mom put it in her jeans pocket, but she'd since lost track of it and figured it had likely gotten mangled by the washing machine. She appreciated his intentions, but no one understood her habit as well as she.

KYLE SHOWED UP at the get together with his boyfriend Donald, a surgical technician at the Medical Center in Torrance. Donald was also a guitarist and played on the weekends with a local funk band called Charlemagne, and he brought with him a twelve-string Takamine electric/acoustic with the black-and-gold sunburst body and solid ebony fretboard.

My mother thought she'd lose continence right there on the living room floor when he took it from its case, it was so beautiful, two thousand dollars on the low end, the Rolls Royce of acoustic guitars. She reached for it like a newborn, her eyes glazing over with a musician's lust. "May I?"

"I'd be honored." Donald offered it over.

He was a slender black man in his early thirties, clean shaven and sharply dressed, his hair sculpted in a perfect flattop fade. He and Kyle had been together for eight years, and though Kyle was a stocky blonde white guy with a very limited fashion sense, their years together had somehow made them look alike. The most interesting thing about them, my mother thought, was their plan to adopt a two-year-old little girl from Thailand. They were in the final phases with the adoption agency, and it was all Kyle ever talked about at work.

"Kyle tells me you're a phenom," Donald said to Mom, "made a hellacious name for yourself around the southwest, so maybe some of that'll rub off on me if you play around with it long enough."

"He's exaggerating," Mom said from her seat on the opposite couch, the Takamine wrapped in her arms like a lover. She plucked arpeggios and tested the action along the frets with lightning fingerwork.

"Exaggerating, my ass," Miranda said, lighting up a cigarette as she took a seat next to Donald. "Her old band played The Regal Blue last summer and blew the roof off the place. Your hubby tells no lies."

Mom looked up at Donald and gave him a sly grin and cocked an eyebrow. "You're gonna have to wrestle me to get this thing back, you know that, right?" She chuckled to herself and strummed a pretty chord. "Man, what a gorgeous thing you are," she uttered to the instrument. "You wanna come live with your Auntie Jo-Jo? Trade places with that Gibson over there?" She tipped her chin to her own twelve-string leaning in its stand by the fireplace.

Donald laughed and swigged his beer. "I'll tell you what. Teach me some of those licks you're doing right now, and I'll trade you for the weekend."

Mom gave him a preposterous glance. "You don't have to do that, I was joking."

"Hey, I know where to find you now. The offer's always open if you want it."

Rachel, Deliah, and Kyle came out of the kitchen, carrying bowls of salsa dip and tortilla chips and cold beers.

Rachel saw Mom with the Takamine and smiled. "New toy?" She

looked at Donald. "You know you're not gonna get that thing back for the rest of the night, right?"

"I'm considering babysitting it until Monday," Mom told her with a crooked smirk. "The next best thing to a new puppy."

Rachel eyed her sideways and spread napkins on the coffee table. "We're not getting a puppy."

Pink Floyd's *Animals* album was playing on the stereo, and Mom strummed along and did little improvised solos, marveling and gushing over the Takamine's lush, vibrant tonality. She offered Donald the Gibson, and the two of them played a spontaneous duet while everyone chatted about work and school.

Kyle told stories about his and Donald's trip to the orphanage in Nonthaburi, just northeast of Bangkok. He said they chose Achara the moment they saw her and even got to share an afternoon playing dolls while an interpreter mediated and worked up all the documentation. It was an expensive undertaking, and Donald would have to be the primary sponsor; he made more money than Kyle, and they hadn't yet divulged to the agency the nature of their relationship.

Rachel found the whole thing intriguing, and she tugged at my mother's arm. "We should think about that when we get ourselves settled. Once you get your career going, and I find a job with a publisher. I wanna have my own kids, but later we should look into adoption. Down the road, maybe."

Mom nodded. "Down the road. Once we have our shit together again. We've got a hole to climb out of right now, but yeah, someday that'd be nice."

Rachel kissed her cheek and went on to tell the story of how she and my mother met, the night she soaked Mom's lap with a trayful of top shelf liquor. She censored out all the drug memories and recounted only the good things, their adventures in Tijuana, hot air balloon rides over the New Mexican desert, and the bright yellow aspens in the Colorado Rockies.

Everybody already knew the worst of what had happened. Tonight they wanted to focus on the better moments, and so Rachel gave my mother a suggestion.

"I think you should play 'Rise' for them. Remember? You played it in Albuquerque at The Arroyo. It's your best piece."

Mom looked unsure, self-conscious and hesitant. It was a complicated song, and she still felt a bit rusty, but Rachel draped an arm across her shoulders and nuzzled persuasion into her neck.

"Baby, please?" she whispered. "It's my favorite, and Miranda's never heard it." She kissed my mother's ear lobe. "Please? For me?"

"People didn't come here for a concert, honey," Mom said. "They came to hang out. Besides, I need my capo for that. If it's not upstairs in my guitar case, then I'll have to go looking for it, and we have company."

"Then look around for it. They won't mind." Rachel kissed her again. Then she said to the others, "You haven't heard her play until you've heard her play *that*. At The Arroyo—standing ovation. The place went *nuts*, no shit." She turned back to Mom and lobbied again. "Come on, baby, you guys are already playing. You've been playing for the last half hour. Since when did *you* become so shy?"

By now, everyone else was prodding her to perform, and so she took the last drag of her cigarette and a swig of beer and conceded. "Okay, all right. Fine. Lemme go take a piss first, and I'll be back." She kissed Rachel's hair and then headed up the stairs.

THE BATHROOM. IT was her least favorite place in the house now. Everything about it was a trigger—the shiny black shower curtain with its giant lily print, the wooden toilet seat, the black shag bath mat. She could still smell Rachel's hair spray and perfume lingering in the pores of the eggshell plaster, the only pleasant thing the room had going for it. She'd been showering and doing all other business in there for the past month, and still, she couldn't quite shake the cravings it seemed to generate.

It made her sad, angry that she'd ruined this simple space meant for cleansing and solitude. Such a stupid disappointment, she thought. How absurd. But if she could've peed in the kitchen sink and showered with the spray nozzle, she probably would have preferred that now. She zipped herself up and went to the sink to wash her hands.

In the mirror, she saw a much healthier woman than she once did, and that was good. Her color had returned, and her cheeks were fuller. The bags beneath her eyes were stubborn, but the hazel had gotten its sparkle back, making her long lashes pretty again, and she liked that. She stood there examining her reflection for a long time, and after a while she found herself thinking of Yvette, the medical assistant from St. Thomas. She could still hear her, speaking through the Ativan fog in ICU: "Be back on your feet before you know it, *mujer*. Change your life around, make a big comeback . . ."

Mom shut the water off and dried her hands. "I sure as hell hope so," she said to her herself and then headed out into the hall.

IN THE BEDROOM, she went straight to the closet and pushed aside the hanging clothes where the Gibson case stood leaning in the corner. She dragged it out and dropped it onto the bed and opened it. Bright red velvet. String packs and spare picks. Her electric tuner. She found her thumb pick in the flip-top compartment, but no capo. She put the case back and went into the spare room where the Fender case was propped against the wall beside Rachel's desk. The Stratocaster was still in it, so she laid the instrument aside and fumbled around through those compartments as well. Nothing. She sat crouched on the hardwood, thinking. Then she put the Fender away and went back into the bedroom.

She remembered having an extra equipment bag that should've been on the closet shelf if Rachel hadn't moved it, so she searched around again and found it, a black padded gig bag, no bigger than a shoebox. She hadn't used it much while in LA, but it was worth a shot.

She unzipped it and found another tuner, a spare vibrato bar for the Stratocaster, two more string packs, and a ziplock baggie full of extra tuning pegs. There were solid chrome pegs and pegs with dice patterns and a full set of gunmetal gray ones that she'd forgotten all about. It was a good find, and she set them aside, but there was still no capo.

The bag had one more zippered pocket that she hadn't yet checked, and so she opened it and stuck her hand inside and felt around. She fished out its contents and then stood there, staring at a soft leather glasses case. Something quivered in her gut.

Downstairs, Miranda and Kyle laughed aloud, and everyone was talking while Donald played something that sounded like Hank Williams. It clashed terribly with the Alice In Chains drifting from Wade's apartment across the breezeway.

My mother took the little brown case and went over to the bed and sat with it, feeling suddenly apprehensive and very dismal. The case was meant to contain sunglasses, the fifty dollar aviator shades she'd purchased on Haight Street in San Francisco last June. But now that was pretty much a coin toss. She unsnapped the leather flap and breathed a miserable sigh because she knew herself very well; she knew herself much better than Rachel ever would.

She tipped the case sideways and let everything fall into her palm—the clean stainless steel spoon, an extra tourniquet, the brand new unsoiled rig still in the packaging, and a ball of Black Tar heroin about the size of a grape, about four doses worth, wrapped and twist tied in a slick sheet of cellophane. Many months back, there had been a prophetic moment in which she'd thought she was thinking ahead, doing herself a favor. A junkie's frantic treasure hunt in the throes of desperation needed a prize, and she had just found it.

"Well, now," she said lowly.

She sat holding the little ball of Tar between her fingers, staring at it in the dim bedside lamp light, thinking for a very long while about nothing. She listened to her guests and her girlfriend chatter about whose staff had the laziest workers and which managers played favorites. It all sounded like they were speaking Chinese, and the bedroom seemed to be getting smaller, and the eightball of heroin in my mother's hand felt like an explosive device, as if she were holding down some safety lever to keep it from turning her to pink mist.

She should get rid of it, the whole damned thing, just put it all back in the case and chuck it. Fifty-six days. It wasn't four years, but it was a start, their fresh new start. They were going to buy a house one day, with a wraparound porch and floor-to-ceiling picture windows, and they'd fill it with children, maybe two or three from Rachel and another few from Thailand, or Malaysia.

My mother toyed with the needle and syringe. She held them up to the light for a good look and nodded. She should definitely get rid of it, all of it. She flipped open the glasses case and stuffed everything back inside and snapped it shut. Then she shoved it into the waistband of her jeans and covered it with her t-shirt. There was a garbage chute at the end of the third floor hall. It would be impossible to retrieve it; once it was gone, it was gone. She got up from the bed and started for the stairs. She could do this. She would do this.

"Hey, babe. Find your guitar thingy?" Rachel asked as my mother came through the living room.

She kept going and didn't answer.

Rachel frowned and called after her. "You okay?"

"Yep." Mom gave her a quick smile from the doorway. "Couldn't find it. Just gonna go check the car." And she shut the door behind her.

It was very easy. Just seventeen steps to the far end of the hall. She pulled open the receptacle lid and dug the pouch from her pants and stood at the black empty hole in the wall, a grimy steel tunnel, disappearing down into the back dumpster. She held the trapdoor with one hand, the dope stash in the other. After a moment, she lay the case at the edge of the chute and let it sit there.

Now, just drop the lid. Go on, let it go. Let it swing shut and be done with it. For Christ's sake, don't be stupid, you've got guests, fifty-six days and counting. She stood looking at it for a long time. And then she did it. She shut the lid and walked away and left it to tumble down into the darkness for good.

When she got halfway down the hall, she stopped. She turned around and stood there, thinking, music and voices coming through the walls. She went back to the chute again, and when she opened the lid, it was still there. Maybe it just needed a little push, or a good toss.

She grabbed it up and looked at it for a very long while, listening to the muffled television of the adjacent unit, a dog barking in the one next door to that one. She opened the trapdoor again, stared deep into the darkness, and then shut it. Then she tucked the case back into her waistband, covered it with her t-shirt, and headed back down to the apartment.

chapter twenty-four

SHE NEVER SAID a word. She turned herself into a dream and vanished so meticulously, it was as if we had never even happened. I can't remember if I'd said I was sorry. I can't remember if I was sorry. I remember her calling my name. I remember her hands. I remember porcelain and huge white lilies and the scent of opium and leather, her purse on the bathroom floor, water running in the sink.

She wasn't supposed to be there, I remember that. God only knows why. A cancelled class, maybe. An early exam day. A useless speculation now. She performed her final rites, washed away the blood, set my head upon a pillow. She had stumbled into a catastrophe and took it for what it was and went about cleaning up the debris, emptying the dresser drawers, the closets, the nightstand, and when she was finished, there was nothing left of us but the things I would remember, moments encased in glass, each one floating in its own little snow globe.

When the finance company came for the Nissan, I would remember driving to Hollywood and Vine the previous week and waiting there until 3 a.m., working up petitions and making resolutions in my head because I could fix us, if only she would listen, if only she would give me another chance—if only she had been there. She was already gone, Miranda said at the driver's side window, back to Ohio, back to her life before me, and I would remember absolutely nothing after that until they turned the electricity off. Then I would remember making an afternoon of something bill collectors call skip-tracing; you try the obvious first, long-distance 4-1-1 for the nearest relative, but all I had was her mother's name, and that was unlisted, so I asked for a list of Akron's cleaning companies, but I needed to be more specific and had no idea how. No such listing for a Cole's Cleaning. Sonya's Cleaning? SC Cleaning, maybe? "I'm sorry, I have no listing for either. Is there anything else I can assist you with today?" A local skywriting company might be useful, I said before I hung up, and I'd have done it if things had been different. I'd have begged for forgiveness from 10,000 feet above the Akron treetops, all my love and sadness evaporating in a blue Midwestern sky.

Funny, amid all this remembering I had forgotten many things. I had forgotten to go to work, and so work had forgotten about me. I had forgotten it was almost January and that the lease was up. I had forgotten what it felt like to be in love, to be in pain, to be buried in a shit-ton of *addicted trouble with no one left as an ally except for Wade next door. I had $574 to my name and a decision to make. I chose poorly, but Wade was a sympathetic soul, and what did it matter now? Seventy-two hours before they'd change the locks, so said the yellow notice on my door, but that was time enough. Wade knew people, and he had a contact with a pickup truck and a thousand bucks, and the guy wouldn't have gotten a better deal if he'd won a contest. His name was Robert, and Robert helped Wade carry the Pioneer and its five surround speakers down to the curb, and he loaded the kitchen appliances and my guitar amps and Rachel's writing desk into the truck bed, too, and padded everything with blankets while Wade boxed up the CDs and VCR tapes. Robert took the Stratocaster and left me the 12-string and five $100 bills. He came back the next morning for the living room suite. I stuffed clothes and pictures and journals into trash bags and dragged them over to Wade's and went back out for the other $500 at the open tailgate of Robert's truck, and then it was done. I had secured nearly a month's worth of Black, and now Wade had a new roommate.*

On Valentine's Day I would remember the last Valentine's Day, when dusk was falling across the San Bernardino Mountains, our eastern balcony view from Author's Row at the Mission Inn in Riverside. Red gladiolas spilled through the wrought iron balustrades, overlooking the Spanish Patio with its Carmine umbrella tables and trickling marble fountains. We were under-dressed, but we didn't care. We took dinner on the Patio in our jeans and hemp shirts and drank too much Port wine and sat dreaming aloud of all the possibilities at our disposal, the glittering fortune we stood to make if everything played out. She had placed herself in my undependable hands. She was gathering false hopes, laying up disillusions, nesting in a home built on quicksand. And on that same evening we would make love to the sound of our own lovemaking, composing the sentimental melodies of us, a mezzo-piano adagio that lasted for hours until she lay sleeping in my arms, and I would remember holding her there, thinking how fortunate I was that she would take me as is, that she hadn't lost faith in us, and that all I needed now was to believe as thoroughly as she.

I spent the one-year anniversary of that night discovering things about myself that I would never understand until months later. I might be inclined to call it desperation, but that would imply a certain justifiable helplessness, like necro-cannibalism when one is shipwrecked and marooned, or shooting the neighbor's dog because it has a 2-year-old by the throat. To clarify all this in proper context, I should explain first that it had taken three weeks after moving in with Wade to slam $1000 into my left thigh, as the last reliable vein in my wrist had finally collapsed and vanished. For the week after that, he extended me $200 credit and *called it a belated Christmas present, but then that was gone, too. His trust and hospitality were remarkable for a guy whose affections had been hitting an unrequited wall over the past year. I slept on his couch, ate his food, watched his television, listened to his stereo, smoked his cigarettes, smoked his weed, drank his beer, threw my clothes into his laundry basket and washed them in the basement with a $10 roll of his quarters—I'd been there for almost a month, and he never touched me, so the laundry was the least I could do.*

It was three days before Valentine's Day when I had no choice but to trade him the 12-string for another gram. He didn't like the idea and instead saw himself as a kind of personal pawnbroker, promising to sell the instrument right back for $80 whenever I could spare it. In what future would that have been possible? Neither of us knew.

Valentine's Day was uncomfortable in every sense. Wade had gone out on a delivery that morning, and he came back with a single white rose in a red crystal bud vase and placed it on the coffee table with a satisfied smile. "No reason to feel like shit today. At least you haven't chased me off yet." He was trying to be charming, and if I were a straight woman, it might have gone over nicely . . . if I were a straight woman who wasn't quite so strung out, and unemployed, and penniless, and about a half day away from getting dope sick. Just how long could this go on? How much was his chivalry really worth, and how long before his charity expired and I found myself rattling in the stairwell of a downtown hotel? As I said before, to call it desperation would be inaccurate—it was calculated, premeditated manipulation meant solely to keep him in play. I had a habit to feed and he kept the treats locked in an antique steamer trunk at the foot of his bed. Wouldn't you? He was a drug dealer who had opened his home to a junkie, a thief in the making, a traitor just waiting to happen. It was unheard of and, to my estimation, a provisional arrangement even under the best of circumstances. He was doing a favor for a friend until he wasn't, and I now had only one thing left of value that would undoubtedly change the definitions of "friend" and "favor," but he was in no condition to refuse, and neither was I.

His surprise was palpable but brief, much like the sex itself, and for the next two weeks I became the dope man's girlfriend for fifty bucks a ride. I had wrought my own financial destruction, witnessed the death of a dear friend, endured the estrangement of my family, suffered the loss of a soulmate, spent two days in a coma, and shuffled through the halls of the state sanitarium, and still, I would not hit bottom until the morning I glanced into Wade Tyson's bedroom mirror and saw a smack whore. All my accomplishments, the awards, the scholarships and grants, the honors and medals and trophies had culminated into that singularly defining moment, and I remember being transfixed, as if I'd never seen my own reflection before, sitting naked in a mound of blankets while he pulled on his jeans in the corner of the room. He came around and kissed my temple and left a ball of dope on the nightstand, then went out into the kitchen and started a pot of coffee.

Of course he tried to stop me when he came back to the bedroom and found me shoving clothes and other belongings into a gym bag, apologizing for everything, for leading him on, for using him, for pretending to be someone he could trust, but I had to go. I couldn't stay there, not another moment, even when he said he loved me, particularly when he'd said that. What other words could I offer in return except "I'm sorry"?

I went to the front door with blinding lucidity, frightened and sick to my stomach because I had no idea where I would go, out into Los Angeles with empty pockets and a gym bag full of dirty clothes and packets of photos and a stack of notebook journals. Wade followed me all the way down Franklin Avenue, calling after me from the open window of his Buick LaSabre, pleading his case, insisting I let him give me a ride, if nothing else, but the more he begged and lobbied the sicker I felt, the more vivid and saturated were the avocado palms, the pink stucco apartment buildings, the orange blinking crosswalk signs at Vermont where I crossed north toward Los Feliz and then lost him in the traffic at the intersection. Just walk. Go, or you'll lose your nerve, I remember telling myself, and it wasn't until I'd reached Finley Avenue that I realized where I was headed. I'd stored the address somewhere in my subconscious, I suppose, and when I finally came upon my destination, I had walked six miles, all the way into the city of Glendale.

I hesitated at the double doors. My head was empty now, but there I was, staring at my stunted reflection in the glass. A woman at the information desk saw me standing there, rethinking this, walking it all back in my mind because I suddenly wasn't ready, it was too tangible now, entirely too real, but she came around the counter anyway and opened the door and stood looking me over as if she knew something I didn't. She was a stout woman my mother's age, short salt-and-pepper hair, blue-eyes, thin lips pressed tight with an intuitive half smile. "This is just a shot in the dark, here," she said to me then. "But I'm guessing you look a lot more lost than you actually are." She said her name was Noreen, and she held the door for me as I stepped inside the Cedarbrook Center for Substance Abuse and Family Services.

I had no money, but I still had the Medi-Cal and a Blue Cross insurance card in my wallet, and they accepted all that just fine. I was given what they called a bio-psycho-social evaluation. They took my vital signs, assessed my mental state—distressed, disoriented, despondent—they asked a lot of questions about my ethnic and family background, where I grew up, my parents' occupations, my education level, my future goals, how I'd learned about the Cedarbrook facility, what was my drug of choice, how long had I been using, when was my last dose. They drew blood from my thigh to be tested for STD's. They gave me a wristband like the one at Westlake. They offered me Xanax to edge me through the withdrawals and took me to a private room on the second floor with a single bath, a recliner, a twin bed, and a television set, and I don't remember much after that except the overhead bathroom light, the bathroom fan, baby blue floor tiles, white porcelain and stomach pain, muscle pain, psychological pain, fury, regret, terror, hopelessness. Shit and vomit, blood and sweat— the same old enemies offering the same old misery.

By day four, I was through the worst of it, but now there were many other factors to consider—the relentless cravings, the relentless depression, the relentless uncertainty, the new me, which, by the second week, turned out to be a very unforeseen and unexpected variation of the old me. The blood tests had come back negative for HIV, hep-B, syphilis, gonorrhea, staph, everything except hCG. I hadn't had a period since December, and it was March, so I couldn't understand how it was possible. But according to the Cedarbrook nurse practitioner, the chemical interruption of a woman's monthly cycle does not necessarily make her infertile.

They took me to a private office and gave it to me straight. They offered me pamphlets that outlined all my options. They sat and counseled me on the effects of diacetylmorphine on an unborn fetus. They provided a list of OB/GYNs that took Blue Cross and Medi-Cal, but I had been using at the time of conception and for days on end thereafter, so the most practical decision now was to abort. I could go with Noreen in the morning and be back to the facility by lunch, pick up where I'd left off, get a do-over, a take-back, move on with my life and put these kinds of reckless blunders behind me. After all, I had acquired this condition under duress, I wasn't thinking clearly, it wasn't me; it was heroin that had done this, heroin and Wade Tyson, that's who the real parents were. I wasn't even a heterosexual, a fact which certainly doesn't disqualify one from giving birth, but that had always been Rachel's dream, not mine. I was quite content to hold her hand through delivery and pass out the cigars when it was over, and now it was me with a kid on the way? I was going to need some time to process this, and so that's what I got, as much time as I needed, they said.

That was last Thursday afternoon, and as I write this now, it's Monday morning, March 19th, 1994. I haven't slept very well, and I don't expect I will for a while. Insomnia is a dreadful symptom of post-withdrawals, but it's given me a chance to think and to write and to recount as much as I can of the past few months. I've got a room to myself now; the roommate I did have graduated to a Sober Living community yesterday, and she was a crack cocaine addict who talked incessantly, so I'm enjoying the quiet at 6 a.m.

Springtime has come early to southern California. All the sparrows and cardinals and finches are out welcoming the sunrise from the pepper tree outside my window as the smell of pancakes and bacon drifts up from the downstairs kitchen. I don't have much of an appetite, these days, and I suppose I'll need to see about a remedy for that. But first I want to get all this down while it's still fresh, while I've got some time alone to illustrate every detail of this complicated morning, because this is the morning when I have decided I'm going to keep you. My name is Jolán, Jolán Elena De Carlo, and I am your mother.

You and I have certainly got some obstacles to overcome, I'll tell you that—me, for starters. I am an irrefutable mess right now. I am two weeks clean from an eighteen-month heroin addiction, and because of that I have compromised your well-being already, before either of us even knows whether you are a boy or a girl, and for that I am profoundly remorseful. Carrying you to term will be a challenge for us both. You've got a 4% chance of having a major birth defect. You are more likely to be born prematurely and are susceptible to low birth weight. You are one of approximately 10,000 babies who will be born to heroin-addicted mothers over the next year. You have inherited my addiction and will, at some point, go through your own withdrawals, if you haven't already. But there's one thing I can tell you for certain—when I am thinking of you, I am not thinking about using, and that is, by far, the most difficult hurdle, so maybe we'll just do this thing together. I don't have much of a plan right now except to get through the rest of the day, and that's the best advice I can offer you as well—just hold on to me, and I'll hold on to you, and then we'll see where we are at lights out.

You were not immaculately conceived, not by any stretch, so I imagine you'd like to know about your father. And I imagine he'd like to know about you, too, but that is a prickly matter now. He represents things I'll do best to forget, all the death-defying catastrophes I should put behind me forever if you even hope to survive, so I'll tell you that his name is Wade Tyson and that he would have loved you, and I'll leave it at that. He has a kind heart, but he is a drug dealer by trade, and I am a drug addict by default, a disastrous combination that ultimately ended in chaos. The only good thing that ever came of our acquaintance was you, and since I know he would want me to do everything in my power to protect you, my primary job now is to protect you from myself, and your father's presence in our lives would make that utterly impossible. So again, I apologize to you both, but it is truly for the best.

I've made many terrible, terrible mistakes over the past year, and some might be inclined to think you are one of them, but don't you ever listen to a word of that. We just might save each other's lives, here, if all goes well enough, although I can't exactly say I know what I'm doing, because I don't. I have no idea how I'm gonna get this right, and the one person who might have had a better sense of direction, a steadier maternal hand, a lighter touch, is gone now, and that is my fault. She would have loved you, too, because she loved me more than I ever deserved. Maybe she still does, but I made it too difficult, and so she did what anyone in their right mind would do; she left me right where she found me last—slumped and drooling with a needle in my leg, lying half-naked in the middle of our bathroom floor. And I miss her. God, how I miss her. Now, especially. I miss the sound of her voice, I miss her hands, I miss the lines of her lips, the way she'd look at me first thing in the morning, as if I alone had made the sun come up, and I loved her like I love the sun. But those were moments shared long before I set out to ruin everything with all my toxins and meanness and self-regard, before I'd broken nearly every promise I ever made, before the drugs made a liar and a disappointment of a well-intended young musician, and I will have to atone for that.

Now, as I sit here in recovery, my future—our future—dangling by a proverbial thread, I'm thinking maybe you are that atonement, my white sheet, my marrow bones, an extraordinary opportunity for redemption. You are the one thing I could do right if I tried hard enough, and so I would be honored to have you . . . if, of course, you would be willing to have me.

RACHEL KNEW BEFORE I did. Mom told her over dinner on their second date after they reunited at Giovanni's, and for a moment, Rachel didn't know whether to walk out or reach across the table and slap my mother's face. She did neither. But she wanted to know whether it had happened before she left, if that was why my mother spent so much time with him. Even after sixteen years and a marriage of her own, it was galling, tragic, unfaithful somehow. She understood it but she didn't, and a part of her resented being privy to something so unentitled, a secret not meant for her ears, but for my mother it was a necessary release, the first step toward reparations for pushing Rachel out of her life so long ago.

The original plan was for Mom and Dad to sit me down together, sometime after Christmas, but when that fell through, Dad was left to do it himself, which he did, the weekend after I'd gotten the pictures and videos from Rachel and Uncle Cam. They all feared my mother might do precisely what she'd done and confess to my notorious conception somewhere within the pages of those twenty-year-old journals. So, before I discovered it during a break between Geometry class and P.E., Dad took me down to Piedmont Park where we walked the trails around Lake Clara Meer as he explained his puzzling place in my life.

The truth was boggling to me. I thought I'd had everything figured out, I thought I understood what had gone wrong between them, it was all supposed to make sense. I was left-handed, and so was he. I had his forehead, everyone always said. I was supposed to have inherited my disdain for onions directly from Benjamin Edmunds; he hated them, too. How many times had my mother, my grandmother, my uncle said, "You're just like your dad. You get that from your father"?

Well, which father? Had they been speaking of Wade Tyson all along, perhaps, and left me to presume otherwise because what difference would it really make? They wanted to wait until I was old enough, Dad said. There were so many dreadful, extenuating stories that he and my mother figured they'd make it a package deal, address the "say no to drugs" conversation, the sexual orientation conversation, and the truth of my own beginnings all in one sitting. But now it was just Dad and me, dressed in our sweats and windbreakers, strolling the park on a Sunday afternoon in January, 2007, a month after my mother's unexpected death. We found seats at the picnic tables, overlooking the lake as Dad went on to tell me the rest.

He said he'd known my mother since grade school, that they'd lived just two streets apart for years and that he'd developed a hopeless crush on her by the time they'd gotten into junior high. He'd ask her to the movies, to go ice skating, invite her to his birthday parties. Sometimes she went, sometimes not. He even offered to mow my grandparents' lawn every other Saturday with hopes my mother might stroll past a living room window, or better yet, wander out onto the front porch for conversation about biology homework or the latest MTV video. It was 1985 then; he was thirteen, she was fourteen.

"It was pretty pathetic, really." Dad chuckled, gazing out across the Clara Meer.

We sat with our bottled water and dried banana chips from the Farmer's Market and watched the people jogging, walking their dogs, stretching in the grass for their weekend yoga classes.

"Every one of my friends told me I was a dolt, but I just couldn't get her outa my head." He grinned at the memory of his foolishness and laughed a little. "God, she was beautiful to me. And you'd think after three years of rejection, it'd wear off, but no," he confessed with a distant smile, lost in his own Bensalem childhood, the summer after eighth grade. "Time only made it worse. And when we finally got into high school, I remember thinking I could impress her with this new dirt bike I'd bought off a friend." He laughed, embarrassed by it now. "The thing had been rebuilt, slapped together with a bunch a rusty pipes and bolts. I didn't even know how to ride it, but I was damn sure gonna learn, see if maybe she'd let me take her for a spin, I dunno. But she never did. I couldn't figure your mother out for the life of me, just couldn't get a handle on what it would take . . ." His thoughts trailed off, and he just sat looking out at the tree line, his hands clasped between his knees. I guess we both know the answer to that riddle now, and he said he knew it even then, but he thought it was a phase, just another way to tease all the other guys who'd gotten in line behind him.

"And when she came home from LA, four months pregnant with you," he recalled, "I figured I must've been right, that it was an adolescent thing, like we all thought, some kind of experimental kick she'd finally outgrown."

"So, when did you find out everything else?" I asked. "Rachel told me about a lot of it last week, about the drugs and stuff. When you guys met again after college, did you already know about . . . you know . . . rehab and all that?"

He swigged his Evian and replaced the cap. "It took a few conversations, but yeah, she eventually told me all of it. That was the one thing we could always do, we could always talk, never had a problem there. I'd heard she was back home from my dad, actually. I'd just graduated from Syracuse, myself, so my folks were having a big barbeque, invited the De Carlos, a few other neighbors. I came out onto the back deck, and *boom* . . . there she was. I'd done a little dating around in college, dated some pretty nice girls. But man, none of 'em were Jolán, not even close. She'd been through hell and back, been through all that shit and still, she was as pretty as the day she left."

"Were you nervous?" I asked.

He chuckled at that and nodded. "Yeah. I was." He picked at the label on his bottle, thinking back. "I had no idea at the time what'd happened to her out there, not yet. She seemed a little distant, though, a little out of place, I remember that. Like she had something heavy on her mind, but she loosened up after a while, and we spent some time catching up. I knew she had a band; I'd seen them play, actually, when I came home for Christmas break during my junior year, but I had no idea they'd taken the act all the way out to the west coast. Pretty gutsy. It's a hell of a long way back if things don't work out."

He stopped and just sat thinking, his nostalgic smile waning a bit, and I wondered which version of her he missed most—the one he'd fallen in love with back then, or the one who'd passed away only a month ago.

"Didn't it bother you?" I asked. "The truth. All those things she did. Rachel won't even let me read half of those journals yet, so there must've been more. You were still in love with her after all that?"

"Your mom got herself lost. She just got turned around, that's all, and she was vulnerable. She needed someone she could count on, someone who knew the real her, who wouldn't judge and who'd take care of her, take care of *you*." He glanced at me with a little smile. "So I volunteered to be that guy. She'd been home for three months, and I just went for it. I got your grandfather's blessing and asked her to marry me on August fifth, 1994. She said no, of course, but your nanna and pap were pretty adamant about it."

For a moment, I thought that was odd. What was there to be adamant about? It was her life. They weren't living in Saudi Arabia or seventeenth century Europe; she wasn't obligated to marry anyone, much less Benjamin Edmunds, but then I thought about the divorce and the way my grandparents railed against it for months. I thought about what Pap had said at my birthday dinner, that my mother seemed to prefer single parenthood and how he and Nanna were too old to keep bailing her out.

At the time I thought they were talking about the consequences of divorce, but now it made a whole different kind of sense, and I looked at Dad who was looking at me, waiting to see if I'd put it together.

"Your grandparents gave your mom an ultimatum," Dad explained. "I can't say I was in favor of their methods; they were pretty ruthless. But once they knew she had a suitor, of sorts, they made her a pretty overwhelming proposition. There were issues about the family name, your grandfather's reputation at Penn, a bunch of bullshit, really. But to them, a child born out of wedlock to their only daughter, and with a history like hers, all the circumstances around her getting pregnant in the first place— she risked losing them altogether, the whole family."

"Even Uncle Cam?"

"Nah, your uncle was still away at college then, but he knew what was happening, and he didn't like it, not one bit. It's one of the reasons why he never left Atlanta, never went back. He didn't speak to your grandparents for two years after that."

"So, what was the ultimatum?" I was almost afraid to find out, but I waited while Dad gathered his thoughts.

"They told her if she chose to have you out of wedlock and raise you by herself," he finally said, "then they would cut her off completely, thus cutting you off as well. Forever. They would no longer acknowledge her as their daughter, and they would not accept you as their grandchild." He gazed out into the park, remembering. "Man, it was a hell of a thing. For both of us. I didn't want her to marry me that way. But I was the only one asking, and she was facing a pretty lonely road, otherwise. A hard, lonely road. And you know your mom—once she makes a decision, it's cast in iron, and she never looks back. I figured she'd just go it alone and make do, so I withdrew my proposal and started looking for jobs around the country, took it as a loss and moved on."

"Yeah, but you didn't," I noted. "You obviously married her, so how'd you get her to change her mind?"

"Well, your mom kinda changed her own mind."

He motioned for us to go walking again, and so I got up and followed him back out to the trail that led down toward the gazebo.

"She did it for you," he said as we passed the Noguchi playground.

It was one of my favorite places when I was little, and I watched the kids swinging high on the tall triangular swing sets, chasing each other through the sand and up into the cylindrical sliding board tunnels.

"Deep down, I always knew that. But I thought if I gave her a good life, gave you a good home, then I dunno—maybe she'd grow to love me. I mean, *really* love me," he said, mostly to himself.

"You were friends," I tried to encourage. "Lifetime friends. I'm sure she loved you on some level. She sure played it off pretty well if she didn't. At least I never noticed anything. Not until the divorce, anyway."

Dad nodded slowly, taking it all into account. He was quiet as we walked, his hands shoved into his jacket pockets, his eyes fixed on the distant city skyline just beyond the sycamores. He didn't say anything else about that. Instead he told me, "The most important thing at the time was you. Your mother and I both put your future first. We got married at the Philadelphia courthouse, had a small reception at Nanna and Pap's with a few close friends, and she went back to school at Curtis until a week before you were born. She took a semester off to take care of you while I looked for a better job. Then she went back and finished her Masters in '95. With a little help from your uncle, I finally got hired on at LMI, and we moved down here to Marietta when you were just a year old."

"And I guess the rest is history." I gave him a little smile.

"That's right. The astounding misadventures of Edmunds and De Carlo." Then looked at me and said, "Maybe we should've joined the circus. We might've fit in a little better."

I smiled and linked an arm around his and leaned against his shoulder as we walked to the parking lot and headed back to the car.

WHEN WE GOT to Jackie's that night, I went straight to my room and took out the 1994 journal from the ones Rachel let me keep, the one I'd started reading first when I'd found them in Mom's closet. It was thinner than the others, and the entries were sparse, sometimes several weeks apart, but she had just gotten home to Bensalem from LA, and there was a lot going on. She'd spent her twenty-fourth birthday with Dad. He took her into Philly, to the Copacabana down on South Street where they ordered overflowing plates of nachos and sizzling fajitas. It's probably where I got my taste for Mexican food, as she was eating for both of us then, and I smiled at the little takeout menu she'd slipped between the pages, a keepsake from a day she wanted to remember.

Everything about home seemed to be giving her strength, even when my grandparents commandeered her freedom like wardens in a Turkish prison. They had discovered her stint at Cedarbrook through an insurance statement that had come in the mail, and so Nanna and Pap made a mid-April trip to Glendale and stayed at the Hilton until Mom was released in May.

They brought her back to Pennsylvania and set her up in her old room. They screened her phone calls and intercepted her mail, including four letters and a call from Rachel, which my mother never knew about, not until she and Rachel met again, years later. They monitored her diet, her hygiene, her mental health, accompanied her to Narcotics Anonymous meetings and took her back and forth to the doctor. They dragged her to mass every Saturday at St. Rita's and gave her the keys to Pap's old Honda for transportation to Curtis—school and back, nowhere else; Pap even checked the odometer at the end of each day and jotted the mileage into a little notepad.

They had made a prisoner of her and tolerated nothing. She hated them for it but loved them just the same because she needed the austerity, the structure, the lockdown on her life that would ultimately save us both.

She needed to forget as much as she needed to remember. She needed new everything. A new school. A new view from her bedroom window. A new future from which she could never look back. She picked up her violin and never picked up another guitar again—she couldn't, it was an alarming trigger, and there was too much at stake; it would be ludicrous to tempt fate, to test her own resolve so boldly after she'd come so far.

She renounced her time at Berklee and called herself a graduate of the Curtis Institute instead. She told herself that Rachel Cole had been a delusion, a daydream from a past life, and she let her die away into a history of regret. She would forget her. She would give her up to God. She would never love another woman as much as she had loved her. And so, on September first, 1994, she took a drive into Center City Philadelphia, knocked on Benjamin Edmunds' apartment door, and accepted his proposal on three conditions.

She asked that he never tell a soul about her troubled past, that he give her space, time to get used to being a man's wife, and that he love and care for her child like his own. If he could consent to those terms, then she promised to be good to him, she would be faithful, and she would honor their friendship by honoring her marriage vows.

And yes, she did it for me. I would likely never know my biological father. I would never know his parents or whether he had siblings I could call aunts or uncles, and if my mother had chosen to raise me on her own, then I would've never known her parents, either. We would've been each other's only family, and we would've struggled.

She would have taken whatever work she could find between loans from Uncle Cam and might have foregone a music career altogether because kids are expensive and demanding and needy, and she said she wanted more for me than a hundred dollar a week babysitter living two apartments over, secondhand school clothes, food stamps, and free lunch programs. She wanted fourth of July fireworks at Penn's Landing, Pocono Christmases, and birthday parties, summer weekends at the Jersey Shore, Crystal Cave, and New York City. She wanted me to have the life my grandparents had given her, and so she sacrificed herself.

She became someone else entirely. She changed her address, her career, her demeanor, even changed her name and called it a clean slate, but some things leave an indelible residue, a permanent silhouette behind all the bright new lights and beautiful embellishments. Some things follow you, and some things you carry around inside, lifelong truths lying dormant for years before they finally come calling again.

She believed she had done us both the best turn, and for a time, I think she had. Jolán De Carlo had reinvented herself and fled away to Marietta as Mrs. Benjamin Edmunds—wife, mother, daughter, sister, friend. She had become a success, and the illusion was working. Until it wasn't, anymore. Until I began to grow and change and bear her own uncanny resemblance in ways that made her shudder.

Gone was the baby fat, the red satin pigtail ribbons, the play dates at Chuck E. Cheese; the braces had come off, and so had the training wheels. Soon it was all bras and maxipads, college plans and boys on the telephone, trapdoors and landmines everywhere. I was thinking for myself, and it frightened her. It reminded her where I had come from, and a thirteen-year façade was finally wearing away, wearing her down with unprecedented guilt because a lie is a lie, and just how many more could she live with, when every glance in my direction was another glance into Wade Tyson's bedroom mirror?

I was half Jolán De Carlo and half a mystery. It was why she had begun to cry every day, why she couldn't get out of bed for weeks at a time. The truth was calling—my truth, her truth, our devastating bond. So, once again, she did what was better for both of us and gave my father back his name so she could breathe again, so she could think, focus, learn how to live without affectation, without stigma, and without regret, so she could be the model that I really needed, the example of a woman who would turn her whole life upside down to remain true to herself, a woman who would not settle.

They'd determined the cause of death to be residual heart damage from the cocaine and heroin of her youth; her choices had come back around to collect payment, to close the circle, once and for all. Rachel gave me the rest of those journals the week after my high school graduation, and

I've read them through a dozen times since then, learning her, memorizing her, piecing her together so I might finally understand the woman who'd raised me, who saved my life by saving her own, her greatest achievement for which she will have my deepest love and respect forever.

Seven years ago, today, I broke her heart, and she forgave me. It was the most important lesson I had ever learned. Forgiveness. She needed it from all of us but mostly from herself.

She was a woman in distress who'd found rescue. She was a woman in need of redemption who'd found true love again. She was a woman hoping to reconcile a thousand mistakes with a heart full of kindness, and desire, and penance. She was Jolán Elena De Carlo, and she was my mother.

About the Author

Carole Wolf is from Allentown, PA and currently lives in Columbus, GA with her partner Yoko Hirose. She has a B.A. in English Literature from Columbus State University, and she has been writing for twenty-five years. Her goal as an author is to write novels that address sensitive social issues, which not only affect lesbian women but all women, and she hopes this will help open up lesbian fiction to mainstream readers. Carole's other passion is music; she is a music producer and has been playing the drums since she was eleven years old. She has played with three local bands and has produced music for several aspiring singers. She has two four-legged children—a German Shepherd/Rottweiler mix named Caesar and a Tabby cat named Jewel. Carole is currently working on her certification to be a Drug and Alcohol Addiction Counselor.

www.ingramcontent.com/pod-product-compliance
Lightning Source LLC
Chambersburg PA
CBHW020500020726
47493CB00001B/112